EAGLE'S NEST

STEPHEN FRANCIS MONTAGNA

Copyright © 2023 Stephen Francis Montagna.

All rights reserved. No part of this book may be reproduced, stored, or transmitted by any means—whether auditory, graphic, mechanical, or electronic—without written permission of both publisher and author, except in the case of brief excerpts used in critical articles and reviews. Unauthorized reproduction of any part of this work is illegal and is punishable by law.

ISBN: 979-8-88640-806-5 (sc)
ISBN: 979-8-88640-807-2 (hc)
ISBN: 979-8-88640-808-9 (e)

Because of the dynamic nature of the Internet, any web addresses or links contained in this book may have changed since publication and may no longer be valid. The views expressed in this work are solely those of the author and do not necessarily reflect the views of the publisher, and the publisher hereby disclaims any responsibility for them.

One Galleria Blvd., Suite 1900, Metairie, LA 70001
1-888-421-2397

*This book is dedicated to a very special person in my life
Someone who stood behind me even when I drove her crazy
My Mom whom I love dearly*

PROLOGUE

The war in Iraq known to the world as 'Operation Desert Storm' began in earnest on January 17th, 1991, and it was fought to place a quick end to the terrible oppression of the Kingdom of Kuwait and her people by the invading Iraqi Armies.

The war officially ended with the last action of the war being fought on March 6th, 1991. On what was soon to be branded as the 'Highway of Death', outside the capital of Kuwait City. The war was short in duration and extremely costly for the demoralized invading Iraqi Forces, who were soundly routed by the combined troops of the Coalition Forces, who stopped President Saddam Hussein's mad conquest to rule over the Middle East. Then, the Iraqi world before it had a chance to flourish and heal its war wounds and place the war behind them and after many months of pounding by Allied aircraft. Hounded and destroyed on the ground by Coalition Forces tanks, artillery and attack helicopters. The Iraqi troops had zero options left opened to them, and they gave up in the hundreds and even the thousands to any Allied Forces they came across.

If the chilling words written long ago in the Holy Bible are correct, the world has to be extremely wary of the second coming of the long feared anti-Christ, roaming the earth in all its evil attempt to destroy mankind. The Coalition Forces placed the dreams of this latest anti-Christ off track, but only for the time being.

Even though the war between Iraq and the Coalition Troops ended on March 6th, 1991, someone obviously forgot to inform the crazed madman running Iraq of this fact. Because of the continuing threat to his neighbors in the Middle East, and to world peace in general, the Coalition Forces were forced to remain intact. To keep a present vigil on Saddam Hussein's ambitions, and his blinding want to be the master of the entire Middle East, or become the destroyer of the world's sanity and peace. Saddam Hussein's most uncontrollable thirst for blood, coupled with his want for revenge and world conquest and domination, caused his unfettered wrath to fall upon his own good and innocent peoples of Iraq. Mostly the unarmed, unprotected, unaware people who did not understand the attacks were coming by this mad dog murderer.

With the memory of his releasing a repulsing and devastating chemical attack on the poorly armed and unsuspecting Kurdish people in Northern Iraq in 1988. President Saddam Hussein turned his tanks and warplanes, along with his military might loose on the poorly defended Shiiti Muslim people in the south of Iraq. The oppressive Iraqi President ordered the renewal of the slaughter of the Kurds in the northern section of Iraq, forced the good nations of the world with a conscious, to create a no fly zone between these two sections of the nation of Iraq.

In an attempt to try and help protect the poorer people of Iraq from their own despised leader of the country. But the United States and the United Kingdom found themselves shouldering the full burden of protecting the innocent peoples of Iraq, with most other nations hiding behind the United Nations flag of indifference and greed.

Increasingly savage attacks aimed against these poorly protected areas of Iraq, caused the Coalition Forces to attack the well dug in SAM Surface to Air Missile sites and radar installations, along with many other military targets spread throughout Iraq over the coming years, since the ending of the Desert Storm war. Allied Forces maintain a constant flyover of these certain areas to help guard the defenseless Shiiti's and Kurds from further attacks by the well armed and feared Republican Guard Units of Saddam Hussein's elite troops.

Separate actions were forced to be carried out against the headstrong President Hussein, to curb his wild ideas of destroying his own people, or threatening the other peaceful peoples of the Middle East lands. Year after endless year, at one point or another, Saddam Hussein had to be beaten back inside his little rathole in the ground, destroying much of the remaining military might of his country in the process by the Allied warplanes.

The hated and widely feared Iraqi President Saddam Hussein used any and every foul excuse in his warped and twisted mind, to increase the constant probes and attacks on the will of the Coalition Forces. In their ongoing attempt to maintain this protection of the innocent and defenseless Iraqi peoples, and the world from this crazed madman and his distorted beliefs, wants, and demands to destroy anything in his path. Steadfastly, the Coalition Forces stuck together, and attacked Saddam Hussein's every evil attempts to rid his country of anyone not following the lead dog in the race, and that dog was President Saddam Hussein.

Nothing Saddam did, could, or would shake the steadfast will and belief of the free world from stepping back, and allowing him to once again threaten the peace of the entire Middle East region. As he did when his military forces invaded the tiny Arab nation of Kuwait, and destroy another defenseless country in the name of his mad quest to rule over the Middle East first, and then the entire world after he had conquered all the Arab lands.

The Desert Storm War spanned the course of three different American Presidential Administrations, with one of them being elected to the honored post twice. Now, with the fourth man soon to be in command of the Presidency of the United States, Albert Cole, Iraqi President Saddam Hussein's mad illusions of being a world power again, surfaced in all its ugliness with new intensity and desire.

The crazed madman of Iraq believed in his mind what with this new American President taking the helm of the United States affairs of his nation and the world. The new President was bound to be much more concerned with the many problems currently facing the American public. Than he was with worrying about what he was doing in the Middle East.

Saddam Hussein was dead wrong in this deformed assumption, because President Albert Cole was going to be the most heavy handed of all the previous American Presidents, when it came to dealing with the madman from Iraq. President Cole wanted to place a final end to Saddam Hussein's wild dreams of conquest of the entire Middle East, and to stop the Iraq problem from draining off so much of the United States tax money once and for all, taxpayer's money that should be spent on schools, the drug problem, and children with guns facing America.

President Albert Cole was soon forced to go to the United Nations many times in his young Presidency, to fight against the lifting of the stifling sanctions imposed against the nation of Iraq that were asked to be lifted by the nations of Russia, Germany and even France. To continue to punish Saddam Hussein's steadfast refusal to relinquish any and all of his feared hidden weapons of mass destruction, and to give up his mad quests of being the master of the entire Middle East region. And, to have the United Nation's sponsor more inspection teams having free reign again, inside the borders of Iraq. To search for these buried or otherwise hidden weapons of mass destruction believed to be within Saddam Hussein's control and borders. The new American President spent so much time in the air between Washington and New York and the United Nations building; he soon branded his great aircraft of Air Force One as, EAGLE'S NEST.

CHAPTER ONE

SATURDAY, JUNE 5th, 1999, THE ROLANDS MOTEL, WASHINGTON D.C. 3:30 A.M. EST

Three young and extremely angry Arabs gathered in a one room apartment of the rundown dilapidated Roland's Motel, on East 57th Street in the downtown area of Washington D.C. Here, the soon to be group of Iraqi terrorists decided to bring the plight of Iraq to the world's eye, by attacking something so cherished by the American people within their own country's borders.

In their warped young minds, each of them felt if they attacked a strategic target within the United States, especially in their capital city of Washington D.C. It would force the American people to demand an immediate end to the sanctions constantly strangling Iraq and its people. The soon to be attackers did not consider the illusions for one minute that President Saddam Hussein was the cause of these terrible sanctions in the first place. The group hung on to, and they believed with their heart every word spewed out of the mouth of the evil President Hussein, of his hatred of the civilized world and all it stood for.

Each of the young Arab men and one lone Arab woman had different targets locked in their minds to attack, and together they threw them all out on the table, to try and single out the best possible target of the lot to strike out at. That they thought could or would finally break the fine and steadfast spirit of the American people, and snap the strong will of the

Coalition Forces to remain intact and still attacking their homeland years since the Desert Storm War.

Iraqi born, Jebril Briegheeth was the one who had assembled the other two Arabs together to pick out and then attack the target they all finally set their eyes upon. He was an active soldier in the well feared Nebuchad Nezzer Republican Guard Unit of Iraq. He suffered greatly through the crushing defeat on the so called road of death leading out of Kuwait and back to Iraq, as the retreating Iraqi Forces crumbled under the relentless attacks aimed against his troops by the Coalition aircraft, as he led what was left of his tank column out of Kuwait City.

When the American warplanes came, he ordered his troops out of the tanks, and then the fleeing Iraqi soldiers streamed out into the vastness of the great desert. As his troops fled the terrible carnage for the safety of the Iraqi border, Captain Briegheeth remained lying on a nearby sand dune, and he stared in stunned disbelief at the savagery befalling his once great and proud Republican Guard Units and their military equipment. Any Iraqi troops that did not flee the military vehicles immediately ended up a charred corpus trapped inside those destroyed war machines of death. He continued to stare in disbelief as thirty Russian made tanks turned into infernos of flaming death. Lying on that sand dune, Briegheeth swore to himself on the bodies of his fallen troops, he was going to make every American living in the United States, regret what they had just visited upon his once mighty and feared troops.

Three times in the past few years, Captain Jebril Briegheeth tried in vain to get his hands on either some chemical or biological weapons of mass destruction. He contacted numerous Russian scientists and other contacts he was friendly with, and he tried desperately to acquire these illegal and cheap to produce weapons of mass destruction. But Iraqi Captain Briegheeth could not get his hands on any of these banned weapons. Since his failure of finding any chemical or biological weapons, he lowered his sights and successfully located a much smaller target to aim himself at, but one that would cripple the American government just as completely.

At every meeting of the soon to be Arab terrorist cell, the younger Iraqi Captain Briegheeth was always in favor of hitting an easy Saudi Arabian target stationed within the United States' borders. He felt if he could damage a Saudi target in America, not only would he thoroughly embarrass their present government. But he could also sow the growing seeds of discontent between the United States and Saudi Arabia, and a number of other Arab nations in the Middle East also. Thus destroying the Coalition Forces once and for all, and at the same time freeing up the staggering yoke of stifling sanctions placed upon Iraq's neck for all these passing years by the hated United Nations members under the direction of the United States.

Mamdouh al-Qassan, the youngest of the three soon to be Iraqi terrorists, wanted to hit just American interests in their attacks. His anger was locked on them, and he blamed the elderly Senator John Hopkins of the Senate Oversight Committee, the most for supplying the monies the American military used to support the continuing attacks aimed against Iraq.

Farseeha al-Mana, the third and the only woman member on the Iraqi terrorist team, and the most fanatical of the bunch, demanded they go after the very heart of the United States. Farseeha wanted to hit the White House with a shoulder launch rocket attack, hopefully killing the new President of the United States, his wife, and their children during the attack, and thus destroying what the American public held most dear to their hearts and minds. She considered the White House as the true seat of the American government and leadership. As she put it time and time again to the other Iraqi's, the head of the snake the evil eye of the great Satan.

At every meeting of the small terrorist group, she hotly demanded without waving in her demand, this one target be given their top priority by the group of Arab terrorists. Farseeha had the dream of going to Paradise with the head of the American President locked so proudly in her blood soaked hands. She always wanted to hand the head of the hated fool to Muhammad, who she was sure, would welcome her home with open arms and a smile on his lips, if she were to die in the attack aimed against the American President.

As fanatical as she was over this dream, Farseeha was a smart and cunning woman, who had no intention of dying in any attack she intended to aim against the United States. She wanted to commit a hit and run operation, and then live out the rest of her life in Iraq as a hero to the cause of Saddam Hussein's wild desires. Even though the terrorists did not agree on any one certain target as yet, for the past five days Farseeha used her time keeping the White House under constant surveillance. She made a detailed log of the comings and goings of the American President, his family and friends from the massive building grounds. She even included the many names of visitors she recognized from the local newspapers. It would add to her attack, if she could get a number of Senators, and other leading American officials in her assault against them.

She was able to get so near the White House by setting up a sort of umbrella stand, selling all kinds of small American trinkets to the countless numbers of sightseers crowding the streets of the capital of the United States. Over the passing weeks, she actually spotted the President six times. Once, she even had an easy shot at him, if she was armed and foolish enough, she could have taken the American President out herself, if she wanted to commit suicide. Farseeha took the time to make up a number of small hand printed maps of the area around the White House; and at times she was even challenged by the local police officers and Secret Service Agents always protecting the grounds and surrounding areas.

She wrote down the known names and descriptions of all visitors to the White House, and she committed everything to paper once returning to the privacy of her small hotel room. Farseeha showed up so much at the grounds of the White House area that the police officers and agents soon grew accustomed to seeing her hanging around and hawking her wears, and they no longer challenged her near as much as they once had. Twice, some of the special agents even bought some items from her table. This added to her growing confidence at getting near enough to the American President, to kill him when the proper time arrived for her to do so.

As the disgruntled Iraqi terrorists sat in the dim lit room and went over their plan of attack on the United States and her leadership. Farseeha al-Mana was the first one to speak up at this latest meeting between the soon to be terrorists. As she rose to her feet, Farseeha tossed the papers she drew up of the White House area, along with the list of visitors to the building on the table. Then she stared hot at the Iraqi Captain and snapped at him at the same time. "Captain Jebril Briegheeth, I demand that we go after the god cursed hated American President..."

"By Allah's powerful hand, please, not this again Farseeha, my ears are still full and burning from the last time you have brought this target up to our attention, foul woman. I already told you that your target is most impossible to get at successfully, foolish female. I went over this with you time and again, and I have pointed out the impossibility of getting near enough to make a successful kill against the hated American President to you already, woman. I like the pick and hope to go after a Saudi Arabian target in the American States; here the security is not as intense. Remember Farseeha, all we want to do is embarrass the foolish American government, and create a number of cracks in the loathsome Coalition group to get some of the pressure off our country and President, so Iraq can once again live in peace wither worthless neighbors.

"Once the support from the Arab countries of the Coalition crumbles, the United States will be totally helpless to continue their foul attacks aimed against our country. Then, President Saddam Hussein will be more than free to pursue his dreams of making Iraq the center of the Middle East, and we can seek proper revenge aimed against the United States, England and France, for what they have done to our country. When the Coalition Forces break up, we can release our youth against our enemy, and they can go to Paradise with the souls of hated American and English soldiers, as an offering to Muhammad. I beg of you woman, put this crazy idea of killing the American President out of your worthless mind once and for all. I don't want to hear of this want ever again from your god cursed lips, Farseeha. It takes away the true reason for our meeting here today, woman. To carry out our mission and find a much more logical target to attack."

"Huh Captain Briegheeth, I cannot believe President Saddam Hussein would ever allow someone as weak minded as you, to control this attack cell for him, fool. We're terrorists are we not, Captain? We should be willing to do anything in our power for our country and our people's sake. If we want to get at the heart of the United States and bring world attention to the ongoing plight of the innocent people of Iraq then we have to go after the very head of the great Satan, and that head is their foolish American President." Farseeha hissed angrily as she suddenly threw her hands in the air, and she actually angrily turned her back on Captain Briegheeth.

"By the angry revenge of Almighty Allah once again Farseeha, you're responsible for the total upsetting of this god cursed meeting between us, foul woman. We have much more important matters to discuss here, if we ever plan to attack any worthwhile target before the Americans destroy Iraq completely against us. If you're going to insist on being so pigheaded about your want to kill the hated American President, I'll send a message to Iraq, and demand that you be replaced with someone more open minded for our need and aims. By the great gray beard of the Prophet Himself, we have to work as a god cursed unit if we're to be successful for Iraq and our President's sake, woman." Captain Briegheeth snapped hotly at the back of Farseeha.

She suddenly spun around and glared harshly in the eyes of Captain Briegheeth for a long moment, as she allowed her right hand to lightly rest threateningly upon the handle of her nine mm Colt pistol, as she suddenly snarled at him. "And, by the sacred chin whiskers of the Prophet also, Captain Briegheeth. I bid you, report back to Baghdad for all the good it will do you, you great fool of fools you. Captain Briegheeth, before your report is answered by anyone who might lend you an ear to complain in, you eyes will be staring the death stare."

"By the five sacred prayers of the Holy Qur'an, are you daring to threaten me with death here, Farseeha? Me, your fellow Arab brother in arms you now wish to harm, worthless woman? We cannot be reduced to fighting and snapping at each others heels like the lowly jackals of the hot, burning sands of the endless desert. This is a terrible insult you have just displayed against me, to be threatened by you, a sister in this Islamic Jihad."

"Fool of fools that you are I'll be willing to threaten the devil himself to get at the Americans who are destroying my country. Because no one is safe from my great wrath, until the mother Satan is mortally wounded, and is no longer able to bring death to Iraq and her people."

"I suggest you threaten the wrong man foolishly, Farseeha. I'm a well respected Captain in the Iraq Republican Guard in case you might have forgotten my position in this god cursed drama. Threats leveled against me, are the same as if they were leveled against President Saddam himself, woman. Especially if that threat is backed up with disgusting moves to a weapon, as you're doing here against me. How dare you threaten an Officer in our service with a weapon and death, lowly female fool? One word from my honored lips and your foul bones will be bleached white in the desert sun, lowly witch." Captain Briegheeth snarled at the young Arab woman.

Farseeha refused to back down one bit as she replied nastily to the supposed leader of the Iraqi terrorist cell. "And, you seem to forget who I am as well, Captain Briegheeth. I'm a Colonel in the Secret Police of Iraq, and we have complete jurisdiction over all you stupid and useless soldiers. Especially if one of those fools is a lowly coward to carry out the mission he was sent here to the United States to accomplish for his President. One word from me, and not only you would be staked out on a sand dune, and then you'll find yourself waiting for the small jaws of the desert scavengers to rip your god cursed body apart. But your entire worthless family will also join you in your foul fate in this very slow death, Captain Briegheeth.

"So I suggest you be extremely careful with who you threaten, Captain Briegheeth. At any time, I can assume control over this god cursed little terrorist cell. The reason you're still in command of us, is because you were in the United States first. I was sent to assist you, and to make certain the target you chose is the best possible one for our needs, Captain. But if I don't approve of the target you settle your worthless eyes upon, it'll be I who'll report to Baghdad with a request to have you relieved of command and sent back to Iraq to face the wrath of Saddam."

Iraqi Captain Briegheeth refused to give an inch to the young and very pretty Iraqi woman either. He debated himself whether or not he should dispatch this always angry and most upsetting woman and then report to his control she was killed by the American police. Once they discovered her hanging around the White House as she was ordered not to do by him.

He fumed at being called a coward by this nasty woman, but knew if he challenged her there would be no settling on any worthwhile target at this meeting. Time was growing short for them to act, and his Commander back in Iraq was waiting for action to begin. To get locked in a battle of words with the worthless and most uncontrollable Farseeha would solve absolutely nothing for him, and it would also add more time and stress to their mission. Captain Briegheeth wanted to leave the United States as soon as possible, because the American customs and foul beliefs sickened him so to his very stomach. The Iraqi Captain could not understand what the infatuation with naked women, brought to the foolish American male's delights.

He longed to walk upon the clean pure desert sand of Iraq, and leave the United States to destroy itself by slowly ripping itself apart. Gang killings, murder in the streets of all major cities, rape, slaughter in schools of their children and the war against the police. How he truly loathed the United States and all she stood for. Captain Briegheeth understood why the Arabs thought of the United States as the great Satan of the world. Only a country controlled by Satan, could possibly slaughter its own people without thought or mercy or regard.

Captain Briegheeth let out his breath slowly, confident of his next words to the upsetting female Iraqi, and the effect they would have on the always angry woman glaring at him with hatred locked in her eyes. "Farseeha, true you work for the Secret Police of our country, and you're responsible to Saddam Hussein for your actions, woman. Since President Hussein is not in charge here, it falls on my shoulders to command this cell. This action is being carried out by the Republican Guards, woman. Saddam is not even aware of our being in the United States, he thinks he could break the Coalition by aiming his radar at their foul warplanes in hopes the damage to Iraq, will weaken the resolve of the other Arab members of the Coalition. He thinks forcing the aircraft to attack his radars that the Arab supporters will withdraw their support.

"We soldiers in the Republican Guard, see this as a serious mistake on President Saddam's part, foolish woman. The hated American Arabs are most willing and pleased to see Saddam's military strength be eroded by the worthless American warplanes. They're pleased to sit back on their worthless arses, and wait until Saddam's forces could no longer protect their interests in the Middle East. Then, the foul fools will make a move on our country and take it over. We'll be forced to the will of the Saudi's, and may Allah forbid, Iran, and their god cursed Shiiti Muslims and their foul and foolish beliefs. Can you imagine Farseeha, Israeli's walking upon the honored lands of Iraq without fear of death, because they're friends of the United States."

Farseeha stared at Captain Briegheeth, while weighing his words carefully, and then she replied. "Captain Briegheeth, I agree with your assumption of the beliefs of Saddam Hussein and his misguided actions of late, sir. You're most correct to believe this, I report directly to our President, and this mission ties my hands behind my back, because he's not truly sanctioning it. I caution you though Captain Briegheeth, because President Hussein is not sanctioning this action, does not mean the foul

Army is in complete control of the operation. There are others powerful in the government who believe this action is correct. That is why I was made part of..."

"Alhamdulilah, Praise be to God, are you telling me there's a possible coup waiting within the government of Iraq, Farseeha? If this is so then aim me at the lowly jackals, and I'll happily slice them into small pieces once they have suffered the slow death of a thousand cuts. Saddam Hussein is the President of Iraq, and he shall be until the Prophet himself deems otherwise, by bringing Saddam home to his bosom for the eternal rest and honor, woman."

"Ahhh... spoken like a noble lap dog, Captain Briegheeth. There is no coup I know of in Iraq, leastwise, not yet that is. But if Saddam doesn't correct his way of thinking, and takes the initiative in striking at our enemy in a more productive way, I cannot guarantee what the future might bring to Iraq. The sand's shift brings constant change to the desert, and perhaps Iraq, fool."

Stunned by Farseeha's threatening words, Captain Briegheeth stared angrily at her for several moments before speaking to her again. "By the power of the mighty shammals (sand storms) that rip the desert apart, I don't know how to react to this idea of a possible coup changing the government of Iraq, foul woman. After all we have been through in the name of Saddam's desires, only to see it change now would be most disturbing for me to absorb, woman."

"Fool, I'm not here to talk about the future of the Iraqi government. I'm here to plan an attack against our enemy's government one that'd surely break the back of the god cursed Coalition Forces, Captain Briegheeth." Farseeha snapped angrily back at the Iraqi Military Officer.

"Huh, are you now going to demand to take over command of this working cell, woman?"

"Only if you don't listen to the words of my logic then I'll take over, Captain Briegheeth."

"Very well then, I shall listen to your words of wisdom you offer me, woman. What were you able to find out about your selected target that is of any new information, Farseeha?"

The standoff continued, until Mamdouh al-Qassan suddenly cleared his throat loudly.

"And, do you have something to add to this conversation, you young fool al-Qassan?"

The younger Iraqi man tried a smile on Captain Briegheeth; it was wasted on his comrade. Seeing no way to lighten the tense mood, he replied in a sharp tone to his Commander. "Captain Briegheeth, Farseeha, I thought we were sent here to the United States to locate certain targets of opportunity for our country to attack. With three targets accepted by us in case we fail to hit one, we had the two others to drop back on, sir. To hear you two speak so, it seems you have already decided on one target and one target only, whether or not that target's obtainable. What happened to our original mission? One we were certain would succeed for us." Al-Qassan lost his trend of thought and where he was heading, so he just put his head down and stopped speaking.

Farseeha, refrained from speaking, but Captain Briegheeth replied right away. "Ahhh... out of the mouths of our youth, woman. I praise the Almighty Allah for giving you the wisdom to see things so simply, young one. Al-Qassan, you're correct with your wise words you address to me. Yes, we were sent here to the United States to pick out three separate targets, and we shall do just as we were instructed to do. We'll keep these three targets under constant surveillance until we decided on which one to hit first. Do you not agree with this plan I offer you, Farseeha?"

Fighting to control her raging anger, Farseeha was forced to nod her head yes in response.

"Then I believe this is settled between us, we'll bring forth our targets then we'll pick the one best to act against. I'll begin with my offering. I favor an attack on a Saudi Arabian target here in the United States. I have picked the Saudi Arabian Embassy for my interest. We can wait until we see the Saudi Ambassador returning from his usual visit in New York City.

"If we can shoot him down like a common animal in the streets of downtown Washington, think of the embarrassment we'll cause to the hated god cursed Americans, Farseeha. Think of the favorable reaction we can bring about by such a wise course of action in the hated United States, woman. We can ask our fellow Arab nations what worthwhile protection the Americans can possibly offer to their worthless allies, when their Ambassadors are killed like the lowly dogs they are in the streets of Washington. It'll surely break up the Coalition quicker than any other attack we can think of on American soil. I truly favor this course of action, Farseeha?"

Drawing in a breath, Farseeha hissed between clenched teeth. "I must admit, it sounds like a target to arouse our interest. But I think an attack on the American President will do more to destroy the Coalition, and the will of their public than any other target we can come up with, sir."

"Perhaps you might be correct with your faithful words to me Farseeha, but we're not going to overlook any targets in this conversation, woman. We know of your target, but there's one more that has something to offer us here, woman." Iraqi Captain Briegheeth offered as he turned to the younger member of their terrorist cell and moaned at him. "Al-Qassan, I believe you have picked out a target for our approval. What target do you have in mind, young one?"

"Yes Captain Briegheeth, I have a target in mind sir. I have leveled my eyes on the American Senator, John Hopkins; he's the Chairman of the Senate Oversight Committee supplying money for the military to continue their attacks against our country of Iraq. If we kill him, it'll place Congress in mayhem, stopping the attacks on Iraq. He's an easy target because I know he enjoys private walks in the garden by the Capital Building. He takes cuttings from many of the plants, trying to root them in his own garden. He's an old fool who walks Washington with little if any security surrounding him. I guess this is so no one witnesses his cutting of the foul plants. If we wait and take our time with this cursed target, we should be able to kill him and escape before the hated police arrive on the scene. That makes this target the most likely of our three."

"Hummm... it seems you have done your homework on this worthless man, al-Qassan. It's one target that demands our further consideration." Captain Briegheeth turned to Farseeha and saw her seething and offered. "Farseeha, as it stands, we have three targets in mind. All will get the job done and stop the attacks on Iraq, but which one is the most important for us..."

"For how long I ask you Captain Briegheeth? For how long will it stop the attacks against Iraq? True, the targets have the ring of stopping the hated air attacks against our country, but I see the only attack that'll stop them for the longest period of time, is the one that I have concentrated my efforts on. Yours are too foolish. What good would it do to attack a Saudi

Ambassador in the United States? True, it'll cause momentary anger in Saudi Arabia against the United States, but I don't believe it'll be enough to break up the Coalition ties to one another.

"With all the deaths occurring in the United States, one Arab's death, I don't believe will amount to anything more than a momentary halt to the attacks in Iraq. Once the Ambassador's body lies rotting in the cursed ground, the attacks on Iraq will begin again, maybe with a new intensity, Captain. Especially if the fools believe an Iraqi was responsible for the death of the Saudi politician. No Captain Briegheeth, I demand that we go after the President of the United States and place an immediate end to the attacks against our country for good. Even if their foul public blames an Iraqi for the attack, the brazen way we'll do it, will cause them to reconsider their effort in Iraq, fearing more attacks aimed against their foul leadership, sir."

"There, you're doing it again Farseeha. I already told you to get off that cursed target you want to hit, worthless woman. Your mind is clouded over and confused with the death of the American President. A target that I truly feel would be most impossible to reach and destroy successfully. How many American Presidents were killed in the past times in the history of the United States, woman? Not very many I'm afraid to offer you, they're too hard a target to get at. I..."

"They're not that hard a target to get at Captain Briegheeth! Look, look to the past and you'll see what you refuse to witness with your own worthless eyes and my faithful words, fool of fools. A worthless madman crippled of mind and good sense, successfully shot President Ronald Reagan. A foolish actor not worth his salt killed another foolish American President..."

"This is true Farseeha. The madman did not kill him, and the actor killed Lincoln only because there was not enough security surrounding a President in their past history, woman." Captain Briegheeth interrupted, angry Farseeha dared to interrupt his words moments before.

"True as spoken Captain Briegheeth that was because he was not of military in nature and untrained to kill properly, sir. We're properly and highly trained in countless military ways and attacking abilities. We know well how to shoot a weapon correctly, and where to shoot anyone to be a lethal hit, and how to get our target in a position to kill him, Captain. If a lone madman can get at and then wound a powerful American President with little thought or true effort, just think of the success that lies at the ends of our fingertips, Captain Briegheeth. If we use time, our patience and intelligence to kill the current hated American President, sir."

Captain Briegheeth stared harshly at Farseeha for several long moments, seeing the wisdom in her words. He had to agree if they were patient enough, and smart enough, they might be able to get at the American President and kill him after all. Leaning back in his chair for a second, the Iraqi Captain rubbed his chin and thought. In his mind, he knew killing the American President was the one statement he was truly looking for, the one action that would surely cause the most problems for the United States, and their foul Coalition friends and fellow murderers.

The Iraqi Captain looked up and saw the steel blue burning eyes of Farseeha drilling a hole in him, and he mumbled at the angry looking woman. "Farseeha, weighing your words carefully for the moment, I believe your suggestions are most convincing to get Iraq out from under the terrible attacks she's suffering through from these filthy jackals of this country. In the past few days, you spent much time stalking this loathsome American Leader. Give me what you have amassed on this fool so far, woman. So we might make a proper decision on his future fate."

Farseeha let out her breath in a deep sigh of victory as she placed out her notes before her and read from them. "On May 31st, Monday, day one, President Albert Cole came out of the White House at exactly eight thirty a.m. surrounded by his usual security guards, and also a number of worthless Senators and other people I did not know who they were who are with him to kiss his behind. They got in a limo and headed south on Pennsylvania Avenue. They returned in three hours, just the American President and his security detachment. I noticed two cars of security both following and leading the President's car. I believe the car is one of armor protection, with windows darken to make this American President a much harder target for snipers to hit. The American President left the White House again at three ten p.m. on the same day with his foul security guards in tow. At this point Captain Briegheeth, I'd deem it nearly impossible to get a clear shot at the fool, without it turning into a suicide mission.

"If we decide to kill the great fool, we'd be forced to wait until he exits the foul car to be vulnerable for our attack. The American President returned to the White House at eight oh one p.m. and remained inside the building for the full night. At no time did I see any other members of his worthless family. I believe they remained in the White House all the day. Tuesday, June 1st, the American President left the White House building at nine twenty a.m., and he was gone for the entire day. His wife and one child left the building at ten thirty one a.m., and they were driven by their usual group of security guards. They returned to the White House before three p.m. though. I believe the car his family rode in, was also of the armored type, Captain.

"At all times, security was present with the god cursed American family, making them an extremely hard target for us to get at. The cursed President returned at six oh five p.m., and he was surrounded with his usual security guards, they shield his body well. It was impossible to find a good attack angle against him. Again, I feel it'd be highly impossible to get and kill the President before his security personnel could react and shield him from our attack. Wednesday, June 2nd, the hated American President left White House at seven a.m. surrounded with seven security personnel, and a few men who I did not recognize or could identify becau..."

"There, you see Farseeha it is as I have offered to your worthless ears all along then woman. Everything I have told you about this target that you have leveled your foul eyes upon, makes it completely impossible for us to get at and kill the great fool who leads this country of lowly jackals. Your own words attest to this fact I have been telling you about all along, woman. Although the American President would serve our purposes very well, I feel to make an attempt against this man would be most foolish on our part. I have no intention of laying down my life on these foolish targets offered at this meeting, woman. I want to remain alive to fight with President Saddam Hussein when he finally drives the great Satan from our lands..."

"Captain Briegheeth, if you'll allow me to finish my report, you'll see what I have discovered on the fourth day of my observing him, about this target I have leveled my eyes upon."

The Iraqi Captain thought for a moment, and then he nodded slightly and replied to the rude way Farseeha had just offered to him. "Yes, you may continue with your god cursed foul words to me woman, you have my undivided attention, foolish one. Enlighten me on what you have observed on the next day of your surveillance of this foul target, Farseeha."

"On Thursday, June 3rd, the god cursed American President, along with seven of his usual security guards left the White House in three different vehicles this time, Captain Briegheeth. On this one day, I chose to follow them all the way to their final destination. Police cars soon joined the caravan of vehicles with the American President as they traveled through the streets of downtown Washington. I followed the fools to what they call Joint Base Andrews Air Force, where the worthless American President met with a number of other fools of his foul government, and then they all boarded Air Force One..."

"I hate to interrupt you Farseeha, again you tell us the American President is constantly surrounded by his security people, woman. How do you plan to overcome this great obstacle?"

"If you'll allow me to continue with my words without further interruptions, you'll see where I'm going with this, Captain Briegheeth." Farseeha offered to the Iraqi Army Officer.

Captain Briegheeth nodded, and then sat back in his chair again and seemed to relax a bit.

"Thank you Captain Briegheeth, I followed the American President to his private aircraft called Air Force One parked in a sequestered area on the massive airfield. I watched the great fool as he climbed the stairs, and at one point he stood fully out in the clear. An easy shot if one was positioned properly to take advantage of the situation when it is offered to that one, sir." Farseeha stared back at Captain Briegheeth as if she had just won the war with him.

"Yes Farseeha, if one was in the proper position to take the shot at the exact moment the American President is boarding the aircraft. I have been to Andrews Air Force on numerous occasions, thinking of the same attack you have just suggested to me. I have never found a good position in which to station myself to make the shot and kill. Again, I offer you there is no way this side of Paradise to get at the American President while he's in Washington, woman. Perhaps, if we were aware of where he was landing, we might set up something on that end."

"Betray not the sacred sands of Mecca fool, because you see out of the eyes that remain closed to all suggestion and sense, but the ones you have leveled your foolish eyes upon. How could you possibly think clearly of any attack on the American President with your mind closed to such an attack, Captain? In my eyes, I see a possibility of killing him in this manner. It seems at one point while boarding his precious aircraft he was most vulnerable and open to our attack. The guards have to give him room to walk up the steps without becoming a danger to him. It's at this point it gives us our attack angle. We have to take full advantage of this fact if we hope to kill this man. Captain Briegheeth, I beseech you to think of what I'm offering you. If we can kill the foolish American President, we'll free Iraq from the attacks by the United States warplanes."

The Iraqi Captain let out his breath in a disgusted sigh as he snapped nastily at the Arab woman. "Farseeha, I'll give your plan some further consideration, but I feel you owe it to us to listen to our suggestions, before we decide on what targets we'll hit, woman." Captain Briegheeth stared at Farseeha until he saw in her eyes, her giving into his latest suggestion.

"Yes, I'll listen, although I'm already aware of the foul targets you will offer, Captain."

"Thank you for this consideration Farseeha, though I must admit woman, my target is not of the same importance as yours might be. I think al-Qassan's offer has merit. It might be easier for us to get a Senator, rather than the President. I think we should look closer at his offer."

Farseeha shrugged and stared off into nothingness, as she tried to control her anger.

"Yes, I fully understand and I also see and feel your anger Farseeha, but you must give us your undivided attention as we listen to the other targets we want to speak of at this meeting between us." The leader of the small terrorist group barked at the female member of their group

"I promise you that I'll listen to every word spoken by either of you two fools, Captain." Farseeha hissed again.

Captain Briegheeth realized he was not going to get anywhere with Farseeha, and he gave up as he turned to al-Qassan and asked him. "Al-Qassan, I see that you have settled your eyes on this American Senator, err..."

"Yes you are correct Captain Briegheeth; I have selected this old American Senator John Hopkins as a possible target for our attention, sir." Al-Qassan offered quickly.

"Yes, Senator Hopkins you offer to me, and you believe this foolish old man is the power behind the American attacks lead against our country, young fool?" Captain Briegheeth inquired of the youth as he held him in his gaze while waiting for his response.

"Yes sir, I certainly believe that Captain Briegheeth." Al-Qassan replied confidently.

"Why do you believe this is as you have offered to me young al-Qassan? Please enlighten me of the fact you have amassed about this old fool young one."

"Because I studied this worthless man ever since I have first heard his name mentioned in conjunction with the ongoing bombing of our country, Captain Briegheeth. I had also read a number of articles written of this man from the GAO…"

"The GAO?" Captain Briegheeth interrupted quickly and then added. "What in Allah's great name is this GAO thing you speak to me of al-Qassan? I have never heard of these letters mentioned to me before this god cursed day, you young fool."

"Captain Briegheeth, those letters stand for the United States General Accountability Office, sir. This foul office releases many different reports about their foolish government and its inner most workings and wasteful ways of spending their taxpayer's money. It was here I discovered this worthless Senator Hopkins was in command of the Senate Oversight Committee that is funding the air attacks aimed against our country. Since first discovering this information sir, I have trailed the old fool on many different occasions, and discovered his walks in the gardens of the Capital, where he then steals cuttings from plants.

"Every time the old fool wanders about into the vast gardens, he's virtually without any real protection surrounding him. The security guards I have witnessed near him were a passing police officer who worked inside the evil Capital building. He nodded to the elderly Senator, and then the guard continued on his way. Evidently, everyone who works inside the Capital building is aware what the old man is up to, and they allow the great fool the privacy he needed to carry out his minor larceny of the flowers. I could have done away with the old fool many times while I kept him under surveillance, sir. The true reason this old man still breaths, was because I did not have your blessings to destroy him." Al-Qassan took a quick breath.

CHAPTER TWO

"From everything I heard uttered between both you and Farseeha. I see this target as the easiest one of the three to get at by us. Granted, he's not of the same great important as the American President is to our cause, or a Saudi Ambassador might be of more importance to our sacred mission. But this hateful old worthless American Senator seems to be our easiest target of the three for us to get at successfully. As Farseeha stated, Baghdad is growing impatient with our constant stalling to bring the continuing attacks by the hated American and English aircraft against our country to a final conclusion, sir. I don't wish to have the fearsome wrath of our great leader fall upon my worthless shoulders because of indecision we suffer over this mission..."

"Nor do I wish that event to ever happen to my head as well, al-Qassan." Captain Briegheeth offered with a smirk to the younger man.

"If not, I suggest we get to work on this Senator. Kill him, and see what the future has to bring forth." Al-Qassan smiled at the Captain, but Farseeha continued starring off in the distance.

Captain Briegheeth turned back to Farseeha, and he noticed the look on her face and chose to ignore it as he growled at her. "Farseeha, I think al-Qassan has picked the right target for us to concentrate our efforts against. One I'll witness myself, and if it is as he states. We'll go after this old fool of a worthless American Senator. If I discover this target is not such an easy one to get at then we'll weigh your suggestion once again. Will this satisfy your desires, woman?"

Farseeha snapped her head around in anger as she instantly exploded at the Iraqi Captain. "Faithful followers of the true Prophet's sacred words should not waste their valuable time with such small and worthless targets as you have suggested to me. I care not one bit if this stupid old worthless Senator sits upon a bench while waiting for death to finally visit his loathsome carcass. I say we still go after the hated American President, if we truly wish to stop the constant air attacks aimed upon our great country, fool. Anything short of killing the foolish American President is going to be nothing but a worthless waste of our time and efforts, and it'll also expose our terrorist cell to possible discovery by the disgusting Washington police authorities.

"I say we go after it all, or nothing at all Captain Briegheeth, and not waste this active cell on an ill gotten attack that'll net us not what we truly desire, or what we were sent to the United States to accomplish for our great President's wants, sir. Captain Briegheeth, if you chose to go after this great fool of an old worthless Senator. I'll not be part of your foul and misguided plan. I'll contact my control, and request a new terrorist cell be added to ours, and we'll go after the American Leader on our own and you can destroy this foolish Senator, Captain."

"Farseeha, you're truly at liberty to contact whomever the devil you may please to make contact with back in our country. But remember this foolish woman, at all times while this cell is operating in the United States. I'm the only one who is in command of this terrorist cell, until I'm told otherwise by my Commander in Iraq. It'll be as I have stated to your worthless ears, woman. I offer you this, I'll accompany al-Qassan, and I'll observe this foolish old Senator and his actions with my own eyes. If he's so open to our attack, we'll pick him out for our target, and see what happens after his worthless death. If I feel he's as hard a target as the American President, we'll drop back to your original plan. This is all I'm going to offer you, woman."

Farseeha's shoulders sagged, and Captain Briegheeth understood she just agreed to his offer without her saying so. He again turned his attention to al-Qassan and said. "Young al-Qassan, tomorrow I'll accompany you to the Capital Building, where I'll observe this old Senator. If I find him an easy target as you have offered, we'll kill him and then report to Baghdad for further orders and possible missions. I think we remained together for longer than is wise. Farseeha, you'll leave first, we'll meet the day after tomorrow here, once we had a chance to observe this old Senator's actions. You may leave woman, be aware make certain no one is following you. Don't draw attention to yourself, and disappear in the morning. One thing Farseeha, I don't wish you to appear anywhere near the White House any longer, until we settled upon our target..."

"But Captain Briegheeth, I was thinking of keeping my vigil on the American President for..."

"You will do no such thing, god cursed woman! You'll remain in hiding until the day after tomorrow, and that is a direct order to you and you shall obey that order, Farseeha!" Captain Briegheeth interrupted as he snapped at the proud looking female terrorist.

"A thousand pardons for my harsh words offered to you before sir. I'm afraid there's no sense for you and the foolish young al-Qassan to go anywhere near the foul Capital Building tomorrow morning, Captain Briegheeth." Farseeha warned her Commander with a smirk on her lips, as she placed her hands on her hips and then she stared angrily at Captain Briegheeth.

"And why is that, angry woman born from the hot desert sands? I warn you god cursed woman, I have no time or patience to argue any further with you on this most foul of days, Farseeha. Persist any further against me with your most upsetting words and resistance against me and al-Qassan, and your eyes will not see tomorrow's sunrise, woman. I'll tie hot bags of ash to your god cursed face, until you beg for death to wrap her icy fingers around your foul and god cursed throat, and bring an end to the torment I'll do to your worthless body. If you persist with your constantly bringing up your wanted target to my exhausted ears and burning, woman!" Captain Briegheeth glared hotly at the young Arab woman standing before him with her hands still resting on her hips in an angry and threatening fashion, while staring at him.

"Don't dare to try and threaten me like that, you great fool you. Because I fear not your empty words and worthless threats leveled against my person, or your thought to be in complete power you think you hold over us. Tomorrow is Sunday fool, and unless I miss my guess, there are never any foolish American Senators hanging around the foul Capital Building on this day, sir. Most of the great fools are trying to get their foul faces on the local television programs, Captain." Farseeha leaned back and then gave Captain Briegheeth a huge grin of triumph.

The Iraqi Captain continued to glare at his young female terrorist for a long moment, knowing he forgot about tomorrow being Sunday. It was embarrassing for him to be caught in the middle of a mistake such as this one was, especially because he was supposed to be the leader and controlling the actions of this small terrorist cell. Being caught in a mistake as he just was, usurped his command of the other two young terrorists from his cell.

Fighting to get his raging anger under control, Captain Briegheeth angrily turned away from the smug looking Farseeha and placed his attention and anger loose upon al-Qassan's head as he howled at the young man. "This is entirely your fault you young fool of the desert sands! I should cut your foul throat with my Jambiya blade for allowing me to be made the fool of. Why the hell did not you remind me tomorrow was Sunday, young fool? Am I supposed to think of everything for this god cursed terrorist cell to operate properly with? Remember everything we have to do in order to accomplish our mission for our President and country, young fool? Al-Qassan, I'll remember this terrible error on your part, and at the proper time. I shall seek my revenge upon your foul head for your failure to the security of this cell."

Al-Qassan put his head down and then he stared at the floor, fearing for his life and the anger of the upset Captain being aimed at him. He knew well of Captain Briegheeth's unfettered anger and ruthful, and what he was capable of doing to anyone who he believed failed him.

Farseeha came over to the younger al-Qassan's aid as she offered in his defense to her Commander. "Captain Briegheeth, it is not al-Qassan's fault for this minor mistake in the least, sir. It truly is no one's fault I offer you, Captain. Many times in the past, I have forgotten what day it was myself, or the time of day it was as well, sir."

Captain Briegheeth took Farseeha's aid of the young man as a sign of weakness in her person. Feeling he was again excreting his command over the terrorist cell, he barked nastily at her. "Farseeha, we'll meet again on next Tuesday at exactly four thirty p.m. At that time woman, we should have all of what we need to make a decision on which target we'll go after."

The still angry Iraqi Captain did not wait for her reply as he turned to al-Qassan and warned him hotly. "Monday, I'll meet with you by the small mail box across from the god cursed Capital Building at nine a.m. sharp, fool. We'll observe this old Senator you have suggested for death, together. We'll make like we're visiting the seat of Satan in Washington on vacation. Carry no weapons on your foul person for this god cursed visit, or anything else that might identify you as an Arab or a possible terrorist. You have your driver's license with you, al-Qassan?"

"Yes sir, I shall be waiting for you to arrive there patiently at the position you have ordered me to wait for your arrival, my brother Captain Briegheeth."

"The driver's license that identifies you as an American visitor from Ohio, you young fool of a pup?" Captain Briegheeth glared at the young Arab man, while waiting for his reply to him.

"Yes Sir I have it with me at all times as you instructed Captain Briegheeth. I'll make certain I have those identifying papers on my person with me when we meet at the Capital Building, Captain." The youngest member of the terrorist cell replied to the leader of the group.

"Good, make certain it is with you on Monday as I ordered, fool. Bring your cameras with you, and wear clothes the police are used to seeing worn by the foolish visitors to Washington."

"Yes, I'll do as you have ordered me Captain Briegheeth." The young one replied.

"Farseeha, I believe it's time for you to leave our presence at this time, woman. Remember foul woman, the date and time for our next scheduled meeting to take place. It's Tuesday, at four thirty p.m., we'll meet here at that time as ordered, woman." Captain Briegheeth stared angrily at Farseeha, until she turned and quickly left the small and filthy room.

Farseeha rose swiftly, nodded and then she left the apartment without uttering any further words to either of the other two other members of the terrorist cell.

Captain Briegheeth waited for more than fifteen minutes to pass, before he dared to order the young al-Qassan to leave the room next. He wanted to make certain Farseeha had left the area, and there was no trouble from the local police as she left the filthy apartment. He was going to remain behind for another hour, before he dared to leave the apartment himself. This was a precaution he was taking, to safeguard himself and the rest of his fellow terrorists from the cell. He did not want to be captured, if the local police authorities were following either of the other two terrorists he was involved with.

MONDAY, JUNE 7th, 1999. 9 A.M. EST, WASHINGTON DC. THE CAPITAL BUILDING

The commanding Iraqi terrorist Captain Jebril Briegheeth, walked casually away from Independence Avenue, and he headed straight for the east front area of the massive Capital Building. Mamdouh al-Qassan already informed Captain Briegheeth that Senator Hopkins always enjoyed his private little walks in the West Garden of the Capital grounds, and he usually rested for a while on a bench under the American elm tree with the brass Good Templars Tree plaque, nailed to one of the oldest trees in the vast garden. This tree stood almost by itself, but there were a few clumps of gathered trees on either side of it, a short distance away from the bench with many avenues of escape, if they were to kill the elderly American Senator while he was in the garden grounds. To the left of this well aged tree, were ten other but younger trees, some thick bushes and walkways on which to successfully flee the area if they decided to kill the Senator.

Captain Briegheeth walked down the path to the Capital Building. He was acting like anyone else who was visiting the beautiful building and area. He stopped when he saw the mail box and al-Qassan waiting for him looking more like a sightseer than most visitors in Washington. The younger terrorist was snapping pictures and did not notice the Iraqi Captain coming at him from the narrow footpath. The Iraqi Captain walked up to al-Qassan before he even noticed him. The young one lowered the camera and quickly closed the gap between them.

"Where is this old fool of an American Senator you have chosen for death, hiding at, al-Qassan? I see no one who even looks like this important man." Captain Briegheeth demanded hotly to know as soon as he was able to ask the young one a question,

"Captain Briegheeth, the old fool should be coming out of the god cursed foul building near eleven a.m., sir. He usually makes his rounds through the worthless garden at around that time every day he is here, especially after a weekend away from the loathsome building of jackals, sir. I guess he wants to see what grew while he was away over the weekend, Captain."

"I hope this is true, al-Qassan. I don't particularly want to waste my time, if he does not show up as scheduled. I don't trust Farseeha one bit, the lowly witch is capable of committing any crime she desires, young fool. Especially when the sand witch is out of my sight and control."

Without speaking further to al-Qassan, Captain Briegheeth turned and walked towards the area he was informed this Senator Hopkins headed for on his daily break, al-Qassan followed him in silence with his head hanging down. The two used the pedestrian walk that circled the target area. They walked until they came across a bench just off the footpath, resting under the Bradford Pear Tree honoring Representative Olin E. Teague, planted on March 23rd, 1979. The bench rested at a crosswalk that went under the overpass for vehicles to use in the area. It was a perfect place for them to wait, to see what the Senator did when he was out on his break.

From this position, the two Iraqi terrorists had a clear view of the bench usually used by the unsuspecting elderly Senator. Captain Briegheeth opened a book as al-Qassan continued to snap pictures of the area like many other tourist were doing. Two police officers on foot passed and smiled as al-Qassan snapped their picture. The Iraqi Captain thought this was good, because what terrorist would dare expose himself to the local police by taking their picture.

The time passed slowly, with the Iraqi Captain trying to keep his interest in the book, while constantly looking over the rim of it, to see if the Senator might come out earlier than expected.

Like clock work and as al-Qassan had offered, at eleven a.m. sharp, many Senators came marching down the wide stairway of the Capital Building. Then they quickly fanned out, with each going their own way. Captain Briegheeth closed his book and stuffed it under his arm, and then he crossed his legs as he stared at the powerful men and women separating from each other. He kept an eye on them until he noticed an old man in an expensive suit and obviously important, cut across the lawn with no one yelling at him for doing so. He held his breath as he studied the elderly man as he moved, stopping just long enough to check the condition of a bush in blossom.

Al-Qassan snapped a picture of the massive stairway and then mumbled. "That is the Senator."

"I gathered that much for myself, young fool born from camel piss. Who are those other people with the old fool? Are they going to stop him from damaging the god cursed plants?"

"I don't know who the others might be with the foul Senator, sir. This is the first time anyone has ever followed the old fool out of the cursed building. We'll have to be patient Captain."

"I don't like this one bit al-Qassan. It looks like they are security guards walking with the old man, fool. I thought you told me no one ever followed the old man around the worthless gardens. If they are security guards then this worthless target is out of the question for our needs, fool."

"Please Captain Briegheeth, I beg you be patient, I'm certain the guards are not following him."

"Maybe, and I hope for your worthless sake they are not guarding this foul old Senator you have marked for his death, you young fool you." Captain Briegheeth snarled nastily at the other terrorist as he trained his eyes on the old American Politician. The guards followed the elderly Senator closely to the park bench, and they waited as he opened the bag and removed a sandwich. The Senator ate in silence and alone. The guards took up positions around the bench, and they watched everyone moving about the large garden. One of the guards actually looked at Captain Briegheeth, who pulled the book from under his arm and fanned through the pages.

When he returned to his book, the security guard instantly lost interest in him and his actions, and he shifted his attention back to a young man and woman walking and talking together, while pushing a baby carriage. The Iraqi Captain watched as the guard then spoke into his sleeve and shifted his eyes to where the guard was staring.

Two other security guards came from out of nowhere, and they stopped the two young people walking with the baby carriage. One guard spoke to the man, while the other faked interest in seeing the infant child in the carriage. Once the security guards were satisfied the couple were no threat against the Senator's life, they quickly disappeared into the surrounding area. After seeing the security suddenly surrounding the elderly Senator, Captain Briegheeth immediately removed the Senator from his hit list, after witnessing the security guards surrounding him now. If this old Senator was so well protected with this much security, he would be possibly a harder target than the American President himself for them to kill the man.

The Iraqi Captain shifted his harsh glare at al-Qassan and hissed angrily at the young man. "Son of a lowly jackal, you told me this old man always walked around the worthless Capital Building without any security around him? You embarrassed me greatly with this blunder, fool."

"Please Captain Briegheeth; I don't understand what has happened on this god cursed day, sir. Every time I have watched the worthless Senator in the past, he has always walked around the gardens by himself, sir. No security surrounding him, never once in the many times I watched him, sir. Something must have happened to change the protection of the Senators."

"Fool born of a camel piss, don't dare to talk to me like a bazaar merchant trying to sell me on their pack of lies and worthless wears. Evidently young fool, the security was always there, it is just you who have failed to observe it before this hated day. I warn you young fool, I'll make my report which will not be in your favor I assure you, dog of the cold night."

"Shall we leave the area before someone takes notice of our presence sir?" Al-Qassan asked.

"Don't be so foolish as to try and compound your pointless error, by making more worthless suggestions to me, foolish jackal. Continue taking your foul pictures of the surrounding area. If you were to flee now, you'll surely draw much attention to yourself and to me by the security of the Senator, young fool." Captain Briegheeth growled nastily as he returned to his book and then completely ignored the younger Arab man standing so near to him.

FARSEEHA

Retaining her anger at Captain Briegheeth, Farseeha walked into the Libyan Embassy, and she showed her identification card to the soldier manning the front desk. He barely took any notice of her presence as he stared at the red star printed on the top of the card. Shaking, he rose while staring at the ID and offered to the young woman. "One moment please Ma'am."

Within seconds, the shaken young Libyan soldier returned, followed by a second but much older soldier, obviously an officer. The guard stopped by his desk as the officer walked around it and loudly snapped his heels together, and then he bowed politely to the young and pretty woman as he offered her his hand. Once they shook hands, the Libyan Officer said nothing more to her, as he moved closer to the Iraqi female, and then quickly and expertly searched Farseeha's exquisite body, taking special care when checking around her breasts and rearend, for any possible hidden weapons or listening devices hidden on her person.

Farseeha knew the Libyan guard was taking liberties with her body, but she needed this lowly dog's assistance, and she was prepared to allow him the little pleasures he was enjoying.

When the officer finished his search of her body, he stepped back and then announced in a commanding tone to her. "Good morning Agent Farseeha al-Mana. I'm Captain Badawlhmed Nabih Khamis, of the Libyan Secret Police. I'm sorry for the search of your body, but one has to be very cautious these days. I was warned in advance by your contact that you might be making connection with me in the near future, woman. Would you like a cup of tea al-Mana?"

"Is that what you call what you did to my body, Captain Khamis. The way you searched me, I thought you were trying to guess my weight, sir." Farseeha offered with a smirk as she nodded in the positive, knowing the Libyan Captain wanted to get her out of the eye of the public, and well away from the main door to the Libyan Embassy as quickly as possible.

Captain Badawlhmed laughed over the female Iraqi Agent's remark, and then he turned without further words and headed for a private office. When Farseeha entered it, he immediately closed the door behind her, and then he walked over to his desk as he pointed towards a chair sitting across from him. When she was seated, the Libyan Captain flipped on the intercom and said into the machine. "Halima, bring tea in, two cups please."

The two sat in silence as they waited for the tea to be delivered. A youngish Arab woman entered the private office without knocking, placed a tray on a side table and then left quickly.

"Please, help yourself Farseeha. I'm certain you'll find the tea to your liking, young lady."

"Can I pour you a cup of tea to enjoy as well, Captain Khamis? I'd be please to do so for you."

"Please do that would be pleasant Farseeha." Captain Badawlhmed waited to be served by the beautiful Iraqi Agent, and when she was seated he grumbled. "Why have you come to me?"

"I'm in need of weapons to carry out a mission for my country, Captain Khamis."

"For what mission do you speak before me I ask of you, Farseeha?"

"I'm on a sacred mission for my country and for my President, Captain Khamis."

"I'm aware of that much myself, woman. What is this mission you speak of Farseeha?"

"It's secret at this time Captain." Farseeha snapped as she glared hard at the Libyan, insulted he tried to get what her mission was. Something no one supporting a terrorist action would try.

"My dear Farseeha, there are no secrets between fellow Arabs working for a common cause."

"I understand this Captain, but I still cannot inform you of my mission, sir." Farseeha insisted.

Captain Badawlhmed leaned forward in his chair and placed his cup on his desk, and growled at the Iraqi Agent nastily. "Huh, and you come here expecting me to supply you with weapons, yet you refuse to inform me of what your intended target in the United States might be, woman? Nonsense, if you wish to keep your god cursed worthless target secret from me. Then I suggest you find another supplier to support this mission for your worthless country and leader."

Farseeha knew if she wanted to enlist the support of the crafty Libyan Officer, she was forced to confide in this Captain of her future plans. "Captain Badawlhmed, I want to kill the American President, I believe with his god cursed death, it'll cause a stop to the hated attacks aimed against my country by the American aircraft, sir. But the fool running this cell is intent with wasting his foul time going after some useless old Senator of this country. I know with the lowly Senator's death, the Americans will not change their ways and beliefs against Iraq. But, with the American President dead, I'm certain they'll have a quick change of heart towards my country, sir."

Captain Badawlhmed eyebrows arched with surprise. He knew this woman was correct, if she truly wanted the bombing stopped, they would have to set their eyes on a large fish. And what larger fish was there than the American President. The remark of the leader of the cell wasting his time on another target flew over his head as the Libyan remarked. "Err... your decision to go after the hated American Leader is most correct Farseeha. If he's your main target then you can count on any help from my government. Farseeha, what is it I can do for you and your cell?"

"Captain Badawlhmed, I have much need of a number of weapons to carry out my attack against the American President successfully, sir."

"Your attack you offer me woman? Of course, yes, yes you do at that, don't you woman. But why did you not go through your normal contacts to receive these much needed weapons for this sacred mission you speak of before me, Farseeha?"

"That's a slight problem with my normal contact here in the United States, Captain Badawlhmed. Anything coming into the United States from Iraq, is extremely scrutinized lately sir. We're certain American custom agents are going through items sent from Iraq under the protection of the diplomatic pouch as well, sir. The items free of searches are the items brought to this country carried by our diplomats on their person only, Captain. But even there, these items are sent through their god cursed X-ray machines, and the contents carefully searched that way, Captain Badawlhmed. This is why it's necessary for me to beg your country for help, sir."

The Libyan Captain Badawlhmed was well aware of this procedure usually carried out by the American Customs Officers he was informed by his people stationed in Iraq. He was made aware of this woman coming to him seeking his help on their orders. The Libyan Officer was ordered to give any and all aid to Farseeha, if she showed up at his office requesting his assistance.

Captain Badawlhmed swiped at his brow at the sweat threatening to burn his eyes, as he replied in a harsh tone of voice to the young Iraqi woman waiting for his reply to her request for help. "Farseeha, I assure you woman it's my privilege to assist a fellow Arab country being raped by the lowly American jackals. What weapons do you seek from me, young lady?"

"I don't know of the weapons I'll need to carry out my mission successfully, sir. I hoped to draw upon your expertise in this case, sir. I do know what I want though, Captain."

"Good, good, perhaps if I was made aware of your intent, I can better determine what type of weapons would serve your needs most correctly, Farseeha." Captain Badawlhmed wanted as much information as he could gather about this upcoming attack on the American President.

Farseeha knew she did not have a choice in the matter. She had to tell this filthy Libyan dog, everything about her future mission, if she was going to draw upon his help. She slowly went over her plan to kill the American President as he boarded Air Force One with the Captain.

As she went over her idea with the concern Libyan Officer, Captain Badawlhmed pulled a weapons book from his top desk drawer, and then he thumbed through it. Finding the weapons he searched for, he interrupted the young female terrorist as he offered her. "Farseeha, I have many weapons at my disposal resting in the Embassy. The first weapon I shall offer to you is a Russian made RPG-7 (Rocket Propelled Grenade). This weapon will destroy the entire aircraft, as well as eliminate your target at the same time, and all those foolish enough to be with him."

"Captain, I did not plan to destroy the entire aircraft itself, and all the fools with the American President. I fear such a powerful attack would only serve to strengthen the resolve of our enemy against my severely damaged country, sir. What is the range of this weapon you offer for my needs, sir?" she asked the Libyan Officer with concern in her tone.

"Not very much I fear woman, only three hundred and twenty eight yards I believe it is. And, it also leaves a well telltale trail, which would lead the survivors' of your attack and the President's protector's right to your hidden position, Farseeha."

"Then I must refuse this weapon's use Captain. I don't want this to be a suicide mission, sir."

"Ohhhhh, I thought you were well prepared to enter Paradise with the head of your god cursed enemy locked within your faithful hands for Muhammad's enjoyment, Farseeha?" The Libyan Operative replied rather smugly to the female Iraqi agent as he allowed a smirk to his lips.

"No not at all Captain Badawlhmed, this is not a suicide mission in the least, we want to live in order to fight on for our country's freedom and needs, sir. Iraq needs all the fighters she has and more, to continue their sacred fight against the great land of sin and lust, sir. What purpose would it serve me, to die in only one attack aimed against our hated enemy? A good and true soldier is smart enough to carry out his mission, yet live to fight on for another day for his country and President's sake, sir. What other weapons do you have to offer?"

"Yes, of course, I see what you're saying young woman, and I agree with you completely. Well Farseeha, I have the latest in snipers' weapons available to me, usually employed by our hated enemy on the battlefield. It's well known as the MacMillian Model M-88, fifty caliber weapon that fires the same ammunition as does the Browning fifty mm M-2 machine gun. It's accurate after fifteen thousand yards, and well beyond that yardage as well, woman."

"This sounds like a better weapon for my need Captain, is it a heavy weapon to use, sir?"

"Yes, I fear this is so woman, and it's hard to conceal, Farseeha. It's a weapon to be carried while in combat whole, not broken down for concealment and such sniper attacks, woman."

"Then I'm sorry to offer Captain Badawlhmed, but again I find myself being forced to refuse the weapon you offered for my use in this attack, sir. I'm searching for a weapon that can be carried easily, concealed completely until needed, yet have a long enough range and accuracy for me to complete my mission successfully against the hated American Leader of this country, sir."

"Huh, I don't mind saying for a terrorist, you're making this rather hard for me to be of proper assistance for your unending needs, young woman. Any terrorist would give his bladder for the weapons I have just offered for your needs. I'll continue searching my list of weapons until I locate one that suits your fancy perfectly woman. But I warn you woman, don't be so fussy about this situation, Farseeha. My patience and support will wan quickly if I feel you're wasting my time and you are here just fishing to know what weapons I have at my disposal, woman."

Flipping through the many pages further, Captain Badawlhmed settled on a weapon he was certain was not going to be agreed to by this young Iraqi female agent. But he offered it because he wanted to keep the pressure on her, and forcing her to pay attention to what he was offering her. "Farseeha, here is another such weapon I see, it's a Russian made one used mostly by the worthless Hungarian soldiers. A sniper's weapon it is also, woman. If it's good enough for our Russian friends and their worthless allies then it has to be well suited for Iraqi terrorists and their needs." Captain Badawlhmed offered sarcastically to the young woman.

Farseeha overlooked the Captain's obvious smug and nasty tone he employed against her this time, as she leaned forward and looked at the picture of the weapon. She could easily tell it was heavy, but she allowed him to make his little speech to her before she refused the weapon.

Captain Badawlhmed moved the book so Farseeha could get a better look at the offered weapon as he announced proudly to her. "It's called the Destroyer. It's fourteen point five mm recoil, semi automatic rifle; it has an effective range of one thousand, two hundred yards. Huh, I can see by the expression upon your foul face that you're not very interested in this weapon I offer for your use as well, woman. Perhaps, I can find another to your likes, but what I have is very limited I fear. I think it'd be a good idea, if we use a Russian built weapon to kill the hated American Leader. It'll help keep the searchers in a state of constant confusion, on whom to try and fix the true blame on for the attack against the American Leader, Farseeha."

"I agree, but can we look a little further in the book perhaps, Captain Badawlhmed? I truly need a weapon that would make my mission successful."

Without replying to Farseeha's last words, the Libyan Operative continued to flip through the remaining pages of his weapon's book, finding another weapon for her needs he mumbled to her. "Ahhh... here we go, this cursed weapon has to agree with your needs completely, woman. It's an English made foul weapon, used for sniping and taking out heads of government without causing much secondary damage. It's the A 196- A 1 sniper's rifle. It has a seven point six two round bolt action with a Bender six by forty two scope. Arrr... it's a very limited weapon, with an effective range of only one thousand yards. This one is no good for your needs I fear woman. I should have known, the foolish and useless English, bah."

Captain Badawlhmed flipped through the next few pages of the book in anger this time. He already knew of the weapon he was going to force Farseeha to settle on for her use on this mission. But he was taking his time getting to the weapon. The wise Libyan Officer stopped searching the book now, his finger holding the pages separated as he looked up at Farseeha, and then he snapped at her in a hot tone of voice. "Young woman, this next weapon I'll offer for your needs, is the last one I have available to me here at the Embassy. It's the one you must settle upon I'm afraid, Farseeha. I believe it'll properly serve your purpose quite well though, woman."

Farseeha leaned forward on the desk and then waited for the Libyan to open the book again.

This time, Captain Badawlhmed did not offer Farseeha a good look at the picture of the weapon, as he opened the book and read the specifications of the weapon to her. "Before I start Farseeha, I must warn you young woman, this is a heavy weapon to use in the field, that requires a tripod to fire the weapon true at your intended target, woman. It's the only weapon that offers a break down feature that enables the weapon to be easily hidden and transported..."

"Hmmm... I want to know how much the weapon weighs, Captain Badawlhmed."

"Thirty pounds I fear woman, but this weapon has an effective range of over two thousand, seven hundred and fifty yards. It has a muzzle flash suppresser, and it's a silenced weapon as well which offers you stealth on your faithful hunt. It comes with a seven round clip and it's the fifty inch Barrett rifle, a fifty caliber weapon with a reputation of clean kills at ranges of over one thousand, seven hundred yards, used during the American invasion of your great country woman. This weapon is guaranteed to deliver massive injury to the target at greater range than most other weapons used in this field. It employs the Leupold and Stevens ten x scope. I suggest you place this weapon on a hard surface, because the muzzle brake will send a cloud of dust up, and make it possible for you enemy's support teams to locate your position before you can abandon the weapon. How far away from your intended target will you be setting up shop for the kill, Farseeha? You do have the location already picked out to kill your target, right woman?"

"Captain Badawlhmed, I picked out an abandoned old water tower off the American Airbase for our base of operations, sir. It's over one thousand and fifty yards away from the target, sir."

"Then this weapon will serve your purpose perfectly I offer you, Farseeha. What other weapons in the way of support will you be requiring from me and my country, woman?" Captain Badawlhmed displayed the scorn most Arab men displayed towards the women of their culture when dealing with them. Even thought Farseeha was a terrorist equal with the men of her cell, the Libyan Captain Badawlhmed still regarded her as a lowly female in her country's employ.

"Captain Badawlhmed, I fear you're in a far better position to offer me the support weapons I'll need for this operation, than I can request from you, sir." Although Farseeha knew the weapons she would need and wanted, she still offered a compliment to the Libyan Officer.

Captain Badawlhmed nodded politely over the kind compliment just offered him by the female terrorist as he replied pleasantly. "Farseeha, I'll supply you with the M-16 Colt Commando with a retractable stock, and the nine mm Heckler and Koch MP-5 sub machine gun for your extra firepower. How many weapons will you be requiring from me, woman?" This was another way for Captain Badawlhmed to glean information from the Iraqi terrorist by her telling him how many weapons she needed, she would inform him of how many persons were in her cell.

"Captain I'll have need of one of the sniper rifles, two MP-5s, and one M-16, sir."

"What! You mean to tell me you only have four members in your working cell, woman?"

"Yes sir, we have decided to travel quite light on this sacred mission Captain, to better enable us to hit hard and then disappear quickly, before anyone can figure out what had just taken place, sir." She lied, she knew full well if she admitted to having only three members in her terrorist cell, the wise Libyan Officer might balk, fearing they will be easily overwhelmed by the President's personal security staff, and be taken prisoner by the American authorities.

"Four fools you are working with in all! What are the precautions you have set in place in case you foul fools are taken prisoners by the hated American security forces, Farseeha?" Captain Badawlhmed did not want the small group of terrorists captured, fearing under drug induced interrogation, the fact Libya supplied them with the weapons they needed might come out.

"We carry cyanide and are not afraid to lay down our lives for the sake of our country, sir."

"Very well then Farseeha. I suggest you come back tonight alone, after nine p.m. woman. I'll have the weapons you need ready and waiting here for you. I'll also include enough ammunition for the weapons to entertain a strong firefight before taking precautions of not becoming prisoners by the authorities, Farseeha." Captain Badawlhmed was warning Farseeha in no uncertain terms no one from her cell better be taken alive, if their operation went sour on them.

Farseeha bowed politely and then she quickly left the office. As she was leaving, she turned back and barked at the Libyan Operative. "I shall return at nine as I was ordered, sir."

When she was out of the office, Captain Badawlhmed immediately picked up the phone and he placed a secured call out to his contact in the Secret Police operating in Iraq.

CHAPTER THREE

THE ROLANDS MOTEL, ROOM 17, WASHINGTON D.C.
MONDAY, JUNE 7th, 1999. 4:30 P.M. EST

Captain Jebril Briegheeth and al-Qassan remained on the Capital grounds until late, before daring to leave the area for fear of arousing any suspicions, because the security surrounding the building and grounds was still very heavy as they left. The Iraqi Captain drove back to their motel, and then ordered al-Qassan to meet him there. He left his book resting on the park bench because he wanted to talk to the young terrorist privately, before having to deal with the always firry Farseeha again. Captain Briegheeth desired to come up with some kind of excuse for his shifting his attention from the Senator, and locking his eyes on Farseeha's selected target now.

The two Iraqi terrorists entered the shabby, rundown terrible smelling room in complete silence, al-Qassan following his leader in. When he was in the room, he sat down on the couch with his eyes cast down towards the floor, waiting for his fuming Commander to really lace into him. But the scolding never came as Captain Briegheeth entered carrying two cold beers. Al-Qassan took the offered beer as if it was his last offering, before he faced the firing squad.

Captain Briegheeth saw the slight tremble in the young man's hands and laughed, proud his mere presence could bring the young al-Qassan so much fear, as he grumbled at the youthful man. "Fool of foul fools, I'm not that angry with you, jackal. It was a mistake, one unforeseen and unavoidable I believe. Something must have happened for the security to tighten so strongly around the god cursed elderly Senator. Now, all we have to do is try and convince the loathsome Farseeha that I have changed my mind to her target because I had a change of heart, and I now believe the foolish American President is the proper target for us to aim our efforts against."

"What do you want me to tell her, Captain?" Al-Qassan asked with concern in his tone.

"Fool of an camel's ass, you shall tell her I saw this worthless old fool of a Senator you wanted to kill, and after viewing his foul existence, I have decided he was not a worthy target for our aims after all, fool. To kill such a foolish and worthless old man of little importance, would not interrupt the many air attacks being carried out against our country for a single day."

"Do you not think she'll believe such a tall story as this one that you shall offer her, Captain?"

"I don't care one worthless grain of sand from the vast desert of our country what she believes or does not believe, young al-Qassan. She's operating under my direct orders, young fool. As much as she'd like to believe she's the one truly in Command of this god cursed terrorist cell and operation, she's not. I am, and I curse the sands of the burning deserts for giving women the power to even think. It should be as it was in the past times of our lands, al-Qassan. Women should be attentive to their husband's needs and wants, and not wasting their foolish time trying to be a man. If Allah wanted women in his Army, he would have given them the spout to piss with, so they don't have to squat in the sands to piss. I'm going to register a strong complaint with my control to have her removed from this cell. She adds mass confusion and anger to my way of thinking, something I don't need if we're to be successful in our mission."

"You must be very wary of her most upsetting presence I fear, Captain Briegheeth Sir? I warn you Captain, Farseeha has extremely important friends in very high places back in Iraq, sir. She might be a very formidable enemy to cross swords with I fear, sir."

"The day I have to fear a lowly woman's presence standing before me, is the day I shall knock upon the Gates of Paradise with my penis resting in my god cursed hand. Al-Qassan, do you have your foolish story straight why we have decided to use her target instead of your pick, fool?"

"Yes Captain Briegheeth Sir, I'll not make another mistake for a second time, sir."

"You better not young fool, because I'm not a very forgiving man for a second time if you fail my needs. It's only because I have future need of your foul assistance that I'll not complain to my control of your most stupid of errors with the worthless American Senator, al-Qassan. Finish your foul beer before it gets warm on you, Jackal." Captain Briegheeth drank his beer, he had no idea Farseeha had made contact with the Libyan Officer in search of their needed weapons. If he had, he would have killed her on the spot, for daring to go over his head in this manner.

THE LIBYAN EMBASSY

The wise and cautious Libyan Captain Badawlhmed Nabih Khamis immediately placed a call to the Iraqi Ministry of Special Police stationed in the Iraq capital of Baghdad, and he asked to speak to an old friend he had dealt with many times in the past. He waited for a few moments not so calmly waited for until they finally located the man he wanted to speak with.

"Yes Captain Badawlhmed Nabih Khamis, what is it you want of me, sir? I'm a rather busy man at the moment, sir. The god cursed American warplanes are again over the skies of Iraq, and they are attacking my forces in the southern zone of my country, and I must move my missiles to avoid their cursed weapons and destruction, sir. At any other time Captain; I assure you it would be a great pleasure to speak with you of past times we have enjoyed together, my old friend."

Ignoring General al-Zahar's rush to stop speaking with him so fast, Captain Badawlhmed spoke quickly, as if he was the first one to offer words in this conversation. "A thousand pardons for this most untimely interruption of your many problems General Hassan al-Zahar. I have just spoken with a young female who claims to be an active Agent from your great country, sir. Who was in search of weapons from me to carry out an assassination attempt in the United States, General? When I spoke with her, she bantered about names most impressive to my foul ears, sir. Your name was the first one on her list she dared to display before me, General al-Zahar.

"At first, I wasn't going to entertain her foul presence in my office a foul woman in charge of a terrorist cell is most unthinkable General al-Zahar. But these trying times make for desperate measures to be taken, this I understand all too well, my Arab brother. When this foul woman first mentioned your name, I decided to see her. I'm calling you to make certain she's truly in your employ, and she is not a foul Agent for the hated American government as I believe she is, sir."

"Yes, go on my old friend, because you have captured my attention, Captain Badawlhmed. As far as I'm aware, there are only two terrorist cells in operation in the land of Satan, sir. Both cells are sleepers at the moment. No one here issued them permission to activate themselves. They were to sleep until I activated them personally, sir. What was the name of this lowly woman who turned up on your front doorstep, my Arab brother?" General al-Zahar placed a lesser Officer in charge of moving the missile sites under pressure from the hated American and United Kingdom warplanes as he continued speaking with the Libyan Officer. His agents in the field were more important to him than his missiles, and if one of his terrorist cells was going active, he wanted to know about it and why they activated. He was furious he was not informed by the cell manager, before they dared approach the Libyan fool. He felt extremely suspicious and angry.

"Yes my faithful Arab brother of many years past, her lowly name is Farseeha al-Mana, sir."

Letting out his breath in a disgusted sigh, General al-Zahar growled harshly into the phone this time. "Yes, that one, she's an Operative of mine, Captain. But she's not the one who is truly in Command of any terrorist cell I know of, sir. Allow me a moment until I find out the name of the supposed Commander she's supposed to be working with, sir."

Badawlhmed heard General al-Zahar fishing through papers and waited for him to finish.

"Yes, yes here it is my old friend the one in Command of the terrorist cell is Captain Jebril Briegheeth, sir. I pray Allah nothing has happened to the great fool, and Farseeha has not taken over the Command of this small terrorist cell I Command, sir. Although she's a good fighter and Agent, her temper overrules her better judgment most of the cursed time I fear, Captain. The great Prophet Himself has cursed her with the weakness of a woman's god cursed mind, to battle with in a man's world. That's the reason she'll never be in full Command of any terrorist cell as long as I'm alive, sir. She is a wildcat, careless and one who sees out of eyes clouded over with hatred and blind rage and anger. Did Farseeha happen to mention Captain Briegheeth to you sir? If he's still in Command of the god cursed cell I personally sent into the United States, sir?"

"No General al-Zahar, she had made no mention of this man you just spoke of to me, sir. The way she spoke to me, made me certain and believe that she was the one who was truly in fill Command of this terrorist cell operating in this god cursed country of lowly jackals and fools. What do you want me to do about the weapons she has begged from me, General al-Zahar?"

"I wish I knew if Captain Briegheeth was alright and still active and part of this cell, sir. How many weapons did this foolish woman request from you to support this foul cell's operation?"

"The worthless woman has demanded three assault rifles, and one heavy sniper weapon was the weapons requested by the worthless woman, General al-Zahar."

"Hmmm... then that means all three of the foul members in the cell must still be alive, sir."

"Three terrorists in this working active cell! General al-Zahar, this foul woman has lead me to believe there were four in her cursed cell, and the reason I placed this call to you, was to request you add a fifth fighter to this lowly terrorist cell, sir. I wanted to make certain this foul woman was working for you as she had offered to me, General. You know we like to have a five man team when a terrorist cell is activated. May Allah curse all women who walk in a man's world."

"Captain Badawlhmed, I had changed this attack cell to a three man hit unit, because I had requested them to locate a target that would cause the stoppage of the ongoing assault aimed against my country, by the hated Coalition Forces and their god dom warplanes..."

"Well my Arab brother, this woman's aiming at the right target to accomplish this feat, sir."

"What is this you offer me Captain Badawlhmed? You're aware of her intended target, sir?"

"Yes, General al-Zahar, I am at that General al-Zahar. I know of her intended target, sir."

"By Allah's great anger, what is becoming of this lowly terrorist cell of fools, I'll have Captain Briegheeth's worthless hide for a prayer rug for his foul errors with this evil woman, Captain. Since when do any cell members inform anyone but me of their intended target? I'll have this woman Farseeha's head on a stick, and her body feeding the flies of the vast desert for betraying her operation to you, sir. I'll have her entire family placed at the point of the sword, and slowly die the death of a thousand cuts for her foul waggling tongue. It seems the only one I can trust from this foul cell, is the young pup al-Qassan. I'll have her begging for a swift dea..."

"Please my wise but very angry Arab brother, allow me to inform you I forced Farseeha to divulge her intended target sir. Her need for weapons overrode her wise sense and the secrecy of her operation. I see what you mean by this woman is too impetuous to Command her own cell, sir. What do you want me to do about her, and her request for assistance from me, sir?"

"What target did she offer you for this attack in America, Captain Badawlhmed?"

"She had offered up the head of the hated American President to me, General al-Zahar."

"The American President you say Captain Badawlhmed?" Al-Zahar mumbled aloud.

"Yes, a very worthy target in deed to aim her foul sights upon at that, General al-Zahar Sir."

"If this foolish terrorist cell is going after the hated American President in this unauthorized operation then you're instructed to supply them with the requested weapons the foul fools need for their mission's success. I'll skin her worthless carcass alive when she has the misfortune to return to Baghdad and stand before my eyes again, for daring to offer her target to you though, Captain Badawlhmed. When she returns tonight to your presence, I want you to question her further about Captain Briegheeth's whereabouts and of his foul health. If he remains alive and well then I'll demand from Farseeha the true reason behind her getting in touch with you and requesting these weapons. Rather than having Captain Briegheeth carrying out his duties to this cell and his country, Captain Badawlhmed. Believe me sir, I'll settle up with her when I next..."

"General al-Zahar, I'd feel much better if you'd appoint another Operative to help control this obviously out of control terrorist cell of yours that seems to have completely broken down their security, sir. I don't like hearing of one Agent going behind the back of the other, especially the one who is the one supposed to be in Command of this cursed terrorist cell of yours, General. If they have no religion for each other then how in Allah's world can they possibly work as a Unit together, and finish their operation successfully, sir?" The Libyan Captain Badawlhmed smiled, knowing full well he was trying to force his will upon the well known and feared Iraqi General, while sticking his nose in his country's business at the same time.

"You're most correct with this request Captain, because it seems no one is in control of this foolish and out of control cell any longer, sir. I'll send someone special I have trust in to reshape this obviously out of control terrorist cell back to respectability, especially if they have found a way to get at the American President, Captain Badawlhmed." General al-Zahar hid well his rapidly growing anger for this disliked Libyan Officer, and his foul words of direction to him.

"Who will you send to shore up this cell's broken backbone, General al-Zahar Sir?"

"There's only one Operative I know of who can reshape this terrorist cell, and get them back on the right course and operating properly again and who can also carry out their original..."

"You mean you're thinking of sending Colonel al-Adwani here to the United States, General al-Zahar Sir?" The surprised Libyan Operative offered with excitement in his voice.

"Yes, you're correct with that assumption Captain. Colonel Abdulaziz Majd al-Adwani, the operative who was behind the attacks on the hated Jews in their foul country during the war we carried out against the Coalition Forces, sir. If anyone can shape this worthless terrorist cell back into the proper working order, he surely can. I'll order him to leave for the United States the moment I'm off the phone with you. He's present at my command station come to think of it."

"If you're going to place Colonel al-Adwani in Command of this foolish terrorist cell then this cell will get all the help they require from my government I assure you, General al-Zahar." The wise Libyan Captain Badawlhmed offered proudly to the Iraqi Officer while smiling again.

"I thank you for this needed assistance to my government and my foolish terrorist cell, my wise and helpful Arab brother. My government will repay you many times over for this kind and mush needed assistance to my operative, Captain Badawlhmed Sir." With that said General al-Zahar broke off the connection and then he immediately screamed for Colonel al-Adwani to report to his office. The American bombs searching for his SAM missile systems, stop falling and quiet had once again returned to the great sands of the vast desert in Iraq.

In moments, Colonel al-Adwani reported to General al-Zahar's office as ordered.

Captain Badawlhmed rose from his chair and headed for the basement of the Libyan Embassy. He passed by a number of attentive security guards on duty, and pulled two of them from their present post to assist him. They opened the massive armory door of the Embassy and followed Captain Badawlhmed into the dank dark chamber in the basement of the building. He produced the list of weapons he wanted carried up to his office, and handed them to the guards. The one quickly scanned the list and without word, he began to search for the requested weapons.

The security guards quickly collected the weapons and needed ammunition. Captain Badawlhmed then ordered the guards to carry the items upstairs, and he followed them out of the armory. Once back in his office again, the Libyan Captain directed the guards to disassemble the weapons to their smallest parts, and store them in their carrying cases. He then ordered a guard to remain behind to help Farseeha get the weapons into her vehicle. When this was accomplished for him, he then settled down and waited for Farseeha to arrive back at his Embassy.

Time past slowly for the slightly excited and concerned Libyan Captain Badawlhmed, and Farseeha refrained from making contact with Captain Briegheeth at this time. She knew he must have returned to his apartment at the filthy motel he was staying at by this time. Although she was dying to find out how he made out with observing the old and worthless American Senator he wanted to kill, she refused to give into her troubling thoughts, by calling her Commander for fear he might order her to return to his apartment before she had the time to collect the wanted weapons and had them in hand for their use to complete their mission as ordered.

Not being able to control herself any longer, Farseeha left her room and headed for the Libyan Embassy before the scheduled time. She needed the weapons, she wanted the weapons, and she made up her mind to go after the American President, even if she had to go it alone against him. Right now, the weapons were more important to her than her fellow terrorists. She drove through the Washington streets carefully and cautiously, taking different roads when she noticed a police car on the road she traveled. All detours she used, took more time than she had allotted for, and she finally arrived at the Libyan Embassy a little behind schedule. She climbed out of her car once inside the secured Libyan compound, and she was instantly picked up by the Libyan security guards stationed on duty outside the building at all hours of the day and night.

The two Libyan Embassy security guards escorted Farseeha to Captain Badawlhmed's private office after searching her body again. The Libyan Captain was already waiting for her to arrive, and he rose and extended his hand to her as he offered pleasantly. "Ahhh... Farseeha, it's so good to see you again, an Arab seeking retribution against the lowly infidels of this evil land. Tea?"

"Do you have the weapons I had requested, Captain Badawlhmed Sir?"

Seeing what General al-Zahar meant by Farseeha's temper and impatience. The Libyan Captain hid his smug smile, as he pointed towards the corner of his office, where a lone armed guard stood. His AK-47 resting across his chest, yet he held it in a threatening manner, his eyes drilling a hole into the chest of the young female Iraqi Agent as he openly glared angrily at her.

"Farseeha, although you're a terrorist, there's no reason to be uncivilized with me. I offered tea, and you did not reply. Am I to take that as your not wanting to share a cup of tea with me?"

Farseeha nodded as her cheeks flushed with embarrassment. Captain Badawlhmed was correct even though she was going to kill in the near future. She was in the presence of a civilized Arab person as she offered him. "Forgive me please Captain Badawlhmed, because I fear the pressures of this foul mission are beginning to weigh very heavily upon my mind and body. The United States is still tearing my country apart, and I'm helpless to stop it, but not for long. Once the American dog is dead, his god cursed people will think twice before challenging the might and power of Iraq for a second time, sir. I'd be most pleased to share a cup of tea with you, Captain."

As the pair sipped tea, Captain Badawlhmed studied Farseeha's fine face and shape. She was a beautiful young woman, her olive complexion highlighting her penetrating eyes, her nose and mouth finished her exquisite face. She was thin, had large breasts and no waist, her rearend was what Arab's longed for, plump, round, wide. Good for sharing long lonely nights with. The way he was staring at her, made him very uncomfortable, she could actually read the lust in his eyes.

The Libyan Captain held his cup as he continued to stare at the Iraqi female, and then he finally offered. "Farseeha, I was wondering, what is the fate of Captain Briegheeth? I was led to believe that he was the one in Command of the terrorist cell that you belonged to, woman."

Farseeha had to place her cup down and hold her hand with the other one to stop herself from shaking before the Libyan Operative. She understood this Libyan Officer must have surely had a conversation with General al-Zahar while she was not in his presence. She cursed herself for not thinking he would contact the Iraqi General in Baghdad when she left his office. She drew in her breath and then she informed him with a meek tone of voice. "Captain Badawlhmed, Captain Briegheeth is alive and well, and he is still in complete Command of our terrorist cell, sir. I'm afraid he's rather busy checking on another possible target we have selected, if we're unable to get at the hated American President and kill him as we planned, sir. He has given me permission to make contact with you, and to acquire the weapons we need for our mission to be carried out successfully, sir. I'm only trying to take some of the pressure of leadership from his strong and capable, but weary shoulders Captain." She was too far into her lie to back out of it now.

"Huh, you offer he gave you permission to make contact with me? If this is true, I have no further respect for this worthless fool. Since when does a true male leader of a terrorist cell, allow his subordinates to speak for him. This foolish man is not a good and wise leader, and I see why your terrorist cell is in utter chaos, Farseeha. Enough of this foolish and confusing talk you have answered my question to my complete satisfaction woman." Captain Badawlhmed decided not to inform Farseeha that Colonel al-Adwani was on his way to the United States, to take over their out of control terrorist cell. The Libyan Captain stared at her for a second time to see if she had something to add in her defense. When she offered no further excuses, he cast his eyes towards the stash of weapons stacked against the wall of his office. She followed his glaze to them.

"There in the corner are the weapons you have requested from me and my government, young Farseeha. That security guard standing there shall assist you with getting the weapons out to your vehicle. Err..." Again, Captain Badawlhmed openly leered at her and her exquisite body.

"I fear I must warn you Farseeha. I believe it'd be in your best interest to remain on my good side. Err... I have been away from my home for longer than I care to remember and admit to, woman. I miss my wife dearly Farseeha, I miss lying in bed with an honorable Arab woman, who knows well how to please her husband, or mate. Do you know how to please a male, my young Farseeha child?" Captain Badawlhmed asked her with a leer plastered on his lips.

"I don't think I like where this conversation is heading off in, Captain Badawlhmed. Why is it in my best interest to remain on your good side, Captain? All you have to do is supply me with the god cursed weapons I have need of to complete my mission successfully, and then you'll never have to see or deal with me ever again in your future, sir."

"Farseeha, to remain on my good side will have me come to your aide, if what you told me about Captain Briegheeth is untrue, foolish woman. I know your control in Iraq would have you skinned alive, if you dared to lie to me about Captain Briegheeth, or you have tried to take over the working terrorist cell without his permission first, young woman. It's both good and wise for you to have a very close working relationship and friend as powerful as I am on your side if things happen to go wrong for you with this god cursed operation you are here to carry out, Farseeha. A mere word from my lips would do much to soothe over any anger from your control back in Iraq. Especially, if I told your control I felt you were the right person to control this terrorist cell operating within the borders of the United States at this time, young woman." Captain Badawlhmed continued to openly leer at her face and body at the same time.

Farseeha caught the stern warning the Libyan Officer was trying to convey to her in this ugly conversation, and she replied simply to the wise

Libyan Operative. "And, what would it cost me to remain on the good side of you, Captain Badawlhmed Sir?"

"Just a few hours of your precious time will seal my loyalty to you forever I believe, Farseeha." Captain Badawlhmed picked up a pencil from his desk and absentmindedly began to twirl it between his fingers while returning Farseeha's angry stare, with one of his own.

"To do what?" Farseeha snapped nastily, growing angrier as she now glared at the Libyan.

"To have sex with me of course, foolish woman from the sand of the vast desert of Iraq."

"I'm afraid I don't have the time to lay with you, Captain Badawlhmed. Once my mission has been completed and successful might I add. I'll then be pleased to return to you, to enjoy your pleasures for the night." Farseeha snapped while staring deeply in the Libyan Officer's evil eyes.

"I didn't know you were so much in demand for this ordered mission, Farseeha. If you don't have the time to spare to lay down with me then perhaps maybe you can take me in your mouth, woman. That'll not take much of your precious time, and it'd do vast wonders for me for now, woman." Captain Badawlhmed glanced towards the stack of needed weapons and the guard still protecting them. As if it was a warning of doing what he had just requested of her, or she was not going to get the weapons she needed for her mission's success.

Letting her breath out in a rush, she snapped hotly at the Libyan Operative in a disgusted voice. "Is this the only way I'm going to be able to get the god cursed weapons I have so much need of from you for the success of my mission, Captain?"

Captain Badawlhmed did not reply, he just shook his head and then grinned at her again.

Without further word from her, she merely rose and walked around the side of the large desk, and then she knelt before the grinning Captain Badawlhmed's knees, as she opened her blouse, and pulled it away from her shoulders. She was willing to do anything in the world to get her hands on the weapons she needed to assassinate the American President.

When she approached Captain Badawlhmed, the security guard automatically tightened his grip on his weapon, but he relaxed when the Captain gave him a slight reassuring nod.

The Libyan Captain could not open his pants fast enough for his needs, and once he was out of his pants, he roughly attacked her slightly swaying breasts with both his hands. She got him to come quickly, but Captain Badawlhmed refused to allow her to pull off him as he came. She was forced to swallow and she hated this man more for what he just forced her to do with him, to get the weapons she needed for her mission.

"Ahhh... Farseeha, I see you truly know how to please a worthy Arab man. I believe I'll enjoy you and your treasures and abilities of the art of making love to a man again, in the not so distant future if you don't mind and have any further need of my government or my protection for you, young woman." He boasted proudly as he quickly fixed his pants and stood at the same time.

Colonel Farseeha fixed the front of her blouse and then she headed for the stack of weapons, completely ignoring the Libyan Captain's rude remarks. She made up her mind she was going to find a way to kill this hateful, god cursed Libyan Jackal. She picked up the two boxes containing the weapons. The guard rested his weapon against the wall and picked up the others and followed her out of the office. Captain Badawlhmed picked up the boxes of ammunition, and followed the two out. Outside, her car was pulled in an underground parking lot, and the trunk opened and surrounded by a horde of other security guards. The doors to the garage were closed so no one might see what they were doing inside the underground parking lot of the Libyan Embassy.

Farseeha placed her boxes in the trunk, as did the guard and Captain Badawlhmed. All identifying markings were removed from the weapons and boxes, and were steam cleaned in an effort to erase any fingerprints from the Libyans. Captain Badawlhmed and the guard wore gloves while handling the boxes after they were cleaned. When the trunk was full, the Captain grabbed her lightly by the shoulders and stared into her eyes as he offered in a smug voice.

"Ahhh... Colonel Farseeha, I fear you'll be forced to wait for a little while longer, before daring to leave the Embassy grounds for your safety, woman. I have other vehicles leaving before you must leave, woman. In this way, if anyone followed you to my Embassy, woman. They'll not know which car to trail once all the vehicles leave before and after your vehicle leaves. Two other cars will follow you out of the compound, and they'll head down different roads away from you. I believe this time gives me a chance to enjoy your educated mouth again, Farseeha."

"It is written, Allah favors the compassionate. Don't be so foolish and presumptuous of me, Captain Badawlhmed Sir. I'll not repeat my act upon you inside this filthy garage. The next time you'll enjoy my pleasures, it's going to cost you dearly, my dear Captain." She had to force herself to display a fake smile aimed at the Libyan Officer grinning back at her.

"Oh? And what will the great sum of money be to my person to enjoy your sexual abilities for a second time, my dear young Farseeha?" He snapped nastily, as he suddenly stopped laughing and stared directly into the ice cold eyes of Farseeha's, while he waited for her to tell him of the price it will cost him to share her pleasures once more.

"Captain Badawlhmed, the next time you'll enjoy me, it's going to cost you a romantic supper, and a room with a clean bed and window." She snapped with venom in her tone, and then she added under her breath. 'And, that'll give me the opportunity to seek my final revenge upon your worthless and foul head for this terribly indecent act you had just forced upon my body, fool'.

He laughed happily as he smiled at her and then offered. Yes, yes Farseeha, it'll be my great pleasure to take you out to supper one night. I don't mind tenderizing my meat, before indulging in the pleasures you shall offer to me in the future, young lady. I believe that you have a date with me then, my lovely Farseeha. When will you be accomplishing your faithful mission, so I know how to better prepare for our long night of making love to each other, woman?"

"Within the next two weeks will be enough time for my cell to accomplish what we have planned for the leadership of this evil country, Captain." She nearly hissed the words at the Libyan Captain as she tried to keep the hatred for the man out of her eyes.

"Fine then I'll be waiting for you to return to me, and to then live up to your side of the bargain just concluded between the two of us, Farseeha." The Libyan Captain offered smugly as he dared to slap her lightly on her plump rearend, further insulting her, especially doing this insult in the presence of so many other men standing around her vehicle.

"I fear that you have again taken great liberties with me and my person, Captain." She snapped angrily back at him. 'And, I shall be looking forward to the day when I can separate your worthless head from your foul shoulders, fool of an Arab Captain' you are'. Farseeha thought, as she quickly climbed into the car, and then she pulled it out of the under building parking garage. She noticed the other cars leaving the grounds through the main gate of the Libyan Embassy before her as she began to leave the area herself, and the other vehicles took different roads away from the Libyan Embassy entrance, at the same time she left the building as well.

The fuming Iraqi Colonel Farseeha al-Mana pulled slowly out of the Libyan Embassy main gate, she was followed closely by a number of other Libyan vehicles that headed in other directions she was going to travel off in. She gassed the car and moved forward slowly and kept driving within the city speed limit. The last thing she wanted or needed to happen, was to give any police officer a reason to stop her. When she arrived back at her apartment, she parked the vehicle and quickly emptied the trunk of the weapons. She placed them under her bed in her apartment and dropped on to it and gave out a deep sigh as she stared up at the ceiling. She wondered how she ever allowed herself to become so involved in this line of filthy work.

The harsh and mannish conditions she was forced to live under for her entire life, along with the terrible strain she was constantly working under, while trying to kill very influential people of other countries, was taking an extremely heavy toll upon both her mind and body. She did not realize it until she finally allowed herself to relax a little that her body was actually trembling from the strain. She slowly drifted off to sleep, not bothering to undress. She was angry as hell she was forced to give pleasure to the hated Libyan dog of a Captain. She hated men, and the world they believed they owned and controlled. She was a female lion about to roar, and when she did, the man's world was going to be forced to pay close attention to her bellow.

CHAPTER FOUR

WASHINGTON D.C., THE ROLANDS MOTEL, ROOM 17. MONDAY, JUNE 7th, 1999. 8 P.M. EST

Captain Jebril Briegheeth and Mamdouh al-Qassan remained inside the tiny and filthy motel room for the entire time until their scheduled meeting with Farseeha was to take place. Both men were thoroughly exhausted from their most trying ordeal of following the elderly American Senator around the Capital Building grounds. The two terrorists engaged in some small talk once Captain Briegheeth felt he had certainly successfully enlisted al-Qassan loyalty in his scheme to make Colonel Farseeha al-Mana believe he decided on her target after all. They filled their time by watching TV and drinking beer until falling asleep for the night.

Farseeha was extremely anxious all night, and she did not sleep soundly for a moment, and when she woke early she jumped out of bed. Without bothering to check with Captain Briegheeth first, she headed for her little portable trinket stand near the White House grounds, even though she was ordered by Captain Briegheeth to stay well away from the White House grounds and the American President. Until they had a chance to speak further about her selected target again. She was there when the American President came strolling out of the White House, and he was surrounded with his usual entourage of heavy security personnel and the other hanger ons.

The young Iraqi female watched patiently as the American President climbed into the second idling vehicle of the caravan. She stopped opening up her tchotchkes stand, and prepared to follow him to his latest destination. As the vehicles speed passed her stand, she latched the lock shut and then headed for her car. She trailed the American President's vehicle, until it ended up parked at Andrews Air Force Base. She parked her car in the shadow of the water tower not realizing this was the place where she was going launch her attack on the President from.

Colonel Farseeha watched attentively as the President followed a number of security people up the stairs to the waiting aircraft. She studied his every movement discreetly, and she noticed at least three different times while he was climbing the steps to the aircraft, or he stopped and spoke with the others with him, she could have easily killed the American Leader. As she stared at the President's massive aircraft watching the action taking place outside and around the plane, she did not notice a military jeep pull up behind her parked car until it was too close to make her escape. She was extremely quick on her feet and she forced herself to start crying when she realized the people in the jeep were out of the machine and they were approaching her vehicle.

By the time the security people walked up to her parked vehicle, their weapons were already held at the ready and she was quite visibly upset. The large black guard rapped lightly on her side window with his flashlight, and then he growled at her at the same time. "What the hell are you doing in this highly restricted area, young lady? Give me your damn license and registration please, and then get out of the car, and have your hands held in plain sight as you get out of the damn vehicle, Ma'am. Hey, what the hell's your problem here anyway Ma'am? Why are you crying, it ain't that bad little lady? If you're not up to something wrong here, you'll be on your way before you know it. C'mon, let's get out of the car please." Her tears made the guard's harsh stance against her easy up as he waited for her to get out of her vehicle.

She gave the large and rather angry and demanding black officer her driver's license from inside the car, while she tried to hide the fact she was crying from him now. She was stalling with getting out of the vehicle, because she felt she was more venerable outside it.

"You were ordered to get out of your damn vehicle. So get out of the fucking car before I pull you out of the damn thing by your fucking hair, you!" The second officer suddenly snapped angrily at her, keeping his weapon leveled right at her chest all the time he growled at her.

"C'mon Bill and back off her some will ya please, it looks like she has a problem here, man. Back off until we find out who the hell she is, man and what she's doing here. Christ, I hope she didn't come here to do herself in. I wouldn't like that shit on my damn patrol." Carl offered in a confused tone as he opened the door for her, and then he waited for her to get out of the car.

"What the hell are you doing Carl, bucking for the fucking bleeding god damn heart of the year award or something dealing with this bitch? You know the fucking standing orders buddy, get her ass out of the god damn car before I drag it out for her, dammit. This is a secured area!" Bill growled nastily at his concerned partner while glaring angrily at him.

Farseeha slowly got out of the vehicle, and the second officer rushed around it, and roughly grabbed her by the arms and slammed her hard up against the side of her vehicle. He held her there by the hair, as he callously began to search her person with his other hand.

She allowed herself to weep more, as the cop roughly assaulted her body with his hands.

"C'mon Bill and back off some on her will ya for Pete's sake. You're scaring the death out of the poor little thing by treating her so roughly man." Carl snapped angrily at his partner as he made a move to stop Bill from roughing up the young lady.

"Not until I find out what the fuck this little bitch is doing parked here in this highly restricted area, will I back off any on her, dammit. Who knows what she was up to here." Bill snarled back at Carl as he continued to search her body for any possible hidden weapons or cameras.

Carl stepped back and allowed Bill to finish his manhandling search of the young woman's body, as he looked at the picture printed on her driver's license, and then he compared it to the woman's face standing before him, and asked her patiently. "Brenda Wilson huh, why the hell are you parked in this highly secured area, young lady?"

"I'm truly sorry if I did something wrong by my parking here, Officer. I had no idea I wasn't allowed to park here, sir. I just found out my husband of ten years is cheating on me with a much younger woman who I once thought was my closest and dear friend, and I'm pregnant also sir. I don't know what to do now sir. I feel so all alone and deeply betrayed by him and my once girlfriend, sir. So I did the only thing I could think of doing, and I jumped in my car and I drove until I couldn't drive any longer, Officer. I stopped here to do what all girls do whenever they are hurt and upset by the man they thought loved them. I wanted to cry in private, sir."

Carl handed the registration and license over to Bill, and then he ran the plates with his command center, while Carl continued to question the young and upset woman further.

"Why the dirty sonofabitch, he should have his ass kicked in for himself. Hurting such a pretty little girl like you is a terrible thing for him to do to you, Ma'am." Carl was being very friendly with the upset acting Farseeha, until Bill returned and he gave him the look, as he took over the questioning of the still sobbing and shaking Farseeha.

"Look bitch, I don't give a fucking rat's ass what the hell's happening in your god damn wasted life, sister. You can't fucking park in a damn restricted zone for nuthin, not even to cry Ma'am. We're supposed to take in anyone we find hanging around any of these fricking areas you know. Put your damn hands behind your back and keep your damn mouth shut tight, and don't make a scene on us, or it's gonna go that much tougher on your purdy little ass when we get you down to our headquarters for processing, honey."

"C'mon Bill and cut her some slack here will ya please. Can't you see she's been through enough already today, and she's pregnant to boot Bill? We got her damn plate number and her license. She checked out okay, or you woulda had her lying on the damn floor by now and hooked up for transport. Look at her Bill she's shaking like a damn leaf in the wind, man. I say let's give her a break and let her get lost. We'll escort her out of the area until she's gone."

"I swear sir I didn't know I was doing something wrong by parking here, Officer. I just wanted to get away from my husband and my once girlfriend for a little while, and have myself a good cry before deciding what I was going to do about my future life, sir." She cried in her defense as she offered her arms out to the cop holding the handcuffs and her by the hair again.

For the first time since the two security officers stopped to check out the parked car, Bill suddenly softened his harsh stance against Farseeha a little. She was a real good looking dish to look at, and she did seem to be genuinely upset while he stared at her for the moment. Then Bill growled at her in an angry tone. "You didn't see all of the fucking restricted signs posted all over the damn place out there, lady? They're on just about every post in the area, dammit."

"I might have seen them Officer, but I'm so terribly sorry sir. I was too upset to pay attention to what was printed on the signs I passed." She carried out her deception against the two police officers by dabbing at her eyes with her shoulder, her hands were still pinned tightly behind her back, suddenly feeling she was going to be let go by the two officers. She knew if these police officers took her down to the station, her target of the American Leader was going to be placed off limit by her Captain, and she would have to pay the price for getting caught by the police, and placing the terrorist cell and their mission in jeopardy. She had no fear of the police officers keeping her plate or license number, they were okay, just made out to Brenda Wilson. The name she used while she was living in the United States since first entering the country.

"Okay Miss Wilson..." The large white officer began to say, until she interrupted him.

"Mrs. Wilson sir." Farseeha corrected as she looked directly at the large security guard now.

"Yeah, right, whatever you say lady. Look honey, I'm gonna cut you some fucking slack this time around and let your purdy little ass go. If I ever catch you parking in a restricted zone again, you won't like what I'll do to your damn body, before dragging your pretty little ass down to the damn station, honey. Cheating husband or not, I'm gonna be keeping my fucking eye on your ass, step over the damn line again, and you're gonna do some hard time in our jail, honey. Beat it now before I change my fricking mind and I run you in just for the hell of it sister." The still rather angry Police Sergeant released the handcuffs, and then he shoved her registration and driver's license back in her hand, and then he glared angrily at her, in his attempt to get her moving out of the restricted zone as quickly as she could possibly get out of the area.

She did not say a word as she rubbed her wrists and scrambled in her car and then drove off, never once looking back. She was scared and angry at herself for getting caught so easily.

The officers watched her leave the restricted area, and then they got back in the jeep as Carl complained at his partner. "Man Bill you were kinda heavy on the poor little girl you know."

"Yeah, but if she wasn't crying like she was, we mighta got us some for letting her go, Carl." Bill grinned at his partner as he rubbed his crotch to show Carl what he was talking about to him.

"Man, one of these days that stinking dick of yours is gonna get you in more trouble than you can get out of, man. You don't wanna get caught fucking round like that while on duty, Bill. They'll nail your damn ass to the cross for it man." Carl warned his younger partner as he placed his jeep in gear and the officers when back to patrolling their area of responsibility again.

"Yeah, whatever you say Carl." Bill moaned back at him as they continued with their rounds.

Farseeha fought to get her shaking body under control. Even though she almost blew her assignment, she confirmed to herself that the American President was vulnerable to assassination while boarding his precious aircraft of Air Force One. She stopped crying and then carefully guided her car through the heavy late afternoon rush hour traffic. She wanted to get back to her apartment, and wait until it was time to meet up with Captain Briegheeth and al-Qassan.

ROOM 17, THE ROLANDS MOTEL, WASHINGTON D.C. TUESDAY, JUNE 8th, 1999. 3:10 P.M. EST

Captain Jebril Briegheeth, along with Mamdouh al-Qassan remained inside the small and filthy motel room while going over the many different ways they came up with, to try and get at the so well protected American President successfully for most of the day. They both knew of Farseeha's plan to assassinate the President while he was boarding the aircraft known as Air Force One, and they had a number of maps of the massive Joint Andrews Air Force Base, along with the surrounding area spread out on the floor, while they were searching the maps for a safe perch from which to try and kill the American Leader.

Captain Briegheeth wanted to be well briefed by the time the always troublesome female terrorist arrived for their scheduled meeting in an hour at the hotel.

Both Arab men stopped drinking beer long ago, and now they drank coffee to make them more alert for the scheduled meeting with their always upsetting female counterpart. The Iraqi Captain was dreading the meeting with the firry and always angry female Colonel, knowing full well she was going to be a force to be reckoned with, because they were going to drop back to use her suggested target now. He knew she was going to see through any excuse he could possibly offer her, and he also understood this was going to make her impossible to deal with, once she realized she was right in the first place about the target they should level their eyes on.

Captain Briegheeth hated having this crafty and extremely dangerous Arab woman in his terrorist cell. The Iraqi Captain was so involved with his thoughts that he did not realize the time, until Farseeha came storming into the small room and she plopped down heavily on the unmade bed, and then she glared hotly at him and barked her words in a hiss. "Well, how did you make out with this foolish old Senator you two fools picked for our intended target, Captain?"

Upon seeing Farseeha's face distorted by the anger she was feeling, Captain Briegheeth offered lamely to her. "Errr... Farseeha, after thinking about it more carefully woman, I have come to believe that you have picked out the right target for us to level our eyes upon after all, woman. What good will it do us to kill some worthless feeble old American Senator, woman? I don't think his god cursed foul death would stop the bombing of our country for a single day. As it is written in the sands of our vast desert, I believe if we're going to place ourselves in serious danger, we might as well go after the most powerful target within the hated United Stat..."

"Hummm... I wonder what truly has forced you two fools to change your worthless minds, Captain Briegheeth. I see many different reasons for this sudden change in your opinion, sir. Could it be as simple as this old and feeble Senator you have concentrated your time so hard on, was too well protected by loathsome security guards after all, to make him an easy mark for our wrath and aims?" She interrupted him while carefully studying Captain Briegheeth's face for any sign of what he truly meant by this sudden change of heart in her favor.

Captain Briegheeth was in no mood to get involved in a long drawn out battle of words with Farseeha and he snapped hotly at her. "Whatever the reason is, it has been done and there is no need to analyze my decision any further in this conversation, upsetting woman. It has been changed, and that should be more than enough for your interests and your ego, Farseeha."

"Very well then Captain Briegheeth, I'll let it go for now sir. Then I shall listen to how you intend to go forward with my plan and target, Captain." She growled smugly at him, while wearing the sneer of knowing he had successfully avoided speaking the truth to her.

The angry Iraqi Captain ignored the extremely upsetting look on her face and he snapped back at her with anger lacing his voice. "What have you been doing all day, Farseeha?"

"Huh, while you two great fools were wasting your precious time following a useless old man around Washington all day, I was busy following the American President to Join Base Andrews Air Force, and I have discovered he's most vulnerable while the great fool is boarding his god cursed precious aircraft. This is the second time I have watched the great fool board the god cursed plane, and I observed at least three different times when I could have killed him easily. Alhamdulilah, (Praise be to God) I have also found the right position in which we can setup, and get a good sight at our foolish target when he is..."

"Farseeha! Did I not order you just yesterday in fact to stay well away from the god cursed White House and this worthless American President while we checked out the lowly and foul Senator as our target?" Captain Briegheeth growled angrily, feeling a little relieved he could change the conversation away from the American Senator and their failed attempt to get position on him to make the old man an easy kill for his terrorist cell.

"Yes you did at that Captain Briegheeth Sir." Colonel Farseeha announced shyly, while ignoring the harsh way the Iraqi Captain chose to address her in.

"Then what do you have to say for yourself, and of your actions of today, Farseeha?"

"Captain Briegheeth Sir, I carried out my orders faithfully to get a target worthy of stopping the daily god cursed bombing of our sacred country by the hated Coalition aircraft. I'll do everything in my power to carry out my orders as received, even by going against you and your worthless orders of hesitation. If you have a problem with my attitude and aims, I suggest you call your control back in Baghdad and bitch at him about my actions and want of a target, Captain. I'm most certain he'll not be as angry as you are, especially when I make my report to him, informing Command that you have wasted much valuable time and Iraqi lives, by chasing after a worthless old Senator to kill." She glared harshly at Captain Briegheeth this time around.

The Iraqi Captain controlled his temper the best he could, because he wanted nothing more from life than to be allowed to place a bullet in Farseeha's brain, to stop her always angry and constant interference of their future mission in the United States. The Iraqi Captain glared harshly at Farseeha for several long moments, before he finally replied rather heatedly at her. "Whatever, we'll discuss this disobedience further, once we have accomplished the mission for our country's sake, Farseeha. I have maps and pictures of Andrews Air Force Base, compliments of our worthless Russian Allies and friends, upsetting woman. If you'd be so kind as to show me where this perch you have discovered today, lies upon the god cursed map Farseeha."

She did not want to argue with the military officer any further either, but she was not going to allow Captain Briegheeth to threaten her in any way, shape, or form and get away with it so easily. She moved nearer to the table and looked over the maps and picked out the secluded area she parked in, when she was accosted by the security people protecting the airbase from attack and she offered the Captain. "Here is where I was parked when I observed the foolish American President boarding the foul aircraft like he was a God, Captain Briegheeth. There were three times during his boarding of the cursed aircraft where I could have very easily killed the worthless fool. If I was in possession of weapons and prepared to act against him, sir."

Captain Briegheeth rubbed his chin absentmindedly, he saw the outdated water tower printed clearly on the map, and he asked Farseeha. "How tall is this tower you have located, woman?"

"It's at least twenty five feet above the ground, Captain Briegheeth. It has what looks like a narrow barrier, and a heavy metal walkway surrounding the entire water tower where we can set up, and wait for our target to arrive. If we arrive before the American security people make their rounds, we'll be well shielded from their view until it's time to act. From what I believe, the security personnel setup a week in advance, before the lowly American President arrives at the Airbase for his foul trip. This could be another way for us to know when he's planning to use his cursed aircraft. They'll never see us on the water tower until it's too late for them to try and stop our mission." She flashed a smile of victory as she stared at Captain Briegheeth.

"Security people making their rounds of the area you just offered to my god cursed ears, Farseeha? What do you mean security guards?" Captain Briegheeth asked her sharply.

"Yes, while I was staking out the hated American President and his god cursed aircraft, I happened to notice a small jeep driving on the dirt road surrounding the massive Airbase. The two guards were well armed, and they seemed to take their job very seriously, and they were observing the surrounding area extremely carefully sir." She lied, but she dared not inform Captain Briegheeth she was stopped the police she was speaking of.

"The security guard did not happen to see you watching the foolish American Leader boarding his cursed aircraft, did they Farseeha?"

"Don't be such a fool Captain, I'm a professional. Do you think for one moment that I'd be so foolish and careless as to allow myself to be discovered by any worthless security personnel of this miserable country of jackals, sir?" She glared at Captain Briegheeth again.

"Good work I offer to you woman, you said something that makes absolute perfect sense to my foolish ears, Colonel Farseeha." The Captain actually smiled at her for a change.

Farseeha nodded to Captain Briegheeth, accepting the compliment he just paid to her.

"Yes, yes, and this means we might be forced to spend up to an entire week set in position while waiting for the foolish American President to arrive at the cursed Airbase, woman. How will we know in time to setup for attack against the great fool, before the extra security personnel begin prowling the area in concern and stop us from setting up against their President Farseeha?"

"Captain Briegheeth, the stupid news reporters of this god cursed country will surely release this information for us long before the American

President, or his foolish security people make the first preparations needed for his protection, sir. The reporters place their foolish President's life in the jaws of death every time he chooses to leave his White House, and they don't even realize it sir, or care they are doing it, Captain. This foul dog deserves what he gets, just for this reason, let alone his ordering the massacre of thousands of Iraqi soldiers and innocent civilians, guilty of trying to protect their country from the lowly infidels and their god cursed bombs, sir."

"I'll accept this explanation from you for the time being woman, but you must remember this for the rest of your foul life, Farseeha. If all does not work out as you have offered me on this day, it'll be your worthless skin that President Saddam Hussein will use for a walking rug in his office. Yes, now we have the location to strike out from, the next things we have to get our hands on are the foul weapons we'll need for this god cursed operation. I'll spend the entire day of tomorrow making contact with the Libyan Embassy. My control has informed me that Libya is more than willing to supply us with the weapons we'll need and use on our mission to make it a complete success for us to carry off, woman."

She began to sweat at this point, because she did not need Captain Briegheeth making contact with the nasty Captain Badawlhmed Nabih Khamis stationed at the Libyan Embassy, and finding out she had already made contact with him, and she had received the weapons they needed from him. She knew the Captain would lose control, and he would kill her on the spot for usurping his authority over the terrorist cell. He would be within his right to kill her outright, and receive no punishment from Baghdad, and his control as she tried to offer him in a clam tone of voice. "Errr... that'll not be necessary at this time I believe Captain Briegh..."

The suddenly concerned Iraqi Captain cocked his head to the side as he interrupted Farseeha's words angrily. "No! And why is that not necessary for me to be worried about at this time, Farseeha? I was ordered by control to make direct contact with the Libyan Embassy, and acquire the weapons we'll need for the success of this mission. Those are the direct orders and I shall follow them faithfully, woman. You know Baghdad cannot supply us with the weapons we'll need for this operation, without the hated American security discovering the transfer of the weapons, and successfully stop us before we're able to kill their foolish President, Farseeha."

"Captain Briegheeth, I was in the United States for many weeks, before you had arrived to better organize our cell, sir. Through my many contacts I established, I was able to acquire the needed weapons from my usual and trusted supplier here in the United States before you arrived, sir. I sat on the weapons ever since first receiving them, sir. I have the weapons and ammunition that'll make our mission a success against the foolish Leader of this worthless country."

"What in the name of Allah are you trying to hand me here, Farseeha? I don't believe your foul and lying words for one god cursed minute, fabricator of the truth. You know we were supposed to receive the weapons we'll employ for this operation from the Libyan fools and no one else, to force the finger of blame away from our country. You're telling me that you were supplied with the weapons we need from our own people and country, woman? I don't believe this for a foul minute from you, woman. I'm concerned over your troubling words." The instantly upset Captain snarled as he waited for her clarification of where she got the weapons from.

"Captain Briegheeth, I don't remember saying anything about receiving the weapons from our Iraqi sources, sir." Colonel Farseeha blasted back, as she glared hotly at the terrorist cell's leader.

"Then where from the devil's armpit did you get the needed weapons from, and what type of weapons are they, woman? Have you made certain they'll well suite our needs on this faithful mission we are ordered out on, Farseeha?" Captain Briegheeth demanded nastily from her as he cast a wiry eye at Farseeha, while waiting for her to reply to his last question of her.

"Captain Briegheeth I had collected the god cursed weapons from a certain supplier at work within the foul borders of the United States and I…"

"I do not like this little game you're playing with me in the least, Colonel. You did not answer my question satisfactorily over where you were able to find the weapons we need to complete our mission successfully, Farseeha." Captain Briegheeth interrupted nastily, and then continued with his angry words. "Unless you can do much better than that woman, I'll place this entire mission on hold, until I get to the bottom of where you have received these weapons from, Farseeha."

"Captain Briegheeth please, I don't believe my unit has to give up our sources to you. You understand the Secret Police of Iraq have our many sources and they have to be protected above all else sir. As you have just stated, let's say they are here and ready for use, and let it go at that. The weapons are impossible to be traced back to us, and I have complete trust in everyone that I was forced to deal with, in acquiring these needed weapons for our mission, Captain."

"Huh, I better not find out you went over my head, and you have acquired these god hated weapons from other sources than where we were ordered to get them from, Farseeha. Anything that foolish could very well place our entire mission in jeopardy, woman. If you dared to make such an ill error, it'll not only cost you your worthless life. But it also place the lives if your entire family in danger also, fool. Our President's wrath has no bounds to them, woman!" Captain Briegheeth warned as he cast his eyes off Colonel Farseeha's face for a moment.

"Captain Briegheeth, I have done nothing wrong, or that would place our mission in danger of discovery, or even threat sir." She put up her back to drive her point home.

"I hope not for your god cursed sake, woman. Once again I shall ask you, where did the god cursed weapons come from, Colonel?"

"Nice try Captain, but as I said before sir, I'll not give up my sources to you for any reason." She smiled at her Commander, letting him know his last ploy did not work on her either.

"The hated Russians? I hope you did not go to them great fools for these weapons, woman."

Colonel Farseeha did not reply to his inquisition, she just smiled back at Captain Briegheeth.

"Huh, I'm correct am I not Farseeha? I hope you were not foolish enough to be supplied with their below grade Russian made weapons for our mission, woman?" Captain Briegheeth bellowed loudly, he wanted to use the weapons employed by the American security people. In this way they would be much harder to traced back to Iraq's shadow on the sands of the desert.

"What the devil difference does it make to you at this point, Captain Briegheeth? Allow the finger of blame to be pointed at the foolish Russian dogs if Allah wills and allow it to be so sir. Even though they're no longer a super power, they still possess many nuclear weapons, and the means to deliver them onto the very shores of the hated United States, sir. These great weapons will keep the worthless American government from reacting too harshly against the great fools, sir. As long as the United States is a country, they would never dream of bombing any Russian cities over the assassination of their worthless President, Captain."

"The god cursed Russian's are our only Allies at this point besides the worthless French, foolish woman. If we hang them out in the open like this, by allowing the finger of blame for the assassination of the hated American President to be aimed at these great fools. The worthless fools might pull their needed support of our future operations and country. I'm quite certain our great President will not be very pleased with us, if we lose a faithful ally such as Russia over this god hated mission, especially one who has helped us so much in the past."

"You worry too much about things that should not concern you in the least I fear, Captain Briegheeth Sir. Again, you must think me a worthless fool that I would dare place such a necessary ally as Russia in harm's way. The weapons I have received are American made and they have come from an American supplier, Captain Briegheeth. Allow their foolish investigators discover where these weapons have come from sir. The worthless fools would only have to look to their own supplies if they want the true source of the god cursed weapons we shall employ to kill their foul President, sir." Farseeha snapped hotly, again, flashing a smile of victory.

"You mean to tell me you have good sources working here inside the United States, who are more than willing to aid Iraq in her desperate time of need and assistance, Farseeha?" The stunned Captain offered, surprised at his own words even as he announced them.

"Once again sir, you request I give up my sources, and I will not do that for any threat or reason from anyone, Captain Briegheeth. I, as you, would rather face certain death at the hands of the lowly infidels of this worthless country, than give up my private sources to anyone, sir. I assure you Captain, not every American is pleased by what their god cursed government is doing to Iraq and her people, Captain Briegheeth. There are numerous calls growing from within their own ranks to stop the continuing aerial bombing of our lands, and lift the staggering sanctions from our sacred country, sir. There are many fools living here in the United States who are more than willing to assist us in stopping the bombing. Allies, fellow Arabs who lived in the United States too long, and they desire to once again walk upon the pure desert sands of Iraq, sir."

Colonel Farseeha lied to the leader of the terrorist cell she had no allies planted in the American government. But she was willing to do anything in her power to stop Captain Briegheeth from making contact with the Libyan Captain who supplied her with the weapons.

"There are many American people willing to go against their own government in dealing with Iraq or her people, Farseeha? I trust you're not talking out of the side of your foolish mouth again, trying to make me believe the impossible to believe here, woman." Captain Briegheeth asked with hope, his eyebrows arching with surprise over her words. He felt he might have underestimated the power controlled by this fearsome and very upsetting woman.

"I have the god cursed weapons at hand for our needs, do I not Captain Briegheeth? And, there is no further need for you to be worrying or concerned yourself about where we'll accumulate the weapons we need for this operation to become a success for us, Captain Briegheeth." Another small smile of victory slowly crossed her lips.

"Huh, you give me gray hair woman and a terrible pain in the pit of my stomach, Farseeha. But you are correct at this time woman. Let's leave this conversation for the time being, and complete our plans on how we're going to kill this foolish American President. Now that we have the location, and we're in possession of the weapons we're going to need to make this operation a success for us, woman. Our next worry is going to be on how we're going to know when to setup to kill this foul and hated American Leader of this god cursed nation of fools. Do you have any other ideas set in that foul mind of yours on how to accomplish our mission, Farseeha?"

"That is much simpler than you might think it is to discover, Captain Briegheeth." Farseeha offered smugly as she leaned back on the bed and enjoyed her moment of triumph over this fool.

"You seem to have all the answers to the countless problems we're facing on this foul mission all of a sudden, Farseeha. Are you now the great Prophet reincarnated in the form of a lowly female? Perhaps, you'd be so kind as to enlighten this true follower of Islam and Allah's sacred words, on how we're going to know when we have to set up to kill this great fool running the hated American government, woman." The Iraqi Captain barked hotly as he glanced at Mamdouh al-Qassan, smiling at the confrontation taking place between the other two terrorists.

"What is so funny with you, mister? Are we entertaining you with the battle we are engaged in between the Colonel and myself, young fool?" Captain Briegheeth demanded hotly from the much younger member of their terrorist cell, once he noticed he was smiling at him.

"Nothing is funny that is taking place between my other two fellow Arabs, Captain." Al-Qassan said as he instantly lowered his head and then stared at the floor.

"Then wipe that foolish grin off your foul face, before I have it sliced from your worthless lips by the edge of a sword, young fool. Farseeha!" Captain Briegheeth turned his attention back to the woman terrorist of their group, and then he waited until she turned her attention back to him.

Farseeha cocked her head to the side and then she waited for Captain Briegheeth to speak further to her once he was finished with the other terrorist.

"You mentioned something that it might be easier than I though on setting up against the hated American President for his cursed death, Farseeha. I order you to explain to me just how we're going to accomplish this great feat, woman. Inform me on how we're going to know when to set up to kill this great American fool, woman with all the answers to my problems?" The concerned Captain tapped his foot on the floor to show he was losing patience with Farseeha.

Without losing a beat, Colonel Farseeha snapped back at her Commander of the terrorist cell with anger lacing her voice. "Captain Briegheeth, all we have to do is be patient and rely on the United States stupid news reporters and their worthless newspapers as we usually do. The great fools will proudly inform us well in advance when the lowly dog of an American Leader is planning to use his phallic symbol to take him on a trip. It seems the American fools have to know where their foul President is at all times of the day and night, or they cannot sleep well at night. Once we know the right time the foolish American Leader is planning to leave Washington, we can quickly set up on the water tower beforehand, and then we can assassinate him when he arrives to board his precious aircraft. Simple, no Captain Briegheeth?"

"Simple yes Farseeha, almost too simple for my likes, woman. Anything that sounds this simple to accomplish usually is not simple, and everything we're trying to do, happens to blow up in our foolish faces, woman. I see I'll be forced to pay much closer attention to any more of your foul suggestions in the future, Farseeha. You seem to have everything already worked out well for us to accomplish this mission, woman. Now, I'd like to view the god cursed weapons you have received from your so called American contact, Colonel Farseeha. I find this statement still extremely hard to believe, young desert woman. Perhaps, we'll explore this source of yours a little further, once our operation has successfully been completed, and the hated American Leader is dead, woman." Captain Briegheeth mumbled as he stared into the glaring eyes of Colonel Farseeha, and he waited for her to reply to his angry words aimed at her.

"Again sir, that's extremely simple to accomplish, Captain Briegheeth. I have the foul weapons waiting in the trunk of my car outside, sir. I'll get them for you if you'd like, Captain."

"No, that'll not be necessary, Colonel Farseeha. I want you to maintain your strength for this upcoming mission, woman. Allow the foolish young al-Qassan to retrieve the foul weapons you have secured for our use. It'll give the lazy fool something else to do besides grinning at us like a foolish schoolboy who has just seen his first naked woman. Al-Qassan, go and get Colonel Farseeha's car keys from her and bring the foul weapons to the apartment. Make certain you're careful, and no one sees you bringing them into the foul building, fool. I cannot believe I must think of everything for this god cursed mission." Captain Briegheeth moaned at the young man.

"Errr…" Colonel Farseeha hesitated for a brief moment as she stared at the Iraqi Captain.

"Errr… what is it now for the love of Allah's great will, Colonel Farseeha? You have something else to add to this foul and endless conversation, woman?"

Colonel Farseeha smiled at Captain Briegheeth as she replied to his demand of what else was on her mind. "Captain Briegheeth, it's still light outside, and I think it'd be extremely foolish on our part to try and start shifting the weapons from my car into this building in the light of day, sir. Even though the weapons are being stored inside unmarked boxes, and I have them wrapped in cloth, to better hide them from any possible prying eyes from discovering what they are, sir. I believe if a nosy Police Officer happens to see al-Qassan moving the foul boxes from my trunk, he might become interested in what he was doing, and move over to see what he was removing from the trunk of the foul car. The police authorities of Washington seem lately to be on sharper guard for anyone who even looks like Arabs these days, sir. I fear that he might be discovered moving the weapons from the car into the building in the light of day, sir."

Captain Briegheeth let out his breath in a rush as he stared intensely at Colonel Farseeha for several long moments, knowing she was absolutely correct to take such wise precautions on moving the weapons from her car into the building in the light of day. He cursed himself for not waiting until it was dark outside, without Colonel Farseeha having suggested it to him first. He understood she was going to make this suggestion. At first he considered changing his order to the young al-Qassan, but since Colonel Farseeha already said something about it, he was bound to inquire as to her slight hesitation now.

"Once again I find myself being forced to agree with your latest suggestion aimed at my person, Colonel Farseeha. I fear this is becoming a bit of a bitter habit for me to live by and disgest, foul woman. I warn you Colonel Farseeha, I don't like agreeing with you so much all of a sudden over our faithful operation, woman. I shall pray to the Almighty Allah this will not become a tendency in my foolish life, woman. I believe it will be a far better idea for us to wait for the cover of darkness as you have just suggested, too shift the weapons to our apartment from your vehicle. We'll also be patient, and wait until the worthless American reporters inform us of where and when the god cursed foul American President intends to leave his seat of power in Washington, and we can then successfully get at and assassinate the great fool, woman."

Colonel Farseeha nodded slowly at the concerned looking and extremely stressed out Iraqi Captain, as she attempted to make herself a little more comfortable while resting on the filthy and dilapidated small bed of the sleazy little motel room. She knew better than to refer to Captain Jebril Briegheeth as Captain outside of the privacy of the room where she spoke with him. Both Colonel Farseeha and Mamdouh al-Qassan were under strict order never to refer to their military rank while in the service, where anyone outside of their terrorist cell might hear it mentioned, and they report them to the local police authorities. She also knew they had to be extremely careful about themselves at all times now that they had a working plan in mind.

CHAPTER FIVE

WASHINGTON D.C., THURSDAY, JULY 8th, 1999. 9 A.M. EST, THE ROLANDS MOTEL

The three soon to be active Iraqi terrorists were fast becoming bored to death while waiting for the American President to finally use his private aircraft to visit another city within the United States, or any other nation of the world. The small group of terrorists took to using the motel room more and more lately to meet, and then wait for any news of when the foolish American President planned to leave Washington on his aircraft. Captain Briegheeth could not understand why the American fool was remaining in place here in Washington for so many days in a row lately. It seemed before they picked him for certain death, the foolish American President left Washington two, to three times a week almost every week. But now he was remaining at the White House and forcing the small group of terrorists to wait longer before attacking and killing him. The small group of Iraqi attackers was fast becoming rather placid with their time while waiting for their chance to act against the powerful American Leader.

Colonel Farseeha al-Mana was out of the tiny motel room buying breakfast for the group, and Mamdouh al-Qassan was in the bathroom with the Playboy magazine to fill some of their time.

Captain Jebril Briegheeth knew what the young man was doing in the bathroom with the book that displayed so many naked women on the pages, but he did not care in the least. As long as the young man was amused and not complaining about the downtime they were forced to endure, while waiting their chance to assassinate the American President. Captain Briegheeth would not have cared if he even brought a female into the room, to help relieve his terrible boredom. He also knew the young man would have never dare request this great a favor from him, because it would cause him his life to dare even think about bringing a woman into the room.

The Iraqi Captain was taken aback by the way Farseeha charging into the small room. She dropped the McDonald's food on the table, allowing the contents of the bag to spill out, and she rushed over to the bed where she quickly spread out the latest edition of the Washington Post. Captain Briegheeth was about to yell at her when she spoke to him, announcing.

"It is stated in the newspaper that the great American fool is scheduled to leave Washington for New York City on the 27th of this god cursed month, Captain Briegheeth Sir." Colonel Farseeha turned and looked up at the Captain, and she smiled a beautiful grin at him.

"What are you talking about this time for the love of Allah, Farseeha?" he moaned at her.

"Please, look for yourself at the news article printed in the worthless newspaper, Captain Briegheeth." She pointed to the article she wanted her Commander's attention drawn to.

Captain Briegheeth looked over her shoulder, as she pointed to the article printed in the Washington newspaper, and he barked at her. "Give me that damn page, woman!"

She pulled the page from the newspaper and handed it to the angry Captain Briegheeth. He dropped on the bed and he read the article. 'July 8th, Washington D.C., the President's Press Secretary announced President Albert Cole, the First Lady and their children, along with Vice President Mary Hirshfield and certain other members of his Cabinet, have been invited to a private screening of Midnight, the new thriller staring Michael Douglas in New York City. The Press Secretary informed this reporter, the First Lady and her two children will travel to New York by car. This itinerary will enable the First Lady some extra time to visit her mother and father living in New Jersey, before arriving in New York City to meet her husband the President.

'She's scheduled to meet President Cole in New York City on the evening of July 28th, for the special viewing of the movie. The Vice President will see President Cole off, and she'll soon follow him to New York City also by car. The President and Vice President are not permitted by law to fly in the same aircraft at any time. This is because if Air Force One develops mechanical problems, the second leader of our country will not be involved in the same situation, but will be ready to assume power over the country, if the President somehow becomes incapacitated for any reason whatsoever. President Cole is scheduled to leave on Tuesday morning of the 27th. He's scheduled to be boarding Air Force One at eight twenty p.m. at Joint Base Andrews Air Force Base, and is scheduled to arrive in New York City at nine ten p.m.

'President Cole will be staying at the plush Trump International Tower and Hotel on his latest visit to New York City. It was reported the President will mix a little business with pleasure, by attending certain meetings with local governors and state leaders, on how to better have communications between the States and Washington. Expect traffic in New York to be very..."

Captain Briegheeth angrily crumbled up the one page of the newspaper in his hands, as if he was angry with it as he looked at Colonel Farseeha and admitted. "Farseeha, it's as you have stated all along. The foolish American reporters and their worthless papers think nothing of placing their foul President's life in danger, by publishing his schedule to the world. You'd never see such articles of this sort printed in the Iraqi newspaper, Al-Jumhourlya. If the great fool of an editor dared to place such announcements in his foul newspaper, he would find himself visiting the lowly inquisitor at Abughraib Prison in Baghdad, while waiting for his death to slowly visit his worthless carcass. This is why the cursed American fools and their bombs have not harmed President Saddam Hussein in their foolish ongoing attempts to kill our President.

"The American hunters never know where our President is going to be until it is too late for them to react against him. Allah must be working with us. What a stroke of luck, and what a target you have leveled your eyes upon for our faithful cause, woman. May Allah always give you such wise wisdom for our country and President's sake, woman." Captain Briegheeth smiled at Farseeha, whose chest swelled with pride over the compliment.

"When shall we prepare to assassinate the hated American President?" Colonel Farseeha asked as she bowed to the Captain's last words.

"That's a good question from you Farseeha. Let me see, today is the 8th, day of this foul month. The newspaper reports the foolish American President is scheduled to leave Washington on the 27th day of this foul month. The extra security goes into effect as you have offered two weeks before the foolish President visits his precious aircraft. This will give us nineteen days in which to make our final preparations in our attempt to assassinate the great fool commanding this foul and evil country. We'll have to store enough food and water at the water tower to sustain us while we wait for our worthless pigeon's arrival before us. Today is not too early to begin our preparations and I want you and al-Qassan to store the food. Remember, everything we need will be carried on our foolish backs, so make it light Farseeha. I'll go over the weapons once again, to make certain they're in the proper working order for when we have need of the foul thing, and all the cursed ammunition is with the right we..."

"And bathroom?" Farseeha asked, and then wanted to bite her tongue for the stupid question.

"Yes Farseeha, we'll have to do our business where we hide on the god cursed water tower. We cannot possibly move about freely in the area, to have the luxury of a pot to use. Farseeha, we're soldiers for our country and Allah, and as true soldiers we'll do whatever we have to do, suffer any indignities that need to be suffered for our just cause, woman. If this is too hard for you to accept then you're free to remain behind and allow us men to carry out their duty for their country and President." Captain Briegheeth sneered at Farseeha, pleased he felt he had discovered a weakness in the powerful and dangerous Iraqi woman from Iraq's Secret Police.

"I spit in your foul face for daring to assume I'm nothing more than a weak willed woman. May Allah cause you to go blind, but not before we carried out our mission for our country, Captain Briegheeth Sir." Farseeha glared at the sneering Arab leader of their terrorist cell.

The Iraqi Captain returned the harsh stare before his face broke out into a wide grin. Forcing her to smile, and then Captain Briegheeth laughed, and he was joined by the young Mamdouh al-Qassan, and then Farseeha. In their mind, they believed they would be the driving force that would stop the god cursed American bombing of Iraq, and save the lives of the innocent in Iraq.

"It's time for us to begin our preparations to assassinate the great American fool." Captain Briegheeth declared proudly as he got up from the bed and began walking around the tiny room.

Farseeha and al-Qassan nodded in compliance with their Captain and commander's words, and then the two terrorists headed out of the apartment without further words, to accomplish their orders. Captain Briegheeth walked to the closet and stared at the weapons still packed in their boxes. He reached in and removed the sniper's weapon and flipped open the latches to the box.

WASHINGTON D.C., JULY 9th, 1999.
THE ROLANDS MOTEL

Iraqi Captain Jebril Briegheeth was sitting alone in the small motel room, when there was a light knock on the apartment door. He automatically reached for his pistol, and he carefully slid the slide back, and chambered a round in the weapon as he stared at the closed door, trying to see through it. Cautiously, he rose from the bed and pushed the box containing the M-88 sniper's weapon under the bed. He had no place to go, and if it was the Washington police authorities waiting for him on the other side of the door, they were not going to take him in alive. He knew the hated Americans employed truth drugs during their interrogations of any terrorist prisoners, and he had no intention of giving up the other members of his cell to the lowly infidels.

As if his hand weighed a ton, Captain Briegheeth slowly reached out and grabbed for the door knob as he moved the pistol behind his back, and then he called out to the unseen person standing on the other side of the door. "Yes, who is there please?"

"Open the god cursed foul door at once my long lost brother for too long, it is I, Abdulaziz Majd al-Adwani. I'm here to pay you a surprised visit that has been much too long in the coming I might add for you, my faithful but very foolish brother from the land of sand."

Deeply relieved by hearing the very familiar voice, Captain Briegheeth's shoulders released their tension as he replied to the voice. "How do I know it is truly you, my older brother? It has been far too long since the last time you have chosen to pay me a visit you know."

"Caution is the very wise and intelligent course of action to carry out at all times, my foolish younger brother. Please, allow me to prove to you who I am to this cursed door that hides my brother's face from my eyes. Briegheeth do you remember when we were in the desert and you came across the young Israeli female, and we took her captive. I was the one who introduced you to pleasures an infidel woman could offer one with her foul mouth, and we did..."

"Ahhh... it is truly you my brother from the burning sands of our sacred country, because there is no other person living on the face of this earth that could recall such a delightful day as that one was, my faithful brother. It is a great pleasure for me to be within your presence again. I thank the wise and merciful Allah for guiding you safely to my side once again, my brother." Captain Briegheeth moved his hand away from the doorknob and then he quickly released the dead man bolt securing the door closed. The door immediately flew opened.

When the two terrorists saw each other standing in the doorway, they both hugged as Colonel al-Adwani kicked the door closed with his foot. When they released their hug, Captain Briegheeth looked in al-Adwani's face and offered proudly. "Allahu Alkbar my faithful Sunni brother, why have you come to me here in America? Has there been a change in our orders?"

"Allahu Alkbar Captain Briegheeth, allow me to inform you why I was ordered to meet with you here in the United States. I was dispatched here by General Hassan al-Zahar himself, Captain. It seems Colonel Farseeha al-Mana has gone out of her prescribed orders, and the foolish witch had made contact with those who were yours to speak with, my wise desert brother. Libyan Captain Badawhlmed was most concerned your terrorist cell was coming apart at the seams, and he spoke personally with General al-Zahar in Baghdad. In his great wisdom, the wise General chosen to dispatch me to you to make certain everything was in proper working order..."

"God curse that evil lowly woman to the fires of hell for all eternity. I knew she did not get the weapons from the Americans, as she stated my brother. I'll take great pleasure in flaying her foul skin from their worthless bones, but not before I pissed in her mouth for daring to lie to me."

"My faithful Arab brother, don't be too harsh on her, because she did wise. From what Captain Badawhlmed has informed me of the meeting held between them, he felt she was taking pressure off of your proud shoulders, Captain. I see its good I'm here, the constant raids by the Coalition warplanes are weighing very heavy on my weaken shoulders. We're completely helpless to do anything against the foul enemy attacking aircraft. When we light up our attack radars for a firing solution, our SAM missile sites are instantly pounded with a rain of America's smart weapons and bombs. Whatever, soon, we'll be the ones who'll place a quick stop to these hated attacks upon our sacred lands of Iraq by these hated infidels. I was pleased to be offered the chance to leave Iraq, and help take Allah's revenge out on the head of the evil leader who is ripping our country apart. Is everything ready for us to begin on this foul mission, Captain?" Colonel al-Adwani sat down on the filthy bed, and then he waited for Captain Briegheeth to report.

"Yes Brother al-Adwani, we have the needed weapons and perch from which to strike out at the very heart of the United States from, Colonel al-Adwani Sir. We only endure time to slowly pass as does the shifting sands of the great desert we'll soon rid ourselves of this criminal American madman who is happy to be killing Iraq's innocent children and mothers, Colonel al-Adwani Sir." Captain Briegheeth saw the look on al-Adwani's face and became silent.

"I fear I carry some bad news for your ears, my brother Captain Briegheeth. You're no longer in Command of this terrorist cell. I was ordered by General al-Zahar to take over Command of your cell, and make certain the death of the foolish American President is accomplished..."

"Am I being punished for some reason by General al-Zahar, because of what Farseeha did behind my back, Colonel al-Adwani?" Captain Briegheeth interrupted the Colonel cautiously.

"Quite on the contrary my foolish Arab brother, it should be deemed a great honor to work with me once again in your life. Do I detect a trace of anger in your tone of voice, Captain Briegheeth? You no longer want to take orders from me, Captain? We have all but suckled from the same teat of a mother's breast, while we were growing up together back in Baghdad, my foolish brother." Al-Adwani smirked as he stared at the slightly younger Arab man.

"No! I love you my brother as I have always have, and I'll follow you to the gates of hell if so ordered by your mouth, Colonel al-Adwani. It's only I feel this sudden change in my orders and Command are the result of Colonel Farseeha's constant meddling in to and against my leadership of this foul terrorist cell, and trying to take control of my cell as she always tried. Ever since first coming to me in the middle of the night. I'll have my revenge on her foul shoulders once this mission is completed, and we have returned to the safety of Iraq once again, my brother."

"Then remove the hatred of revenge that is slowly eating away at your very proud heart and mind, my desert brother. It is not Farseeha's fault that you were replaced by me. It was the Libyan Captain Badawhlmed who dared to place the words of concern within General al-Zahar's mind. He told General al-Zahar he felt a three man terrorist cell would not be able to accomplish the great target you have selected for your attack cell. General al-Zahar had agreed with his foul assumption, thus I have showed up at your doorstep to take Command my desert brother."

"How much do you know of my intended mission, my brother Colonel al-Adwani?"

"I know of your intended target, and I happen to agree with your wise choice my brother."

"Colonel al-Adwani, how the devil did you find out about my target, sir? We just decided on it ourselves, and I have not made my report to my control back in Baghdad as yet. Ahhh... Farseeha! She has dared to inform the lowly Libyan dog of our intended target. Colonel al-Adwani, you must allow me to dispatch her foul presence on this earth when we're done with our mission here in the hated United States, my wise and faithful brother of countless years past. She has broken the first rule of our terrorist cell, to expose our proposed target to anyone not part of our cell before we have successfully destroyed it, is unthinkable of her Colonel. She has placed the entire mission of ours in serious danger. I'll skin her foul hide for thi..."

"You'll do nothing but follow orders as I give them to you my brother. Farseeha is not your concern any longer Captain Briegheeth, she is my problem to handle now, and I'll take great delight in handling her worthless being, Captain. I have already decided what will befall her foul evil head. I agree in this case with you, Captain Briegheeth. She has placed this entire mission in danger, and she'll be dealt with when the proper time comes for it to take place. How soon will you make your move against the hated American President, Captain Briegheeth?"

"On the 27th day of July. We have discovered on this day where our target will be at that time. I fear it's the only time when he'll be most vulnerable to attack, Colonel al-Adwani Sir."

"Very good Captain Briegheeth, I should have known better. If this mission is successful, you'll be very well rewarded on this earth by our President in Iraq, or in Paradise, if Allah chooses to call you home after you have completed this mission for our country and President and his people. Show me what you have worked out for this operation so far, and if I like your plan. I shall give you the final go ahead for the mission to continue, my brother."

The Captain spread out the maps of Andrews Air Force Base on the bed, as he explained the plan to the new commander of the operation. When he finished his explanation, Colonel al-Adwani nodded as he remarked. "It is a go Captain Briegheeth. Where is Farseeha at?"

Captain Briegheeth smiled, feeling Farseeha was going to get her just dues in the future, and the Captain quickly informed Colonel al-Adwani where he would find Farseeha. He hoped Colonel al-Adwani was going to remove her from the cell, and then use him to replace her.

"Again my wise Arab brother, you have done very well on your orders and choice of target. When the young fool Mamdouh al-Qassan returns to the god cursed smelly room, have him remain here until I had a chance to speak with him. I'll being leaving to speak with the troublesome Farseeha, and I'll straighten out her wild and extremely dangerous ambitions, or I'll kill her with my bare hands." Colonel al-Adwani rose from the filthy bed, and then he hugged Captain Briegheeth then left the apartment. He had his own transportation.

It took Colonel al-Adwani fifteen minutes to reach the room of Farseeha. He knew she was home because he saw the car he personally rented for her when she first came to the United States. He was the man who began her on her way with this cell. He was her main control, the one she reported to. The Colonel was something else to Farseeha. He smiled as he headed to the rooming house. He looked for apartment fifteen, and when he found it, he tapped on the door.

Colonel Farseeha was just coming out of the shower, and she had a towel loosely wrapped around her exquisite body, and she was still soaking wet. When she heard the light tapping on the door, she rushed to a drawer and removed her pistol. She drew in her breath deeply, and then she commanded as she aimed the pistol at the closed door. "Who is standing at my front door?"

"Open the foul door at once Farseeha. So I might once again set my eyes upon your great beauty, my dear and only beautiful sister." Colonel al-Adwani said from behind the closed door.

"Al-Adwani!" Colonel Farseeha yelled excitedly as she immediately flung open the door. When she saw Colonel al-Adwani standing at the door, she immediately flew into his arms. Colonel al-Adwani's hand pulled the towel from her body and he cupped her breast. Colonel Farseeha feverishly pulled at his belt buckle as she tried to lead him deeper into the room.

"Err... perhaps you should allow me to enter your room first, before you dare to do that to my body my foolish and very wayward sister of the sands of the desert of our ancestors." Colonel al-Adwani offered as he tried to move Farseeha back in her room so they could have a private meeting between the two of them.

Farseeha pulled him into the room by the belt, and closed the door behind them and continued to work on his pants with shaking hands. She led him to the bed and pulled his pants down around his ankles. He sat on the unmade bed as Farseeha drew his hard member in her mouth.

"Ahhh... that feels so good my sister, it has been too long since the last time I had the pleasure of your lips wrapped around my shaft. You have been a very naughty little girl I fear, Farseeha."

Farseeha pulled off his shaft with her mouth and she mumbled as she looked into al-Adwani's black and staring eyes. "I thought you like it when I'm naughty my lover?" She went back to pleasing him with her lips again. She was surprised the Iraqi Colonel was in Washington, but she refused to ask him why he returned to the United States. The last she knew of him, he was fighting against the allied warplanes still ripping apart Iraq with their no fly zones.

"That is not what I meant, my foolish young Princess of the dark Underworld."

Farseeha stopped again and asked him. "Am I in displeasure with you Colonel al-Adwani?"

"Not with me my pretty little sister. Please, continue with what you were doing. It has been far too long since the last time I saw you and you have pleased me so well, young woman."

"Then who have I crossed my lover?" Farseeha asked as she took him in her mouth again.

"You almost caused the foolish Captain Briegheeth to suffer a god cursed heart attack by your actions of late my sister. He's aware that you went behind his back to visit Nabih for..."

"But..." Colonel Farseeha interrupted as she stared deeply into the Iraqi Colonel's eyes again.

"But nothing, please continue with what you were doing for me young woman." Colonel al-Adwani guided her head back to his waiting shaft, and then added. "I care not one foul grain of god cursed sand from our great desert for what Briegheeth believes or feels. I don't like him in Command of this mission, I never did woman. He's a stupid fool, too damn cautious my lovely sister. How were you able to talk him into going after the target I ordered you to take out?" Colonel al-Adwani understood if this terrorist cell went after the American President, it certainly amounted to a suicide mission on their part, and he wanted to share Colonel Farseeha's sexual pleasures for one last time, before she died going after her intended target.

"I argued with him many times over this mission, he's far too cautious as you have just admitted to me Colonel al-Adwani. He wanted to go after some worthless old American Senator as his prime target. I pointed out his death would not stop the bombing of Iraq..." She would have went on with her words of complain, but she was interrupted by the Iraqi Colonel again.

"Neither will the death of their foolish American President do it." Colonel al-Adwani corrected the dangerous female terrorist.

She looked deeply in Colonel al-Adwani's eyes and then said in a confused tone of voice. "Then why are we going after the great fool if his death will not accomplish our wishes?"

"Because I want the great fool dead, President Saddam Hussein wants him dead. If Saddam Hussein could have his way, he would order me to aim your terrorist cell at the ex-President George Bush. He's the one Saddam hates more than the devil himself, my lovely little daughter of the sands." Again, he tried to guide Colonel Farseeha's head back to his waiting shaft.

"All of a sudden, I feel we're being ordered on a suicide mission, my Brother al-Adwani."

"Don't be so foolish as to believe that for a moment my sister. I'd never allow anything bad to happen to you. When you return to Iraq, you'll become my wife. Yes my sister that's the way to please me properly. Ahhhh... you're so good at whatever you do for me, my lovely sister."

"Then you'll finally be leaving your wife, Colonel al-Adwani?" She paused for a second.

"No Farseeha, poor me. Alas, my beloved wife was killed in one of the many allied attacks against our country. I don't know what she was doing so near one of our missile sites. Someone told me she had a message in my name." He lied he had no intention of leaving his wife ever for Farseeha. He was stringing her along until she was killed on this her final mission. Colonel al-Adwani gave her a quick wink as returned to his shaft with vigor this time.

"Ahhh..." He moaned as he arched his back, Farseeha did not pull off him.

"I fear no one can give such great pleasures of the body like you can offer, Farseeha." Colonel al-Adwani watched as she wiped her mouth on the filthy bed spread, and then complained.

"Colonel al-Adwani, I must report that I was forced to please the ugly Libyan dog in much the same manner as I have just done for you, before he gave me the god cursed weapons I demanded from him. I'll seek revenge on his foul head, once I completed this mission my lover."

"The son of a milkless whore reared by a camel's arse and his foul urine." Colonel al-Adwani growled nastily, hiding the fact it was he who told the Libyan to enjoy Farseeha's special talents.

"I shall kill him for that terrible insult against your person, Colonel al-Adwani."

"Yes, of course you will my foolish young daughter, and I'll be in attendance when you do so to the filthy dog of the desert. I might piss on his foul body for insulting you in this foul manner, my lovely sister.

I'll spit in the face of the lowly foul jackal, as he lay dying at your feet, until your revenge is complete against his foul being, Farseeha." It was Colonel al-Adwani who had actually picked the target Farseeha was to offer Captain Briegheeth and Mamdouh al-Qassan. He knew if the order came from his headquarters, Captain Briegheeth would have complained to his control, and there would have been a war of words raging between the two services that were in control of the operation. Something Colonel al-Adwani wanted to avoid at all cost, because he was only going to lose one of his operative on this dangerous mission, not two.

"Colonel Farseeha, when you set up for your attack against the American fool, I want you to be well prepared to leave the area the instant the worthless American President is dead by your hand. You are ordered to leave the other two fools behind, in case they're attacked by the hated Secret Service of this foul and evil country. I want you to get out of the United States alive my love. Who is going to be the shooter on this mission?" Colonel al-Adwani offered to her as he smiled reassuringly at her to reassure her he was truly worried for her.

"I am, my brother and lover. I have trained too long to allow one of the fools to take the shot." The female terrorist replied proudly over the honor of being the shooter for the mission.

Colonel al-Adwani nodded pleasantly, knowing full well that Farseeha was as good as dead already as she offered him she was to be the shooter on this operation.

"You're not going to be with us on this sacred mission I take it then, Colonel al-Adwani?" Farseeha asked with much concern lacing her tone of voice this time.

"No my beloved sister, but I'll be an observer from a short distance away, and I'll act as your backup so I know you'll live through this mission, my sister. I'll register the kill for you. You just worry about getting out of the area alive, so we can be together forever after this god cursed mission is done with, Farseeha." Again, Colonel al-Adwani was lying. He was not going to be anywhere near the shooting.

CHAPTER SIX

TUESDAY, JULY 27th, 1999. JOINT ANDREWS AIR FORCE BASE. 10:30 A.M. EST

The cramped and extremely irritable Iraqi Captain Briegheeth shifted his rearend for the umpteenth time while trying to get comfortable on the narrow metal grate he was resting on. It was two weeks since the three terrorists last showered, shaved, or relaxed properly. Even their sleep was constantly interrupted by the ever roving security patrols that became intensive over the past two weeks, and the ever present mosquitoes also interrupted their peace and rest.

At one point during the night, a bright light was shined at the water tower, it crossed over the shelter they used for an observation post, it was the old pump station for the water tower. It was just large enough for the three terrorists to hide in. Captain Briegheeth was deeply worried the three security guards were going to climb the metal ladder and check the tower out closer. But the light went out and the roar of the engine of the small jeep leaving the area, assured the Iraqi Captain and terrorist as good as the security for the American President was it was not perfect.

For the past three days since the terrorists assumed position on the old water tower. The flood of security personnel on the airfield increased dramatically, an armored military type vehicle was pulled up alongside the well sequestered aircraft resting in what the Americans labeled the penalty box of the airbase, that separated the military end of the base for the President's needs. Captain Briegheeth watched as a flood of police officers dressed in black uniforms took positions around the aircraft and airbase. All air traffic taking off towards the President's aircraft was shifted towards the other end of the massive base, even though this forced the other aircraft to take off with the wind, instead of against it. Security at the terminal was maddening with a flood of armed personnel watching everyone moving about the structure on the base.

Even though the President was not going to come anywhere near the terminal building, it was basically closed to the general public. One look at the many soldiers openly carrying weapons, informed everyone there the soldiers were prepared to shoot anyone who made a stupid move against them. It was mostly American soldiers walking around inside the building, and the civilians felt extremely threatened by the security guards who seemed to glare at everyone.

A pair of fast moving military helicopters appeared from the south end of the base, and landed away from the massive aircraft. Eight officers poured on the field, but remained near their crafts.

Captain Briegheeth watched everything taking place on Joint Andrews Air Force Base. He knew when it was confirmed the American President was on his way to the base. The helicopters would take off and remain airborne, and escort the massive aircraft down the runway. Four F-18 Hornets slowly taxied up to the President's aircraft, stopped, and were checked out by security personnel. The Hornets were topped off with fuel, and the pilots remained inside their aircraft while surrounded by the small army of Secret Service representatives. The horde of security guards actually aimed their weapons at the pilots at all times. Captain Briegheeth shook his head slowly, not believing the security guards did not even trust their own American pilots.

Every muscle in Iraqi Captain Briegheeth's cramped body tightened up, as he watched the security personnel taking up new positions all around the massive aircraft and airbase. For some reason, the water tower was never really scrutinized closely by the gaggle of security agents. He felt they believed it was too far away from the airbase to be a possible threat against the President or any of his staff. He turned to his two fellow terrorists and announced in a commanding tone at them. "We'll take the time to eat now, and then discard the rest of the food we have. I want everyone alert and ready to act. Today, the God of our Father's land calls us to our glory. We must be prepared to answer His call, and carry out His bidding for the good of Iraq and Allah."

For the rest of the day, both Farseeha and al-Qassan tried their best to try and relax and gather their strength, but Captain Briegheeth kept a constant vigil on the massive airfield and the massive Air Force One aircraft. As the moments slowly ticked away, the security teams seemed to be growing at a fast rate, and becoming much more alert and active and searching the area constantly with their eyes. For the first time since the three Iraqi terrorists arrived at the old and abandoned water tower, Captain Jebril Briegheeth spotted a number of police officers armed with long range rifles taking up positions on any knoll or building surrounding the massive airfield. There were a number of fighter aircraft also making constant passes over certain areas of the airbase now, swooping in low and fast. He did not know the smaller F-18s were taking pictures that were instantly transmitted to the terminal, and then gone over by the secret service members.

Farseeha stared at the back of Captain Briegheeth's head because she decided she was going to kill him right after she successfully dispatched the hated American President.

At seven twenty p.m., it began to get dark and the terrorists were more on the alert, staring at the road that would bring their intended high value target to his waiting death. A constant flow of military vehicles, and unmarked security cars parked in the area now. Captain Briegheeth felt every police officer and security personnel in all of Washington was now gathered on the airbase. He was wrong, with each passing minute, more vehicles pulled onto the airfield. What he had not noticed was the military and civilian aircraft coming in, or taking off from Andrews, were now stopped or stacked up in the air, and the base was as quiet as a church. Just as the clock turned to eight p.m., a new rush of speeding vehicles rapidly approached the huge airbase. It was no doubt in his mind it was the President's private entourage as he called out. "Farseeha, he arrives."

Farseeha wiggled her way up the few feet to the small hole she had drilled in the wall in the side of the building she was hiding in, and then she carefully slid the weapon's long mussel out of the tiny opening she cut into the thin metal skin. She paid no attention to all that was going on around the rest of the massive airfield, she concentrated all her energy on the door of the Air Force One aircraft the American President had branded Eagle's Nest, and the number of security guards she could see standing out in the opening of the aircraft. It was the others of her cell's responsibility to make sure no one interfered with her shot at the President until she took it.

Captain Jebril Briegheeth was amazed at how well the security had tightened up even more around the aircraft and base. He was a little worried if there would be enough room for the bullet to pass by them, as it sliced through the air on its way to the intended target as he called out. "Farseeha, ready, the foul vehicles have stopped at the stairs of the cursed aircraft, and the people are getting out of the foul vehicles now. You know what our target looks like, woman?"

"Fear not, he's as good as dead the moment I lay eyes on the great fool of the American Leader, Captain." Farseeha hissed as she stared into the scope of the weapon.

The Iraqi Captain Briegheeth returned to observing the long line of parked vehicles sitting by the massive aircraft. The American President got out of his vehicle quickly, after all the security guards had climbed out of the other vehicles first, and they instantly surrounded and protected him. The American Leader reached back in the car and he took the hand of the female Vice President, and then he helped her out of the vehicle carefully. On the other side of the long black limo, two other people got out, one was the National Security Director, Norman Griffin, and the other was the Secretary of Defense, Jerry Richardson.

The Iraqi Captain had no idea who these two men were, nor did he care. From the other limo, more people came out and there were hugs and shaking of hands and general laughter and conversation going on by the ever growing group of people bunching up by the aircraft.

He grumbled to himself bitterly, trying to actually will the American President to carry out his will. "Come on you great fool of a man and go up the god cursed steps so we can finally finish this long awaited drama. That's it, go up the foul steps dead man. Farseeha, the fool's heading up the foul steps it is time for Paradise awaits her heroes. Tonight, you'll sleep in the very pits of hell for all your crimes you have committed against the good people of Iraq, Mr. President."

Farseeha stared in the scope of her weapon and she easily picked up her slow moving target. The American President was nearly impossible to get a clear shot at for the time being, because of the small mob of people trying to suck up to him, as the President slowly headed up the metal steps leading to the waiting aircraft.

Captain Briegheeth saw the problem she was having getting a clear shot at the President and he called out to her in a commanding tone. "Farseeha, are you going to be able to get a shot at the great fool? If not, go through anyone standing in front of the fool. With the weapon you have at your command, the bullet will easily travel through three bodies or more to get at its target."

"Shut up fool, I'm trying to concentrate on our hated target!" Farseeha hissed angrily at Briegheeth, refusing to take her eyes off her target for an instant, as the American President moved up the steps to the waiting door of the huge aircraft. Once she almost squeezed the trigger, but a female suddenly moved in her line of fire when she was ready to take the shot. She did not know it was the Vice President she wanted to walk with the President until he boarded the aircraft, and then she was going down the steps. The President was half way up the steps now.

The American President Albert Cole did not like the heavy crush of people surrounding him. He never liked any sort of a crowd. He could not see his feet in front of him as he climbed the steps to Eagle's Nest, so he hesitated for a brief moment, to allow the people in front of him to move a little further up the steps, and give him some extra room to move. The ones following him knew what the President was up to, and they slowed their pace down some.

Farseeha smiled as she waited for the American President to get to the top step. The female Vice President suddenly joined him there as they shook hands, and hugged again before she left him standing alone on the platform. The Vice President then turned and smiled at a man who quickly came up the steps behind her. She and the President waited for this man to catch up to them. The Vice President stepped slightly aside and then she blocked Farseeha's easy shot at her target. The assassin cursed and waited again. She knew if this man got up to the top step before she was able to fire at her target, this man would totally block her shot on her. The President would escape his death by being escorted into the interior of the aircraft by this other man.

Sweat poured down her face as Farseeha held her breath in an attempt to try and calm her trembling nerves down, and then she pulled the trigger of the weapon. She felt this was going to be her best shot at the American Leader, and she took her shot. At the same exact instant as she pulled the trigger of her weapon, there was sudden movement on the steps leading to the aircraft's interior. The Vice President moved again, and the man who was standing on the steps jumped up and onto the small platform at the same instant the bullet arrived for its target.

The back of the head of the National Security Director exploded, sending brain matter, blood and bone fragments flying over all the people standing on the platform along with the stunned President, and in the doorway of the aircraft. But the bullet did not stop its death flight there. The instant the bullet was fired all eyes went searching for where the loud sound came from. Mary Hirshfield, the Vice President of the United States looked towards the sky, thinking it was possibly a sudden clap of thunder as she moved across the President's path. The bullet struck her in the right shoulder, and came out deflected by her collar bone near her neck.

Many excited and unseen hands instantly grabbed at the stunned and not moving President of the United States, and they roughly yanked him into the aircraft's interior, nearly lifting him off his feet in the process. While other security personnel fell on top of him, protecting his life from further rounds fired at him. One of the agents accidentally kneed the President in the groin. A second agent went to get by the President lying on the floor, and he accidentally stepped on his hand. The special agents and others gathered on the steps to the aircraft tried to run down them, seeking cover and safety. It instantly turned into a rolling mass of bodies tumbling down the metal steps, as gunfire erupted from all around the secluded aircraft; all weapons were firing in the direction where it was thought the sniper's bullet came from.

Inside Air Force One, the angry and hurting President tried to push the sudden crush of bodies off the top of his body. When he was able to crawl out from under the pile of secret service guards, he looked at the staircase and saw the fixed and staring eyes of his Vice President, as she lay helplessly on the top landing of the portable steps, and he roared at the nearest agent to him. "Get my fucking Vice President the hell inside this fucking aircraft immediately, god dammit. Is she still alive for the love of

God! Who the hell did this to her for Christ sake?" President Albert Cole growled angry at his security agents as he watched them jump into action.

As the fuming President screamed, hands dragged him deeper into the interior of the aircraft for his own protection. The sounds of jeeps and cars starting up and then roaring away from the area could be heard from outside the aircraft, along with the roar of the attack aircraft and helicopters taking off or closing in on the aircraft as well. Gunfire burst forth around the President's aircraft as more hands pulled the wounded Vice President Hirshfield into the waiting plane. A loud noise just to the right side of the aircraft scared the President as he yelled at the people helping with his injured Vice President. "Is she still alive, god dammit!"

The sound of something inflating drowned out his cry and demand. A number of hands roughly pulled the President back to his feet while ignoring the position of the most powerful man in all the United States. The President was dragged and then shoved towards the right side of the massive aircraft, and then he was unceremoniously thrown down the rubber slide. Heavily armed soldiers waiting at the bottom of the inflated ramp, immediately pulled the President from it, and they literally tossed him head first into the waiting armored vehicle that had pulled up alongside the slide ramp of the aircraft when the weapon fire started.

"God dammit, someone answer me for Christ sake! Is Mary fucking alive or what, god dammit!" President Cole snarled again as he allowed himself to be manhandled by his agents.

An excited secret service agent jumped on top of President Cole, and he replied to his demand. "Yes Mr. President, the Vice President's alive. She was breathing on her own when I last saw her sir. She's in a helluva lot of pain, but she's conscious and is trying to talk, but the wound was making it impossible for her to speak properly sir. The medic's taking good care of her at this time sir. No if and or buts about it sir, you're out of here sir. Are you alright sir?"

"The hell with me for fuck sake, take your damn hands off of me, mister. I'm the fucking President of the United States, and I simply refuse to be treated and handled like this for a moment longer for Christ sake. I want to see my Vice President, dammit!"

"Sorry for the rough treatment Mr. President, but I'm in charge of you now sir. No can do that sir, you can't see the Vice President under any circumstances right now sir. Driver, get us the hell outta here pronto mister. Head for the White House." The agent had to actually place both his hands on the angry President's chest to force him back in the seat, and then he tried to strap him in for his own safety, but he refused to be restricted by the seatbelt.

As the armored car rapidly pulled away from Air Force One now known as Eagle's Nest, it was instantly surrounded by a flood of police and unmarked cars. The small convoy of vehicles drove forward while crashing into other squad cars that accidently ventured into their way, or could not get out of the armored vehicles way in time. Two attack helicopters took position over the car, and they escorted and guarded it on its way back to the White House.

"I missed the great fool Captain! Damn the hands that guide fate was not with me on this god cursed night. I have missed the great fool and hit some other fool who was with him, and he is still alive and is now safe." Farseeha shouted out to warn the others of her failure.

"There's no time to worry about that now Farseeha. Discard your sniper weapon and take your automatic rifle in hand; the lowly jackals obviously know where the bullet came from, and they are rapidly attacking us now, woman. I take sanctuary in Paradise, my brother and sister." Captain Briegheeth yelled out as he watched a sea of people wildly charge at the water tower.

An attack helicopter arrived first and hovered over the tower, and it started to blast away at the tall structure with its heavy machine guns. Military vehicles slid to a stop before the legs of the water tower, and the soldiers poured out of the machines and they fired up at the shape wildly.

Mamdouh al-Qassan was the first one to return fire at the horde of security guards firing at them, and he was instantly ripped apart by a string of bullets slamming into his body from the low hovering helicopter. Captain Briegheeth glanced around his position, looking for a better place to hide in, or to try and make his escape from. When he saw none existed, he drew in his breath and then fired at the first police officer trying to climb up the ladder to get at them. His fire brought weapons trained on the tower firing at him. He died before he even exhaled.

Farseeha wiggled into the narrow spot from which she fired at the President from, and she opened fire at the soldiers and police officers and special agents surrounding the water tower against her. Hundreds of weapons fired as one, literally ripping the metal structure apart. The firing did not stop until there was not enough of the structure left to hide a rat in. A second fast attack helicopter arrived on scene, and four SWAT Officers rapid repelled down the ropes and the officers landed on top of what was left of the ripped apart water tower.

The officers cautiously crawled on their bellies to the edge, and spotted the bodies of three terrorists lying on the landing, and they pumped a few more rounds into them, to make certain they were no longer a threat against them. Once they were certain the three terrorists were dead, the SWAT Officers climbed down the side of the slowly crumbling water tower, splitting up on the narrow landing, with two officers working their way around from each end of where they landed. They moved extremely cautiously, when the first officer saw the head of a terrorist, he fired at it. The body jumped from the round striking it in the middle of the forehead and from the way it moved, the officer knew immediately the body of this man was already dead.

The heavy weapons firing from below the tower stopped the instant the SWAT team arrived on scene. Security agents on the ground put up their weapons, and set crime scene tape out, and watched the other officers check the bodies. One officer signaled the men on the ground with his hand, informing them three were spotted, and three were down. Two secret service personnel jumped on the metal ladder, and climbed up to the shattered landing. Water poured out of the thousands of bullet holes ripped into the light metal skin of the water drum, making it extremely dangerous to climb up the ladder, or to move around on the narrow metal landing of the tower.

When the SWAT Officers saw the special agents heading up the ladder, they pulled away from the bodies of the three dead terrorists, so as to not mess up the crime scene any more than it already was on them. The special agents were in control of any investigation as always to be carried out when there was an attempted assassination on a seated President's life.

THE DRAGOON ARMORED PERSONNEL CARRIER

The heavily armored vehicle with the President being bounced around inside it, ripped through the streets of downtown Washington while heading back for the White House at breakneck speed, plowing into any civilian cars that ventured into its path, as it went through red lights and stop signs at will. The traffic was heavy, mostly with police, military, and unmarked secret service vehicles, all heading for Joint Base Andrews Air Force Base. When the alarm shots were fired at the President of the United States went out, every police unit throughout Washington and Maryland immediately activated. Police cars stopped the flow of all side street traffic, until the President's vehicle passed their positions. The fast moving caravan protecting President Cole was picked up, and followed by every type of police vehicles in the surrounding area.

Inside the bouncing and speeding armored Dragoon vehicle, the President of the United States was fit to be tied. He screamed at the agents as they kept their eyes glued to the gun ports, to make certain there was not another attempt on the President's life, while was under their charge.

"What the fuck's going on out there for the love of God, dammit? How the hell is my Vice President doing, someone find out how she is for Christ sake! You're all fucking fired, every last one of you bastards are gone from your damn jobs! Was anyone else hit in this damn mess tonight? I want the fucking skins of the lousy bastard's who did this, hanging on the Oval Office door by this time tomorrow morning, or asses are going to fry, and you'll all be looking for new jobs by tomorrow morning. How the hell is Mary doing I asked, god dammit?"

The co-driver of the Dragoon vehicle glanced back at the extremely upset American Leader as he offered in a contrite tone to the man. "Mr. President Sir, we were just informed by radio that they got all the damn shooters already, sir. There were three of them, two males and one female, and all three are dead, sir. They didn't want to give up to the officers, sir."

"Fuck them where they breathe, I want to know how Mary is doing for Christ sake."

"With the greatest respect Mr. President Sir, I'll make contact with the hospital and see if I can find out what's up with the Vice President, and how she's doing for you sir."

"You do that mister, not a half an hour from now, and not even five minutes from now. You will do it right this god damn minute mister! You should have done this crap already for me dammit. Was there anyone else hit in this damn attack obviously aimed at us, mister? Where was all this damn security at that was supposed to be protecting me at all times? How the fuck was these damn assholes able to get this close to us?" President Albert Cole was not able to see what happened before him. When the shot was fired, someone instantly grabbed him by the collar of his coat, and roughly pulled him into the safety of the aircraft. All the President knew was, there was fresh blood all over his suit, and if it was Mary's he feared she had to be dead. As he waited for a reply from the driver, the President picked a flake from his suit and studied it carefully. When he realized it was bone fragment, he dropped it like it burned him and he gagged.

The co-driver of the armored vehicle looked at the President, and when Mr. Cole saw the look he feared Mary died in the attack against him, and he barked one word at the man. "What!"

"With all due respect Mr. President, the Vice President is in critical but stable condition, sir. The sniper's bullet entered her right shoulder area, and it came out by her neck, sir. She's breathing on her own, but she's in a helluva lot of pain sir. The Doc's are very hopeful sir. If she survives, they don't know if she's going to be able to speak again though, Mr. President."

"Dammit to hell!" The President growled in a shaking voice and then he added to his angry words. "Was there anyone else hit in this mess?"

"Fraid so, Mr. President." The driver offered as he took a quick breath in for himself.

"Well give it to me mister, dammit!" he snarled back at the young driver.

"Yes Sir Mr. President." The soldier said shocked at the uncontrolled rage that was in the angry President's tone. "Mr. President, the National Security Director, Mr. Griffin's dead sir. He was hit in the head by the round, sir. He was dead before he hit the floor sir. Sorry sir."

"Shit! Can you make contact with the Chairman of the Joint Chiefs of Staff on that damn thing for me mister?" the President asked as he tried to calm down some.

"Yes Sir Mr. President, but I'm afraid it might take me a few seconds to do it though sir."

"Good, get General White on that damn thing this instant, and tell him to report to the damn White House, STAT. I want him there before I arrive, mister. Errr… you better wake up that big Native American friend of the General's as well, mister. I want his ass at my office too. We have to respond to this shit immediately for the love of the good Christ Child." President Cole stopped growling, and suddenly rested his head in his hands, thinking about Mary and Norman.

The extra driver knew who the President meant, and he replied to his Commander in Chief. "Mr. President, I believe the CIA Director John Raincloud has already been informed about the attempted assassination on your life, sir. From what I have been able to pick up from the radio chatter sir, he's already on the crime scene conducting an investigation himself, sir."

The President was stunned he did not realize this was an attempted assassination on his life until this very moment. He drew in his breath and then let it out slowly as he moaned. "I don't care where the fuck he's at right now you just find the man and tell him to report to the White House immediately. He's to drop whatever the hell he's doing and report to the Oval Office, period. I'm not going to stand for this crap for a god damn second I assure you, mister. I want heads resting on spikes, and that's what I'm going to have, dammit."

"Yes Sir Mr. President Sir." The driver did as ordered by the American Leader.

The President finally settled back and closed his eyes, allowing the vehicle to bounce him around like a rag doll. Every time someone blew a horn in the streets, he thought someone else was trying to shoot him. He wondered who would have dared to try and kill him, and why.

It took the heavily military armored vehicle fifteen minutes to reach the White House area. When the machine turned onto Pennsylvania Avenue, the drive was locked down. His vehicle had to stop until a massive Abrams A1A2 main battle tank was moved out of the way. The entire block of Pennsylvania Avenue was ringed with heavily armed soldiers, all ready to kill anyone who dared to even look at them cross eyed. The heavy metal White House gate was closed and heavily guarded by Marines, and huge dump trucks loaded with yards of sand in the dump bodies blocked the entrance. Again, the President's vehicle had to stop, until the dump trucks were moved away from before his waiting vehicle, and the gates then slowly opened.

Once back on the White House grounds, tens of heavily armed Marine soldiers lined up protectively along the long and winding driveway to the main structure of the White House. When the armored vehicle passed the soldiers, the Marines moved back in the road to block anyone else from getting any nearer to the White House than where they stood. Three attack helicopters patrolled the air over the White House. The upset President looked to the roof of the White House, and he noticed it was swarming with heavily armed special agents and soldiers. Most of them were speaking into portable radios locked in their hands. Machine guns were set up, all aiming in different directions on the property. Not even a bird could approach the White House with this much armor and soldiers hanging around, and survive the attempt.

When the armored vehicle pulled up to the main entrance of the White House and stopped, another horde of special agents immediately swarmed around it and then waited for the shaken President of the United States to step out of the war machine. They instantly moved in and shielded the shaken President with their bodies as he was quick marched to the entrance of the building, complaining all the way. "I want to speak to Mary right this fucking minute, dammit!" He bellowed the instant he spotted his White House Chief of Staff aide coming towards him from inside the building with an extremely worried look on his face.

The young man stopped dead in his tracks and responded in a calm tone. "I'll see what I can do about your last request, Mr. President Sir. I can't promise you anything at this tim..."

"I didn't tell you to see what you can do about it I told you I wanted to speak to Mary right now, dammit! If I can't speak to her by phone, I don't give a rat's ass what these fucking Agents and damn soldiers have to say about it. I'm heading for that fucking hospital myself, and your job here is fucking history, mister." President Cole glared hotly at the young Chief of Staff aide, until he jumped into action and quickly disappeared back inside the doors to the White House.

"That's better, dammit." President Cole barked at the back of the young man. He was cursing up a storm, and it did not matter if any female staff was within earshot of his flood of angry and upsetting words. He was fuming and uncontrollable and very concerned about his Vice President's condition, as he marched down the hall to the Oval Office. He crashed into the doors like a line backer trying to get at the quarterback on the football field.

THE WATER TOWER NEAR JOINT ANDREWS AIR FORCE BASE

The SWAT Officers cautiously approached and then checked out the bodies of the three downed terrorists, they were bullet ridden and very dead. The SWAT Officers pitched the dead bodies over the side of the rail from the water tower, and allowed them to crash to the ground some fifty feet below them. They were dead, and there was no need being careful with the bodies from this point on. When the terrorist bodies hit the ground with a sickening thud, a horde of special agents moved in and they began to strip the bodies of their tattered clothes. They checked the woman's private places for any possible hidden explosives, or hidden identification. The agents carefully checked out the bodies of the two males of the assassination team as well.

Then the agents left the naked bodies of the terrorists uncovered lying on the ground. A horde of reporters tried to get around the special agents and security tape to get some pictures of the dead attackers, and what the agents was doing to their bodies. The reporters were roughly shoved back behind the crime tape set up to keep everyone out of the agent's way and area.

The SWAT Team Officers remained checking out the landing of the old water tower, as a number of more special agents joined them. They carefully picked through all the debris littering the narrow walkway surrounding the water tower. The agents picked up the weapons used by the three terrorists, bagged and tagged them as evidence and then they passed them down to other agents waiting on the ground to be properly taken care of and secured. The officers picked up food wrappers and urine cans, and looked for any possible receipts to try and determine where the items were bought. The special agents ordered the police officers down from the landing as they now assumed complete command of the ongoing investigation.

Once the agents took over the investigation from the police, it was determined there had to be another terrorist involved in the attack, one they did not get. On a slip of paper discovered in the litter on the walkway of the tower, a lone name was written printed out on it, al-Adwani. Agent Winters was handed the small slip of paper and he scrutinized it. The agent who found the paper mumbled to him with concern lacing his tone. "Sir, I examined the weapons of the terrorists and they're American sir, they'll be rather hard for us to trace sir. They could have come into the country with the damn terrorists, or they were picked up at any local gun show, or from any of the many underground suppliers, sir. The numbers on the weapons have been pretty well ground off, but I'm certain the lab boys should be able to raise the numbers so we can read them, sir.

"It looks like we have one more shooter out there someplace, sir. I think he might be the one commanding the other assholes here sir. He made certain he kept his fricking ass well out of the line of fire, sir. He probably directed them from a safe place. We found a small portable radio in the mess he must have used it to communicate with the other terrorists on the tower, sir."

"How's that?" Winters snapped as he stared at the agent and held on the paper with the name.

"The way I see it sir, this paper was in the possession of the female terrorist. We found it in the area where she took the shot from, sir. From what we can tell, she was the shooter, and the males were her backup and protection. The positioning of the male shooters, informs me they tried to protect the female, and hold us off until she took her shot, and they make certain her target was out of the picture. That informs me the shooter was to report to this al-Adwani when the deed was carried out. It was her first mistake I thought these terrorists were better trained than this sir. To take the name of your control to your shoot is plain nuts. It gives us a path to take, sir."

"You're smart, perhaps too fucking smart. Pay that much attention to your duties, and skip all the smart remarks will ya. Were you able to trace the radio freq back to this control, Agent?"

"No sir, the control broke off contact immediately sir, as soon as the first shot was evidently fired off. He's a smart one, he made certain we couldn't trace him back that easily, sir."

"I agree with your assumption, mister. I believe we have another fricking shooter out there on the prowl on the streets of Washington somewhere, and until we find the fucking prick, the President's life is still in danger. I'll inform General White we have a loose cannon in Washington he can take it from there. He's the man to take over this mess now I take it. Has the damn Doctor arrived on scene yet sir?" Agent Winters moaned as he glanced down towards the ground and saw an old man approaching the bodies as if he was afraid they would do him harm.

"Ahhh... there's the little prick now I guess sir. Hope he can determine who these bastards belong to for us. Seeing the name al-Adwani printed on that small slip of paper, makes me believe we're dealing with more fucking Arab terrorists on this one, sir. Now, all we have to do is determine whose stable the bastards belong to and half the battle's done, sir." Winters grumbled at the young agent standing at his side as he watched the doctor cautiously moved in.

A youngish and very cautious doctor carefully approached the bodies of the three dead terrorists as if they were still alive, and he carefully rolled one on his side and took a vile of blood from each body. He placed the blood in a small kit and shook it rapidly in his hand. Then he placed the vile into a portable computer and separating system. Within seconds, the doctor was able to determine the fountainhead of the assassin's origin. Once he had this evidence in hand, he yelled up to the controlling special agent, and informed him of his test results.

"Agent Winters Sir, from all the tests I just performed on the blood of the three dead terrorist's sir. They're certainly Arab terrorists, sir." The doctor quickly reported to him.

"No fricking kidding, but that don't tell me jack fucking shit where the damn terrorists came from, mister! We have already determined that much just from the fucking evidence we have located in this mess up here sir. I need to know what fucking Arabs they are, Doc?" Agent Winters bellowed back at the doctor as he cupped his hands around his mouth.

"That'll take me a few more seconds to determine that evidence with any certainty, sir."

"Then stop bugging my fucking ass until you have that damn information I need, Doc." The agent snarled nastily, and then he went back to picking through the litter on the landing of the nearly destroyed water tower, placing spent shells in the evidence bags after examining each one of them carefully. Each agent wore plastic gloves and booties, and they made certain where they stepped to preserve any possible evidence on the scene. The doctor went back to his computer and beat on the keyboard. Seconds later, he called out to the agent again.

"Agent Winters Sir, all evidence I have points to the purps being of Iraqi nationality, sir."

"Are you god damn certain about that fucking decision, Doc?" Agent Winters again glared down at the upset doctor from where he stood on the nearly destroyed landing of the water tower.

"Ninety nine point nine percent certain of it, sir." The doctor replied calmly to the agent.

"You're busting my fucking horns again here Doc, and you better place a quick end to it if you like your damn job mister. I'm not here to split fucking hairs over this shit with you Doctor. That's not what I fucking asked you. Are you certain they're fucking Iraqi's there Doc?"

"Yes Agent Winters, they're unmistakably Iraqi's in their origin, sir. The blood history confirms this as to be the fact as far as I can tell without having a lab to properly work with to make absolutely certain of my findings, sir." The doctor shot a smile up at the angry agent, in an attempt to stop him from yelling at him so much and loudly. But the smile did nothing to soothe over the angry agent's mood, as he continued to glare down at the now very upset doctor.

Without responding further to the doctor's words, Agent Winters lifted his arm and then spoke in his mike hidden in the sleeve of his jacket. "Yes, this is Agent Winters, you want to inform Director Raincloud that these birds are definitely Iraqi pricks we have on our hands here, sir. Also, inform the Director there's another shooter still on the loose out there somewhere, sir. No sir, we didn't get them all when we hit them, sorry sir. The cell's control wasn't with the damn shooters we got here, sir. Yes, you'll contact Director Raincloud for me sir? Thanks much."

CIA Director Raincloud was in his car heading for the White House as ordered, as fast as the Washington traffic would allow, dodging police and military vehicles flooding the roads when the call came in. "Director Raincloud, our Agent in the field reports the shooters were identified as

Iraqi terrorists, sir. e stated there's another one that they didn't get during the attack, sir."

"Shit. Is he positive they're Iraqi terrorists, sir?" the Director asked the agent with concern.

"Yes sir, he's positive of that in his report, sir." The agent replied to Raincloud over the radio.

"Crap, that's going to be a serious problem for us to work around this time, dammit." He replied as Director Raincloud's car stopped at the beginning of the road leading to the White House, and he had to wait until the massive Abrams tank started up and slowly moved out of his way, before he could enter the White House ground. The surrounding area of the White House looked like a heavily armed military camp, with tens of extremely threatening and armed soldiers, and special agents hiding behind anything they could get behind.

Countless military jeeps and armored personnel carriers were parked all over the front lawn of the White House, and heavily armed helicopters hovered like a swarm of angry large bees over the ground. Everywhere Director Raincloud looked, he spotted either a soldier, or a special agent, or a police officer standing or locked in a firing position, and they were all heavily armed and looked like they were just daring anyone to look at them the wrong way.

CIA Director John Raincloud spotted a number of his special agents running around the White House grounds, dressed in their black body armor and hoods, and was heavily armed and ready for anything to come their way. All other soldiers and police officers and special agents were likewise dressed in their bulletproof vests, and they were prepared to defend the grounds and the President and his staff against any possible intruders who might be trying to get at their leader.

Director Raincloud's staff car pulled up to the main doors of the White House, and he got out and entered the locked down structure. He was greeted by one of the White House aides, and then escorted to the Oval Office and waiting President by an armed special agent.

INSIDE THE OVAL OFFICE

When President Albert Cole attacked the doors to his office as if he was personally angry at them, he found General John White, the Chairman of the Joint Chiefs of Staff, already waiting in the office for him to arrive. He was startled by the way the President entered his office.

"Oh, I see you're here already thank you, General White Sir. This is good, very good in deed sir!" the President snapped harshly at the seated General enjoying a cup of coffee.

"Mr. President, you were the one who ordered me here to use your own words, STAT sir." General White grumbled as he went back to sipping his coffee. He was upset over the fact there was an attempted assassination on the President's life on his watch, but he was a professional and hid the fact he was so upset. He did not want the President to see he was so angry.

"Who the hell were these bastards that tried to pull this shit off against me, General White Sir? The sonofabitches tried to take me out, assassinate me like I was some kind of a fucking criminal or something right here in my country, dammit. They killed Griffin, and wounded Mary for the love of God. For that, I'll have their fucking balls for tie god damn tacks, sir. General White, John, I want you to take Director Raincloud and the both of you are to make a..."

"We have already positively identified the terrorist cell as Iraqi terrorists, Mr. President." Director Raincloud announced in a commanding tone, as he entered the President's office.

President Cole heard a noise behind him and turned and saw Director Raincloud entering his office, and he snapped angrily at him. "How the hell do you know they were Iraqi attackers for a fact so quickly, I just found out there was an attempt on my god damn life, for Christ sake."

"Mr. President, a Doctor in the field ran a quick DNA run on the bodies of the terrorists, sir, and he discovered their blood chemistry was compatible with that of the Iraqi bloodline, sir. He's going to run a much more detailed scan on the blood when he returns to his lab, to make certain of his findings out in the field, sir. With all due respect Mr. President, I have to inform you that there's a strong belief another shooter, possibly the actual control for this damn terrorist cell, is still out there someplace and moving around against us, sir. That means you're going to be forced to endure house arrest so to say, until we successfully capture the missing bastard, sir."

"The Iraqi's tried this shit against my ass, dammit. If I find out that damn madman Saddam Hussein and his pissant thugs were behind this assassination attempt on my life. I'm going to bomb his ass all the way back to the days of Ali Baba and his forty thieves. I want to see Mary, let her know that I'm with her." The President suddenly roared as he walked around his massive desk, and then he plopped down in his chair and stared back at Director Raincloud.

General White continued to enjoy his coffee, more than pleased to allow Director Raincloud, to field the questions and demands from the angry and rather upset President.

"Sorry sir, no can do that sir. As I stated Mr. President, you're at this time theoretically under house arrest until further notice sir, or we have captured this last terrorist, sir. That means Article Three has been instigated against you for your own protection, sir. You're not going within three miles of the wounded Vice President until we get this last shooter sir, and we know there are no other terrorists hanging around out there still hunting you, Mr. President." Director Raincloud tried a quick smile on the still extremely upset and exhausted American Leader. It was wasted, and Director Raincloud had to absorb the harsh tongue lashing from the angry President.

"Now you look here Director Raincloud, how the hell long have you known me mister?" President Cole growled angrily at the CIA Director this time.

"Oh, I don't know Mr. President, somewhere around ten years I'd imagine now sir."

"Fine, then you know damn well that I don't like being told what I can and cannot fucking do around here, especially in my own god damn office and country, buster. I intend to see Mary, and I don't think I need your damn permission to do so either, mister." The President snarled at his powerful CIA Director as he continued to openly glare at him.

"With all due respect Mr. President Sir, I understand perfectly how you must feel about this order and situation, Mr. President. But I have to insist you stay far away from the Vice President, until we get our hands on this last terrorist, and this present situation has ended, Mr. President

Sir." Director Raincloud remarked, and then he smiled for a second time at the President.

"You have to insist you say to me mister. You do have fucking brass Bravos (balls) to say that to me and expect to live, Director Raincloud Sir." The President snarled, and then he relaxed some, knowing the large Native American was correct and he moaned. "When can I see her?"

"Perhaps some time on Monday in the afternoon at the earliest sir, by then we should know where this last missing terrorist is hiding at, and we'll either have him in custody, or he's dead sir. Hopefully sir, he'll be in our custody and then we'll find out for certain who was truly behind this attempted assassination against your life, sir."

"Fine Director Raincloud, you obviously won this round I guess, mister. Let's talk about the, err... what did you just call them sir?" the American Leader replied as he let his breath out in a rush, and then he seemed to relax a little more.

"Shooters Mr. President Sir." The CIA Director replied to the President's last question.

"Yes, the shooters. You said they were positively identified as Iraqi terrorists, Director Raincloud Sir." The President mumbled as he calmed down a bit more now.

"Yes Sir Mr. President, we're certain of this much about the shooters so far sir." Raincloud replied as General White refilled his cup with coffee. This caught the President's attention.

"General White, I'm so glad to see that you're taking this assassination attempt on my life so causally and calm, mister. Please enjoy your coffee there sir!" President Cole suddenly glared angrily at the seated General, waiting for him to respond to his heated words aimed at him.

"What do you want me to do, Mr. President? Jump up and down on one foot and rant and rave like a lunatic while beating my chest with both fists, sir? I will if you'd like that sir, but what the hell good would that do anyone around here, Mr. President. All I know is, you're safe and sound Mr. President, and there's another shooter out there somewhere looking to take your life sir, and he's probably stalking you as we speak in this office sir. He'll have to be some kind of magician though if he's going to try and get through the defenses I have set up around the White House and you, Mr. President. I have enough elite and specialized troops out there, to stop

EAGLE'S NEST

World War Three from taking place at this point, Mr. President Sir. I even dare him to make another attempt on your life sir." Now it was General White who tried a smile on the fuming President.

"Don't give me any of that shit, mister! I don't like being shot at while I'm boarding my..."

Their conversation was interrupted by Senator Wilson, who came charging into the President's office. His expression showed he was extremely worried he was going to be told the President was killed in this assassination attempt. When the President saw the expression on the worried Senator's face, he smiled as he offered to the elderly politician. "Please relax I'm not dead, sorry for scaring you like this Senator Wilson Sir."

"Thank the Good Lord for that much Mr. President Sir. I was at a special meeting when the word there was a shooting at Air Force One came in. I'm afraid I though the worst for you sir."

"Have a seat Bob. How's Eagle's Nest, Director? Did she suffer any damage in the attack?"

"I don't know that for certain sir, checking on the plane was the furthest thing from my mind."

"Thank you for that much concern sir. I'll accept that remark for the time being Mr..."

Again their conversation was interrupted, this time by the Secretary of State, who was being quickly wheeled into the Oval Office by the young White House aide. Seeing Maria Hernandez's concerned and stunned face, made the President feel like he was finally safe and protected in his office. He nodded to her slightly, and then barked at the White House aide at the same time. "Did you do as I ordered you to do for me mister?"

"Yes sir, I sure did Mr. President Sir. I was informed Mary was rushed to surgery sir. What I got from the Doctors who would speak with me was, she's holding her own very well, but she's far from out of the woods at this time, Mr. President Sir."

"You keep on that for me every second she's still in the damn hospital, mister. I want constant updates on her condition, the second you become aware of them. I want to know the moment when she's out of surgery as well and how she is and when is the earliest I can speak to her. You're free to interrupt any conversations I'm engaging in, if you have any new information for me about Mary's condition. Get out and get back over to the damn hospital then keep me informed every ten minutes, mister."

"Yes sir, I'll do that Mr. President Sir. You can count on me sir."

Everyone waited until the White House aide was out of the office, and then Maria spoke as she took the President's hand in hers. "Albert, I can't tell you how happy I am to see that you're okay sir. I was so scared when I first found out there was a shooting by the aircraft involving you."

The President leaned forward and he kissed Maria lightly on the forehead tenderly, as he wiped a tear from her cheek and then offered pleasantly. "You're always in my corner Maria."

"You know I'm always there for you Albert. That's where I belong, Albert." She kissed his hand, and held it up to her cheek and added. "Who did this terrible thing against you Albert?"

"Director Raincloud's quite certain it was some Iraqi terrorists who tried to assassinate me today, honey. I don't know what the hell was behind their screwball way of thinking and attack, but I'm sure as hell going to find out though I assure you, young lady."

"Do you think it could be because of the continuing bombing we're still carrying out against President Saddam Hussein's unholy regime, Albert? You know we have discussed these ongoing situations in many of our conversations in enforcing the pair of no fly zones over Iraq, and we always felt it was only a matter of time before that mad dog tried something against us or our military forces, to try and stop the bombing of his country, Albert."

"Maria, I'm afraid this isn't the time for that conversation to be rehashed, honey. If the SOB wanted the bombing stopped, all he had to do was stop probing our resolve, and give up all his damn weapons of mass destruction. He's the damn ass in this picture, not me, young lady." President Cole snapped as he pulled his hand from Maria's grasp, and then he sat down on the edge of his desk and looked down at her. He loved Maria she was with him ever since he first ran for the Presidency of the United States. She was his staunchest backer, willing to defend his every decision, even if she was not very pleased with them. It tore his heart apart to see her being slowly eaten away by Muscular Dystrophy. When he first started out, he could not keep up with her when she walked with him, now, she had to be wheeled around wherever she went. To see this so strong a woman reduced to a cripple, took his breath away.

The American President drew in his breath, and then stated hotly to all gathered people in his office. "Look people I don't intend to hide behind the intercourse of diplomacy on this one. I'm going for his fucking, err... excuse me please Maria. I'm going for Saddam Hussein's god damn throat this time, if he's the bastard behind this assassination attempt on my life, dammit. If he was the one behind this attempt then I'm going to level his stinking regime right before his god damn eyes. I'll have his ass dragged back to the United States, so he can stand trial for the attempted assassination of an American President."

The Speaker of the House was next person to rush into the Oval Office. The President stopped speaking until Edward Gordon calmed down and took a seat, and then the President offered him. "I'm fine, thanks for the concern Mr. Speaker. The bastards hit Mary and killed Norman."

"Norman's dead, Mary's hurt, Christ sake sir. When you're ready to go after these bastards, give me a damn weapon and I'll get them for you sir. The sonofabitches killed a very good man, and hurt an outstanding woman and leader..."

The President laughed as he retorted. "Ed, you're sixty seven years old for Pete's sake sir."

"What the hell does that have to do with the price of tea in China, sir? Someone dares to hurt any Americans and tries to assassinate my President and friend on my watch, and as long as there is breath left in my body, sir. I'll get the sonofabitches."

"You know, with all the interruptions I'm constantly being hit with, I think it's about time I get my backside on the air waves and let the general public know I'm alright. While I'm doing this General White, I want you to order what's left of my Cabinet here, sir. Err... have your Joint Chiefs of Staff respond to my office as well General. Err... General White, what's the present situation with your specialized Rapid Response Strike Force? If it goes the way I think it will, we might have need of those outstanding soldiers you formed into this special attack force, sir. Better get in touch with your Commander, and have him place an order out for all Rapid Response Forces to stand by. I want to be ready to respond in any direction

I choose to go off in, sir. I'm not going to stand for this crap, especially taking place on American soil, General White.

"We're going to discuss exactly what we intend to do about this situation over the attempted assassination on my life sir, when I get back from my announcement to the general public, General. Exactly how and when we're going to respond to this attempt on my life. It's going to be a military response, General White Sir. All we have to determine is how strong a military response it will be, sir." President Cole leaned back and pressed the button to his intercom.

"Yes Peter, I think it's about time I take time out and address the public and let them know I'm fine and am still in command of my office. What time is it anyway? Nine thirty, okay, let's wake everyone up and have them respond to the press room A-SAP. I want to be able to speak to the public at ten sharp. Set up a conference for thirty minutes from now. Yes, all stations are to be interrupted by my broadcast, Peter. It's going to be a nationwide address this time. Did you find out anything else on Mary's condition for me, mister?"

"I'm afraid she's still in surgery, Mr. President Sir." The young Chief Aide of the White House announced cautiously, as he spoke to the concerned President.

"Dammit to hell and back." The President moaned as he stared at the young man.

CHAPTER SEVEN

COLONEL ABDULAZIZ MAJD al-ADWANI

Iraqi Colonel Abdulaziz Majd al-Adwani watched the attempted assassination on the American President's life from a safe distance away, as Farseeha took her shot at him. He was a little over a mile away from the old water tower, parked off the side of the road stationed where he could best see the water tower and the President's aircraft at the same time. He actually heard the report from Farseeha's weapon, and smiled as he aimed his field glasses at the American aircraft, hoping to see the President tumble down the steps, dead. He saw the one man's head explode, and the woman standing on the platform drop, obviously wounded by the same bullet. He cursed as he saw the American President being pulled safely into the interior of the large aircraft, and then disappeared from his view. From the way he moved, the foreign Colonel realized the American President was not even wounded by the round his shooter fired at him.

Angry over the failed assassination attempt, Colonel al-Adwani aimed his glasses back at the water tower, and waited for Farseeha to begin pounding away at the massive aircraft with random rounds, in hopes of hitting the invisible President now hidden inside the huge aircraft. His anger rose when she did not fire again at the American Leader. Then, the entire area around the water tower erupted with heavy weapon fire and glaring bright lights, mostly hitting the tower.

A harsh sneer slowly crossed his lips, when he realized the security personnel assigned to the protection of the American President's life, must have discovered where his people were hiding. The way the police and secret service agents were firing at the water tower, it assured him they were not the least bit interested in trying to capture his terrorists alive. Colonel al-Adwani was pleased no one from the cell was going to live to possibly inform the Americans who was behind the assassination attempt on their foolish President's life. He knew if Farseeha and the others had survived this attempt and escaped, he was under orders from his Commander in Iraq to dispatch the three of them, and then he was to return to Iraq. When the helicopter showed up by the water tower, and began to wrack the upper end of it with heavy weapons fire, he realized immediately that Colonel Farseeha and the others with her were surely dead.

The wise Iraqi Colonel remained stationed at his position for as long as he dared to remain while watching what was happening at the tower. When the weapon fire stopped, and the police began to climb the ladder to the top of the tower. The Iraqi Agent decided to leave the area before he was discovered, and classified as a suspicious person and arrested by the police running wild in the area of the attack. He slowly walked over to his parked car casually and then placed his communication device to the terrorist cell under the rear tire of his car, and started it and sped off, shattering the small radio under the wheel. He was passed by many police cars responding to the situation taking place at the airbase, so he decided to head in the same direction.

Something inside forced him to make certain his terrorist cell was dead. He knew he could ill afford to have any suspicions aimed at Iraq or his President. He understood once the three terrorists were dead, it was going to be nearly impossible to discover the terrorists were Iraqis. He continued towards Andrews Air Force Base until he reached a roadblock, and was forced to take a secondary road leading away from the air field. A thought struck him and he headed for Farseeha's apartment, he wanted to erase all traces of his being in the room. He cursed himself for giving in to his weakness of enjoying a woman's treasures. Her room was the only place where he had removed his gloves, the only place where he could have left any fingerprints in.

Colonel al-Adwani was prepared to set fire to the entire apartment if needed, if he could not be certain he successfully removed all evidence of his ever being there. He did not kid himself in the least he knew his fingerprints were on file at FBI headquarters. He attended enough parties in the Capital to arouse suspicion he might be an agent for Iraq. Being thought so, the American Intelligence Agency would have surely found a way to lift his prints from something he touched at the party. The Iraqi Colonel took a number of side roads to the apartment, and parked his car two blocks away from Farseeha's apartment, and then he walked down the road acting like a sightseer. He wanted to make certain the police were not already ransacking the room.

Colonel al-Adwani waited a few moments across the street from Farseeha's apartment, and he took the time to light a cigarette, and continued to watch the front door of the building and road for any signs of police coming for the apartment. When he waited long enough, he walked across the street and hesitated by the front porch and then rushed inside the building. He took the stairs instead of the elevator, not to bump into anyone renting a room in the building.

He went fishing through his pocket as soon as he stood before the locked door to her apartment and removed the key. He unlocked the door and entered the room cautiously. He rubbed both sides of the door knob with a rag. He found the newspaper he read, and ran the rag along the headboard of the bed, and any surface he might have touched while visiting Farseeha. He checked the garbage pails to make certain he did not drop anything in them. When he was satisfied there was no trace left of his being in the room, he left, going down the stairs again. When he reached the first floor, he hesitated for a second time. Just at that exact time, a horde of police officers suddenly rushed into the building, and they charged at the elevator wildly. They were grumbling to each other as they waited for the elevator to arrive for them.

The Iraqi Colonel looked around the area he was standing in for another escape route, he felt like a trapped rat. He spotted the narrow window on the landing above where he stood. He ran up the steps silently and forced the window open and then crawled out and dropped down to the ground. The narrow alley he ended up in was pitch dark, this enabled him to easily blend in with the many shadows and to cross the wide yard and come out on the other block.

The police waiting for the elevator were angry, and the Commander looked at one of the other officers and bitched at him. "What the hell are you doing here? Get up them damn steps and make sure no one's trying to escape down them. We'll meet you on the second floor. Be careful, you never know if the one we know escaped could be hiding in this bitch's room." The officer took off like he was being chased, his pistol held at the ready as he charged up the steps.

Colonel al-Adwani hid in the shadows of the alley while watching the end of the alley, and when he saw no police hanging around it or coming down the alley, he decided to leave his protection and walked down the street like he did not have a worry or care in the world. He was certain his forged driver's license and Social Security card were going to be enough to get him past any police checkpoints. He crossed the street where Farseeha's apartment was, and then he headed down the next street until he finally located his car.

The Colonel sat in it for a moment and lit another cigarette, and he took his time starting the vehicle's engine, he then pulled away from the curb. He did not want to bring attention to himself by speeding away from the area like he done something wrong. A slow driving police car nearly stopped, as the officer shined the spotlight on his face, as he drove passed the car.

Colonel al-Adwani nodded at the officer with the light aiming at him as he fought to get his breathing under control, and he smiled at the officer. Before the police car turned down his road, he wiped his face with a rag. He knew if any police officers saw him sweating for no reason, they would immediately pull him over and find out what was his problem. As he drove away from the area, he kept a close watch on the police car slowly moving behind him, checking to see if the officers were going to turn around and come after him.

He headed across town to get far away from the scene of the assassination attempt, and Farseeha's apartment. He had a safe house there, and planned to hide for a week before venturing out. He wanted things to die down, and Washington to get back to normal before he tried to leave the United States for the safety of his own country. He knew the only safe place for him after this failed assassination attempt on the American President, was Iraq. He could lose himself in the vastness of the deep desert, in case the Americans discovered he was behind the attack, and they send their soldiers to arrest or assassinate him. He planned to surround himself with enough Iraqi troops to protect him against anyone they might send to try and capture or kill him.

Colonel al-Adwani understood no matter how careful he was, somewhere he was certain he left some evidence the American investigators would find, and piece together he had something to do with this assassination attempt. He drove carefully, stopping at all the red lights and stop signs, and staying a few miles under the posted speed limit. Any time a police car with its lights flashing turned down the road he was on, he pulled way over and allowed the squad car room to speed past him safely. He only started breathing normally again when he finally spotted his safe house in the distance. The Iraqi Colonel did not know his name was printed on a small slip of paper and found by the secret service where they slaughtered his assassination team.

THE WHITE HOUSE, WASHINGTON DC. 9:35 P.M. EASTERN STANDARD TIME

The Chairman of the Joint Chiefs of Staff, General John White watched as the extremely upset President left the Oval Office to prepare for his latest press conference. When he was gone, the General went right in action. His first call was aimed at Colonel Bruce Leadbetter, the Marine Commandant stationed at Camp Lejeune, in Jacksonville North Carolina. He was in command of the General's so called Rapid Response Force troops. He actually put off calling in the President's Cabinet until he finished speaking with his Marine Colonel first. He had to wait a few moments, before the phone was answered by a sleepy and very grumpy sounding Colonel.

"Yeah, unless you're an incredibly beautiful blonde, I'm going to hang up this phone, dammit. Who the hell are you and what the hell do you want from me this late in the damn day?"

"I'm not blonde but will I do for your needs, Colonel Leadbetter Sir? You sound like you're in one of your usual good moods I see, sir." General White snorted into the phone.

Colonel Leadbetter instantly recognized the powerful General's harsh voice on the phone, and he sat up on his bed and swung his feet off his rack as he replied. "Sorry General White Sir, I have an early morning meeting set for Zero, Six Hundred Thirty Hours, and I was trying to catch up on some of my sleep, sir. What's up over there at Fort Fumble these days, General White Sir?" Colonel Leadbetter used the ground soldier's slang for the Pentagon.

"I'm not at the fucking office mister. And, what the hell did I tell you about calling that place by that damn name, Colonel Leadbetter Sir? Keep it up mister and you're going to find your ass shooting at the god damn camels in the fucking desert for a living, mister."

"Yes Sir General White, but I'm certain you didn't call me this late, to threaten my ass, sir. What's happening that you might have need of me and my specialized troops, General White?"

At first, General White felt like ripping into his insubordinate Colonel, but the situation made him override that decision as he barked at him. "You're damn right I have need of your pack of screaming squirrels, Colonel Leadbetter. We have a situation rapidly developing in Washington, sir. Some damn asshole just tried to assassination the President and your boss and there is..."

"Jeeesus Christ Almighty, is he alright sir?" Colonel Leadbetter interrupted the General.

"He's fine, but he's fit to be tied though. Mr. Griffin was killed in the attack, and the Vice President was seriously wounded in the attempt as well, Colonel. The reason for this call to you is the President wants me to order you to place your pack of criminals on a twelve hour standby alert order. Once we know who is responsible for the damn attempt on the President's life, he wants eyeballs and assholes, Colonel." General White paused to take a quick breath.

"I take it the whole Unit's to be activated, General White?" Leadbetter asked, as he allowed his eyebrows to arch a little with surprise over the assassination attempt on the President's life.

"The President didn't say for certain, but you better get the whole lot of them asses up and on standby, just in case this shit storm turns into a full scale situation on us, Colonel."

"Roger that General White, anything else to offer sir?" the Colonel asked in the phone.

"That's about all I have for you at this time Colonel. I'll be back to you the moment the Boss makes up his mind about what he wants done about this mess. Get your people hot mister."

"Will do sir." The Colonel replied as he heard the connection terminated from the other side.

THE ISLAND OF MARATHON IN THE FLORIDA KEYS

It was Fleet Week down at Key West, with the Nuclear Powered Aircraft Carrier CVN 71, USS Roosevelt, and her many escort ships moored at the old Navel Base stationed at Key West. Thousands of sailors were let loose and they flooded the streets of the tiny Island in search for women, booze, and some fun. Many others moved up the lower Keys in search of women. Some of the Sailors found their way to Marathon, the middle Key in the chain of a hundred Islands.

Tuesday, July 27th, was the birthday of Lieutenant Robert Walker who was better known to his fellow troops as Road Kill. He, along with his lady, Sergeant Dorothy Ramirez, the Mutt, Lieutenant Frank Hall with more troopers from his elite group of special operations soldiers, celebrated his special day. Since the bars opened, the group of soldiers made the rounds, saving the best for last. The Mermaid Club was the only strip joint on Marathon, and it started hopping after nine p.m. The elite group of soldiers entered at nine forty p.m., and they took over the tables to the rear of the place. In their training, the soldiers always wanted their backs protected, this time they were using the wall of the building for their protection.

The only way anyone in the bar knew this group was soldiers, was by their Unit's tattoo on their right forearms, and their haircuts. When the soldiers were seated, the beer started to flow, along with rude remarks the soldiers aimed at the three women stripping to a song by Aerosmith. The Mutt scanned the bar and noticed a mess of swabbies hiding in a corner of the bar, and they were glaring at them. The anger between the services was still alive and well.

When the swabbies saw the obvious special ops soldiers enter the bar, and noticed their Unit tattoos, one of them snapped nastily. "Something smells rotten in here all of a sudden."

"Why you lousy sonofabit..." The Mutt growled, but he was stopped when Walker grabbed his arm and then warned him hotly. "You betta relax some buddy, we're not here for a long time, we're here for a good time. We'll bury him when the time comes."

Blind Date, Sergeant Regina Raphael saw the terrible look between the two soldiers, and knew right off the Mutt was in search of a fight, and she grabbed his hand and smiled warmly. The Mutt got his tag name because he had a white mom, and a black dad. Regina was on loan to the elite Unit of soldiers from France, and when the Mutt's lover was killed in Operation Sandstorm, she stepped in to fill his void. He saw the smile and cooled off. The party was going well, with one soldier calling out to the strippers. "Hey, that bitch has more tits than enuf man."

McNip next yelled out at one of the strippers. "Hey lady, sex is like a pizza, when it's good, it's great, when it's bad, it's still pretty damn good." The special soldiers broke up with laughter because of the bantering they were doing with the strippers, but the swabbies continued to glare angrily at the new intruders to the bar. They had been plying the strippers with drinks since they first entered the bar, and were taking the soldiers as a threat to their future plans with the girls.

"Hey baby, you betta remember my name cause you'll be screaming it out later on in the stinking dark, honey." The massive No Neck called out, as he took a seat next to Walker.

"Hey guys, I warning you guys and remember no trouble in here, or I'll bounce the lot of ya outta here faster than a queer's ass from Fort Bragg." The bartender warned the group from behind the bar, when he noticed the threatening looks being passed between the two different groups of service men and women in the bar.

The excited Mutt looked at the blonde stripper with a good pair of tits and then he called out to her. "Here honey, here let me clean a place for you to sit down on." The Mutt then ran his hands over his face and this action caused Walker's group to roar with laughter again.

"Huh, ten thousand comedians out of work in the United States, and you're trying to be a funny man, asshole." A Sailor growled nastily at the Mutt. It seems he had gained their anger.

"Fuck you and the horse you rode in on, you fucking swabbie asshole you." The Mutt retorted hotly, and then he flipped the bird at the young Sailor bothering him.

Lieutenant Walker grabbed the Mutt's arm, while the Sailor in charge of the swabbies, grabbed the man's arm who just growled at the Mutt, and he pulled him back down to his seat.

"Unless you're growing, you betta sit back down sucka, I hate that fag ass hair cut anyway, buddy." The Mutt added angrily at the Sailor and he continued to glare at him, and then he snapped at him again. "You keep eyeballing me like that sucka, and I'll snatch the damn thing out of ya stinking face, and I'll serve it up to you for fricking supper, buddy."

"What's the matter soldier boy? Did the damn hamster fall off the wheel again on ya, man?" The Sailor growled back at the Mutt as he kept staring at him nastily.

"Hey buddy, you need to take yourself a serious shit, swabbie. Cause every time you open your stinking mouth, that's what comes out it on ya man." The Mutt snorted back at the Sailor.

"I warned you birds once already, keep it up and you're all outta here toot sweet. Why don't you chumps do the girls a favor here and pay attention to them and let it go at that." The bartender warned the soldiers for a second time.

"Hey pal, unless you're a stinking hemorrhoid, stay the fuck offa my ass, man." The Mutt aimed this warning at the bartender, as he stared at the man, daring him to keep busting his horns.

"You're pissing up the wrong tree there buster. Any more shit out of your ass, and you and the rest of your pals are out of here for life, buddy." The angry bartender stared at the Mutt, daring him to say another word at him. The Mutt finally got the message, and he tipped his beer at the bartender, and then he went back to watching the girls doing their thing on the stage.

Walker leaned over to the Mutt and hissed at him. "Hey Mutt, what do you want from life?"

"I wanna die and come back as a seat on a girl's bike, man." The Mutt retorted with a grin.

"You're impossible you know that dog man. I don't know why I keep putting up with your ass all the time." Blind Date moaned as she punched the Mutt in the arm.

"Because I'm the best lay you can ride on, baby. But I'll be fucked to hell and back again, if I'll allow some stinking swabbie banjo picking sonofabitch to get the last laugh on my stinking ass, honey." The Mutt went back to staring angrily at the Sailor doing all the bitching at him.

Neck (Sergeant Robert Abbott) was drooling over the blonde dancing on the stage, and he finally called out to her. "Hey blondie, wine me, dine me sixty nine me."

"Enough of that kinda talk there, big guy." The bartender grumbled, not bothering to look up from what he was doing at the bar. He knew where the comment came from.

Neck jumped up from his seat and began to beat on his massive chest like a gorilla in heat, while howling and laughing at the same time. The bartender allowed this because it seemed to have relieved some of the tension in the bar, as everyone in the bar joined his laughter.

Ramirez whispered to Walker. "I guess it ain't easy being sleazy for the big jerk, huh?"

Walker laughed, but he kept his eye glued on the Mutt. He was thinking of getting the guys out of the bar before something happened. He knew you could not mix swabbies with other soldiers.

"Hey man, look at that, I can see her no no places man." Mother Flanagan (Sergeant Richard Flanagan) grunted as he sucked on his beer. Mother got his name because he was always stuck with the new recruits to join the unit until they knew what they were doing with the elite soldiers.

Just as Blood Clot (Sergeant Richard Burnbach), the Unit's medic caught up with Walker's group and he entered the bar. The Mutt angrily snapped back at the Sailor still staring at him. "Whatsumatter Swabbie, my damn fly open or sutten, scumbag?"

"Relax Sailor he's just a dumb shit. Mutt, knock it off man will ya." Walker warned him.

"Don't defend him to me buster." The Sailor snapped then slapped sticks with his friend.

Mutt tightened the muscles in his body, and prepared himself to attack the Sailor, but Walker grumbled at him. "Let it go man, they ain't worth the sweat from our stinking balls, Homes."

"Hey buddy, if your friend fell down and broke his head open, nothing but a bunch of empty beer cans and half eaten pussies would tumble out of it." The Sailor said, trying to insult the Mutt. But he took it more as a compliment than a knock, and let it go sailing over his head.

Baby Tee, (Sergeant Teri Dorland), who got her tag name because of the small size of her breasts, saw things were starting to get carried away between the two servicemen, and she yelled out. "I can suck dick so good, it'd force a homeless man to build a house to get himself some." She was three sheets to the wind and barely able to stand on her own.

Everyone in the bar turned and stared at the young female soldier, no one knew where her last comment came from. Neck started everyone laughing again by clapping his hands.

The swabbie still making it hard on the Mutt noticed the pin on his shirt. 'Desert Storm Vet, will work for food will kill for sex'. He shook his head and grew even angrier at the young and good looking soldier. He knew with all the commotion the soldiers were making in the bar, the strippers would want to be with them instead of the group of Sailors when they closed down the bar for the rest of the night. He simmered as he continued to glare at the Mutt.

The Mutt decided to place a quick end to all the tension in the bar, and he began to strip in front of one of the women strippers. Walker's group egged on his wild dance soldier, and when he got down to his skivvies, the group really got on him, daring the Mutt to drop his drawers in the bar. Even the strippers started to clap and urge the Mutt on. One of the strippers made a number of daring moves towards the Mutt, in an effort to try and make him drop his drawers.

"Huh, if you don't think I'll do it, you're dead wrong baby." The Mutt grinned from ear to ear as he ripped off his drawers, and swung his dick at the strippers and yelled at them. "Here baby, put a lip lock on this here weapon will ya." The Mutt roared and grabbed his dick again.

Walker rushed over to the Mutt's side and barked at him. "What the fuck are you doing here for crap sake man? Hide that god damn black snake of yours for Pete's sake."

"I don't know, I guess it was one of those fricking sperm of the moment things, Homes." The Mutt slurred, the drink starting to get the better of him, and he began to slow down some.

"That's a fricking asshole if I ever saw one man." The same Sailor shot back at the Mutt.

Walker turned to the swabbie making all the trouble for the Mutt, and he snarled at him. "Hey pal, if I want anymore shit outta your stinking ass, I'll squeeze your fucking head buster. When the crunch time comes a knocking, you'll be shivering in your frigging boots, like a fucking turtle trying to dry hump a bone dome (Helmet), asshole."

The Sailor flipped Walker the bird, and then laughed at the large and very dangerous soldier.

"Is that your IQ, or the number of white parents you got mister?" the Mutt fired at the Sailor.

Walker also snarled at the Sailor. "Fucking with me is gonna get real expensive on your fricking hospitalization, fella. Why don't you sit your ass back down and enjoy the broads."

"I see a streak of pure asshole in your buddy there, friend."

"Mess with me and you'll wish your daddy never proked your mama." The Mutt snapped at him as he hunched up and took a linebacker's stance against the Sailor.

Again, the Sailor flipped the finger at both Walker and the Mutt this time.

"You wave that finger in my face again, and I'll bite it off for ya ass." Walker warned him.

"I warned you people twice now, this is the third and last time I'll warn any of you in the bar. One more threat from you birds and everyone's going out of here on their ear. Why do you people do yourselves a favor, and sit down and enjoy the show, or get out of here and let the rest of the people enjoy the girls. Hey pal put your damn drawers on before we get raided, will ya."

Everyone in the bar laughed as the Mutt quickly struggled back in his pants, and the bartender gave a quick nod to the girls, to get them started dancing on the stage again.

"That's it, C'mon baby I'm moist with anticipation here honey. Shake those lovely little puppies of yours for me baby." No Neck yelled out at the top of his lungs, as he ripped off his shirt and allowed his massive frame to be exposed to the three female strippers. It was easy to see how Neck, (Sergeant Robert Abbott) got his Unit tag name. His chest was so large it made it seemed like his head was resting square on his massive shoulders.

The soldier known to the Unit as the Ghost came strolling in the bar, and he sat down with Walker. Sergeant Walter Casper got his tag, because when he was in the jungle, he moved like a ghost. He picked up the tension in the bar and offered. "Hey man, what's going on in here Walker, and is there any way I can cause a stinking problem for ya, man?"

"Those damn swabs over there are busting the fucking Mutt's horns, man. I'm thinking about dragging his stinking ass the hell outta here, before all hell breaks out on us Ghost."

"Fuck that bullshit man, you're gonna allow some stinking swabbies run the stinking Mutt outta a titty bar, Walker?" Casper glanced at the swabbies a few tables away from them and saw one staring at him and growled at the dude. "Hey man, who the hell peed in your gene pool pal?"

The swabbie gave him the finger, and then ignored the Ghost after that.

"That's right asshole, fuck with me I dare ya. You fuck with me and you'll never be too dead for me to stop pounding on ya damn ass, buster." Casper snorted as he went to rise, but Walker stopped him by grabbing his arm and forcing him back in his chair.

The swabbie waved him off with a simple flip of the hand, and a disgusted look.

"That's right man, you're looking for more hell than a little bit, sea shit." Casper snapped at the back of the swabbie's head, and moved his hand like he was masturbating at him.

"Hey man, you gotta watch your fricking mouth around here man, or Oprah's gonna quit on us Homes." Mother Flanagan said through a drink induced haze and bloodshot eyes.

"Come again." The swabbie said, thinking he heard an insult that was aimed at him again.

"I didn't know I came the first time." Neck grumbled as he got into the mounting tension.

"You're getting loud again people." The bartender warned as he wiped a glass with a towel.

"Cool it Casper, we're getting the frick outta here before the shit hits the fan." Walker offered.

"Hey, I just got here I wanna see some stinking tits bouncing around for a little while man."

"Then shut the hell up and enjoy the damn show will ya man." Walker growled at him.

For a short while, things were pretty quiet in the bar until the Mutt happened to notice the swabbie give him the mad dog and forcing him to bitch at the guy. "Hey little Sailor boy you trying to intimidate me, Homes?

Fuhgedaboutit man, my mama has more fucking attitude than your fag ass does, dickhead."

"You betta give it up, Mutt will stay on your face longer than a blackhead." Neck grunted.

"He's lucky its black history month or he'd be stinking history by now man." The Mutt said as he took a pull of his beer, and then smiled at one of the strippers who caught his eye.

The swabbie stared at Neck for a moment then grumbled nastily. "Huh, it's true what they say, you can spend the whole damn day polishing a turd, and you'll still end up with a turd stick."

Neck was in such a good mood he ignored the rude remark, but the Mutt was in no such mood as he growled at him. "Keep talking like that and you're gonna put me in a fucking panic, pal."

"I'm gonna break you in fifty pieces and ship a different part of you to every state in the damn union, buster." The Sailor warned the Mutt as he tensed up, openly looking for a fight now.

"My heart dos quiver with fear, shit licker swabbie." The Mutt fired back at the Sailor.

Lieutenant Walker realized it was going to end up in a pier sixer, and he announced to his small group of troops. "C'mon pukes let's let the salt water taffies have this stinking dump."

"Ha, ha, Christmas might be over, but not all the ornaments are back in the damn attic."

"Hey swabbie, I don't give a shit if you wanna tempt faith by rattling the Mutt's cage, but if you go fucking with my tree, I'll fall out of it and land on your throat with both feet, sucka."

"Suck my dick soldier boy." The Sailor fired back at Walker angrily.

"Naw, I won't suck your stinking dick swabbie. But I tell you what I'm gonna do for ya pal. I'll break the damn thing off for ya, and stick it up your friend's ass over there. From what I hear about you damn tail gunner turd pusher types, that's the way you people like it anyhow, man." Walker growled as he placed his hands on his hips and then he glared back at the Sailor now.

Then a number of the Sailors stood and took threatening stances aimed against the specialized soldiers. They out numbered Walker's group two to one. Neck moved over to Walker's side and complained at him. "There are more of them than us man."

"That's cause it takes three fricking Sailors to lace the stinking boots of a real fucking soldier, Homes. If their numbers make you nervous, don't fucking count the bastards man."

"I got the one doing the fucking talking Walker. I wanna snap him in two like he was a stinking Slim Jim, man." Neck grumbled as he moved to the front of the line of soldiers, and assumed a linebackers stance against the Sailors at the other table and waited.

"I had it with you people in here, I told you boys to put a lid on it and you jerks didn't listen to my warnings. So get the fuck out of my bar before I call the cops, and have them drag you people the hell out of here kicking and screaming, dammit." The bartender lifted a baseball bat from behind the bar and then aimed it at the two groups of servicemen squaring off for a fight.

The strippers did not know what to do, and only reacted to the bartender's silent signal, and they began to dance again while trying to head off a possible fight in the bar.

One of the strippers called out to the Neck. "Hey big boy, how do you like these here babies?" She lifted her breasts in both hands, and wiggled them before his face.

"Sorry baby, I don't have the time to chew the fat, alls I got time for is to come and go honey." Neck replied, refusing to take his eyes off the larger group of Sailors in the bar.

"Hey big man, here is a few bucks. Why don't you go and buy yourself a fucking neck."

Casper moved over to Neck and said. "Was it wrong, I was aroused by that stripper, man?"

Walker had to stop himself from laughing over the Ghost's last comment. He wanted to get involved in a bar fight like he wanted to have his balls beaten flat with a wooden mallet. But he felt his troops had taken enough crap from these rude dudes in the bar, who had invaded his private little Island and his good time.

"People, people, people, I have the cops coming. So I suggest you people beat feet and get the hell out of my damn bar before they arrive and all hell breaks out for you guys." The bartender warned the soldiers as he slapped one hand with the baseball bat, and he glared at the two groups of angry service people facing off in his bar at the same time.

Walker glanced at the bartender, and was instantly hit in the side of the head with a glass. Sergeant Ramirez saw who pitched the bottle at Walker, and she was on him in a flash. She had the Sailor in a head lock against her hip, and she was pounding his face with her closed fist.

"Go get the bastard Raz!" Blind Date yelled as she leaped on his back and helped Ramirez beat him to the floor. The rest of Walker's people charged the swabbies like raging bulls.

Two Sailors grabbed the Mutt, while a third one smashed him in the face and sent him flying back. The three strippers quickly disappeared as did everyone else not involved in the fight.

Walker saw the Mutt go flying back, and he helped him back to his feet.

"Shit, I shoulda hit him with my stinking right for crap sake Walker." The Mutt complained as Walker pulled him back to on his feet.

"Hey Mutt, that's a pretty hard punch to throw while lying flat on your ass on the damn floor, man. I liked the way you tried to break that other dude's fist with your stinking jaw, Homes."

Walker and the Mutt then charged into the wild fracas that erupted in the stripper bar, and both soldiers were sent flying back and landed on the floor together.

"Hey Mutt, you ain't doing so good in this one, are you man?" Walker smirked at him.

"Yeah, the fucking sun got in my stinking eyes." The Mutt replied as he got back on his feet.

"Yeah, I heard it hit ya like a stinking haymaker buddy. You know, there was a time in your wasted life when you hit someone and he stayed fucking hit, man."

"You sit back there and watch my fricking act, Road Kill." The Mutt warned as he again leaped up to his feet, and then charged back into the small war taking place in the bar.

"That's it Mutt, kick him in the slats. Break his fricking leg man bite his fucking nose off Homes. Yeah, yeah, you hold him there and I'll kick him in the fucking balls for ya man."

"You ain't kicking anyone in the fucking nuts, mister." Someone from behind Walker warned him as he suddenly grabbed him by his shirt.

Walker turned as someone grabbed him from behind by the collar of his torn shirt, and he squeezed his throat with his other hand. He saw a large cop followed by a second one with his weapon out. He turned back to the fight just in time to see the Mutt get smacked over the head with a chair, but he remained standing on his feet and still fighting like he wasn't hit by the chair. He did not see the Neck get smashed over the head with a bottle and go down hard to the floor. It hit him right in the temple and opened a good size gash and knocked him out.

"Okay children, you had enough fun for the night, everyone get up against the damn wall and pull out your military ID's." The cop holding Walker growled at the beat up soldiers. Ten more police officers circled the rest of the fighters. Shore Patrol from Key West arrived at the bar next, and they took charge of the Sailors. That left the deputies dealing with only Walker's group.

Sergeant Dorothy Ramirez was sitting on the floor nursing a bleeding nose and black eye. Walker pulled away from the cop and rushed to her side. The cop saw what he was up to, and allowed him to get over to the female fighter to help her out some.

"How is she doing?" The officer asked he was a little concerned over Ramirez's condition.

"She's fucking pregnant Homes and these flaming assholes betta not have hurt our kid or I'll fix the lot of them." Walker snapped back angrily at the cop.

"And she's fighting in a damn bar, that's pretty stupid on her part soldier?"

"She's a fucking soldier first and a mother second, man." Walker fired back at the cop.

"Well soldier that don't make much sense to me, arrr… the whole lot of you people are under arrest. So line up, we have a truck coming to take all you birds down to the cages."

"Can we put up bail so we can get the hell out of the stinking can tonight, Homes?"

"Yeah, but only after you go up before Judge Becker, soldier. I'm warning you buster, she a no nonsense type judge. Act cool with her and you'll be home by tomorrow afternoon. Come in with the case of the ass before her, and you'll find yourselves cooling your damn heels off for a sixty day vacation in the bird cage at the Island's expense, mister."

"What the hell are you arresting our asses for man? e didn't start the damn fight you know. What are the charges against us anyway, man?" Blood Clot asked the cop.

"Oh, so you're this mess's attorney, huh? Fine with me buster! You're being arrested for D and D, and that's Drunk and Disorder, fighting, destroying private property. I'm certain if I look around here a little more, I can find a few more charges I can tack on your ass just for some shits and giggles, if you'd like, buster?" The cop gave Blood Clot a smirk.

"Naw Homes, that'll do good enuf for the time being." Blood Clot replied as he looked down.

Walker helped Ramirez to her feet, while Blind Date helped the Mutt out. She left the busted chair hanging around the Mutt's head, as they were led to a pickup truck. The group was in the back of the truck, and drove over to the small Marathon jail. There, they were processed.

CAMP LEJEUNE, JACKSONVILL, NORTH CAROLINA

The instant Colonel Bruce Leadbetter was off the horn with General White, he placed a call to Walker's residence. When he received no answer, he called the other soldiers he knew were on the small Island with him, or on the other Keys. Walker was allowed a number of phone calls, and he called a few soldiers to bail them out. When Colonel Leadbetter finally got a hold of Just Bob, (Sergeant Robert Bozzelli) living on Grassy Key, he just finished speaking to Walker at the jail and informed the Colonel he was going to bail out the group.

Colonel Leadbetter wanted to know why Lieutenant Walker's group was arrested on Marathon, and Just Bob informed him it was some kind a bar fight they were in with a bunch of fleet fags visiting the Island from Key West. The fuming Colonel hung up with Bob while cursing up a storm, and then he placed a call down to the local Sheriff's department on Marathon. Here, he was informed it would take an act of Congress to get the soldiers released, before they went before the judge. He broke off the connection and phoned General White at the Oval Office, to inform him his specialized troops were in a pail of shit down on the small Island.

CHAPTER EIGHT

10 P.M. EST, WASHINGTON, THE WHITE HOUSE.
JULY 27th, 1999

The still rather shaken President stepped before the podium in the press room of the White House packed full with many news reporters attending the conference, knowing something serious had happened on this night, but they were unaware what it was all about. They held their breath and waited for the President to begin speaking to them. "Ladies and gentlemen of the press, and my fellow Americans, I called this press conference together to inform the American people what has transpired at Joint Andrews Air Force Base a little earlier in the day."

At the same exact instant the upset President of the United States began to speak to the American public on the TV, reporters transmitted their stories of the incident of the attack at Andrews, and the Fox News channel began their own special report on the situation that took place at Andrews, before the President interrupted the transmission on them, and he continued speaking to the gathered news reporters and TV cameras.

"This is Fox News reporter Gloria Hamelton reporting. We were just informed about some kind of shooting that has taken place at the Andrews Air Force Base. First reports in stated the President of the United States, and certain members of his entourage were involved in the deadly altercation at the military airfield. As of this moment, we're still unsure if this was an assassination attempt on the President's life. We have our sources out, and they're trying their best to bring the story to you as quickly as possible, but for now..."

Their broadcast was interrupted, and anyone watching the program, found themselves suddenly staring at an upset and disheveled looking President, already speaking to them.

"At or around eight ten p.m. Washington time tonight, an attempted assassination on my life was perpetrated by a number of unknown assassins. As you can see, I'm alright, so there's no need to wonder about who is running the office of the President of the United States. I'm still in full Command of the office. A number of terrorists attacked Eagle's Nest, err... excuse me please, that's my pet name for Air Force One. It was determined I was the terrorist main target on this night. They missed me, but in the ensuring gun fire, the National Security Director, Norman Griffin was killed in the altercation. Mary Hirshfield, the Vice President of the United States was critically wounded in the deadly exchange of gun fire. She was hit in the right shoulder, and she is in extremely critical condition and is undergoing surgery as I speak."

"Mr. President, Mr. President, please Mr. President." Shouts from the gathered reporters filled the press briefing room, as the President's face was showered with blinding lights from the many flash bulbs going off. It rattled the still shaken American Leader, and it was his wise Press Secretary, who announced there was to be no more pictures taken of the President at this time.

"Please, allow me to finish with my statements first, and then I'll be most pleased to answer a few of your questions before concluding this press conference for the day. I'm terribly exhausted as you can well imagine. I don't know how my Vice President is doing at the time, and I'm extremely concerned about her physical condition as you all can well understand and I want to get back to my Cabinet. I'll tell you everything I know about the terrorist incident. The investigation's continuing as we speak. I assure every American citizen watching me at this moment that steps have been initiated to protect the life of their President now, and in the future.

"From what's believed, there's an assassin who successfully escaped the police response to the attack against my life, and he might be stalking me as I speak to the American public this very minute. Three of the terrorists were known killed in the response by our police departments and by the Special Agents assigned to protect my life. All airports have increased their security and scanning of anyone attempting to leave the United States, and the borders of the United States have seen more police officers and security tightening up their borders, because of the search for this missing terrorist. This has been ordered by me, to prevent the assassin from escaping his just punishment for this horrendous assassination attempt against my life, and the killing of the National Security Director, and the terrible wounding of my Vice President.

"That's about all I know of what has transpired tonight I'm afraid. There'll be more information released to the general public as soon as it becomes available to the investigators. This new conference was ordered by me, to assure the American public that their President is still alive and well, and I'm in complete Command of this great country of ours at this time. I had to address the American public, because I didn't want any false or unbelievable stories started that weren't true about the present situation and about my physical condition, and before I knew it, rumors of my demise would be wrong. I also wanted to let the ones behind this assassination attempt on my life, to know that their hired killers have failed to accomplish their orders of killing me in my own country. At this time I shall answer a few questions for the press, and then I'll call this press conference to a..."

"Mr. President, please Mr. President." Was frantically shouted out again, as many gathered reporters hands shot in the air, and other reporters lifted their notepads and phones.

President Albert Cole looked at the first news reporter, she was from the Fox news station, he recognized her, and he liked the way she always conducted her questions to him. "Yes Cathy."

"How is the Vice President doing Mr. President Sir? And, what hospital was she taken to sir?" The female reporter asked with genuine concern lacing her tone to the President.

"That is a very good question Cathy, and I thank you for your concern for my Vice President's physical condition, Ma'am. As I have already stated at this press conference, she's reported to be in extremely critical condition and the Vice President has been taken to Bethesda Naval Hospital for treatment and emergency surgery. The last report I had received about her condition, stated that she's in emergency surgery and is listed in extremely critical condition, sorry for repeating myself here but I'm exhausted as you can well see for yourselves. It has been brought to my attention that

Vice President Mary Hirshfield was conscious when the doctors brought her into the operating room. I'm taking that as a pretty good sign to hold onto for the time being. All we can do right now is pray that she's going to be alright. Next question please?" President Albert Cole looked at a news reporter from the Washington Post, and smiled at him as he nodded at the reporter this time, and then the President waited for his question of him.

The cries of "Mr. President" were shouted once again at him, as the reporter from the Washington Post rose and then he offered the American Leader. "Mr. President Sir, what are you going to do for the Security Director Norman Griffin, sir?"

"Director Norman Robert Griffin will be afforded a full state funeral, along with full military honors and all that goes along with this great honor to his memory. He has lost his life in the line of duty for his country and for the office of the President of the United States, and that makes him a prime candidate for Arlington National Cemetery. His body will lie in state in the Capital Building, and then he'll be moved to the Cathedral of Saint's Peter and Paul, better known to all as the Washington Cathedral. Once the service is completed there, Director Griffin's body will then make its final journey to Arlington for proper burial.

"It's a very sad day for our country when a great American Leader like Mr. Norman Griffin, loses his life in the service of the United States. I promise all gathered here tonight and watching me on their TVs that the killers of the National Security Director will suffer the United States' great and unfettered wrath for this terrible attack and the deaths it caused, next question please. Let's move this thing along a little bit quicker please, so I can get back to my people and find out what's happening here in Washington and with my Vice President, people."

The shouts of "Mr. President" began anew from the many gathered reporters.

President Cole scanned the sea of excited faces of the reporters, until his eyes rested on an old friend from Channel Two news. President Cole smiled at him as he gave him the nod.

Peter rose swiftly to his feet, and nodded politely to the President as he began speaking. "Mr. President Sir, first, let me state how pleased I am to see you're alright sir, and I want to tell you how sorry I am about Mr. Griffin's death, and the wounding of our Vice President, sir."

"Thank you very much for those kind and concerned words for the Vice President, Peter. Your question please sir?" President Cole replied as he continued to smile at his old friend.

"Mr. President, do you have any idea who might have been behind this attempted assassination against your life, sir?" The old and very crafty news reporter asked next.

"Yes, there was certain evidence discovered at the crime scene that points the finger of blame at a certain faction of well known terrorists, sir. As soon as we can make certain the information we have discovered is beyond reproach, then we'll quickly make that information available to the general public." The President gave out with a deep sigh.

The reporter remained standing, and he asked a second question of the President, before any other reporters could interrupt, or cut him off. "Please Mr. President Sir; do you happen to know who was in control of the terrorist group operating inside the United States, sir?"

"Yes I do Peter, but at this time I'm afraid I'm not at the liberty to divulge that particular bit of information to the American public just yet, sir. Anything we let out prematurely, might damage the ongoing investigation on us, Peter. First off sir, we have to make certain the ones believe to be behind this assassination attempt on my life, are the true conspirators in this terrible act, before we act against them and their host nation as well, sir. Once we're absolutely positive about this gathered information, I assure you and everyone else living in the United States, Peter. We'll act accordingly, I believe the same as President Reagan did, I'll deal with terrorists, but only in the harshest of terms possible to be employed against them sir."

"Does this mean you're contemplating going after the host country believed to be sponsoring these new groups of terrorists, Mr. President." The reporter shouted out over the new cries of "Mr. President" coming from the other reporters gathered in the press room of the White House.

"You're damn right I am. The American people and I demand this from me and our military, and I'm not going to stand for one moment of having some third world country attempt to destroy the great leadership of the most powerful country in the free world. If we allow anyone to kill any American President and we don't react as seriously as the attempt assassination on my life was. Then what the devil kind of message will we be sending to any would be terrorist in the world in the future? If we don't go for the throats of all involved in this most contemptible and evil crime committed right here on the United States soil, any second rate would be killer who wants to make a name for himself, will try to kill other heads of governments throughout the rest of the world. Forgive me please I seem to be getting a little carried away with myself here."

A female reporter jumped to her feet and she snapped at the exhausted looking American President, while cutting off the other reporter from speaking further, as she called out. "Mr. President Sir! I have a question for you if you don't mind, please sir."

President Albert Cole did not recognized the young lady and he could not read her press ID from this distance away from her to discover what newspaper or news channel she worked for, but he allowed her to speak and he gave her a nod.

The reporter started to speak the instant she got the nod from the President. "President Cole Sir, I'm a reporter from the New York Post, sir. From your last words stated sir, I gathered you think the terrorists were Arabs in nature, behind this assassination attempt against your life, sir." The young lady smiled at the still shaken and upset American President.

The President's eyes instantly narrowed to mere slits as he glared angrily at the pretty young woman reporter as he snapped curtly at her. "Well young lady, I don't seem to remember saying anything about my believing this latest group of terrorist were as you just put it, Arab in nature, or any other nationality for that matter, Ma'am. This is why I chose to address the American public in the first place tonight, young lady. I don't need any of you news reporters putting your own spin on this failed assassination attempt against my life. If I didn't address the American public as quickly as I chose to, I'm quite certain by this time tomorrow morning, I'd be reading, or at least hearing stories greatly publicized that I was wounded or even killed in this failed assassination attack against my life, Ma'am."

The reporter blushed slightly, because of the President's tongue lashing he leveled against her as he continued to glare at her. Then, she gathered her thoughts and fired back at him, refusing to allow any other reporters to cut on her questions to the President off on her. "Mr. President Sir, please excuse me for the poor choice of words I addressed you with sir. The only reason I asked if you though the assassins were Arab terrorists behind this attempt on your life sir. Was because you made mention of third world politics being behind this attack against you, Mr. President.

"I'm terribly sorry Mr. President, but I must ask you if you have any leads on the identity of the person or persons behind this attempt on your life? Also Mr. President, how many terrorists were involved with this attempted assassination, Mr. President Sir?" The female reporter drew in her breath quickly, and then she stared back at the President while waiting for his reply.

"I'm sorry to offer you, but as I had stated a little earlier at this press conference, I'm not at liberty to give out any further details about this ongoing investigation, than I had already made mention of before you, Ma'am. Err... I think that's about it for this question and answer time, gentleman, and ladies, and I thank you all for your time and patience over this matter."

The President nodded at the reporter as he included ladies in his words, and then added to them. "I'll have my Press Secretary made available, and he'll be pleased to inform you and the public, about any new information we discover throughout the rest of this exhausting night. I'm sorry, but any further questions you might have, will have to be directed at my Press Secretary from this point forward. I thank all of you for attending this press conference ladies and gentlemen." The President smiled pleasantly at the horde of reporters staring at him, and then he rushed away from the podium without answering another further question that was still being called out at him. The still highly upset President was instantly surrounded by a heavy crush of his security people, and aides who assisted him with the news conference.

President Cole ignored the reporters as they called out after him, trying to ask more questions of him before he disappeared where they would not be able to ask any further questions of him. The President rushed down the hall leading to the Oval Office, and the Cabinet members he ordered to wait his return. He was fuming over the mind rattling questions put to him by the female reporter. It certainly upset him more than he already was. The upset President cursed her and her newspaper, but he was really cursing himself, because he made the slip of the tongue about the third world countries being involved in the assassination attempt on his life.

The concerned security guards tried to stay up with the President the best they could, yet remain out of his way, as they nearly ran down the hall leading to the Oval Office. Again, the President attacked the doors to his office as a linebacker attacked the defensive line of the opposing team, as he charged in his office. He was still fuming over the reporter's question, and he vowed he was going to have her White House press credentials taken from her, so he would never be forced to answer her questions in the future. The American Leader was that upset with her and himself. All he wanted to do at this moment was to find out how Mary was doing in surgery, and what was going on with the investigation about the assassination attempt.

He entered his Oval Office just as the Chairman of the Joint Chiefs of Staff General White, answered the call from Colonel Leadbetter, stationed at Camp Lejeune. President Cole took his seat behind his desk, and decided to use this time while the General spoke to someone on the line, to gather his thoughts and calm down a little. The aide rushed to the President's side and whispered to him. "Mr. President, Mary's out of surgery, and the doctor's think she's going to be alright, sir. The next few hours will tell the tail for us, sir. I'm terribly sorry sir, but they still don't know if she'll be able to speak properly, Mr. President Sir. The bullet did some major damage to her neck and shoulder and the Doctor's are concerned over her speaking abilities, sir."

"Oh thank Christ for that much, you just made the rest of my day, young man." The President mumbled as he placed his hands to his head, and then he rubbed his temples slowly. Then he looked at the people still gathered in his office and nodded to them.

General White was fuming Colonel Leadbetter dared to call him at this time, knowing he was at the White House. Especially because the President just returned to his office. "Yes Colonel, this better be god damn important sir, or I'm going to skin your damn ass alive for daring to interrupt me at this time, mister. Did you get those damn screaming squirrels of yours placed on full ready alert yet, Colonel Leadbetter Sir?"

"That's what I'm calling you about, General White." The Colonel offered calmly.

"Jesus H. Christ, what did your pack of criminals do this time, dammit? I can tell by the tone of your voice those kids are in some kind of trouble again, Colonel." General White kept his voice low, knowing the soldiers well enough to realize this call was about them being in trouble.

"General White, it seems Lieutenant Walker's crew bumped into a bunch of Navy pukes out trying to make a name for themselves, sir. Well sir, Walker being Walker, he couldn't leave well enough alone, and the soldiers with him on his damn Island in the Keys ended up cracking a few eggs. So the lot of them are resting their heels in the can sir. I spoke to the local Sheriff and he informed me it was going to take some fancy foot work to get the soldiers released from jail, sir. It seems the Sheriff's plenty pissed off at our guys down there sir, it looks like Walker's crew ripped up the bar some sir, and they want to make an example of our people, General White."

"Did the police arrest the miserable group of Sailors who were involved in the damn fight as well as they arrested my people down there on that damn Island, Colonel? I know the Navy has some pull on those damn Islands because they have that large Naval Base stationed at Key West, sir." The General asked, already softening his stance against these elite soldiers.

"Shore Patrol handled the Sailors, General White Sir. The Island's deputies took custody of Walker and his people, sir. What do you want me to do about this situation, General?" Colonel Leadbetter asked his commanding officer while trying to keep the smile off his lips.

"Jesus Christ mister, are you trying to inform me the damn Sailors involved in this little fracas on that Island walked out of this mess Scott free sir? Yet Walker and his pack of lunatics are going to be sucking eggs over this, err... slight misunderstanding, Colonel Leadbetter?"

"All I can say for certain General White Sir. Shore Patrol has the Sailors in their custody, sir." Colonel Leadbetter tried to insert again, but he was cut off by the angry General.

"Are you suffering from a recital cranium inversion, Colonel? Get your fucking head outta your damn ass will ya please! You know damn well Shore Patrol released those Navy pukes long before they got back to their base with the pukes, mister. I won't allow them to walk away from this mess, yet have Walker and his fools picking up the tab..." The General's words were cut off by the President, as he asked his officer what seemed to be upsetting him so on the phone.

"Is there a problem General White Sir? You seem to be getting slightly upset with whomever you're speaking with on the phone, sir. Can I be of any assistance to you, General?" President Cole asked with concern, as he lifted his head and looked at the military officer trying to control his temper the best he could while speaking on the phone.

"Hold on for a moment will you Colonel Leadbetter. The Boss is speaking in my other ear." General White placed his hand over the receiver, and turned to President Cole and announced while holding on the receiver in his other hand. "Mr. President, it seems Lieutenant Walker's group got themselves into a mess on that damn little Island of his sir, and all of them are cooling their heels off in jail, sir." General White knew this was going to anger the President further, so he tried one of his widest smiles on the staring President as he looked back at him now.

"Nice try there General White, but your sheepish little smile isn't going to cool this mess off so damn easily this time around, sir. We need those kids General White, and we need them right now. I want the bastard who escaped, caught and brought back here to the United States if he's able to get out of the country before we get our hands around his neck, and bring him in for justice. I want to look in his eyes, before they pull the switch on the bastard, General White."

"Mr. President, there's no proof the last terrorist was able to escape the country, sir."

"Quite right General White, but you know the bastard's not going to surface again until the heat is off him, and he can make good his escape from our country, sir. I don't think we have a prayer in the world of capturing him while he's still running loose in the United States, sir. That is why I want your specialized soldiers ready for when they have to go to Iraq to catch this man. What's it going to take for you to gain the freedom of these kids down on that damn Island, General?" the President rose and began to pace behind his desk while cracking his knuckles.

"Mr. President, Colonel Leadbetter informed me he was warned in advance by the Island Sheriff that it was going to take an Act of Congress to get my troopers out of jail, sir."

"Well sir, do you think a Presidential Order will do the trick for you, General White?"

"Are you kidding sir, with a Presidential Order I can have Walker and his people treated like Kings on that damn Island of his, Mr. President Sir." Another smile crossed the General's lips.

"Then you have it General White. I want you to get your backside down to Joint Andrews Air Force Base and climb on Eagle's Nest Two and take her down to the Island, and get those damn kids of yours the hell out of jail tonight, sir. If you have to, pay for their damages to the damn bar. I want them kids heading for...err... where sir?" the President stopped speaking as his eyes narrowed, and then he stared at the General.

"Camp Lejeune, Mr. President Sir." General John White offered as his smile grew larger.

"Right General White, get damn kids out to Camp Lejeune and start their training, sir. Inform the Colonel he's to work out the damages you'll pay for while you're on this Island, out of their rearends. I want them primed and ready for anything that comes their way, when we know for certain where this terrorist is going to surface." Now, it was the President who smiled at the General, because he knew the Colonel was going to work Walker's group like they were never worked before, but would not place any extra duty on them for getting into a minor fracas.

"You got it Mr. President." General White hung up the phone on the Colonel, and left the office like he was farting sparks. He wanted out of any further conversations about how, and who they were going after. He was a soldier, not a politician, his job was killing, not talking.

The Chairman of the Joint Chiefs of Staff General John White made it through the heavy security surrounding the White House, and the mayhem still flooding the streets of downtown Washington, until his vehicle parked on the tarmac of Joint Andrews Air Force Base still a mess from the attempt assassination on the President's life. He had his driver parked the staff car next to Air Force Two. He glanced up at Eagle's Nest One and saw it was flooded with police and special agents, looking for missed evidence, and cleaning up the damage caused to the aircraft by the assassin's weapons. General White started up the steps, and was warned the President informed the flight crew he was on his way to the airport. The co-pilot informed the General they submitted their flight plan and had clearance to the tiny Island of Marathon's airport.

MARATHON AIRPORT, THE ISLAND OF MARATHON IN THE FLORIDA KEYS

Even before the Chairman realized it, he was in the air heading south for the Florida Keys. It took the aircraft just under four hours to reach Marathon Island. General White looked out the window and for the first time, he was scared. He did not think the small airport could possibly receive the huge 767. The General watched as the emergency vehicles worked swiftly at removing other parked aircraft, and the police cars lined the airbase for his arrival.

All the Marathon Sheriff's department was informed of, was Air Force Two was landing on their Island. They had no idea who was on board the aircraft, but until they knew for certain, the Sheriff was going to have his people act as if the President himself was landing on the Island.

When the aircraft finally rolled to a stop, it was immediately surrounded by the horde of squad cars and officers. The Sheriff greeted the impressive plane in person. General White saw his expression fade when the Sheriff picked up a mere General was walking down the steps. The Sheriff put out his hand and General White shook it and nodded at the Sheriff.

"Errr... General err sir..." The Sheriff offered as he put out his hand and waited.

"White sir. General John White, I'm the Chairman of the Joint Chiefs of Staff, Sheriff, err..."

"General White, it's a pleasure to meet you sir. I'm Sheriff Edwards, General White Sir. What brings a four star General and the Commander of the Joint Chiefs down to my small Island, sir?" Sheriff Edwards asked the powerful military officer.

"It's good you're here Sheriff Edwards. It saved me the trouble and time of having to hunt you down on the Island, sir. I'm here to get my soldiers out of your jail, Sheriff. I was informed by Colonel Leadbetter that my soldiers were arrested for disturbing the peace or some other bullshit like that. I have immediate need of these specialized soldiers sir, and I can't replace them with any other soldiers in the service, sir. So it's imperative I get the damn kids released as quickly as possible, Sheriff. I have a letter here from the President of the United States, sir."

The Sheriff took the letter and glared at General White as he complained at the military officer. "Disturbing the peace you say! General White, these so called soldiers of yours nearly took apart a local bar down here, stick by stick with their bare hands, sir. There are plenty of people on the Island who want to tar and feather them, and run them off the Island on a rail, and I can't blame them, sir. We don't have this type of trouble on Marathon Island, sir. It was a peaceful Island until your soldiers arrived that is, General." The Sheriff opened the letter.

"Consider yourself very lucky then Sheriff Edwards, if these kids left any of the bar still standing sir. Their training should have had them not stop until there was nothing left of the place, sir. These kids must be slipping a might, but I'll sure get them hot again Sheriff."

The Sheriff's look tuned to one of anger, as he stared at the General because he was not very impressed by the General's last comments. When he climbed in the car, the Sheriff growled at the military officer hotly. "General White Sir, before you get your people out of my jail, I want a few minutes with them privately, and then sir I'll hand them over to you."

"You're not going to lay a hand on them sir!" The General asked as he stared at the Sheriff.

"Of course not sir, what the hell do you think we are down here, General White Sir? I just want to scare the shit out of them before releasing them to you, that's all, sir. Then you can have these err... so called specialized soldiers back and get them off my Island until everyone here relaxes and forgets what these damn kids did on the Island, sir."

"Good luck with trying to scare these nuts under my command, Sheriff. These kids I trained don't get scared of anything very easily, sir. Sheriff Edwards, I assure you sir, anything you're going to threaten against these kids, has been tried on them before, sir. Without much luck I'm afraid to offer. This pack of screaming squirrels are not much when it comes to manners and respect for anyone in command, Sheriff." General White offered to the upset looking officer.

"That maybe so General White Sir, but your presence here on the Island is going to give me a high card in this game I plan to employ against these damn kids of yours, sir. I'm going to beat them over their heads with your presence before I finally release them to you sir."

"Ahhh... I see you have a reason behind your madness, sir. Have fun with them Sheriff. Let me know if your plan works. I was instructed to pay for any damages to the bar by the President that these soldiers might have created on your Island, sir. I'm quite certain you heard there was an assassination attempt on the President's life last night." General White offered as he lit a smoke.

"Yes I did General White, that's why I thought it rather strange Air Force One was landing on Marathon, sir. How is the President's health sir? He wasn't wounded in the attempt, was he General?" For the first time since they met, the Sheriff allowed a slight smile to cross his lips.

"That's Air Force Two, Sheriff and no, the President wasn't wounded by the attempt on his life, the bruises you saw on his person were caused by overly protective Service Agents, sir."

"Oh. I wasn't aware of that General White Sir. It's good he only received those few minor injuries during the attack, sir." The Sheriff moaned as he cast a quick glance at the aircraft resting on his airport surrounded by his deputy cars. It took less than five minutes for them to reach the jail on the small Island. General White was offered a cup of coffee, as Sheriff Edwards went in the room that allowed him to enter the main part of the jail.

Lieutenant Robert Walker's group was being held in a large secluded room in the jail area. The Sheriff did not want to mix the extremely dangerous group of specialized soldiers in with the other inmates he was holding in his jail. He did not know what type of reaction it might cause between the two different groups, and he did not want the soldiers fighting with the common people of his Island. The entire group of elite soldiers except for the one branded No Neck was there; he was in the Fisherman's Hospital getting stitched up and medically looked after.

Baby Tee was sitting on a cot with no shirt on, and her breasts seemed to be smiling. The soldiers was not separated by sexes, because the Sheriff knew these people were part of the elite Special Forces group, and they would not take kindly to being separated. When the Sheriff entered the room, he did so without saying a word to anyone, he looked from one soldier to the other. He had to stop himself from smiling at the ragtag group of bloody and battered soldiers, when he saw one of them still wearing a busted chair around his neck. When the officers tried to remove it, it nearly caused a riot with the other soldiers. For some reason, they somehow had adopted the chair as a sort of symbol. The Sheriff went from one soldier to the other, until he found the one he was looking for, the obvious leader of the group of young misfits. "You!" He barked hotly at the soldier and then glared at him while waiting a response from him.

"Yeah! What sir?" Walker snapped back at the equally as large police officer.

"Are you the ring leader of this mess in here, mister?" the Sheriff growled, as he swung his arm out to encompass the entire group trapped in the room with the soldier he spoke to.

"Yeah, I'm the head fucking cheese of these guys if you wanna call me that, Sheriff. Why?"

"What's your name mister? And keep a civil tongue in that mouth of yours while you're at it."

"Walker, Robert P." Walker smirked as he stared in the eyes of the angry looking Sheriff.

"Your rank also, mister? Since when does a damn active soldier offer his name without adding his rank at the same time, young man?" Sheriff Edwards then placed his hands on his hips, and he stared at Walker for a long moment until he replied to his last question.

"Civilian, why sir?" Walker again smirked at the Sheriff on the other side of the bars.

"Cute, real cute wiseguy. Well Mr. Civilian Soldier, I have some bad news for ya to hear, you're not a civilian any longer, mister. It seems this little war in the bar of yours reached the ears of the President, and he sent down a four star General, with enough salad pinned to his chest to feed all of South Africa for a year. To eat you people alive and then spit you people out while leaving a bad taste in his mouth at the same time mister." The Sheriff placed a wide grin on his face, as he stared at Walker who suddenly turned green right before his eyes.

"Hey man, this stinking warlord (slang for officer in command) didn't give you his damn name, did he sir? It wasn't General White, was it Sheriff?" Blind Date cried with her French accent as she moved up to Walker's side and stared at the Sheriff with fear in her eyes.

"Yes young lady, that's the name he gave me, why?" The Sheriff now smirked at the soldiers.

"Gees Sheriff, who do I have to blow to get out of this jail cell, sir?"

"Back off some Blind Date!" Walker snapped angrily as he fired a harsh glare at Regina.

"Hmmm... it seems your female friend over there doesn't want any part of this here old General, Mr. Civilian. Well he's here, and he wants you. I'm going to serve you people up to him on a silver platter, and I'm going to stand by while he dismantles the lot of you, mister."

"Is there any chance we can make a break for it?" Ghost said as he stared at the smiling cop.

"Try it mister, and I'll have your ass filled to overflowing with a load of buckshot for your trouble, buster. Civilian Walker, I'm going to let this General have at you now, my friend. Is there anyone on the Island you want me to notify when he finishes with you people in there?"

"You're a real fucking Jerk Benny I see, huh Sheriff! Don't enjoy this shit too fricking much buddy. I know the General, and if he's down here, he ain't down here just to chew on my fricking ass, sir. So go get the fucking General in here will ya, and stop trying to beat me over the damn head with his presence, sir."

CHAPTER NINE

When the Sheriff disappeared, the complaints started, mostly aimed at Lieutenant Walker.

"Hey Walker, I'd rather take the fucking chance of having my ass filled with buckshot, than spread my cheeks and let the stinking General have at me for this stunt." Casper moaned as he shook his head and looked Walker in the eyes, trying to figure out what the General wanted.

"Hey Walker, whatdaya think has the stinking General coming down here for man? We ain't that fucking important to anyone in the world, to get the hot shot General outta Fort fucking Fumble, to come the fuck down here, to chew on our asses a little, for a stinking bar fight we enjoyed, Homes." Buckethead complained as he stared at Walker and waited for his reply.

"Beats the fuck outta my stinking ass what the hell he's down here for, man. I guess we're gonna hafta just wait and see what the stinking General wants with our asses, man. I know he's not down here because we got our asses in a fight with some fleet fags, man. Something big musta happened someplace in the world, and he needs us to respond to the trouble man."

"I hope you're right." The Mutt snorted, not showing any fear of the approaching General.

"If the stinking hot shot General's down here, we musta beat the crap outta some fucking big shot snot nose special Navy shitter in that little bar fight of ours, Homes. Maybe one of those pukes we stomped into the fucking ground was a fricking Admiral's kid or suttun man." McNip added, he then moved to the rear of the pack of soldiers in the back of the jail cell.

"C'mon you guys are getting all worked up over nuthin. What can he do to us, he can kill us yeah, but he can't eat us that's illegal." Walker snapped at the complainers in the cage as he shifted his weight and waited for the General to come into the room and get on them for the fight.

Everyone quieted down the instant General White entered the large room the soldiers were being held in. Without saying a word to them, he looked at the many grime covered and bloody faces staring back at him through the bars of the cell. General White smiled when he saw Baby Tee without a shirt on as if it was not anything to her. He saw Sergeant Dorothy Ramirez and could see her showing the first signs of being pregnant. He was surprised she was involved in the bar fight because of her condition. She looked a real mess and he could see the shiner she was supporting around her left eye, and he knew she was right in the middle of it with Walker and the rest of the soldiers when the shit hit the fan. When he saw the Mutt staring at him with the broken chair still wrapped around his head, he shook his head and then stared at Walker.

Walker smiled at the General and he shifted his weight from one foot to the other.

"Wipe that shit eating grin off your slimy puss, mister! Before I take a giant dump on your puss for ya! Jesus, Mary and Joseph, why am I not surprised to find the pack of you flaming assholes stuck in the can? I'm not in the least bit impressed by your stupid stunt here, people. I thought you assholes were better trained than you obviously are it seems. Looks like I'm going to have to change your training a might on you pack of criminals. You fucks embarrassed the shit out of me big time on this hair brain little stunt of yours, people. You pack of jackasses couldn't have picked a worse fucking time to display how lack of intelligence you and this bin of God's lunatics don't control. Jesus Christ Walker, what the hell am I going to do with you and the rest of your fruitcakes you're supposed to have fucking Command over, mister?"

"Why is that General White Sir?" Walker replied as he lit a cigarette and then added to his words for the powerful General. "It wasn't no big deal here sir, we just kicked ass on some rather inconsiderate swabbies. It ain't nuthin for you to be overly concerned with sir."

"I didn't give you permission to smoke, mister! Or to talk to me for that matter! Anything you asses do, concerns me Lieutenant. Whatever you people do, reflects on me all the fucking time, mister. You people are my pet project, and I'm responsible for the lot of ya, dammit. The President jumped all over my ass when he found out about your fight with the Navy shits, mister. Remember stupid, the President was Navy." The General growled as he snatched the cigarette from Walker's hands, and began smoking it as he barked at the rest of the soldiers. "Stand at attention while I'm addressing you pack of flaming assholes, dammit!"

Immediately, everyone in the jail cell snapped to attention before the fuming General.

"I don't know if you people are aware of this or not, shithead. But I have a real fricking cock stiffener to lie down on your slimy ass. Last night, a small pack of flaming assholes tried to assassinate the President of the United States right in Washington D.C."

There was a grumbling of anger from the specialized soldiers in the cell, as they moved a little closer to the bars in an effort to hear the General's words better, and then Lieutenant Walker asked his commanding officer with concern. "The President's okay, right General White Sir?"

"Yeah, he's fine Walker, but the Vice President took one in the shoulder, and she's in critical condition. She's expected to survive, and the National Security Director was killed in the attempt against the President, buster. Washington's now an armed military camp and completely closed down. It seems one of the damn terrorist had successfully escaped our response to their attack, and there's a massive turd hunt on for the missing prick right now, mister. How the fuck did you jerks end up in here anyhow, dammit? You people look like a bunch of asses trapped in there."

"General White Sir, everything was going okay with us in the damn bar until one of us tried to steal some of the lousy furniture from the dump we wrecked last night when we went afta the swabbies, General." Walker stopped speaking and glanced at the Mutt who still had half the broken chair hanging on his shoulders, and then added to the officer. "C'mon General, you gotta get us outta here sir. We gotta get this prick before he tries it again, or he tries to get outta the United States before we get his ass, sir." Walker pleaded as he stared in the General's eyes.

"That's why I'm down here buster. I'm going to get you people out of this damn birdcage. Then, you assholes are to report to Lejeune and wait. Colonel Leadbetter's expecting you..."

"Yeah, out of the fucking frying pan and right into the stinking fire I guess, huh General White Sir?" Weird Bill, Sergeant William Molinari complained at the officer outside of the bars.

"Can that crap buster before I wipe up the damn floor with ya ass mister. Mutt, get rid of that damn chair around your neck, or I'm going to make you eat the damn thing. Hmmm..." The General slowly rubbed his chin as he looked at each of his troops, and then he added to them. "Speaking of necks, where the hell's that poor excuse for a gene experiment gone haywire on us, No Neck? He was down here with the rest of you asses, am I correct Walker?"

"Arrr... they hadta take his ass over to the hospital to close up a cut from a broken bottle, sir." Walker replied as he continued to stare at the powerful General over the news he told them.

"What's this shit mister? What the hell's this shit about! I can't believe this shit I'm hearing from that sewer you call a mouth for a damn second. You pack of assholes allowed a Navy puke to place one of your people in the damn hospital? How many of the salt water taffies are with him in there? It better be every damn puke who was involved in that fight or heads are going to roll, mister. We don't leave our wounded behind, and we don't allow anyone to put any of us in the hospital, without them paying big time for it, Lieutenant Walker." General White snapped, pissed over one of his soldiers was hospitalized over the bar fight his troops were involved in.

"He caught a stinking cold sir." Blood Clot smirked, trying to lighten up the General's mood.

General White shot a harsh look that would have melted butter at the smirking medic.

"Hey General, we were outnumbered three to one by the water shits, sir. The damn saltwater swabbies did a masterful job of staying out of our clutches while taking shit shots at us, sir." McNip, (Sergeant David Nirajima) offered lamely to the well respected military officer. He got his tag name because his mother was Irish, and his father Japanese.

"Phesss, that's good fighting odds for how you people were trained. What the hell were you people trained for dammit, a one on one situation, or going up against the odds and surviving, mister? What the hell is the matter with you assholes anyhow; you people getting soft on me or something around here?" General White was trying to insult his group of elite troops now.

"We'll get the lousy bastards betta the next time we go at them good and proper, General White Sir." Buckethead offered from the cot he was sitting on. Sergeant Vincent Lombardo got his tag name, because of the size of the helmet he had to wear to cover his massive head.

"Another fucking country heard from I take it. Get on your damn feet when you're addressing me, oak tree. Before I fill your skivvies with termites and face me right as well, mister! Who the fuck told you to rest in my presence, mister? I was forced to leave Washington at this extremely crucial time to come down here to this hot ass little Island of yours, and then drag your sorry asses the hell out of this damn birdcage. I have a good mind to bust the lot of you asses back to fucking Privates, and allow you people to start all over from scratch to regain your rate and your damn standing in the service, I shou..."

"Poor threat there General White." Hunter, (Sergeant Frank Whitcomb) offered sarcastically.

"Is zat so wiseguy? And how is that pray tell, mister?" the General snorted at the soldier, as he turned to the second of the pointmen from the unit. The Ghost (Sergeant Walter Casper) was the other, and the General knew these two were the most dangerous of the lot. Any time someone had to take the point position for the group, the most dangerous position in the entire unit, and protect the rest of the soldiers. These two troopers were always picked for the detail. They were the best of the best he had in the unit.

"Cause General White." The Hunter retorted with a smirk as he leaned against a concrete support column of the jail before continuing with his words in a sarcastic tone. "Everyone knows to be part of the Special Forces you gotta be a fucking Sergeant or betta, General White."

"You think that's a fact, huh hot shot? Well you listen to me asshole, when you're addressing me mister, you better added the "Sir" before and after each sentence you aim at my ass for one. You also better watch your damn mouth when speaking to me that's two, buster. Or I'll have your balls for marbles, mister. I don't give a shit if you're dressed in your skivvies or a military uniform. I'm still Sir to you at all times, you got it mister! You're not dealing with Colonel Leadbetter here, buster. I don't care how you speak to him, but you'll respect me at all times if you know what's good for ya ass, mister." General White snapped, angry at the disrespect these elite soldiers were showing him as they all stared at the General from inside the cage.

"Sir, yes sir." The Hunter automatically went to attention stance as he stared at the General.

"That's better shithead, now to answer your last remark mister. You're forgetting something important here, buster. I set the ground rules for the damn game, and if I want to bust your ass back to Private, yet keep your ass in the Special Forces. All I have to do is cut the orders, and it's done that simple, pal. Do you have anything else to add to this conversation?" General White growled as he took the stance of a linebacker and threatened the Hunter through the bars.

"I didn't hear you shithead?" the General roared at the fearsome Hunter.

"Sir, I have nothing else to add to this conversation, General White, SIR. And yes sir, I understand you set the rules for the damn game, and it's what you say that goes around here, sir." The Hunter offered as he straightened up more before the fuming General.

"That's better shitbird. Walker, the President wants me to get you people the hell out of here. Heaven knows why though, dammit. I'd as soon let you people rot in this damn birdcage. Maybe it'll teach you people a lesson. Arrr... I seriously doubt it. All kidding aside Walker, the President wants you people ready for immediate action. He wants to get the terrorist able to escape the failed assassination attack against him, and those who were sponsoring him. That means you might find your asses back in Iraq, soldier." The General took a quick breath.

"You think the fucking Iraqi shits were behind the assassination attempt on the President's life, General White Sir?" Walker growled as he allowed his anger to show up in his voice.

"No Walker, we know it for a fact..." The General began to offer to his young Lieutenant.

The General was interrupted by an extremely angry Mother Flanagan as he hissed at his commanding officer. "That muthafakka will never learn sir. His fricking mother of all wars died in labor sir and here he is again, trying to flex his dick, General. It's about time he and all his stinking assholes that follow the dumb ass to get turned into crispy critters, General White Sir."

General White completely ignored Mother Flanagan's bitch, as he continued speaking with Lieutenant Walker. "Lieutenant, there was some evidence discovered at the damn crime scene mister. I happen to agree with the President in this case, he doesn't feel this last terrorist is going to surface again until he makes it back to his damn rat's nest in Iraq, where he might think he's safe from us and I'm going to use you poor excuses for solders to show him the error in..."

"General White Sir, is everyone from the outfit going in on this next mission to get this missing terrorist, sir?" Sergeant Ramirez asked as she stepped forward and looked at the General.

General White knew the reason why she asked him that question and he replied in a flat tone of voice. "No Raz, only a few of these flaming assholes are going in on this one, Sergeant. I want the terrorist caught, and brought back to the States in one piece, so he can stand trial before the American public and receive his just deserts, but I have no intention of invading Iraq in force, Sergeant. Now don't get me wrong here Sergeant Ramirez or the rest of you assholes. I don't care if this ass is bent up a little, as long as there's enough of him left to try and then fry.

"Things might change once we hash over the evidence we discovered, and see if Saddam Hussein was the suck ass dick deep in this shit, and issued the orders to assassinate our President. I believe if the Boss discovers this as a fact, he's going to level Iraq once and for all, Lieutenant. He threatened he was going to bomb Hussein and his thugs back to the days of Ali Baba and the forty thieves. I think he's angry enough to carry out this threat this time around, mister. The President was really pissed enough to chew on rusty nails and enjoy it I tell you, Sergeant." General White saw the unasked question in Ramirez's eyes and offered.

"I'm sorry honey, but you don't come up in the equation this time I'm afraid. In case you forgot, you're pregnant young lady, and that omits you from any active mission the rest of these shitheads are sent out on, until you have your baby that is, period Sergeant."

"But sir..." Ramirez began to plead in her defense, but she was cut off by the General.

"Period I said Sergeant Ramirez, so don't give me any further shit over this matter, huh. I don't intend to get involved in a battle of words over this shit with ya. That's my decision, and you have to live with it plain and simple. It's for your own damn good, and the kid's as well, Sergeant." General White snapped, and then felt bad when he saw the hurt look etched in her eyes and he added. "Yeah Raz, I understand how you must feel and you're missing a big one here, but them are the breaks young lady. Next time you'll make sure this ass fires off in the air."

A bunch of 'Oorahs' followed the General's words aimed at Sergeant Ramirez.

"What do you have to do to be cocked, locked, and ready to rock, Lieutenant Walker?"

"When?" Walker fired back, speaking for the entire group standing behind him now.

"Two days from today will do, Lieutenant. The latest Intel put the spin out this missing bastard will most likely stay in hiding in the States until the heats off his ass. I don't think you'll need any extra training on this one just a little tune up will do for the ones going in after this prick. Once the heat calms down a bit, this ass will try and make his escape from the States. I have Colonel Leadbetter getting the troops spread throughout the country to report back to Lejeune. That's why I'm giving you at least the extra fucking day to get up to Camp Lejeune, mister."

Lieutenant Walker knew why the General said only a few elite soldiers from his element might be heading for Iraq this time around. He felt that remark was meant more for Sergeant Ramirez's benefit than what the other soldiers were really going to do about this missing terrorist, and he asked the General. "The whole group's going in on this next mission sir?"

"Didn't I just answer that damn question for you, shithead? Ten to twelve of you shit bags will is more than enough to enter Iraq and get this lousy bastard and that's all, if we have to go this route that is Lieutenant. More if you think you might need a little extra support on this possible upcoming mission, mister. If it turns into a mission at all that is, Walker. There's always that one chance in a million the dumb ass bastard might be captured in one piece, before he can flee the country. But I'm activating the entire Multi National Rapid Response Force, and having all the soldiers reporting back to Camp Lejeune, just in case things go sour on us and this damn mission ends up going tits up on us, Lieutenant Walker."

"General White Sir, you give me ten to twelve of my fucking troops, and I'll finish the stinking job the god damn Coalition Forces started, with these fricking sand swimming camel jockey scumbags, sir." Walker offered angrily, as he stared into the General's unblinking eyes.

"Ahhh... spoken like the true killer you are Mr. Walker. What do you have to do to be ready to bug out?" General White asked his young officer as he smiled at him for the first time today.

"All I have to do is close up my place, and inform the stinking Sheriff I'm leaving the damn Island, and they'll keep an eye on the dump until I return home, General White Sir."

"You think the Sheriff's going to be on your side, what with all the heat you caused his ass yesterday, mister?" General White asked as he shook his head, not believing Walker would dare to think the Sheriff department would help him any after all the grief he just caused them.

"Shit yeah General White Sir. We know most of them personal, and as long as we don't give them too much shit while we're on the Island, they'll support us sir. I'll have the Mutt close up his place as well. The rest of these shitbirds are either staying with us, or they're renting apartments on the Islands, General White. It shouldn't take me too long to get everything..."

"Errr...Walker." Sergeant Ramirez offered in a low contrite tone to her lover.

All eyes went to Sergeant Ramirez, and the concerned soldiers waited for her to speak up.

"What's up baby?" Walker asked he could not help feeling bad for her missing the mission.

"You seem to forget something about this mission, Bobby. I'm being forced to remain on the Island while you and the rest of the young and useless here are traipsing all over the globe, soaking up all the glory in this mess, Robert. That means you're not going to have to close up the house this time because I'm going to be stuck here worrying about you people."

The General placed his hands on his hips and allowed an angry look to cross his face as he stared at Ramirez, and then he snapped at her. "Sergeant, do you think for one god damn second I'm going to leave your little ass down here devouring time stacking pencils, (killing time) sister? No way in hell soldier. Yes, I told you you couldn't go along on the mission, but as long as you're part of this mixed up crazy ass Unit, you're to respond to any call up, even if you have to shit that baby of yours out somewhere along the way, Sergeant. You understand me young lady?" General White growled as he informed Ramirez she was activated also with the rest of the Unit.

"Yes sir, I sure do General White Sir. Thank you for the order General White."

"Don't thank me I didn't do you any favors here. You're part of this Unit, period sister."

"Soldat Dzhein." Siberia, one of the female Russian soldiers mumbled just loud enough for the rest of the group to hear her. Sergeant Taras Zarugnaya, was on loan to the group of elite soldiers from Russia, as part of their commitment to the rapid response force organized by many nations to combat terrorism, no matter where it reared its ugly head in the rest of the world.

"Hey bitch, what didja just say?" Walker growled he still did not get along well with this Russian babe. Every chance Siberia got, she teased Walker sexually or got him in fights.

"No let shit hot on you, big shot America soldier you. I call Sergeant Ramirez GI Jane in Russian. She good fight, better than most you men in you outfit, big stupid you."

"Here's some fucking Russian back at ya baby. Pissoffski on her stinking ass, bitch." The Mutt hissed at the Russian soldier, feeling she was dumping on Ramirez.

"I do no have much pleasure be near so to big America Pig, who think they Rambo cock fight man all time, please. In Russia, all soldier good as you special warrior think you be in America."

"Oink, fucking oink, yeah Commie Bitch, that's why Russia's fricking swimming around in its own shit right now, huh baby? Get your Commie ass back in line so we can get the fuck outta this miserable dump will ya." Mother Flanagan griped angrily, as he entered the conversation for the first time, also feeling the Russian was taking uncalled for shots at his fellow soldiers.

"Cut the shit out before I make each one of you asses lick the shit knife. We're all part of the Unit of the best fighting men and women in the damn world, and we don't go and fight amongst each other period. There are plenty of bad guys out there to fight with, without you people going at each other's fricking throats." General White snarled from outside the cell as he stepped up to the Russian soldier, and stared her right in the eyes for several long seconds.

"You star no impress me much General. I answer only to my General back in Russia."

"So you think you're a hard nose little Russian shit, huh bitch? Well, let me inform you of something here and now. I have the power to send your ass back to your own country. Then, you can have the pleasure of explaining to your General how you gave me grief, while he's standing your ass before the firing squad for embarrassing Russia by disrespecting a Commanding Officer. What's it going to be, you going to be part of this solution, or part of the problem?"

Siberia cast her eyes down as she mumbled barely over a whisper. "I good part of Unit, General." She knew the officer was correct, if she was sent back to Russia, because she gave a problem to the commanding officer. She would at the least be disgraced, at the worst, killed.

"That's better young lady." General White growled as he turned back to Walker and ordered him. "Have these poor excuses for soldiers clean up. You're getting out of here as of now, mister. I expect everyone on these damn Islands to report to Camp Lejeune on there own accord by no later than Zero, Six Hundred Hours, on the 29th of July, Lieutenant. There are enough of you jackasses on the damn Island for me to have a C-17 Globemaster dispatched to pick the lot of you up. That thing you people call an airport on this damn Island should offer some rather interesting entertainment to the pilots of the Globemaster. Let them try their damn skills at trying to land on a postage stamp for a change and do some touch downs and go again landings. You're free to make it back to Camp Lejeune on your own as well, Lieutenant Walker. Either way, make damn certain you're at Lejeune by the time ordered, or you're going to be branded AWOL, and then I'll have you hunted down and shot on the spot for sport. Got it people?"

"Yeah sir, your voice carries sir." Walker replied as he straightened and saluted the General.

"Deputy, I want out of this damn birdcage immediately dammit." General White bellowed at the deputy who had followed him in this certain section of the jail.

A young female deputy opened the door as she offered politely to the military officer. "General White Sir, all you had to do was open the door, it was never locked on you sir."

"How the fuck was I supposed to know that, dammit!" When General White barked at the young female deputy without thinking who he was barking at, he regretted his words. He allowed the pressures of the attack on the President, and the trouble these young soldiers gave him, to rule over his usual good nature. He bowed slightly to the deputy as he mumbled at the thoroughly embarrassed female deputy. "I'm terribly sorry for snapping at you like I just done young lady, you're not one of my soldiers, Ma'am. Forgive me please."

The deputy nodded politely at the powerful General, and tried to hide her smile.

"Are these shits free to go Ma'am?" the General asked the deputy as he followed her.

"Yes General, and Sheriff Edwards informed me the bar has offered to dismiss the charges, and forego reimbursement. The owner said it was the least he could do for soldiers of America."

"That's fine, well, and good for him young lady. But I have every intention of paying for all the damages to his establishment caused by my so called soldiers, Ma'am. I need a bill for the damages so I can write out a check for the bar owner, please."

"Yes sir, will you follow me please General White Sir."

General White went to leave, and suddenly he turned back to Walker and warned him in no uncertain terms. "Lieutenant Walker, you'll get these soldiers the hell out of here, and collect that fricking missing link of yours, and prepare them all to get over to Lejeune. Report earlier if you're able, Lieutenant." Then the General was gone as quickly as he had arrived.

"Whew, well that was painless enuf I guess people." Walker said as he grabbed his ripped shirt and let out his breath in a rush. The soldiers followed Lieutenant Walker out the door. They collected their wallets and personal stuff from the deputy who handled these items, and then they headed for the Fisherman's Hospital to collect the injured Neck.

FISHERMAN'S HOSPITAL ON MARATHON ISLAND, FLORIDA

Lieutenant Robert Walker's group entered the quiet hospital as if they were an invading Army. The Mutt called out Neck's name, while Walker spoke to a nurse who was at the front office.

"Hey baby, I'm here to pick up Sergeant Robert Abbott's fat ass from this dump, honey."

"I'm afraid the man you're speaking of is under arrest, and he can only be released by the Sheriff and Doctor, sir. If you can't be quiet, I'm going to be forced to ask you to leave the hospital immediately sir. We have sick people resting in the hospital and they need…"

"Yeah, yeah lady, you do that will ya please. Where the hell's he hiding in here honey?"

"Neck!" The Mutt screamed out at the top of his lungs, and then listened for a moment.

"Here! I'm down here people." Neck called out from his hospital room just as loud.

"Where the fuck's here man?" the Mutt replied as he looked down the long hallway.

"Down here stupid in one of these small ass rooms they have me stuffed into, guys." Neck replied as he tried to get out of the bed and meet the excited soldiers outside.

"Please sir, you must be quiet while you're visiting the hospital sir. There are patients here who are very sick, and you're upsetting them with your calling out like that sir. If you can't be a quiet, I'm going to be forced to call the Sheriff, and have him remove you and your friends from the building at once, sir." The nurse picked up the phone as if to enforce her threat aimed against Walker and the rest of the soldiers with him to call the local cops.

"Just try it lady, and it's gonna be like Friday night at the fights in here, sister. I gotta letter from the major puke on the Island, releasing Neck to me. Here, read it for yourself honey." Walker shoved the letter from the Sheriff at an angry nurse, who took over the conversation.

"I don't know who you're talking about sir. There's no one in here by the name of Neck, sir. That's a rather strange name for anyone to have sir." The nurse offered as she read the paper. "Oh, you mean Mr. Robert Abbott, sir. The Doctor finished stitching him up, but he wants to keep him for a few days for observation, to make certain he didn't receive a concussion in the bar fight he was involved in the other day, sir. He was struck on the head, and there's a good chance his skull was cracked during the fight and the Doctor wants to make certain he's alright and..."

"Hey baby, it'll take a One, Oh, Five, Howitzer round to crack his stinking skull on..."

"Hey guys, I'm down the hall here man." Neck yelled out as he struggled into his pants.

"I got the fuck Walker." The Mutt cried as he and the others charged down the hall.

"Please sir, you can't go down the hall of the hospital without an escort... Oh, hell. Mr. Walker, go get your friend, and leave the hospital. But only if the Doctor releases him first sir, I'll page the Doctor, and have him meet you and your friends at Mr. Abbott's room, sir."

"Hey baby that's the first time anyone called me sir, without adding I was making a stinking scene someplace." Walker smiled as he snatched the release form from the nurse, and then he charged after the rest of his group already moving down the hall.

"But you are causing a scene Mr. Walker." She called out after him as she paged the doctor.

Walker turned the corner and saw his group stopped from entering Neck's room by a Sheriff standing guard by Neck's room. The deputy's hand was resting threateningly on his pistol.

"Back off dude I got a stinking letter from your big shot, man. Neck's released to me pal." Walker hissed as he handed the paper over to the officer standing guard. The Doc caught up to the soldiers and cut through the group and saw Walker speaking to the deputy and said to him. "I take it you're the one in charge of these, errr... people, sir?"

"Yeah, what's it to you fella?" Walker snapped angrily at the man dressed in white.

EAGLE'S NEST

"Because I'm the Doctor in charge of this patient..."

"He ain't no patient Doc, he's the fucking Neck, sir." The Mutt offered with a wide smirk on his lips as he grinned at the concerned looking medical doctor.

Neck now stood in the doorway struggling to get in his clothes as he spoke to Walker over the shoulder of the deputy who was actually blocking the door. "Hey Road Kill, you hear some fricking schmucks just tried to off our stinking President last night on us right in the middle of his country man? We gonna go get the fricking lousy little pissants or what, Homes?"

"Whatdaya think I'm doing out here organ donor. We got us some new stinking orders from the head warlord, man. C'mon big man, we gotta get the hell outta this here stinking dump, and get on our damn horses and head for Lejeune ten minutes ago. We got the deal to clean the clocks of the dopey ass marmalukes who just tried to do the Boss in last night. We got ourselves a real, ever loving fucking vengeance mission on our damn hands again, man." Walker replied as he forced his way by the deputy, who now stepped aside and allowed the soldiers to enter the room after reading the release form from the Sheriff. The doctor followed the group into Neck's room as the soldiers spread out to give the doctor room to work on Neck.

"Mr. Abbott, you have to sit down on the bed, so I can examine you again please sir." The doctor ordered as he pulled Neck's arm, and tried to lead him back to the bed.

"Hey Doc you have to understand suttin here, he ain't no mister, sir. He's a gene experiment gone haywire on us, sir." Blind Date offered as she bumped the Neck with her hip.

"That maybe so, but I still have to examine him before I can possible release him from the hospital and our care, Ma'am. Here Mr. Abbott, please follow the light closely with your eyes. Don't move your head with the light just follow the light with your eyes for me please."

The Mutt got alongside Neck, and stared at the pen light with him, and then he asked Neck. "Whatdaya see in there man, you see any naked women dancing around in there, Homes?"

The doctor stared at the Mutt for a second as if he had a screw loose. The massive Neck shoved him away with his shoulder, and the rest of the soldiers broke up with laughter. In the hall, a number of patients gathered to see what the hubbub was about. Then they shared a laugh with the soldiers as they watched the doctor check out the injured soldier.

"Well Mr. Abbott…" The concerned doctor asked his young and massive patient.

"Look Doc, if you wanna get along with me betta then you're doing right now sir then you're gonna hafta start calling me Neck. When you call me Mr. Abbott, I don't know who the hell you're talking to sir. I'm not usta being called by my real name by these slugs, Doc."

"Very well Neck, it seems you have a slight concussion, sir. I see a trace of blood behind your eyes, son. I'd like to keep you for a couple of days for observation and…"

"I'll observe the big guy for ya good and proper, Doctor." Bouncer, (Sergeant Carol Burnhart) offered with a grin as she lifted her shirt and stuck her breasts in Neck's face, and he gave her a bronskie. Bouncer nearly smothered him with her breasts. Neck made god awful noises as he slobbered all over Bouncer's breasts. She got her tag because of the size of her breasts.

"Please young lady I can't have that kind of thing going on in a hospital, Ma'am."

"Eat it Doc, if you want this big guy well and offa his damn duff, this is the only way its gonna happen for you sir." Bouncer helped Neck to his feet, and buttoned up his shirt for him.

The people standing in the hall clapped over what Bouncer was doing to the massive patient.

"I'm afraid I can't possibly release him in his present condition, in all good conscience, Mr. Walker sir." The concerned doctor offered as he placed the pen light back in his pocket.

"In a pig's fucking ear you can't Doc. Look here sir, there's not enuf fucking cops on this stinking Island to stop me if I wanna go somewhere, sir. I'm as fit as a fucking fiddle man, and I got a few fricking bad guys to deal with Doc. Any stinking prick who tries to off my fucking Boss, has to answer to me, real personal like you know Doc. If you can't release me Doc then I'll sign myself outta this dump myself, sir. I gotta be with my stinking people if they're heading for any action Doc." Neck offered as he steadied himself on his feet.

"Very well then Mr. Abb… err… Neck. I'll allow you to sign yourself out of the hospital on your own accord, sir. But I'll add to your report your release is against AMA, young man."

"What the fucks does that shit stand for Doc? It sounds like I belong to some kinda fucking medical group all of a sudden, sir." Neck growled as he pulled free of Bouncer's grasp, and he followed the other soldiers out of the room.

"It means you're being released Against Medical Advice, young man." The doctor replied.

"Yeah sure Doc, anything you say Doc. You just put down whatever the hell you wanna on my stinking report, sir. I don't give a flying shit if you put down I'm fricking pregnant sir. I'm getting the hell outta this stinking place right now sir." Neck complained at the doctor this time

The doctor followed the group of soldiers back to the main desk of the hospital, and then he wrote something down on the report.

The Mutt looked at the Neck and asked him as serious as he could speak to the man. "You're really not pregnant are you man?"

"Fuck you shithead." Neck growled angrily back at the clowning around Mutt.

"Yeah, I was wondering how a stinking beer bottle crashed over that stinking bone dome of yours, could possibly put you in a place like this, man. I thought it hadta be something else that got you stuck in here, dopey. Hey Raz you betta make room in that bed of yours, when you're gonna have your kid, honey. I think the stinking Neck's gonna be sitting next to ya in it, baby. I thought he was putting on extra weight while soaking up that good life down here. But I never thought he was pregnant." Casper offered as he lit a cigarette, and grinned at the big man.

"You fucking bullet stoppers ain't gonna let it go until I get pissed at the lot of you, and have your damn carcasses replace mine in this here stinking dump." Neck hissed back at them.

"Sir, there's no smoking allowed inside the hospital area, please sir." The head nurse at the station said, as she tried to grab the cigarette from the scary and rather huge man's hand.

"What the hell are you gonna do honey, give me a god damn bad report for smoking in school or something? Hey baby, whatdaya hafta do to become the head nurse around here anyhow?"

The doctor turned to the injured soldier, displaying his anger in his eyes as he snapped at Neck. "That'll be just about enough of that kind of talk around here, mister. I have put up with an awful lot of shit here today for the sake of you people, and I gave you people the benefit of the doubt because you're soldiers. But any more of that kind of talk, and I'll have the police throw the lot of you out of here on your god damn ears. I won't stand for anyone insulting my nurses in this hospital. Mr. Neck here are your papers, keep them with you for a week or two. I want you to take it easy for as long as you possibly can son, and if you feel yourself getting dizzy or your stomach gets upset on you. You're to see a Doctor immediately, and give him these reports so he knows what's bothering you sir. It could save your life for you young man. This is a serious injury you received in that bar fight and you aren't completely healed as yet, young man."

"Hey Doc, he's always fricking dizzy, or puking up his stinking guts all over the damn place, especially when he's on a ship, or a submarine, sir. You shoulda seen him heaving his guts out on that fricking tub taking us to Iran during Operation Sand Storm, Doc. He was worse than a god damn school girl on her first date." One of the soldiers called out from the group.

"What's this fucking shit about people, pick on the big dumb jerk day or something around here for crap sake? I'm hurt, and you people aren't supposed to be picking on me so much you know. Can't you people cut me some damn slack, not flack?" Neck complained bitterly as he stared at the many smiling and concerned faces of his friends.

"There's an awful lot there to pick on you know, speed bump. Who the hell was it that was trying to break all the bottles in the bar with his stinking noggin last night, man?" Walker replied as he joined the laughing soldiers still attacking the injured soldier.

The doctor's eyes did not leave Neck, until he responded properly to his last question.

Neck turned to the doctor and said. "Yeah Doc, I hear you loud and clear sir. If I get fucking dizzy or I start to puke some, I gotta go and see a medic pronto, sir. Can I leave now sir?"

"You better, it could mean your life if you ignore any of these symptoms too long young man."

"Yeah, yeah Doc, I hear ya loud and clear sir, I got ya sir. Can I go now please Doctor?"

"Yes, go with God's speed and protection young man." The doctor smiled at the large man.

"Thanks for everything you did for me Doc. You did a real banged up job fixing up my ass for me, sir." Neck saluted the doc, as he and the other soldiers poured out of the hospital.

"Whatdaya wanna do now Walker? We still got us some stinking down time to kill off, before we hafta report back to fucking base man, and I wanna tie on one last friggin jag, before we go active and we can't have another stinking party until we complete our next fricking mission, man." Mother Flanagan offered as he took a smoke from Casper.

"Dunno man, I kinda like to have us a little bash or something before we hafta report myself."

"Let's go down to Crage Key and have us a keg party." Baby Tee offered the others.

"Sounds like a stinking plan to my ass, people. You guys head out, me and the stinking Mutt will pick up a few kegs of beer and meet ya there." Walker pulled on the Mutt's arm and they were gone as the rest of the soldiers with him piled into cars, and headed for the south end of Marathon Key for the twenty six acre island of Crage Key. Sergeant Ramirez called the rest of the soldiers on the Island, and the surrounding Keys, to inform them there was a party on the go.

CHAPTER TEN

By the time Walker and the Mutt arrived on the beach, the party was going hot and heavy. Casper rolled up a fist full of joints for the other soldiers, and he passed them out to his people. Some of the girls from the Unit stopped at the local food store, and brought a ton of burgers and franks, and already had them cooking. It was getting to be late afternoon, and Baby Tee and Siberia were dancing topless for the male soldier's enjoyment.

Buckethead had his boom box and tunes blasting away. The group of specialized soldiers had permission to crash on Crage Key by the owner any time they wanted to use the property to get away on. The local police allowed the soldiers to take over the small Island feeling if the soldiers were there, they could not be causing any other problems elsewhere on the small Island, and they basically left the soldiers alone. The deputies knew the soldiers were on call, and they could lose their lives in the next action and because of this, they allowed them get away with certain things they normally would have busted them for.

By the time the sun was starting to set, everyone in the group was feeling pretty good. The magnificent sunset caught their attention, and everyone stopped what they were doing, and they stared at the golden globe as it slowly disappeared from sight. The women soldiers made suggestive sounds as they stared at it. Once the sun was down, the party turned serious with the soldiers pairing off, each with a girl from the group. Most of them made love under the stars and soft warm breeze. Walker and Ramirez were on the sand doing it, she held onto Walker as if it was going to be the last time she was going to see him alive. Every time they went out on a mission, Ramirez felt one of them was not going to return home alive. This time, without her going along on the mission, she felt more than ever she might lose Walker to the next action.

Lieutenant Walker rolled off Ramirez, and he stared at the star filled sky. He lit a smoke, and turned back to his lady. He saw she was softly crying and he knew the reason why. He caught a tear in his fingernail, studied it carefully for a second and then he placed it in his eye.

"What the hell are you doing Bobby?" Sergeant Dorothy Ramirez asked her lover.

"I'm keeping the tear for ya. When I return, I'll give it back to you with interest, baby."

"You sonofabitch, how well you know me Robert." She punched him in the arm.

"Hey baby, how many times do I gotta tell ya there ain't no fricking bullet made on the stinking face of the earth that's fast enuf to cap my ass on me, honey. I'm afraid you're gonna be stuck with me for the rest of your lovely life, honey." Lieutenant Walker smiled as he stared into the stunningly beautiful eyes of Ramirez, and then he smiled lovingly at her for a moment.

"Oh, poor little old me, say Walker I love you so much dammit. You better come back to me in one piece from this damn mission, my lover. We're going to have a child, and the child will need the both of us to help raise him or her." Sergeant Ramirez said as she returned the loving look from Walker with one of her own and hugged him to her as tightly as she could hold on to him.

"I gotta, you got my kid in ya honey. I want to see him and show the world there is gonna be two Walker's loose in this crazy ass world. I wanna see how the fucking world's gonna react to the two of us." Walker said proudly with a wide grin on his lips as he smiled at his lover.

"I love you so much Bobby." Sergeant Ramirez hugged Walker, as if her life depended on it.

The Mutt crawled over the sand on his hands and knees, because he was too drunk to try and walk right, and he saw the moment and decided to break it up on the two love birds. Blind Date was right behind him and the both of them were naked and high as kites.

"Any chance I can get me some of this fricking love making action around here, Raz?"

Walker looked up and saw the drooling Mutt and asked him. "Some of what stupid?"

"Hey man, Raz gives the best stinking face outta the whole damn Unit, Homes. I can sure use some head right about now man."

Blind Date punched the Mutt in his ribs and hissed at him with her heavily French accent. "And what the hell do you call what I just gave you, mista? Next time you can blow yourself."

"Don't get all fucking touchy and upset on me baby. I was trying to get these two stinking people to smile again. Look at them, they both look like they're walking down the last fricking mile or something, baby. Man, they should be enjoying the last days we have to ourselves for a change honey." The Mutt complained as he tried a smile on all three of his closest friends

"C'mon Mutt, if you don't mind making love to an ugly fat woman, join in and lets have one last fling before you guys head off on this next mission." Ramirez offered him.

"Hey baby you can never look fricking ugly to my ass Raz." The Mutt offered kindly to Walker's girlfriend as he and Blind Date joined Walker and Ramirez lying on the warm sand. They shared a four way, until the breeze slowly picked up, and they were forced to abandon Crage Key, for the warmer surroundings at Walker's home on Tingler Island. The temperature was scheduled to go down to the low seventies on this night, not very cold for the Island, but a little too cool to be outside running around without any clothes on for long.

BETHESDA NAVY HOSPITAL. 0130 HOURS EST, JULY 28th, 1999

The President of the United States, Albert Cole's small entourage arrived at the emergency entrance of Bethesda Naval Hospital, and he was quickly ushered into the building amongst extremely heavy security. Even though the Congressional Laws forbid the President to meet with the Vice President under these conditions President Cole enforced his will on his people, and had his security teams setup the meeting to take place.

The President left the White House through the back gate with the armored blocker car and six special agents inside the vehicle, the armory car with another six agents in the car, along with much heavier weapons stored in the car. In case they came under a sudden terrorists attack again, and a second unmarked armored Chevy suburban carry all, that the President sometimes used to travel the streets of Washington in secret. The suburban had six more secret service agents surrounding the still extremely upset and exhausted American President.

Upon entering the hospital, President Cole was quickly escorted to the third floor, where two special agent guards waited outside Mary Hirshfield's private hospital room. There were two other armed security guards stationed at the four elevators that serviced the floors of the hospital, and as the President walked into the hall, he instantly spotted two more special agents sort of just hanging around by the door leading to the stairwell of the floor. The President could only imagine every staircase leading up to the third floor of the building, had similar security guards posted at all of them. He breathed a deep sigh of relief, realizing the security protecting his injured Vice President was well entrenched and ready for anything that came their way.

The President entered the room silently and alone and instantly saw Mary lying on the bed, her neck and shoulder was heavily bandaged. The special agent who accompanied the President on his secret trip to the hospital, immediately took up positions with the other guards standing just outside the hospital room, to allow the President the privacy he needed and demanded to speak with his severely injured Vice President. A number of wires and tubes came from her body here and there, and they were hooked up to different monitoring machines surrounding her in bed. The still fuming President shook his head sadly as he stared down at Mary, angry as hell with what happened to her all because she was offering him a good trip to New York City.

President Cole moved a little deeper into the room as quietly as he could move, trying his best not to disturb Mary's seemingly restful sleep. He just had to prove to himself she was alive and doing well as could be expected under the circumstances. He was constantly kept up to date on her physical condition, but he had to see for himself first hand that she was truly okay. He stopped at the edge of the bed and carefully studied her face for a moment. Her hair was a mess, it seemed dirty, matted, but he washed it off as to the doctors being more concerned for her health, than her appearance as it should be. There was a dark chemical stain on her neck that turned it dark red. He saw some traces of blood on the bandage, and cursed under his breath at the terrorist who hurt his Vice President during the attempted assassination aimed against him.

Even though the terribly wounded Vice President was heavily sedated, the sudden movement in her room made her open her eyes. Seeing Albert standing so near her bedside, she immediately smiled up at him. The smile made her wince slightly from the pain it caused her. The Vice President tried to reach for her neck, but the one hand was taped down to a heavy rubber plate, this was so she did not move her arm suddenly, and possibly pull the needles and wires free of her body that were keeping her alive.

President Cole took Mary's hand in his and patted it gently as he smiled and offered pleasantly to his Vice President. "Please, don't try to say a word young lady. You just lay there and let me look at you for a few moments, please. Gees, I'm so damn glad you're alive I was so worried about you honey. When they pulled me out of Eagle's Nest, the last vision I had of you, was you lying on the top step of the ramp, bleeding and staring back at me like you couldn't see me dammit. Jesus Christ young lady, I thought you were dead, god dammit." The President kissed her hand. He could swear he heard her purr sweetly at him.

She tried her best to speak to the concerned looking American President, but her words came out so slight a squeak he was barely able to hear them, and the attempt to speak caused her more pain and discomfort, and it also served to set off a buzzer in the monitoring machine. A nurse reading her vital signs from outside the room, immediately rushed into the room and quickly adjusted the pain killing liquid constantly dripping into her arm, and then the nurse warned the Vice President not to try and speak again before leaving the room, she barely acknowledged the shaken and concerned looking American Leader watching her work on Mary.

"Dammit to hell and back, perhaps it wasn't such a good idea for me to come to visit you after all, Mary. I should've listened to everyone telling me to leave you the hell alone, dammit. But you know how I am, a thickhead and all that other crap. I just had to see for myself how you were doing, and nothing this side of judgment day was going to stop me from visiting you today, honey. I think I'll leave you for now and let you catch up on your needed rest, young lady. I'll be back to see you when you're feeling a little better sweetheart. Maybe next week I'll sto..."

The President's words were cut off by Mary grasping his hand and holding onto it for dear life.

"Hummmm... I take this as you don't really want me to leave your side just yet, honey. Am I right with this assumption, young lady?" President Cole smiled down at his Vice President.

She squeezed his hand tightly for a second time and tried to smile up at him again.

"Okay pretty lady, I'll stay with you until you get sick and tired of my ugly face, honey."

A tear escaped her eye as President Cole sat down in a chair while still holding on to her hand. They sat in silence with the President stroking her hand gently, before she finally nodded off to sleep, because of the pain medications were taking effect on her again.

When President Cole felt her slowly release his hand, he carefully rose and kissed her on the forehead. He took the time to adjust the sheet over her body, and then he left the room as quiet as a church mouse. As he entered the hallway two nurses walked by him, both nodded to his presence and then they attended to Mary's needs. The nurses were waiting outside the room, giving the President the time to be alone with the severely injured Vice President.

A large special agent rested his hand lightly on the President's shoulder, adding pressure as he directed the American Leader towards the bank of elevators. None of the other agents wanted the President to go to the hospital in the first place. They were more concerned about the terrorist still on the loose in Washington, and until he was captured, the missing terrorist was still a serious threat against the President's life.

President Cole allowed the agent to lead him to the elevators as he offered weakly to him. "Don't worry about it Sam. I assure you, no one is going to find out about this little visit of mine. I made certain everyone involved, sworn to me they'll keep my visit to Mary a secret."

"I'm sorry Mr. President but I have to log this excursion of yours in sir. Then my buns are going to be deep fried over an open pit by Director Raincloud, sir. You know you were under strict orders not to come any where near this damn hospital, sir. Director Raincloud made it painfully clear to all of us under no conditions, were you allowed to leave the White House for any reason whatsoever sir, especially to visit your Vice President, sir. Director Raincloud has little compassion for anyone who goes against any of his orders out in the field sir."

"I'll protect you Sam. You know how I am when someone tells me I can't do something around here." The President offered with a smile, as he moved towards the elevators.

"Yes sir, and that's why I voted for ya in the first place, Mr. President Sir."

"Thanks, I'll take care of any problems you get into over this little stunt of mine, Sam. I just had to see her for myself to make certain she was going to be alright, dammit."

"I understand completely Mr. President Sir. That's why I consented to this little visit of yours in the first place sir. With all due respect Mr. President, I have to get you back to the Crown (code for White House) before anyone realizes you're gone and calls out the dogs hunting for you on us, sir. I don't want Director Raincloud running all over Washington searching for ya, sir. Besides sir, you have a meeting scheduled for later on today if I remember correctly, sir. We barely have enough time to get you back to the Crown before it starts. Please sir, let's get going sir." The agent stopped the elevator door from closing as the President entered the car.

WASHINGTON D.C. THE WHITE HOUSE. 0500 HOURS EST. JULY 28th, 1999

General John White, the Chairman of the Joint Chiefs of Staff returned to Washington the night before from Marathon Island in the Florida Keys. He spent some time with his wife before reporting to the White House the following morning. He was informed when he landed that the President called in his troops for an early morning meeting before he had to address the American public for a second time. To update them on how the investigation into the attempted assassination was going, along with the search for the missing terrorist. The President set the press conference for nine a.m. sharp, and he wanted to be caught up on what was being done about capturing the missing terrorist. Or what further evidence was discovered at the scene.

Air Force One was again cleared for duty the night before, and she was in the hospital hanger being cleaned up, and repaired of the minor damage received from the round fired meant to kill him. The President wanted to inform his staff on the present condition of his Vice President.

General White was at the White House ten minutes before five, he was ushered into the Oval Office. To his surprise, President Cole was already seated behind his desk waiting for his people to arrive. General White came to attention and snapped off a fine salute to the President.

"That's not necessary under the circumstances, General White Sir. Hang the damn formalities for the time being sir. How the hell did you make out with your troops down in Florida, sir?"

The General was shocked and concerned over the physical condition of the President. He looked very haggard, exhausted in fact, his hair was a mess and his suit seemed like he slept in it last night, and he was in a desperate need of a shave, and wore no tie. Something General White had never seen him go without before in all the times he was meeting with the powerful and well respected President since he took over the office.

"Fine Mr. President Sir." General White replied pleasantly as he took a seat on the couch, and then continued with his report. "It was no big deal sir, the kids got into a fight with some Navy puk... Excuse me sir, Sailors." General White corrected himself, remembering the President was ex Navy man himself. "No one was hurt, and the fight seemed to have bolstered their moral some, sir. I have them letting off some steam on the damn island. Then, they're ordered to report to Lejeune tomorrow at Zero, Six Hundred Hours to begin training to capture this nut if he makes it back to Iraq before we get our damn hands on his ass, Mr. President. If the lousy bastard gets out of the States, we're going to be forced to sit on our thumbs and wait for the prick to surface wherever he's at, and claim responsibility for the assassination attempt on your life sir."

"Dammit General White, please allow me to ask you a question, sir?"

"Sure thing Mr. President, shoot away sir." The General offered with a slight smile.

"Do you think it might be a wise idea on our part to let these young troops of yours free on the streets of downtown Washington, General White? You know why I ask you this question, to hunt down this missing terrorist, and anyone else he might have been working with that we don't know of as yet, sir. This way we can capture the lousy bastard while he's still here in the States, and we don't have to go through with placing your brave young soldiers on Iraqi soil searching for this one, General. I'm not very comfortable with having your soldiers infiltrate Iraqi soil you know, sir. Even though Saddam Hussein's Army is severely crippled at this time, it's still a very active and strong force to contend with that knows what it's doing in the field of battle, sir. I'd sure hate to think what will happen if your outstanding soldiers run into a good size unit of soldiers from the Iraqi Republican Guard, who would come out on top, General White?"

"I assure you sir my specialized troops will come out on top without a doubt about it, Mr. President!" the General hissed confidently as he shook his head, and then he finished the President's question of him. "Gees sir, you want Lieutenant Walker and his group of screaming squirrels roaming the god damn streets of downtown Washington, with loaded weapons no less, with a real purpose in mind at that sir? Wow. I don't know about that one Mr. President you're not going to control these kids like you do the local police departments, sir. Once these kids are out on a vengeance patrol, they'll not stop until they get their man no matter what, sir. No matter who they have to walk through, over, or under to get at him Mr. President Sir."

"I understand that General White. We held these conversations many times in the past about allowing the special operation force troops hunt down some damn drug dealers and more dangerous criminals roaming around the streets of the United States, sir. We can see how they work on the streets by allowing them to go after this terrorist, General White. Use it as a test so to say to see how the troops do if we decide to allow them loose on the streets of Washington."

"Yes Sir Mr. President, and with all due respect sir, I'm still dead set against using these highly trained and extremely dangerous troops, killers if you will sir. As some form of god damn peacekeepers or police officers, sir. Who will the soldiers answer to sir, the police, me, or yourself? They're soldiers who are trained to kill with anything they have at hand, Mr. President. To have these troops dealing with damn civilians and criminals I know they hate. No way in hell sir. I don't agree one bit with that dangerous thought, sir. I don't know what would be the larger wrong of the two evils, the criminals, or Walker's bunch of crazies roaming the city streets thinking they're doing the United States a favor by killing all its damn troublemakers off, sir."

"They'll answer to you alone General White! If we use the troops to reclaim certain streets in the United States, you'll be the one in complete command of the soldiers at all times. General, you know damn well what my election promise to the public was, sir. To get the streets of the United States free of crime, even if I had to turn the military loose on those street to accomplish this feat, sir. Safe for God fearing good women and children to walk on at any time of the day or night, and I'm damn well prepared to accomplish this promise, even if I have to use these elite troops of yours to get the job done for me, dammit." The President offered with anger creeping into his tone, as he stared at the General sitting across from his desk.

"Mr. President Sir, my specialized troops are just a phone call away at all times for any emergencies any State in the Union suffers, sir. The troops can be out on the streets of any city in the United States, within eleven hours at the longest, Mr. President. If things get that bad, I can have the troops good to go quicker than the time I just offered you, sir. To have these troops roaming around on the streets of the United States looking for some trouble is plain nuts, sir. I'd rather have the troops sitting on their duffs then respond to an emergency call up only if, and when we have need of them, Mr. President. I'm still against using these specially trained troops in any other way, shape, or form for civilian use, unless things are that far out of hand on us where we might be forced to send the troops into a certain area to restore law and order, sir."

"General White, I guess now is not the time for this conversation to take place, sir. What you're telling me is, if we locate this missing terrorist, it'll take at the most, eleven hours to have your troops respond to the situation if they're needed to lend any support to the local police departments, General?" the President asked of his military officer in an exhausted voice.

"Less time then that I assure you Mr. President Sir. Once these kids are stationed at Camp Lejeune, and set on full standby alert. It'll take the troops less than a few hours to be on the streets of downtown Washington, armed, and ready to respond to any possible situation they're assigned to correct, sir. The troops are already foaming at the mouth with wanting to get at this terrorist turd that went after you, Mr. President Sir. It seems the troops are taking it kind of personal that some damn nuts tried to assassinate you here in the States, sir. The troops understand that, and my soldiers want revenge on the terrorist's head who tried to assassinate you, sir." General White replied as he smiled at the President for a brief moment.

"And, that's the way it should be with your troops, General White Sir." The President leaned back in his chair and let out his breath in an exhausted sigh.

"Err... Mr. President, with all due respect sir, I heard some serious scuttlebutt floating around town about you sneaking out on us last night, sir. Is that rumor true sir?"

"Zat so General White Sir? What did you hear sir?" the President gave him a sneaky little sort of smile that informed the wise General he was caught dead to rights.

"How is the Vice President doing anyway sir?" the General asked as he smiled back at him.

"How well you know me I see, Mr. White. Mary looks like death warmed over dammit. But she's doing as well as can be expected, sir. She's got a ton of tubes and wires connected to her body, and I think she's going to speak okay because she's already making some damn noises, General. I had to fight through a mess of Doctors and my own security staff to get to her though. But I was damned to hell and back if I was going to be blocked from seeing her I tell you, General White. When do you think this missing terrorist will make his move to leave the States?"

"If he doesn't try and make another move on you again that is. Mr. President Sir."

"Yes, quite right General White Sir." The President agreed with his military officer.

"Mr. President, I think this damn terrorist who escaped us will lie low for a week, maybe ten days or even a little longer, sir. Then, the missing terrorist is going to sure as hell try and make every effort to get out of the States alive. He knows it's too damn hot for him to hang around here for any length of time. The longer he remains here in the States, the more likely someone will recognize, or even turn his ass in for the reward we're offering for the lousy prick, sir. I'm going to make it a helluva lot hotter for the rotten little bastard, by placing military types hanging around all civilian airbases throughout the States. I doubt much he'll make a second attempt on your life, Mr. President Sir. But we have to be prepared just in case he does go against the norm. He'll have to be a fucking ghost though to try and get at you again, sir."

"A week to ten days you say, General White Sir?" the President asked the military officer.

"Yes Sir Mr. President, that's the way we figure it sir, and that's why I allowed the troops to take an extra day for themselves, before they report back to Lejeune for special training, Mr. President Sir. I don't think we're going to see hide nor hair of this scumbag until he's safely back in his little rat's nest where he can surface, free of reprisals for his actions here sir."

"Reprisals against him, General White? So I guess we're going to be forced to place your troops in Iraq to capture this SOB, and bring him back to the States to stand trial and reap his just deserts, sir. General White, I want it impressed on your troops that I want this man brought back to the States in one piece, so he can stand trial before the American public, sir. Bent up a little is just fine with me sir. But he has to be in one piece and still alive and kicking, General White. I want to be the one who pulls the god damn switch on his damn ass, sir. You know sort of payback for Norman's death, and what he did to my Vice President, General. I can't believe Norman's gone. He was a good and wise man. I needed him and his wisdom, dammit." The exhausted President let out his breath in a sudden rush of air and ran his hands through his hair.

1171 EAST NORTHFORK DRIVE

Iraqi Colonel Abdulaziz Majd al-Adwani acted like a caged wild animal while hiding in the safe house since the attempted assassination of the American President. He hid behind the door with his weapon constantly held at the ready in hand. He was ready to kill anyone who tried to enter the room without him knowing or inviting the intruder in first. He swore to himself that he was not going to allow the Washington police authorities to take him in alive. Now, his driving force was to take as many American police officers with him as he could, before he breathed his last breath in this world. Colonel al-Adwani had a hand grenade also tucked in his pants, along with three extra clips for his pistol, to be used as the last ditch effort to try and kill any American Officials he could before he died by their hands.

Colonel Abdulaziz Majd al-Adwani began his second full day of hiding in the secluded safe house. He did not have a thing to eat since he first arrived at the safe house. He was angry as hell his failed terrorist cell did not accomplish their mission and kill the American President as they were ordered. The Iraqi Colonel and terrorist also fumed because he found himself trapped in this dark and dank basement of this filthy building, waiting for death to visit him. He felt as if there were a thousand eyes glued to his every move, as he unlocked the front door of the safe house yesterday when he first entered the building.

As yet, his safety net had not showed up to meet with him, or to explain how he was going to get out of the United States alive and in one piece. This made him more upset with his position. His support was supposed to be waiting for him when he first arrived, ready to help or die with him if he was confronted by the Washington police or any of the agents assigned to protect the President. Colonel al-Adwani was not only cursing the American President for surviving his assassination attempt on his life, his security people, and his own terrorists who had failed him, but he was also cursing Rasha Ali Abulfath, his safety net controller as well.

The Iraqi Colonel's stomach growled in hunger, and he placed his hand on it to quiet it, and for the first time since entering the safe house. He took some chances and began to search the building for something to eat and drink. His hunger forced him to act and he came out of the basement as if death hid behind every door in the old building, and he cautiously moved to the kitchen area. As he rummaged for some food, there was a sudden and soft tapping on the door.

He immediately dropped down to the floor, his nine millimeter Colt pistol held in a death grip in his hand, aiming at the closed door. The Iraqi Colonel cautiously and ever so slowly inched his way across the filthy floor, using his powerful legs to propel him forward. His eyes shifting all over the kitchen, looking for extra weapons, in case he was forced to use up his ammunition against the person knocking on the front door of the apartment. The light tap again, with al-Adwani seeing no weapons of worth in the room, he hunched his shoulders and rose to one knee before the door. He aimed his pistol at what he felt was the intruder's waist and waited.

After a series of third tapping, a sweet sounding young female voice called out barely over a whisper to him from behind the closed door. "My foolish lover, I am here to visit with you, but I'm afraid I cannot stay for too long on this day."

He released his breath in a rush as he replied through the door. "Does your foolish husband know you were coming to visit with me today my love?"

"Yes, although he does not approve of my visits, he allowed me to come to you."

Colonel al-Adwani rose from the floor and then quickly opened the dead man's bolt on the door, and then he slid the chain backup lock free. He unlocked the door and opened it just wide enough for Rasha to squeeze into the dimly lit room. When she was inside the room, al-Adwani attacked her in all his anger, as he slammed the door closed behind her. He was fuming that she was not there to meet him when he first arrived at the safe house, and in desperate need of her protection and information about what was presently going on in Washington, over his failed assassination attempt against the American President.

Colonel al-Adwani pulled Rasha in the room by her hair and spun her around by it. He held on her hair and bent her head painfully down, as he kicked the door closed behind her with his foot, and snapped the locks in place with his free hand, and then he pulled her up by the hair. He stuffed the pistol in her face and threatened her with death before removing it and placing it back in his pocket. The raging Iraqi Colonel slapped Rasha hard across the face as he hissed at her. "Where the hell were you all this time you bitch of the desert sands? You were ordered to be waiting for me when I found out how our assassination operation turned out, god cursed woman. You compromised my position and my life by not being at your post as ordered. You failed me, and you failed your country, your President, and Allah. Allah might forgive your mistake, but I have a long memory, and I have no intention of forgetting this foolish error on your part, Rasha."

All the time he yelled and slapped Rasha around, he pulled her by the hair and bending her head backwards painfully by it so he could slap her face freely. She was not able to protect herself, nor did she try against the terrible assault on her body by the irate Iraqi Officer.

"The god cursed operation being worked by incompetent fools, blew up in my god cursed face. The sons of a worthless camel were unable to kill the American fool who commands this foul country. The worthless fools allowed him to sneak away from them unharmed. How the devil do you think I felt entering this building without you here to assist me? I knocked, and when you didn't answer my call, I had no choice but to enter a dark building, not knowing who might be waiting for me. I hesitated outside, further compromising my position, witch of the sand. I didn't know if I was walking into a trap. Not knowing if you sold me out to the American authorities. Wait until I get you back in Iraq. I'll have your skin whipped from your hide until you beg for death to visit your body. Where were you that you weren't in position when I arrived, bitch?"

Colonel al-Adwani finally released his death like grip on Rasha's hair, but not until he flung her to the floor by it, and then he swiped at her side with his foot as a further insult to her.

The badly beaten Rasha did not reply to Colonel al-Adwani's question as she easily dodged his weak kick at her. She remained sitting on the floor with her head down while trying to catch her breath and absorb the pain. She wiped a small trace of blood from the side of her mouth, and then she glared up at the Iraqi Colonel as she cursed him under her breath.

"Don't dare to look at me that way, bitch of a camel's pleasure! It's your fault you received my wrath on your cursed head, witch of the desert sands. I asked you where you were, I'm waiting for your answer witch!" He rushed her and kicked Rasha hard in the stomach, causing the woman to cry out in pain for the first time since he began his assault upon her helpless body.

"Where were you, whore born from a camel's prick!" He growled angrily at her again.

"Colonel al-Adwani, I have been busy following the orders given to me by General al-Zahar, sir. When I was informed the American President survived your assassination attempt on his life, I set out to get you a new passport, and a new identity, sir. So you can escape this country of disgust, for the safety of Iraq. I have all the papers you'll need to escape with me." She cried out between gasping for air while holding on her ribs, trying to absorb the pain in them.

"Huh, give me the god cursed papers you offer me, lowly daughter of a sand flea! And, I'll see if your efforts were successful or not, worthless woman who should have her back opened by the lash." Colonel al-Adwani put out his hand and wiggled his fingers, waiting for her to hand him the papers he demanded from her. He savagely pulled the papers free of her trembling hand, and made a motion to hit her with them, and then he grinned over the fear his presence caused her.

She ducked from the threat of being hit again by the angry Iraqi Colonel as she continued with her report to the military officer. "Colonel al-Adwani, I have Ahmed bringing a makeup case, so I can change your face to match the picture perfectly printed on the new passport, sir. As you can see for yourself, I made it an Israeli passport for your use, sir. They're the only ones who come and go to this cursed country, without being scrutinized as severely as anyone else visiting this foul country of sinners, sir. I'll be traveling with you Colonel al-Adwani, because the loathsome American fools are looking for a lone terrorist. They'll not be looking for an Israeli man traveling with his wife, and leaving this foul country to visit the Middle East, sir.

"Colonel al-Adwani, I was forced to go this way sir. If I was to give you an Arab passport, you would have surely been stopped at any airport you chose to use to leave this miserable country of sin from, sir. I checked, any Arab, or anyone even resembling an Arab, is being detained by customs and the police, and they are checked over extremely thoroughly, sir. Five of our other operatives were arrested on charges, because the American government knew they were in their country to create problems for the great fools. Many of our people went underground, until the American authorities relax their security around the country." She tried to get up to her feet, but the pain drove her back to the floor and again she held her ribs to try and ease the pain.

Colonel al-Adwani smiled as he carefully studied the passport. The picture staring at him did not look very much like him. He was lucky he had the type of face that could pass for an Israeli, Arab, or even an American. He allowed himself to relax, and he let his temper wan a bit. He looked down at Rasha still sitting on the floor, and then he pulled her up to her feet by the arm with little effort. The Iraqi Colonel then looked her deep in the eyes with a threatening glare, as he snarled savagely at her.

"Rasha! You seem to have a rather good excuse for me not to have you, and your entire family put to death when we return to our faithful country, woman."

That was as close to an apology as he had ever come in his life. He turned his back on the suffering woman, and headed for the kitchen to eat something. He barked over his shoulder at the shaking woman. "Rasha, get in here and make something for me to eat before I beat you again, worthless woman. By the gray whiskers of the Prophet himself, I'm starving filthy pig."

She dashed to the icebox and removed some food from it. Within seconds, she had a steak cooking for the angry Iraqi Colonel. All the while she cooked a meal for him she held her head down, afraid to possible insult Colonel al-Adwani by allowing her eyes to meet his.

"Daughter of a lowly camel spider, do you have something I can eat now? I'm starved to death I told you, useless woman." Colonel al-Adwani barked angrily at her as he kicked her on the rearend, nearly knocking her into the hot stove.

"I have some bread and cold tea I can fix for you quickly, Colonel al-Adwani Sir." She offered in totally fear of her life, as she remained with her back towards the extremely upset Iraqi Military Colonel, and she continued to attend to the steak cooking on the stove.

"Yes, that'll do fine until you fix me a proper meal to fill my gut with, woman. Bring that to me before I beat you for sport, witch!" Colonel al-Adwani warned as he glared harshly at the young and running Arab woman, and he allowed himself a quick smile when she held out the tea and bread before her. Instead of taking the food, he rudely ran his hand in her blouse and roughly fondled her breasts. He knew he was thoroughly embarrassing her, and he took great delight in her obvious discomfort. When he had enough of her breasts, he nastily pinched her nipple until she actually had to actually cross her legs, to stop herself from crying out in pain.

She understood if she cried out, he would use this as an excuse, and attack her again without mercy for a second time. One beating from him was more than enough to last her for a lifetime.

The angry Iraqi Officer removed his hand from her blouse and took the offered tray and food, and then crudely dismissed her with a nasty flip of his hand, followed by a harsh glare as he growled at her again. "Get back to your god cursed stove before I forget that I am a good Arab gentleman of Iraq, and I beat you further for your insolence displayed against me since you have first come to me, daughter of a milkless whore you are."

She bowed as she rushed for the stove, glad she was still alive and to be out of striking range of his powerful hands. When the steak was done, she brought it over to Colonel al-Adwani. He stabbed it as if it was his enemy, and then he slammed the steak down on his plate. He made certain he took the entire steak and left none for her to enjoy.

She sat at the table watching the Colonel gnaw his way through the meat like the savage animal he was, and she shook her head slowly over his ugly display of eating and manners. "Wine! Get me some wine to drink with this foul meal you have prepared for me, worthless woman!" He spat out nastily, while pointing the tip of his knife at her chest, and then he shoved a chunk of steak in his mouth, and made god awful noises while chewing it.

She carefully poured the wine for the Iraqi Military Officer, and then she tried to get out of his sight, but he stopped her flight by saying to her. "Where the hell do you think you're going, daughter of a whore's nightmare? Sit down and speak with me while I eat this foul meal you have prepared for me that is unfit to be eaten by a lowly dog, you filthy pig you. I have many questions that need answering by you, worthless pig born to the sands of our endless desert." He pointed at her with the fork with a piece of steak stuck on it this time.

"Yes Colonel Adwani Sir, your wish is my command. What are these questions you have need of answers to, sir?" She was unable to hide the anger that was rising in her own tone.

"Be very wary of how you dare to speak to me, you daughter of the lowly night crawlers. For it is within my power to have you slowly put to death by the nightmare of death by a thousand cuts. Is there any way I can leave this loathsome country of lowly infidels immediately?"

CHAPTER ELEVEN

"I'm afraid that's totally out of the question Colonel Adwani. The American security agents and authorities have all airports locked up under heavy surveillance. All water ports are likewise blocked off by the American Coast Guard, and customs ships and security guards. Any ship that could make it to the shores of Iraq is thoroughly checked like never before I must report for your ears. I have word some ships heading for Iraq had been stopped on the seas, and were boarded by armed Coast Guard and military servicemen. I heard reports that state the borders to Mexico were supported by countless extra border guards and special agents and the likes. I believe it'd be impossible to move you safely across the country, to get you out of this god cursed country through Mexico until the Americans stand down and relax their surveillance, Colonel Adwani."

"Have you spoke to General al-Zahar yet, you god cursed bitch? Does he know what happened with my cell, woman?" He snarled at her as he continued to eat his prepared food.

"Yes, yesterday in fact sir, it was through his contacts that I acquired the passport, Colonel."

"Did the General have orders for me to follow, sand witch of the burning desert?"

"Yes Colonel Adwani, General al-Zahar has ordered me to inform you that you were not to be taken alive by any American security people under any circumstances, sir. He has ordered you to commit suicide if the need arises, sir. The General wants you to kill as many lowly foul American fools as you possibly can, before you breathe your last breath, Colonel Adwani Sir."

"I didn't need him or you for that matter to inform me of what I have to do, if anyone tries to arrest me from this miserable country, woman. Any Police Officers foolish enough to come anywhere near me, are going to be dead before they know what hit them, bitch. Those are the only orders he had for me, camel eater?" He barked harshly at Rasha as he glared at her again.

"No Sir Colonel Adwani. General al-Zahar has informed me to instruct you to remain at the safe house for at least a ten day period of time, sir. In that time Colonel, he feels the foolish American authorities would have no other choice but to believe that you have by this time, successfully escaped their worthless attempts to capture you, and you're no longer in their foul country, sir. General al-Zahar has also instructed me to protect your life with that of my own at all costs sir, and to remain by your side at all times until you're safely out of this god cursed lowly country, sir. It's my only desire to see you safely back on the sacred sands of Iraq again, Colonel Adwani, and far away from this great land of sin and greed, sir."

"Yeah! Is that all our Control had to offer me, a bunch of worthless orders I could have figured out for myself, bitch of the hot desert sands?" The still upset Iraqi Officer snorted angrily at the young woman as he continued to hold her in his harsh glare.

"Yes Colonel Adwani Sir, the General has further ordered you to sit tight, and if you happened to be discovered by the local police authorities, you are to kill yourself as I had already stated to you. I have the same orders, to die by your side if needed sir."

"I didn't need you to repeat my worthless orders to me, daughter born of camel spit. I believe that it's time for you to show me the proper respect I believe I have earned, by adding the 'al' to my proper name when addressing me, lowly camel filth. Give me more wine and retrieve a local newspaper, bitch. I want to read who died in our attack against the hated American President, and what the foul police are doing to capture me. The fools are so stupid, they publicize their police efforts, and it makes easy for us to elude their foul attempts to capture me. The lowly infidels will never realize what they offer to those who try to destroy them in this foul world, woman."

"Yes Colonel al-Adwani Sir. Any particular newspaper you wish to read on this day sir?"

"Yes filthy pig, get me the Washington Post. Is there a TV in this foul place, woman?"

"Yes Colonel al-Adwani, it's in the next room, the large one to your left, and there's a changer for the TV resting on the side table where you will sit in the room, sir." She replied to the angry sounding and acting Iraqi Colonel as she stared back at him.

"Put the foul thing on before you leave the worthless apartment to carry out your latest quest for me, put it on CNN news channel. They're even bigger fools than their worthless reporters are. They'll probably have maps of Washington on the air for us to study, woman."

Rasha ran in the next room out of fear of the Iraqi Operative and she placed the TV on loud enough for him to hear it clearly from the kitchen area. She put on a number of lights and tried to make it seem like the house was a normal home.

He watched attentively as Rasha turned on many lights, and she even opened the shades in the room he was not seated in. He knew why she done this, and he nodded in approval of her actions, but nevertheless he kept his angry scowl set in place on his face. He continued to glare at her until she was completely out of the building. He was not going to give her any satisfaction over the fact she was doing everything expected of her to protect his life.

WASHINGTON D.C., THE WHITE HOUSE, 0510 HOURS EST, JULY 28th, 1999

Just about everyone the President wanted to attend the meeting, was assembled in the Oval Office. President Albert Cole realized the CIA Director John Raincloud had not arrived as yet, and he was angry he was late for the meeting. The President glanced at General John White, and the military officer knew why the look and he stared at the door to the Oval Office, trying to will the powerful Director to arrive, before the President grew any angrier at him.

No one gathered for the special meeting dare to sit in Norman Griffin's usual seat for the meeting. Secretary of Defense, Jerry Levenhagen sat nearest to Griffin's place he was his closest friend and collaborator. Secretary of State Maria Hernandez sat away from the facing couches, locked in her wheelchair. The Deputy Secretary of Defense, Harold Clifton stood behind Maria with his hands resting protectively on her chair. He looked like a huge black cloud hovering, while guarding over the frail and older woman. Most of the Chief of Staff was assembled in the chairs surrounding the back section of the large office. Everyone wore the mask of anger, depicting the reason for the meeting with the exhausted American Leader.

Director John Raincloud drove like a wild man through the streets of downtown Washington leading towards the White House, he had to wait at his office to get the file on the man whose name they found printed on the slip paper at the crime scene of the assassination attempt against the President a few days before. The CIA Director was at his office all night, waiting for the report to come in. It did not finish arriving until four, fifty five a.m., and that made him late with the President and others of his staff scheduled to attend the meeting.

The CIA Director pulled up to the main entrance of the White House, and jumped out of his car, and allowed the parking steward to park his car for him as he rushed inside the building. Director Raincloud passed by Peter, the young Chief of Staff aide of the White House in a rush, as he nearly ran down the corridor leading to the Oval Office in the East Wing of the White House, swinging his briefcase like a parachute behind him. Completely out of breath, he grabbed the doorknob and opened the door, with Peter rushing behind him in an effort to catch up to the powerful and well respected CIA Director, so he could properly announce the Director's presence to the President and the others waiting in his office.

When Peter saw he was not going to catch up to him in time, he pulled up and allowed him to enter unannounced. He was relieved he did not have to go before the President again.

Director Raincloud entered the room under the harsh glare of the President. He walked over to the couch and nodded to the President, and he took a seat next to General White.

"I take it you're late for this meeting because the traffic must have detained you, Director Raincloud?" the angry President snapped at the man as he glared at him from his chair.

"I'm afraid not exactly Mr. President Sir. I had to stay in my office longer than I intended sir." The still out of breath Director announced to the President with a smile.

The President's eyebrow arched slightly in surprise over Director Raincloud's explanation for his tardiness to attend the meeting.

Director Raincloud completely ignored the queer look from the President as he began to report to him and the others in his office. "With all due respect Mr. President, I have the complete file on this terrorist named Colonel Abdulaziz Majdal al-Adwani with me, sir. It took all night to receive the report through from Interpol and assembled for your review, Mr. President Sir. The Brits are extremely slow on their paperwork when they want to be, sir. I had to promise them I wouldn't bring them into this damn mess in any way, shape or form for fear of any possible reprisals carried out against the United Kingdom, by followers of these damn terrorists, sir.

"I wanted to make certain that you were well prepared for your upcoming press conference scheduled for a little later on this morning, Mr. President Sir. I figured the more information you had available for you the better you'd be able to answer any reporter's questions at the conference, sir. We know you're going to be assaulted by a flood of questions by the excited news reporters on who was behind this assassination attempt on your life, sir."

"Outstanding Director Raincloud, I believe you're correct with your last assumption, sir. The damn reporters are going to be out for blood on this one, my blood I'm afraid to offer you, sir. I have the latest report on Mary's condition to inform the reporters of at the conference also sir. She's doing a helluva lot better than first expected sir. I feel knowing who this bastard who tried to assassinate me, is half the battle sir. That's going to help me with some of the reporter's damn questions. How did you get this file assembled so quickly, Director Raincloud?"

"Mr. President, I informed you we had discovered a small slip of paper at the crime scene with the name al-Adwani printed on it, sir. We felt the woman terrorist was ordered to report the success or failure of their attempt to assassinate against you Mr. President, to this man when the attack was over with, sir. It was by a sheer stroke of luck that the damn slip of paper remained lying on the all but destroyed landing of the water tower where it did, and we were able to find it sir. I was also able to place a face to the name, and I have assembled everything anyone knows about this man with me, Mr. President Sir."

CIA Director Raincloud went fishing in his briefcase, and when he found the report he was searching for he removed an eight by ten photo of Colonel Abdulaziz Majd al-Adwani from the file, and handed it to the President, and offered at the same time. "Mr. President Sir, this man is thirty nine years old, and he's full blooded Iraqi, and a Ba'ath Loyalist member. His mother came from the north of Iraq, and his father lived all his life in the capital of Baghdad, sir. He has two brothers and a sister and all are reported to likewise be loyal members in the feared Republican Guard Units one way or the other, sir. All believe fanatically, as does this Colonel al-Adwani that the United States should be lying dead in the dust, sir."

"He looks rather young for his chosen profession, who the hell is he, Director Raincloud?"

"Mr. President, he's Colonel Abdulaziz Majd al-Adwani of the Iraqi Secret Police, sir. He belongs to the vicious and the most feared Nebuchad Nazzar Republican Guard Unit, and he's also part of their Intelligence Division of that Unit as well, sir. It's believed he's the one who masterminded the suicide attacks organized against Israel during, and after the Desert Storm Operation had ran its course inside Iraq, Mr. President Sir.

"This Colonel al-Adwani is well trained in the use and planting of explosives where they'll do the most damage to their intended civilian or military targets. He's a marksman, believed trained in Cuba, and has been known to carry out assassinations personally in Saudi Arabia, Jordan and Syria, sir. Assassinations seem to be his main thing to carry out, Mr. President Sir. He's known to be able to change his appearance, until even his own mother would have a serious problem recognizing him in a lineup of one person, sir. He's well traveled, a rather likable and agreeable man, very intelligent, and is extremely dangerous and has been known to visit the United States on many different occasions in the last three years, sir. His visits were always hiding behind the diplomatic courtesy we offer to all other nations of the world, Mr. President Sir."

Director Raincloud took a quick breath, and then went on with his report to the American Leader. "Mr. President, this Colonel al-Adwani has been observed in the United Kingdom, France, Italy, Libya and Spain in past few years, sir. It seems where an important government official's assassinated in any country, this man was seen in the area before the death was recorded by the authorities, sir. He's known to be a real bastard when on a mission, who'll turn on his own mother to forward his operation, and once given an assignment, sir. This Iraqi Agent never backs off while on that mission, until he completes it one way or the other, Mr. President.

"We've known about his terrorist activities for the past two years, but he's wise and we've been unable to pin him down to any crimes, because he's usually the one controlling the other terrorist cell sir, and he stays well out of attack areas. This is the first time we've been able to link this man to any terrorist attacks here or abroad sir. Mr. President, if this is the missing terrorist we're talking about then your life is in serious danger, and I must insist you don't take any more late night visits to Bethesda sir, or anywhere else for that matter, for all our sakes..."

"Uh-oh, you know about my, err... little trip over to Bethesda I take it, Director Raincloud Sir?" the sheepish President interrupted and asked at the same time.

"Mr. President Sir," Director Raincloud cocked his head to the side and gave the President a sly smile and then went on with his words. "I knew about your little trip even before you left the White House, sir. Most of the Doctors you saw walking around on the third floor of the hospital were my people, sir. Believe me Mr. President they were all well armed and ready to protect your life if this nut tried something against you on your let's say little visit, sir. Mr. President, I must insist, until this man is captured or killed, and this present situation is over with, you have to give yourself to my people for your own protection, sir." Director John Raincloud stared at the President, politely demanding a reply to his last request.

"Yes, yes of course Director Raincloud Sir, you're absolutely correct to make that request of me and anything you say for the time being goes with me as well, sir. Do you have any fucking idea who the other god damn terrorists in this cell were, who attacked me, sir?"

"Yes Mr. President Sir, we were successfully able to place a definite identification on each of the terrorist subjects killed in the assassination attempt against you by their fingerprints, pictures, and prior terrorist activities carried out by them throughout the world, sir." Director Raincloud took a second, and passed another picture over to the concerned looking President, one of a pretty, young, dark complexioned female, and then he continued with his report for the council. "Mr. President Sir, ladies and gentlemen, the lone female terrorist and supposed shooter of the assassination group, was identified as a Colonel Farseeha al-Mana. She was the hardest to identify, and was believed to be enlisted in the special police section of Iraq, Mr. President.

"She has been known to have used many different aliases in her past, but this is her true identity and name, Mr. President. She was a real hard nose fanatic who did most of her dirty work in and around the State of Israel, sir. Colonel Farseeha al- Mana has been known to work for a one Iraqi General Hassan al-Zahar, Commander and Chief of the Secret Police of all the Republican Guard Units. We have massed evidence that this man is Colonel al-Adwani's main control sir, and it has been suggested that Colonel Farseeha was Colonel al-Adwani's sometime lover, and has worked with him on other terrorist activities over the past ten years, sir. This confirmed our beliefs that the missing terrorist is positively this Colonel al-Adwani, because Colonel Farseeha al-Mana was involved in this assassination attempt on your life sir..."

"I still can't believe someone actually tried to assassinate me right here in the United States for the love of God, Director Raincloud." The President moaned as he interrupted the Director.

"Yes Sir Mr. President Sir, I can certainly understand how you must feel over this attempt, sir. It has to be extremely upsetting for you to understand you were signaled out for an assassination attempt, sir. This is the first time Colonel Farseeha al-Mana has ever been noted doing her work outside the Middle East region, Mr. President Sir. That means someone extremely powerful had to have ordered this attack against your person, sir. This Colonel Farseeha al-Mana was twenty five years old, and she had fifty known kills under her belt already Mr. President. No one placed an exact number of deaths attributed to the bombs and ambushes she placed in and around the nation of Israel, and a number of Arab nations as well in the Middle East sir.

"It's been suggested she was responsible for planting the bomb in Jordan, in an attempt to upset the improving relations between Israel and Jordan during their recent peace talks, sir. Thank God it didn't work Mr. President. She has been active in terrorist activities since the age of eleven, when her mother and two sisters died in the Israeli attack on the nuclear power plants in Iraq, Mr. President. Her father's alive, but he isn't believed to be part of her activities, sir."

"It's a crying shame, such a waste for one so young and pretty, to be so filled with hate and dead before she even began to enjoy, or knew what life had to offer her, dammit." The President grumbled as he passed the photo over to General White, who merely glanced at it, and then he passed it on to the next member of the meeting.

CIA Director John Raincloud totally ignored the President's last remark as he flipped a page in his note book, and then he began speaking again as he handed a third photo to the American Leader and added to his report. "Mr. President Sir, the second man you see here was positively identified as Iraq Captain Jebril Briegheeth, sir. He was forty three years old sir, and has been active on many different terrorist attacks of Iraqi interests. It was no surprise he was in the United States, most of his underhanded terrorist activities were carried out abroad though, Mr. President Sir. This isn't the first attack on the United States credited to this man, sir. No one truly knows how long this man was active in this terrorist field, but we have been after him for over seven years now, sir. It's believed he had something to do with acquiring the explosive chemicals used by the Twin Tower bombers, Mr. President Sir.

"We've known about this man for that many years now sir, but he's been rather successful in eluding all our attempts of capturing him over the past years, sir. He's a fanatical Ba'ath Loyalist member, and he's very attuned to the more fanatically wants of the madman still running Iraq. This Captain Briegheeth has been known to and has mastered the ability to impersonate a number of State Diplomats, and other powerful political figures, Mr. President Sir. It's a feather in our caps to have erased this one man from the rolls of the terrorists, sir."

Director Raincloud stopped speaking just long enough to take a sip of water, and allow anyone at the meeting a chance to ask any questions of him, or give their own opinions to the other members of the meeting. When no one spoke up, he continued with his report again. "Mr. President, the third member of this terrorist cell is a relatively unknown man to this field of this sort of activity, sir." Director Raincloud passed the fourth picture over to the President, and then he allowed him a few seconds to look at the photo before going on with his report.

"Mr. President, it's believed he was a new comer to the world of terrorism, sir. Thank God we were able to stop this man before he carried out any of his dirty deeds against us, or any other freedom loving nation of the world, sir. His name was Mamdouh al-Qassan, he was the hardest of the terrorists to identify, because of his newness to this field of dirty work sir.

"I think he was actually recruited primarily for this one mission that was aimed against you, Mr. President Sir. We don't know how old he was, but the coroner believes he was in his late teens, or early twenties at the oldest, sir. Since we started investigating this one, we have discovered he was seen hanging around the Capital Building, along with a second man believed to be this Captain Briegheeth, as recently as last month, sir. We believe he was hunting out a secondary target, maybe a Senator, or Representative, sir. Our computers and whiz people placed the mostly likely target of these terrorists was most likely Senator John Hopkins..."

"Senator Hopkins! Now why in the good Heaven would any of these lousy bastards want to kill that poor old man for, for the love of God, Director Raincloud? He's as harmless as a damn church mouse, Director. I can't believe this, what the hell kind of god damn savages do we have roaming around in this world of ours, dammit?" the President hissed as he interrupted Director Raincloud for a second time.

"Mr. President Sir, Senator John Hopkins seats the Senate Oversight Committee supplying the funds to keep the air attacks on Iraq continuing, sir. That's why our computers picked his name out of the hat as a possible target from these latest terrorists, sir." Director Raincloud offered in an attempt to try and explain why the Senator was picked as a possible target.

"Yes, yes of course he does, I knew that sir. What are you doing in the way of protecting this fine old man's life, and the lives of the other Senators and Representatives Director? I don't want him assassinated next." The President sat forward in his chair, and stared directly at Raincloud.

"Mr. President Sir, we have dramatically increased the security around all the Senators and Representatives living in Washington and the surrounding area, sir. We also have a number of Special Agents protecting their private residences and families throughout the United States, sir. We have also bolstered up the security in and around the Capital Building, as well as any other buildings the Senator's are known to frequent or use, sir. They're as well protected as you currently are sir. We're increasing the security surrounding all the monuments in Washington for the duration of this emergency situation of the assassination attempt on your life, sir."

The President nodded as he sat back in his chair, satisfied with the Director's explanation.

CIA Director Raincloud went on with his report to the American Leader without missing a beat after the minor interruption. "Mr. President Sir, we have successfully discovered where the terrorists met in Washington, while planning their assassination attack on your life, sir. The Rolands Motel, room seventeen to be precise Mr. President Sir. It's a rather sleazy little filthy dump frequently supplying drug addicts and prostitution a place to operate and carry out their illegal activities from, sir. We thoroughly ripped the place apart, and found some added evidence pointing to the fact that these terrorists used this room as their sort of safe and organizing place, Mr. President. We also found Colonel Farseeha's hotel room, and we discovered a cash of extra weapons and a number of explosives hidden inside the room.

"There was also a number of bomb making material stored in the basement of the building this woman was renting while she was preparing for the operation aimed at your life, Mr. President Sir. Iraqi Captain Jebril Briegheeth's apartment was also discovered and searched sir, and it has been established the young Mamdouh al-Qassan was sort of living with him, sir. We found numerous papers identifying them both as Iraqi loyalists, as well as other weapons and explosive equipment hidden inside his room, sir. It seems if they successfully assassinated you sir, they had further intentions of continuing their terrorist activities until they were either captured or they were ordered out of the country by their main control, Mr. President Sir.

"That was if they were to survive the assassination attack on your person, Mr. President Sir. Finding these extra apartments the terrorists were living and working out of sir, makes us believe the filthy little room they rented in the Roland's Motel, was being used by these terrorists as a special meeting room to work out the finer details of their assassination attempt planned against your person, Mr. President Sir."

"Good work Director Raincloud. Now, to ask the question on everyone's mind. What are you doing to capture this Iraq Colonel while he's believed to be in the United States, Director?"

"Mr. President Sir, I assigned two hundred extra Special Agents to this case, sir. That's not including the hundreds of local and Federal Police Officers and other investigative personnel, already working on this case with us, sir. We're with information many Police Officers off duty, are offering their services up in hunting down this animal, sir. We even had a number of Officers from other Police Departments from all over the country, offering their Officers and Investigation services for our help with trying to locate and tracking this missing terrorist down, Mr. President Sir. It also seems everyone wants to help out wherever they can, sir. As of this moment Mr. President, we're raiding all known safe houses and hangouts, commonly used or visited by would be terrorists operating in Washington, Virginia, the District of Columbia and Maryland..."

"Gees Director Raincloud, are there that many damn terrorist operating in the United States at this time, Director?" Secretary Levenhagen asked with much concern in his tone of voice as he placed a stunned look on his face and he stared at the CIA Director.

"No, not exactly Secretary Levenhagen, although it might seem like we're heavily infested with a number of terrorist organizations here in the States, sir. It's believed there are only fifty active terrorists units working in and around Washington as of this moment, sir. We have identified most moving operatives already sir, along with the host nations they're affiliated with, and if they step out of line against us, we're going to drop on them like an old building, sir. Most of the well known terrorists are under constant surveillance at this point here in the States, thus they're rendered harmless to their usual activities and affiliations, sir.

"We intend to get this bastard before he's able to escape the States sir. As of this moment, we're quite certain Colonel Abdulaziz al-Adwani's still within the limits of Washington. With the flood of police and Special Agents on the roads the instant this assassination attempt on your life was tried Mr. President, we're certain he went in hiding in a safe house somewhere within the limits of Washington, and this terrorist Iraqi Colonel is currently more than likely waiting for the heat to die off a bit, before he makes his attempt to leave the country, sir."

"What happens if this Iraqi Colonel al-Adwani is able to make it out of our country safely, Director Raincloud? What then sir?" the President asked as he slowly sat forward and began to twirl a pencil in his fingers, his favorite habit lately.

"Well Mr. President then it becomes a difficult problem for us to solve at that point, sir. If Colonel al-Adwani's able to escape the States' in one piece and makes it back to Iraq. Then I'll be forced to rely heavily on General White's specialized troops, to capture him. If he makes it back to Iraq safely that is, sir." Director Raincloud offered to the President of the United States.

All eyes went to General White, seated next to the standing CIA Director, as soon as Director Raincloud mentioned the General's name in the conversation.

General White picked up the ball and he began to speak as soon as the President's eyes met his. "Mr. President, once we're positive this miserable asshole has successfully fled the country, sir. We'll be forced to sit tight and wait until he surfaces in Iraq somewhere, sir. When we know of his location then I intend to send in a small force of my Tier One Asset Special Operations Troops, ten to fifteen NFT (No Fail Team) soldiers on a KCO sorry for using these terms, this one means a Kill, Capture Operation, and have them stalk this lousy little bastard, until they can get at him and snatch his ass, Mr. President Sir. Their orders will be to take him captive, and drag his ass out of Iraq, and back here to stand trial in the States if possible, sir. But if the Tier One Assets are unable to get their hands on him, their orders are to go over to kill the bastard and anyone protecting his backside, and then get the hell out of that damn country, sir."

"What makes you believe he'll surface in Iraq, and make himself known once he reaches his own country, if and when he gets safely back in Iraq, General?" The Secretary of State asked.

The Chairman of the Joint Chiefs of Staff, General White shot one of his best smiles at the crippled but well liked Secretary of State, and replied to her question politely. "Maria, he's a man, and being a man and a terrorist, he suffers from the same ego problem as does most men on earth do, Ma'am. This sonofabitch has just tried to assassinate our President in his own country, Ma'am. I don't see him sitting on that information for a long time, Ma'am. It'll drive him absolutely nuts trying to keep his actions quiet for very long. The missing terrorist has to want to brag to the rest of the world of what he tried to accomplish against our President, Ma'am."

"Well stated, General White." Maria returned his smile with one of her own.

"Errr... excuse me for interrupting you, General White Sir. But what the hell happens to the mission if your Tier One Troops can't get near enough to this man to take him captive, sir? What are the ground soldier's orders after that point, sir?" the Deputy Secretary of Defense, Clifton asked this time as he stared back at the rather large, black military officer this time.

"Secretary Clifton Sir, my people will be operating under extremely strict guidelines during this entire operation sir, if and when they're ordered to invade Iraq to get this SOB, sir. Their orders will be to capture him alive if at all possible, and if they're unable to accomplish this order as received. As I stated prior, their secondary orders are to take him out, period. We can't allow this man to remain safe, no matter where he tries to hide in the world, sir. I'll assure you sir, either way my no fail troops will get this man wherever the hell he tries to hide on us, sir."

CHAPTER TWELVE

President Albert Cole sat back in his chair to take a moment to collect his thoughts, and get comfortable in his chair again. When he did, everyone in the Oval Office stopped speaking, to allow the President to think for a few moments. CIA Director Raincloud understood it was getting late, and the President had to leave for the second scheduled press conference. They watched as President Cole rubbed his eyes with the palms of his hands and let out his breath in little puffs. He stretched and looked at each person as if he tried to find answers in their gaze.

Maria Hernandez knew the exhausted President better than anyone else in the office, and she spoke up after giving the man a few moments to think. "Albert, I believe it's getting near time for you to head off for your scheduled press conference, sir. I'm quite certain that you have enough information to see you through your speech to the public at this point sir. Anything else you want to discuss with the rest of us I'm quite certain can wait until you finished speaking to the American public, and had a chance to rest a bit for yourself, sir."

"Yes Maria, you're absolutely right, I have to change my clothes and take a few seconds for myself to collect my thoughts and prepare for my speech. I hate like hell to meet with those damn reporters. Their questions and other crap always end up turning my stomach and pissing me off at the same time, dammit. Thanks for reminding me about the press conference. Okay people, if there's nothing else I need to know, or we have to discuss before I leave the office, I guess I'm going to leave you for the time being. I'd appreciate it if anyone has anything else of importance we have failed to go over at this meeting, wait here until I return. If not, you're free to carry out your other duties of office. Thank you for meeting me like this ladies and gentlemen."

President Cole clapped his hands together loudly, and stood and left the Oval Office without further word to anyone at the meeting. When he entered his private walkway, the President was greeted by Peter who ushered him to the elevator leading to his private living quarters on the third floor of the White House. He assisted President Cole in picking out his suit, shirt and tie and once dressed, Peter supervised the combing of the President's hair, as well as his makeup by the many assistants. When he was ready to greet the public and reporters, Peter escorted the President to the main elevators to take him down to the waiting press conference area.

Even with the heavy makeup he wore, it was easy for the reporters to see the sheer exhaustion, and anger still etched in the President's eyes as he made his way slowly to the podium.

Surrounded by a wave of flashing cameras and questions rudely called out almost hysterically by the reporters gathered in the press room, the President waved at certain reporters he recognized. For the most part, he ignored questions yelled at him as he waited for the clapping to end before beginning his speech to the gathered. The blinding glare from the flash bulbs hurt his eyes, to the extent where he was forced to put his hand out before them for protection. Already, he was getting a pounding headache from the reporters and the commotion they created.

President Albert Cole had to wait a few moments before he could speak over the reporters constantly yelling questions almost angrily at him. The Press Secretary held up his hands and threatened to call off the conference if everyone did not quiet down, and allow the President the opportunity to speak. This threat forced the horde of reporters to stop calling out their questions so loudly, and wait and hear what the President had to offer.

President Cole smiled at the reporters. He was addressing the public more than the reporters in the room, as he started his speech. "Good morning ladies and gentlemen of the press. I called this unusually early morning press conference to inform the concerned public of our country of the condition of their government and Officers. By now, everyone in the United States, as well as the world, must know there was an attempted assassination on my life, when I was boarding Eagle's Nest two nights ago.

Err... excuse me, Air Force One for New York City. I use the phrase Eagle's Nest for my own benefit and pleasure. I'm proud to inform the American public that three of the known terrorists were killed at the sight of the assassination attempt against me. Only one of the terrorist made good his escape, and he's presently loose in the Washington area.

"But I assure everyone listening to my words of this unusual event that the missing terrorist is expected to be arrested before he can flee the country. I wasn't hurt in this failed assassination attempt, but for a number of minor bumps and bruises. But the National Security Director, Norman Griffin was killed in the attempt on my life, and Vice President Mary Hirshfield was critically wounded by this horrendous act perpetrated against my life, and your government and leaders. I'll be attending Security Advisor Norman's funeral tomorrow morning, and then I'll begin considering to replace Mr. Griffen as the new National Security Adviser."

The President had to wipe at his eyes, he was that upset over Norman's unconscionable murder. Most reporters felt the President was fighting back tears while speaking of the murdered Security Director, and they respected the President for his display of friendship and loyalty for his fallen comrade. It took a few seconds before the President was composed enough to continue with his words to the reporters and public. "I wish to take this time to inform the public that Mary's doing fine, better than believed she would. The Vice President's a strong willed woman and is determined not to allow this attack against us stop her for long. She's expected to be released from the hospital by the end of next week, and I'm looking forward to Mary resuming her responsibilities of the office of the Vice President, by the end of the week she's released.

"The kind prays and concern from the public has been answered, and I thank everyone for praying for Mary's health and well being, and for her full and complete recovery from these terrible injuries she received in this attack. I want to assure everyone in the United States that everything possible is being carried out in the attempt to capture this lone surviving terrorist throughout the United States. I want to take this time to assure the American public never will any sitting President ever, and I mean absolutely ever be forced to deal with a batch of terrorists that threatens the leadership of this great and proud and powerful nation of ours ever again.

"No civilized nation will ever accept such deplorable activities carried out on their lands by a few people who live and work without honor, without punishing these vile perpetrators, and their sponsoring nations who act against the civilized people of the world, with all the anger civilized nations can muster against the loathsome terrorists. The public will be safe in their homes, and on their lands of the United States. This I guarantee to all listening to my words here today. I issued orders once it has been determined where these terrorists originated from, that sponsoring nation will feel the full wrath and weight of the United States' military might and vengeance.

"I'm more than prepared to place all military and investigatory assets available in the United States and elsewhere, in action in the ongoing search for these wanton criminals crawling their way in the backstreets of any nation. I'm committed to fighting terrorism no matter where it might rear its ugly head here within the United States, or throughout the rest of the world at the same time. I'm afraid that's all I have to say at the moment, but I'll make myself available for a few of your questions, and then I have to leave this conference."

President Cole looked to his Press Secretary, and covertly put out five fingers where he was the only one to see them, informing the secretary he wanted to be interrupted in five minutes instead of ten, and be taken away from the meeting. So the news reporters could not get more information from him. The Press Secretary gave a slight nod, informing the President he got the message from him. President Cole did not want to be forced to answer too many questions for the reporters, for fear of giving out certain information he might mistakenly let out.

When the President stopped speaking, the loud calls for questions from the reporters began anew. It was sheer mayhem at best at the conference, with many of the excited reporters screaming out their questions in an effort to be recognized over the other reporters. It upset the President to see the actions, but he allowed it to continue because as long as they argued between themselves, the reporters were not pressuring him with troubling questions.

General White still seated in the Oval Office with the others, waited until the President was out of the office before collecting Director Raincloud, and then the two men left for his office back at the Pentagon.

He wanted to see how his specialized troops were doing assembling at Camp Lejeune, for their training in capturing the missing terrorist.

The exhausted President fielded a few questions from the excited group of reporters, careful not to give out a too direct answer to them. This action made the reporters get even more excited and loudly press their questions further in the need of information and possible news scoop from the President. The fighting between the reporters to ask questions of him, used up most of the allotted time the President offered, and at exactly five minutes into the question and answer time, the Press Secretary walked up to the podium and then he whispered something in the President's ear. The American Leader nodded in response to the Secretary's timely interruption.

When the President and Press Secretary spoke in private, the reporters quieted down to see if there were any new developments in the situation that almost claimed President Cole's life.

After whispering his thanks to the Press Secretary for his timely interruption, President Cole turned to the reporters and held up his hands to silence their incisive questions and said. "Ladies and gentlemen of the press, I'm terribly sorry for this untimely interruption, but it seems I have an important call I must attend to immediately. I'm forced to place an early end to this press conference. Please forgive me for this inconvenience, but I must leave the room immediately. I want to thank all the reporters for showing up and listening to me, and I'd especially like to take a moment to thank the public for inviting me into their homes, and allowing me to take up so much of their valuable time on this day. I'll report to the public the instant when any new information surfaces over this present situation. I thank you all for your time and patience, and for your concerns for me and my injured Vice President's health."

Without any further words to the gathered and still excited reporters or public, President Cole walked away from the podium amidst many questions still being shouted out at his back from the many reporters. The President laughed along with the Press Secretary as they both walked out of the conference room. "When the hell are those people ever going to learn for Pete's sake? It's better to remain in your seat and raise your hand calmly, so I could pick and chose the damn reporters I want to answer their questions then for them to be shouting their questions out like a pack of nuts, and my not picking on any of them to speak to. I can't believe in all that time, I only answered a few of their questions."

President Albert Cole was not lying either, ever since the attempted assassination on his life was perpetrated by the Iraqi terrorists, his phone has not stopped ringing. Nearly every head of nations called to see if he was alright, and to see what he intended to do against the attackers who just tried to kill him. Many nations offered him their elite troops to help track down, and bring to justice the murderers of the American National Security Director. At this moment, the President of Russia was on the phone waiting to speak with him over this very matter.

JULY 29th, 1999, CAMP LEJEUNE NORTH CAROLINA. 0600 HOURS EST

Lieutenant Robert Walker was the first man off the aircraft as it landed at the civilian airbase so near the massive military base. He looked around for the bus scheduled to pick up the soldiers and bring them down to Camp Lejeune. As he hunted around the area, the rest of the specialized soldiers gathered around him to see what was up.

Sergeant Dorothy Ramirez leaned against Walker because she was exhausted from her condition when she spotted the bus turning onto the tarmac of the airport. "There it is Walker. It looks like they're going to pick us up right from the aircraft, Bobby. That's good I'm too damn tired to walk all over the place looking for our ride back to the base, lover."

"Yep." Was all Walker growled as he moved towards the bus as it pulled up before him and the rest of the other soldiers. He was in his usual bad mood whenever he was ordered to report for active duty from the base.

Mutt, (Lieutenant Frank Hall) caught up to Ramirez and grumbled. "Man, what's his problem sister? His jockies riding up his crack or something, he seems more pissed than usual, baby."

"Naw, he always gets like this whenever he's heading back for base and a possible military action. You know how Walker is he's perpetually in a bad mood, Mutt."

"Honey, how you stand big dumb jerk soldier when act like this I no know how do it you?" The dangerous and wise Russian Sergeant Taras

Zarugnaya, (Siberia) added as she followed the other soldiers as they quickly piled onto the waiting bus.

Sergeant John Kirkpatrick, Colonel Bruce Leadbetter's right hand man and go for, was waiting for the troopers on the bus to arrive on base. When the elite soldiers saw the Colonel's henchman glaring at them, one of the soldiers complained at Walker. "Man, it fucking figures this POS (Piece Of Shit) would be waiting for our asses to arrive on the damn base, pal. He's so far up the fucking Colonel's ass he can tell what the lousy little prick had for lunch, man."

"Yeah, Colonel Leadbetter couldn't do a fricking column left without snapping that mother fucker's nose off his damn face, people." The massive soldier branded No Neck added as he glared angrily at the young Marine Sergeant, his head pounding him from getting the beer bottle broken over it a few days ago.

Sergeant Kirkpatrick got on his toes in an effort to see over the other soldier's heads, to try and locate the ones dumping on him from the group. The Sergeant's face was a mask of anger, and he wanted the bitching soldier's ass so he could get back at him for his nasty comments.

Lieutenant Walker saw the look and warned the other soldiers with a snap in his voice. "Okay you pack of walking sandbags cut the fucking shit out will ya. The Sarge isn't that bad a stinking Joe. Remember Mutt, he helped get your sagging ass outta that fucking mess back at Port Said in Egypt way back when, man. I'm warning everyone here, get offa his fucking ass, or you'll answer to me when I get my damn hands on ya asses. I keep telling you screaming squirrels to lay offa the little prick and I mean it, dammit. Enuf already for crap sake."

Walker turned back to the Sergeant and offered in an angry voice. "I wanna pitch a bitch at ya, Sergeant. What's the fricking deal man? You hafta know what the hell's going on around here."

"How you making out Lieutenant?" Sergeant Kirkpatrick said as he offered Walker his hand.

"Just fucking dandy I guess Sarge. What the fuck's up man?" Lieutenant Walker replied hotly once again, as he shook the Sergeant's offered hand. He did not demand to be saluted by the Colonel's Sergeant, he was not able to order him around, because he was working directly for the Commanding Colonel of the massive military base, and that made him more powerful than Walker or any of the other soldiers from the special operations group.

"We have no new information about the damn slug who tried to bump off our Boss. So the Colonel wants everyone on base ready for anything, if and when it comes our way, Lieutenant Walker. I guess we'll be forced to take a wait and fucking see stance for the time being, until this missing prick decides to surface, and then we can get at the scumbag and bring him in, sir."

"Are we heading for fricking sand land in the arm pit of the damn world again, Sergeant?"

"I'm afraid I don't know that for certain just yet Lieutenant Walker. It seems General White's still holding out some kind of hope of finding this missing puke before he successfully escapes the States, sir. But I can guarantee you this much though, Lieutenant. If this asshole gets out of the damn States, we're going out for his hiding place no matter where he is in this fucking world. Even if we have to go to fricking sand land to get his damn ass and bring him back to the States to stand trial Lieutenant, so you pricks better be prepared for anything coming your way, sir."

"Hey jerk, in case you haven't noticed it yet, I'm no prick like most of the rest of these guys are around here. There are a good number of female soldiers involved with the rest of these slobs around here, mister." Baby Tee, Sergeant Teri Dorland complained, as she slowly ran her hands over her breasts, and then she stuck her chest out as far as it would go.

"Can the shit Baby, I have more important questions needing answering by the stinking Sergeant, honey. Whatdaya gonna do if we find out this mutherfucker is still hiding here in the States, Sergeant?" Walker asked the Colonel's private henchman.

"I don't know that for certain either I'm afraid, Lieutenant Walker. I heard some recent scuttlebutt that you guys are going to be armed, and possibly sent out into the damn streets of Washington to get the lousy bastard, if he's discovered still hanging around there like the bigwigs believe he might be doing. Like I just said to you sir, we're going to go after this lousy little turd no matter where the hell he's hiding on the earth, sir. Personally Lieutenant, I don't think we're going to find the fucking prick here in the States, sir. If I were him, I'd lay low until the heats off some, and then I'd make my bird for home base, Lieutenant Walker."

"Holy shit Sarge what fucking Easter egg hatched that fucked up idea, because that means we're gonna be fricking armed, and let lose in the stinking streets of downtown Washington, man?" the Mutt asked as he moved a bit closer to the Sergeant and Walker.

"It sure looks like that way if it comes down to that, dog man. That's what I heard anyway Lieutenant." The Sergeant offered back as he turned to the Mutt, to reply to his question.

"Hot shit man, I'm gonna finally get me a little fricking payback with some of the damn local bars of Washington that kept tossing my stinking ass outta them stinking places like I was a pain of dirty diapers, when I was just starting to have a good time in their damn dumps, man." The Mutt added as he slapped his hands together, thinking of the first bar he was going to seek his revenge on, once he was turned loose in the streets of Washington.

"I heard that's exactly what General White's worried about, Lieutenant Hall. It seems the President wants you guys out in the streets of Washington, until we know for certain where this lousy little missing prick is hiding at. But the General's resisting the President's request for the time being, sir. I'm under the impression the Boss and General White went round and round about arming you screaming squirrels, and then allowing you pukes to walk around downtown Washington armed and hunting for bear, or in any other city of the United States for that matter, Lieutenant. The President wants to trust you guys no matter what, but the General's afraid some of you guys might get a little carried away with yourselves, and do the things just like the dog man just offered moments ago, Lieutenant Walker Sir. I think the General knows you people a lot better than you guys know yourselves, sir." Sergeant John Kirkpatrick grumbled as he looked at Lieutenant Walker first, and then over at the Mutt.

Lieutenant Robert Walker cast a quick glance at the Mutt, and then he added to the concerned looking Sergeant. "Yeah, I see what you mean about what the General's worried about, Sarge. Don't pay any stinking attention to the damn Mutt. He's been this way ever since he discovered he can't leave a bar with furniture wrapped around his god damn neck, Sarge. It seems the owners really get pissed off when you try and steal a chair from their place, man."

The Sergeant ignored the remark about stealing a chair from a bar, not knowing what Lieutenant Walker was referring to. He had no idea about the bar fight that got most of the troops standing before him, dumped in the can back on the Island of Marathon.

"Lieutenant Walker, I heard the General's planning to make a fucking mock up of a civilian city on base, a sort of shoot house if you will, equipped with fricking computers and all the little goodies that go along with it. Then he's going to have you guys trained in urban terrorism tactics and civilian riot control situations. He informed the President once you guys have the proper training in dealing with armed and unarmed civilians behind you. Then he might be willing to consider allowing you stinking slugs lose in the more dangerous sections of the States with god damn weapons, to help bring law and order back to these regions that are sort of out of hand..."

"Shoot house?" The Russian female soldier Siberia (Sergeant Taras Zarugnaya) interrupted as she struggled to the front of the group of specialized soldiers, and then she stared at the young Sergeant for a long moment, and then added to her words of confusion to the NCO. (Non Commissioned Officer) "What this shoot house you speak of to me mista? I never heard shoot house word or what means before day, fool."

"Yeah." The Sergeant replied nastily at the foreign female soldier, not liking her Russian accent in the least, or the stance she was taking while speaking to him. "I don't recognize you honey, so you must be one of the stinking Russian bitch warriors we got our asses stuck with for the Unit, baby." Sergeant Kirkpatrick groused at the woman warrior.

"Da Sergeant. I good Russian soldier stuck with sloppy America outfit sure thing you know."

"Fine, you don't like me and I don't like you in the fucking least, I can live with that alright sister. You keep fricking eyeballing me like that, and I'm going to nail your damn tits down to the fricking deck, and them I'm going to take some pock shots at your stinking ass sticking out in the fucking breeze, bitch." The usually calm Staff Sergeant snorted at the female Russian, and then he snarled at her further. "I'll fucking explain this once, so pay close attention and if you don't follow my words, interrupt and I'll explain more carefully for ya. That's only because I think you don't understand our fucking lingo properly, baby. All you people have to understand is in which direction the General's heading with you soldiers.

"The Chairman of the Joint Chiefs of Staff, General White realizes we're fast running out of real, combat wars, the time of massive tank columns and overwhelming invasions of battalions of heavily armed soldiers, armor, and aircraft invading a country, are fast becoming a thing of the past, and the next generation of wars are going to be fought on a much smaller scale. It's now believe the next wars are going to be fought in low intensity conflicts in small towns, villages and even cities, where terrorist and rampaging civilians are creating serious problems for their governments and civilians.

"We're going in after the damn terrorists and troublemakers no matter where they are, before they can forward their lousy ideals of destruction and death to other civilians of the cities under attack by them. We understand if the terrorists are successful in their evil attempts, they'll start a possible shooting war between neighboring nations spread throughout the world, and our job will be to stop the damn assholes dead in their damn tracks, before they can create a war between other nations and possibly involving the rest of the stinking worl..."

"Yeah, yeah this is all fine, well, and good Sergeant. But this stinking commercial is wearing a little thin on my stinking ass man, and its still not answering what a fricking shoot house is for us, fucker." Wacko, (Sergeant Salvatore Tomassi) interrupted angrily, as he glared hotly at the Sergeant. Tomassi got his tag name because he always got nuts whenever he smoked a joint. A good many soldiers knew what a shoot house was, with some of the troopers already having a little training in assaulting a civilian, or terrorist controlled building.

Sergeant John Kirkpatrick glared hard at Wacko because of the way he interrupted him, and then he hissed at Wacko in no uncertain terms. "Okay wiseass, a fricking shoot house in this case is a three story building with separated rooms and countless little nooks and crannies built in it for the supposed enemy to hide in. There's going to be everything in the rooms from TVs, couches, furniture that's commonly used in all normal civilian life and other crap like that.

"Everything that's found in a civilian's room and terrorists can use the items as cover, or even obstacles hindering us from getting at them, and freeing any possible hostages the terrorists might have in their control, will clutter the rooms of the damn shoot house. There are also going to be a number of hostage dummies, along with the supposed terrorists and civilian trouble making dummies in some of the rooms as well. Everything humanly possible in an attempt to simulate a strong terrorist situation, and a strike force intrusion will be present.

"These dummies are going to spring up at you people when you least expect an attack from anything in the compromised room, so keep this in mind whenever entering the shoot house and or one of the other rooms inside the building. There's also going to be computers and sensors spread throughout the structure, and even on the dummies themselves, that'll help grade your action when entering and taking out the damn hostiles. Video tapes will be made of every forced invasion, so we can go over them later on, to help with making more efficient entries into hostage situations, people. The sensors will detect any hits scored on the terrorists, and any possible hostages you people might mistake for some of the stinking bad guys in the rooms.

"Simulated intrusions will be carried out with live ammunition, stun and smoke grenades, and other instruments used in gaining a hot entrance into a hostile building or situation. There's going to be some times when you people will be using the laser hit weapon systems, and their detection belts when it's not a live ammo intrusion of the in question structure. At these times, you people are going to be fired at by live terrorists, or civilian troublemakers likewise armed with the laser tag weapon systems, and when your belt goes off, you're out of the picture. I warn you people, you don't want to be taken out too many times in any of these intrusions, or you're going to find your ass possibly dumped from the damn Unit." The Sergeant warned the elite group of soldiers who were taking in every word he was saying to them.

The Sergeant took a slight breath, and then he went on while commanding the soldier's full attention to his every word. "Everything possible to cause you people any grief, and possibly force you guys to make mistakes and errors in your better judgment, or your actions in the shoot house, are going to be thrown at you one way or the other, until you guys can recognize these situations in your fucking sleep. Even some simulated terrorists are going to act like some of the damn hostages and arming the hostages with empty weapons, to try and help confuse your asses, when you burst into the compromised structure. You guys are going to have less than a fricking heartbeat to pick out the differences between the damn hostages, and the bad guys in most of these situations, people. The better you slugs get at being able to pick out the fucking terrorists from the hostages, the tougher it'll get detecting them in any future exercises.

"Colonel Leadbetter's going to be trying to driving you people absolutely fricking nuts over this new training program, so you're going to have to keep your eyes open and your heads on a swivel for anything possible going down in the shoot house. I saw the first drafts of the damn building and training scenarios, and it seems like it's going to be a damn good training structure to learn from, people. I heard some other scuttlebutt if it works out like expected, other shoot houses will be constructed on other military bases for urban, and terrorist training of the troops. We're going to draft Units for this special training crap, so it's not only going to be dumped on our shoulders alone. I think the General's planning to include this training for all military types in the near future as well people. I take it as the more, the merrier for our purpo..."

"It seems like the fucking brass is turning their stinking attention to using our troops in the damn streets of the United States. I wouldn't mind this new training crap, anything we can pick up can be useful for us in any terrorist situation, Sarge." Lieutenant Walker interrupted and took the cigarette from Mother Flanagan and began smoking it himself.

"Yes sir that's true Lieutenant Walker Sir. But I heard some other crap your troops, once trained in this field might be farmed out to certain other nations of the world. In an attempt to try and help them with hostage, or terrorist situations in those troubled countries. I was informed just the other day by Colonel Leadbetter if the training went well enough, you people might even make it to Russia, to help them out with the rash of Islamic terrorist bombing taking place against the civilian apartment buildings in downtown Moscow. I can't understand when the damn Islamic types go after something, it always involves stinking civilian targets, dammit. I don't know why if they have a beef with their governments, why they don't go after military targets..."

"That's because the fricking military targets can shoot back at the dumb fucks hitting the damn civilians, Homes." The huge soldier branded Buckethead grumbled with a smirk.

The troops broke out with a chorus of 'Oorahs' and laughter in their agreement with Bucket's assessment of why the terrorists always went after the civilian targets on their terrorist attacks.

"You're right on the bull's eye with that remark, can head." The Sergeant offered then added. "Look people, we're not only going to be offering your services to our allies, but to our stinking antagonists as well. It's going to be the only way we can keep our stinky finger in every fucking boiling pot throughout the damn world, people. We're going to do everything possible to try and stop the stinking spread of terrorism, and civil unrest no matter who requests your damn help."

"That's fucking jack Homes. I hate this bullshit with a passion man. We're gonna now find ourselves playing fricking peacekeepers all over the damn world, huh? That's tight, look Sarge, if I wanted to be a stinking peacekeeper, I woulda joined the pussy ass fucking Peace Corp crap, or the Salvation fucking Army, man. I'm a stinking soldier bred for killing and creating pure mayhem against our stinking enemy wherever we find the scumbags, man. I'm not made for keeping the fucking peace in some God forsaken rat infested country that I can't even pronounce the fricking name of." The Mutt snorted hotly as he glared at the Sergeant.

"Look dog man, I got some bad news to inform your sagging ass of, buddy. I'm telling you and you can take this to the stinking bank with you, man. If you people are ever sent anywhere, to any other nation of the world to keep the fucking peace for that nation. You people will be given permission to install that peace in any fashion that'll make it happen, and happen with the least amount of casualties dealt out to the peace loving innocent civilian populations of the damn world. Our only responsibilities are going to be saving the stinking innocent civilian lives and their structures and homes, and installing law and fucking order in any of these troubled areas of the world, period soldiers. I know damn well you people are born killer's and that's the way we breed and trained ya to be, and if and when you people are sent out into a possible terrorist situation. You guys will be free to use your own judgment on how best to get a hostile situation under fucking control, and quickly while you're at it people.

"I can assure you people that the General made it known to the President and the other members of his Cabinet that any time his troops are sent out into any urban zone to install peace or end a terrorist situation. The soldiers will be on a free fire mission, and he's going to be the only one who'll answer for any mistakes you slugs happen to commit while active on the damn mission. The General's placing his dick in the fricking vice, because he don't want any of you pussy lappers second guessing yourselves, or hesitating in the least for any reason when you're dispatched out in the field. You all here understand and have been trained extensively in this type of judgment, one stinking moment of even slight hesitation on your part, can possible cause causalities in your troops, and that's an unacceptable fucking scenario for our unit, people.

"General White will skin the hide off any of you shits who hesitates in the least with taking out a hostile target while on an active operation anywhere you people might be sent out to. You guys will not be targets on the hooves for any fricking asshole who wants to take out an American soldier. If you people go in, you have to go in understanding this is a terrorist or an unruly civilian situation, with innocent civilian lives held in the balance, and is to be handled as if you were going against any enemy of your country. With extreme intent and violence, people.

"Anyone suspected of being a possible threat mounted against you, or any of your fellow troops out in the field, is to be dealt with, and dealt with extreme prejudice while you people are at it. For you flaming assholes not very familiar with the last term I just used on you people, it means anyone thought to be a possible fucking threat against you asses, is to be splashed without the slightest hesitation, whether that target's a man, woman, child or animal. It's to be killed just as any other stinking enemy of the United States, or any other of our allied nations, or our Unit would be eliminated people.

"I know General White's not going to allow what happened to our nation's police officers, happening to any of you people. Having your damn hands tied behind your stinking backs and be afraid to react to a life threatening situation because of public fricking opinion, or some stinking bleeding fricking heart politicians. We have surely learned our fricking lesson in Vietnam about not going in hot and heavy at the damn enemy, and allowing them to slowly wear us down in return out in the field.

"From now on whenever we go in on any stinking situation that is getting out of hand, public opinion be damned and isn't to be a stinking concern of ours, it means that the situation is out of control and we have to bring it back under control in a fast hurry it up. You people are highly trained professionals and you will be allowed to respond to a justified situation just as you have done in the jungles and deserts of any damn war the United States was involved in. Period! No if and or buts about it people. Well people, Colonel Leadbetter's waiting for ya, if you have any further questions, I suggest you people bring them up to his attention. We better get a move on it before he sends out the dogs for us. He's probably fucking eating the leg of his desk by now if I know him, and believe me, I know the man."

The group of specialized soldiers grumbled and complained about everything and anything, as they slowly fell in line behind the young Sergeant Kirkpatrick, as he quick marched them over towards the old grinder or marching field on the massive military base, situated right in front of the Colonel's private office and living quarters. One of the soldiers from the group suddenly complained out loud from the ranks at anyone who would listen to his gripes.

"Yeah Homes, I'm gonna go and ask the fricking Colonel a stinking question alright. In your stinking dreams I will because I happen to like the way my fricking balls are swinging between my stinking legs. Asking the fucking Colonel any stinking questions, puts them at severe risk of an attack by the man, pal. I know damn well how he likes to answer any stinking questions we grunts might have for the man."

All the soldiers, including Sergeant Kirkpatrick laughed over the last comment made by a soldier as they continued their march over to the so called grinder of the base.

CHAPTER THIRTEEN

WASHINGTON D.C.,
THE WHITE HOUSE, JULY 30th, 1999.
INSIDE THE CAPITAL BUILDING, 9 A.M. EST

The President of the United States spent the entire day preparing for the National Security Advisor, Norman Griffin's funeral. It was a terrible thing to be forced to go through, especially for the still shaken President from the assassination events of a few days ago. The pain of seeing one of his best friends lying in a copper coffin dead, angered him to no end. The President's mind was filled with revenge and hatred, not only for the killers of his dear friend, but also for the host nation that had aided the terrorists in accomplishing their evil act inside the United States. In the back of President Albert Cole's mind, he knew damn well that it was Iraq who was solely responsible for the attempt assassination on his life the other day, evidence discovered at the crime scene and elsewhere conclusively pointed to this fact, and he was so angry that he wanted nothing more in life than to finish off what the former Bush Administration had began with the rebel Iraqi madman, and his out of control Arab country.

To wipe that nation off the face of the earth, and then erase the constant threat of Saddam Hussein once and for all from the entire Middle East region. The American President had to force himself to get his breathing under control, as he slowly entered the Capital Building. There were masses of people crowding the steps of the building, and also waiting inside the structure.

President Albert Cole nodded politely too many of the dignitaries gathered in the massive Rotunda of the Capital Building. Once he completed the political end of his office, the President walked up to Norman's body lying in the casket, and lightly touched his ice cold hand and whispered to him. "Norm, I swear to your memory by everything that's Holy. I'll get the lousy sonofabitches that did this to you and Mary." Then he stared at the lifeless face of his long time friend in silence for a long, silent moment. His thoughts were suddenly interrupted by a murmur of surprised voices behind him, by those gathered in the Rotunda of the Capital Building and he looked around to see what the commotion was about. To his surprise, the still terribly injured Vice President, Mary Hirshfield was seated in a wheelchair, and she was being pushed through the long lines of mourners by a medical aide from the hospital.

All who came to view Norman's body lying in state stared at the injured Vice President as the wheelchair headed for the coffin resting in the center of the Rotunda. The four Marine Guards snapped to a sharper attention as Mary's wheelchair approached them and the casket.

President Cole did not know how to react as Mary was pushed up to the coffin by his side. He too ended up staring at her sitting in the mobile chair, and shook his head slowly. He was thoroughly amazed she would make the superhuman effort to visit the funeral and pay her last respects to Norman. All he could do was step aside, and allowed her to view Norman's body as close as she could be wheeled up to it. President Cole stared at her, her face was white as snow, and she seemed completely exhausted, like it was a major effort for her to just breathe. Her hair was fixed nicely, and she wore just the right amount of makeup, but she was dressed in a hospital robe and slippers. A white towel rested across her lap and it went up to her shoulder. Obviously, in an attempt to try and hide the heavy bandages still covering the terrible wound she had received in the attempted assassination on his life a few days before.

As she was pushed through the hordes of people towards the coffin, she acknowledged the many faces she recognized in the crowd. But when she saw Norman's body in the coffin, she could not help herself and she grew upset. Unashamed tears rolled down her face, and she did not try to hide the fact she was crying as she took hold of Norman's hand and kissed it. She hated seeing him this way because he was a man she always looked up to, and respected dearly for his strength of character and work ethics.

Then, surprising the President further, she summoned up her strength and she wiped a tear on Norm's hand and said barely over a whisper. "Here Norman, please take this tear with you. It'll help keep you company, and it'll remind you of me forever. It'll also force me to remember you for the rest of my life. It's the only thing I have I can possibly give to take with you on your long journey home. I love and I'll miss you dearly my old friend. Go with God in peace, you're in His hands now. He'll protect you now from all who wish you any harm, and He will make you comfortable for all eternity sitting by his side, my old friend."

When she finished paying her private respects to Norman, the President stepped up to her side and moved the hospital aide aside, and he took the handles of the wheelchair as he grumbled low at her, so only she could hear his angry words. "Young lady, what the hell are you doing here anyhow, god dammit! You should've told me you were planning to visit Norm on this day. Jesus lady, you're too weak to be out of bed so early, honey. You need rest to help you get better for me, young lady. Dammit to hell, you should've told me you were planning to come here. I would've stopped you if I had to have you tied to your damn bed I would've stopped you, Mary. You're such a head strong young woman. Here is not the place for someone convalescent from such a terrible wound as you had received a few days ago, honey."

She reached up painfully and lightly rested her hand on the President's hand, and she smiled weakly up at him. She knew President Cole was right, but this was something she knew she had to do no matter what the effect would be to her.

The President could easily see the terrible pain etched deeply in her sad eyes, and where the needles to keep her alive penetrated her hand and arm. There was some black and bluing from them, and this added to his anger against the terrorists.

"Albert, do you really think I could lie in bed in peace, knowing this was the last chance I would ever have in my life at seeing Norman again in this world? Don't you think I knew if I was to tell you I wanted to come see Norman one last time, you would've stopped me from coming here one way or the other? Yes, I'm head strong at that Al, but only for those who I hold so dear to me. Please Albert, don't be angry with me, I had to come see Norman one last time." The Vice President cried to the concerned President as she tried to smile at him this time, and she instantly paid the price by another wave of terrible pain assaulting her body.

"Angry with you? No way in hell, how could I ever be angry with you that is the last thing I could be with you, young lady. I guess I can't blame you for coming here Mary. I know what Norman meant to you, and I respect that. I just wished to hell you would've informed me you planned such a foolish stunt today. I would've cleared the way, and made it much easier for you to travel here to see Norm." The President smiled in the concerned eyes of his Vice President.

"You seem to forget I'm the Vice President of the United States Albert, and when I speak, people jump just as high for me as they do for you, mister. You could not have done more for me to make my traveling any easier to come here. The Doctors and security guards have been jumping through hoops for me, and they've been wonderful about this situation, Al. Bending over backwards for me just to fulfill my every wants and needs Albert. This need was the most important one to me in my entire life, Albert. I must make a mental note to thank Director Raincloud for the great efforts he has displayed in making it possible for me to visit with Norman one last time, my dear. He's really a good man to have working on your side, Al. One who only thinks of your best interests at all time Albert."

"Jesus young lady, you mean to tell that damn fool knew you were planning to come here today, and he didn't inform me about it first, dammit. Was he the force behind this crazy idea of yours? When I get my damn hands around that thick neck of his, I'm going to squeeze it until his damn eyeballs pop out of his head, and then I'll use the damn things for marbles, young lady." President Cole snorted as he tried his best to hide the anger he was suffering for being deceived by both Director Raincloud and his Vice President at the same time.

"No you won't Albert. I'll not allow you to be angry with him for my coming here for one moment. You can't believe how torn up inside he was over this decision of mine to come here today, fighting his loyalty between you and I. He knew he should inform you of what I was planning to do today, but I stopped him from doing so, Al. You can't blame John for this move because it was I who swore him to secrecy over this matter. I'm too weak to argue with anyone at the moment, Albert." She suddenly patted the President's hand lightly that was resting under hers, and she gave him a weak smile. Then she moved her hand to the side of her neck and winced in terrible pain, caused by her trying to speak so much to the President.

"That's it young lady, you're in too much pain to be here any longer and you're heading right back to the damn hospital toot sweet, young lady. You know I'm only thinking of your health and well being. You have to get better for me and our citizens, I need you back at my side again, honey. I hate looking for you at every meeting and not finding you standing by my side there, knowing you are still suffering because you're associated with me, dammit." President Cole began to wheel her out of the gaze of the hundreds of people staring at the slight confrontation taking placed between the two powerful leaders of the United States.

"Come on with me young lady. I'm going to get you the hell out of here and get you back to the hospital, so you can get well for me. I don't want these nosy bodies gawking at you like they're doing, honey. You have a lot of work ahead of you that you need to catch up on, young lady. Just because you're enjoying your little sabbatical from your office, it doesn't mean the rest of your office is vacationing with you. I warn you honey, your work's piling up on your desk, and it's going to be waiting for you when you return to work. If you think I'm going to do your work for you, you're sadly mistaken young lady. Your office is your office to control, and your work is your work to do, Mary." The President tried to lighten up the moment with a slight joke.

"You swear you're not going to get on Director Raincloud's case for helping me Albert?" She was almost to tears worrying about Director Raincloud's fate. She knew how the President got when he was angry at someone, and it was her fault Director Raincloud went against the President's wishes, and not informing him of what she wanted to do for Norman.

"How could I ever get angry with anyone guilty of helping my Vice President like this, Mary?" The President replied, giving into his Vice President's lovely charms again.

"Thank you Albert. You don't know how much this means to me. I guess you're right, I think it's time I get back to the hospital, I'm tired, exhausted in fact Albert, and I'm in some pain also. Besides Albert, you're right I don't particularly like my public seeing me in this terrible condition. I must look a fright to them." She suddenly ran her good hand over her hair as if to empathize the fact she was still unable to properly care for her looks for herself yet.

"That's exactly why you should've missed the funeral, honey. No one would've blamed you in the least for not showing up to see Norman off like this. He and everyone else know your heart's with him today, Mary." President Cole snapped in a sort of angry tone at her as he hurried her towards the privacy of an office set up out of the gaze of the civilians gathered inside the building. Hundreds of pictures were being taken off the disabled Vice President when she was being wheeled up to the coffin, and then speaking with the President.

"No one but me would have blamed me that is, Albert." She replied the best she could under the circumstances, and the pain she was still suffering through.

"You're impossible do you know that Mary? I don't know what I'm going to do with you and that stubborn ass mind and will of yours, young lady. You're so damn hard nose all the time." President Cole replied as they entered a private room just off the Rotunda, followed closely by the concerned hospital aide and the President's support people. To his surprise, there were three doctors and Director Raincloud waiting in the office for them. The doctors instantly surrounded Mary and checked out her vital signs. One doctor looked at the President and stated.

"President Cole, the Vice President's doing very well so far, but I think it's time she gets back to the hospital, and catches up on her rest and medications, sir. I don't want her getting too exhausted this early on in her rehab, sir. It could set her recovery back some week's I'm afraid sir. She's not supposed to be speaking like she's trying to do all the time either, sir."

"That's what I was afraid of happening, dammit." The President nearly roared at the concerned doctor, and then he added. "Don't waste your time talking to me about it then Doctor. Bring her back to the hospital PDQ. If anything happens to her, you're going to find yourself looking after sick people in Africa, mister." President Cole could not hide the anger in his voice held against the doctors for allowing his Vice President to leave the hospital and come to the funeral.

The doctors took the threat from the President seriously, and they began to wheel Mary out the rear door of the private room and out to the waiting ambulance parked just outside the secured door. They were stopped by Vice President, who held up her hand and tried to turn around in an effort to see Albert's face again, as she wanted to say something else to him now.

"God dammit! What the hell is it now Mary? You have to get your pretty little can back to the hospital and rest, dammit. You're too weak to take on so much activity this soon after being so badly injured, young lady. Didn't you hear your Doctors? They want to get you back to the hospital pronto. Prove to me how stubborn you are when you're feeling much better, honey." The President snorted as he gave out with a disgusted sigh and he quickly moved to the front of the wheelchair and he stared down at the very sad looking Vice President.

Fighting exhaustion, she struggled with her words which hurt her when she tried to speak. "Albert, have you given any thought to who you're going to replace Norman with?"

"Now is not the time to discuss that situation honey. Don't you go off and start worrying yourself with problems facing me about my staff now, Mary. You just worry about getting better for me, and getting back to your workstation as soon as possible young lady. There's plenty of time once you're well, to start discussing who I'm going to replace Norm with, honey. I have my eyes leveled on a few people who can fill his position properly, Mary." The President shook his head, fighting with himself over how she was concerned with his office than getting better.

"I know how you are Albert, and I also know deep down in my heart, you already have the replacement locked in your mind, mister. I have someone in mind as well, and I want to see if we both agree on Norm's possible replacement at this time Al. I have given this problem much thought while lying in my hospital bed, Al." She pleaded with the President with her eyes.

President Cole knew he could not win a battle of words or wills with her, whenever she looked at him that certain way with her jaw set and her lower lip sticking out a bit as she was doing at this moment. He let out his breath in an exhausted sigh, and then he replied after giving into her request completely. "You're not going to give up on this damn thing I see are you Mary? I don't know what the devil I'm going to do with you."

She knew he was really angry at her because he was using her first name now, as she shook her head no. She was almost too weak to reply with words any longer.

"If it's going to get you back to your damn hospital bed any faster today, young lady. Then I guess I'm going to get stuck in a conversation I don't really want to be involved in at this time, Mary." The concerned looking President of the United States smiled at his Vice President again as he shook his head slowly at her.

"It will. Just because I'm flat on my back for a few days, it doesn't mean that I'm not going to get my nose involved in matters that concern you and your Administration, Albert. I have many certain responsibilities no matter what my condition might be, mister." She mumbled barely over a whisper as she looked at the President with eyes that would melt butter

President Cole looked to the doctors who shook their heads, while trying to hurry him along some, so they could get her back to the hospital where they could look after her much better.

Again, he gave a deep sigh and then he grumbled at her almost in a whisper so not to upset her any further. "I'm going to remember this one young lady, and how you made me go against my better judgment in dealing with you honey, and when you get back to your office. I'm going to make you run around like you have never run around the office before."

She smiled the best she could while fighting the pain still assaulting her battered body, at the concerned looking President of the United States.

"Very well then young lady, since it seems I have no other alternative in this matter, but to give into you as usual. Yes, I gave this subject some serious thought young lady, and I think I'm going to replace Norman position with Bill Blaylocke. He has been by my side ever since I first decided to run for the office of the President. I don't think I'd be President if it wasn't for his diligent and untiring work on my behalf behind the scenes. It's about time I reward him for his steadfast loyalty over all these years. Honey, I'm going to remember this and those lovely eyes of yours. You won this little battle, but I swear to you I'm going to find a way to defeat those beautiful eyes of yours so I can control you once in a while, instead of the other way around."

Again, she smiled as she strained to speak again. "Forget it Albert, you love me too much to defeat me in anything, you know it and I know it. But I happen to agree with your pick though. He's a good man, if it was up to me I would've suggested him myself to you, Al."

"Thank you for agreeing with me so quickly on my pick for Norm's replacement honey, that means a whole lot to me. You know how much I value your opinion, young lady. Now honey, do you think you're about ready to get back to the damn hospital, and leave the running of my office to me for the time being, Mary?" He gave her one of his looks, which informed her he had enough, and he was beginning to become extremely upset with her now.

She nodded ever so slowly back at the President of the United States.

The extremely worried President gave a quick head movement, and the doctor standing directly behind Mary and resting his hands on the handles of the chair, instantly moved the wheelchair towards the rear door of the side room. President Cole walked alongside her, and he held her hand all the way as she was slowly wheeled towards the waiting ambulance parked just outside the security door of the Capitol Building, with its lights constantly flashing and the motor idling for a fast get away from the building.

"Err... do you mind if I ask why you have agreed so readily with me on Bill replacing Norman, Mary? That's not really like you to agree with anything with me so quickly, young lady. I was scared to death we were going to get into a real brouhaha like we usually do, whenever I make a decision without consulting you first, honey." He asked as he looked down at Mary as she was being wheeled towards the ambulance again.

The doctor automatically stopped the wheelchair from moving forward, to give the Vice President a chance to reply to his last question. He knew he had to stop the chair, or she would remain angry with him until she was finally able to answer his question.

She looked deeply into Albert's eyes for several long moments, while quickly collecting her thoughts and then she announced with a slight smile on her lips. "No wars this time around Albert, he's a very smart man who only has your best interests in his heart and mind at all times. Besides, he reminds me so much of that small actor I like so much you know."

The President cocked his head, trying to see in his mind's eye that she was referring to.

Mary saw she just confused the President and she quickly added for him. "Al, you don't think Bill looks a lot like Danny De'Vito. If I didn't know any better, I'd swear he could pass as his twin brother. That's why I like the little man so much, Albert."

President Cole could not help himself and laughed as he saw Bill's face and stature in his mind's eye. She was right; Bill was the spitting image of the smallish famous actor. Until now, he never linked the two together as she done. Bill stood just over five feet tall, balding just like the actor, an older man and a little thick around the waist, and proudly owned Danny's fine nose and many of his wildish mannerism. Thinking about it a little closer, he had to admit that it was almost comical when Blaylocke grew angry over something he was involved in, or he was trying to get his point across to someone he was speaking with. He did act so much like Mr. De'Vito.

"I see you agree with me Albert." She said as she smiled weakly at the President again.

"Yes honey, after you pointing this fact out to me, what other choice do I have but to agree with you, young lady? But I warn you honey, I'm going snitch on you and tell Bill what you had to say about him, my little one. Knowing him, he's going to have a little something special to say to you when you finally take over your office and get back to business again, sweetheart." Again, President Cole turned to the doctor still standing behind Mary, and he was sort of resting his hands on the arms of the wheelchair now, and the President gave him another slight head nod, informing the doctor he wanted her out of the area, STAT.

The doctor nodded back at the President, and then he pushed the chair to the ambulance.

President Cole was still laughing over her thoughts of Bill, when the CIA Director John Raincloud joined him, while he was watching the ambulance as it pull slowly away from the orange painted curb. CIA Director Raincloud joined the President in his laugh.

When President Cole realized someone was standing alongside him, he stopped laughing and turned to face the person. Instantly, the laughter left his mood as he growled at the massive frame of Director Raincloud. "You! I have a damn bone to pick over with you mister."

Director Raincloud pointed to his chest and then arched his eyes at the President.

"Yes you, and don't you dare give me any of that poor innocent little old me look either, mister. You know damn well what you did to me today with this move you conspired with my injured Vice President, and you're going to answer to me over it, buster. I can't believe you helped her leave the damn hospital in the terrible condition she's in, mister." President Cole warned the big man as he aimed his finger directly at his face.

Director Raincloud tried a quick smile on the angry President, but it did not work and the President's facial expression did not change one bit against him as he barked at the Director while still holding him locked up in his angry glare.

"Stick your damn smile where the sun doesn't shine, mister. I want to know why the hell you didn't think it was necessary to discuss with me first that Mary was planning to attend the funeral for Norm today, mister. This is definitely something I think I should've been informed about well in advance of it taking place, Director Raincloud. You know damn well I'm not very fond of any damn surprises being played out against me you know, especially when it concerns my injured Vice President, sir." The President growled at the still grinning CIA Director.

"I'm terribly sorry Mr. President Sir. But I didn't find out about her plans to visit the funeral, until she was already up and out of bed, and she was busy bullying the poor Doctors, nurses and my Special Agents around helping her leave the hospital, sir. I received a number of rather frantic calls from one of my Agents assigned to protect the Vice President while in the hospital, sir. He informed me what she was demanding and up to, and he didn't know how to respond to her request to visit Norm one last time, sir. I dropped what I was doing and rushed over to the hospital, and I try desperately to talk her out of going to the funeral. But you know her and how she is and how she gets, and when she sets her mind to somethin..."

"Yes, I certainly do know that for a fact, Director Raincloud. I've been on the receiving end of how she gets when she sets her mind on something." The President interrupted the CIA Director, and then he added to his words to him in a much calmer tone of voice this time around. "And, that fact alone is the only thing that's saving your ass from the damn frying pan, John. I know you were sworn to secrecy by Mary, but I think your loyalty to me usurps any allegiances you might have to anyone else in my office or Administration, mister."

"I warned her I was going to inform you of her intent, Mr. President Sir. But she got angry as a wet pup in a thunder shower, and she swore me to secrecy, sir. She warned me if I told you about it before she showed up here sir. I was going to find myself looking for spies molesting polar bears up at the North Pole, sir. She even went so far as to threaten my manhood on me, sir. The Vice President can be an extremely persuasive young lady when she really wants to be, Mr. President Sir." Director Raincloud offered in his defense and then added. "Besides sir, I heard her when she told you not to be angry with me, sir. I warn you sir, you pick on me and I'll tell her about it, and you'll then have to face her wrath, Mr. President Sir." Director Raincloud was trying everything in his power to try and keep himself out of the President's dog house.

The President knew the threat to tell Mary about him being angry at Director Raincloud, was only a joke and he replied in a much better humor and tone of voice this time. "I have news for you Director Raincloud. The many times I saw Mary being rather persuasive, she was acting everything but a lady, mister." The President laughed at his own joke, deciding to let the whole mess fall out of his mind. He knew he had much more important items on his addenda, than to worry about this small breach in communication between himself, and the CIA Director.

"I was only trying to be kind to the Vice President, sir." Director Raincloud offered him.

"I thank you for that much and I understand the reasons for keeping her secret from me, John. Damn, Mary was speaking pretty damn good there wasn't she? I didn't think she'd be able to talk this soon after her terrible injury and the damn surgery. By the way Director, how's General White doing with his specialized troops down at Camp Lejeune, sir?" President Cole decided to change the subject and get back to something more important to him and his Administration.

"Yes Sir Mr. President, the Vice President was speaking very well today at that sir, and about General White, sir. I'm afraid he's in a much better position to make that report to you than I am, Mr. President Sir. I happen to know the elite soldiers ordered to report to Camp Lejeune, are all present and accounted for at the military base, sir. I'm also aware the shoot house is well under construction, and it should be completed later on today at the earliest, sir. The General has informed me his troops currently stationed at Camp Lejeune, should be starting their first urban training on the structure by no later than August One, sir.

"The General's really pushing like hell to have his troops hot and ready to go after this lousy little missing prick, no matter where he might turn up in the world, Mr. President. The General's on the ball with his troops, and his ideas on how to capture the missing terrorist, sir. General White has further informed me how he plans to seek revenge on the sponsoring nation of this terrorist cell, sir. I'll tell you this much Mr. President. I wouldn't want the General angry and planning against me, sir. He has a very evil mind when he wants to have it, Mr. President Sir."

"I kind of heard that about the man myself, and that's why he's part of my office and current Chairman of the Joint Chiefs of Staff, Director Raincloud Sir." The President mumbled as he thought over what Director Raincloud just told him, and then he added to his words. "Excellent, that's the way it should be all the times in my Administration, John. I don't know what I'd ever do without you and General White standing by my side, sir. I thank God for the likes of you two people." He offered politely as he signaled for his car to be brought around by the exit by raising his arm and waving his hand, so he could return to the White House. His horde of security guards had formed a wide and kind of loose circle around him and Director Raincloud, to give him the privacy to speak to the CIA Director and the Vice President in private.

"Mr. President Sir, I just received a new press release from Iraq earlier today..."

"What does that damn fool have to say this time, not that I'm the least bit interested in anything that piece of trash has to mumble about, mister. I swear to God Almighty, the second we have positive proof he and his nation was the one behind this assassination attempt on my life, Director Raincloud. I'm going to send everything I have available to me, out to put a quick end to his evil regime in Iraq once and for all, that's something that should've been done a helluva long time ago before I came to office, dammit." The President snapped angrily as he watched his bulletproof limousine slowly pull up to the curb for him now.

Director Raincloud reached in his breast pocket and removed a slip of paper and unfolded it.

"How long have you had this damn report on you John? I should have been informed of this the moment you discovered it." He asked as he stared deeply into the eyes of his CIA Director.

"For a few hours more or less sir, it came in over the open UP lines around six a.m. our time, Mr. President Sir. We intercepted it at that time sir. I have Iraq being monitored at all times, in case we missed this damn terrorist sir, and he makes it safely back to his miserable country in one piece, Mr. President Sir." Director Raincloud replied to the President of the United States as he returned his harsh stare with a smile, trying to get the President in a better mood.

"Okay John, you peaked my interest in this damn report you have their sir. What the hell does the damn madman have to say this time around that's going to prove to the world he's out of his mind, sir?" He said with a sort of smile as he returned the Director's smile.

"Mr. President Sir, it's quite a most interesting statement at that from the Iraqi madman, sir. Yet somewhat confusing as well, like most of the damn babble this nut has to offer us, sir. With all due respect Mr. President Sir, allow me to read it for you sir."

"You know something John, you're starting to get too much like General White lately mister, with all this constant stalling and other crap you keep aiming at me, Mr. Director. Just get to the nitty gritty of the statement for me please, so I can get back to my office with you, sir. I don't mind telling you though John, with this last terrorist still on the damn loose here in Washington someplace. I'm not very comfortable standing out here in the open like this sir." President Cole said as he watched a security guard open the door of his limo for him, and then he step away from the car and waited for the President to enter it.

"Mr. President Sir, I assure you sir that you're being extremely well protected anywhere you may choose to go now, sir. Not even a damn fly could get anywhere near you this time sir, before my Special Agents and the Special Agents from your usual security forces reacted against any new or possible threat aimed against your person, sir. My Agents will put a quick end to any possible threat leveled against you sir, especially after the failed assassination attempt on your life, sir. Mr. President, I'll read some of the crazy ass report, the rest I'll omit for the obvious reasons, because it's just more of his usual mindless ranting and raving of the troubled man, sir." Director Raincloud announced proudly to the President this time.

"C'mon John, I'm not patiently growing any older here, waiting to hear this damn report of yours, mister. Can we get on with the report, so I know what is being said by this nut, sir?" the President snapped as he placed his hands on his hips and then he glared at the CIA Director, in an attempt to move him along with reading the report from Iraq.

"Yes Sir Mr. President, by all means, I'm sorry for wasting your time like this Mr. President Sir. The jest of the rather long winded and foolish statement from President Saddam Hussein reads as follows sir. 'Iraq deplores any and all such terrorist attacks aimed at any rival government official throughout the world. Iraq will refuse any and all aide to any known and active terrorist cells working for their own evil gains and profits in the world. Although Iraq is still at odds with the United States and its people, Iraq chooses at this particular time to air some of those differences before the United Nations' members for their judgment of the military actions still being carried out by the United States aimed at my country.

"Iraq is not a rebel country that has to lower itself by dealing with the hated and evil terrorist organizations and the likes from the foul world. Iraq has the most powerful Military Army every created in the entire world. The next time the United States or any of her worthless allies chooses to try the might and will of Iraq's Army, America and or her allies will find themselves in the mother of all wars. Thousands of American parents will see their children slaughtered in the sands of my vast deserts on their news channels'. Arrrr, yada, yada, yada. It goes on from there Mr. President Sir, and gets even worse yet with all his usual clap crap, sir. The same added threats and all the regular bullshit coming from a madman, sir."

"Someone better inform the damn fool that his first mother of all wars died while in labor, John. Dammit, I don't know what to think any longer, John. It's not like Iraq to not take the credit for any possible attacks against us or the United States. I hate to say this, but perhaps Saddam Hussein wasn't involved in this damn assassination attempt after all, sir." The American Leader offered as he went deep in thought for a few seconds.

"Mr. President, do you really believe for one moment that the damn terrorist cell might have been working independently, sir? I find that awful hard to believe myself, sir. The damn terrorists never do anything without being well paid for it, or put up to it by someone else who was in powerful positions, sir. With all due respect Mr. President Sir, I think you're dead wrong with this way of thinking, sir. No terrorist cell carries out an attack unless the attackers are ordered by their higher ups to do so, sir." Director Raincloud replied as he stared at the President for a quick moment while he waited for his reply to what he just informed him of.

"Is that so John? And what the hell makes you think I could be so far off the mark here with my thoughts, sir?" the President asked his CIA Director as he cautiously eyed him for the moment and then he waited for his reply.

"With all due respect to you again Mr. President, I assure you sir. It takes a shitload of preparation and mighty good intelligence work, for anyone to make an attempted assassination on a seated President of any nation, especially one as powerful as our nation is for any terrorist aiming himself at you, sir. A helluva load of support, financial aid as well as arms are needed for any successful murder attempt or just attempt against you, sir. The terrorists had to have a flood of the latest up to date information pouring in for them at all times if they wanted to be successful with their attempt on your life, sir. Picking up your daily routines, habits and the likes, Mr. President Sir, knowing where you might be at any given time, to act against your person sir.

"No independent assassins or group of terrorists will ever going to be able to amass such valuably needed information sir, without a helluva lot of outside support systems standing behind them, and supporting their evil actions at all times, sir. The last reason for my belief that it was sure as hell the leader of Iraq behind this assassination attempt on you is; these damn terrorists had to have a helluva motivation for them to make such a desperate attempt on your life sir. No independents are going to take it upon themselves to go and take out a leader of a government on their own. Especially one as powerful as our country is, Mr. President Sir. The damn terrorists had to have been ordered to do this assassination act by someone who was much higher up in the damn food chain of nuts than just the leader of the terrorist cell was, sir."

"Very well put John. I think all the damn terrorists belong to the same chain of nuts at that, Director Raincloud Sir. Why else would they try and carry out their evil and appalling work aimed against any other country of the free world, sir? Hmmmm... I'm beginning to see what you're driving at here though, Director Raincloud. Perhaps I was a little bit off base with my last assumption these damn terrorists might have been working independently, sir. But mind you Director, you didn't hear me second guess myself here though, sir. Okay John, we'll keep with the original plan still intact until some other evidence comes across that might point the accusing finger at someone else, sir. I think I might want a few of our Aircraft Carriers and their support ships moved over to the Middle East and Mediterranean, a sort of show of force if you will to inform these people we mean fucking business against them this time around, Director."

"I believe you have already issued that order, Mr. President Sir." John said with a laugh over the President refusing to admit he might have been a little wrong with some of his thoughts.

The President did not say another word to the powerful CIA Director, as he leaned forward and then climbed into the rear seat of his limo. He was followed by John in the vehicle. Within seconds, they were heading for the White House under heavily armed escorts and other police protection both before and after his vehicle.

A good number of extra police squad cars picked up the President's entourage, as it headed through the streets of downtown Washington. The American Leader remained silent for the most part during the entire drive over to the White House, as he stared out the window, and tried to collect his thoughts, and tried to figure out why and how this attempt on his life happened in his country in the first place.

CHAPTER FOURTEEN

CAMP LEJEUNE, NORTH CAROLINA.
JULY 31st, 1999, 6:23 A.M. EST

Colonel Bruce Leadbetter noticed Lieutenant Robert Walker hanging around the outside of the soldier's barracks, before anyone else was up, and he complained at him. "Hey Walker, I wanna see your ass right the fuck away, mister. Do you hear me Foot Slogger?"

"Yeah Colonel." Walker fired back as he looked to see who was jumping on him this early.

Colonel Leadbetter waited for a moment until the young Lieutenant caught up to him, and then he walked with the Lieutenant as they started to explore the new shoot house construction, before the other elite troops were allowed to work out their first attack scenario against the building, and the supposed hostages and terrorists there in.

"Christ sir, someone did a bang up job on getting this building completed so quickly Colonel."

"Yeah Lieutenant, them damn Navy Seabee pukes can do a good days work, if they're properly motivated, mister. I wanted everything ready for this fricking slimy turd hunt we're about to go out on, Walker." Colonel Leadbetter growled angrily as he watched a few of the Seabee electricians hooking up the last of the computers and sensors systems to the main bank of command computers he and the rest of his people would use, when they were monitoring the Special Operations troops assaulting the makeshift shoot house building.

"Properly motivated Colonel Leadbetter Sir?" Walker asked with a grin on his face.

"Yeah Walker, you'll be surprised what a little good old size eleven boot motivation sure helps plenty good enough for them damn Seabees, when you really want them to move their damn asses a little quicker for ya, mister." Colonel Leadbetter snorted as he kicked at the air before him, and then he grinned back at Walker.

"I've been on the receiving end of that kinda motivation myself a few times more than I'd like to admit to Colonel, done that and got the tee shirt for it, sir." Walker replied as he grinned at his commanding officer again.

"Yeah Lieutenant fucking wiseass, I guess you were at that mister. I remember the many times of having my leg buried up to its damn knee in your stinking ass, Mud Slapper." The Colonel growled as he began to point out some of the many different traps set up spread throughout the training building. They were meant to help familiarize the elite troops with any and all possible, life threatening situations hidden within the building when they attacked it.

"You seem to be preparing us for a fricking bloody war with this damn building, Colonel."

"You don't want to go walking into hell not looking for the fucking fight of your damn life, do you stupid? We don't know where this lousy turds going to pop up on us, and we have to be damn well prepared for any possibility when he finally shows his damn head again, Walker."

"I'm getting kinda tired of traipsing all over the damn place looking for these flaming assholes who think they can rule the damn world, sir. I think I wanna miss this one if you don't mind, Colonel." Walker grumbled as he started to look over the building closer with the Colonel.

Colonel Leadbetter stared deeply into Walker's eyes for a minute, trying to read in them if he was serious or not about his last statement. Then he noticed the sort of smile on his face and he snarled at the young officer. "Keep fucking around with my damn ass like that mister, and I'm going to jump on your chest and stomp it until you fart out the Star Spangle Banner, buster. Where's your fricking missing link hiding at around here anyhow, Walker?"

The Lieutenant knew the Colonel was speaking about the Mutt and he replied smugly. "I think he's off to see the stinking Wizard, Colonel. He should be coming round soon enuf though, sir. He was up and breathing and fricking moving around when I left him at the damn barracks, sir."

"Dammit to hell, is he fucking drunk again Walker?" the Colonel hissed angrily at Lieutenant Walker this time as he waited for his reply.

"The Mutt's always drunk one way or the uther and you know it, Colonel Leadbetter Sir." Walker replied with a smirk.

"He's getting that bad lately huh Walker?" the Colonel asked with concern lacing his tone.

"Colonel, I've seen the Mutt so drunk he was walking around with a snake, while trying to kill a stick, sir. But he was still able to carry out his responsibilities to the best of his abilities, sir. I think he works best when he's drunk if you were to ask me, sir."

Colonel Leadbetter could not hide the smile that crossed his lips, as he drifted into another room of the shoot house while grumbling at Walker who was following him through the shoot house. "Maybe so mister, you two birds must have been born under the same slimy rock, buster. Walker, I want every one of you jackasses sober as a judge for this upcoming turd hunt, buster. It's up to you to keep everyone off the damn sauce and grass from this point forward until we have completed this mission, mister. Follow my fucking drift, Lieutenant?"

"In Technicolor, I got it loud and clear Colonel Leadbetter. I was planning to give that order out myself sir. I want everyone in top notch condition for this upcoming turd hunt mission, Colonel." Lieutenant Walker replied to the other officer with a sharp snap in his tone, knowing the Marine Officer was right with his last order.

There was a slight noise from the ground floor of the shoot house that interrupted their conversation, and Colonel Leadbetter and Lieutenant Walker both looked down the staircase, and they spotted the Mutt coming up towards them with a shit eating grin on his face.

"Arrr... speak of the devil one and it shows its ugly head all the time, dammit. The few the proud the insane. Walker, here comes your twin brother from another mother. You better be ready to control his ass, or I'm going to chuck his stinking ass out the damn window, and leave his rotting carcass out there for food for the worms." The Colonel warned the Lieutenant.

"You can't control what's meant to be wild, Colonel Leadbetter Sir."

"You better try to Walker." The upset Colonel warned seriously, and then he complained in the same breath. "Why the hell do I always get stuck with the cream of the crap, dammit?"

"You're lucky I guess, Colonel Leadbetter Sir." Walker smirked at the Colonel.

The Mutt walked up to the two officers and then remarked with a smirk. "Hey Colonel, you got any friggin cheese to go along with that stinking whine of yours, sir? What's up Homes?"

"I'm warning you in no uncertain terms buster, you don't want to go fucking around with my ass today dog man. I'm in no damn mood for any of your wise cracking bullshit today, buddy. I'll tell you what the hell's up, you self propelled sand bag you! We're going over the traps I have set up inside the shoot house against you flaming assholes, mister. I'm warning you buster, you and any of your screaming squirrels screw up on these training exercises, I'm going to bounce the lot of ya asses the hell outta here so fast you won't see where you're going, so pay attention, and keep your damn mouth clamped shut while you're at it, mister."

"Is it wrong, but I was aroused by that last bitch, Colonel? Who the hell peed in your gene pool today Colonel?" the Mutt asked his commanding officer with some heat in his tone this time.

"You, and the rest of the mucked up pack of asses you prowl around with, buster." The Colonel fired right back at the Mutt.

"Whew, you need a new fucking hobby or something, Colonel Leadbetter Sir. You're starting to get real stinking bad in your old days, sir." The Mutt countered.

"I have one wiseguy, it's trying to shape you people into the elite fighting Units you're supposed to be around here, dog man." The Colonel snarled back at the Mutt.

"We're the best trained soldiers you ever had, or will ever have to work with, Colonel Leadbetter. So get off the damn bitch train for a little while, sir." The Mutt snapped back, allowing his temper to surface a little again at the Colonel.

Colonel Leadbetter stared at the Mutt for a second, and then he snorted nastily at the young soldier. "Yeah, sure buster! Whatever the fuck you say."

"Hey Colonel Leadbetter, be gentle with me will you please sir. I was once a virgin you know sir." The Mutt added to his aggravation for the military officer.

"In your fricking dreams you once were Mutt. I believe you were fucking your mother's kidneys before you came shitting out of her ass, mister. Follow me and shut it up asshole."

Walker took a back seat and allowed the Colonel and the Mutt to go at it.

"Christ Colonel Leadbetter, if I didn't know any betta, I'd swear you don't like me because I'm part black." The Mutt remarked as he now openly glared back at his commanding officer.

Now it was the Colonel who allowed his temper to surface and get the best of him, as he growled back at the Mutt. "You poor excuse for a fucking soldier. You can accuse my ass of being a lot of crap in this world of ours, but a fricking bigot, naw that boat's not going to sail on my fucking Ocean, mister." Colonel Leadbetter growled at the Mutt as he pointed to his chest.

"You two betta knock it off or I might get confused and believe you two birds like each uther or something around here, man." Walker remarked as he started to follow the Colonel to another room of the building to see what was waiting for him in that room.

"Fuck you and the damn horse you rode in on Walker, and who the hell gave you permission to smoke around me, scumbag." Colonel Leadbetter barked nastily at the young Lieutenant, and then he snatched the cigarette from Walker's lips and began smoking it.

The Mutt belched, and then let out his breath in a rush before the other two soldiers.

"Holy shit man, what the hell were you eating last night, Mutt? You smell like something crawled in your damn mouth on ya and it died, and is now rotting in there, man." Walker complained at him as he stared at his lifelong friend and fellow soldier.

"Pussy Homes. Nothing but pussy I eat my friend." The Mutt retorted to Walker.

"Wow, who knew masturbation could make a person so fricking witty so early in the damn morning. Enough horsing round and listen up you two birds." Colonel Leadbetter grumbled.

"Who the hell were you eating anyway Mutt?" Walker asked the Mutt, trying to bust the Colonel's horns a little further.

"Three Martines man." The Mutt replied proudly with a huge grin.

"Fuck you man, her damn legs are corked tighter than a moonshiner's jug, Homes. Remember when she first linked up with our damn outfit, man? You just brushed up against her purdy little can in the stinking showers, and she came running out of the head screaming like a banshee that you tried to rape her sagging ass in the damn showers, man. She almost killed Baby Tee by crashing into her as she was dressing, and she nearly had you lynched by the other women of the group, all because of her stupid bitch, man. I got some uther bad news for your ass as well buster, she doesn't like the stinking brothers too much either, man."

"Well, I got some news for you too Walker. She likes this half ass brother now Homes."

"I warned you two ass already to can the shit and pay attention on what I'm telling you two misfits about this damn shoot house. If I have to repeat myself again to you two shitbirds, I'm going to start taking numbers and fucking asses." Colonel Leadbetter warned the two young soldiers angrily, he hated to admit he was enjoying hearing how the two young troopers were getting along together. (Numbers is a military slang for a life)

Walker and the Mutt followed the Colonel up to the third floor of the makeshift shoot house. The Mutt leaned a little closer to Walker and then he mumbled at him. "Man Homes, I think I had a little too much fish to eat last night."

"Is that what you two were drinking?" Walker retorted, meaning the Mutt and Blind Date.

Another harsh glare from Colonel Leadbetter cut their conversation short as he barked at them. "I warned you two assholes once already, you two shitbirds better start paying a whole lot better attention to this damn shit. The third floor of this damn building is going to be the hardest floor for you war wacky buzzards to save any possible hostages before the damn supposed terrorists have a chance to react and kill them off on you assholes." Colonel Leadbetter pointed out the many different ways Walker's crews might attack some of the supposed entrenched terrorists, or civilian troublemakers in this compromised room. As he explained further, his words began to get drowned out by more of Walker's troops as they started to show up, and began to explore the shoot house structure on their own.

Colonel Leadbetter grew furious with the ongoing commotion the other soldiers were creating downstairs, and he stuck his head out the third floor window and yelled at the lot of them. "You damn shitbirds better get over to the mess hall on the double quick and choke some shit down before I start your training exercises right now, dammit. You slobs won't have anything to eat until the exercise is completed once it starts. Move it out on the double quick before I change my damn mind, and I make you damn fools work on an empty stomach, people!"

The Colonel stared at the troops, until one by one they headed off for the mess hall.

"What about us Colonel? I'm kinda hungry myself you know, Colonel Leadbetter Sir. I didn't eat shit since I woke up." The Mutt asked as he smirked at the Colonel.

"What about you what, dog man! I don't care one shit if you're hungry mister. If you're too stupid to go and get yourself something to eat when you're hungry then starve to death for all I care. Besides dopey, I thought you just said you were eating some poor woman who gave you a little attention, buster." The Colonel snapped back at the young Marine Lieutenant.

"I'm still kinda hungry no matter what you say or who I was eating earlier, Colonel." The Mutt quickly informed the military officer.

The Colonel slowly rubbed his chin for a moment as he milled over the Mutt's words, and then he moaned at him. "Yeah, I guess you're right at that dog man. There's no sense going over this crap now that those other pukes have upset my damn thoughts, mister. I think it might be better served if you guys went and got some on the job fricking training, rather than my trying to explain this shit to you thickheads like this. Shove off and go eat and get your asses back here by Oh, Seven Thirty Hours, and be prepared to work your asses off for the rest of the day after that time, busters. I'll have your equipment shuttled out here, so you people don't have to report back to the damn barracks to get dressed in the crap."

Walker and the Mutt left the shoot house as if their asses were shooting sparks. Laughing all the way as the Mutt announced to Walker over his shoulder. "Hey man, Colonel Leadbetter's a fucking real Crankinstine this morning, Walker. He betta go and get laid or something real quick like, before he ruptures something vital on his damn ass, man."

"Yeah, he wants to get this damn turd almost as much as we want to get the bastard, Mutt." Walker replied as they entered the mess hall, and they both headed right for the group of elite soldiers who took over the rear fifteen tables of the large eating room. The regular soldiers gave Walker's crew a wide birth. No regular soldiers wanted to associate with the Special Operations troops because of their terrible and hard hitting reputation for their uncivilized code of military conduct actions, or their willingness to kill without thought or hesitation against the enemy forces they were engaging on any field of battle or operation.

Lieutenant Walker paid the other soldiers no mind because he liked them not bugging his troops. The specialized soldiers chowed down, and by Zero, Seven, Ten, Hours, they were ready to head back to the shoot house. He told the other troopers they did not have to return to the barracks for their equipment. The troops followed Walker out of the mess in silence. They were already preparing their minds and bodies for action in the shoot house structure.

Colonel Leadbetter pulled an open back Humvee up near the front entrance of the makeshift shoot house structure, and he stood on top of the machine as the specialized troops approached the installation. The returning soldiers began to gather around the angry and glaring Colonel, and waited for him to address the soldiers.

"Listen up you screaming squirrels. This is the start of the fifth day since the assassination attempt on the President's life, people. The Pentagon's prophets believe this missing turd's probably preparing to make his move to try and escape from the United States within the next few days or so, you birds. We want to catch this dirty little bastard while he's still trapped here in the United States, dammit. It'll make our job a helluva lot easier to accomplish for ourselves, if we can get him while he's still in the States.

"We have a shitload of crap to go over, and precious little time to accomplish this feat and understand what the hell we're trying to teach you cruds in so short a period of time. So I intend to work you Rambos and Pambos to fucking death, until you know every way possible to get at this missing little prick, and take him in alive for our Boss. Once we know exactly where this can of shit comes from, we're going to teach his miserable country not to go fricking around with the United States. Your stinking crap's stacked over there people."

Colonel Leadbetter pointed to the armor body plating and weapons the elite troops would use, and then he snarled at the group of specialized soldiers. "You sleazbags have ten fucking minutes to dress and be ready to nibble on the big shit sandwich for today. The time starts now people. Any shit not ready by this time will answer to me."

As the elite soldiers quickly dressed in their extra gear, Colonel Bruce Leadbetter climbed off the back of the jeep and then he walked over into the makeshift command center of the shoot house, to make certain all the sensors and dummies set up inside the shoot house were activated for the upcoming training exercise. Everything was up and on line and working properly.

"Okay Sergeant Kirkpatrick, we're going to see just how good Lieutenant fucking Walker and the rest of his damn misfits truly are today, mister. Set up the intrusion exercise. We'll keep this exercise confined to just the first floor of the damn shoot house, with a close quarter entry this time around. I can't wait to see these stupid asses tripping all over themselves trying to gain entry into the fricking building on this damn exercise. Once I see how good or bad they do, we'll open the second floor next to their training exercise. I'll get the damn troops moving faster, you get the sensors and computers ready and up and running, Sergeant. We'll make this exercise using five terrorists, and nine hostages. Make two hostages kids. It's way too early so this exercise won't be a live ammunition maneuver, so set everything up with the IWESS. (Infantry Weapons Simulation System, a laser tracking base simulation training device). I don't need any of these flaming asses shooting one another on the first fucking try, Sergeant."

"Yes Sir Colonel Leadbetter, consider them up and on line, sir."

"Yeah buster." The wise Marine Colonel barked hotly, thinking his Sergeant was a good ass kisser. He left the control center to jump on his troops, but to his surprise, Walker's people were dressed and ready for the first exercise to begin. The Colonel smiled as he snapped at the waiting specialized troops. "Okay you sacks of shit, if you think I'm going to give you lunatics a well done, you're sadly mistaken, people. In my beloved world, no one gets a pat on the fucking back for doing his or her job. Besides, a pat on the back's only twelve inches away from a damn kick in the rear, so remember that one for the rest of your wasted lives, people.

"This is going to be a close quarter entry people, so try not to trip over each other's damn feet in here, huh. It's going to be a graded exercise, so keep your damn eyes open, and your mouths clamped shut. I want you pack of criminals to quick march your asses over to damn supply and requisition yourselves the IWESS systems. I decided to use this device for the first few entries of the building, until I feel I can trust you dopey shits with a live ammo exercise. Get a move on it, you troops have fifteen minutes to get the IWESS, crawl into them and muster back here double quick. Anyone late for the muster will find themselves standing extra watch after the exercise in the damn boondocks, getting eaten alive by the fucking mosquitoes while they're at it." The Colonel glared harshly at the troops this was more than enough to get the soldiers moving.

1171 EAST NORTHFORK DRIVE, WASHINGTON D.C. AUGUST 1st, 1999 10:30 A.M. EST

The Iraqi terrorist identified as Colonel Abdulaziz Majd al-Adwani, could not hide his impatience as he paced the apartment in a wild rage, waiting for Rasha Ali Abalfath to return to the building with his ordered cigarettes. He turned into an ugly person hiding in Washington like a coward, until he could safely escape to Iraq. Al-Adwani thought himself a hero to Iraq and the rest of the Arab world, and to the beliefs of Islam, even though his assassination attempt on the American President had failed. His failed attempt has rose Iraq from the ashes of defeat, and it elevated her back to the most powerful nation in the Arab world of the Middle East.

Iraqi Colonel al-Adwani had no doubt in his mind everyone knew Iraq was behind the assassination effort leveled against the American President, but this fact did not bother him as much as it should have. He beaten Rasha numerous times over the passing few days for the slightest infraction committed against him, or what he conceived as an infraction. He wanted to be back in Iraq so bad because he knew once he returned to his country he was going to start the waves of revolution aimed against President Saddam Hussein. Colonel al-Adwani saw in his eyes, the true

EAGLE'S NEST

reason the invasion of Kuwait had failed his troops, Saddam Hussein. Backed by the prominence of his action against the American Leader a few days ago, was going to ensure the following of every officer and soldier in Iraq to his cause.

Colonel al-Adwani was furious as hell when he heard over the radio that President Saddam Hussein had denounced the attack against the American President. He felt Saddam was pulling back like he usually did whenever he was trying to confront the hated Americans. He spat on the floor, thinking again the great Iraqi fool had hung him out to dry, and he was prepared to say he knew nothing of the assassination attempt against the American Leader's life. When in reality, Saddam was the main driving force behind the attack in the first place. Maybe not so much as actually taking command of the attack, but as sure as the desert was covered with sand, he gave the order to go ahead with the assassination attempt against the American Leader.

Al-Adwani was further angered with the Iraqi Leader, because he felt if Saddam gave the Iraqi troops occupying Kuwait the military support they truly needed, and he would have reacted long before the American Forces had the chance to form up, and strengthen the Coalition Forces into the mighty war machine it rapidly became. Iraq would own not only the nation of Kuwait by now, but also Saudi Arabia, and Iraq would have destroyed by now, the troubling and untrustworthy Fundamentalist Muslim Shiite nation of Iran, and the entire Middle East would then be forced into following one the true religion of Islam, the Ba'ath Sunni.

The Iraqi Colonel knew in his heart the only reason Saddam hesitated with his opening attack on Saudi Arabia, until the Coalition Forces became the undefeatable behemoth, was solely because he thought just by his reputation of being a military giant alone in the Middle East, would have been enough to have the Coalition Forces quaking in their boots.

Colonel al-Adwani was in the Intelligence Division of the Republican Guard and knew better, and he tried to warn the great fool ruling Iraq of what was taking place around him. That the United States and her fearless young warriors, were just itching for the chance to bring the supposed fearsome Arab antichrist down to his knees, and they were prepared to stop at nothing to accomplish this feat. The then American President, George

Bush hated Saddam with a passion, and he was going to make an example of him to the rest of the Arab world.

The Iraqi Military Officer remembered with a black heart how he tried to pressure Saddam into attacking Saudi Arabia before the United States had the chance to place their military bases on the Saudi land and strengthen them. He understood once the American Forces had operational military bases on Saudi soil, they would be impossible to defeat on the field of battle. He cursed when President Hussein removed him from office because he would not let it go, and Saddam thought he was correct and would not listen to Colonel al-Adwani's voice of reason for one moment in the opening days of the war aimed against the nation of Kuwait.

Nothing was going to convince Saddam his logic was in error, and the great fool would not admit it even while his mighty and once feared Republican Guard troops were being slaughtered by the hundreds while hiding in their foxholes, or surrendering to unarmed, unmanned American reconnaissance aircraft. Colonel al-Adwani remembered the terrible scowl etched on Saddam's face as he witnessed his troops giving up in the thousands to small columns of American war machines, and even unarmed news reporters in helicopters. He remembered Saddam's reaction to the surrenders, he did not blame himself. No, he blamed his exhausted and battered troops, and then he issued orders to kill the families of any soldiers who surrendered.

This was Colonel al-Adwani's sole driving force for the want to overthrow Saddam's foolish Presidency over Iraq. The deplorable condition of Iraq's once so well feared Republican Guard Units was inconceivable to behold. The Iraqi Army once indescribable and thought of as a human war machine, now, was thought of as the Army that surrenders to unarmed American news reporters and aircraft. Colonel al-Adwani drew in his breath in sheer anger, wanting to get back to Iraq so he could begin the task of overthrowing the great Fool of Baghdad. His troubling thoughts were interrupted by the series of light knocks on the door to the safe house.

Forgetting himself he surrendered to his uncontrolled anger, he forgone his usual precautions, and he savagely yanked the front door of the room open, and then he roughly grabbed Rasha by the throat, and literally dragged her into the apartment. He actually flung her to the floor by her throat and then kicked at her trembling body in a wild rage. Rasha tried her best to protect her vital spots on her body with her hands, arms and legs.

She had no idea why Colonel al-Adwani was reacting so violently against her this time. But the intensity of the unprovoked assault on her helpless body left her no doubt in her mind that he was actually trying to kill her by beating her to death. A hard kick to her solar plexus brought a sharp cry of pain from her lips, as she crumbled to the floor in a heap. The cry seemed to have backed off his attack on the defenseless and shaking woman for the moment.

He stared angrily at Rasha as she lay on the floor in the fetal position in terrible pain. She was bleeding from the mouth, nose and right eye. In pure disgust, he turned away from her and then he headed in the room with the TV, forgetting about his need for cigarettes.

Rasha tried to get her breathing under control while she laid on the floor in pain and fear, and all she could say was, 'Oh God' in her efforts to get to her feet. She truly believed al-Adwani was going to stomp her to death with the rage he was in. Painfully, she released the death grip of a hug she held on her chest, and she slowly rolled over onto her back. A new wave of pain engulfed her entire being, and Rasha brought her knees to her chest to slacken the intense pain some for herself. Nothing she did relieved any of the pain though. Her body reacted to the pain by completely shutting down on her, and forcing her to lose consciousness.

Colonel al-Adwani allowed Rasha to lay on the floor for over an hour in her unconscious state, only his need for a cigarette caused him to get up and check on her condition. Her body lay motionless stretched out on the floor. In disgust, he kicked her in the ribs, doubling her over on the floor in her unconscious state. Her eyes flew open with the wave of new pain assaulting her body. Again, she struggled to catch her breath as she moaned at the angry Arab man. "I beg to the merciful Allah. Please, no more beating from you Colonel al-Adwani, please."

"Allah is merciful, but you'll find the opposite with me, bitch of the desert. Get up pig of the sands before I kill you. By the five prayers of the Holy Qur'an, where are my cigarettes at?"

Fearing for her life, she rolled over on her side and painfully struggled up to her feet. Try as she might, she could not stand straight as she reached in her pocket with a trembling hand and she removed the crushed pack of

American made cigarettes, and then she handed them cautiously over to her still extremely angry Arab attacker.

Colonel al-Adwani stared at the crushed pack for a moment, and then he glared at her again, driving her fear of him to new heights.

The look from al-Adwani forced her to flinch in fear of her life. She aimed her eyes to the floor and hunched her shoulders, fearing he was going to beat her for the crushed cigarettes.

"Huh daughter of the god cursed devil, it's wise you fear for your loathsome life so before me like this, worthless woman. It might serve to keep you alive for another worthless day. Are you prepared to get me out of this loathsome country of lowly infidels and jackals, defiled one?"

"Colonel al-Adwani, do you not believe it's still too early to dare expose yourself to possible capture by the American police authorities, by attempting to leave this foul country at this time, sir? You must take a little more time to get comfortable, once the hated American police authorities have given up their search for you. I swear by the Ten Prophets of Islam, I'll get you safely out of this foul and loathsome country safely, Colonel al-Adwani."

"Foolish woman who dares to council me when I need no such counseling from a lowly and filthy woman, my prayer rug is the only thing that comforts me any longer in this hatful world. Don't dare try and speak to me as if I were a lowly camel merchant trying to sell a lame camel to a fool of the desert sands. Alhamdulilah. Praise be to God, how long do you think I can possibly keep my sanity locked up like this inside this god cursed foul apartment? When I should be back in Iraq helping to decide the true future fate of my country." The irate Iraqi Colonel complained bitterly at the young and pretty woman assisting him.

"I beg of you Colonel al-Adwani be at ease and allow a little more time to pass, so the hated Americans give up their search for you, Colonel al-Adwani." She begged as she straightened up the best she could while still fighting off the terrible pain he caused her body.

"Ansh Allah, if God wills it to be so, I shall be captured by the great fools of this foul country, but I assure you I'll not be taken alive by the lowly jackals. What cannot be avoided must be written on the sands of the desert, witch born from a camel's arse. At least I'll give up my life in the attempt to bring some glory back to our country's name and pride,

EAGLE'S NEST

worthless woman. Come with me my young daughter of Iraq and I'll lead you down the true path of Allah. Fight me as you have been doing of late bitch, and you'll die a slow and very painfully by the death of a thousand cuts, handed out by the fabled sword of Damascus." Colonel al-Adwani glared at the still cowering Rasha for several long moments while waiting for her reply.

"What will you do once you're in Iraq that you could not wait longer to begin, Colonel al-Adwani?" She ignored his threat, she knew he had the disposition of a scorpion if upset.

"By the great gray beard of the Prophet himself, woman. I'll fan the mighty winds of a great Shammal to action against the worthless President Hussein, a sandstorm that'll quickly remove the foul fool of our country from office once and for all time to come. Once the new government of Iraq is firmly installed in our nation, we'll get down to business and deal faithfully with the hated Americans and their capitalist enslavement, and imperialist aggression in the Middle East on a new footing. We must destroy the United States god cursed aims if we're ever to survive as a nation of free thinking Arab peoples of the Middle East, bitch." Once again Colonel al-Adwani glared harshly at the still suffering young Arab woman.

"Colonel al-Adwani, you intend to remove Saddam Hussein from power in Iraq? Are you not thinking of too great a step to free Iraq of his evil control, sir?" she asked with surprise as she stared deeply in the eyes of the Iraqi Colonel and terrorist.

"By the great Prophet Muhammad's all knowing wisdom and guidance. I'll take the greatest of pleasure of slicing the grand fool into many pieces too insignificant to even be fed to the smallest of the lowly loathsome desert scavengers, Rasha. The evil and stupid fool who believes he's still in complete control of a defeated Iraq has turned his back on me and what I have tried to accomplish in his name and here I, Colonel Abdulaziz Majd al-Adwani sits, rotting slowly in the hated land of the foul infidels of the world. I'll not allow my country to continue down the same foolish path that Saddam Hussein has lied out before it and our country's faithful followers. We act like a filthy horde of lowly jackals, snapping and fighting at each other haunches, rather than fighting the true enemy of our country and the Arab world, the United States. Saddam Hussein has turned his people into a lowly wandering band of filthy Nomads without true government or direction. It's time to place a quick end to his indirections and foolishness over our nation."

"Colonel al-Adwani Sir, I beg of you not to betray the sacred sands of Mecca. How will you ever accomplish the great feat of President Saddam's death as you offer to me, sir?" She cried because she was actually stunned at what she was hearing coming from the angry lips of Colonel al-Adwani. Although she did not fully agree with the way Iraqi President Hussein was running her country of late. She never dared to dream of trying to overthrow his evil regime, and freeing Iraq and her people of his madness.

"It's much simpler than you might believe my questioning young daughter of the sand dunes. With one cast of the blade of truth, we'll succeed in our quest against the great fool in Command of Iraq. I know there are many in our country who believe as I do since Saddam Hussein chose to display his milkless backbone again towards the god cursed foul American soldiers, by denying our existence. He has made his last mistake running our country. I pray Allah for revenge on the heads of all who stand in my way." He hissed nastily as he lit his second crushed cigarette.

Seeing no other way out of her present dilemma, she totally gave in to everything the feared and powerful Iraqi Colonel was ranting and raving about standing before her like he was. She knew Colonel al-Adwani's mind was impossible to change once he had made it up against something he wanted to do. She bowed her head slightly to him, and then offered correctly to save her life to the fuming military officer. "Good fortune in your sacred quest to set Iraq free of all who wish to keep Iraq's face buried within the hot sand of the vast desert. May Allah grant you the life of a thousand years and the wisdom of the ancients, Colonel al-Adwani."

"And may you live a thousand years and grow smarter with every breath you draw within your body, my faithful young daughter of the hot desert breath. Come with me, we must make further plans to leave this foul land of the lowly god cursed jackals and infidels, my faithful desert daughter. This time the American reporters will not report their news of conflict from atop the Al-Rashid Hotel in downtown Baghdad against us. This time they'll cry out their words of death from the very streets of the country of our hated and sworn enemy." Colonel al-Adwani reached out his hand, and Rasha took hold of it and allowed him to lead her to the TV room.

CHAPTER FIFTEEN

CAMP LEJEUNE, NORTH CAROLINA. AUGUST 1st, 1999, 1:30 P.M. EST

Lieutenant Robert Walker's elite troops began their first attack on the second floor of the so called shoot house complex constructed on the grounds of the massive Marine base of Camp Lejeune. The three previous attacks on the first floor of the structure went mostly without any problems, with the special ops troops destroying the supposed terrorists before they had a chance to harm any of the supposed hostages they were in control of. Each engagement netted an eighty percent or higher probability of successfully saving all the hostages, and killing the terrorists taking over the building. Anything over a fifty percent hostage save was an acceptable number for what the troops called breakage, when dealing with a terrorist situation. The second floor of the shoot house structure was going to prove a little more difficult for the elite troops to operate against. Colonel Bruce Leadbetter was going to do everything in his power to make certain this training exercise was going to tax the soldier's resourcefulness to the fullest.

Lieutenant Walker and his troops were bunched up in the parked Humvee vans along with their equipment a half a mile away from the makeshift shoot house waiting the call to duty.

Colonel Leadbetter placed six of the fake terrorists in three separate rooms of the shoot house this time, giving each supposed terrorist's complete control over five hostages. This was so it would cause more problems for his attackers to get at the terrorist before they could ice off some if not all the hostages. This attack was going to incorporate the IWESS laser combat systems. The Colonel had every intention of pushing the pace of the training for his specialized troops up, because he had certain time constraints to get these troops as sharp as they could possibly be in as short a time he could accomplish it. The crafty Colonel was not concerned with overloading the soldiers with the new training program and information. They were that good working units.

If the two attacks went well employing the IWESS systems on the second floor, he intended to shift over to a live ammunition exercises on the third floor of the structure, and the next training exercise to take place against the shoot house and supposed terrorists. The wise Colonel looked at the Sergeant operating the computers, and snarled angrily at him. "Sergeant, push the fucking button on the fricking troops, dammit."

Walker was just lighting up a Marlboro cigarette when the light flashed in his idling van. He ditched the smoke and picked up the mike and roared in it at his troops. "Head Hunters!"

"Lieutenant Walker, this is Sergeant Rosco at the Command Center, sir. The Trump Tower has just been invaded by an unknown number of terrorists, sir. They're believed to have taken up shop on the second floor of the structure, sir. You're ordered to move in with all the troops you have at your disposal and gain the release of said hostages, and splash all terrorists discovered operating inside the compromised building, sir. Over Lieutenant."

"How many hostages and terrorists are we talking bout over this takeover of the structure, Sergeant?" Walker snarled into the radio, trying to glean as much information as possible from the concerned sounding reporting Sergeant, before engaging any of the terrorists supposed to be operating inside the shoot house structure. He issued orders with a number of swift head movements and hand signals while remaining on the mike to the rest of the soldiers, who were going to be involved in this next attack against the shoot house.

"That's unknown at this time Lieutenant. You'll have to determine that in the field, sir."

"Roger that last Sergeant, no interest in taking any possible prisoners on this mission I take it?"

"Negatory on that last, Lieutenant Walker. This is a TNP (Take No Prisoners) operation, sir. When you go in, all talk is out, sir. There's no chicken switch (abort button) for this entire exercise, sir. You'll have to see it through, no matter what the outcome of the action is stacked up against you, sir. Good luck on this one Lieutenant, get her done soldier, Ooorah."

"Roger that last Sergeant, on the move out, Ooorah." Walker pitched the mike back on top of the radio as he turned and saw his troops in the humvee already busy struggling into their so called chicken plating. (Protective armor) He grinned at them, and then snarled at the soldiers while trying to get them hot and ready for immediate action.

"Okay Bullet Stoppers as reported, we have an unknown number of fucking organ donors, (enemy) holding same number of Straphanger. (Useless people, hostages.) The exercise has been given the code name of Trump Towers. It's a TNP operation as ordered. Let's go get this fucking thing done with troops, because I want to be back in the barracks before the five o'clock news starts. Ooorah people."

"Walker, we got it made on this one, man. You and Raz are already familiar with the damn Trump Tower layout, Homes." The Mutt wise cracked as he shifted his weight under his equipment while struggling to get comfortable inside the slow moving humvee.

Walker glared at the Mutt, and then snapped at him. "Can the shit will ya dog man, and suit up for Christ sake. What the hell makes you think this dump's gonna look anything like the fricking Trump garbage can we did our stinking act in a few months ago, man. C'mon people time's a wasting on us, and lives depend on us to get them outta there alive. Paint it up people. We got a hot mission to command. Ooorah. Unass yourselves people. We got ourselves some stinking turds to stuff into mummy bags on this training exercise, troops."

"Back off some will ya Walker. Don't allow playing fucking soldier go to your stinking head on us, Homes. Ooorah, I have me a need for some stinking I and I, man." (Intercourse and Intoxication) The Mutt complained, trying his best to add levity into the situation.

"Keep it up dog man, and I'm gonna fricking hop you right square in the fucking ass, buddy." Walker warned his lifelong and close friend as he checked his weapon for action.

"Man, I could sure use me a little bit of B and B (Beer and Broads) myself, Homes." Neck offered with a grin as he shoved his head in the heavy Kevlar helmet and then checked his radio mike inside the helmet by blowing into the small crystal mike and the end of a wire hanging by his mouth. It worked fine and he next checked his weapon before engaging the terrorist.

"Am I gonna start having trouble with your ass too, big man? Look Neck, I don't want you hanging around with the fucking Mutt anymore. He's starting to rub off on ya ass, tree trunk. By the way big man, how's your stinking noggin doing? Are you having any trouble, seeing any stinking stars or getting dizzy on me, asshole?" The concerned Lieutenant growled as he latched his armor in place, and then moved his weapon into a better firing position near his body.

"Don't worry bout me Walker, I'm doing fine, man. I'm, hot, locked, and ready to fucking rock man. Besides Walker, I don't want the stinking Mutt hanging round me any and my getting any of that mixed up brother shit getting under my stinking skin on me, Oooooorah." Neck complained, and was instantly hit in the helmet with the butt of a weapon by the laughing Mutt.

"Shit Homes, if you gots you a little bit of this mixed soul and Mick blood injected in your fat ass, you'd have to start beating the chicks offa your stinking back with your new, and longer crank, man." The Mutt announced, proud of the fact he had a white mother, and a black father.

A chorus of 'Oorahs' filled the air as the troops got themselves hot, and ready for action.

The radio came to life again with the Sergeant barking in it. "Lieutenant Walker Sir!"

"Here. Send your traffic. Over." Walker growled in his radio as he waited for the report.

"WST soldier? Over." (What Status Troops?) The Sergeant replied to Lieutenant Walker.

"Cocked, locked, and ready to fucking rock Sergeant. Moving out now, Oorah. Over."

"Streets are clear to move out in tight formation, sir. You have a direct line open to the Tower, and present hostage situation. Over." The Sergeant in the control room offered over the radio.

"Roger that last as stated. Understood all as offered and received. Over." Walker replied as he waved his hand out before him, and the first large troop carrying humvee started up and quickly moved towards the sand road leading straight towards the shoot house structure. As he waited in the van, he checked his helmet radio while struggling with the IWESS training system. "Walker to all Head Hunters. Check in with my ass immediately people."

Walker listened as each soldier involved in the latest exercise called in.

Sergeant Dorothy Ramirez was unable to fit in her tight fitting body armor any longer because of the pregnancy, but Colonel Leadbetter did not let her off the hook that easy for the training exercise. As long as the female Sergeant was stationed on his military base, she was subject to be involved in any training exercises the rest of the troops entered on the base. The wise Colonel stuck her inside the shoot house with a check off chart. She was going to help grade the efficiency of the elite troops as they tried to free the hostages, and take out the supposed terrorists trapped in the same action.

Colonel Leadbetter went outside the command trailer because he wanted to see this attack better, and he stared down the road and saw the unmarked convoy of troop carrying humvees heading for the shoot house at breakneck speed. He ordered a number of trucks and cars parked around the supposed target building, making it look like any structure occupying space in the congested heart of New York City. The Colonel also ordered regular Army and Marine troops milling about the shoot house like packs of nosy civilians, along with other soldiers acting like responding police and fire department personnel. It was sheer mayhem at best around the intended target building area. The Colonel smiled as the first military van plowed into a parked vehicle, the heavily reinforced bumper and grill easily shoved the smaller car out of its way, without sustaining any sort of damage to the powerful military vehicle.

Leadbetter stared as the elite troops piled out of the first machine, and they took up a defensive posture around the front of the compromised building, while waiting for the other elite troops involved in the exercise to catch up with the leading element of the group of invaders.

Walker was the first soldier out of the stopped truck, as he usually was in all actions he was part of, and he bellowed at the other soldiers to form up around him. When they were there, he dished out a bushel of orders at them. "Buckethead, you and Mother Flanagan are our rear guard in this fucking action. If we get caught up in the shit, you two spudheads are to break the back of the checkmate, and pull our balls outta the stinking fire. Mutt, you, McNip, Neck, Wacko and Snatch are in the first room with me. Siberia, Baby Tee, Roach, Sun Tan, CoCo-G and Just Bob take the left room we got the right one covered. The Ghost and Hunter, you two Alpha Hotels (AssHoles) are going in first, and get us some up to date recon and information of the situation we'll be facing inside this friggin dump. I need to know how many turds we're going up against in there, troops. We're not going to move out until you two slugs report in on the exact number of these human trip wires (enemy) operating inside this stinking dump."

"We're off and hunting as ordered Walker." The Ghost shot back as both he and the Hunter made for the front doors of the shoot house. The two soldiers knew the first floor of the building was not compromised on this training operation.

Walker and the rest of his troops hunkered down and waited for the first reports from his two pointmen to come in. The outside troops used this time to make certain their weapons and radios were in the proper working order, and they try to catch some movement in the building.

The Hunter and the Ghost check out the first floor carefully anyway, because they did not trust the Colonel of not placing a few of the supposed terrorists on this floor. Then the two soldiers made for the second floor, after checking the hallway out for any signs of terrorists lurking about, or setting up an ambush against them. When they were certain no terrorist were in the hall, the two extremely dangerous soldiers next scouted out the area before them, until they located what they were looking for. Just to the left of the staircase, there was an air shaft that went up to and through the ceiling to the second floor, and continued to the third floor of the structure. The Hunter stood guard while the Ghost pried off the light metal grate.

The Ghost made a mental note to carry a multi tipped screw driver on any missions he was involved in, because he was having a problem using his K-bar knife to loosen the screws holding the grate to the wall. A screw driver would have made his life much easier, and it would have also increased his speed of their entry. Once the grate was off the shaft, they both disappeared in the shaft and then they cautiously worked their way into the narrow crawl space, checking on the six offices through the grates cut in the ceiling offering fresh air to the offices.

The first two rooms the soldiers surveyed were empty. Silently as a cat, the two deadly soldiers worked their way towards the third office on this floor. There, they saw what they took to be six terrorist dummies, they knew they were serious threats against them, because each one of them had a weapon strapped across their chest, and they had the IWESS laser straps wrapped around them haphazardly, and they seemed to be waiting for Walker's troops to make a forced entry into the room. The Ghost counted five hostages also piled up near the outer section of the compromised office, and spotted another one inside the room.

The Ghost lightly tapped his helmet radio, and then he blew into it and whispered his report back to his commander for this latest operation. "Hey Walker!"

"Go Ghost. It's about friggin time you finally got back to my ass, man. What the fuck do you have for me in there? Over."

"Walker, I got six fake turds set up waiting for you to enter the room marked two, three, on our funny papers, (Maps), sir. Over." The Ghost reported as he continued to scan the interior of the small target room.

"Got it man? Give me the number on hostages trapped inside this room, soldier? Over."

"I have a good MOE (Mark One Eyeball) on five tent pegs the terrorists have packed to the outer left side of the fucking target room. The hostages should be well outta the way when you make your hot entry into the stinking room, man. There's a lone straphanger with a clipboard also in the damn room, man. I guess he's the fricking dude that is gonna grade your fucking hot entry into the compromised room, Homes. Keep your fucking eyes open for the dopey slug and don't clip him on the entry, or we're gonna lost the intrusion. It won't look too good on his stinking score card for us if you go splashing the fucking ass in the training exercise. It might get him a little pissed off at us, and he could possibly fail you just for that mistake, man."

"Out fucking standing report Ghost, thanks for warning on the damn grader, Homes. Go to the next room, scout it out and report back to me on your findings in that room, Ghost. I want to know everything we can about this damn mission before we jump off against them, ooorah."

"Working." The Ghost broke off the communication, and then crawled to the next room on the third floor. The scene was virtually the same in this office, with six terrorists and five hostages gathered in the small room. He reported this to Walker, and then the Ghost headed off for the fourth room on the floor. Again, it was the same scenario there, but with one difference here though. The hostages here were positioned so they actually stood between the door and the group of supposed terrorists. The supposed terrorists were using the hostages as a sort of human shields in this room before them. The Ghost reported this new move to Walker as well.

"Shit! We're gonna get our damn asses a little bloody on this fucking hot entry, Ghost. Fucking Leadbetter's really putting it to our stinking asses on this one, dammit. Check out the next two rooms on the floor and report back to me A-SAP..."

Their communication was interrupted by the Colonel, as he growled in Walker's mike.

"Whatsumatter Walker? Are you afraid of a little fucking challenge mounted against you and your pack of jack rabbits during this operation, sonny? You people are supposed to be fucking profession soldiers, mister. So why don't you people start acting like it, and get your fricking ass in there and free them damn hostages before they die of old age for this training exercise mister. If you're capable of any such a task assigned to you that is, mister." Colonel Leadbetter was enjoying ribbing Walker, before he entered a mission. He was trying everything in his power to help confuse, or rile him up some so he would make some mistakes during the exercise.

"Fuck you in the god damn ear, Colonel. We'll get the stinking job done no matter what you have stacked up against us, sir. Over." Walker growled back angrily at the Colonel.

"It's a damn good thing you remembered to add the 'Sir' to your fucking bitch at my ass, sonny. Stop dicking around out there will ya Lieutenant, and get your damn ass in there and free those damn hostages as you were ordered to do on this exercise, mister. Sixty thousand screaming Chinese were born in the length of time you people are dicking around before engaging the enemy inside the damn structure, mister. You people have a mission to complete, and I suggest you to haul ass and get her done toot sweet, Walker. I intend to have the terrorists begin executing the hostages in five, and I repeat to you, five fucking minutes mister.

"So if you don't want to lose every stinking hostage to this fucking hostile action in there then get your ass humping wiseguy. Ooorah!" Colonel Leadbetter broke off the communication with the angry sounding young Lieutenant, and stared at the computer screens covering the interior floors and rooms inside the shoot house structure, with the terrorists hiding in them from where he was standing in front of the control room command center.

The Ghost reported as soon as Colonel Leadbetter cleared the radio frequency with Walker. "Hey Walker, the other two rooms are empty as a bird's nest in fucking winter, man. I put it at eighteen terrorists and fifteen hostages in all for this exercise."

"Good, errr... look Ghost, I'm gonna use you and the stinking Hunter in a different way on this mission, buddy. I think I want you two birds to keep your eyes locked on the fourth room of the structure. I'm going to use you two guys to gain entry into said room when we jump off against the rest of the damn supposed terrorists inside this lousy structure. Since they have the hostages packed in the way of our hot entry of the fucking room, they won't be expecting an over the top deployment aimed against them fucks. I want you and the stinking Hunter to clear the fourth friggin room for us while we do in the rest of the asses inside the structure." Lieutenant Walker informed the Ghost working over the third floor of the shoot house.

"Gotcha Walker. When we hear the first crash bangs (grenades) pop off, we'll drop down from the fucking ceiling and splash the suckas in the room when we crash down on the asses, ooorah. The fourth room's our fucking Easter egg to hatch, Homes."

"Sonofabitch! This lousy little bastard has just dicked me up the damn ass, the sneak little bastard he is for fuck sake. He must have learned this crap when he was a kid ripping off fucking gas stations back in the real world, dammit. Walker's going to get the jump on the room I set up as a no possible win situation against him and the rest of his fucking troop's hot entry into the damn building." Colonel Leadbetter growled at his Sergeant as he punched the air before him, after realizing how Walker had just skillfully worked his way around the trap he had set up against him and his troops inside the shoot house structure.

"That one's sure on the damn ball, Colonel." The Sergeant moaned back at the officer.

"Fuck you and keep your eyes glued to that damn computer screen, before I use you for one of those damn dummies in there, mister. If Walker thinks for one second he got by me by the shot hairs that easily on this damn training program, I'll fuck him to death somehow before I'm done with him." The Colonel snarled as he studied the layout of the terrorists in the shoot house.

Walker and his assault group charged up the steps leading to the second floor of the shoot house. Once they were on the landing, the troops put their backs against the walls, and inched their way forward towards the rooms with the terrorists hiding in them. Walker, Mutt, McNip, Neck, Wacko and Snatch, (Sergeant George Weaver) was on the right side of the hall. The invading soldiers singled out the first room to be entered by the gather troops. Siberia, Baby Tee, Roach, (Sergeant David Burgwald), Sun Tan, (Sergeant Clifford Saldinger), CoCo-G and Just Bob, (Sergeant Robert Bozzelli) was against the left wall of the hall, and they aimed them themselves at the second room containing another group of terrorists and hostages.

Mother Flanagan and Buckethead, (Sergeant Vincent Lombardo) remained in the center of the hallway, and they stood ready to lend a hand to either team that might get bogged down during the attack into the two compromised rooms. Both backup soldiers carried the heavy M-60 machine guns with the laser senders attached on them, to detect any kills they scored in the high risk entry they were involved in the shoot house structure.

When everyone in the two groups of attacking soldiers was ready to go in action, Lieutenant Walker got in front of the door to the room his group was to enter, and raised his foot in the air and aimed it at the closed door. CoCo did the same for the second room the soldiers were going to enter. Walker nodded to CoCo, and then he crashed his leg into the door, which sent it flying off the hinges, and the power of the kick sent the door crashing into the center of the small room. Walker went along with his momentum, and he fell into the room and then he dropped to the floor and rolled off to his left, just as the Mutt and Neck pitched two stun grenades into the room, and they readied another pair to backup the first two grenades going off.

Wacko, (Sergeant Salvatore Tomassi) charged wildly into the room like a madman, and he was screaming and firing at the same time at the supposed terrorists, he quickly moved to his right once inside the room. Snatch followed him into the small room, doing the same thing Wacko did as he moved to his left. Both soldiers were using their screams and wild actions to help confuse the supposed dummy terrorist actions. Walker and the Mutt fired at the terrorists they sighted in from the floor. Walker made certain no hostages were hidden terrorists. He kept them covered as Snatch called out, "Clear on the left man." Meaning the terrorist in his responsibility zone was out of the picture. Wacko called out next. "Clear on the right."

The tension built up in the soldier's bodies, lessened as they got control of the supposed terrorist situation inside the shoot house. The Mutt made certain the terrorists dummies received the final death shot, by firing one round into each through the supposed head. By the time the smoke cleared in the room, six terrorist dummies were lit up like Christmas trees. One hostage was hit and glowing. None of the intruders were hit in the action by the so called terrorists, or their own controlled firing at the supposed terrorists trapped in the small room.

CoCo-G, (Sergeant Milton Pettibone) kicked down the door to the second room, at the same time Walker and his team attacked his compromised room, and he fell into the floor and rolled off to his left side. He covered his follow on troops from the floor position as they entered the room. Siberia, (Russian Sergeant Taras Zarugnaya) followed next in the room tossing two stun grenades she removed the pins from. Sun Tan went to the left side of the door, and remained standing in the room controlling his fire at the supposed terrorists trapped in the room.

Just Bob went to the right of the room, and remained standing and firing at the supposed terrorists hiding in the room. This way the soldiers had the room completely covered from the floor, and from the standing position at the same time. The Roach tossed another pair of stun grenades into the suddenly overcrowded room, to add to the confusion and smoke flooding the room. By the time their action was completed, all terrorists trapped in the room were classified as dead, and none of the hostages were hit by this hard hitting action.

Mother Flanagan backed Walker's group on their intrusion into the room, and stood in the doorway with his M-60 held at the ready, in case any terrorists were somehow missed on the initial splash and splatter entry in the compromised room. Buckethead stood almost filling the entire doorway, where Siberia and her group entered the other room through. He too was ready to mow down any supposed trapped hostels that might have been left alive in the other room.

When the Ghost heard the first stun grenades go off in the other rooms, he kicked the ceiling grate out of the duct they were using for their hot entry into the compromised room, and the Hunter dropped down in the room, firing at the six terrorists as he fell to the floor. The Hunter ended up landing behind the terrorist dummies, and picked them off easily, they were unable to move and turn around, or fire on him from their position. The Ghost added to the Hunter's fire power, by firing from the hole in the ceiling at the supposed terrorist dummies in the room below. No hostages were hit in this action either. It was impossible for the dummies to turn or react against the soldiers dropping down from the ceiling behind them.

Colonel Leadbetter was steaming over the way Walker's troops controlled the hostage/terrorist situation, he thought he had Walker locked up in a no possible win situation in the last compromised room of the shoot house building. He wanted to prove to the young Lieutenant and the rest of his troops, they were not as invincible as they might have thought they were, and they could be placed in a no win situation at any time during any operation assigned to them. Where all the hostages would be killed before he and his troops could get at any supposed terrorists controlling the hostages. He never gave a thought to Walker having his people attack the room from a ceiling position. Now, he knew it was almost impossible to have his troops placed into a no win situation, if they used their heads and acted as a working unit.

The surprised Marine Colonel especially liked the crafty way Lieutenant Walker collected his real time information on the supposed terrorists and their hostages trapped inside the building, by utilizing the two dangerous pointmen the Hunter and the Ghost, as his advance units for their intrusion into the already compromised building and floor. It showed good thinking on his part, and the Colonel was really proud of Walker and the actions of him and the rest of the elite troops under his command.

Colonel Leadbetter picked up the mike and stormed over it. "Buster, Buster. All hostels are considered splashed at this time. You walking sandbags did a good job this time, but remember people you didn't hear that crap coming from my lips. It looks like I'm going to be forced to be a little more devious in my next scenarios against you people. If I want to teach you pack of pudheads a fucking lesson in humility that is. Walker collect your shitbags and get out of my building and assemble them before the HQ pronto, mister. I want to analyze this last action closer for you people. All spotters are to report to the front of the building. I want your input in this debriefing immediately, so we can have a round robin skull secession of this latest rather successful intrusion into the fucking building flooded with terrorists and hostages."

The group of elite troops took their ever loving time leaving the shoot house structure. They were in no big hurry, and Colonel Leadbetter could not do anything to them for wasting time like they were doing. They had a good excuse this time. All they had to say was they were mopping up the last situation, and Colonel Leadbetter had to accept the line of bullshit from the elite troops, even though he knew they were just busting his horns again.

Walker made the most of getting under Colonel Leadbetter's skin for what he believed was a trap set out by the Colonel against him and his troops on this exercise. He lit up a smoke and looked for Sergeant Dorothy Ramirez inside the building somewhere. He found her and she rushed in his arms and kissed him and offered. "Walker, everyone did real well on this last action, honey. I spoke to the other spotters, and they all agreed the troops did an outstanding job on this exercise, honey. Colonel Leadbetter has to give you credit for this one, Bobby."

"Honey, I'm not in this thing for any damn credit or medals. If I want credit, I'd deal with Sears. How you doing anyway baby, ooorah?" Walker looped his arm protectively over Ramirez's shoulder and they started walking together.

"I doing fine I guess, I'm proud of you but I'm broken hearted I can't be with you and the rest of the troops when you guys go after this missing turd who tried to assassinate our President, Robert. This is the first mission I'm going to miss with you, Bobby. I'm not going to be there to protect you." Sergeant Ramirez replied to Walker as she smiled at him.

"Hey baby, you're the one who wanted to get pregnant, remember honey." Walker taunted Ramirez as he returned her lovely smile with one of his own.

"I know that so don't rub it in on me mister..." She mumbled at her lover.

"I'll rub it in more than you can possibly believe, if you POS (Pieces Of Shit) don't get your asses in gear and get outside this damn building on the double quick, buster." Colonel Leadbetter snorted from behind the small group of elite soldiers, as he glared at the troops bunching up in the room, jaw jacking (Talking) with each other.

"Crankinstine's at it again I see, dammit." Walker bitched as he remembered the word the Mutt branded the Colonel with earlier in the day, and then he hustled passed the Colonel and outside the shoot house building.

CHAPTER SIXTEEN

1171 EAST NORTHFORK DRIVE, WASHINGTON D.C., AUGUST 2nd, 1999 SEVEN A.M. EST

The day went by slowly, with Rasha following Colonel Abdulaziz Majd al-Adwani's orders on making it possible for him to be ready to leave the United States safely undercover within the next few days. The Washington hordes of police and special and FBI agents were still crawling all over the State, looking for any sign of the missing Colonel al-Adwani, and anyone else who might be helping or protecting the most wanted terrorist in all the world at the moment.

She understood Colonel al-Adwani had to leave the United States as soon as possible, or he was going to do something foolish that would surely result in his being discovered by the American law officials, and then killed by the flood of special agents and police officers still involved in searching for him. His face was being flashed on every TV for the past two days.

She employed all her resources, and was able to set up a civilian car to be used to pick her and Colonel al-Adwani up the following day, and then drive them secretly to South Carolina, where they would board an aircraft for Canada. The support group she worked with, informed her the small Carolina airport, would be the least covered by the increased security agents and police officers and FBI agents. The special agents there rarely checked anyone heading for Canada. It was the only airport they dared to pick to handle Colonel al-Adwani's escape from the United States, because of its smallness, and had the lack of any beefed up security.

Colonel al-Adwani was making Rasha's life a living hell with making constant and many unattainable demands and requests of her, and the terrible beatings he gave her when she was unable to fulfill any of his demands or wants. She feared Colonel al-Adwani was slowly losing his mind, and during these terrible fits of uncontrolled anger and rage, he might kill her out of plain meanness, and his want for revenge against the rest of the world. She wanted to be rid of the extremely dangerous Colonel al-Adwani, as much as he wanted to be away from her at the same time. Last night she did not sleep a second, worried Colonel al-Adwani was going to visit another terrible beating on her body, for no other reason than her just being there.

She was thoroughly disgusted when he demanded sex from her, while treating her like dirt under his filthy feet. She rapidly grew to hate him for his terrible actions and crimes committed against her person and mind. This morning she was forced to take care of him with her mouth. She was furious he did not even bother to wash, before he forced her to perform for him. It informed her of the true hatred he held for all women.

She stared at the clock, trying to will the hours away with her mind. She knew once she was safely in Iraq, she would find a successful to pull away from Colonel al-Adwani's overpowering influence, and she would complain to her control of the deplorable way he had treated her while in the United States, and the foul and deplorable demands he forced upon her person. She was also going to demand never to work with Colonel al-Adwani ever again, even if it meant she would lose her present standings with her controller back in Iraq.

Two Arab Americans working closely with Colonel al-Adwani's terrorist cell were scheduled to arrive at the safe house later that afternoon with their vehicle. They were going to spend the night at the safe house, and then take off tomorrow morning for the small South Carolina Commercial Airport. These Arab men worked in the United States for many years, and had successfully established flawless reputations while doing so for themselves.

Rasha purchased flight tickets for Canada, and their flight was scheduled to leave the airport at eleven thirty a.m. the following morning. She was going to act as Colonel al-Adwani's wife on this upcoming excursion. Once across the Canadian border, she would purchase tickets that would get them safely to Iraq. Canada lifted its restriction on flights to

Iraq last year, and the country never reinstated them after the assassination attempt on the American President's life.

She tried to hide herself the best she could in the kitchen all this day and she only moved out when Colonel al-Adwani bellowed out for her assistance for any reason. She made his meals, and cleaned his clothes and bought makeup, the newspapers and a number of packs of cigarettes for him as they waited to leave the safe house.

Colonel al-Adwani smoked two packs of cigarettes a day, which seemed to make him more irritable and nervous and angry at her for no other reason than she was in the building with him. It appeared to her that Colonel al-Adwani could not get enough of reading about his failed attempted assassination against the American President, or of all the precautions the police and special agents did in protecting the President from any further possible assassination attacks aimed against him. Or what they were doing in the search for him.

She heard Colonel al-Adwani laughing from the kitchen, and was tempted to go into the living room of the safe house to see what suddenly placed him in such a rare good mood. The decision was taken out of her hands when she heard him call out for her.

"Rasha, get your ass in here and read this god cursed newspaper article for me, woman."

She painfully got up from her chair as if she had the weight of the world pressing down heavily on her shoulders, and she cautiously headed in the room Colonel al-Adwani was using for his private living space. She moved towards the chair and waited for him to point at what he wanted her to see and read for him from the newspaper.

"Here you pig of a lowly whore, read this foul report if you're smart enough to read at all that is. See bitch, I told you, Allah will protect all those who are right and just and at peace with Him. It's our sacred duty to raise the foot of the United States from the necks of the honorable peoples of Iraq, worthless woman you are. Allah's greatness has giving us the flag of freedom to wave, until all hated American bones are being bleached white in the vast deserts of all Arab lands they chose to invade, once the god cursed scavengers have finished with the fool's bodies."

Rasha took the newspaper, and read the small article tucked on the tenth page of the newspaper. 'The FBI and CIA are stumped in their current search for the missing terrorist'. The small print read, 'It's believed the lone terrorist able to survive the unsuccessful assassination attack against President Albert Cole's life, has by this time successfully fled the United States, and he was now believed to be back in his host nation. Enjoying the protection that government offered its terrorists and other world criminals. Although it's believed the terrorist is no longer within the United States, the local police and FBI Agents will keep up their present level of alert, until the terrorist surfaces elsewhere. The federal government is pulling some of their special agents working on the case, and assigning them to other matters'.

Colonel al-Adwani had no idea the article in the newspaper, was a plant ordered up by CIA Director, John Raincloud, to try and see if they could possibly flush out the missing terrorist, or cause him to make his first mistake since he fled the crime scene. Director Raincloud wanted to make Colonel al-Adwani feel most of the heat was off him, and hopefully cause him to make a foolish move to get out of the United States. The CIA Director knew if the terrorist believed this story, he would make his move to try and make good his escape from the United States, and make it that much easier for them to trap him in the open.

While she read the news article, Colonel al-Adwani undid his pants and he removed himself from them. He was excited, and when he was stimulated, he wanted sex. When she finished reading the article and tried to hand the newspaper back to Colonel al-Adwani, she saw his condition and sighed deeply. She knew he was going to force himself on her body again. Use her as if she was nothing more than a lowly whore working on the backstreets of Baghdad, and not as a freedom fighting activist, trying to free her country of the sphere of hatred and mistrust forced on her nation by the hated Americans and United Kingdom military.

Colonel al-Adwani reached out and roughly grabbed her hand and savagely pulled her to her knees by it. She tried her best to resist his efforts, and when he bent her hand backwards, causing terrible pain in her wrist and arm. She had no other choice and she had to go along with the pressure, or risk having her wrist broken by the sneering Iraqi Colonel.

The instant she was down on her knees al-Adwani grabbed her by the hair, and forced her head to his shaft. He grabbed himself and forced his member roughly in her mouth. She offered little if any resistance, but was defying his demands of sex by not helping him in any way in his attack against her. The Colonel's free hand reached out and ripped her blouse to shreds, and once her breasts were exposed, he roughly manhandled them. Pinching and twisting the nipples and causing terrible pain to her out of his meanness. It seemed everything he did to her, was to cause severe pain to the young Arab woman obeying his every demand.

She merely went through the motions of sex, but she refrained from getting involved in the pleasures she offered al-Adwani, and her lack of emotions caused the Iraqi Colonel to grow angrier at her. He pulled her off him by her hair, and he stared deeply in her unseeing eyes, and then he shook her head violently by her hair and snarled in her face, sending spittle flying over the side of her cheek. "You better do this god cursed act the best you ever have done it before in your worthless and foul life, pig. I'm happy today, and I want to be pleased properly by you lowly pig. If you fail to give me the pleasure I seek from you, daughter of a whore, I'll slit your worthless throat and leave your body to rot in the unholy land of Satan."

Colonel al-Adwani was not fooling with his threat directed against her life, as he slowly removed his razor sharp Jambiya blade, and he laid it out threateningly across his legs below his bunched up pants. Once he did this, he glared at her again, and applied more pressure to the back of her head, again guiding her mouth towards his waiting shaft.

She saw the deadly blade lying just inches away from her face, and she picked up the very threatening warning it caused, and she went back on Colonel al-Adwani's shaft with a new vigor. Within seconds, she had him squirming all around in the chair. She tried to pull off of him when she felt he was about to come, but the angry Iraqi Colonel was still treating her like a piece of dirt under his feet, and he held her head fast by the neck and hair, and she did the only thing she could possibly do, she swallowed.

"Arrr... filthy lowly bitch of the burning sands of the vast desert of our ancestors, you have a very special way with the tongue and mouth, pig. For that fine effort will allow you to live for another day, whore. I need help with my god cursed makeup, if I ever hope to get passed the police security authorities of the loathsome airport. So I can leave this foul land of sin and lust once and for all." Colonel al-Adwani carried out his terrible insult leveled at Rasha further, by wiping the end of his shaft on her face, and then he released the death like hold he had on her head, and allowed her to stand. She wiped her face on a cloth, and then without being ordered to do so, she left the room to retrieve the small makeup kit she brought with her to the safe house for Colonel al-Adwani's use.

For the next two hours, she successfully changed Colonel al-Adwani's facial appearance. She lightened up his skin tone to try and make him look more European than Arab, and she cut his hair shorter, and added a light touch of gray over his ears and here and there on his head. She had Colonel al-Adwani shave carefully making certain he did not nip himself while shaving, leaving a well trimmed slight goatee and mustache, trimmed to perfection in a European manner. She even gave him a small mole on his right cheek, and a pair of glasses. She plucked his eyebrows to thin them out to enhance his European look, and help erase his overpowering outstanding Arab features. When she was finished, she handed Colonel al-Adwani a hand mirror.

He nodded slowly, greatly pleased and impressed over her expert handiwork on his appearance. Next, she worked on the Iraqi Colonel's stance and mannerism. She had him soften them to hide his military and his usual arrogant Arab demeanor. She even told him to move his shoulders forward a bit more, not back like a cocky military agent.

She had the Iraqi Colonel walk across the room a few times in front of her while correcting his gate as ordered by Rasha, until she was satisfied with his movement. When he stood still, she had him rest his hands on his hips, or place them in his pockets, or even read a newspaper while he stood waiting to board his airplane. She wanted him to look nonchalant, even bored as they waited for the aircraft to leave the United States. Next, she worked on his Arab accent. Unable to hide it successfully and completely, she gave him a fist full of hard candies, and told him to place one in his mouth when he feared he was going to be questioned by anyone. It helped a lot.

She next fumbled through the many items of false identification and papers she had acquired over the years of her covert work for her country. She selected the one that she had modeled, and most resembled Colonel al-Adwani's fine looks, but showed him as a slightly younger man. This allowed for changes she was unable to accomplish or hide on his face. It informed the reader al-Adwani's name was now Alfred Rosenberg, a Jew from South Carolina, working for the IBM computer company for fifteen

EAGLE'S NEST

years. She next placed a sheet of paper in the typewriter, and issued orders for the supposed Mr. Rosenberg to travel to Canada to setup the powerful T441 M computers usually employed for airline security at most airport terminals throughout the world.

She felt if Colonel al-Adwani carried the papers confirming he worked for airport security, any investigators checking up on him would never aim a suspicious eye at al-Adwani. She handed him a license with the same picture printed on it, after she doctored it up to agree with his present looks. She was a master when it came to falsifying documents of identification and papers.

Rasha was to dress as Colonel al-Adwani's wife for the flight to Canada, but this work took most of the day up for her, and when a light rapping on the front door came, it made Rasha jump and turn. Colonel al-Adwani removed his pistol, and moved into the narrow doorway separating the kitchen from living room area of the small apartment. He was out of sight and well hidden by the shadows of the hall, but he was still easily able to see the front door. With a swift head movement, he motioned her towards the front door so she could open it for him.

As she headed for the front door, she removed her clothes and wrapped a towel loosely around her body. She had the clothes she was going to wear accompanying Colonel al-Adwani to the airport, hanging on a kitchen cabinet knob. When she reached the front door, she called out cautiously to the person on the other side of the door. "Yes." Then she moved slightly away from the front door to give Colonel al-Adwani a clear shot at anyone outside, if they were American police officers or special agents still searching for him.

"Is this the home of my dear and lovely sister whom I have not seen in well over a year's time I ask?" The voice on the other side of the door asked.

"I'm afraid that depends on who your sister is, stranger knocking at my door." She replied in a teasing manner to the voice, knowing this was their planned password between them. Her shoulders released all their tension.

"That's my lovely little sister from New York City. I can tell by your voice, even though I'm unable to see your lovely face through this heavy wood door standing in my way. Cathy, it's I, your brother William from North Carolina. Open this door at once, so I might again see the lovely face of my pretty and beloved little sister after all these passing years."

"William!" She suddenly cried out as she flung open the door and actually jumped in the arms of the stranger waiting to be allowed to enter the apartment. This was to take any suspicion away from the neighbors who might be listening to their conversation.

"Ahhh, it's truly good to see you again, sis. But is this the way you usually answer the door in Washington, young lady?" Admad al-Taai said, also for the benefit of the neighbors.

"William, I just stepped out of the shower when you knocked on my door. Come in my dear brother, you must be starving. Mother told me you might be coming by to visit me soon." She pulled al-Taai into the apartment as the second man followed him in without a word.

Once they were in the first room of the safe house, al-Adwani came out of the shadows of the doorway, placing his pistol in his pocket, and al-Taai and he embraced. They kissed, and then al-Taai pulled away from him, and introduced the second man assisting him to al-Adwani.

"Ahhh... my Iraqi brother of many years, Colonel Abdulaziz Majd al-Adwani this man with me is Saad Ihsaan. He's an Egyptian who is in compliance with the plight of our country against the hated American soldiers who have invaded our country, sir."

Colonel al-Adwani nodded slightly at the stranger, but he kept him glued in a suspicious stare. All three men watched as Rasha stepped out of the towel, and she quickly dressed right in front of the three men, so she was dressed properly for their flight out of the United States, and the group could leave the safe house and head for the small Carolina Airport.

Admad al-Taai leaned closer to Colonel al-Adwani and whispered in his ear, so only he could hear his words. "At first my foolish brother, I felt bad for you being cooped up in this foul place for so long a time, fearing for your life. But seeing this pretty naked woman standing here makes me understand I was in error for my worry over you. I wish I was locked up with such a beauty as this one for many days and nights, my foolish brother of the sands." Al-Taai jabbed al-Adwani softly in the ribs with his elbow, and gave him a quick wink of the eye.

"Huh, if you want to enjoy what the filthy pig Rasha has to offer, step up to her and take what you want from her worthless body. She's here to serve me, and all who aide me faithfully, and she does have special ways to please a man's sexual desires I assure you, al-Taai. But the foolish whore has committed many mistakes that'll surely be answered by her, once we returned to the safety of Iraq and her great deserts, my brother and friend."

Al-Taai did not reply as he continued to stare lustfully at her exquisite body, as she was busy stuffing her well endowed breasts in an ice blue lace bra and he offered to the pretty young Arab woman. "I'd be most pleased to assist you getting those golden breasts of yours in the restricting cups, Rasha." This ignoring of Colonel al-Adwani's question reaped a sharp jab in the gut of al-Taai by Colonel al-Adwani's fist. Al-Taai nearly doubled over, catching his breath he offered.

"Colonel al-Adwani, I have the vehicle that'll take you safely to South Carolina. Rasha has already purchased the airline tickets for your use, so that much has been completed already. This airport we're heading for is very lax in their security behaviors and precautions. Besides, I heard the foolish American Leaders now believe you have already fled the foul country, and this should make it easier for you to escape. But just in case, we intend to stay in the air terminal, and if anyone challenges you, we'll place a quick end to their suspicious ways. Then we'll get you to another terminal and another safe house in Florida. We have weapons and enough ammunition to hold off a small American Army if needed. I have a second, clean car parked at the airport already, in case we have to make an escape from this terminal, sir. Fear not my faithful brother of the great deserts of our ancestors everything is well taken care of for you, sir." Al-Taai smiled as he turned to Rasha stepping into matching panties of her outfit.

"Must I pluck your worthless foul eyes out of their god cursed sockets and hold them in my hands to keep your attention to this conversation, fool for a whore? I'm not done speaking with you al-Taai." The Iraqi Colonel barked at the man assisting them leaving the United States.

"Please Colonel al-Adwani, it has been many long and boring months since the last time I shared a bed with my loving wife. Allow me to enjoy what I have been missing all these many months for a few moments longer, before it's removed from my worthless eyes, sir." Al-Taai cried as he continued to stare at Rasha while she was getting dressed.

There was not more al-Adwani had to go over with al-Taai, so he leaned against the kitchen wall, and he also enjoyed the slight show Rasha was offering to the three of them.

She was thoroughly embarrassed by the lowly fool's remarks, and she did not reply to al-Taai's disgusting offer. She knew it was her own fault for bringing her clothes out to the kitchen, that she must now endure the lingering leers and ugly remarks from the three lowly male members of the new terrorist group staring at her as she dressed. But this was done by her to enable her to keep out of Colonel al-Adwani's cursed reach and his deplorable demands for more sex from her. Now, she was trapped, because she knew no one from the group was going to be allowed out of the sight of the others, until Colonel al-Adwani was finally safely out of the United States and on the airlines heading for Canada in a few hours.

She struggled into the skin tight dark skirt, zipped it up and moved the skirt around until the zipper was behind her back. Next, she slid in an almost transparent, light blue tinted button down shirt that matched with her skirt. She knew what she was doing she was offering anyone who might question them the show of their worthless lives. She hoped to glide through the airport security because of this look she should be displaying before all. Rasha was told many times in her past by her control, that the foolish Americans are so easy to beguile by merely exposing enough, but not too much skin of her body to their foolish eyes. Besides, it was common knowledge that any respectful Arab women would never allow their cherished bodies to be seen by anyone other than their honored husbands. To be so forward in her appearance would help to lend to the belief that they were not Arab persons in the least.

Once she was in her clothes, and she was now fussing with her hair, the three Arab men quickly lost interest in her and they began to speak amongst themselves. Colonel al-Adwani did not know the second man, so he was receiving a chilly welcome from the well feared Iraqi Colonel, while he spoke mostly to al-Taai. The three male terrorists slept in the chairs in the living room, and Rasha was the first one up before the others. She prepared coffee and some snacks, and then moved her and Colonel al-Adwani's bags nearer to the door. She did not know, but Ihsaan kept his eye and pistol on her constantly, all the while she moved about the room. When she stopped to pour coffee, she noticed Ihsaan's eyes open, and locked in his hand, the weapon and it was aimed right at her. Anger instantly replaced the smile she tried on the Iraqi man, as she hissed at him will all the venom she could possibly muster in his voice.

"What is the meaning of this god cursed foul insult you aim at me, you filthy camel spider you? How dare you level a god cursed weapon at me, you fool. I'll have your foul head separated from your god cursed worthless shoulders for this terrible threat leveled against me, and then I'll have the children of my village use it for a piss pot as they play with your separated head. I'm an honored Officer in my government's service, and I deserve better treatment from the likes..."

"Stop wasting your breath on my ears, daughter of the desert before I blow your head off. You think because you're an Officer in the Secret Police of Iraq that you're above suspicion and investigation? My dear whore of the night wind, no one from Iraq is above suspicion." Ihsaan hissed nastily as he moved his pistol more out in the open as a further threat against Rasha.

"No you foul fool you, I'm never above any suspicion just as you are not, but an Officer of higher rank is the only one who can aim a weapon at me, and hope he can keep his worthless head still resting on his cursed shoulders for doing so." She fired angrily right back, pleased she was finally able to get some of her anger out of her system.

Ihsaan did not reply immediately to Rasha's stinging words and threat she had just spat out of her mouth at him, he merely aimed his weapon at her chest a little more carefully, and then he actually cocked the hammer of the weapon back and continued to sneer at her.

This further warning instantly informed her and the others in the room with her, that this man was obviously an officer of higher rank in the Iraqi Secret Police himself. Even though he was an Egyptian man, he must have been enlisted by General Hassan al-Zahar himself, her boss for the duty he was carrying out for the remaining part of the terrorist group.

She immediately backed down on her angry stance she was directing against the man, and then she lowered her head in total submission to the obvious officer from her country.

"That is better, filthy whore of the desert sands. If I were to tell General al-Zahar how you were responding to this situation, I'm quite certain he'd make life extremely hard for you. The General has informed me you were to do as you're told, and nothing more, woman. You'll not make a move unless someone is with you at all times, or you inform me or Colonel al-Adwani first before you dare move is that clear woman! I have no time to waste on the likes of you!"

She nodded in the positive, wondering why she had to dress the day before her mission started. Now, she felt she was in need of a bath, and she also wanted to change her clothes again.

Colonel al-Adwani had to have some minor touch ups on his disguise, and he barked at Rasha. She moved to his side and repaired what she done the day before. When she was near his ear, she whispered softly to him. "Colonel al-Adwani Sir, do you not think it would've better served us if we waited until today to dress for our departure from the hated United States. I feel like a mess already, and worry I'll now draw special attention to us because of this bad feeling sir."

"Normally, I would've agreed with you Rasha. But I had decided to have us dress yesterday, because I didn't want to look too perfect when we arrived at the cursed airport in this country, woman. I've been in many airport terminals in the past years, and few people waiting to catch a plane, look their best when boarding the aircraft, woman." Colonel al-Adwani replied and he was also trying to whisper. The two other Arab men with them were paying no attention to the two of them speaking together at the moment.

"Ahhhh... I see what you mean by that order, Colonel al-Adwani Sir. But do you not think if we look like too much of a mess, we might draw even more attention to ourselves when boarding the god cursed aircraft, than if we were looking at our best, sir?" She was still fishing for the Colonel's approval for the concern she was displaying for his safety, as she straightened up and then she smiled at the well feared and powerful Iraqi Colonel.

"Huh! I fear even the great wisdom of Allah would have trouble having all the answers to the countless riddles of life and death, Rasha. Now, I don't truly know what to think any longer."

Al-Taai butted into their conversation by offering with a snap in his voice. "Either way sir, it's far too late to consider changing your clothes now, Colonel al-Adwani Sir. We don't have the time to and besides, I think the both of you look like god cursed American travelers, sir."

Colonel al-Adwani glared at al-Taai, but he did not respond to his last words.

Al-Taai did not like the ugly stare from the Iraqi Colonel, and he looked down and made like he was checking his watch. It was four thirty and they had about a four hour drive over to the small Carolina International Airport, depending on the flow of traffic. Al-Taai then looked up and offered to the Iraqi terrorist. "Colonel al-Adwani, I suggest we get moving about this time sir. We can always stop along the way and get something to eat if we get hungry along the way, sir. I say if you have to use the bathroom, do it now and not wait until we start our trip, sir."

"I have no need for the use of the foul bathroom, Al-Taai. Do you Rasha?"

She shook her head no, as she looked back at Colonel al-Adwani.

"Fine I believe we should leave this foul apartment now. I'll pull the car to the front of the building. You'll remain hidden in the safe house until we're certain no one is setting up a trap against us." Al-Taai offered the Colonel, to get out from under Colonel al-Adwani's harsh glare.

Colonel al-Adwani watched attentively as the two Arab men disappeared from the living room, and carried his and Rasha's bags out to the waiting car. The Iraqi Colonel stayed by the door and heard the car start. He saw the lights go on, and the car as it stopped in front of the safe house. Ihsaan stepped out of the car and opened the rear door for them. Both Rasha and Colonel al-Adwani rushed out of the building after making certain they left no evidence behind they were there. He did not take the time to lock the door behind them, from this moment on this safe house was abandoned for any future use by any other terrorist group operating in the United States. They jumped into the car, Ihsaan closed the door behind them and he raced around it and climbed into the passenger's seat. Al-Taai gunned the engine, and then he pulled away from the curb.

CAMP LEJEUNE, NORTH CAROLINA. AUGUST 3rd, 1999
4 A.M. EST

Lieutenant Robert Walker and his crew of specialized troops just finished their second night time intrusion of a simulated occupied terrorist situation inside the makeshift shoot house structure. If he only knew how close his wanted target was going to be to him and his troops within the next few hours, he would have gotten sick over it.

Colonel Bruce Leadbetter ordered the elite troops to gather outside by his control trailer before him, so he could evaluate the last exercise's success with the soldiers. The troops were thoroughly exhausted and all they wanted to do was get out of their body armor and sleep for a week. They were not in the mood to hear the Colonel rip them apart for something they did, or did not do correctly on the last training exercise inside the shoot house.

Colonel Leadbetter did not care how tired they felt, or how exhausted they were. He was going to speak to them. "Eyes!" The angry Colonel bellowed from the top step of the command trailer, as he glared at the soldiers with his hands resting almost threateningly on his hips.

The upset and exhausted soldiers took their time assembling, and they were also carrying on their own conversations and ignoring Colonel Leadbetter.

"Listen up you pack of pussy lappers! When I say eyes, all eyes better be looking directly at my ass if you know what's good for your asses. Any eyes I don't see staring back at my puss will end up sitting in my trophy case, where they can stare at me all day long, every day of the damn week. That's better you puds, I knew there was some kind of damn intelligence locked up somewhere in those thick noggins of yours. Lieutenant Walker, you could've knocked me over with a pubic hair, at how well this last action went down inside the shoot house, mister.

"The people up there at Fort Fumble, has listed anything over a sixty five percent survivors rate, as acceptable odds to any forced intrusion of a hostage situation involving a group of terrorists, Lieutenant. In case you people aren't aware of it yet, you pack of shitbirds have been averaging over eighty nine percent survival rate for the damn hostages on these last three intrusions of that shoot house building. That's outstanding for our line of work I'd say! I particularly like the way you shitbirds head upstairs, placing a hand on the back of the soldier in front of you, to help guard against him falling backwards on your asses. I also like the way you soldiers are protecting each other's backs as you ball sacks were doing on these last assaults of a compromised building. That shows me some real smarts being displayed by you pack of screwballs. Where the hell did you people pick that crap up from?"

"From Cops." Buckethead grumbled as he sat on his Kevlar helmet, and glared at the Colonel.

Another tired soldier called out that he did what the little voices in his head told him to do.

"Cops huh?" Colonel Leadbetter grumbled at the exhausted soldiers, and then he went on with his words aimed at the soldiers. "You fucking people never cease to amaze me. I can't believe you flaming asses waste your time watching that show? They can't show the real shit that goes on in the mean streets of this country, only the mild stuff." He groaned as he ignored the stupid comment from the other soldier, and then he looked for the one who spoke. Seeing Buckethead sitting on his bone dome, he got angry and thundered at him. "Hey stupid, that helmet isn't for sitting on it's not a damn seat you asshole. It's for protecting your damn noggin. Unass yourself before I come over and show you the errors in your ways of thinking, pudhead! You fuck it up again on me, and I'll make you eat the damn thing for the hell of it. You're no pussy get on your damn feet and stand like what you're supposed to be, Soldier!"

"Take it easy Colonel Leadbetter after all I was only put together with one screw you know sir." Buckethead laughed at the Marine Colonel as he stood up as he was just ordered to do.

"Hey, hey, Buckethead couldn't find his stinking dick with both hands in broad day light, Colonel Leadbetter." The Mutt yelled out as he shoved Bucket in the back with his arm.

"You people better can the crap before I ring your fucking necks for the lot of ya assholes. This ain't no game we're playing here troops. We're going after this lousy little turd who tried to assassinate your Boss, soldiers. Let's get back to evaluating the latest training exercise, so we can put an end to this day's exercises. Mother, how the hell did you know I placed a terrorist you capped in that hallway closet on you, mister? Can you now see through walls, mister?"

"Fuck if I know Colonel. I guess I just played a hunch on it, that's all sir."

"Well mister, your damn hunch paid off well for ya this time. You see people, it's not only good soldiering that makes you people what you are today. It's the ability to use your noggins once in a while for more than a damn hat rack when you're on a mission it's called independent thinking, troops. That's why I keep telling you lunatics to use your heads all the fucking time. Whether Mother knows it or not, his hunch was his using God's gifts and his own instinct for survival. This is what I mean to keep your heads on a swivel when facing a hostage situation. Remember Murphy's Law of combat thirty two. Professional soldiers are predictable, but the world is full of amateurs who don't know what the hell they're doing. Good work Mother."

"Hey Mother, remember this buddy, a stinking pat on the back's only twelve inches away from a kick in the fucking ass, man. That little bit of wisdom comes right from the Colonel's own lips, man." Wacko warned as he shoved Mother Flanagan on the back with his forearm, forcing him to take a step forward.

"Mother Flanagan's getting to be a real cheese dick lately man." (slang for a soldier sucking up to the officers) A soldier called out from the ranks, almost causing a near riot.

"Fuck you, I'll turn you into a fricking crispy critter (Burn victim) if you don't back offa my ass, sucka. Show yourself if you got the balls to step forward, and I'll snap you in half like a Slim Jim, fucker." Mother Flanagan hissed as he balled up his fists and took a fighter's stance.

"My heart dos quiver with fear." Neck growled as he stepped forward from the group.

Colonel Leadbetter was about to jump on both soldiers when Walker growled at them before he could respond to their horn busting. "I'm gonna beat the fricking snot bubbles outta both you shits if you don't step off some. Neck!" Walker called his name as if it was a four letter word. "You keep fucking up like you did in the damn shoot house, and I'm gonna break you apart and piss on all the pieces. I about had it with you and your not listening to my damn orders, straphanger. I told you to stay out in the stinking hallway with the damn sixty, and standby to lend any backup support to any insertion team that might get trapped or hung up in a situation. But nooo, you had to enter the fricking room with us, stupid. You fucked up big time in there and you coulda gotten all of us into one helluva fucking fire fight in there, stupid. You better get your head on straight and get your act unfucked, before you're dumped from the stinking outfit, you asshole. Follow your order next time shithead."

"Whaddaya expect from a damn Y chromosome Walker? You know he would forget his own name if he didn't hear it called out at least twice a day." Baby Tee called out this time.

"Hey Walker, I heard something the other day about the Neck taking an IQ test, and it came back negative, honey." Blind Date offered as she moved nearer to the Mutt for protection, in case Neck lost it and he went after everyone busting his horns. She enjoyed getting on the men for any mistake they might have committed whenever she could.

"Oh great, now the damn bitches are gonna get on my stinking case I see. Here you foreign rope swallower, you wanna flap your stinking jaws on something. Why don't you put a damn lip lock on this shaft here?" Neck grabbed his crotch through the armor.

"Don't worry about him baby sister, the Neck has enough trouble getting into his own pants, let alone trying to get into yours, Blind Date." Another male soldier offered her.

"Hey Baby, Neck will stay in your pretty face longer than a fucking blackhead." Dock Rat, (Sergeant James McNulty) fired off with a grin. He was standing next to the smallish woman.

"Hey Rat Man shouldn't you be off shoplifting some fricking watermelons or something for yourself, man? It looks like the damn sewer pipe musta backed up while you were still being percolated in your mama's gut, big mouth. You sure your stinking daddy used the right fricking hole to make you? You sure your mama didn't shit you outta her backside, man?" Neck growled at Dock Rat in an angry tone, trying to repay him for getting on his ass like he was doing in front of the rest of the elite troopers.

"Are you trying to intimidate my stinking ass here, Homes? You betta fuhgedaboutit man, my mama has more fricking attitude than your big ass does sucka." Dock Rat replied, not giving into the massive Neck's angry prodding.

Baby Tee was not afraid by Neck's nasty gesture, and she made some mouth movements.

"He bitch, I haven't seem movements with a pair of lips like that, since the last time I gave my stinking dog a fricking tootie roll to eat." Dock Rat offered as he stared at Baby Tee's face.

Tee shoved him across the chest with her weapon, causing the other soldiers with her to roar with laughter as he almost tripped over his own feet from the shove Tee just gave him.

"Gees, I need a fucking aspirin." Colonel Leadbetter moaned at no soldier in particular in the group, as he rubbed his temples with the palms of his hands, giving up on the specialized soldiers for now, as he added at them. "Crap, there isn't enough fucking aspirin in the whole damn world to cure the headache you sacks of shit give me every damn day I have to deal with you bag of nuts, dammit. Yeah, it looks like I got myself stuck with the cream of the crap here alright."

The Colonel realized it was impossible to speak to these soldiers when they got like this, and they were really dumping on each other now, as he went on with his words to the troops. "I'm not going to stand here while devouring time on the likes of you damn shitbirds here. But there's something I have to inform you shitbirds about before I'm done with you slobs. The poets of propaganda at Fort Fumble have leaked a story about our FBI and Special Agents backing off some on their search for this missing ball sack. They're hoping to cause this missing turd to make a damn mistake, and come out in the open where we can get our damn hands on his ass.

"If the dumb ass plan works, it looks like the police might do our job for us, troops. Look people, I'm not fond of placing you soldiers out in the field flooded with crazy ass civilians running all over the damn place. If the police can't get the damn job done then we'll go to the ends of the damn earth searching for this lousy little prick. Get down to the mess hall and get yourselves something to eat, and then hit the fricking racks while you can. The next training exercise is scheduled at exactly Zero, Ten, Thirty Hours, and it'll be a graded one, troops."

Groans filled the air around the gathered soldiers, as they started to move out as ordered to go and get something to eat before the next exercise started. Most of the elite soldiers wanted to lie down and get some rest more than they wanted to eat something.

The Colonel was not in the mood to let anything further escape his wrath, as he barked at the slow moving soldiers. "Listen up you ball sacks. There are two things you people can do about it, nothing, and like it. Anyone not here at that time will have to answer to my ass, personally. Get your asses in gear before I start kicking any asses I still see hanging around here, people."

More grumbles filled the air, as the soldiers picked up their gear and headed for their barracks. Moss (Sergeant Cathy Stillwater) headed for the barracks she was more tired than hungry.

EAGLE'S NEST

Colonel Leadbetter watched the soldiers leave, and Sergeant John Kirkpatrick joined him on the steps of the trailer and announced. "That's one helluva bunch of soldiers you have there sir."

"Yeah, when they get back to the shoot house for the next exercise, I want a live ammo intrusion set up for this exercise, Sergeant. This time we're going to place terrorists inside two rooms on all three floors of the structure. I intend to make the soldiers work their asses off for their stinking money for a change around here, mister. Get moving on my last orders, Sergeant."

"Gees Colonel, you ain't got no heart for the poor slobs, sir." The Sergeant offered.

"You have a problem with that, or my training program of these soldiers, mister?" He turned to his Sergeant and placed his hands on his hips, as he waited for his reply to his question.

"No sir, not at all Colonel. The training of the troops is going great for us, sir."

"Fine Sergeant Kirkpatrick, I didn't think you did. Setup for the next training exercise, and have Sergeant Ramirez placed on the third floor for grading purposes on this one. That's going to be the hardest room to get any hostages out of this fucking situation alive. If you think I'm being kind of hard ass on these lousy puds, that girl won't cut these pud fuckers any slack at all."

"Will do sir." The Sergeant offered as he went about his business, setting up the exercise.

CHAPTER SEVENTEEN

HIGHWAY I-95, NORTH CAROLINA. 8:10 EST

Al-Taai kept an eye on his watch and the speed of his vehicle at the same time. He was pleased they were making such good time while traveling on I-95. He decided to take a quick break, and get something to eat for the group. He saw a sign offering a McDonald's restaurant just off the side of the road, and he aimed his car for the exit.

"What the devil are you doing now, you foul fool? Why are you turning off this god cursed road for?" Colonel al-Adwani hissed from the rear seat of the car.

"Colonel al-Adwani Sir, we're currently well ahead of our schedule, and besides sir. I'm rather hungry and I figure we can take a little time to enjoy this minor luxury and have something to eat, and then relieve ourselves if need be, and still arrive on time for your scheduled flight out of this foul country, Colonel."

Al-Adwani looked at Rasha and she nodded as she offered to the Iraqi Military Officer. "Colonel al-Adwani, I'm terribly sorry sir. But I'm afraid that I do have to go to the bathroom. It would also be good to stretch our legs for a moment and have something to eat, sir."

Colonel al-Adwani looked at the back of the head of the driver and then grumbled nastily at him. "It's wise you're suggesting this break in our driving, al-Taai. I guess I can do with a little something to eat myself, fool. Let's take the time now then." He stared out the windshield as the car slowly pulled into the parking lot. When it stopped, Rasha climbed out of the car first, and she headed right for the female restrooms on the side of the building.

Ihsaan got out of the car and followed her to the restrooms. He did not think twice about entering the female bathrooms with her. He stared at her as she went in one of the stalls to relieve herself. He relieved himself in a sink, and then he waited for her to finish up and then come out of the stall. When she did, she glared harshly at Ihsaan, he sneered back at her and she followed him out of the bathroom. As they were leaving the restroom another female entered, and when she saw Ihsaan she snapped hotly at him. "Hey, this is the ladies room, mister."

"You show me a lady in here woman, and I'll bow to her presence, you filthy pig."

The woman glared at Ihsaan, as he and the young woman left the bathroom.

"Ihsaan, do you not think it would have better served our purpose, to be a little more polite to a stranger, than by drawing even more angry attention to yourself and the rest for us by challenging anyone you come across in this foul restaurant, fool?"

"You mind yourself and your own foolish actions, and I'll take care of mine, desert pig."

She hated this man more with each passing second she was forced to be in his ugly presence, and she rushed back to Colonel al-Adwani and al-Taai who had already ordered food for them. She sat down by Colonel al-Adwani's side directly across from al-Taai. Ihsaan took the seat across from Rasha and he openly glared at her all the while he prepared to start eating his meal. They all ate their food in silence.

The woman Ihsaan insulted moments ago in the bathroom, entered the restaurant and went to her boyfriend and whispered to him. When they stopped speaking, the young man rose from their table and walked over to al-Adwani's table with a swagger in his walk, and he hissed while looking directly at Ihsaan. "Hey pal, you have a fucking problem with my girlfriend?"

"I have no problem with her, she is a lowly pig." Ihsaan snarled angrily at the concerned man, not bothering to turn to face the young stranger snapping at him.

"How would you like it if I ripped your fucking head off your lousy shoulders, and then I pissed down your fucking throat for you, wiseguy? That's my girl you're cursing buster and I don't like it." The young man took a threatening stance against Ihsaan as he waited for the man to reply.

"I don't think I would like that very much I believe young man. But I do know you'll not try that foolish mistake against me, young fool." Ihsaan hissed as nastily as he could possible speak as he finally turned and looked up at the angry young boyfriend.

"Yeah, and why is that buddy? You think your friends here are going to help you fight me?"

"No friends, just one of my friends will help me fight you, young fool." Ihsaan leaned a little to the right and removed the Glock 9 mm pistol and laid it down on the table before him, and then he snapped at the young man again. "I am Police Officer, and this woman is under arrest, fool. That is why I followed her into the woman's bathroom if you must know about my business mister. I'm sorry if I insulted your lady but she opened her mouth and I responded, young man."

The younger kid stared at the weapon lying on the table for a long moment, and then he quickly turned on his heels and he rushed back to his girlfriend seeking revenge for being insulted by the stranger in the woman's bathroom moments ago. Ihsaan watched out of the corner of his eye as they both whispered excitedly together again for a few moments and then they quickly paid their bill and left the restaurant as fast as they could leave.

Ihsaan handled the incident well, but Colonel al-Adwani was angry as hell there was a confrontation in the bathroom in the first place, and he leaned forward and growled harshly at the young Arab man. "What the hell is the matter with you foolish self, Ihsaan. I have to keep a low profile here if I ever hope to leave this miserable country of sin and lust in one piece, you fool. I don't need you making any further problems for us than we already have following us, you fool. I shall report this serious mistake on your part to your Superior Officer when we are safely back in Iraq, and then your insolence will be handled properly by your control."

"You can report anything you please to whoever will lend a cursed ear to hear your worthless complaint, for all the good it shall do you, Colonel al-Adwani." Ihsaan glared hard and long at Colonel al-Adwani, displaying absolutely no fear of the power the terrorist thought he commanded back in their country over him.

Colonel al-Adwani knew he could ill afford a war of words in a public place with the upsetting Ihsaan, and he decided to let it lay for the time being. He finished eating his meal, and then he kicked Rasha lightly under the table, and she finished eating her food quickly. Al-Taai left the restaurant first and he filled the car with gas.

Rasha, Colonel al-Adwani and Ihsaan got up and they slowly walked outside the restaurant after paying for their meals so they did not draw any special attention towards their movements. It was a beautiful day out for early August, warm, but not too hot yet. The trio headed for the car and al-Taai. Once everyone was inside the vehicle and comfortable, al-Taai gunned the engine and then he pulled onto the road. He took the entrance ramp and shot out onto I-95 heading south again. The rest of the trip was completed mostly in a very strained silence, with Colonel al-Adwani answering any questions put to him, by either of the two men riding in the front seat of the car, or by Rasha with a sharp response and not engaging in further conversation.

Rasha rested with her head leaning against the back seat of the car. But before she settled in to try and take a quick catnap, she carefully straightened her dress out the best she could in the vehicle, and then she fussed around a little bit with her hair and when she was satisfied with her appearance again, she closed her eyes to sneak in a little rest.

CAMP LEJEUNE, JACKSONVILLE NORTH CAROLINA. 10:30 A.M. EST, AUGUST 3rd, 1999

Colonel Bruce Leadbetter stood on the top step of the command trailer with his hands resting threateningly on his hips, as the elite group of troopers slowly assembled before him, dressed in their full body armor and carrying their weapons like they weighed a ton. He could see most of them were still suffering from a serious lack of sleep and food and exhaustion and he smiled. He felt this time the troops would screw up real bad inside the shoot house, and he would then have a chance to get on their backs and bust their horns over their failures. As the Colonel glared at the gathered soldiers, his assistants set up the dummies to be slaughtered by

Lieutenant Walker's assault crew, and Sergeant Kirkpatrick checked the connections for the computers and sensors to the dummies. The Colonel knew they were falling a little behind their schedule and were not ready for the troops to enter the building just now, so he decided to do a little stalling, by speaking to the troops before letting them go in action for this training exercise.

"Okay people listen up this is important dammit. I want to go over a few things with you asses before we start, so you people know exactly where the hell you stand, and what you're going to be facing in the future. This urban fighting crap's a load of new shit for most of us to absorb, so there are some rules you must keep in mind at all times. If you're sent out to any other nation, or city of this country, you're to act as if you're fighting a fricking guerrilla war. And make no mistakes about it people, it's a stinking guerrilla war you'll be fighting, but against a bunch of fucking amateurs this time around, people. That makes these nutty little bastards the worse fucking problem fighters we'll ever be going up against, dammit.

"Let me explain why I say this is going to be a guerrilla war. In a guerrilla war, ground doesn't mean jack shit to anyone involved in the action, it's all about punishing your fucking enemy with extreme malice to make them suffer and absorb terrible causalities. Until they reach the point where the assholes have to stop the bleeding, and they can't continue on with their quest and they finally quit fighting. These flaming assholes who want to call themselves terrorists will fight all night long, but when the sun comes up and we can see them, they're not going to be stupid enough to stand and fight with a Unit of professional soldier's toe to toe and nose to nose, people. The terrorists wouldn't last ten fucking seconds against real and tried fighters such as you troops are. The terrorists thrive in the fucking background, the shadows, they do they best work in the dark. So we have to use different tactics when dealing with shits like these.

"Once you people are active and out in the field, if and when any of these asses attack, you'll simply adopt the tactic of withdrawing from the area and lead them into traps you have set up before you advanced into the trouble zone in the first place. Once they get chopped up in a few heavy crossfire's, they'll withdraw sure enough, and that's when you people will advance again and really cripple or just wipe them out in that action. Simple enough people.

EAGLE'S NEST

"When you people are sent in on a surgical strike such as this one might turn out to be for us, and you have to take a fucking prisoner in a hostile land, and bring him out of the area alive. You're going to be forced to work in reverse of your usual training. You'll own the night, and hide during the day. You'll stalk your damn targets until you know how they act and breath, and then you'll determine the proper time and place to make the snatch of your intended target. You'll drug the sonofabitch up, blind fold the lousy bastard, and then you'll drag his ass out of his miserable nation of flaming assholes. You might even be forced to have troops act as trailers, to lay down a suppressing fire against anyone who might be trying to free your target, or attack your group's flanks as you disconnect your involvement with the damn terrorists.

"Once you people have your target secured, I'll make damn certain you people in the field have enough air and other support assets in the surrounding area, in case the shit gets too thick for you people to handle with the weapons you have available for your use. I'll also have an emergency E-vac system set up in case you have too many of his friends trying to get him back from you people. I can pull this air cover from the aircraft performing picket duty over the two no fly zones in fucking Iraq. Once you have this shitbird under your control, I want him taken out of Iraq in one piece, so he can stand before the President of the United States, and the President can kick him right square in the fucking chops if he so desires. I want this lousy little bastard in one stinking piece, but if you can't get him, or you're taking causalities, ice the dumb fuck and then evacuate the area immediately. Execute him immediately, film it so the President can see his revenge was carried out on the lousy asshole.

"Then, you people will change hats in the middle of this possible mission, and you'll make it to the EX, (Extraction Rendezvous) point that's marked clearly out in purple on your damn funny papers, (maps) for immediate removal post haste from the host nation. This mission is being classified as a SAS, a Spot And Snatch mission. But at any time during the mission, if conditions call for it, it can go over to an ASP mission, Aim, Sight and Pull. If this shit happens and you carry out this part of the operation, you people will go into an EAE (Escape And Evasion) mode and FBEP. (Fall Back to Extraction Point) Before entering any of the three purple positions marked on your maps as EPs, (Extraction Points) one soldier is to do a creep and check out the surrounding area of any EP before the rest of you enter the damn extraction zone.

"If any hostels happen to be spotted in or near the Extradition Point, that soldier will realize the area is compromised and he's to call an EXFIL, Exfiltration. For any of you birds who might have slept through this class, it meaning rescue help to possible hot Extraction Point, possible enemy troops waiting for Unit in the safety Extraction Zone. Then I'll turn this end of the fucking mission into a SLAM operation, that's a Search, Locate, and Annihilate Mission, taking out any and all possible threats aimed against you and your troops, Walker. Once we're certain this slug worked for the Iraqi government, all bets are off and I'll turn them all into gun chum. Look here troops, these low intensity conflicts engaging terrorist activities, are nothing more than dirty little wars that violates all normal and respected rules of military conduct and engagement.

"We must act accordingly against them if we intend to place a quick stop to any further such attacks carried out against our or any of our Allies soil. If they want to act like fucking shit then we're going to wallow in the crap along with them to get at the lousy bastards and set them straight. Make no mistake about it people for one fucking moment, this is a shit magnet mission, and we're going to end up eating some garbage before its conclusion I can tell you troops that much. While we're training here, anyone's free to ask for any special skull secessions at any time of the day or night, if you want anything clarified for you pack of criminals. I don't need anyone second guessing themselves in A-rab land, or being confused about their parameters for this damn mission. This is my Head Shed, (HQ) and I'll be here for any questions and answers at any time they crop up for any of you people both day and night."

A wave of a hand by one of the assistants drew Leadbetter's attention, and he informed him the shoot house structure was ready for immediate action. The Colonel instantly bellowed at his troops. "Okay troops, let's get hot, the fucking game starts as of this time dammit. AMC(At My Command) ATT, (Advance To Target). Move it out people."

The soldiers left singing a desert song, 'Rudolph the red nose camel', thinking they were going to get stuck going back in Iraq for the Christmas holidays. Colonel Leadbetter smile, pleased his troops were in this type of good and confident mood.

Lieutenant Walker's troops moved out as if warned about the terrorist takeover of the training building. This was the first training exercise scheduled to involve every floor of the entire shoot complex this time as a compromised situation. The first floor was attacked by the troops with silenced weapons, to avoid informing the other terrorists they were taking over the complex. Walker had Neck and Buckethead with him, and they plowed into the first office with Walker dropping to the floor and banging the first two terrorist with weapon fire. Neck splashed the other two supposed terrorists caught inside the room while Buckethead stayed ready to erase any possible leakers. One hostage was classified wounded in the hard hitting action.

All the while Walker and the rest of his following troops cleared the first floor of the training building of any would be possible terrorists. Mother Flanagan took the rest of the Unit up to the second floor of the structure. A Blackhawk helicopter hovered over the complex in whisper mode, and the soldiers Dock Rat, Blind Date, Snatch and Wacko tossed the eighty foot ropes out both sides of the helicopter, and then they fast repelled down to the roof of the supposed compromised building. They were going to infiltrate the third floor of the shoot house structure from the roof area, and then coordinate their attack with Mother Flanagan's hit team working over the second floor of the training structure.

Colonel Leadbetter was enjoying watching the fast and hard hitting action taking place inside the shoot house immensely. He particularly liked how Lieutenant Walker set up the hits on the compromised building from both the ground and air. Although he knew the dummies did not respond as quickly as real terrorists normally would, the Lieutenant made a real show of getting to the hostages better than any Pentagon bigwigs believed was possible. He knew it was by his orders, that the helo was being used in this operation, but it was him calling the shots in the field, and he was making the best use of his assets and troops on the ground.

Once Walker's group successfully cleared the first floor of the shoot house structure of all supposed terrorists and they freed the simulated hostages on that floor, he quickly assumed the follow on role of protecting the leading element of the assault team working on the second floor of the structure. Mother, the Ghost, Hunter, Siberia and Caviar, a Russian Sergeant on loan to the United States for the hit team, picked the first office they knew the terrorist were hold up in along with a number of hostages. McNip, Nentendo, (Sergeant Nasayoshi Nakamura), the Mutt, Baby Tee, Roach and Hardon, (Sergeant Leslie Horner) spread out and protected the doors to the offices they knew other terrorists and hostages were supposedly stationed in.

The soldier branded Coco-G stayed in the center of the hall with the M-60 held at ready as backup for the attacking troops. Sun Tan was the second heavy, armed with his M-60. Just Bob, Weird Bill, Three Martines, (Sergeant Cheryl Grantham) and Plus Ugly, (Sergeant Jerry Rudnick) broke off, and they headed for the third floor to help support the roof penetration team.

The first office hit on the second floor of the shoot house building, classified as the terrorists main headquarters, once this room was neutralized, the infiltration troops prepared to hit the rest of the rooms at the same instant on the same floor. The attack went off like clockwork for the invading troops, with all the terrorists being splashed at almost the same instant as the troops smashed into the compromised rooms. Nine of the thirty so called hostages were classified as wounded during this part of the fast and hard hitting operation, with just two hostages being classified as hit bad enough to be rated as killed in the wide sweeping intrusion. Twenty three other terrorists armed with various weapons were also classified as splashed in the action.

Only one room on the third floor was where most hostages were wounded or killed by the rapid intrusion troop's actions. It was being observed and rated by Sergeant Ramirez, and she was not being kind to the penetrating troops in this fast moving action. Even hostage dummies that were not directly hit by rounds fired in the room were marked down as wounded by Ramirez. If she felt any bouncing rounds came close enough to them to have hit them. She also judged this by seeing the movement of the hostages in her mind's eye, if they were normal breathing and scared persons, moving into the incoming rounds as nature would have deem them to do, to try and save their lives when her soldiers attacked the terrorists inside her compromised room.

This room was a set up from start to finish by Colonel Leadbetter, and he had wisely dumped nine terrorist and five hostage dummies in this one room. Again he wanted to create a possible no win situation for his invading troops on this training exercise, and this was done to ensure this situation, and he placed Ramirez inside the bulletproof enclosure inside the room, knowing she would be the hardest on judging the elite troop's latest actions during this training exercise. He was correct in his way of thinking about the female Sergeant.

Snatch, (Sergeant George Weaver) and Blind Date, (Sergeant Regina Raphael), on loan to the United States hunter team from France, checked Ramirez's score card, and they started to bitch at her staggering tally of kills and wounded delivered to the supposed hostages trapped in this one room. The two extremely upset soldiers tried everything in their power to convince her she erred in her tally of the wounded and killed hostages in the room, before Colonel Leadbetter came up and reamed the soldier's new assholes for killing and wounding so many of the supposed hostages. Sergeant Ramirez ignored all their complaints, and only when Walker stormed into the room, did the other soldiers finally back off their attack on Ramirez.

His harsh glare was more than enough to back the complaining soldiers off the female Sergeant, as Walker went up to Ramirez and opened the protective divider she was secured behind. He kissed her, and growled at the same time. "What the hell was that crap about, baby?"

"Lieutenant Walker, they're pissed off at me, because I rated some of the hostages not hit outright by their rounds, as being wounded by their wild fire in my estimated judgment."

"How the hell is that shit you got going down there Raz? I thought if the fricking dummies didn't take a direct hit by us, they weren't to be classified as wounded in the action?"

"Look Bobby, when the assault team first came charging in the room wildly shooting as they did, they sprayed rounds all over the place without truly aiming at their supposed targets. Mind you Robert, I'm not saying it wasn't controlled fire offered by the attacking soldiers, but they could have been a little more careful with their expenditure of rounds, and their aim as well inside the room, Bobby. They know and understand full well that they're not to SAP (Spray And Pray) any rounds during a hostile intrusion when hostages are involved in the military action. There were so many rounds flying about in the room, I decided some of the supposed trapped hostages would've normally ran into some of them, while trying to get out of the soldier's direct line of fire, in an attempt to try and save their own lives during the hot intrusion of the American troops into the compromised room. I'm really sorry but that's the way I saw it go down Bobby."

"C'mon baby, you're being a little heavy handed on the dumb shits here, why not cut them some slack, not flack will ya. You know if Colonel Fuckface sees this many wounded and killed hostages in this one room. Then we're all gonna find ourselves stuck running another fucking assault action on the shoot house structure sometime today. Most of my people are already dead on their feet as it is. If we're forced to run another assault action on the god damn shoot house building, there's gonna be an outright fucking slaughter in here, and we're all gonna loose our rating we racked up on these fucking training exercises, honey. If you change your score card just a wee bit, I'll give you one helluva mustache ride tonight, honey." Walker offered a little bribe of sex, knowing how Ramirez loved whenever he got his face down between her legs.

She giggled, but it was cut off by someone bellowing at them from behind them.

"Hey shithead! It's Colonel Fuckface Sir, to you mister." Colonel Leadbetter snarled as he stormed into his set up room, followed closely by Sergeant Kirkpatrick, carrying the stack of score cards already collected from the other rooms and raters in his hands.

"Let me tell you something mister, if Ramirez changes anything on her fucking score card to make you slobs look any better than you shits were on this training exercise. Then she's going to end up having that little bastard she's carrying in her gut by the side of a snow dune, while pulling extra duty at the North fucking Pole, mister. No one in this damn Unit changes any reports for any reason around here, once it's written down on fucking paper. Stand down and back the fuck off her Lieutenant Walker. Ramirez, lemme see your damn score card will ya." Leadbetter held out his hand and wiggled his fingers and Ramirez turned over her rating card.

Ramirez moved over to the side, as Colonel Leadbetter scanned the hits she scored on her card and mumbled to the Sergeant, and the soldiers who followed him into the room. "Hmmmm... I never took in consideration any hostages might move into the line of fire, while they're trying to save their asses in this action, Sergeant. Good work there Sergeant Ramirez."

While Leadbetter read over Ramirez's score tally, Walker kept busy scanning the interior of the room, and when he realized how the Colonel had set him up in the room, he grew pissed as he fired angrily at the Colonel. "Hey Colonel, I think you set us up on this fucking room, sir. Seeing the way the supposed terrorists were packed in this god damn room, you made it completely impossible for us to do any better than we did in here, sir. Shit Colonel, ain't our fricking job hard enuf already, without you making it even worse on our stinking asses by setting up some impossible winning scenarios on our fucking asses, sir?"

The Colonel turned to Walker as he handed Sergeant Kirkpatrick Ramirez's card. He drew in his breath as he studied Walker's face staring at him for a few moments, and then he grumbled at the excited soldier. "Look Lieutenant Walker, you have to be prepared for anything taking place against you during any and every hostage situation event you and these troops are involved in, buster. This ain't no fucking game we're playing here mister! You think a terrorist is going to play by the usual rules of combat when you engage them?

"No way in unholy hell would they ever, Soldier. There are going to be times when you're going to be expected to enter a room with only one hostage, and ten terrorist or more in it, and be anticipated to bring that one fucking hostage out alive, bug eater. Look here Walker, in case you're not aware of it, your pack of shits sticks did far better than I dared thought possible. This damn room was classified as a death room, meaning no one was expected to survive in it when your troops entered this compromised room. Quite frankly mister, I'm fucking amazed any of your people were able to save two of the damn supposed hostages trapped in here, mister."

Colonel Leadbetter checked his watch again, it was already eleven thirty and he saw the exhaustion etched deeply in Walker's tired eyes, and he decided to give the troops some slack time to catch up on some of their rest and feed out. He knew he was pushing his people beyond their endurance, but he had orders from General White to get his people ready for anything coming at them. He was going to follow his orders to the letter, even at the expense of his soldiers. The Colonel let out his breath in almost a hiss, and then he ordered the troops to break off from the training exercise, and go and get some hot food, and then some needed rest. He watched as the soldiers prepared to leave the shoot house area.

COLUMBIA AIRPORT, NORTH CAROLINA, 10:35 A.M. EST. TUESDAY, AUGUST 3rd, 1999

Al-Taai pulled his vehicle in the hourly parking lot of the small South Carolina Airport, and he jammed the car in park. Ihsaan was the first one out of the machine, and he rushed for the rear door and opened it for Colonel Abdulaziz Majdal al-Adwani to exit the vehicle. The Colonel got out of the car and Ihsaan went to the rear of the vehicle and opened the trunk for them. Rasha was left to her own and she slid across the rear seat of the vehicle and got out while Ihsaan emptied the trunk of their luggage. He carried al-Adwani's bags to the airport terminal, while allowing Rasha to carry her own luggage. As the group reached the sidewalk, a sky cap appeared with a cart and took the bags for the two would be passengers.

Colonel al-Adwani glanced at his watch, it was ten thirty a.m., and their flight was not scheduled to leave the airport until eleven thirty a.m. It was good they arrived an hour before their scheduled flight was to take off. The South Carolina Airport was small, and it was only because al-Adwani's passport identified him as working for the airport security, that enabled him to get a flight out from this small airport over the Canadian border at this time.

The pleasant young sky cap followed the three men and one woman to the American Airlines ticket counter, and they waited to get taken care of. The female boarding clerk asked for his airline tickets, and Colonel al-Adwani passed the folders over to the young woman. She glanced at the seal printed at the top of the folder and knew this man standing before her worked for the airlines. She smiled kindly at the Iraqi Colonel as she pulled up the information and asked him kindly. "Do you have a current photo Identification please, sir?"

Colonel al-Adwani offered the doctored up drivers ID to the pretty young clerk next.

The attendant looked at the picture for a moment, and compared it to Colonel al-Adwani's face with a quick glance as she offered. "Mr. Rosenberg, Flight Four, Fifty, Four is on schedule sir."

When the sky cap heard the flight number announced by the young woman, he quickly disappeared with their luggage.

Al-Taai remained standing with the car and weapons, in case he had to assist Colonel al-Adwani in an escape if anything went wrong with his boarding the aircraft.

"Mr. Roseberg, you may wait for your flight to take off in Lounge Seven if you'd like sir." The flight clerk offered in a sweet voice and she continued with her advice. "It's mainly reserved for friends and family of the airlines, sir. Flight Four, Fifty, Four will be departing from Gate Three, Mr. Roseberg Sir. We request everyone scheduled for this flight, be gathered by the Gate fifteen minutes before the scheduled departure time, sir. I wish to thank you for choosing American Airlines to fly with sir, and please have a good flight, and remember to always fly American when you need to be someplace and be there on time, sir." The young female flight attendant offered Colonel al-Adwani his ticket folders back, and then she smiled a smile that would have melted butter on the table.

"I always do young lady." He replied smugly, as he stuffed the tickets back in his breast pocket. As he waited for the flight attendant to finish up dealing with Rasha's tickets, he scanned the smallish terminal for any possible special agents lurking about it. His military eye picked out three undercover police officers checking the faces of everyone reporting in for their flights.

Rasha did likewise, and when she picked up two other obvious plain clothes security guards checking people out in the terminal with their eyes, she undid her jacket and pulled it off her shoulders and looped it over her right arm. Every male eye in the entire air flight terminal went to her outfit and body. The bra barely covered her nipples, and the brown crown was able to be seen over the rim of the small half bra she wore. The effect was exactly what she planned for when she first picked out this outfit to wear for her flight.

Every male eye followed Rasha's movement as she slowly and sexily walked over to the VIP Lounge. Some of the more brazen men even followed the three young people into the lounge. One agent decided to follow them, not out of suspicion, but to enjoy a closer look at the view this stunning young woman was offering them. When the trio entered the Lounge, all suspicion of them being part of the terrorist group, was erased from their presence. Each special agent knew what the VIP Lounge meant for anyone entering it.

Colonel al-Adwani ordered a Pepsi without ice, Rasha ordered a cup of sweet tea, and when it arrived at their table, they began sipping the liquids in silence. Ihsaan continued to scan the entire lounge area for any possible problems cropping up against them, his fingers drumming nervously on the table surface.

Rasha was the only one who smoked, and was doing so while waiting the call for her flight to be announced. The three Arabs engaged in small talk and sipped their drinks, waiting for their flight to be called. The agent that followed the three into the lounge area grew bored after a short while, and he left to watch over the rest of the terminal.

When no one from his team rushed out of the terminal, al-Taai finally allowed himself to relax, and he began to fuss around with the car to have something for himself to do, while he continued to wait for his partner to come out of the terminal so they could leave the area. A police car slowly passed by him, the driver staring at al-Taai as he drove by, and then continued on with his patrol without bothering him.

The hour flew by quickly, and when the announcement for all passengers scheduled for Flight Four, Fifty Four finally came to begin to assemble at Gate Three. Colonel al-Adwani quickly rose, followed by Ihsaan. Ihsaan shook hands with Colonel al-Adwani, and then he kissed Rasha on the side of her cheek and walked them over to the gate, to make certain nothing went wrong with their boarding of the aircraft. Neither Iraqi Colonel al-Adwani nor Rasha had any carryon luggage with them, their luggage was already checked in for the flight.

Ihsaan walked with al-Adwani until they stopped by a steel gate, a metal detector frame, and an X-ray machine. Three armed police officers were on the other side of the security gate, along with two other men dressed in expensive suits and ties.

They checked everyone out as they went through the security gate and checking machines. Colonel al-Adwani removed his keys, loose change and a pen from his pockets, and placed them in the offered tray. Then he walked through the metal detector while holding his breath, fearing the machine might scream out a warning signal, and alert the security guards to his presence at the air terminal. It remained silent. Rasha walked right through the machine displaying not a care in the world expression on her face. Her outfit had no pockets in it, and she already placed her purse in the X-ray machine. It was waiting for her on the other side of the boarding gate.

As Colonel al-Adwani retrieved his items, one of the men dressed in the suit approached and asked politely of him. "Sir, do you mind if I ask you where you're heading today, and what is the reason for your flight, sir?"

Colonel al-Adwani did as Rasha instructed and instantly stuffed a small hard candy in his dry mouth, when this man asked him a question. The Iraqi Colonel knew this man had something to do with airport security, and he answered him pleasantly. "No not in the lease sir. I'm heading for the Montreal Airport today sir, to try and correct a slight malfunction in one of their main airport security computers, sir. Why do you ask this of me sir? Is there a problem sir?"

The candy had the desired affect, it nearly hid his Arab accent completely, and it made it hard for the security agent to understand what Colonel al-Adwani was saying to him.

"No reason at all sir, so I take it you work for the airlines then sir?" The concerned agent asked Colonel al-Adwani.

"No, not really sir, but if you must know a little more about my business on this day sir, I happen to work for IBM. It's one of our main line security computers that's causing the Canadians some fits up there, sir." Al-Adwani was well coached by Rasha, and he knew when to add a bit of sarcasm in his tone of voice, when he was forced to answer any questions for the security agents of the airport.

"Oh, I see, sir. Well sir, please enjoy your flight then. I take it that is your wife traveling with you today, sir?"

"Yes sir if it's any of your business, we intend to take some time for ourselves on this business trip, for a little pleasure while we're at it, mister. Use it as sort of a second honey moon I guess. Why are you asking me all these personal questions, sir? Do you happen to work for the airlines as well sir? If not I'm going to report you to the airport security and have them check you out, sir." Colonel al-Adwani asked and then warned the man questioning him as he allowed a slight concern come into his tone as he popped another candy in his mouth.

"Cough drops sir?" The agent asked as if an afterthought, as he ignored al-Adwani's last questions, and continued to eye him cautiously for the last time.

"No, I'm afraid it's a childhood weakness, just candy sir." Al-Adwani replied to the agent.

"I understand the weakness perfectly sir. I have a few of them kind of weaknesses of my own sir." The obvious special agent snapped as if he was suddenly bored with Colonel al-Adwani's uninteresting response to any of his questions. He stepped aside and allowed the two strangers to board the aircraft. The agent stepped in front of the next passenger, and then he began to ask him a series of questions also.

Rasha caught up to Colonel al-Adwani, and grasped his hand and gave it a light squeeze as she leaned up against him and whispered so only he could hear what she was saying to him. "You did wonderful, Mr. Roseberg. There's no way he can possibly be suspicious of you now."

Outside the boarding gate, when the man dressed in the suit approached and blocked al-Adwani's way, Ihsaan tensed up as his hand covertly checked his weapon. He stared at the man questioning Colonel al-Adwani, not removing his eyes from the man for an instant, until he stepped aside and allowed al-Adwani to proceed with his boarding of the aircraft. Then, he rushed out of the terminal as fast as he dared move. Ihsaan never expected to see any special agents hanging around such a small airport. He realized the FBI played a mind game with them, when they announced they were cutting back their security precautions at many of the airports. He rushed to the car and jumped in it and instructed al-Taai to leave the area quickly.

When al-Adwani and Rasha were shown to their seats over the left wing of the aircraft, he let out his breath in a deep sigh and wiped his brow and offered. "Rasha, you were most wise about the god cursed candy trick. That idea has completely erased your many mistakes of the past while we were on this mission for our country. If it was not for you and your wisdom of the security precautions employed by the god cursed Americans at their foul airports. I'm certain I would've been arrested by that lowly man questioning me. I'll make such a report known to your superiors when we're safe in Iraq. You have earned yourself the ranking of Colonel First Class on this foul day Rasha, and I'll make certain you're awarded that when we're safe back in the lands of our great ancestors." Colonel al-Adwani turned to the window and watched as the aircraft was loaded with luggage, and a horde of airport personnel went over every inch of the outside of the aircraft as they waited for takeoff.

Rasha smiled, she did not tell Colonel al-Adwani she was a Colonel of the first class in the secret police already. All of a sudden, all the terrible experiences and beating she endured at the hands of Colonel al-Adwani, did not seem all that bad to her now as she warned the Iraqi Officer. "Mr. Roseberg, you must remember to remove the words we use in our country while we're in transit, until we reach the pure sands of our country." She then closed her eyes and leaned her head back in the seat, and she also sighed deeply and allowed herself to relax a little.

In what seemed like hours to Colonel al-Adwani, the aircraft finally started its engines, and then it slowly pulled out onto the long and narrow runway. He waited while the aircraft aimed itself in the wind, and then it shot down the runway at breakneck speed, while increasing its speed for full takeoff power. He grinned when the jetliner slowly climbed in the clouds, it then make a slow turn towards the north. Now, he knew he was home free. Once safely out of the hated lands of the United States, he felt no one would ever again challenge him as the worthless American authorities have done before he was able to escape their evil country.

He turned to his side and looked at Rasha, already sound asleep on him. He looked at her sitting there, she obviously straightened out her dress, and she must have fussed with her hair a bit, because it looked almost perfect again. He smiled at her, thankful for her warning about using words that would prove to the world he was an Arab as they traveled.

Now, he realized what she meant. If he was to judge her, he would swear she was nothing more than a thoroughly exhausted American traveler, waiting for her trek to finally end for her. Giving into the needs of his body, he rested his head against the seat and then he closed his eyes and willed himself to fall off to sleep.

CHAPTER EIGHTEEN

WASHINGTON D.C., AUGUST 4th, 1999, 630 A.M. EST. THE PENTAGON

General John White, the current Chairman of the Joint Chiefs of Staff, was furious as hell that their plan to bring the missing terrorist out to the surface, by making him believe the police and special agents had truly scaled down their search efforts for the elusive Colonel al-Adwani here in the United States, did not work out for them. General White entered his office earlier than usual on this day and he immediately dialed CIA Director John Raincloud's private number. He knew he would be able to reach the Director at this number no matter where he was on the face of the earth. When the phone finished ringing, and a loud beep filled his ears, the still angry General punched in his private number and then he hung up the phone.

Mary, his secretary entered the office early as usual, just as John hung up the phone carrying a cup of coffee for him to enjoy.

"You're a real doll you know that young lady. I don't know what I would ever do if I didn't have you looking after me as well as you do, Mary."

"If I wasn't here, you'd replace me with some young bimbo with big tits and nice ass, so don't hand me any of that crap it won't work on me mister. John, you look exhausted already, what the devil are you doing here so early this morning, General White?"

"I may ask you the same question there young lady. What the hell are you doing here this early in the morning?" John replied kindly, as he smiled

EAGLE'S NEST

over what Mary just complained to him about. He knew he was very lucky to have her as his secretary.

"I came in early today to finish up some of my paperwork that had slipped through the cracks on me yesterday, if you must know why I'm here, General." Mary tried her best smile on John. But he easily saw through it as he said back at her.

"Now who's trying to blow some smoke in the air around here, young lady? You knew I was upset about this missing terrorist, and I was going to come to my office early today. Right?"

"I'm afraid I'm guilty as charge, General White Sir." Mary smiled at the General.

"What the hell's this crap General White shit about Mary? Am I in trouble with you or something, you're being so damn formal today, young lady." John looked into the beautiful blue eyes of his secretary to see if she was upset at him for some reason.

"No, not really, I'm not upset with you in the least, but I do wish you'd look a little better after your health, that's all John. You're not sleeping or eating right, and I don't like it one bit if you must know, sir. You haven't been ever since this terrible assassination attempt on the President's life happened, General White."

"Arrr... this damn thing's really got me by the balls, Mary. Err... I'm terrible sorry Mary, please excuse my vocabulary today. I guess I'm a little more exhausted than I first believed, young lady. Why don't you grab yourself a quick cup of Java and join me, while I wait for the damn Chief to return my call, and we can get down to some brass tact's today." General White offered to his pretty secretary as he sipped his coffee again.

Mary knew General White was speaking about Director Raincloud. He was the only man in all Washington, who could dare call him the Chief and remain in one piece. She went out of the room and got herself a cup of coffee. While she was out of John's office, his phone rang.

"Yeah, and if this isn't a gorgeous looking young blonde woman then I'm hanging up on ya." General White warned, already knowing it was Director Raincloud on the other end, by his caller ID system.

Director Raincloud tried his best to make his voice sound like that of a woman, as he squeaked over the phone. "Oh John, I want you, take me, take me now. Oh God I want you so much."

293

"Can the shit John. What's the latest crap you have on this missing turd for me, sir?"

"Nothing much I'm afraid. This little prick made like a ghost, and he has successfully disappeared on us, John. My Agents and Intel can't locate this lousy bastard anywhere in the United States, General." Director Raincloud complained to the military officer.

"Shit! Dammit! How long before you can make it over to my fucking office today, John? I need to speak with you." General White asked the CIA Director with concern lacing his voice.

"I'm just outside the building as we speak sir. I was already heading for your place when you bugged me on the damn horn this morning, General." Director Raincloud replied as he smiled in his phone receiver.

"Then get your can up here on the double wiseass, we have to talk mister."

"On my way John. Obviously you have something on your mind, and I needed to speak with you as well over this latest situation, sir." Director Raincloud replied as he broke off the connection while his driver parked in the North lot of the Pentagon.

Mary returned to the General's office carrying two cups of coffee for the men, because she knew Director Raincloud was on his way to the General's office. General White looked at her, and smiled as he offered. "How the hell did you know he's here already, young lady?"

"Because I'm your secretary General White, and I know everything that happens in my office, mister. I'll make myself busy outside your office, so you two can speak in private, sir." Mary replied, knowing their coffee break was placed on the back burner for the time being.

General White nodded and then he leaned back in his chair and rubbed his burning eyes with the palms of his hands as he let out with a loud growl.

Director Raincloud entered the office without Mary escorting him in, and he smiled at the seated and exhausted looking powerful General. "I got bad news for you mister. You'll never pass for a woman on the damn phone, Chief."

"I don't ever want to either General. I like women the way they are, and me the way I am, sir. What's on your mind, John?" CIA Director Raincloud asked as he settled down in a chair.

"I guess I can ask you the same question Chief. Mary poured you some coffee before you arrived." General White nodded towards the steaming cup.

"She's good, I really need a cup to get my blood moving. John, I believe this damn Iraqi Colonel al-Adwani has successfully escaped the United States by now sir. I don't know how the hell he was able to pull it off safely, or if it's true at all mind you, sir. But I got a gut buster that says the lousy little prick's out of the damn States, and he's laughing his ass off at us as we continued to search for his ass here in the States, dammit." Director Raincloud grumbled hotly, showing General White he was really pissed off about the possibility of the missing terrorist escaping their trap for him.

"I got the same feeling Chief. What's our next move with this sonofabitch? We have to capture this man, or the President's going to use the lot of us for target practice, John."

"I hear that General White. Look John, this is for your ears only sir. I have a pair of deep seated Operatives working over the Baghdad area of Iraq at this time sir. They're sleepers so far, have been since the conclusion of Operation Desert Storm there, sir. I implanted them, thinking we were going back after Iraq, and give her another bloody nose in the near future, sir. In their off time, the two Operatives have been working on locating any prime, and the most important military targets for us, when we went after Iraq for a second time and..."

"Targets? What kind of targets do you have them searching out for us, mister?" General White interrupted the huge Native American, as he looked at him for a moment.

"Yes John, prime targets, such as chemical and biological labs and plants, working on other types of weapons of mass destruction. The Operatives were also instructed to locate where Iraq's hiding her rocket engines and parts. Crap like that, General."

"Were they able to locate any of the damn things for us as yet, John?"

"The sleepers were quite successful with picking up some thirty six extremely interesting hits for us so far, sir. I know if we go after Iraq for a second time, we can completely destroy Saddam Hussein's insane quest to become a nuclear, chemical and or biological threat to his neighbors in the Middle East, or the rest of the world this time around, General."

"All I know is we should go after the lousy prick under just those pretexts alone, John. The last President dropped the ball on this prick, and his nation of nuts. We should've pounded Iraq until the madman dumped all his weapons of mass destruction on the steps of the United Nations building. Shit, I see somewhere in the near future, we're going to be forced to send our countries treasures back to Iraq, to finish the job started and botched up on us. I hate this shit. Arrr... never mind him for the time being what about these damn Operatives of yours working in Iraq, Director? What are the sleepers up to now, John? You seem to be driving at something during this conversation, my friend. Don't hold back on me now, I know the Boss is going to be calling me some time today, to find out any updates about this missing prick al-Adwani."

"General White, I'm going to change their orders and activate them immediately, and then I'll place them on the heels of this lousy little bastard General Hassan al-Zahar, until Colonel al-Adwani surfaces somewhere in Iraq. This little prick won't be able to take a damn shit, without my knowing about it well in advance I assure you, General White Sir. Once we're certain this Colonel al-Adwani's back in Iraq, you're going to have to pick up the ball from there and run with it I'm afraid, General White."

"Director Raincloud, Colonel Leadbetter already has my troops foaming at the mouth to get their hands on this damn prick's little neck. I'm going to make a deal with you Chief, you locate where Colonel al-Adwani's hiding in Iraq, and I'll bring you his damn hide back for a present." General White offered to the CIA Director with a wide grin.

"You got yourself a deal there, General White Sir. You going to report to the President, or are you going to wait until he makes contact with you first, sir?"

"I'm not going to wait for him to make contact with me first I can tell you that much, Director. I learned my lesson about that move I can tell you sir. I'll make contact with the President first and inform him of our beliefs that this damn Colonel al-Adwani has cleared the country safely, sir." General White remarked as he glanced at his desk calendar just to divert his eyes from the Director for a brief moment.

"Good luck on that one, John. I wouldn't want to be the one who has to inform the President our missing target, might have got out of the States alive. He's going to be fit to be tied, my friend." The CIA Director offered and he slowly shook his head no.

"And, what the hell makes you believe you're not going to be part of bringing this shit news to the Boss' table, mister? If I have to place my balls on the table for the man to beat on for a while then I'm going to have plenty of company joining me there, buster. Meaning you mister." General White warned the CIA Director as he held him in his glare now.

"Thanks a shitload General White." Director Raincloud smiled back at his friend.

General White leaned forward in his chair and picked up the phone and said. "Yes Mary, can you do me a favor and get me through to the White House Chief of Staff, STAT please? I have to request a private meeting with the President to take place sometime later on today, at his earliest convenience please, young lady."

"Consider it done General White." Mary replied pleasantly in the receiver.

General White placed the phone back in its cradle. He no sooner did and begin to speak to Director Raincloud again, when the phone rang and it interrupted him a second time.

"General White Sir, I have Peter Waters on the line waiting to speak with you sir."

"Thank you Mary, Pete. How the hell are you today young man?" the General asked him as he nodded to the Director as ne fielded the phone call.

"Trying to keep my head real low today I'm afraid, General White Sir. The President's been up for an hour now, and he's been jumping all over everyone he spots walking by him or caught up in his angry sights, sir. I never saw the President is such a terrible mood as he's in today, General White Sir. Something must really be upsetting him and he's taking it out on everyone working at the white House, sir." The White House aide complained to the powerful military officer.

"His mood isn't going to improve very much either, once I had a chance to speak with him today, Pete. Can you inform the President that I'm requesting a meeting with him, for later on in the afternoon at his earliest convenience, son?"

"May I inquire as to the contents of this requested meeting, just in case the President asks me that is which I'm certain he will, General White Sir?"

"Sure thing young man, we believe this damn Colonel al-Adwani has succeeded with his escape from the States safely, and he's on his way back to Iraq I'm certain."

"Wow, now there's a message no self respecting homing pigeon would want to deliver to the Boss on a day like today, sir." The young man moaned back at the General.

"Sorry you got stuck with the shit end of the stick this time, but you wanted your job Pete."

"No one informed me it was going to be so troublesome and life threatening, before I signed on for the President, General White Sir. I'll inform the President of your request for this meeting, sir. Would you like to hold the line, or do you want me to call you back with the time and place of this requested meeting, General White Sir?" The young White House aide remarked as he laughed in the phone with the powerful General.

"I don't have much to do right now, so I might as well hold on till you get back to me son." The General snipped at the young man over the phone.

"Very well then General White Sir, I'll be back to you as soon as I can, sir. I think I'm going to file for a set of steel pants, to keep the President from eating on my ass so much lately sir." The White House aide ignored the slight snip in the General's voice.

General White chuckled over Peter's remark as he covered the mouth piece with his hand, and said to Director Raincloud in a whisper. "The President's in a real snit today John."

Director Raincloud just shook his head again and gave a half ass smile to the General.

General White was about to add something else in his conversation with Director Raincloud, when he heard a voice on the other end of the phone. The second he heard it, General White straightened up in his chair out of habit, and paid attention to the upset sounding voice.

"General White, what the hell's this sack of god damn bullshit I just heard from Peter, that you believe this Colonel al-Adwani bastard has successfully escaped the United States, Christ sake? What the hell am I paying the lot of you people around here for, dammit? I really wanted this lousy bastard before he was able to flee the States. Now, we have to make a major project out of this damn mess, and cost the taxpayers a bundle of money while we're at it, to capture this assassin, General White Sir. Jesus Christ Almighty General White, you knew how much I wanted this man captured while he was still trapped here in the States. Dammit!"

"I understand how you must feel Mr. President Sir. Evidently, this Colonel al-Adwani prick has had quite a bit of support helping him evade every Agent searching for his ass while he was trapped here in the States and they were able to get..."

"Yes, I know all that crap already General White! I heard it all before sir." President Cole interrupted nastily, and then he went on with his angry words aimed at the military officer. "And, I want the asses of every one of the bastards who assisted this Colonel al-Adwani in his plight from the United States. I want heads rolling around here dammit! And heads is what I'm going to get, General White Sir. Whether they be of Arab or American General's heads mind you, mister. Do I make myself perfectly clear on this subject with you, General White?"

"Crystal clear on this one, I assure you Mr. President Sir." The General offered back calmly to the extremely upset sounding American Leader.

"Fine General White, now we understand each other a little better here, I want you at the Oval Office at nine a.m. sharp. That's nine a.m., and not a second later, General White Sir. I want your god damn partner in crime with you as well, General." The President slammed the phone down because he was so angry the terrorist was believed to have escaped the United States.

"Shit, Peter wasn't kidding about the President being plenty pissed off today, John. He wants the both of us over at the big house at nine a.m. sharp today. You have anything that needs looking after until the meeting takes place, John? I suggest you look after it now, no telling how long this meeting with the Boss might go on." General White asked the large Director.

Director Raincloud shook his head no, and finished off his coffee.

"Fine then we might as well leave for the White House now, and be early for the meeting for a change. Maybe it'll help calm the Boss man down some if we show up early."

"In a pig's ear it will. The only thing that's going to calm the President down at this point is having Colonel al-Adwani's head resting on a silver platter right in front of him, General White." Director Raincloud complained as he rose from his chair and then he followed the General out of his office.

BAGHDAD, IRAQ. AUGUST 4th, 1999, 7:30 P.M.

Colonel Abdulaziz Majd al-Adwani was right, once he and Rasha were safely out of the United States, travel was much easier for them to accomplish. It took the two sixteen hours since they left Canada to reach Iraq. The Iraqi Colonel was forced to suffer through an extremely long and most boring two hour hold over in Canada, before being able to board the aircraft for his home land. It was dark when he walked down the ramp to no one waiting for him. This angered him immensely because he felt he should have received a hero's welcome in his country, for his near completion of the assassination of the American President. Even though the attempt failed, it informed the American public they were not as safe in their homes, as their foolish government would like them to believe. So the attack served some purpose after all.

Not seeing anyone to welcome him home from his government, let him know how scared his President was of the American military presence in his country. The lights of the airport were mostly off with just a few lit the one usable runway, and Colonel al-Adwani knew this was solely because the military feared new attacks from the American warplanes owning the skies over Iraq at this time. Rasha followed two steps behind the angry Colonel al-Adwani.

When he reached the tarmac of the airfield, he scanned the all but still destroyed civilian airbase. There were some signs of the heavy destruction here and there spread around the airport, caused by the attacking warplanes during the so called Desert Storm war Iraq engaged in with the joint Coalition Forces. Planes, both civilian and military destroyed in the bombing of Baghdad, were pushed to the far end of the airbase, and left to rust there.

Many young children of Iraq enjoyed themselves by picking through the rubble of the aircraft in hopes of finding something of worth to sell on the black market. But the military had already removed anything that could possibly be sold or salvaged from the destroyed planes. Search lights continually scanned the sky, keeping a constant visual for any renewed attacks from the ever prowling American warplanes keeping Iraq's airforce grounded, and its military hiding in holes in the ground throughout the country.

When Colonel al-Adwani's civilian aircraft entered Iraqi air space, it crossed over the no fly zone from Kuwait and almost instantly, two sleek gleaming American F-15 Eagle warplanes came up to check out the civilian airliner. Once it was determined it was a civilian aircraft, the two American warplanes dipped their wings in a friendly move at the Captain of the other aircraft, and then they quickly disappeared as fast as they had appeared.

Colonel al-Adwani glared harshly at the pair of F-15 Eagles with the proud American stars painted so boldly on each wing of the deadly warplanes, and the stacks of rockets and bombs hanging ominously from below the wings of each aircraft. The Iraqi Colonel almost smiled when the pilots saluted, and then dipped their wings to the civilians staring at them from within the windows of the civilian aircraft. The way the attack aircraft disappeared in the star studded night with the twin cones of flames emitting from the rear of the planes, instantly forced Colonel al-Adwani to curse the American military, and also the brain thrust still ruling his country. He knew Saddam's time had long ago ran its course, and if he had anything to do with it, Saddam Hussein would soon be nothing more than a bad memory locked in the hearts and minds of all Iraqi civilians and military personnel alike.

Rasha took hold of Colonel al-Adwani's arm almost like she was reading the troubling thoughts he was suffering through, and she squeezed it gently as she tried to lead him over to one of the beat up taxis waiting near the exit of the terminal that still bore the shattered windows from the heavy allied bombing. She saw and understood the anger building in Colonel al-Adwani's eyes. She skillfully led the upset Colonel over to the one cab that seemed to be in the best of condition of the three. But when they climbed into the rear of the cab, the driver announced he had no gas and was living in his car.

Colonel al-Adwani cursed himself as he slammed the door of the cab closed as hard as he could slam it, making dust fall from underneath the dilapidated car. The driver of the cab cursed as nastily as Colonel al-Adwani did, and the Iraqi Military Officer ignored him and headed for a second cab parked a hundred feet away from the first one. Before he got in, he growled at the elderly driver in an extremely angry tone of voice. "Foul and worthless curse of the vast desert sands, you do have petrol for the god cursed machine, do you not, fool of fools?"

"Do camels have fleas? What good would I be as a cab driver, if I had no fuel for my vehicle?" The driver smirked at he looked at the two people with the one speaking to him.

Colonel al-Adwani glared at the older driver, and when Rasha climbed in the car, did he break his stare and growled at the driver. "Take me to One, Five, Seven Mohammed Drive, you fool."

The driver felt an icy chill run down his spine, as he repeated the address over in his mind. He immediately realized he had an extremely important person in the rear of his car, someone who must work for the secret police, or a different department of his shattered government. Shaking, the driver replied in a pleasant tone to his fare this time. "Allahu Akhbar kind stranger, yes my honored brother of the great desert sand, I'll be most pleased to bring you to your final destination, and get you there safely while I'm at it kind sir."

The cab driver slowly pulled from his parking spot, trying not to jog or bump his believed to be important passengers riding in the rear seat of his car, as he picked his way carefully through the rubble covered streets of downtown Baghdad. He stopped at a working red light, but Colonel al-Adwani growled from the rear seat at the driver. "Go through the god cursed foul stop light you worthless old fool you! No one is coming from the other direction as you can plainly see for foul yourself if you opened your god cursed eyes and look down the foul road."

The driver nodded to the man in the backseat, and carefully inched his way into the crossroads, and when he was certain no other cars was coming at him, he darted across the red light. As the cab drove through the poorer section and streets of Baghdad, Colonel al-Adwani saw much of the damage of Iraq's war with the Coalition Forces wasn't repaired yet. People still got their drinking water from broken pipes, or puddles lying in the filth covered streets. The entire area smelled like a large bathroom, with raw sewage invading the puddles the people used for their drinking water.

EAGLE'S NEST

As the cab headed into the better sections of the capital, he saw much of the destruction was already repaired, or at least cleaned away. When the cab turned onto the blocks where President Saddam Hussein housed much of his elite military personnel, there was little if any signs of destruction that ripped Iraq apart during the war with the hated United States.

All these street lights were working properly in this section of downtown Baghdad, and it seemed every house they passed in this area, lights were burning. Colonel al-Adwani heard the sounds of a TV playing and he looked for the house with it on. The streets were well repaired, along with the sidewalks and houses, and in this area there were no naked or half naked children checking the garbage pits for rotted food to eat. Every child he saw seemed like they were well fed and active. They were clean and getting out of the way of the cab as it passed by them. In the lower section, the children got in the way of the cab causing the driver to lay on his horn while the children begged for food or money from the two passengers riding in the cab.

The cab driver soon pulled up to the requested building, and the driver jumped out of the cab, and opened the door for both Colonel al-Adwani and Rasha. The Iraqi Colonel barely took any noticed of the scared looking and acting elderly driver, as he slipped him an American twenty dollar bill. The old Iraqi bowed many times over, as he carried their luggage up to the building's main door. Colonel Abdulaziz Majd al-Adwani knocked on the heavy door, as Rasha took the luggage from the driver who quickly disappeared with his cab into the night's darkness.

The door opened, and a man dressed in a clean Iraqi Colonel's uniform barked at him. "Yes!"

"Fool, you don't recognize who I am standing before your worthless carcass!" Colonel al-Adwani fired back harshly at the man who looked like he was not the least bit interested in anything going on around him.

"No! Am I supposed to recognize who you are, fool? Are you a God, that I should know you by mere sight, fool? Are you an important man that should command instant recognition of your foul presence before my eyes? I don't know who the devil you are, and if you value your worthless life as it is. I suggest you leave here immediately, stranger. Before I show you who I am and the power over life and death I command over your worthless life, you great fool you!"

"Son of a lowly camel merchant who pollutes the very air of Iraq by breathing it for his worthless survival I am Colonel Abdulaziz Majd al-Adwani. I am here to report to General Hassan al-Zahar in person about my mission in the United States, fool."

"A report you say to me stranger with the loud mouth and the manners of a camel in heat? You must think of yourself as a very important Agent to the needs of Iraq and her government. We have many such foul Agents working out in the field, and they realize how unimportant they are to the General's interests in life. Wait here while I see if General Hassan al-Zahar has the time to waste on meeting with you. He's a very busy man you know, fool."

"I don't care one lowly grain of the great desert sand for how busy General al-Zahar might be you just inform him I'm here to see him at once, Colonel." Colonel al-Adwani glared harshly at the other Colonel, as he closed the door in his face.

Rasha moved up to the military officer's side and she offered him in a low and concerned tone of voice. "Colonel al-Adwani Sir, I believe if you were a little more civil to anyone you might meet, you might be better received by them in return, Colonel."

Colonel al-Adwani glared hotly at her, and she immediately backed off him. The door opened, it was the angry Colonel again, and he growled nastily at the two people standing by the door. "General al-Zahar says he will see you Colonel al-Adwani. Come in and wait in the sitting room. The General will be with you shortly I believe, sir."

The Colonel stepped aside and he allowed the two agents to enter the building. Once inside the structure, Colonel al-Adwani found he was facing two heavily armed and threatening Iraqi soldiers. The Colonel walked up behind him, and forced Colonel al-Adwani's arms in the air with a hard shove of his hands, and then he expertly frisked him to make certain Colonel al-Adwani did not have any hidden weapons on his person.

When the Colonel finished with his expert search of Colonel al-Adwani, he then turned to Rasha. She automatically raised her hands over her head and waited to be searched. The second Iraqi Colonel checked her over for any possible hidden weapons. His hands linger on her breasts and between her legs a bit longer than was necessary for his search though, as he skillfully slid his hands up her inner thighs. He even dared to run a finger inside her pants. When he found nothing hidden on her person, he smiled which was more a sneer at Rasha who gave him a dirty look and turned her head away from him.

"What is your foul name Colonel!" Colonel al-Adwani demanded hotly from the Iraqi officer.

"Colonel Hamoodi al-Qaysi. Why do you ask me such a foul and unimportant question, Colonel al-Adwani? If I wanted you to know who I was, I would've introduced myself to you when you first knocked on my foul door, Spy." The smug officer snapped back at him.

"Do you always search all your Agents when they come to report to their control, you foul fool you?" Colonel al-Adwani demanded to know for the other Iraqi Colonel hotly.

"I most certainly do Colonel al-Adwani. I like keeping my job and my General safe at the same time while I'm at it, sir." The Colonel glared harshly back at the Colonel al-Adwani.

"Well you great fool you, I shall inform you that your foul job is in serious jeopardy for the terrible indignities you have just forced upon me and my female assistant here. I'll have your foul skin ripped away from your worthless bones while you still breathe, and I'll order it brought out to the vast desert for the ugly scavengers of the sand to feast greedily upon. Because you don't understand exactly who you're dealing with here, lowly dog of the garbage pits. I have teeth, and when I bite, I always draw blood from anyone who is foolish enough to stand in my way and I shall bite whenever I am forced to deal with the likes of you, fool..."

"Look here Colonel, I fear you not in the least. You can bark at me all day, and I still would not fear you in the least, sir." The General's subordinate hissed angrily as he moved his face right in front of Colonel al-Adwani's, and then he hissed at him again in no uncertain terms. "I fear your bite even less than I fear you, lowly spy why crawls through the foul shadows of the night to carry out your evil work against the innocent of the world. Perhaps, you don't know who you are dealing with here, Agent. If anyone can have someone killed around here, it is surely I. I'm General al-Zahar's right hand man, and I control everything the great General..."

General al-Zahar entered the sitting room with his hand outstretched, and he walked up to Colonel al-Adwani, interrupting the heavy confrontation going on between his two Iraqi Officers and he offered politely to his agent. "Colonel Adwani, it's good you have successfully escaped the great land of sin with all your tail feathers still intact, sir. By the Five Prayers of the Holy Qur'an, if I didn't know you by mannerisms, I would be unable to pick you out of a crowd because of the way you look today, sir. You did a masterful job of changing your appearance. Colonel Adwani, your actions in the United States have again placed Iraq back in the world dominance she deserves to be standing in, Colonel. You must be exhausted from your long trip home. Colonel al-Qaysi, have some tea brought out for my dear friend here, sir."

The second Colonel did not move a muscle, causing General al-Zahar to turn and ask him in a concerned tone this time. "Did you not hear my request of you Colonel?"

"Yes, I heard your request General. But this great fool who prowls the lowly night, was threatening me because I took certain precautions with him and his bitch fellow spy, sir. It seems he resented their being searched by me, General al-Zahar."

"Precautions, what are these precautions you speak of, Colonel al-Qaysi?" General al-Zahar asked his officer as he cocked his head to the side and stared at him.

"Yes sir, as I have just offered, I had their cursed bodies searched for hidden weapons, General al-Zahar." The still angry looking Iraqi Colonel snapped back at his commanding officer.

"And, Colonel Adwani took offense and objected to this search of his person I take it, Colonel al-Qaysi Sir?" General al-Zahar snapped hotly as he turned his attention to Colonel al-Adwani and Rasha standing at his side, and now he stared at them with questioning eyes.

Neither Colonel al-Qaysi nor Colonel al-Adwani replied to the General's last question.

"I didn't think this was a serious problem for him to absorb, sir. Did you inform the Colonel we always search anyone visiting my headquarters? Ahhhh, Colonel al-Qaysi the tea please."

The Colonel nodded at his commanding officer, and then he quickly disappeared from the room. General al-Zahar waved his hand towards a number of chairs set out in a sloppy circle in the small room. The security guards already on station in the room moved behind the chairs, and they remained on the alert. Once seated, Colonel al-Adwani spoke to his General and control.

"General al-Zahar, the great fools you had saddled me with to carry out the assassination attack on the worthless American President, was inept on their foul mission, and they were unable to accomplish their orders successfully, sir. It has caused me much trouble, and great confusion on this mission, General al-Zahar Sir. It was extremely hard for me to escape the great land of Satan and sin with my skin still covering my worthless bones, sir. If it was not for Rasha's expert assistance there, I believe I would've surely been captured by the god cursed American Agents sent out to find me, sir. I should've had better Agents to work with in the United States if my mission was to be a success, General. Perhaps, we would've been successful on our mission with better Agents, and I would have surely been able to..."

"I have news for you sir, your mission was successful Colonel Adwani, beyond your wildest dreams I offer to you, my wise desert brother. It has drawn renewed attention to the terribly suffocating sanctions imposed upon the shoulders of Iraq and her people, by the United Nations and the United States, and her hated allies. Some of our brother Arab countries who have been too long with holding their silence, are starting to rise up their voices in condemning the ongoing sanctions, and the foul animals that enforce them. There are calls for a face to face meeting with our President, and the Secretary General of the United Nations. To discuss the possibility of ending the foul sanctions once and for all, and also allowing Iraq to again join the peaceful nations of the civilized world, and to live in peace with them again in the flow of the worlds pulse. We're patiently awaiting further word from our great President, if he intends to meet with any of the foolish Delegates of the worthless council."

"There is another reason why I wanted to meet with you privately tonight, General al-Zahar. I want to discuss a matter of utmost importance to me and the nation of Iraq." Colonel al-Adwani announced cautiously, overlooking the praise the General was offering him.

"Oh? What do you have on your mind this time, Colonel Adwani? I am open to hear anything one of my Officers has on his mind, especially if it concerns our country and security." The powerful Iraqi General asked his agent with caution dripping from his tone of voice he was using on the Iraqi Colonel.

Colonel al-Adwani briefly glanced at the two security guards standing directly behind them. Trying to inform the General he wanted to speak to him in private.

General al-Zahar followed Colonel al-Adwani's eyes towards the two security guards standing directly behind him, and he instantly understood what he wanted and he offered to the two security guards. "That will be all. You two are dismissed and you may leave my side now. Everything is alright with my Colonel here I assure you." General al-Zahar snapped at the two young and heavily armed soldiers guarding him and the Colonel.

Without a word from his security people, the two guards instantly snapped to attention and they quickly left the room as ordered, closing the door behind them.

Colonel al-Qaysi saw the door close and he did not dare knock on it for fear of disturbing his General and the conversation he was engaged in with the two spies who have just returned to Iraq from this mission in the United States. He did not have the requested tea because a servant was going to bring it in for the General and his agents. Colonel al-Qaysi felt it was beneath him to bring the other Colonel a cup of tea because he hated all spies.

"Now that we're alone sir, what is truly on your mind that you could not speak of it before my trusted guards, Colonel Adwani." General al-Zahar knew what he was doing, and he was omitting the 'al' before Adwani's name on purpose. He was only going to use it if, and when he found himself again trusting the agent who had failed on his mission to assassination the American President. Once Colonel al-Adwani failed his mission, General al-Zahar thought about ordering both Colonel al-Adwani and Rasha killed for their disappointment. He delayed the order because he wanted to hear the Colonel's report before ending his life.

"General al-Zahar Sir, I have to admit to you that I'm not very pleased with the way President Saddam Hussein is running our country of late and his allowing the hated..."

"I'm afraid there are not many of us who are very pleased with Saddam Hussein's actions of late, Colonel Adwani. Do you happen to have something else in your mind to offer me, about this present situation concerning our fool of a President, Colonel?" General al-Zahar interrupted his agent's words coarsely, purposely putting more pressure on his operative's mind, as he waited for him to finish with his words.

"I certainly do General al-Zahar Sir. I purpose we consider assassinating the great useless fool still in command of our country. Then install someone else who has the backbone and wherewithal to properly deal with the god cursed hated American criminals and their British cohorts for the sake of Iraq and her people, sir. We need someone who is strong enough to bring Iraq back into the flow of the world." The Colonel offered to his control.

"And, who do you have in mind to place as our new President of Iraq, if you were able to successfully assassinate the Commander of our country, Colonel Adwani?"

"You, of course I believe is the only person who is better prepared and strong enough and respected enough to run our country of Iraq General al-Zahar. With your strength and knowhow running our country, we shall finally have a person of high standings to better deal with the worthless Americans in the manner of a powerful nation. Not as a nation of fools and cowards who surrender to unarmed helicopters being flown by Amercan useless news reporters, General."

CHAPTER NINETEEN

General Hassan al-Zahar removed his eyes from Colonel Abdelaziz Majdal al-Adwani's face, and he looked at Rasha for a moment, to see if she agreed with what the Colonel was offering to him. Then he asked her in a commanding voice. "Do you happen to agree with what Colonel al-Adwani's purposing before my foul ear, my dear?"

She knew better than to give an answer to the General's question, and she merely cast her eyes down towards the floor, causing General al-Zahar to place a sneer on his face, as he turned back to Colonel al-Adwani and remarked to him almost angrily. "I'm most flattered you believe I can run the affairs of Iraq better than President Saddam Hussein can, Colonel. But I believe you understand I could not possibly run this great country all by myself, Colonel Adwani. Of course I'd need a strong Prime Minister, a number of Ambassadors, and many other Officers to help maintain control over the military and our foolish civilians. I'd hate to assassinate our worthless President, only to fall victim of an assassination myself, lead by a military coup aimed against me. Who would you offer me as the second most powerful man in all Iraq, to be my Prime Minister, Colonel Adwani? Saying I might feel the same as you and believe it's time to rid Iraq of Saddam Hussein foolishness, Colonel." The General asked suspiciously.

Colonel al-Adwani knew he went too far with his words to stop now, and he offered smugly to his commanding officer. "I'd offer the services of myself as your second in command, General al-Zahar Sir. I can from this position, keep a close eye on the military, thus assuring you of no possible assassination attempts being aimed against your life, sir. From the ranks of our own Officers in the Republican Guard, we can pick out your other true and strong government officials we'll need to form our new government of Iraq, General al-Zahar."

"You huh Colonel Adwani?" General al-Zahar offered smugly, as he leaned back in his chair and exhaled, as he thought over what Colonel al-Adwani just offered him.

After thinking about if for several long moments, General al-Zahar acknowledged to his military officer. "I must admit I'm most intrigued by your words of interest and concern, Colonel al-Adwani. Most intrigued indeed I offer you. But how can you be so certain that the needed military leaders will be so willing to follow us in this coup attempt aimed against Saddam Hussein's rule of Iraq? I saw few Officers capable of independent thinking in most of the Guard Units still left intact, sir. Most of the great fools are nothing more than worthless puppets for President Hussein's iron fist tactics and policies."

"The witless ones we can merely eliminate before going forward with our coup easy enough, General al-Zahar. Once they're eliminated from the picture, we can replace these worthless fools with other Officers who think more as we do General al-Zahar. When we own the military, it'll be a small and simple matter to take to assassinate the god cursed worthless fool who thinks of himself as the invincible leader of Iraq. When he's dead, we'll make our thoughts clear to the hordes of civilians of Iraq, and take over the government. Then we can train our eyes upon where they properly belong, on the hated Americans and their cursed allies who continue to attack and punish our great country, sir." The fact General al-Zahar decided to add the 'al' back to al-Adwani's name did not go unnoticed by the agent as he spoke to the concerned General.

General al-Zahar suddenly clapped his hands loudly together as he sat forward, and then he said. "And, who do you think is strong enough to assassinate our once feared President of Iraq when the proper time comes to do so, Colonel al-Adwani?"

"Again General al-Zahar, I'll offer you myself and my services to your new government, sir." Colonel al-Adwani offered proudly to his commanding officer as he shot him a quick smile.

"And what makes you believe you can assassinate our so well protected President successfully, especially when I sent you out on a mission to assassinate the god cursed American President. Yet the great fool still breathes, and you sit before me with no true explanation as to why he still breathes and lives, but to merely blame the ones under your command for your failures, Colonel. Many have tried to kill the wise old fool who commands our country countless times in the past. Even the awesome power of the mighty United States military might was unable to eliminate the great fool from Iraq, Colonel al-Adwani. Do you think our foolish and unwise President is any less well protected than the American President is in his own country, sir?"

"The only reason the American President is still breathing, is because I was surrounded by a ring of fools who were stupid, and unable to complete their mission as I have ordered them to do. If I was allowed the proper assassins, the American President would be no..."

"And, this mission in Iraq will be much better run then I take it Colonel al-Adwani?"

"Yes, it certainly will be, with me in control of it General al-Zahar Sir." Colonel al-Adwani replied confidently this time to his General and commanding officer.

"And why is that this time, you were in control of the last mission were you not Colonel al-Adwani? With you in command of this next assassination attempt, this time against our own President, it will be successful Colonel?" The crafty Iraqi General asked of his agent with a smug expression on his lips, as he continued to toy with the angry looking agent.

This time Colonel al-Adwani smiled at hearing what the respect General al-Zahar offered him, as he replied to his question. "Because General al-Zahar, I'll be the one who'll pick out the other Operatives who I want to work with this time, to carry out this special mission successfully, sir. If you'll allow me that great privilege I mean and request, General al-Zahar. That is the only way I can possibly guarantee the complete success of an assassination attempt against the worthless President Hussein's life here in Iraq, sir."

"Again Colonel al-Adwani, I'm most intrigued by your extremely interesting words you speak to me during our faithful conversation, sir. Just saying I happen to agree with all you have just offer me for the time being, and I allow you to try and assassinate our worthless President. What is the timeline you'll need to accomplish this great assassination, and then free Iraq of the worthless President Saddam Hussein's foul fist crushing Iraq's throat, sir?"

"General al-Zahar Sir, if I'm free to move about our country without concern while searching for a few much needed Operatives to get the job done properly for us. I'd say I'll need two, no more than three weeks at the most, before I'm properly prepared to make the hit on the foolish President Saddam Hussein's worthless life, General al-Zahar Sir. With the Operatives I shall hand pick for the mission myself this time I'm quite certain I can kill the worthless fool of Iraq." Colonel al-Adwani offered with a smug smile of confidence on his lips.

"You're rather sure of yourself I understand and I see, Colonel al-Adwani. Why are you so positive about this action you offer to carry out for our just cause, sir?"

"Because in all my years of loyal service to Iraq, General al-Zahar. I'll finally be able to hand pick those who I would most trust with a mission of such importance as this one I have suggested to you, sir." The overly confident Iraqi Colonel offered to his General.

"Exactly how many other Operatives would you be requiring to carry out this assassination attempt on our foolish President this time, Colonel al-Adwani?" the General demanded to know from his operative as he waited for his reply.

"I'd require five, maybe up to seven trusted Operatives to form my assault team if I want to make certain I can get near enough to Saddam Hussein quicker, General."

"I suggest you take ten Operatives in your hit team then, and get the great fool tomorrow, Colonel al-Adwani!" General al-Zahar suddenly snarled as he held him in his angry glare.

Colonel al-Adwani stared at his control, his eyes begging, pleading tomorrow was out of the question for him to try and assassinate Saddam Hussein. There was no way he would possibly be able to assemble a hit team and go active that quickly.

General al-Zahar noticed Colonel al-Adwani's dilemma he was suffering through and smirked as he added. "Relax Colonel al-Adwani I was only kidding with you, fool. I know it's impossible for you to hit Saddam Hussein as early as tomorrow, fool. Missions such as this one takes many days, maybe even months of constant planning and adjusting before you might be properly prepared to act against our worthless fool of a President. Colonel al-Adwani let me say I agree with what you offer me. But I fear you're little known to our people of Iraq. For me, once I become the President of Iraq, to pick someone unknown to the Iraq people, will serve to make them believe there shall be no changes in the way Iraq's new government will think and act for them. You offer me new and most pleasing problems in which I must conquer in my own mind. I shall pray to the great Prophet Mohammed for His wise guidance in this most troubling matter."

"What problems do I bring to you, my faithful brother of the hot desert sands?" Colonel al-Adwani was already trying to be a politician in his dealings with the powerful General al-Zahar.

"Ahhh... I see you're already quickly learning the most confusing political ways to deal with your new mentors, Colonel al-Adwani. This is most pleasing for me to understand, I see you learn rather quickly, Colonel al-Adwani. The problems you bring before me are as follows my foolish Arab brother: Few of Iraq's civilians know of your existence within their own country, Colonel. The worthless fools know of me from my many years of fighting the hated Jews, and what I did against the god cursed Coalition Forces during that war when they attacked our country. If it was not for my better judgment during that most foul of lowly wars, we would've surely lost two full Divisions of the Republican Guards in the Kuwaiti Theater of War.

"It was by my orders alone that the Rumayalh oil fields in Kuwaiti were set ablaze, and we used the billowing smoke in which to affect our retreat safely from that land of lowly infidels and jackals. My face and military feats are well known throughout all of Iraq and even the Middle East. Yes Colonel al-Adwani, I happen to agree with your assumption that I should be the next true President of Iraq. Arab nations will once again find their backbones when they see me leading Iraq to the greatness she once commanded in all the Middle East region. Yes, I believe many Arab nations will flock to our side when they see a powerful leader such as I, set in place to run Iraq's new government and military for them, Colonel. The problem that you give me is you're relatively unknown to the Iraqi people and the other nations of the Arab world, Colonel."

General al-Zahar held up his hand to cut off Colonel al-Adwani's complaint, as he offered to him in a rush of words. "Yes, yes I know before you bring it up to my attention, Colonel al-Adwani. It's because of your wise covert actions that made you the unknown guiding light of Iraq behind the scenes, sir. It's up to me to bring you to the surface of the light, and allow the Iraqi people see all those who I have surround me with sir, and who'll be running their future government for the worthless fools. Yes Colonel al-Adwani, I shall waltz you out before all the worthless Iraqi people, and then the rest of the world so they can realize the help you have…"

Rasha suddenly shifted her weight in her chair, interrupting General al-Zahar's trend of though so much that he was forced to ask her in an angry voice. "Yes Rasha, you seem to have something you wish to add to this cursed conversation, foolish woman?"

Rasha hesitated for a brief moment, as she again diverted her eyes from the two men.

"Come, come my foolish young child. You'll be an important part of this new government we are discussing here before you, woman. You may speak your mind without fear of suffering the death of a thousand cuts or the bite of the lash. The only way you may lose your foul life with me, is by holding your tongue and not offering what you believe. Speak to me woman!" General al-Zahar snapped at the pretty young Iraqi female agent while waiting for her to talk.

Rasha slowly raised her eyes from the floor and looked directly in the cold black eyes of General al-Zahar, and then she offered meekly to him. "General al-Zahar Sir, please forgive me sir, I don't mean to question your great wisdom in this conversation, sir. But I believe it's impossible for Colonel al-Adwani to come to the surface now in Iraq, and assume a leading role in Iraq's new government you're forming, sir." Rasha shot her eyes back to the floor, for fear of the reaction her words would have on these two powerful and feared soldiers of Iraq.

Colonel al-Adwani turned in his chair, already hunching up his shoulders and balling up his fists, as he glared harshly at Rasha, fearing she was about to betray him to the General.

General al-Zahar's eyebrows arched, and he stared at Rasha with surprise etched in his eyes, while trying to figure out what she meant by her most troubling and disturbing words aimed at him. The General sat forward and snapped harshly at the scared young woman. "Rasha, your words are most confusing to my worthless ears, my daughter of the desert sands. I trust the hot winds of the desert has not scrambled your foul wits on you, woman? Why the devil do you offer to me it's impossible for Colonel al-Adwani to show his face in Iraq at this time, woman?

"Come Rasha, you spoke your mind to me moments ago and then you stopped speaking. I demand you enlighten us to the ways a woman's mind truly thinks for them. I warn you woman, hold your tongue further against me, and I'll have it yanked out by the foul roots and placed in your hand, so it can never betray another of your fellow Officers, woman. If that's what you're truly attempting to do here Rasha, speak now woman! I grow bored and tired by your sudden silence, lowly woman. Speak, or I'll have you removed from this room, and marched to the courtyard and have you shot as a foolish woman who had no business in the world of a soldier."

Rasha looked deeply into the glaring black eyes of General al-Zahar. Seeing the demand blazing within them, she realized she had no other choice in the matter now, but to finish her statement to the extremely powerful Iraqi Military Officer. With great inner strength coming to her rescue, she began speaking again to her Commander. "General al-Zahar Sir, Colonel al-Adwani, I'm fearful you might be overlooking one important issue in this conversation..."

"You're beginning to try my patience most unwisely here Rasha, and that's not a very wise course of action to adopt for your future sake on the face of this earth, woman. For the sake of your well being and for the sake of your foul family living in Iraq, I suggest you come to your point much quickly than you're speaking to me now, woman. I'll be the judge if your offering is an important issue we happen to be overlooking in this conversation or not, foul woman." General al-Zahar hardened his angry glare at the shaking young woman.

"Yes General al-Zahar, Colonel al-Adwani." Rasha made certain she include the Iraqi Colonel in her address to the General, as she continued with her words now. "We know the god cursed hated American authorities and government is well aware Colonel al-Adwani was in part, responsible for the attempted assassination on their foul and worthless President's life, sir. That Colonel al-Adwani was the true control of the failed terrorist cell, and the assault team has successfully killed one of their powerful politicians, and the cell wounded their Vice President in the same assassination attempt, sir. I fear with all my heart if you allow Colonel al-Adwani to be seen standing by your side before the Iraqi public. It might incite the loathsome American military to react against his appearance, and their soldiers make their own assassination attempt on Colonel al-Adwani's life here in Iraq against him sir.

"As of yet General al-Zahar, the hated worthless American fools have no idea where Colonel al-Adwani is hiding at this time, sir. If he's seen with you in Iraq, they'll know where he's hiding, and the American fools will more than likely react against him and even yourself. I only bring this matter up to your attention, in sincere hopes of protecting the Colonel's life, while he's assisting you in your future takeover of power of Iraq and her people, sir."

Colonel al-Adwani's harsh stare softened when he heard Rasha's explanation, knowing she had only his best interests and well being in her thoughts and words to the General. Gone, was any thought of her betraying him before the other Iraqi Officer. Colonel al-Adwani looked at General al-Zahar who was still staring at Rasha, while he thought of what she just offered him. Colonel al-Adwani could tell the General was deep in thought and he remained silent.

Suddenly, General al-Zahar snapped out of his private thoughts and spoke to Rasha in a commanding voice. "By the great gray beard of the Prophet Muhammad himself, woman. Your fear is well founded in this case for your Commanding Officer as it should be at all times, Rasha. I cannot believe I didn't think of this possible threat against the Colonel's life for myself, woman." General al-Zahar turned to Colonel al-Adwani and added while allowing the worry lines to disappear from his face. "As I stated, you have come before me with a full bag of problems for me to try and solve for you and myself, Colonel al-Adwani. How do you suggest we handle this new problem Rasha has just brought up to our attention, Colonel al-Adwani?

"I believe the only way I see out of this dilemma is if you maintain a low profile while you're here in Iraq, until the foolish American authorities no longer want your foul hide for their god cursed revenge. Maybe, it was not such a wise idea to go after their American President after all

I suddenly fear, Colonel al-Adwani. We should've ended the worthless President Saddam Hussein's life first, and then we should have sought a peaceful relationship to develop with the hated Americans and their god cursed allies.

"Judging by their past actions in the Middle East, the foolish Americans seem to have very short memories. In due time, I believe they'll forget about this failed attempted assassination on their god cursed leader's life. Then you can surface and take your rightful position in my future government, Colonel. Especially if we try a peaceful solution to the terrible feeling that currently exist between our two nations at the moment, once we have eliminated the great fool from his command of Iraq, and the world sees us in a different light sir."

Colonel al-Adwani's anger took over his mind, he felt he was being omitted from the future new government of Iraq, and offered hotly to the other Iraqi Officer. "First; I must thank Rasha for keeping my life in the front of her mind. General al-Zahar Sir, what was the purpose of this attack on the American President, sir? It was created to force the cursed American fools to remove the terrible yoke of depression they been drowning Iraq with for all these years, since the close of the Desert Storm war they waged against our country, sir. If we allow the Americans to force me to hide like a lowly jackal within my own country sir, I fear Iraq will never be free of the terrible American oppression the United States is smothering Iraq with, General al-Zahar."

"I assure you Colonel I understand how you feel over what I suggested. What do you suggest we do if you refuse to remain in the background until our new government is established?"

"General al-Zahar Sir, I intend to stand proudly by your side so you can get the foolish Iraqi people use to my appearance before them. Once I'm appointed Prime Minister of Iraq, I don't see how the worthless Americans can possibly perpetrate their revenge on my head. We have to take a firm stand someplace along the line in dealing with the United States and her stubborn people and their worthless allies, sir. Or Iraq will never again be seen as a nation of respect and fear by the world and the other Arab lands of the Middle East, sir. I demand we draw the red line in the sand, and if the foolish Americans come for me and they cross that red line in the sand. There never will be any true peace between our two nations, no matter what we try in our attempt to make peace with the hated fools who think they control the entire earth, General."

General al-Zahar shook his head, half of him wanted to agree with Colonel al-Adwani's complaint. But others in Iraq informed him many times in the past, if he were to align himself with Colonel al-Adwani and his harsh beliefs and anger, his government will never be taken serious by the United States or any of her allies. He wanted to kill Colonel al-Adwani, and easily remove this problem from his mind once and for all. Thinking about it a little further, he felt he should keep the foolish Colonel around for a while longer. Maybe he could use him in the future to form some kind of a lasting deal and peace with the Americans. He wondered if he could offer the Americans, Colonel al-Adwani head trussed up like a stuffed goose, if they would recognize his newly formed government and him as the true leadership of Iraq.

General a-Zahar cleared his throat, and then he offered to the staring Colonel. "Colonel al-Adwani, I like your proud fighting spirit you display before me today, sir. You make me honored to be Iraqi soldier, sir. Yes Colonel, we shall bring you out before the foolish Iraqi people at that. So they can see how well you have served their country and them. Once President Saddam Hussein is dead, I'll indeed appoint you as my Prime Minister of Iraq. When you're a powerful politician for Iraq, I don't see how the Americans can possibly come for you in Iraq. Yes, this is a good idea you have just offered me Colonel and I shall make good use of your offer, Colonel.

"We shall do as you have just offered for certain Colonel al-Adwani." General al-Zahar decided if the not trusted American fools approached him before he came to power, he would quickly hand Colonel al-Adwani over to them peacefully. Then once he was the new President of Iraq, he would call in his favors to the Americans, by demanding they acknowledge him as Iraq's new leader of the damaged nation. He decided he was going to make contact with the Americans himself, and inform them that he had the leader of the terrorists, who tried to kill their precious President in his custody. That way he can claim no kinship to the terrorist actions, and shift the blame entirely on the fool running Iraq now.

"When shall we make our first appearance before the Iraqi people, General al-Zahar Sir? I would like to know and be well prepared before I finally meet the people of Iraq, sir." Colonel al-Adwani asked cautiously, daring to interrupt General al-Zahar's thoughts.

"Yes Colonel al-Adwani, I believe we'll do this introduction to the Iraqi public tomorrow morning. I'll find a most novel way in which to get the cameras to search me out, and look to interview me. You Colonel al-Adwani, shall be standing by my side all the while I'm speaking to the horde of fools, as we begin to spin our web of deceit, laying out the seeds of a coup over our foolish President Saddam. I shall rub you in the noses of the hated Americans for spite and my own personal revenge against the lowly jackals, until they become ill with the taste of you caught in their god cursed throats. I shall prove to the worthless American fools, the future government of Iraq, no longer fears American military power, nor her empty threats leveled against the peoples of Iraq. Yes, this was a good idea I offer you, Colonel. I'm rather pleased you thought of this action, and brought it up to my attention Colonel al-Adwani."

WASHINGTON D.C., CIA HEADQUARTERS, AUGUST 4th, 1999 10:30 EST

When CIA Director John Raincloud and General John White, the Chairman of the Joint Chiefs of Staff parted ways for the day, Director Raincloud headed back for his office. He went to his computer, and made contact with his pair of sleeper agents he ordered working in Baghdad since the conclusion of the Operation Desert Storm War. The Director pulled the two agents from their sleep, and informed them they were to activate immediately, and then trail the Iraqi General Hassan al-Zahar until the missing terrorist, Colonel Abdulaziz Mahd al-Adwani finally made his first appearance in Iraq. The two sleeper agents were ordered to take pictures of any and everyone showing up at General al-Zahar's building, fearing Colonel al-Adwani might be employing a disguised, to help keep the fact he was in Iraq a secret for as long as possible.

When Director Raincloud received conformation from his agents out in the field that they understood their new orders, he broke off their connection. Before he did, he transmitted his latest picture of the wanted Colonel al-Adwani along with a snapshot of General al-Zahar, with the order of activating the sleeper agents operating in Iraq.

EAGLE'S NEST

Director Raincloud had no other choice but to believe Colonel al-Adwani successfully eluded the web he had flung over Washington, and the eastern coast by now, the missing terrorist must have made it back to his country safely. Director Raincloud did not mind this escape, as much as he put on for the President's benefit. Now, once Colonel al-Adwani surfaced back in Iraq, he would know who launched the assassination attempt on the President's life, and have General White and his troops react accordingly against the attempt and the nation of Iraq.

The once pair of sleeper American Agents studied the three picture of the faces of the two Iraqi soldiers the Director wanted them to be on the alert for, committing them to memory then they destroyed the pictures. The two American Arab Agents then began working their way to General al- Zahar's known headquarters. Once there, the two agents quickly set up shop, pretending to be hawking prayer rugs, dates and many worthless trinkets to the civilians walking the street.

The agents bothered everyone passing with their wares for sale, making enough noise to draw attention to their booth. The two agents knew if they did not get in everyone's face, someone was going to become suspicious and challenge them. In Iraq, beggars constantly let the civilians know they were around and had things for sale. The older of the two agents checked his watch, it was five thirty p.m. They discussed and then decided to work until after eight p.m., and then sort of hang around the area begging food or money and watching, always watching.

When the two agents showed up outside General al-Zahar's office and quarters, they took pictures of everyone who entered or exited the building. By six p.m., they took fifteen pictures, and made enough cash to have a good night's meal, and rent a room to sleep.

After six p.m., much of the activity at the target house had stopped, and it became boring to the two agents forced to hawk their wares, until they were almost horse and thoroughly exhausted. By seven thirty p.m., the American Agents considered leaving the area to get something to eat, and rest for the night. But the older agent decided to stay for a little while longer, in case someone turned up late at the building. By eight p.m., both agents closed up shop because they did not want to sell any of their wares too late, for fear someone would ask them what they were up to working so late into the night.

The lead agent watched as the younger and less experienced agent quickly packed up their stuff. He lit a cigarette and then leaned up against a parked car, when he happened to notice a cab slowly coming down the street. He watched attentively as it pulled up before General al-Zahar's headquarters, and then two strangers climbed out of the vehicle. Instantly, the miniature camera replaced his cigarette, as he snapped more pictures of the male, and then the female stranger. The lead agent took four pictures of the male person before he disappeared back in the General's building, not knowing this man was his target.

With the last stranger showing up, the deep cover American Agents decided to remain around the building until ten p.m., maybe later than that if the occasion called for it. No one else entered or left the building for the rest of the night. The two agents decided to eat and then transmit the roll of exposed film to CIA Headquarters, by means of a special miniature radio communication system that turned pictures into a mass of scrambled numbers, letters and lines, and instantly reconstructed them in the CIA lab in the States to the proper pictures and words and numbers.

Director John Raincloud was making a pest of himself, hanging around the office waiting for the first batch of photos to come in. When he was notified some photos arrived from his agents working in Iraq, he rushed to the first floor and entered the lab area of the building.

The technician reconstructing the transmitted photos hung each picture on a drying line hanging before him when they were developed. Director Raincloud and the lead technician closely scrutinized the first batch of photos with powerful magnifying glasses, while comparing each face with the two eight by ten photo of Colonel al-Adwani, one his profile, and the other photo was his face head on. When they reached the photos of the disguised Colonel al-Adwani, they studied them much closer. Both of them agreed out of all the pictures taken by their agents, these four resembled Colonel al-Adwani the closest. The Director scooped all the photos up and then he rushed out of the lab to his car. Once in it, he placed a call to General White, to make certain he was going to be in his office and informed him he was on his way over to him.

It took twenty five minutes to get to the Pentagon building, and Director Raincloud left his car parked under the awning that protected the North entryway to the Pentagon. He rushed in the building and took the elevator up to General White's private office. When he entered, Mary handed him a cup of coffee as he passed through the outer office and headed right for the General's office. He thanked Mary and entered White's office.

"What do you have for me John?" General White asked as he rose half way out of his chair.

"The first batch of pictures came in from my Operatives working in Iraq, General White Sir." The CIA Director reported in an excited voice.

"Great, did they find any sign of the missing sonofabitch in any of the damn photos they sent to us, John?" General White asked him as he got up and prepared to look at the photos.

"I don't know the answer to that question for certain yet, John. I think one set of pictures fits Colonel al-Adwani alright, but I can't be absolutely positive this one man is our missing bird, sir." Director Raincloud replied as he laid out the photos on the General's desk. General White leaned over his desk and carefully studied the photos as the Director laid them out before him.

Director Raincloud had to point out the more suspicious of the photos to the General.

"Jesus Christ Almighty Raincloud, this sonofabitch doesn't look anything like our missing turd as far as I can tell ya. I'm afraid you better got your damn eyes checked if you feel this guy is the one we're looking for here, Chief. I think you're losing it on me my friend."

"I understand that General White, but this one person has the same build, the same facial structure, and the same height of Colonel al-Adwani, John. He's the only one who showed up at General al-Zahar's headquarters that even looks anything like Colonel al-Adwani that my Agents saw all day long, John. I have the lab boys putting copies of the photos through the computer, so they can erase the beard and make his hair longer, and shade in his skin some and also enhance the damn photos a little better for us. I don't know why, but I believe this one person is our missing man, General White." The CIA Director offered to the General as he moved closer to the General and studied the same few photos he was looking at.

"Well, maybe the sonofabitch didn't get to Iraq yet John. Did you ever think of that possibility John? Look Raincloud, as much as I want this lousy prick's ass for the Boss. I don't want to push any god damn panic buttons here, until we're absolutely positive Colonel al-Adwani's back in Iraq and we got him spotted. Who the hell is the damn bitch standing next to this one you feel is our guy? You have anything on her yet John?"

"I'm afraid not yet General. I ran her photo through our CID (Criminal Identification Department), but nothing came up positive on her, she's clean so far, but if that woman is with this guy, then she's as dirty as he is, dammit. Either she was never arrested, or was never under suspicion." Director Raincloud offered as he ignored the way the General was bitching at him.

"Keep after her then. Identify her, and if you discover she's part of Adwani's terrorist group, I'll be forced to agree this bird's our target."

"You got it General White, I'm on it sir. Anything else you want to offer me, General White?" Director Raincloud said back to the General.

"When are you expecting the next batch of photos to come in from your two Operatives working in Iraq?" the General asked as he continued to look at the pictures Director Raincloud dumped out on his desk before him.

"My Agents are instructed to transmit any photos to my office the instant they fill a roll of film. That way, if they're captured, we'll only lose the one roll of film they have in the camera."

"Outstanding Director Raincloud, a good call on your part. Look John, I'm kind of jammed up the damn wazoo with work for today sir. Why don't you head back to your office and wait there for the next roll of film to come in from your damn Operatives. Then, if you think you have something positive to show me, get your ass back here on the double quick, and then we'll submit the picture to the President and see what he thinks of them. I'm getting a little sick and tired of the Boss constantly chewing on my damn ass lately, while we stumble around looking for this missing Iraqi prick all over the face of the damn earth, John."

John nodded in replied to the General's last words, and then he turned and rushed out of the General's office. He left his cup of coffee resting on the General's desk, never once did he touch it.

CHAPTER TWENTY

BAGHDAD, IRAQ. AUGUST 5th, 1999.
8:30 A.M. IRAQI TIME

The two deep cover American Operatives working in Iraq were at their post since six a.m. the following morning on their second day after being activated personally by Director Raincloud. They took three photos of a man leaving General al-Zahar's building earlier. For the past hour and a half, it was quiet. The younger agent tried to talk a passerby into buying his prayer rug at his going price. The buyer wanted to pay half the asking price, and he tried to chew the agent down on the price. The operative was locked in a battle of words and curses with the buyer.

The older agent smiled as he leaned against a parked Iraqi military jeep, and he watched as his partner curse the angry Arab buyer for not wanting to pay his asking price for the rug. He just shifted his weight on his feet when he noticed a car slowly coming down the road. It stopped in front of General al-Zahar's headquarters, and a pile of what he believed to be news reporters, immediately climbed out of the vehicle and they instantly fanned out before the Iraqi General's headquarters. The lead operative realized something big was up, and he pulled the rug out from the younger agent's hand, and he actually gave it to the buyer to end the argument.

The two deep cover operatives spoke between themselves for a few moments, and then the younger one moved to the front of their wagon, while the older agent stayed more or less in the background, and he prepared to take pictures of anyone coming in and out of General al-Zahar's building to greet the gathering reporters. As the two American Agents waited for what was going to take place, more reporters arrived in front of the headquarters, and took over the street and sidewalk, stopping all traffic and people walking in the area. With so many reporters in the area, it made it nearly impossible for the American Operative to get a clear shot at the steps of General al-Zahar's headquarters. The lead agent was certain someone from inside was going to say something to the gathering reporters outside the building.

As the horde of reporters began pushing, cursing and roughly shoving one another out of their way, military police arrived and they made some order out of all the mayhem. The police shoved the reporters out of the road, using the butts of their weapons to move them, and then they set up a number of heavy wood barriers where the reporters had to stay behind. Some of the reporters closed in on the agent's small wagon. The older operative knew he had to react against the sudden crush of reporters, and he cursed and shoved the reporters away from his wagon.

Two Iraqi policemen saw the commotion happening by the small cart, and they made their way over to the wagon. One of the officers fingered the prayer rugs, while the second officer grinned at the two American Agents posing as merchants. The lead operative went to the police officer and he offered him in an excited tone of voice. "Do you like my fine prayer rugs, sir? My lazy good for nothing wife weaves them with her own hands in her spare time. It's the only thing she's good for lately I'm afraid to off to you, sir."

"How many of these lowly rags does your lazy wife make in one day, fool of the desert sand?"

"Three, unless I beat her then she makes up to five, and sometimes even six in a day sir."

"Then I suggest you beat her a little more often you old fool. She should make at least ten of these worthless rags a day, every day of her lazy life, and still have time to see to your pleasures and needs of the rest of the day, old man." he police officer smirked nastily as he continued to finger the fine prayer rug.

The wise agent knew the smug officer just insulted him, and he was bound by honor to react against his nasty words. "Worthless rags you say to me! Alhamdulilah, Praise be to God. Your foul hands have never touched such fine works of art for you to bend your knees to honor Allah, my brother of the sands. Allah would be most pleased if you were to bend your knees upon one of my fine prayer rugs, to pay great homage to Him, you son of a lowly jackal."

"Son of a lowly jackal you say to me old man? I should have you whipped raw for insulting me like this, you dirty old merchant. Along with your foul pig of a wife, filthy camel piss." The suddenly irate Iraqi Police Officer growled nastily as he glared at the operative, and then he dropped the rug he was fingering on the pile of other small prayer rugs on the cart.

"Salam Alaikum, peace be upon you today, sir. Don't be so rash in your judgment of my old and lazy wife and me, my General." The crafty agent offered meekly, now trying to praise the police officer to calm his anger.

"I'm no god cursed General, fool who has his brains scrambled by the heat of the desert."

Some of the reporters began to pay attention to the slight confrontation going on between the police officer and the old beggar, because the two were starting to get loud.

"Please my Sadeeky, (friend) look at the outstanding craftsmanship that went into the making of one of my fine prayer rugs, sir. Just look at the most interesting patterns my lazy wife has worked into the beautiful design, how well they match the rug throughout the work. Allah would be most pleased to see you worship Him upon such fine prayer rugs to honor Him, sir. I'll take your advice and beat my wife more, so she makes more of these fine rugs for me to honor Allah with, sir." The lead operative actually shoved the rug into the young police officer's hands, and then he made him feel the weave again with his fingers and hands.

Some of the reporters shoved closer to the wagon, to see what was happening there.

"Defiled foul ones back off, this is my corner to sell from." The agent balked at the crowd.

"Your corner you say old man? Since when does a filthy jackal from the desert sands claim any part of Iraqi land for his own property, you old fool? Wrap up this mess and leave the area immediately, before I have you arrested and confiscate all your worthless wares, dog born from camel's dung." The police officer ordered him in an angry tone of voice.

"Please no Sadeeky, I must be allowed to continue selling my wears, so I can buy food for my family, and support our government and her fine police officers, sir. This is the best corner in all of Iraq to sell my items from. I woke hours before the sun came up to claim this one place to sell my fine prayer rugs from, Sadeeky. If I'm forced to pack up my cart and leave this place to sell from, my worthless wife and our ten children will surely starve?"

The Iraqi police officer eyed the old looking beggar cautiously, knowing he lied about having that many children, but he also knew what would soothe his anger, and he allow him to let the old beggar remain on the street corner in peace. Without responding to the elderly beggar's complain the Iraqi police officer picked up the rug and allowed it to rest over his arms. When the rug barely sagged in the middle, the officer realized it was fine work at that.

The American CIA Operative knew what would please the officer most, but if he gave in too quick he felt the police officer might become suspicious of his actions, and demand to check his identification papers. Drawing in his breath and acting like he was about to lose his mistress to the affections of another man, the agent and beggar complained in a contrite tone to the officer. "Sadeeky please, allow me to make a present of my lazy wife's fine handicraft to you, sir. It'd bring me great pleasure for you to receive this prayer rug as a special gift from me, sir."

A grin more a sneer than a smile crossed the police officer's lips, as he rolled the fine rug up and then looped it under his arm. He looked at the beggar almost hoping on one foot now, and grumbled at him. "Huh filthy bazaar merchant, you just brought yourself this worthless corner of Baghdad for your use, at least for the rest of this foul day, old fool. If I have any more trouble with you though, I'll have you beaten with the lash old man. Then you'll work on clearing out the filthy slums for a week or more to teach you a lesson in respect, lowly infidel trash."

Reporters shoved the agent, trying to get closer to hear what the officer yelled at the beggar.

This shoving caused the operative to complain again to the Iraqi Police Officer. "Praise Allah, what corner do you offer me to work from, sir? One packed so tightly with a horde of these lowly jackals who receive their worthless pleasure by shoving me around like I don't exist in my own land, sir. I'll not be able to sell a single thing under these conditions with this pack of foul dogs of the desert crowded around my cart, sir. How will my customers ever reach my wagon, to see what I have to offer them with these worthless fools blocking me like they are?" Again, the agent knew what he was doing with the Iraqi Police Officer.

The second police officer moved in front of the first Iraqi guard. This was what the agent was waiting for. When the second officer was near enough to his wagon, the operative picked up a second rug, and he thrust it in his hands. This caused the other officer to grin at him.

"Please Sadeeky, move these god cursed lowly jackals away from my wagon for me. I have fifteen children to feed and clothe, let alone feed a lazy old wife to support."

The second Iraqi police officer nodded pleasantly and smiled, after hearing the old beggar had just increased the size of his family by five, as he began to shove the massing reporters back by barking at them. "Come on, you must give this poor man room to work from. He was here first, and he has staked his claim to this spot to sell his items from. Move back now!"

A rush of curses flooded the area as the reporters were roughly shoved away from the small wagon, and they were forced back behind the wood barricade.

The agent kept nodding and bowing happily towards the officers who ignored him.

There was a slight commotion at the doors of General al-Zahar's building. It instantly got the attention of the reporters as they shoved towards the building. The police formed lines and kept shoving, and now even hitting some of the reporters to keep them behind the barriers.

The door of the building opened and out stepped Colonel Hamoodi al-Qaysi. He stood on the top step of the landing with his hands resting threateningly on his hips, and glaring at everyone crowding the street and sidewalks before the General's headquarters.

The agent snapped a picture of the Colonel he saw him yesterday and sent his picture on.

More people soon gathered behind the angry looking Iraqi Colonel standing on the top steps of the headquarters, and they took up their positions just behind the Iraqi Officers. Try as he might, the American Operative was not able to see clearly all the people standing behind the

329

Iraqi Officer now. A small desk with a number of microphones was hastily setup before the standing Colonel by other soldiers who poured out of the building. Once this was completed, the Iraqi Military Officer stepped aside and General al-Zahar moved forward and sat down before the table. More people moved out of the headquarters, and they stood behind the powerful General.

General al-Zahar did not speak right off as he took some time to scan the many concerned faces of the reporters staring back at him all were calling out questions to him. The General ignored the yelling reporters because he was waiting for silence from them. The reporters soon realized this, and they quieted down to hear what the General had to say.

The agent moved back and forth behind his wagon, covertly snapped pictures of everyone standing on the steps, or near the General. He made certain he got one picture of everyone.

Seven of General al-Zahar's closest military officers followed him out of the building, and they formed a protective circle around him on the steps of the building. A number of servants, along with his private secretaries, and wannabe important people of Iraq, also flooded around the seated and powerful General. Colonel al-Adwani and Rasha were among the last ones to come out of the headquarters. Colonel al-Adwani struggled to move forward through the crowd until he stood nearly right behind the respected and well feared Iraqi General.

Unknown to al-Adwani, two of General al-Zahar's Officers were ordered to shield most of him from view of the reporters and operative snapping picture of the gathered Iraqi soldiers. Rasha was completely blocked out by the much larger male officers gathered on the steps.

When silence replaced the mayhem created by the reporters, General al-Zahar raised his hands and cleared his throat to make certain the microphones were in the proper working order.

After his meeting with Colonel al-Adwani and his female terrorist was completed. General al-Zahar met with Colonel al-Qaysi and a few of his other military officers in private. He was looking for any reason to call for a press conference. It was decided General al-Zahar was going to announce a SAM missile site successfully brought down an American warplane, performing its ordered picket duty in the Northern section of the so called no fly zone of Iraq. Although this was not true, General al-Zahar knew the Iraqi people would be pleased to hear anything good their military was able to accomplish for them. When the mood of the gathered reporters was just right, General al-Zahar began his speech to them.

"Good people of Iraq, your military leaders want to inform you that we're constantly manning our weapons and post's both day and night, defending the borders of Iraq to keep you safe in your homes. Seeking revenge upon the god cursed invaders who freely roam the skies over Iraq, and choose to force on us their own foul and lowly will and orders. August 5th, of 1999, your faithful military warriors were attacked once again by the hated American warplanes in the area the lowly infidels have branded the Northern section of their self imposed no fly zone over our great country. This unprovoked and unwarranted attack against the defenders of Iraq, has netted the worthless American fools dearly for their trouble and efforts, one downed aircraft, and a second aircraft crippled and limped away from the attack, cowardly using the clouds of the sky as cover to escape our wrath and defense against them.

"There was no damage created to the Iraqi missile installation that brought down the American troublemaker. Your proud soldiers have successfully captured the enemy pilot and they are at this moment, transporting the god cursed lowly infidel to Baghdad, so he can be marched through the streets of the city. So the good civilians of Iraq can see the evil American, and all their foul cohorts who are trying desperately to impose their cursed will on the peace loving people of Iraq.

"I pray to the Almighty Allah so He might in His interminable wisdom, give the hated foul and lowly infidels the knowledge to understand the strong and faithful will of the proud Iraqi people. Will never be pounded into the sands of our vast deserts under the threads of their god cursed hated tanks, nor under their cursed lowly bombs and worthless planes of war they continue to attack the innocent citizens of Iraq with. I say let the lying American fools keep coming to Iraq, we have many empty coffins in which to fill with their..."

There was a sudden roar from many of the gathered Iraqi reporters there to hear this press conference from the Iraqi Military Officer that interrupted the General's speech momentarily. The few European reporters remained silent their interest was to report what this Iraqi General was reporting to their country and her people.

The Iraqi General was forced to raise his hand in the air for a second time, to silence the unruly crowd before he continued on with his report to them. After a deep breath, the upset General continued with his words. "People of Iraq, there are countless many who stand behind your proud and well feared Armies, and serve in silence. So they might defend your lives, and make it possible for you to sleep safely at night in your homes anywhere in Iraq. We'll remain diligently standing at our posts until we break the foul will of the hated Americans and United Kingdom efforts to destroy our country, and prove to the world once and for all, that Iraq will no longer be trampled upon by any other nation's wills of the world. At this time, I'll be more than pleased to answer a few questions for the reporters, to help with their story for their newspapers."

Many cries rose from the excited crowd, as each reporter tried their best to be heard over the others. The Iraqi General spotted one of his favorite reporters, and he nodded to him. The reporter instantly asked the Iraqi Military Officer. "General al-Zahar, what type of American warplane was destroyed in today's engagement with our military defenders, sir? And, at what time and where did this latest confrontation take place in our great country of Iraq, sir?"

"Those are very good questions Riyadh al-Obaidi. The invading American enemy warplane I believe was one of their F-15 Eagle fighter bomber aircraft. We saved most of the badly destroyed aircraft, so our military can expertly examine how it was constructed. The foul attack occurred at five thirty this morning. As I stated to you, in the so called Northern no fly zone of our country, set up by our enemy who believe they control the proud will of the Iraqi peoples."

More questions interrupted the General's words, and he decided to answer another reporter. Once the General looked at the man, he called out to him. "General al-Zahar, what type of weapon did we use to bring down this hated American intruder to our land, sir?"

"It was a SAM Gadfly Seven missile. It was built by our Russian brothers and allies, and given to us for the better defense of our nation of Iraq against the hated American and their worthless ally invaders of our sacred lands." The General replied proudly to the reporter.

Another question was shouted out by an unseen reporter from the group. "What is the condition of the filthy American flyer, and was he captured alive, General al-Zahar?"

"I'll answer that question. The reports I read state the invading enemy pilot is in relatively good shape. He has received a few minor cuts and bruises, but nothing life threatening."

"General al-Zahar, will you be releasing the United States pilot back to the Americans, sir?"

"No!" the General growled harshly and then he went on with his angry words to the reporters. "I'll release the foul pilot only to the Red Cross, once we had a chance to question him thoroughly, but we'll never release him back to the hated Americans. There never will be any lasting friendship between our two nations, until the skies over Iraq are free of all allied planes of war, and their evil bombs of death they drop upon the unsuspecting innocent civilians of Iraq. I refuse to be forced to deal with desert rats under any circumstances now."

"General al-Zahar, are you saying the American pilots are nothing more than desert rats to you sir?" A second unseen voice called out from the middle of the crowd of news reporters.

"What else can they be thought of as, fool? The hatful American and English pilots are guilty of acting like desert rats, feasting upon the bones of the dead and dying of Iraq's faithful innocent men, women and children. Yes, it is true that we had invaded Kuwait with just cause, which is rightfully our land in the first place, and was our right to do so. And yes, we received a bloody nose from the god cursed Coalition Forces in that war of honor waged against Iraq. But how long do these foul Armies of lowly infidels and jackals intend to pick Iraq apart, and keep us from rejoining the other peace loving nations of the world? The foul forces that wish to destroy Iraq as a sovereign nation are more than willing to allow our civilians to slowly starve to death, before the very eyes of the entire world and the United Nations.

"The lowly dogs praying Iraq will slowly wilt under these foolish and most smothering sanctions imposed on us, mostly because of the will of the United States? Why? Because they wish Iraq would dry up and be blown out of the conscious of mankind by the desert's great shammals. (Sand storms) War is war, and once that war is over, it's time for all nations involved in that war, to come together as one to allow the healing to begin at the peace tables, and work out their differences to the satisfaction of all nations involved in that war, not just for the United States and the United

Kingdom's satisfaction. Look at the Americans they have made peace with Vietnam, though locked in the hearts of many of their proud warriors, that war is not concluded.

"The god cursed United States is also trying to make peace with North Korea. The foolish Americans try to wine and dine the Chinese, yet they wish to punish the good nation of Iraq for endless centuries to come. Why? Because the United States mighty Armies were unable to break the unconquerable spirit that makes Iraq the proud and strong nation she is today, and the fools resent that fact. The Americans and United Kingdom resent Iraq's very existence upon this earth, because the people of Iraq will not bend their knee and bow to the great America's will and outlandish demands made on them. Iraq is the only other nation unable to be conquered by the great American and English war might.

"We're on an equal footing with the Vietnamese people, yet the United States wish to ignore us, and yet they deal with the Vietnam government openly and kindly. Yes, I believe the foolish Americans are lowly desert rats as I have stated before, and I'll continue to believe this way until the American fools prove otherwise to me, and my great nation of Iraq and her citizens."

"Do you think the United States might form some sort of rescue attempt of their downed fighter pilot, General al-Zahar?" Someone else called out from in the midst of reporters.

"I say let the American fools dare to set one foot upon Iraqi sand, I just dare them try. I'll personally chop it off and feed it to my dogs." The General bellowed as he raised his fist in the air and shook it violently and glared at the gathered reporters. His threat was drowned out by cheering of the Iraqi reporters for his threatening words aimed at the United States.

At the headquarters of President Saddam Hussein, the President of Iraq was glued to his TV. He was locked in a blind rage, fuming because he was not appraised his military defenders successfully brought down an American warplane. Ever since the United States first started to enforce the two no fly zones in his country, Saddam Hussein prayed for his defenders to bring down just one of the American warplanes. Now, his prayers have been answered by Almighty Allah, and he felt he was the last one to know about this great feat. He ordered his staff out to bring General al-Zahar to him when he finished addressing the reporters. Saddam allowed his wrath to fall down upon the heads of anyone in his headquarters as he ranted and raved at the General's face staring at him from the TV screen, and he could not do anything to stop it.

Iraqi President, Saddam Hussein knew there were many in his country who sought his job, and until now, he always trusted General al-Zahar with his life. Now, Saddam wanted his powerful General dragged before him in chains, to answer why he went on the air before the countless news reporters of the world, and he did not inform him so he could be the one to tell the Iraqi people they finally destroyed an American warplane, and then he could reap the rewards of a successful mission carried against the invading American and their allies.

In his blind rage, Saddam ordered his guard to a higher level of alert, in case this Iraqi General was planning a coup aimed against him. He ordered certain members of his government to his stronghold palace to form a ring of protection around him. He wanted them surrounding him when the powerful General was dragged before him, to answer for his foul crimes committed against him and his country. He wanted the select few soldiers around him, so they could not jump him, and lend support to this General suddenly challenging him for his Presidency. He demanded to know which troops were under General al-Zahar's control, and once found out those troops were to be relieved of duty by troops more loyal to Saddam Hussein's rule.

WASHINGTON D.C., THE PENTAGON

The concerned Chairman of the Joint Chiefs of Staff, General John White listened attentively to his radio. He did not have the luxury of a live picture feed to watch what was taking place in Iraq. To see this Iraqi General's sneering face as he reported this false kill of one of his aircraft to his people. He wondered why it was this Iraqi General was reporting the supposed kill to the Iraqi public instead of Saddam Hussein, or his usual staff not reporting the possible coup of the century for his government. The American General fumed, fearing the Iraqi gunners might have finally got lucky, and they might have brought down one of his warplanes.

Calls flooded his office from many different military commands stationed throughout the Middle East, and had anything to do with enforcing the no fly zones over the skies of Iraq, assuring him none of their warplanes were reported missing or unaccounted for over the skies of Iraq. Other officers, Senators and politicians, likewise called the General's office to see if this latest confabulation from Iraq bore any truth to it.

For the most part, General White allowed his staff to field most of the pain in the ass questions for him. But when the General was informed the President of the United States was on the line, and he was demanding to speak with him personally, he answered this call himself.

"Yes Sir Mr. President, General White here sir." The General offered pleasantly.

"For the love of God John, what the hell's going on in Iraq, dammit! Did the lousy bastards finally down one of our aircraft or what, sir? And, if this is a fact General White, why the hell wasn't I informed about this shit, before I had to hear it come over the damn news wire, mister? I need to know about these things STAT, General White!"

"With all due respect Mr. President, as of this time I can neither confirm nor deny any of the Iraqi General's asinine remarks and claims, sir." General White replied with his usual pact answer to anyone he was speaking with, if he truly did not know the answers to the questions he was being asked. He was further angered the President was getting on his case over something he did not know if it was true or not as yet.

"What the hell's that line of shit you're dumping on me now, mister? I'm no damn news reporter who you want to withhold any information from, General White! I'm the damn President of the United States, and I demand an answer to my last question of you, mister. I better get one if you hope to hold onto your job after today, General White Sir. And, I better get it right now at that or else, General White! I needed this news like I needed a hole in the head, especially after some damn fool just tried to blow my damn head off my shoulders a couple of weeks ago, General White!" The fuming and extremely angry American President responded, angrier than the first time he spoke with the General.

"Yes Sir Mr. President! With all due respect, all military units presently involved in the imposition of the no fly zones over the Iraqi airspace both north and south of Baghdad, haven't checked in with me as of yet, sir. This lack of this confirmation is blocking me from giving you a more positive response to your last question either way, Mr. President Sir." General

White shifted the receiver to the other ear, and rubbed his burning eyes with his fingers.

"General White, why the hell do I feel you're giving me a reach around to my question, sir? I'm not use to you responding to me in this fashion, and I'm telling you General. I'm not enjoying your response to me one bit, sir." The President growled at the military officer.

Unseen by General White, the President ran his hand through his hair, and then he turned his head and blew his breath away from the receiver. The pressure to capture the missing terrorist was getting on everyone's nerves, and the President continued with his angry words aimed at his military officer. "It looks like I'm going to be forced accept this line of bullshit you're spoon feeding me for the moment, mister. Christ sake! General, I want to know the first second you can confirm either way if Iraq got one of our damn aircraft sir. If I find out from the media before I hear it from you, sir. I swear to the Good Christ Child General White, you'll walk a post at the North Pole dick deep in snow while dodging Polar Bears, mister."

"Yes Sir Mr. President, the second I'm appraised either way of the possible kill to one of our aircraft, you'll know about it at once, sir." General White smiled over the President's comment about the North Pole, ignoring his threat knowing the President was just kind of overreacting to the possibility of Iraq shooting down one of their warplanes.

"Very well then General White, I guess I have to ask you to give me your honest opinion on this crap, sir. Do you really think the damn Iraqi military was able to knock down one of our aircraft? We know damn well this is one of this madman's orders to his military. Saddam Hussein wants one of our aircraft even more than he wants the lands of Kuwait now you know that for a fact General White." The President's voice sounded a little contrite.

"Truthfully Mr. President Sir?" the General asked the President seriously.

"Damn right truthfully General White! Who the hell do you think you're talking to here dammit, a Senator mister?" the upset President shot right back in anger.

General White responded with one word to the fuming President of the United States. "No!"

"You sound extremely confident over that last response, sir. Why is that General White?"

"Because Mr. President, if the Iraqi gunners got one of our aircraft, we wouldn't have found out about it until they had the damn thing on the back of the flatbed truck, and dragging the damn thing through the streets of Baghdad, and their wild ass civilians beating on it with anything they can pick up and hammer it with, Mr. President Sir."

"Okay General White, I'm going to take your word for that last statement, sir. What? Hold on for a second will you please General White. I seem to have another call coming in that I must respond to immediately, sir." A few seconds later the President was back and speaking with his military officer. "General White Sir, I'm sorry but I have to go, I have the Prime Minister from the United Kingdom on the horn, and he's telling me it emphatically wasn't one of his planes the Iraqi's might have shot down today. If this aircraft was shot down, that means if one is down, it has to be one of ours. God damn, I wish to hell this damn crap was over with already. Let me know when you can confirm it either way, General White."

The White House Chief of Staff aide entered the Oval Office and mouthed the words informing the President the President of France was on the line, wishing to speak with him.

The President nodded at his favorite young aide, and then he waved his hand at Peter as he listened to the General's last words over the phone. The President then he hung up when he knew the General did not have anything else to report to him of any importance.

"Will do Mr. President Sir." The General replied to a dial tone.

General White placed a personal call to every military station supplying warplanes and other military equipment for the no fly zone enforcement of Iraq. He wanted to hear from their Commander's lips, if they did not lose a plane over the skies of Iraq on this day.

BAGHDAD, IRAQ

Iraqi General Hassan al-Zahar sat defiantly in front of his small desk placed on the top steps of his headquarters while wearing the smile of a smug looking man. He reviled in all the attention he was receiving from the news media, as the horde of reporters scrambled to try and hear every word from his lips. The powerful General knew he was backstabbing President Saddam Hussein over this press conference, but he no longer feared his wrath falling down upon his shoulders. He now classified Saddam Hussein as a defeated President who was just waiting for the right man to come along, and drive him from office, and General al-Zahar believed he had the backing from most of the Iraqi military to accomplish this feat.

The Iraqi General al-Zahar enjoyed the complete backing of two of the most feared Republican Guards Units of the six spread throughout the rest of Iraq. The largest, the Hammurabi Unit with well over one hundred and thirty thousand well trained and highly motivated Iraqi troops, along with the Al-Nida Unit. With over one hundred and ten thousand tried and well seasoned Iraqi troops, and the armor and military weapons needed to back any attempted coup General al-Zahar might decide to try against Saddam Hussein's command.

Both Republican Guard Unit personnel were stationed in and around the Iraqi city and capital of Baghdad, reporting to his office their every movement of late. The Units were under General al-Zahar's direct control during the Kuwaiti campaign, he was basically responsible for getting the soldiers out of Kuwait when the Coalition Forces began overwhelming the Iraqi troop occupying that country. These soldiers were not going to forget that General al-Zahar was the one who saved them from the terrible slaughter under the American Juggernaut of a war machine.

With this announcement of the shooting down of one of the United States warplanes today, though false as it was, gave the civilian population of Iraq something good to believe in for a change, and to see that new leadership was being born in their country. General al-Zahar added to his smile, when he remembered what Colonel al-Qaysi warned him of when they spoke privately about offering this press conference to the world. Colonel al-Qaysi was most concerned about the civilian reaction to it, when it was discovered the downing of the United States warplane did not truly occur, that this story was nothing but a lie.

General al-Zahar remembered telling his concerned officer not to worry about it, that they would merely turn the story around and state the lie was born within the President's office. That way, any wrath the population would seek, would automatically be aimed at the fool running the country of Iraq, and not at them. The General took a deep breath, making his chest swell with pride, as he arched his back and gazed at the faces staring at him as if he were a god.

All the while the powerful Iraqi General was addressing the unending questions being fired at him fast and furiously from the gathered reporters of the world. Colonel al-Adwani constantly tried to get his face in front of the milling swarm of military personnel constantly blocking him from the reporter's view. He realized the protective ring that the wise General had set around him, successfully blocked most of the reporters from seeing his face. Each time the concerned Colonel al-Adwani moved to the front of the group of soldiers and others cluttering the steps of the General's headquarters, he was not so politely shoved back to his previous position by one of the military officers surrounding General al-Zahar.

The older American Operative tried his best to get behind some of the pesky reporters, to get in a better position to snap a photo of everyone standing on the top step of the General's private headquarters. The agent found it nearly impossible to get a clear photo of everyone gathered on the steps of the building, so he got some group pictures from a number of different angles. He was on his third roll of film, and so far, no one paid much attention to his antics.

One Iraqi police officer noticed the American Agent moving around behind the crowd of reporters, and it seemed to him the old merchant was taking pictures of the Iraqi General. But he decided to let it go as something the old beggar was doing, so he would have pictures of the powerful General he could sell the next time he set up business some where else on the streets of Baghdad. The officer absentmindedly fingered the fine prayer rug given to him by the old man moments ago as he thought, and then he classified the old man as harmless and decided to allow the old beggar to take his worthless pictures of the powerful General.

He got what he wanted from the old man, and he was not going to stop him from making a little money off some pictures he took of the respected military officer. The police officer knew corruption was rampart in the streets of Iraq, and he was not going to be a fool by not taking full advantage of any situation when it showed itself to him.

When this roll of film was used up, the lead operative decided to transmit what he had already accumulated so far, back to his control in Washington. In case he happened to draw the interest of the horde of

EAGLE'S NEST

police officers suddenly ringing the group of news reporters, standing in the street before the General's headquarters. He walked towards the back of the small wagon, and secretly placed another roll of film inside the tiny camera. Then he placed the machine in the hands of the second and younger agent, while telling him he was going to report to their control and send the pictures he had back to their control.

The younger American deep cover special agent knew he was only supposed to hold on to the camera and protect it with his life, and not dare take any more pictures of anyone or thing happening in the middle of the street before him. The younger agent received orders to drop the small camera in the cup of acid resting on the back of the wagon, if he felt any Iraqi police officers were going to question them over what they were doing so near a military press conference, especially if they were spotted taking pictures of the event.

The lead agent walked down the narrow filthy alleyway to the rubble covered back courtyard of four connected buildings. Broken glass, shattered bricks and yards of crumbled concrete made walking extremely hazardous in the cluttered filled courtyard area. It was one of the many places the Iraqi government had piled rubble from the Allied bombing of their city during the Desert Storm War. Most of the rubble was classified as salvageable goods, thus it was being stored in selected pockets such as these until needed again. The pockets of rubble spread throughout the country, was now the living quarters of many of the homeless of Iraq. This pile of debris was no different from any of the others.

As the lead agent cautiously entered the courtyard, he saw a number of young children instantly disappear under the pile of rubble like a pack of rats running away from the daylight. Then the curses and demands to know what the suddenly invader wanted in their domain filled the air about him. The American Operative ignored the angry calls being aimed at him as he walked around the massive pile of building materials to the section he claimed for his private living space. He removed the piece of corrugated metal he used as a door, and then he crawled into the cave he had drilled in the mountain of loose building debris. With his foot, he shoved a second piece of metal over the opening, sealing himself inside his small tomb, so he could report to CIA Director John Raincloud in private.

The American Operative had no fear whatsoever the Iraqi police would detect his small radio, or his hiding place. It was the latest in the field of covert communications. The radio and transmitter was so small, he was able to hide it from the most determined of searchers easily. It took the agent a few moments to set up the radio and connect the antenna, a strip of discarded electrical wire he had run up the side of the pile of rubble. When he completed hooking up the radio, the agent took a moment to catch his breath and calm his trembling nerves.

Before the crafty CIA Agent began the transmission to his command headquarters back in the United States, he listened to the sounds of life filling the cluttered back courtyard. When he heard children playing in the courtyard again, he dared to send his message to his control in the United States. The all but forgotten children of the capital city were the best warning alarm any special operative could possibly ask for to protect them from discovery. The street wise children knew when soldiers or police were coming, even before they knew it themselves.

The operative placed the first undeveloped roll of film inside the small pocket of the radio, and then he pounded out the location the photos were to be sent to on the miniature palm held key pad. There was a low hum coming from the radio, as it connected to the location indicated. Once the connection was made, the hum turned into a low pitch whine, as the film was instantly sent out to the other station in the United States in a flash of static.

The once American Sleeper Operative knew when the miniature machine was finished transmitting the pictures sent out because the hum stopped. He removed the film and exposed it to the glare from the sun filtering into his narrow tomb. Then the agent inserted the second roll of film into the radio, and repeated the process again. When all three rolls of film were transmitted to his control and destroyed by him, the lead operative disconnected the radio from its makeshift antenna, and returned it to its hiding place under the rubble in his narrow hiding place.

The American CIA Agent then took some time to enjoy a cigarette in peace, and once he finished it, he shoved the bent and jagged metal makeshift door aside with his feet, and then he painfully backed out the extremely narrow hole drilled into the mountain of bomb rubble. Once outside, the agent covered the opening over with the second piece of metal he used to hide his private place in the huge rubble pile. There was something about the countless homeless and poor of Iraq. They would steal anything not bolted down from anyone, but they would never steal a thing from one another of the poor. The American Special Operative believed it was as simple as a matter of honor among thieves.

Once the agent was satisfied he covered his hiding place good enough, he returned to his wagon, and the horde of news reporters still screaming to be heard by the seated Iraqi General. When the operative came out of the alley, he fussed with his robe especially around him crotch area, to make anyone watching him believe he went down the alley to relieve himself. When he returned to the small wagon, the second agent handed him the camera, and the lead operative went back to work trying to get a snapshot of everyone still hanging around in the open on the steps surrounding the General's headquarters.

CHAPTER TWENTY ONE

LANGLEY, VIRGINIA, CIA HEADQUARTERS.
2:30 P.M. EST, AUGUST 5th, 1999

The Central Intelligence Agency Director, John Raincloud sat in his office with his feet resting lightly on the top of his desk, while he was leaning way back in his chair with his hands clasped behind his head. He was sort of daydreaming and relaxing for the first time today. He was thoroughly exhausted from the trying strain of waiting for the next batch of photos to arrive from his two operatives working inside Iraq. He was taking a few moments for himself, when his intercom suddenly startled him. The Director removed his feet from the top of his desk, and then he leaned forward and snapped the button on his intercom and offered into the machine. "Yes!" Was all he growled into the machine and then he waited to hear what he thought was his secretary, had to offer him.

"Director Raincloud, this is Sam downstairs at the Envision Lab Section, sir. I'm informing you that I have just received four new rolls of film from our Operative Sand Flea, Director Raincloud Sir." Sand Flea was the code name given to the operative team recently activated in Iraq by Director Raincloud.

"Jesus why the hell didn't you say so with a little more enthusiasm in your voice Sam, for Christ sake. I swear to all that's Holy Sammy, you wouldn't get excited about a damn blowjob, mister. I'll be right down son." Director Raincloud snapped as he shook his head to the boring sounding response by his lead technician over the next batch of photos to arrive.

EAGLE'S NEST

John shot out of his office with his secretary calling out after him. "I'll hold all your calls until you return to your office, Director Raincloud Sir."

"Yeah, please do that Mary." Was all John replied as he disappeared in the elevator.

The CIA Director entered the lab section as the technician removed the first of twenty four photos from the developing bin. Sam laid them out carefully on the drying table, and Director Raincloud did not wait for them to dry before he began to examine them with the powerful magnifying glass. The worried Director had his fingers crossed he was going to spot the missing Colonel al-Adwani in the new collection of snapshots sent to him by his agents in Iraq. Try as he did to block his agents from losing interest in the case by constantly rotating them from one assignment to another, many of them were growing bored looking for a missing shadow in the United States. He knew sooner or later, the attention from his agents was going to lax, and even if the terrorist was still trapped in the States. He would easily escape with little trouble, when his agents began to feel there was no hope of locating him any longer stateside.

Director Raincloud wanted to locate the missing Colonel al-Adwani terrorist in the batch of photos, because he wanted to know where the Iraqi Colonel was hiding, so he can make the proper preparations for his capture. If Colonel al-Adwani did show up anywhere in Iraq, the problem then became General White's cause to find the solution to, and he would relax some for himself once that was determined.

Sweat dripped from his brow and dropped onto the first batch of photos he was examining. Director Raincloud ignored the drop of sweat as he carefully studied the harsh looking face of Colonel Hamoodi al-Qaysi that seemed to be glaring at him from the photo, and then he complained to Sam with a snap in his voice. "What the hell's wrong with those two asses over there for Pete's sake, dammit? They sent me pictures of this one in the first batch of photos they took of the man. He was already identified as Colonel al-Qaysi, one of General al-Zahar's many flunkies he usually surrounds himself with." Director Raincloud complained to the young lab technician busy working on developing the second batch of photos.

"Maybe because it's another day and they chose to snap his face again for some reason, Director Raincloud. They could have thought they might have missed him the first time around, and they were making certain they had him on film this time, sir. At this point, I'd rather have more pictures of the same person, than suffering the possibility they might have overlooked the one we're looking for, sir." The technician said over his shoulder to the CIA Director.

The Director looked at the back of the young technician, and then he bitched at him in a sharp voice. "Sammy, you're a wealth of wisdom today I see, mister. How the hell many damn shots did the Operatives transmit this time around to us, mister?"

"I believe we received four complete rolls of film, than makes it ninety six shots in all Mr. Director Sir." Sammy replied as he continued to work on developing the next roll of film.

"I can count for myself, wiseguy. Just keep on with what you're doing, and keep your opinions to yourself unless I ask for them, dammit." John snorted nastily as he went back to the stack of slowly drying photos spread out on the reading table. As he leaned over the table, Director Raincloud's cell phone suddenly raised a fuss on him.

"Jesus what now, dammit?" he growled as he nearly ripped the phone out of his pocket. He hated to be interrupted when working. "Yeah." He hissed in the phone.

General White's eyebrows arched at the way John snapped in the phone and he fired back at him. "That's it John, it's nothing but decaf coffee from here on out for you, buddy."

"General White!" the Director more asked than said in the phone.

"Yep, what's up John, you sound pissed off more than usual today, sir. Didn't get any last night, huh my friend?" General White asked the powerful CIA Director over the phone.

"I'm rather busy working right now General White Sir." The large Native American growled back in the phone at the military officer.

"Gees, that's too damn bad, what the hell do you think I'm doing, Chief?" General White snorted back into the phone this time, pissed off at the way the Director just snapped at him.

"Chasing Mary around your office I'd suspect General White."

"Ha, fucking ha wiseguy." The General smirked back in the phone.

"What the hell do you want from me today anyway General? I'm busy at the moment sir."

"Hey Chief, give me a damn break here will ya huh, this fucking terrorist thing's getting on everyone's dick nerve lately mister. I called to find out if any new photos came in from your damn Operatives working in Iraq." The General offered to Director Raincloud.

"I should've known you'd be calling about that, General White. I just received another batch of photos this very minute from my two Operatives, sir. What do you have my office bugged or something, General White? I'm looking at soaking wet snapshots at the moment." Director Raincloud complained at the military officer as he continued to look at the new batch of photos.

"You want me to come over, so you don't have to fight the Washington traffic, John?"

"It'd help me out greatly if you do that for me, General White." Director Raincloud replied.

"I'm on my way John. See ya in about twenty or a few minutes longer, Chief." General White hung up the phone, and then darted out of his office like someone was chasing him. The General was exhausted, and he wanted to go home in the worse way and enjoy one of his wife's home cooked meals, and maybe share her love for the night, and then he would turn in for the night. The idea of seeing a new batch of photos from Director Raincloud's Operatives working in Iraq gave him renewed vigor, as he rushed for his parked staff car.

It took General John White longer than expected to fight his way through the maddening traffic of downtown Washington, to get over to CIA headquarters. By the time he arrived at the CIA headquarters in Langley Virginia, Director Raincloud was already scrutinizing the third set of photos sent to him by his two operatives in Iraq.

General White tossed his hat on the chair and went over to Director Raincloud's side where he was going over the latest photos. Sam came over with the last batch of pictures and handed the General a strong magnifying glass so he could better study them.

He looked up while taking the glass and mumbled at the young man. "Thanks, my eyes aren't what they used to be lately I'm afraid, Sammy. Don't smile at me like that mister, you'll see what I mean when you get to be around my age, mister."

"Aren't all of ours sir." Sam replied pleasantly as he laid the last pictures in the drying bin.

General White turned to Director Raincloud and grumbled almost in a nasty tone at him. "Did you spot the sonofabitch hiding in any of these new god damn snapshots of yours, John?"

"Afraid not yet John, some of the shots are worse than crap though. I can't make anyone out in them very clearly for Pete's sake, sir. They're suffering from sun glare, and other crap like that I guess, General. My damn Operatives must be having a hell of a hard time lining up their shots from what I can tell by the pictures I looked at so far from them, John. From what I can see of the photos, if this Colonel al-Adwani bastard stood right out in the damn open, with the piss poor quality of some of these shots, I wouldn't be able to pick him out if my life depended on it, dammit." Director Raincloud complained as he moved some of the photos around to get a better look at them. By now, many of the pictures were beginning to overlap one another, and it was getting harder and harder to see the ones underneath the other photos.

"How the hell are you seeing what the hell you're doing here for Christ sake, John? With the mess these photos are in, I can't see a shitting thing about them any longer dammit, and you're bitching about the damn quality of the shots? Don't we have a better place where we can lay these damn things out more, and see them any better for ourselves?" General White complained at the CIA Director as he looked at him with angry eyes.

Director Raincloud straightened up and realigned his back by wiggling his hips, and then he groaned as he offered to the General." I suppose you're right John. I guess we can always bring the pictures over to the work table and spread them out better for ourselves there, sir."

"I'm afraid a good many of the photos aren't quite dried yet, Director Raincloud Sir." Sam griped at John over his thought to move the photos from the drying table.

"What the hell's the matter with you mister? You afraid you're going to get stuck cleaning up another work station, Sam? You're getting worse than my wife with your complaining lately." The Director snapped hotly, pissed off that Sam was bringing up such trivial matters to him.

"It's not that at all, sir. But we have certain precautions we must keep in mind at all times, while we're working with any photos being developed in the labs, to better secure the correctness of the photos, sir." Sam grumbled at his boss.

"Fuck the damn precautions Sam. We have to spread these damn things out better so we can examine them much closer, or we're never going to be able to find this missing terrorist, if his ass is in this damn lot of photos, mister." General White barked, and did not wait for the Director and lab technician to finish butting heads with each other. He just scooped up an arm full of the photos and slung them on the larger table and then spread them out so none of the photos were overlapping one another. Director Raincloud joined him and they put the pictures in certain lots. Any that did not resemble the missing terrorist Colonel al-Adwani in the least, were stacked one on top of the other and discarded from the rest of the photos. Even though the pictures were placed aside, they were still going to be added to the file pertaining to any possible future troublemakers from Iraq. Copies of the photos were also going to be sent over to the FBI Security Index Section, which lists all people considered to be possible threats to public officials and the national security of the United States or any of her allies.

By the time General White and Director Raincloud eliminated many of the pictures for consideration sent to them by the two operatives working in Iraq, they were left with a thin stack of group shots to still go through. When General White and Director Raincloud removed many pictures from the lot, they laid the remaining ones out in neat rows so they can see them clearer.

BAGHDAD, IRAQ

The older American CIA Operative could not get a good angle on a few of the men still standing just behind the Iraqi General who was speaking to the gathered reporters, no matter how hard he tried. He felt he was moving around too much and was worried he was going to draw attention to himself, and he decided to wait until the news conference started to break up some. Maybe then he could get a photo of the few persons he might have missed in the other photos. The lead CIA Operative joined his fellow special agent over at the small wagon, and he started to hawk his wears and cursed at anyone who ignored them or just looked at their items for sale.

General Hassan al-Zahar was rapidly growing bored with the press conference changing from what he wanted to talk about. When the question if he though Iraq might have been wrong with their invasion of Kuwait was asked of him by one of the reporters, he jumped to his feet and leaned on the table with both hands resting on the surface, and he barked savagely at the reporter who just asked him the tough question. "Where the devil do you come from, you foul fool you? How dare you ask me such a god cursed foolish question like that."

"The Netherlands sir." The reporter replied, trying a smile on the Iraqi General.

"Then mister reporter from the Netherlands, I suggest you go back to the Netherlands and leave Arab matter to the Arab people to solve for themselves, sir. We don't need any Khawajis (outsiders) questioning what the Iraq people believe, or questioning any of their actions of the past, present, or the foul future. That is it, I'm ending this god cursed press conference right here and now. You worthless fools are not the least bit concerned over what is truly happening to the nation of Iraq. You fools are only interested in what happened in the past times. I can no longer change the past than I can stop the mighty power of the Shammal, nor would I want to change the past. We learned much from our past mistakes, so they'll never happen again to us, sir."

The fuming Iraqi Military Officer turned his back on the reporters in anger and angrily stormed away from the table in a huff. The people standing behind him on the steps parted, so the extremely upset General could walk through them and get back inside the building with little trouble. Most of the other military officers quickly followed General al-Zahar inside the structure, but Colonel al-Adwani decided to remain standing outside the building.

He finally realized this as his first chance to get his face before the many reporters still milling about before the General's headquarters. He began fussing around with a number of papers left lying on the desk the General read from. Some of the reporters shouted new questions out at him, asking him for his name and what he was doing in the building. Colonel al-Adwani ignored all their calls as he continued to stack the papers into a neat pile.

The American Operative realized this man was one of the few persons in the gathering he was unable to get a clear shot of before this time, and he clicked away at him. A second man, a civilian suddenly joined this stranger at the small table, and the operative included him in some of his snapshots he was taking of the mystery Iraqi Colonel.

Colonel al-Adwani nastily shouldered the second man away from him as he looked up and stared at the reporters still hanging around the General's headquarters, to give them a chance to get a good look at him and his face. He had no fear whatsoever over the fact the hated Americans might be already looking for him in Iraq. Since he arrived home, he was constantly being surrounded by a group of heavily armed Iraqi soldiers. His head spun around, and Colonel al-Adwani smiled when he saw the soldiers General al-Zahar assigned to him as his personal bodyguards were still standing their post near his side. In his mind, he was actually daring anyone to try and snatch, or kill him while he was so well protected by his lesser soldiers.

The Iraqi Colonel reasoned if the American soldiers came after him and they failed in their attempt to assassinate him, his standings with the Iraqi people would grow by leaps and bounds. Feeling far superior with the soldiers standing so near behind him, he placed his hands on his hips and straightened up, and glared at the reporters starting to leave the once press conference.

The lead CIA Operative smiled as he mumbled to himself. 'Go ahead and smile for my little camera, you great fool. If you're the asshole my boss is searching for, your worthless days are numbered on this earth, my most unwise friend'. The agent took seven pictures of this man in total. Making certain he got both sides of his profile, as well as a few shots of him straight on. When the agent felt he had enough pictures of this man, he looked for more targets to film.

He took a few more pictures, and then he backed off when he ran out of targets. The agent went to his brother operative and helped him finish a sale to one of the reporters still hanging around in front of the General's headquarters. The lead agent grumbled for the lesser operative to wrap it up for the day. He felt he had a photo of everyone in General al-Zahar's building. Besides, he did not want to press his luck any further then he already done. The older operative had six exposed rolls of film and wanted to get them out of his possession as soon as possible.

When the younger agent had most of the wagon packed up to his satisfaction, the older operative announced for the sake of anyone observing their actions, and listening to what they spoke about, that he had to relieve himself again. Then he headed for the courtyard for a second time on this day. The same scene repeated itself with the young Iraqi children disappearing under the pile of rubble, and the cursing started anew against him as he headed for his radio.

The agent smiled at one of the filthy children who did not seem like he wanted to hide this time, wondering when these kids were ever going to get used to his presence in the cluttered and filthy courtyard. He did not understand these kids were destined to grow up not trusting anyone for the rest of their lives. Thus insuring the hatred Iraq held for the outside world, would continue to grow in future generations. The agent rolled the metal sheet out of his way and crawled inside, moving the second piece of metal in place with his feet. He quickly set up the radio, and then waited for the hum and then he transmitted the next roll of film on its way.

CENTRAL INTELLIGENCE AGENCY HEADQUARTERS, LANGLEY VIRGINIA

The Chairman of the Joint Chiefs of Staff, General John White's back was killing him from bending down so much while staring at the many photos the agents sent them, so he straightened up to try and relieve some of the pressure off his back. He was beginning to believe Colonel al-Adwani was not in Iraq as yet, or at least, he was not bothering to report to General al-Zahar as of this time. The powerful military officer was sort of daydreaming and working on the pain in his back, when Director Raincloud suddenly announced in an excited tone to him.

"Dammit to hell and all the way back again General White Sir, I really think I got the missing fucking bird in this one photo, sir!"

The pain in the General's back instantly left as he leaned forward and studied the picture Director Raincloud held in his hand examining it.

"Look General White, check out the fellow standing next to the one in the Iraqi military uniform. Here, take my glass, it's much stronger than the one you're using there, sir."

General White took the offered looking glass and carefully examined the picture, while Director Raincloud took a moment to straighten out himself. General White squinted, even closing one eye so he could concentrate more directly on the partially blocked face on the photo and then he grumbled. "Ahhhh... I don't know John, I can't see enough of this bird's damn puss to say for sure it's Colonel al-Adwani's mug. Are there anymore pictures with this guy's puss in them? Maybe one that'll show his damn face a little clearer for us, John?"

"Yes, I already put them aside, General White. But I'm afraid this one is the best shot in the entire lot we got of the one man in question here, sir. I can only hope my Operatives can get a clearer photo of this bird so we can be certain it's this damn Colonel we want, sir."

"Dammit to hell Director." General White growled as he tossed the picture and magnifying glass down on the table and bitched at Director Raincloud. "I can't swear this man's this damn Colonel al-Adwani from that shot or not, John. Can you get hold of your Operatives in the field, and order them to concentrate on this one person for us. Maybe get some better pictures of him so we can make a positive identification that this one is Colonel al-Adwani, dammit. I can't go to the President on this one slim shot we're branding as al-Adwani here, John."

"Shit General, I can't make open direct contact with my Operatives in the field now, sir. Evidently, they're right in the middle of this news conference General al-Zahar is holding, sir. If I beeped them now, it might alert anyone near them that my Agent is just that, sir. I'm sorry General White, but I think we're going to get stuck sitting this one out, and hope they use their damn heads, and get this guy in a clear photo for us, sir. They seem like they're doing a pretty thorough job of getting one shot of everyone attending this damn press meeting, sir."

"Shit, I feel we're so damn close to locating this bastard, yet so far away from finding him, Director Raincloud. If your damn Agents don't transmit a clearer picture of this guy, there's no way in hell I can go before the Boss and tell him we got the damn prick. This isn't enough to place Lieutenant Walker and his war wacky bastards on go alert, sir. I need a better picture of this prick, or I can't react against him. I agree with you John, from what I can see, he does look a helluva lot like this Colonel al-Adwani. But I still can't be positive of it from this photo, sir."

"Maybe I can give the photo to the lab boys and see if they can possibly enhance it a little clearer for us, they might be able to bring out the features of this prick's face some more for us. Maybe there's some way they can remove the face blocking our target, and then construct the missing part of the face, so we have a better ID of the man..." Director Raincloud offered with a shrug as he continued to stare at the photo still locked in his hand.

"That's not good enough this time around John. I can't possibly go before the President of the United States with a fricking computer enhanced photo of this lousy prick we want, and tell him beyond a shadow of a doubt he's our missing target, sir." General White interrupted the CIA Director, as he picked up the picture again and stared at the partial face and mumbled more to himself than the Director. "I have to admit though that it sure does look a lot like the lousy sonofabitch we want alright. Can he be that stupid and brazen to expose himself to the public eye so quickly after what he just tried to pull off here in the States, the damn ass?"

General White tossed the photo down on top of the others and shook his head slowly as he continued to complain at the CIA Director. "No John, I can't believe this asshole is Colonel al-Adwani at that. He couldn't possibly be that stupid. He knows damn well if we discovered where he was hiding, we'd do everything in our power to get at him, and take him prisoner and bring him back to the United States, or kill him in his own damn country, sir. He has to understand we'd be looking to make an example out of his ass, to deter any other asshole that tries to take a shot at our President, sir. He just can't be this damn stupid for Christ sake. I can't believe he could be that stupid. It has to be someone else who looks a helluva lot like the lousy bastard, it just can't be him, Director. Shit, I wish we had a better pict..."

"Maybe so General White, but this one in the photo certainly looks a lot like our missing boy alright, sir. Judging by what I can see of his face in the picture, General. Could he be sending us a message? A warning that he feels he's so well protected in his lousy little rathole, that he doesn't care one bit if we know he's there or not sir?"

"What kind of fucking message could he possibly be sending us, John? That he's tired of living for Christ sake?" General White asked as he looked at a second picture with the suspected Colonel al-Adwani shielded by someone standing directly in front of him.

"Could he be trying to send us the message he doesn't care what we could do to get him?"

"In a pig's fucking ear he's doing that crap at us, John. He has to understand if we couldn't drag his ass the hell out of Iraq and back here to the United States, so the sonofabitch could stand trial for trying to assassinate our President. We'd send in our own assassination hit team to frag his damn ass for him where he's staying in Iraq, sir. If for no other reason but to show other would be terrorists we're not without resources to get them wherever they try to hide, if they try to attack the United States one way or the other, dammit."

General White's gripe was cut short by the buzzer, informing Sam more pictures were about to be transmitted to the lab from the two operatives working in Iraq.

"What the hell's that damn racket over there about, mister?" General White snorted angry he was interrupted by the noise.

"That's my Operative's radio linking up with ours here at the lab, General White. The deep cover Agents are obviously sending another batch of pictures to us as we speak, sir. I sure hope to hell they got one clear shot of this prick we're looking at here sir." Director Raincloud replied with a grin as he rushed to the side of Sam and looked over his shoulder, as the blank screen instantly turned into a blaze of scrambled numbers, dots and dashes.

"Is that a picture coming in now?" The Chairman asked and Director Raincloud replied.

"Yes Sir General White, this is the only way we can securely transmit an unexposed picture to home base from our Operatives working out in the field, sir. The computer received these signals in a burst transmission, and then instantly reconstructs them on a negative roll here. Then Sammy develops the negative and we end up with a finished photo, that simple sir."

"What the hell happens to the film your Agent's have in the field, once we have the transfer roll here, John? What do they do with the transmitted film?" General White asked as he followed Sam over to a second machine where he watched a second technician feed the newly acquired information into this computer, and the machine did the rest for him.

"Once our Agent transmits his material to this office and receives a confirmation reply the transfer was completed and successful. He exposes his film to the sun, allowing it to completely destroy the film. Then he buries the exposed roll of film and gets far away from it as quickly as he possibly can, sir." John answered as he felt the General should have known the agent would destroy the film as he joined General White standing by Sam's side.

"That sounds like a plan to me. How long do we have to wait for the first pictures from this last batch to be developed?" General White asked the lab technician

Director Raincloud allowed Sammy to field that question from the Chairman as he stared at Sam and waited for him to reply.

"General White, I should have the first batch of photos ready for you within five minutes, sir."

"If you can beat that time any for me. I'll get you so blind drunk and laid for your effort, my boy." General White said with a smirk as he gave the technician some extra room to work.

"Coffee General White?" Director Raincloud asked, trying to get the General off his technician's back so he could work uninterrupted on the pictures.

"Naw, this is too important to break away from it for any length of time John."

"Well then let's leave my technician alone, so he can do what he does best and gets these damn photos developed for us, General White."

"What Director Raincloud?" the General growled back at Director Raincloud.

"I'm not kidding you General, Sam knows what the hell he's doing without you busting his horns and looking over his shoulder like you are doing while he works on the damn film for us, General. With you hawking his ass like you're doing here sir, it's going to end up costing us added time for him to the developing of the new batch of pictures for us, sir. C'mon General White and back off my people a little will ya please, sir."

"Hmmm... I think I might have that coffee break after all, John. That way we can let Sam do his act with the damn pictures, sir. Besides, my back will love to be straightened up for a little while, Director." General White mumbled more to himself than to the Director as he grinned pleased he was finally able to get a little rise out of the massive Native American.

General John White and the CIA Director John Raincloud watched Sam work as fast as humanly possible on the unexposed film. When the first photos from this new batch were ready, Sam brought them to the table instead of the drying bin. He laid them out carefully on the table and Raincloud and General White attacked them as if it was the last keg of beer at a frat party.

General While quickly spread out the new photos, and then he let his breath out in a rush as he grumbled at the CIA Director. "Jesus Christ Almighty Chief, these fucking things are of the same piss poor quality as the other crap we just looked at. They're fucked up man. I can't see this cocksucker at all in any of the damn new shots, Chief. I thought you said these Agents of yours in the field are good, and they knew what the hell they were doing over there, dammit!"

"They are that good General White. I can tell from the angles of the shots the Operatives took that they couldn't capture this bastard on film cleanly for us sir. The Agents can only take advantage of the opportunities offered to them in the field when they expose those opportunities to them, General. If this guy's smart enough to linger in the background for the full length of the press conference, I don't think the Agents will ever get a clear photo of him, sir. What can you expect from my people, sir? Cut them some slack will ya please for Pete's sake, General."

"Yeah." Was all General White growled as he went back to scanning the new photos. The second batch was finally done, and they did not show the face of the man in question either.

"Shit, I think we're pissing up the wrong tree here, John. Maybe the lousy little prick is still somewhere in the States after all, Director Raincloud." General White moaned as they finished up scanning the second stack of pictures just transmitted to them.

"General White have some patients will you please. Something we learned a long time ago, while working in the National Photo Envision and Interpretation Agency, sir." Director Raincloud replied as he continued scanning the new photos that just came in.

"Is that what you're calling this section of your office now, John? The National Photo Envision whatever the hell it is, Director." The General smirked at him.

"Yep." Director Raincloud shot back at him with a kind of smirk.

The third set of pictures was done quickly, and Sam rushed the new batch over to the drying table while they were still dripping wet. He dropped the photos down before the General one on top of the other. He was still a little upset the military officer was taking cheap shots at him and his workstation with the CIA Director.

General White looked up and glared at the young technician as he walked away.

Director Raincloud understood the action and ignored the show of resentment aimed at the General as he began to pull the wet photos apart before they stuck together with his fingers, and then he barked at the military officer. He could tell the Chairman was angry as hell and he got on Sam's back for his display of insolence against him. "C'mon General and give him a little break please. He's doing his best under very trying circumstances for us sir."

General White returned his attention to the new set of photos, and the first five pictures were more of the large group shots of a bunch of Iraqi soldiers standing on the steps of the General's main building. Each one of them did not help him to identify the one man in question. Two photos were slightly stuck together, and General White carefully pulled them apart. The first was another group shot, the second was of a man standing alone on the middle of the steps of the building, before the small desk resting on the steps.

"Bingo, bingo, bingo! We got the motherfucking sonofabitch dead to rights Director. Look at the dopey little bastard standing there as if he didn't have a worry in the fucking world for crap sake." General White growled as he passed the photo over to Director Raincloud.

General White went after the rest of the photos with a new vigor, two, three, and then four full facial shots of Colonel al-Adwani were present, one face on and two photos of different profiles. The pictures caused the General to wiggle his hips in sort of a dance as he bellowed out. "I need it I love it I have to have more of it. We finally got the dirty bastard balls up John. We have a positive ID that this photo is clearly Colonel al-Adwani. I can go to the President with a clear conscious with these photos and show him the prick who tried to cap his ass on him."

General White let out his breath in a deep sigh, clutching the clear facial shot of Colonel al-Adwani in his hands. He turned back to Sam and announced to the young man. "Sammy, I want these five photos dried immediately, and placed in a holder. Let me know when it's done, will ya? By the way, can you make a number of copies for me? I'd like three sets of each and enlarge them to eight by twelve for me while you're at it if you can."

Sam turned to Director Raincloud and he nodded at Sam. The young man was not about to take further orders from a man ranking on what he did for a living. Director Raincloud answered the General for the young technician. "Sam can make all the copies you need, and he'll enlarge them for you, General White. He'll have them ready before we leave for the White House, sir."

General White leaned closer to Director Raincloud, and bitched barely over a whisper at him. "Man John, I guess I got him plenty pissed off at my ass today, huh my friend?"

"More than I ever seen him pissed off before in my entire life, General White."

"Good, maybe it'll loosen his gray hair manner up some for the stuff shirt."

"You don't ever back off from anyone, do you General White?" The Director complained.

"Not over matters this important to my ass, Chief. Err... you're not out of the woods here either you know, mister. You better be well prepared from a shitload of fucking grief from the Boss. He's going to want to know how this slimy little bastard ever got the hell out of the United States in one piece, with so many of your and FBI Agents searching for the prick." General White lit up a stogie and offered one to Director Raincloud. They enjoyed the cigars while waiting for Sam to finish up with the requested photos. When he was done, the young technician handed the five sleeves to Director Raincloud, and then he went back to finishing up with the other copies of the photos the Chairman had requested from him.

General White laughed as he looked at Sam working and grumbled at the young man. "I see you're still angry with me, huh mister?"

Sam ignored the rude remark, causing the General to add. "Adjust to it fellow."

General White snuffed out the cigar and rose and offered. "I better get these damn things over to the Boss PDQ." He put out his hand but Director Raincloud did not turn over the photos.

"I take it this means you're coming along with me to see the Boss, huh Chief? I really want you with me when I show him these damn things." General White asked the Director.

"Damn right I am General White. I'm going to use these photos to get my ass out of the fire, if it's in it, sir. I don't see how the Boss could possibly be pissed off at me once we turned up Colonel al-Adwani for him, sir." Director Raincloud announced proudly to the military officer.

"Fine then let's get moving on this crap John. If the Boss gives me the green light, I have to activate my specialized troops so they can hunt this lousy bastard down, sir. It depends on how bad the President really wants this bird's ass served up to him on a silver platter."

Director Raincloud followed the Chairman out to his staff car. Once in the vehicle, General White ordered the young Marine driver to take them over to the White House. When the car was moving, General White dialed up the Chief of Staff of the White House aide. After two rings, Peter answered the call.

"White House Chief of Staff. How can I direct this call for you please?"

"Peter!" General White grumbled in the phone at the young man.

Peter instantly recognized the General's voice and he replied to the powerful military officer. "Yes General White Sir, and how are you today sir?"

"Just dandy son. Is the President in the building?" General White asked him.

"Yes Sir General White Sir." Peter ignored the usual course General's tone as he continued. "The President has a meeting scheduled with Senator Williams from North Carolina for later on today sir, and he's just marking off time until the meeting begins, General White."

"Well Peter, you're going to have to have him cancel it for me. I have to see the man A-SAP."

"If you'll hold on for a moment please General White Sir, I'll find out if the President can squeeze you in today for a short meeting, sir. Where are you calling from General White, in case we get disconnected, and I have to call you back sir." Peter asked the Chairman.

"I'm on my way to the White House as we speak mister, so if we get disconnected, don't worry about calling me back, kid. I'll be there before you can reestablish communications with me Peter." He offered to the young aide as he calmed down a little.

"Yes sir, please hold the line open then for me, General White. I'll see if the President will meet with you, sir." Peter informed the General.

In what the General felt was less than a heartbeat the President's voice filled the receiver in a growl. "General White, what the hell is the meaning of trying to see me without going through the proper chain of command sir, as you have dared to put it to my aide sir, A-SAP sir! I'm not at your beck and call at any time you feel like shooting the breeze with me, mister. I do have other matters of state I must concern myself with, rather than holding your hand and chewing the fat with you, General White."

"With all due respect for you Mr. President Sir, we have gathered some new information concerning this Colonel al-Adwani and his present location at this time sir." General White offered while smirking over the President's tone.

There was dead silence on the other end of the phone for a long second, and then the American Leader replied. "Okay General White, you have my full attention now sir, so get over to my office to use your word here, A-SAP sir. I'll cancel my scheduled meeting with the Senator, and hold the rest of my afternoon open for this meeting with you sir. Have you been able to locate this missing Colonel al-Adwani for me, General White Sir?"

"Yes Sir Mr. President we sure did sir, but I didn't locate the bastard sir, Director Raincloud's Operatives found him in Iraq for us, sir." The General offered, hoping to help out the Director's position with the obvious upset President.

"Then I take it Colonel al-Adwani is no longer here in the United States from what you're reporting to me at this time, General White Sir?"

"Fraid that's a correct assumption to take at this time, Mr. President Sir."

"Dammit, okay General White, how long before you can get over to the White House, sir?" The President asked as he glanced at the clock to see what time it was.

General White looked out of the window of his staff car, they were just going over the Arlington Bridge, and he replied in a pleasant tone to the American Leader. "Mr. President Sir, I should be arriving at the White House within the next fifteen minutes at the latest, sir."

"Good, then I'll be waiting for you to arrive, is Director Raincloud with you by any chance, General White Sir?" The President asked hoping the Director was with the General.

"Yes sir, he's sitting right next to me Mr. President Sir." The Chairman added.

"Fine, I'll not have to send for him then I see, General White." The President mumbled as he disconnected the communication with the military officer.

General White dialed up Colonel Bruce Leadbetter's office at Camp Lejeune. Sergeant John Kirkpatrick was in the office cleaning up the Colonel's back log of paperwork and other duties he could remove from the Colonel's back, and he answered the phone. He informed the General that the Colonel was out in the field with the troops forwarding their training.

CHAPTER TWENTY TWO

"Sergeant Kirkpatrick, if you wish to keep your damn stripes for another ten minutes mister, you better get the damn Colonel, and inform him I'm on the horn waiting to speak to him toot sweet son. I don't have much time before I have to meet with the President, and I want to speak to him before my meeting starts with the Boss."

"Yes sir, right away General White Sir." Sergeant Kirkpatrick snapped as he laid the phone down on the desk without hanging it up, and then he darted out of the office for the Colonel.

Colonel Bruce Leadbetter was inside the temporary command post, and he was busy controlling the shoot house activities with his elite soldiers, when Sergeant John Kirkpatrick came bursting into the trailer out of breath.

"What's up Sergeant, someone tell you there was a naked broad in here or something, mister?"

"General White's on the phone and he's waiting to speak with you sir, and he sounds plenty pissed off as well, Colonel."

"When the hell ain't he pissed off lately for crap sake, Sergeant." Colonel Leadbetter growled as he watched Lieutenant Walker and three of his fellow troopers enter a compromised office on the third floor of the shoot house, and the soldiers shoot up the three dummies classified as terrorists in the room, and then he bitched at his Sergeant. "Did he happen say what the hell he wanted from my sagging ass, Sergeant?"

"From what I was able to tell Colonel, he's evidently riding in his staff car, and he reported he was heading for the White House as he spoke with me, sir." Sergeant Kirkpatrick replied as he stared at the concerned looking Colonel.

"Shit, that don't sound too good for us, man." Colonel Leadbetter turned to the second Sergeant in the command center and barked at him. "Any why you can have that fucking call transferred to me over here in the damn command trailer, mister?"

"Easy as shit Colonel Leadbetter." The Sergeant replied as if he accomplished the impossible.

"Then get it done for me mister." Two seconds later, Colonel Leadbetter was speaking with the angry Chairman of the Joint Chiefs of Staff.

"Where the hell were you that it took you this long to get back to me, Colonel Leadbetter? I don't need you traipsing all over that fucking base at this crucial a time on me, sir. Didn't your damn Sergeant inform you that this was an important matter, Colonel?"

"Look General White, you can spend much of this call chewing on my ass as you want, and we won't get anything accomplished with the call, sir. What's the reason for the call sir, I have troops operating in a live fire exercise inside the damn shoot house structure at this time sir, and my attention has to be on them during this extremely dangerous exercise, General."

"Watch your fucking tone when addressing me or it could cost you big time, mister. Colonel Leadbetter, we just received positive confirmation that our missing bird's back at his rat's nest safe and sound in Iraq, sir." The Colonel's commanding officer barked nastily at him over the phone as he waited for a reaction from the other military officer.

"Does that mean we're going active, General White?" Colonel Leadbetter asked the General.

"Damn right it does Colonel Leadbetter. You better get you people ready and hot, Colonel. I'm meeting with the President in five minutes, sir. Once I speak to him, I'm certain he's going to give us the green light to go after this Arab bastard over there in sand land, sir. I'll have the troop transport aircraft in the air later on today for your troops, Colonel Leadbetter. Long before your troops will have any need of the damn things, sir. They'll be landing at the Green Monster stationed at Fort Bragg this time sir. Get your troops over there ten minutes ago, and have them ready and good to go by that time, Colonel."

EAGLE'S NEST

"Yes Sir General White, we'll be hot, cocked, and ready to go and get this lousy bastard for you, General White." The young Marine Colonel replied to his commanding officer this time.

When the General broke off the connection, Colonel Leadbetter hit the buster siren, informing the elite troops operating in the shoot house that the exercise was at an end as of this moment.

The Chairman sat back in his seat as the vehicle turned into the main gate of the White House grounds. The security guards checked the General's ID, and saluted him and waved the car through the gate. Peter was waiting outside the building for the General and Director Raincloud to arrive at the steps leading to the main entry of the White House. When the General's staff car stopped, he opened the door and waited for the two men to get out.

"Where's the President at Pete?" He asked the young White House aide.

"General White, Director Raincloud, the President's waiting for the both of you in the Oval Office. Err... General White Sir, I must inform you that Vice President Hirshfield's attending this meeting also, sir. The President wanted me to warn you in advance about this fact sir, and he wants you to watch your mouth at the meeting sir, and try not to upset the Vice President, if it's at all possible during the meeting, General White Sir."

"Are you insinuating I might have a problem with my fucking mouth around here, Peter?" The smug sounding General asked the young aide with a straight face.

Peter did not know if the Chairman was just fooling around with him or not. But he was not going to answer that loaded question, for fear he was not joking with him. The young White House aide knew the General was well aware he had a terrible vocabulary.

"Calm down some will ya Pete. I was only busting your horns a little on ya son. You better take some time off and get yourself laid young man. It'll do wonders for your disposition sonny. Thanks for warning me about Mary. How is she doing anyway Peter?"

"As well as can be expected I guess under the circumstances General White, considering all of what she's been put through with the assassination attempt on the President, and her getting wounded in the event, sir. She's still in a helluva lot of pain sir. But she's toughing it out pretty well just to attend this special meeting with you and the Director, sir. She was dying to get back to her office, even against AMA, General White Sir."

"She always was a rather tough old bird. What the hell does AMA mean to me, mister?" The General asked the aide, never hearing these three letters before in his life.

"Sorry General White, it stands for Against Medical Advice, sir."

The Chairman and Director Raincloud fell in line behind Peter as he rushed them down the hallway leading to the Oval Office. Peter knocked on the door lightly, and then opened it in the same motion. The President was the only one who rose from his chair, as he waved his hand before him towards the empty couch across from where Mary, and the new National Security Director, Bill Blaylocke were seated in the room. The President waited until the General and Director Raincloud was comfortable, and then he started his comments. "First off everyone, allow me say how happy we are to have my Vice President sitting at my right hand again. Mary, I missed the hell out of you and all your help, young lady. It's a wonder this office was able to function without you standing at the helm with me, honey." President Albert Cole smiled warmly at Mary, and she nodded slowly back at him.

Director Raincloud did the class act and he rose and took Mary's good hand in his, and he kissed it as he offered kindly to the Vice President. "It's great to have you back at work Ms. Hirshfield. I really missed you Ma'am."

She nodded again. General White smiled and he received one in return from Mary.

The President cut in and announced with concern in his tone. "As good as it is to have Mary back at her post, that's not the reason why we're here, people. General White, I believe you have some new information you want to share with me over this missing terrorist, sir? Please General inform us of your latest discoveries concerning this Colonel al-Adwani."

General White shifted his weight on the couch, until he was staring directly at the President seated behind his desk. He removed the file folder he carried to the office from under his arm, and he removed the latest eight by ten pictures of Colonel al-Adwani they had of him in Iraq, and he offered calmly to the seated President of the United States. "I'm terribly sorry to offer this to you at this time, Mr. President Sir. It seems the lousy snake got out of the States on us sir."

"To be quite frank with you General White, I didn't believe we had much of a chance of finding him, while he was still in the States, sir." The President offered calmly as he carefully studied the sneering face staring at him from the photo, and then he remarked. "He's a rather nasty looking bastard, isn't he General White?" President Cole passed the first picture to Mary, and she had all she could do to stop herself from crying as she stared at the photo. Director Blaylocke saw her frustration and he sort of yanked the photo from her hand. The smallish man did not want to see her hurt anymore than she already was.

Director Raincloud stopped himself from laughing at Bill Blaylocke, the new Security Director, for he also knew who the Vice President thought he looked like, and he happened to agreed with her assumption of the man. He really did look a lot like the smallish but great male actor.

"Okay General White, now that we know where the hell this man is hiding, what's our next step in getting him back here to the United States to stand trial for the crimes he committed against our government and myself, General?" the President asked as he stared into the eyes of his respected military officer, as he waited for his reply.

"Mr. President Sir, I placed my troops running exercises down at Camp Lejeune on a two hour alert warning, sir. The next call if you want this man's hide is, Mr. President. Is you're going to have to give us the green light to jump off, and have these specialized troops go and capture the terrorist al-Adwani where he's hiding..."

"I want this man's hide more than I want to be reelected to another term as Vice President, General White! After what he has done to poor Mr. Griffin, he's not fit to breathe the same air as the rest of us civilized people do, General White." Mary interrupted with surprising strength.

The President smiled at Mary as he listened to her strained voice and then replied to her statement. "Well, you heard the young lady, General White. What I want to know from you is. What's the chance of us getting this man out of Iraq alive, and in one piece at that sir? I'd dearly love to have him back here to stand trial for the murder of my National Security Director, sir. Be honest with your response to this question please, General White."

"Better than a seventy five percent possibility I believe at that, Mr. President Sir. Judging on the latest reports I'm receiving on the troops attacking the shoot house structure on my ordered training exercises at Camp Lejeune, sir. Colonel Leadbetter states the troops are accomplishing just about what the computers classify as a successful mission, on just about every invasion of the shoot house building they're involved in, sir." The Chairman replied proudly over the successes his troops were enjoying with their new training program on the military base.

"General White, let us suppose for a minute your troops find this man in Iraq once we sent them to the country that is, sir. But they're unable to get at him because he's being well protected by bodyguards ordered to protect his life. How long will the troops continue to try and capture him, sir? And if the soldiers can't get at him what's their options then, General White?" Mary said as she fought to remain comfortable on the couch, holding the side of her neck with her hand to help her absorb the pain she was suffering with trying to speak at the meeting.

"Madam Vice President, my troops will be allowed twenty four hours in which to snatch and scoot with their intended target. At the end of the twenty four hour time limit set, if my troops were unsuccessful in their attempt to take the Colonel captive, Ma'am. Then their mission will instantly shift over from a snatch and scoot operation, to a search and splatter mission without further communication from me, Ma'am. They have standing orders to kill this man wherever he may be found in Iraq, and to film the action as well. So the President and the American public will see for themselves that we're not fooling around with any damn terrorists thinking about attacking American civilians anywhere on the face of the globe, especially at home Ma'am."

"Search and splatter, oh that sounds so cold General White." Mary cried at him.

"Yes Madam Vice President it certainly is, but you have to remember who we're dealing with over this latest situation, and what caused the situation in the first place we're reacting against. It's the only way to deal with any terrorists, in the harshest terms possible Ma'am." The General replied while trying to keep his anger out of his response for the Vice President.

The President cut the Chairman off, fearing he was starting to upset his injured Vice President a little, and he announced to his military officer. "General White Sir, if I give you the green light to deploy your elite troops to Iraq to get this little bastard. The soldiers will understand their priority is to take this man back to the United States alive, bringing him back here to stand trial so I can see his face when they push the button on the bastard, General White?"

"Mr. President Sir, Colonel Leadbetter has drummed that exact order into the soldiers heads every chance he got so far sir, ever since the soldiers first arrived on the military base, sir."

"Very well then General White, this matter seems to have taken up too much of my time already, sir. I'm not going to hesitate for one moment longer over this situation, sir. General White, you have the green light to deploy your elite troops to Iraq immediately, sir. May God be with them, and give them the guidance to carry out their orders successfully for us this time, and to bring them all back home alive and well General. I'll pray that none of our soldiers get hurt on this upcoming mission, General White." The President explained to the Chairman.

Mary nodded in agreement of the President's words to General White.

The new National Security Director, Matt Blaylocke offered as he got in on the conversation now. "Mr. President Sir, I think it might be a wiser idea if we increase the security at all our airports, and historical monuments spread throughout the United States, sir. As well as on all military bases and United States interests abroad. We should also send out a message to all American Embassies sir, and order them to a heighten alert status on their grounds, in case they get hit by a terrorist group trying to make a name for themselves over al-Adwani's assassination attempt on your life, Mr. President Sir. Once we take Colonel al-Adwani prisoner, or at least erase him from the face of the earth, you can bet the bank on it that fanatical Arab wannabe terrorists around the world will be looking to seek their revenge against us, sir."

The President slowly nodded as he offered in a low voice to his new National Security Director. "That seems like a very good plan to offer to me, sir. I'll leave that order entirely in your hands, Director Blaylocke. Oh, please forgive me sir. Do you happen to know General John White, he's the current Chairman of the Joint Chiefs of Staff at the Pentagon, sir. And John Raincloud, he's the CIA Director, sir."

"I know Director Raincloud, but not the General, sir. Glad to meet you General White."

"Glad to have you on board with us, Director Blaylocke Sir. We need all the brain thrust we can possibly generate when we're forced to deal with any terrorist activity anywhere on the face of the earth, Director Blaylocke." The General replied pleasantly to the new man.

The President suddenly clapped his hands loudly, and then announced. "Now that we have the future of this Iraqi Colonel al-Adwani settled, is there anything else you might need from me, or we have to go over at this time, General White Sir?"

"There is one question I must ask of you, Mr. President Sir." The General requested.

"Please ask away while you have my full attention at this time, General White Sir." The President responded as he smiled back at the respected General.

"With all due respect Mr. President, these soldiers I'm sending after Colonel al-Adwani know only one way to accomplish their mission, the way the troops were trained for, sir."

"What are you driving at here General White? I'm not picking up what you're aiming at in this conversation, sir. I believe you're going to have to take a more direct request if you need something more from me, General." The President asked the Chairman with concern.

"Mr. President Sir, when my specialized troops enter Iraq, they're going to be dumped right in one of the most hostile areas of the world for Americans, let alone United States soldiers, sir. These soldiers will be out head hunting Colonel al-Adwani, and while they're hunting they won't be thinking of taking any prisoners except for the one we have sent them in after, Mr. President Sir. With all due respect sir, if this mission turns into a mini war of sorts, I want to know just how far I can go with it, and if my troops are expendable on this mission, sir?" The military commander asked the President with much concern as he waited for the President's reply.

"General White, no American treasures are expendable assets as far as I'm concerned, especially if they're carrying out my personnel orders, sir. And make no mistake about it sir. These troops are operating under my direct orders, General. If your troops find themselves cut off, or in what do you call it, some kind of fight I believe I'm searching for, sir?"

"A fire fight I think is the word you're searching for, Mr. President Sir." He offered.

"Right, right General White yes a fire fight was the words I was searching for, sir. If your troops get bogged down in a fire fight, you have the liberty to employ all necessary equipment and support troops and any other assets to extract them from Iraq safely sir. Short of firing off any nuclear weapons against that nation giving us any trouble that is, General White." The President's last words made everyone in the office chuckle a bit.

"Let me get this right sir. I'm free to support my troops out in the field with everything I have at my disposal, without any further orders or requests from you or Congress am I correct Mr. President Sir?" He asked the President to clarify his words properly.

"General White, you were never more free to use all our military assets to support one of these covert missions, and the troops carrying out that operation. Then you are on this one mission, sir." The American Leader replied as he turned his attention from the General, and looked back at his scared looking and shaken Vice President, and his heart skipped a beat over her condition.

"No matter how bloody it might get on us, might I add to this conversation, Mr. President Sir?" General White asked with a slight hint of caution in his tone.

The President had to tear his eyes away from his Vice President and he replied to his military commander with a snap in his voice. "General White! I'm not going to cross swords with you on this latest mission, sir. You do whatever the hell you have to make damn certain these brave young men and women of ours get out of Iraq alive, sir. Then you're to report to me after you have done whatever was necessary to carry out this operation successfully, General White. How much clearer can it possibly be for you to understand, General White?" The President stared at the military officer while waiting his reply.

"Thank you for clearing that bit of confusion up for me, Mr. President Sir. I didn't want to have happen to my Special Forces, what happened to those proud young Ranger warriors we sent to Somalia some years past, sir. I swear by the stars on the flag, none of my Special Forces soldiers will ever be dragged through the god damn streets of a hostile nation naked at the end of a rope, and having a bunch of screaming assh..."

The President interrupted the General's angry response because he felt he was beginning to get a little off the mark with this meeting as he moaned at the powerful Chairman. "C'mon General White please. You're dragging up ghosts here sir, and it's doing nothing more than serving to upset my Vice President and the rest of my council attending this meeting, sir. I know how terrible you must feel about that horrible blunder, it was one of our worse mistakes the United States military ever committed sir, and it'll never happen again on my watch I can assure you of that much, mister. But now is not the time to bring up such terrible skeletons, especially before my injured Vice President, General White Sir. That was a helluva mess, one I'll never be trapped into, that's why I'm giving you card blanche on this mission to support your troops out in the field properly with all necessary assets we have in our arsenal, sir. It's all I can do, but I'll do it to the best of my abilities, General White Sir.

"I assure you sir, that scene still haunts me every day of my life General White, and every American in the world sees that nightmare in their eyes. Every time we sent our troops in action, I see that poor young soldier's face, and those damn animals jumping all over his body while they dragged him around by a damn rope, sir. No General White, I assure you sir that'll never happen on my watch, sir." The President cocked his head to the side and he looked deeply in the General's eyes for a long moment before the military officer replied.

"Thank you for your support on this matter and for my troop's welfare while they're on this operation, Mr. President Sir." General White offered proudly, as he nodded politely to the President. His mind was working on overtime already. He was pleased the President was allowing him so much support on this latest possible mission, to hunt down the terrorist who tried to assassinate him a few weeks ago, and the attackers wounded his Vice President.

"Now that's settled with, is there anything else that we have to go over concerning this matter at the present time, General White, or Director Raincloud? I do have some prior scheduled meeting for later on today I must attend to." The President offered them.

Both men shook their heads no as they smiled at the American Leader.

"Very well then General White, is there something you have to do to get the wheels in motion for your troops to head out on this operation, sir?" the President gave the General a moment to think, before he responded to his question, and then he was going to call the meeting to an end so he could get on with the rest of the meetings he had scheduled and bumped for this meeting.

"All I have to do is make contact with my Commander and the troops and their support backup teams currently stationed down at Camp Lejeune, sir. Why do you ask me that question, Mr. President Sir?" General White leaned back on the sofa, and stared at the President as he waited patiently for the American Leader to reply to his last remark.

"I asked you that question because General White, I wish to get off of this so troubling conversation as soon as possible, and then I intend to invite everyone attending this meeting for some tea. A sort of welcome Mary back in the fold if you will, and then I plan to reschedule the meetings I put off to meet with you, General." The President stared at General White for several long moments, while waiting for his response now.

"Well, I guess I can make my calls from here if I have to, and once I'm done with these communications, sir. I'll be free for the rest of the day if you'd like, Mr. President Sir. I don't have anything else scheduled on my plate as far as I'm aware of, and nothing I couldn't put off. Colonel Leadbetter can handle the troops and the transport aircraft to get the soldiers to their deportation center easy enough, sir." General White offered politely to the President as he sat up again, and smiled warmly at the Vice President, watching his every move now.

"Then get it done if you don't mind General White, and if anything else comes up I need to know about immediately, sir. We can always discuss it over some tea in a much more civilized and comfortable manner, General White." The President offered to his military officer as he watched him start to stand and head for the free phone in his office.

General White nodded to the President, and then he rose and quickly headed for the Marine console stationed at the other end of the long hallway. So he could communicate directly with Colonel Leadbetter, the commander of his specialized troops at Camp Lejeune. The concerned Chairman also wanted to get the Marine Colonel and his elite troops on the move as quickly as humanly possible, now that he had the green light for immediate action from the President, so they could get after the missing terrorist discovered hiding in Iraq. He was actually smiling and he was in a great mood to boot, as he thought of his troops hunting the missing terrorist down in his own country, to show the terrorist how it felt to be hunted in his own lands.

In the General's magnificent military mind's eye, he could see his brave young soldiers taking the Iraqi terrorist Colonel in custody, and bringing him back to the United States to stand trial before the general public of this country. Then executed for the crime of attempted assassination he committed against the President of the United States, the wounding of the Vice President, and the murder of the National Security Director Norman Griffin during the same attack.

The proud General's chest swelled with pride over the fact his pet project with the elite soldiers was picked to take the Iraqi Colonel into custody. He knew when, not if his soldiers were successful on this mission, he was going to come out of it smelling like a rose, and the thankful President would be beholding to him, and the rest of his specialized troops. Anything he might need for these specialized troops in the future, the President would trip all over himself to give him what he needed or asked for his troops.

CAMP LEJEUNE, JACKSONVILLE NORTH CAROLINE. AUGUST 5th, 1999, 6:30 P.M. EST

Lieutenant Robert Walker, better known to his elite troops as Road Kill, heard the siren going off and he knew instantly there was an early end called to the latest training exercise. He tapped his helmet radio and blew softly in the crystal mike and warned the rest of the soldiers in his group. "Okay people listen up, someone must have a stinking itch up their ass, and we gotta go and scratch it for him. Colonel Leadbetter just pulled the switch on this damn exercise on us. None of you yard birds betta have screwed up and didn't inform me before the damn Colonel was told of it, or I'm gonna eat you alive and then shit you outta my ass afta mess, dammit. I keep telling you pukes we have to be top notch for these damn training exercises."

"Ooooo, you can start your meal with me Walker baby. I heard many stories about how good you are with that lap dog type tongue of yours." Baby Tee purred sexily in the radio at him.

"Baby Tee, I'll lick you good and proper all over for any damn reason at all, baby." The Mutt remarked proudly, as he snorted like a pig into the radio, and then laughed into it as well.

"Hey girl, you better watch out for that one. The Mutt would lick himself all over if he could bend his neck against the laws of nature, sister." Foreplay, (Sergeant Sabrina Claybrook) added as she joined the fun and ribbing of the Mutt.

Lieutenant Walker ignored Foreplay's remark as he barked in his radio. "Is that you Tee?"

"Guilty as charged sweetheart. What's up honey?" The young and pretty soldier replied.

"Let me tell you something baby girl. I'm so damn good, I scream out my own name during sex at night, honey." Lieutenant Walker laughed into the radio as he headed for the stairs leading out of the shoot house structure.

This remark from Walker made many of the soldiers get into the conversation on him.

"Stop bragging so damn much Walker, you're fogging up my glasses on me, mister. Nobody's that good when it comes to sex, especially a big dumb man." Bouncer added.

"Walker's muscle bound between the ears, Bouncer." Ice, (Sergeant Diane Morrison) offered as she got into the conversation, and immediately dumped on Walker.

"I'm afraid Lieutenant Walker has to shave between his eyebrows and take a bath first, for me to be the least bit interested in giving him a little tumble between the sheets, girls." Three Martinis laughed into her mike as she got in the conversation now.

"Who was that last bitcher shoots jabs at my ass? Who just said that last remark to my ass dammit?" Walker bitched in his radio at the last talker.

"Three Martines honey." The female soldier laughed in the radio at the young Lieutenant.

"Hey man, Three Martinis' legs are closed tighter than two coats of fucking paint, Road Kill. She's so tight I could shove a piece of coal up her ass and pull out a fist fulla stinking diamonds, man." The Mutt offered, taking a cheap shot at the young female soldier who almost got him lynched by the rest of the girls of the group a few weeks back. He was still a little angry at her for making such a scene in the showers, when he accidentally bumped into her butt, causing her to run out of the showers and go crashing head long into Baby Tee who was minding her own business standing by her bunk in the barracks, giving her a helluva bump and a cut over her right eye in the hard collision.

"Fuck you dog man. You're still mad at me because of my mistake in the showers I take it, mister." Three Martines snapped back at him.

"Hey Martini, you better watch yourself when picking on the dog man around here, sweetheart. When the Mutt was first born, his upset father went down to the local zoo, and he started to throw a fist full of rocks at the stork you know, girl." A female voice mumbled into the radio without identifying herself.

"Yeah, when the Mutt was a little bitty baby, he was so mean his mother had to feed him with a sling shot and a stick, girl." Another woman's voice said over the radio this time.

"The Mutt's just plum mad dog mean, and it doesn't look like he's gonna get any fucking betta anytime in the near future, people. He's always ready to sink his teeth or anything else he has on his body for that matter, into someone else's business." A male voice added this time, also omitting identifying himself for fear of the Mutt's wrath.

"Who said that, you stinking ball sack you? Are you a coward you hafta take pot shots at me, without telling me who's busting my stinking horns, man?" The Mutt hissed in his helmet radio, feeling he could go after any guys of the group dumping on him, without causing too much of a stir with the women soldiers of the group, who always seemed to be on his case lately. The Mutt did not understand the women were picking on him to take his mind off losing Fun Bags, Sergeant Barbara Meyerhoff, his original girlfriend in the Operation Sandstorm action in Iran.

"Who said that man? I'll rip your fricking head offa your damn shoulders for ya, and shit down the fucking opening, man." The Mutt growled, getting even angrier this time around.

"I can't beat you in a fair fight Mutt, so I'm not gonna ID myself to your ass, man." The same voice called out and then he laughed.

"That shows how fricking stupid you really are Homes. I don't fight anyone fair, man." The Mutt warned the unidentified speaker.

"Ooooooo... Mutt, you have to watch your mouth a little better, or Oprah's going to quite on us baby." Baby Tee used her favorite phase, as she purred, and she got back on the Mutt's case.

"Hey people, how the hell come did this thing get to be a climb on the big dumb half black man's ass deal around here, huh dammit? C'mon, be gentle with me people, I was once a virgin you know. You people started this fuck-go-round by getting on Walker's fricking ass, if you remember right guys? How's bout getting back on his fricking can for a while, and leave me the fuck alone. I give up, you people win this one I'm guilty as charged." The Mutt said as he caught up with Walker, and started down the interior staircase of the shoot house.

"They're really getting on you this time, so leave me the fuck outta this mess, bro. Didn't you take a stinking shower today Mutt?" Lieutenant Walker asked as he offered the Mutt a butt.

"That couldn't be the Mutt doing all this complaining can it? The only way the Mutt would ever give up anything, was if he was five days dead, and the buzzards were already picking over his fucking bones, man." The Hunter replied, as he decided to get in on the conversation this time, and get on the Mutt with the other soldiers.

"Yeah man, it's so much fun dumping on the dog man's ass all the time, people. After all, he gives us so much ammunition to attack against him with, the damn fool he is. Getting on you is like rolling a pork chop in front of a hungry wolf, and see if he's going to attack it or not, Mutt baby." Jail Bait said as she walked up behind the Mutt and Walker, and swatted the dog man on his ass, and took the cigarette out of his mouth and threw it on the floor and stomped it while she complained at him. "I told you before that shit's going to kill you real fast stupid. How many times am I going to get stuck telling you the same damn thing over and over again, Mutt?"

"How you mother decide ever give birth you Mutt? If one should throw out with sink water. It you surely ass, big shot American soldier boy." Siberia said, as she joined the group now.

"Hey Ruskie, you can't get on the Mutt's case, baby. In case you don't understand it yet baby, you're still a fucking foreigner around here, girl. Let me do it for ya, will you honey. The Mutt's doctor slapped his mother right in the chops when he was first born you know, girl." Mother Flanagan piped in as he lit up a cigarette, and then headed outside the building to relax for a little while. Until they found out why the buster signal was sounded against them, stopping the group of elite soldiers from attacking the shoot house in their latest training exercise on the structure supposed to be compromised by a group of supposed terrorists. He never did leave the building.

"Black is beautiful, tan is grand, but white's the color of the man, people." The soldier branded Weird Bill, Sergeant William Molinar mouthed off, just to have something to say to the other soldiers still dumping on the Mutt's case, while get himself into the conversation at the same time. He was one of the new guys to the outfit, and he felt a little left out on the bantering the soldiers were doing against each other. He was extremely careful, because he did not know how far he could go in busting the other soldier's horns yet. The last thing he wanted to do, was to overstep his bounds and get the rest of the soldiers pissed off at him, because he was not totally accepted by the group of elite soldiers yet. That would come with his first action and his first kill and get himself bloody.

"Will you fucking people get back on Walker's case for a while, and leave me the hell alone please. I have enuf stinking problems to deal wit, without you slugs adding to them like this, dammit." The Mutt moaned as he slugged Mother Flanagan in the guts. Mother's body armor blocked the blow, and it made the Mutt shake his hand, because it was foolish to punch anyone still dressed in the body armor.

"Leave the poor Mutt man alone people. He's truly a nice man and you people don't understand him like I do yet." Blind Date complained at the other soldiers from the unit as she caught up to her new lover, and placed her hand on his rearend and smiled in the eyes of the extremely dangerous young soldier.

"Hey bitch, the only reason you're sticking up for the dopey bastard who didn't know if he wanted to be black or white when he was being put together in his mother's gut. Is because you like how he kisses your belly button, it drives you fucking wild girl." The Ghost said as he now got into the conversation and started right off with getting on the Mutt's case.

The Russian female soldier on loan to the elite multi national forces from the renowned Russian Blue Berets, looked at Mother Flanagan as if he had three heads. Before getting involved with the joke aimed at the Mutt and she snapped at him. "What so special Mutt kiss belly button of woman for, big dumb fool you? How that act drive woman crazy like you say, please? It no do anything my sexual appetite I tell you big dumb soldier you. I no understand ever crazy big America soldier please. If America woman so easy please by have belly button kissed and come in pants, they lose all fun of sex true meaning of enjoy, please." Caviar complained joining the ribbing the Mutt was taking from the rest of the group of elite soldiers.

"That's because you're a fucking Russian babe, and you don't understand how the stinking Mutt does it to you girls, baby. He does it from the inside Ruskie." The Ghost added with a wide grin on his lips.

"Ooooo." Caviar purred sexily as she looked at the Mutt, and then she added as if she believed what the Ghost just said to her. "I must make time allow Mutt dog soldier do me like that please. I want experience same pleasure self. I no think that be possible be done by any man from inside a woman, please."

"It ain't stupid," Neck griped as he cut into the conversation this time and then he continued his bitch at the foreign soldier. "You fucking Russian chicks are so god damn gullible all the time. No wonder your stinking country's in such a fucking mess. You stinking Ruskies gotta come to the twenty first century and catch up with the rest of the world."

"If you believe that line of fucking bullshit Siberia then I have a fricking bridge in Brooklyn I wanna sell ya purdy little ass, baby." Wacko said, now he was getting on the Russian beauty this time around. He liked Siberia, and he was doing his best to try and make her notice him.

"What I want with bridge for in this Brooklyn country you tell me about, big stupid American soldier you? How move dumb bridge when I go back home Russia, fool. What I do with bridge anyway American soldier you? You no take home with you. You keep you bridge for youself, stupid American soldier you."

Siberia's remark made everyone leave her alone, because it was not much fun getting on someone who did not know she was being had by the rest of the group. Besides, not many other soldiers trusted the Russian soldiers, so they did not want to get close to them yet.

"Hey Mutt, did you ever try patting them on the ass once in a while, man. That always seems to drive the girls a little wild for me." Dock Rat said as he caught up with the group now.

"I heard about you and your weird fucking sex games you like playing with the broads, Rat Man." The Mutt fired back at him, trying to get the rest of the soldiers to attack someone else from the group for a change.

"This is fine, as long as you stay the hell off Walker's can, you guys." Sergeant Dorothy Ramirez warned the other soldiers, as she ran to catch up with Walker and the rest of the soldiers, and she looped her arm in his and smiled at her lover and soldier.

The soldiers felt bad Ramirez was not going along with them on the upcoming mission because she was pregnant, but it did not stop them from getting on her either. When she said something, she became fair game to the other soldiers.

"Hey Raz, you have to explain something that has been bugging the living shit outta my stinking ass for the last year or so, baby. Will you really answer this concern for me, little sister? It really has me confused and I don't know what to think about it, sister." Mother Flanagan grumbled as he joined in on the bantering once again, and this time he aimed his zingers directly at the female Sergeant.

"What's that Mother? You know you can ask me anything you want honey. We're all one in this group you know my friend." Ramirez offered to the large man as she shot him a quick smile, and then waited for him to ask her what was bugging him.

"Raz, I wanna know whatdaya ever see in that big dumb slob over there anyhow, honey? You're so damn good looking and got a great shape, and yet here you are and you're wasting your time chasing his ass all over the stinking globe. Look as the big dopey bastard will ya, he walks funny, he looks like shit warmed over on a hot stove and left to dry, and he smells as bad as old shit all the time. Jesus baby, he smells like a three day old fucking corpse left out in the sun to bake. Hell honey, let me tell you something, my grandfather was ninety three years old when he died last year, and by the time I saw him, he was three days dead already..." Mother was cut off right in the middle of his gripe.

"What's your point you're driving at Mother? I'm not reading you yet, soldier." Sergeant Ramirez interrupted him, trying not to laugh at where Mother Flanagan was heading with the shot he was taking at her lover and soldier.

"I'll tell you what my point is I'm trying to make here baby. At three days dead, my grandfather looked and smelt a helluva lot better than your lover does alive and kicking and running round, baby. Raz, didn't you ever notice it honey? People throw stinking darts at him wherever he goes, and mothers hide their daughters whenever he comes to town, and the fathers take up arms against his ass all the damn time. He's ugly enough to turn a fucking funeral up a blind alley. C'mon Raz, I'm telling ya, you're much better off without the big dumb slob." Mother Flanagan offered as he broke up with laughter and he pushed a fellow soldier on his back with his forearm.

CHAPTER TWENTY THREE

Sergeant Ramirez smiled at Walker as she offered to her lover and soldier. "I don't know what's eating Mother so bad today, lover? He's really getting on your case, honey. Did you do something to him in one of your past lives, baby?"

"Envy, poor guy." Walker grunted as he continued walking towards the door of the shoot house without looking back at Ramirez.

"Envy?" Sergeant Ramirez asked as she stopped walking and looking into her lover's eyes.

"Yeah baby, penis envy. I got a bigger crank than he does and he's really pissed off bout it, baby." Walker smirked as he smiled at her.

She squeezed Walker's hand and laughed at the same time, as she leaned up against him as they came out of the makeshift shoot house structure together, and they stepped in front of the group of soldiers gathering just outside the building. Ramirez was a little out of breath, and she was feeling the added weight of carrying a growing person in her body. When the other soldiers noticed Walker come out of the structure, the conversation instantly turned serious with the group and the questions went flying in all directions.

"What the fuck's up the fucking Colonel's ass today, Walker? Why the hell did he just cancel our training exercise on us man?" Danko, (Sergeant Christopher Danko) asked the young Lieutenant the moment he set eyes on Walker and Ramirez coming out of the building.

"I'll answer that damn question myself, you fucking little puke you." Colonel Leadbetter snapped angrily as he joined the rest of the soldiers gathering in front of the shoot house building. "You god damn people finished fucking around with each other yet, or do I have to put a stop to it myself with a little size eleven persuasions applied to your dumb asses? I don't particularly like it when you people are tying up the fucking radios by screwing around with yourselves like this shit. Them fricking helmet radios are for official use and times of emergency only, you bunch of jackasses. I was trying to get through to you shitbirds for the past five minutes, and couldn't get through because of your jerking off with each other on them damn radios, dammit.

"Every damn time I got on the radio, all I heard was you people squaring off against each other like a bunch of fucking kids. This crap better not happen when you jackrabbits are out in the field, or I'm going to have them damn radios removed from your helmets, and you people can communicate like the Indians did, with fucking smoke signals."

When no soldier replied to their commander's bitch at them, Colonel Leadbetter went on with his words for the specialized soldiers. "Before I inform you poor excuses for fricking human beings and elite soldiers, why the training exercise was just called off on you shitbirds, I need to know if anyone encountered any problems you feel I should know about with this last action inside that damn structure. The training mission is the most important item on the fucking plate at this moment and that's what I'm concerned with at this point, people."

The Mutt raised his hand, causing the other soldiers to groan, knowing he was about to bust the angry Colonel's horns over something stupid.

"I should've known your mix bred ass would have a fucking problem with something around here, mister. What the hell is it now dog face? And it better be a real problem or I'll skin your ass alive, buster." The Colonel growled as he glared harshly at the smirking Mutt.

The Mutt lifted his MP-5 machine gun and he complained as serious as he could make his voice sound. "Colonel Leadbetter, I think got my stinking finger caught in my gun again, sir."

Colonel Leadbetter did not reply to the Mutt's joke. Instead, he walked up to the Mutt and stared him right dead in the face. Then he snarled at the young and extremely dangerous soldier. "You keep fucking around with me like this mister, and you're going to find yourself ass deep in the damn swamp, surrounded by hungry alligators, and your damn pockets stuffed full with dead fish. You open your fucking mouth again on me, and I'm going to kick you so hard in the damn ass I'll have to wait until your morning ritual to get my boot back. I don't need any of this shit from you at this time, mister. What am I doing, talking to you is like talking to a fucking foreigner around here, buster. Step back and keep your fricking mouth clamped shut, or I'll fill it with cement for ya. And besides mister, it's not a fucking gun it's your rifle or weapon, asshole. Any other problems I should know about the latest exercise, people?"

"You betta get outta my fucking face for something bad happens to ya ass, big Brass Man." The Mutt suddenly snapped from out of nowhere, actually threatening the angry looking Colonel.

Lieutenant Walker jumped at the threatening warning the Mutt just fired off at their commanding officer, and knew he better do something real quick before the Colonel went off on the Mutt like an angry old junkyard dog. The Mutt was exhausted, and he allowed his mouth to operate without thinking about what he just said and to who he said it to.

The Colonel's eyebrows arched as he digested the threat leveled against him from the Mutt. Then his glare hardened as he hunched over and took a threatening stance against the soldier.

The Mutt did not back down a step as he snarled, and then assumed a linebackers stance himself. "You don't wanna go walking through hell not looking for a fucking fight, Colonel."

Lieutenant Walker stepped between the Colonel and the Mutt, and he tried to shove the angry Mutt out of the Colonel's face while saying. "Hey Colonel, the stinking Mutt didn't spend three years in the fifth grade, because he was the sharpest blade in the drawer, sir. C'mon Colonel, we're all of one blood here, we're one sir. You can't go get on the stinking Mutt's ass because he shot off his big fucking mouth again, because none of us had enuf sleep in the past couple days to keep us alive and acting right, Colonel. Wasn't it you who drummed into us we must always speak our mind no matter what's bugging our stinking asses, sir? You instilled in us independent thinking Colonel Leadbetter, so you can't take it back now sir."

"Don't try and defend this piece of shit to me, Lieutenant Walker. I'm going to disassemble him, and reshape the dopey bastard into a respectable fucking soldier. Something I should've done with him the first time I ever laid eyes on the dumb sack of shit, mister." Colonel Leadbetter snarled angrily at Lieutenant Walker, as he moved to his left, to get around Walker who followed his move to continue to block him from getting at the Mutt.

Blind Date moved to the Mutt's side and looped her arm through his arm, in hopes of stopping what looked to be a sure fight shaping up between the Mutt and the angry Colonel.

Colonel Leadbetter hissed nastily at Lieutenant Walker. "Hey stupid, your fucking halo's a little off the fucking mark again, mister. Back the fuck out of this, this don't concern you in the least, asshole. Anytime you feel fricking Froggy, jump for it Mutt. I'm going to beat your ass until your nose bleeds on you, mister. I'm in just the right fucking mood to handle your ass now, buster. I'm tired of what you call being a soldier, buster." The Colonel hissed savagely, not daring to take his eyes off the dangerous Mutt for a second.

"Hey Colonel, moods are for cattle and sex play." The Mutt hissed, still refusing to back down.

"Colonel Leadbetter!" Walker yelled out as the rest of the soldiers quickly moved in, and they surround the three angry men, as they prepared to stop a possible fight from happening between the two officers.

The massive Neck grumbled at the three soldiers, trying to make light of the dangerous situation taking place before him. "It seems like we have ourselves a minor fucking tiff developing between these two shitbirds, people."

"Minor fucking tiff you say asshole. It looks more like a fricking war about to go popping off on us, man." The Hunter added as he moved closer to the Colonel now. He was prepared to grab the Colonel before any blows were traded between the Colonel and the Mutt.

"It seems like the Colonel took a mild case of the dislikes to the fucking Mutt all of duh sudden, people." Buckethead offered as he stepped in front of the Mutt, and pushed him back.

The Colonel glanced around and easily picked up the movement of the other soldiers, and he knew he might be overreacting to the Mutt's stupid threat against him. He was just popping off like he usually did after any training exercise was completed. He suddenly relaxed his threatening stance and grumbled at his young military officer. "Yeah, I guess you're right at that, I think your dog is off his fucking leash again Walker. I guess

I'll never make a fucking true soldier out of you, mister. Mutt, you just pulled your ass guard duty at the Green Monster until we shove off on our next mission, mister."

Walker's ears immediately perked up as he asked his commanding officer with concern in his voice. "Colonel Leadbetter, we're going active I take it sir?"

"As active as you can possibly get without being on your fucking target, mister. You have one hour, I repeat this for the dumb people of the Unit, one fucking hour to get your personal crap straightened out, and then be prepared to ship out for Fort Bragg after that time, people. General White from his palace at Fort Fumble just ordered a mess of trash haulers (transport aircraft) to pick the lot of ya asses up, and ship you people out to who knows fucking where. I assure you boys and girls the second I find out our destination I'll inform you people of it. I don't like heading out on any fucking mission half ass blind like this. On the fucking double quick, shove off and carry out your orders, people. Err, one other thing before you jackasses leave.

"You people did me justice in this shoot house structure with every training exercise we carried out in there so far, now we're going to see just how fucking well you people apply what you learned here, in the field of reality when we jump off on this latest operation, people. Remember, courage don't make the person, the person makes the fucking courage. Good luck people. I want you to know, I'll be out there in the field along with the rest of you people on this mission, and I'll be looking over your fucking shoulder and ready to apply a little size eleven boot intelligence to anyone who fucks up on this damn mission, move it out people."

"Hey Colonel, thanks for the warning, will there be any beer there sir?" Wacko called out.

"I swear to the good God above me, you pack of shitbirds are going to send me right over the mother fucking falls before I'm done with the lot of you crazy ass bastards. I was hoping to make a bunch of real soldiers out of the lot of you, but there's not enough time in the world to make that happen." The Colonel growled as he watched the soldiers dart off to follow their orders. Some of the soldiers took the time to shoot the bird at the Colonel, and he ignored the rude gesture as if it was a naked orphan.

The soldiers bunched up as they rushed for the barracks to pack their gear, and picked up where they left off with dumping on the other soldiers.

"You know something Walker, that man has no social graces at all left in his stinking body, sir. He's going to grow up into being a nasty old man if he's not a little more careful about the way he is treating us." Baby Tee complained while speaking about the Colonel.

"He almost makes me dislike the lousy motherfucker." Mother Flanagan added to the bitch being aimed against their commanding officer.

"Get outta my stinking face before I knock you three sewers back, thick man. You hit me again with your stinking elbow, and I'm gonna rip the damn thing off for you, and wave it back at ya puss before I beat you over the head with the damn thing, big man." Walker snapped at Neck, who almost ran right over the top of him by accident.

"Calm down a kittle Walker, why the hell are you so pissed off at my stinking ass for, man? I gotta take me a fucking dump, Homes. If I don't get there quick, I'll Code Brown myself man." Neck complained as he tried to get passed Walker and make it to the barracks.

"Hey big man, I got some bad news for you, Walker was born pissed off." Blind Date laughed and then she added to her attack on the Lieutenant this time. "I heard many stories that his mother was afraid to breast feed him when he was a child."

"He's got more balls than brains, people." Another soldier called out from the group against Lieutenant Walker.

"Oorah." Most of the troops screamed out as one as they increased their pace for the barracks.

"You people betta stop flapping your fricking gums so much, and pay more attention to what the hell you're doing around here dammit, times a wasting on us people. We got a set time limit to get packed up and ready to shove off. I don't need the stinking Colonel starting this mission off in a bad stinking mood and getting on our damn cases because we were late shaping up to ship out people." Lieutenant Walker growled as he hit the steps of the barracks.

The elite batch of specialized soldiers stripped down and rushed to the showers to wash off the sweat and grime of the day's training exercises. Buckethead yelled out as he entered the shower area. "Hey man, this thing's filled with a clear, non-alcoholic liquid people."

"You mean water asshole." Fire, (Sergeant Ashely Reeks) laughed as she slapped the massive Buckethead on his naked rearend, making it sound like someone just fired off a weapon in the shower area of the barracks.

"Yeeehhhaaawww that hurt like fucking hell rope swallower." Buckethead griped as he turned and glared at Sergeant Reeks for a moment, as he rubbed his rearend. Fire left her whole handprint on Buckethead's rearend and she was proud of the mark she branded him with.

"Whatsumatter, did I hurt your itty bitty bottom on you big boy? Poor little baby you." Fire smirked as the big man continued to rub his can, and he remained staring angrily at her.

When the soldiers came out of the showers, they began to pack up their loose gear for their trip over to Fort Bragg. No one was too worried about their personal belongings. The soldiers knew the barracks fire guard would protect their stuff with his life. So they mostly concentrated on only the military equipment they were going to take with them on the new mission.

The Mutt naked as usual while packing his equipment up, asked Walker with concern. "Hey Road Kill, were do ya think we're heading this time around man?"

"Don't be a fucking ass, man. Where the fuck do ya think we're heading for this time, dog man. We're heading for fucking Iraq sure as shit, stupid."

Even though Sergeant Ramirez was not going along with the rest of the troops on this operation, she showered with them, and then she stood and offered Walker any help she could give him. She had a towel wrapped around her waist. "I'm going to really miss the hell outta you baby." Sergeant Ramirez whispered to her lover and soldier.

Walker stopped packing for a moment and he kissed Ramirez. The soldiers immediately began making cat calls and hoots and hollers at them, and telling Ramirez to send Walker off with one of her famous blow jobs. She flipped the bird at the other soldiers she saw calling for her to do Walker in front of them.

The Mutt was not going to let her off of the hook that easy, and he leaned closer to Walker and bitched at him. "You know something Homes I've been doing a little fucking thinking lately."

Lieutenant Walker looked back at the Mutt, (Lieutenant Frank Hall) for a moment, and he noticed he was trying to be dead serious this time

EAGLE'S NEST

around, and he fell right into his trap with both feet, but not before taking a few slugs at him first. "That's a fucking surprise buddy. I didn't think you thought about anything but beer and broads all the damn time, man. You didn't hurt yourself a little inside the shoot house building today to make you do this thinking thing, did ya pal? Please brother, you have to enlighten me with these great words of wisdom you thought up for some reason all by yourself that I'm afraid to hear, Homes."

Everyone stopped what they were doing to hear the Mutt's latest words of wisdom.

"You know something Walker I been doing some serious thinking about this shit for a long time now, man. I really believe they should think about renaming the phrase 'blow job' if you were to ask me, man...'"

The troops let out with a groan, and some of them went back to packing their gear.

"No man, I'm being true with all of ya, hear me out for a second will ya huh. I'm on the up and up here this time around, man. This is some serious shit I wanna lay down on you people here, so let me continue so you guys know what I'm talking bout. Don't go tits up on me now people. Just the name of it sucks, blow job, do you feel me people?" The Mutt offered as he kept a serious look glued on his face as he continued speaking to the group of specialized soldiers.

"That's why they named it that way, you fucking asshole you." Neck growled back at the Mutt, and then he continued his bitch at the soldier. "It's supposed to suck stupid." Neck was immediately assaulted with a barrage of pillows, mostly thrown at him by the women in the barracks who took exception to his last words.

"No man, listen up Neck. Did you ever ask yourself why so many women stink at the fucking act all the time, man? It's like stinking work to them, a fucking job. It's gotta be a fricking subliminal thing, a sort of mental block for them and that's why they..."

"Now there's a five dollar word I never thought was in the Mutt's fucking vocabulary, people." The Ghost said as he lit up a joint, and then passed it on to Hunter standing by his side.

"Fuck you man and the horse you rode in on, buddy. I'm trying to be dead serious with you slobs here, and you people are giving me nuthin but lip shit and bad manners. So don't give me a case of the damn ass. Hear me out first will ya before you go off and get on my ass, people."

"Back off some people and let's hear what the asshole has on fucking his mind. Okay Mutt, you have our undivided attention so go ahead with your bitch. I gotta hear this fucking shit out now man, and you two birds betta go light on that fricking crap while you're at it. You know we're not supposed to be hitting that shit while going on active duty, assholes." Walker grumbled at the two point soldiers, as he stared at his lifelong friend.

The Mutt started off again. "Christ sake man, look at the stinking evidence lying out before ya own stinking eyes, man. No wonder a hooker's so good at it, people. It's a stinking job to them, and they get paid for it as well, man. Shit Homes, if you wanna good blow job, you gotta change the stinking name of it and make the ladies wanna give you one and not that they have to..."

"To what do you want to change the name to Spudhead? I'm sure you have a new name in mind man so spit it out." Buckethead asked, getting involved in the Mutt's words now himself.

"I don't know tree trunk. I don't have all the fucking answers to this stinking problem. Maybe change it to blow fun, blow experience, how about a damn blow vacation. Pick one, but the word 'job' has to go if you ever wanna enjoy one again guys. Take a bitch out in an expensive car and get the blow ride of your fucking life..."

"Hey dick stretcher, I seen your stinking car Homes, and it ain't worth twenty bucks, and that's with a full tank of stinking gas in the damn thing, and a new fucking wax job. You want a good blow job then go see Raz will ya. She's about the best I ever saw at the act, Homes. She can do it so good, she can make a homeless man wanna go out and build himself a fucking home, man." The massive Neck moaned, as he went back to packing up his gear up again. His words caused everyone to break up with laughter and another flight of pillows aimed at him.

"Fuck he will, if he ever wants a blow job from me again. He has to learn how to treat a woman better first." Sergeant Ramirez complained as she stifled a laugh at the grinning Mutt.

"Hey Mutt, you ever try any of your relatives. I bet they can do you good and proper man?"

"Hey man, I never dated one of my stinking cousins, that's bullshit and bad manners man. Fucked them yeah, but I never dated any of them, man." The Mutt's last words brought another barrage of pillows flying throughout the barracks, this time most of them were aimed at him, with many women yelling out "Disgusting" at him as they threw their pillows at him.

"Christ sake man, I knew the stinking Mutt way back when you could understand what he was talking about." Baby Tee said, getting back on the Mutt's case again.

"Hey bitch, how's bout you putting some stinking lip stick on my dip stick. If you think you're so stinking smart all the time." The Mutt fire back at the smallish woman busting his horns.

"If you don't relax some Mutt, they're gonna hafta bury your stinking ass standing up, stupid." Neck grunted at him as he stopped what he was doing and smirked at the soldier.

"Neck, I'm telling ya man, I'm not here for a long time, but I'm sure here for a good time man." The Mutt snorted at the huge soldier.

Lieutenant Walker shook his head, Ramirez rested her hand on his shoulder and this seemed to relax him as she whispered to him. "I'm afraid he's about as crazy as they come Walker."

"Don't I know that for certain honey, but he's the best friend anyone could ever ask for, baby." Walker replied as he turned his attention to the Mutt, to see if he was finished talking or not yet.

"Hey Walker, I think I'm gonna hafta get the Mutt one of those stinking mechanical head things from the local fuck shop just off the base, man. That way he can get all the stinking blow jobs any time he wants them, Homes." Mother Flanagan said as he walked up to Walker and whispered his words to him so the Mutt did not hear them.

"You better be a little more careful with the Mutt than that, Mother. Mutt will fuck you to death for that kinda shit, even if it takes him the rest of his damn life to do it, man. He doesn't like fucking round when it comes down to that kinda shit you know, Homes." Lieutenant Walker warned him angrily as he held him under his harsh glare for a few long moments.

"I hear that loud and clear Road Kill. Maybe it wasn't such a good idea for me to pop off like that on him, man." Mother Flanagan griped as he went back to smoking his blunt and finished packing. But not before removing the joint, looking at it for a second and then offering as if an afterthought just struck him. "Man, this shit's so fucking bad it'll put the fucking hump back in a camel's back, Homes."

Lieutenant Walker laughed at Mother Flanagan's last words as he glanced back at the Mutt, and he happened to read what the Mutt had printed on his backpack. 'The driver only carries twenty dollars worth of ammunition for his M-60 at all times'. Again, he shook his head, pleased he was friends with a man he classified as too wild to be mild, and a damn good soldier.

Most of the specialized soldiers in the barracks were dressed and finished packing when Sergeant Kirkpatrick came strolling into the barracks. Jail Bait saw him enter first, and she immediately warned the other soldiers by calling out to them. "Heads up people, we have some covert company infiltrating our stinking barracks on us people."

Sergeant Kirkpatrick shot the female soldier a dirty look, and then he ignored her as he headed directly for Lieutenant Walker's bunk. He was always trying to get the group of elite soldiers to like him, but the specialized soldiers already branded him as Colonel Leadbetter's private little henchman, and they were not cutting him any slack either, whenever he had to deal with the group of soldiers preparing for the operation.

"Hey baby, take the fucking glare out of your stare, or I'll give you something to look at." Jail Bait said as she lifted her shirt and jiggled her breasts at the stunned looking Sergeant.

Walker growled at the soldier getting on the Staff Sergeant's ass. "C'mon Jail Bait, you're gonna give the little puke the shits if you keep doing that kinda crap to his ass." Walker then turned to Sergeant Kirkpatrick and snapped at him. "Whatdaya doing in no man's fucking land, Sergeant? I always thought you didn't want to hang elbow to elbow with the likes of us shits in here for a damn second, Sergeant?"

"That's not true at all Lieutenant Walker. I really respect you and the other soldiers of the Unit, sir." Sergeant Kirkpatrick offered Walker.

"Stick your fucking respect up your fricking ass will ya Sergeant. What the hell's on your damn mind anyway, man?" When Lieutenant Walker snapped at the Sergeant, he was immediately sorry for his outburst. He remembered the Sergeant stuck his dick in the ringer for the Mutt when he set fire to the Cave, the small illegal bar back in Egypt when he gave Fun Bags the flaming send off honor.

"I'm sorry you still don't like me much Lieutenant Walker. I'm not in this thing for a personality contest either, sir. The Colonel sent me here to see how you people were getting along, and to make certain you guys didn't need or want anything special, before we head out for Fort Bragg, sir. Or if any of you had any last minute requests or needs for any special weapons, or any other items or equipment you feel you might need in the field on this mission, Lieutenant."

"That's a good question there Sergeant Kirkpatrick. What about our fucking weapons Sarge? Who's looking afta our weapons and special gear for us, mister?" Walker grumbled as he stopped packing, and he stared at the Sergeant while waiting for his reply.

"Lieutenant Walker, the Colonel has your weapons packed up on a duce and a half already, and it's on its way to Fort Bragg as we speak, sir. Can you think of anything else you might need or want in the field for this operation, Lieutenant?" The Sergeant asked the Lieutenant.

"You know where we're heading I take it, Sergeant? I got a pretty good idea where we're going on my own, mister." Walker asked the snooping Sergeant this time.

"Iraq sir, it's been confirmed your target got back safely to his stinking little rathole there, Lieutenant Walker. It seems Director Raincloud has some CIA Spooks active in Iraq, and they were able to get some pictures of the bastard hanging around some damn Iraqi General. This info was given to the President and he pulled the trigger and ordered General White to send you guys after this lousy little turd, sir." Sergeant Kirkpatrick informed Walker.

"Shit, I was kinda hoping that we might be able to skip going to fucking camel land for this fucking operation, Sergeant. Err... there is something we should have with us for this operation, we could sure use some C-4 explosive, just in case we have to go in after the lousy turd hiding in some stinking building, or other place we hafta blast our way into to get at his stinking ass on this operation, Sergeant." Walker requested from the NCO (Non Commissioned Officer).

"The C-4 explosive is already packed along with three satchel charges, and one bunker buster weapon. I included these items on my own just in case you had to blow down any locked doors, sir. You have anyone in the outfit trained in handling the C-4 explosives, Lieutenant?"

"Yeah, Mother Flanagan and the Ghost can handle the crapola okay for us, man. You know how many of us are going in after this fricking missing turd, Sergeant?" Walker asked the man.

"I know the Colonel's leaving that entire up to you this time around, Lieutenant. You're more than free to take as many troops as you want, or need with you on this mission, sir. I know the Colonel's going to activate the entire group though, and hold everyone you don't take along with you on an Aircraft Carrier scheduled to be stationed in the Gulf of Aden for the duration of the operation, Lieutenant. Just in case the shit hits the fan and they have to be flown in where we can perform a hot extraction of your troops if they run into any trouble in Iraq, sir."

"That means this can be classified as an all out operation I guess, Sergeant?"

"Balls to the fucking wall Lieutenant Walker, Colonel Leadbetter's going to be stationed on the Carrier along with the troops he's going to hold back in reserve, sir. I think he wants in on this mission real bad sir, and the Colonel feels the only way that'll happen, is if the mission goes tits up on you, and we have to commit the other soldiers we have held in reserve to pull you guys safely out of Iraq, sir. The Colonel backs the shit out of your guys you know, Lieutenant. Colonel Leadbetter takes better care of you people, than I saw him help with any other Unit he was ever in command of, Lieutenant Walker Sir." The Sergeant offered to Walker with a grin.

"You say that like it's a fucking bad thing, Sergeant. This is the first fricking time since I hooked up with this friggin outfit that I feel we're gonna finally have the proper backing on a stinking mission, Sarge. I guess it takes an attempted assassination on the President's stinking life, for the assholes over at Fort Fumble to take their job a little more seriously for our asses, man." Lieutenant Walker noticed Sergeant Ramirez staring at him from the corner of his eye, and he growled under his breath, "Shit." As he tried to keep his attention on the conversation he was having with the Colonel's private little hatchet man

Sergeant Kirkpatrick saw the quick slight glance and knew right away what was suddenly bugging Walker's ass, and he offered quickly to the young military officer. "Lieutenant Walker Sir, I know the Colonel's including Sergeant Ramirez in on the mission as well, sir. He's going to employ her as an Agent keeping a close eye on all the reports as they come in from your troops out in the field, once the operation gets on its feet sir, and she'll be taking all AARs (After Action Reports) once you people are back from sand land along with your damn prisoner, Lieutenant Walker. The Colonel told me he was activating the entire unit, and that includes Sergeant Ramirez, sir." The Sergeant shot a quick smile at Ramirez, because he knew she was hanging on every word they spoke together. The female Sergeant could not hide the smile glued to her lips, as she looped her arm in Walker's, and she nodded pleasantly to the Sergeant.

Walker lightly patted her hand and said. "You see baby, we're all still a working unit here."

Sergeant Kirkpatrick glanced at his watch, and then he remarked to the young officer. "Say Lieutenant Walker, you better step it up some, sir. The Colonel's heading for the Grungies as we speak sir. (Grungies-Humvee Jeeps) I know he's expecting everyone to be there when he arrives at that station, Lieutenant. He's in a pretty good mood so far sir, but if he beats you people over to the damn Grungies, you can rest assured he's going to be fit to be tied sir."

"Thanks for the fucking warning Sarge, I don't need the stinking Colonel to get on our asses before we jump off on this next operation. Err... Sergeant, you mind if I ask you a question?"

"Shoot Lieutenant Walker Sir." The Sergeant replied as he looked at the Lieutenant, while waiting for his question to be asked of him.

"You coming along with us on this little old turkey shoot here, Sergeant?" Walker asked as he stuffed a special undershirt in his bag, to be worn under his body armor. He was trying to think of anything he might need for the new mission into Iraq before they headed for that country.

"Damn right I'm coming along with your troops, Lieutenant Walker Sir. I'm hoping to get involved in some of the action as well along with the rest of you guys, sir. It's about time I trade in my damn pencil for a stinking weapon and get some trigger time in around here myself, Lieutenant." The young Marine Sergeant offered to Lieutenant Walker proudly.

"You got that right Sergeant and we can sure use all the extra help we can get for any operation we're sent on." Walker put out his hand and he waited for the Sergeant to shake it.

The Sergeant stared at it for a moment, and then he shook hands with Walker as he added. "Glad to have you on board on this one Sergeant. We can sure use you on this one mister."

Colonel Leadbetter was about to leave his office when the phone rang and stopped him dead in his tracks as he grumbled at himself. "Oh crap, what now for the love of God?"

"Colonel Leadbetter?" the voice on the other end growled in the phone demanding to know.

"Yes sir." The Marine Colonel replied as he settled back in his chair again, because he instantly recognized the voice on the horn.

"General White here sir, I have the green light from the President for you people to go hot. The Aircraft Carrier George Washington's already lifting anchor as we speak Colonel, and by the time you people get deployed, she'll be set on station off the coast of Kuwait, sir. Here's your mission the way it shapes up at this time, Colonel Leadbetter. You're going to be dropped off in Kuwait by transport aircraft, under the guise of a special desert training operation.

"Under the cover of darkness, your troops will be transferred out to the old Desert Storm Special Ops Base, Ramble, situated just outside Al-Athamin in the Saudi Arabian desert, Colonel. From there, your troops will be inserted in Iraq, and then the soldiers will work their way up the nation of Iraq until they reach the small Iraqi town of Dawral. It has been reported by Director Raincloud's Operatives out in the field that General Hassan al-Zahar and this damn Colonel Abdulaziz Majdal al-Adwani were going to move their current operations over to this small Iraqi town within the next few weeks or so, sir.

"It was suggested this move was in conjunction with the Iraqi General al-Zahar putting it to President Saddam Hussein about a supposed downing an allied aircraft from our no fly zone forces operating in Iraq, and the Iraqi General was moving his headquarters out to this little town to get himself and his followers the hell out of Baghdad, so close to the Iraqi President and his revenge for putting it to him the other day. They never did get one of our aircraft, Colonel Leadbetter Sir. The Carrier

EAGLE'S NEST

Washington's going to be equipped with a wing of Osprey tilt wing aircraft on board, in case the troops on board the Carrier have to go in, and forcible extract the your troops from Iraq, if you're discovered and your operation becomes compromised, and your troops come under attack by a powerful force of Iraqi regular troops, sir.

"Colonel Leadbetter, the latest Intel we were able to gather on this missing prick and his damn friends, has placed General al-Zahar and Colonel al-Adwani moving from Baghdad, because of the heavy heat his last press conference placed on them, over to this Iraqi town of Dawral. That makes our target thirty miles closer to the Saudi Arabian border for us. It gives us a fucking break here, because General al-Zahar's complex in Dawral isn't as well fortified as his stronghold back in Baghdad is. He has fewer troops surrounding him in Dawral, and we can use all the damn breaks we can muster on this fucking revenge mission the troops will be on, Colonel.

"As it stands right now Colonel Leadbetter, this mission has been classified as TS/SC, (Top Secret/Special Category). No one but the President and his closest staff, along with you, me and the soldiers who are going on the mission, will know this assignment is in operation, sir. Before you ask me Colonel Leadbetter, yes, the Saudi King's well aware of the operation, but he's the only one from that country who knows shit about the damn thing. I have to inform you that we don't have his full blessings for the mission as it stands, but he's willing to support this operation anyhow. Or at least turn his back while we make use of his damn country to launch this raid into Iraq, if your troops come under attack in Iraq.

"Err... one other thing you have to be made aware of, Colonel Leadbetter while I have your ear, sir. This mission will be a success, no matter what we have to employ or accomplish, to insure that success in the field, sir. The President gave me, and that means you, carte blanche on this damn mission Colonel, to insure the fucking operation's a success, and the successful extraction of our troops and their prisoner from the field at the completion of this operation. The President has also given me the power just short of employing nuclear weapons for commitment, if you people come under attack and you have to fight your way out of the situation, Colonel. That's why I have the Aircraft Carrier Washington moving into the Gulf, air support will be less than five minutes from your people at all times during the entire operation one way or the other, sir.

"I intend to beef up the two no fly zone watch in Iraq, giving the area your troops will be operating in, top priory air coverage and operational support for your operation for the full duration of that action, Colonel Leadbetter. That way air support will be closer than five minutes away from your area of operations at all times, if this mission goes tits up on us, sir. I can't impress on you how bad the Boss wants this fucking man standing before him. To be quite frank with you on this one Colonel, it wouldn't break my heart any if General al-Zahar got in the way of a fucking stray bullet or two if you know what I mean, sir. I have no special care to keep this bastard of a man alive a moment long than he breaths, Colonel."

"Understood your last suggestion as received, General White Sir, what the hell do we do once we're inside the damn building searching for this little prick in Dawral, sir? How far can we go before we switch the operation?" The Colonel asked his commanding officer over the phone.

"Of course Colonel Leadbetter, the President wants to keep the killing of anyone not included on the hit list I just suggested to you, down to an absolute minimum sir. But anyone conceived as a possible threat against your troops is to be eliminated without hesitation from your Tier One Assets, sir. I don't give a fucking rat's ass if it's female, male or animal, Colonel Leadbetter. Erase any and all possible resistance you might encounter in the field of this mission during the entire length of this operation, sir. We're going to take the fucking 'T' out of terrorism if I have anything to do about it. We're going to hit them with impunity, Colonel Leadbetter."

"I read you loud and clear on this one, General White." The Colonel replied proudly to him.

"Okay Colonel Leadbetter, get it done for us then soldier. How close are your troops from heading out to Fort Bragg, Colonel?" the Chairman asked his lesser military officer.

"I was just on my way out to see that for myself, General White Sir. These damn soldiers better be well prepared to shove off for Fort Bragg if they know what's good for them sir." The Colonel offered as he looked out the window out of habit to the training grinder.

"Fine Colonel Leadbetter Sir, you'll have two full days to prepare your troops for this raid into Iraq, sir. I want it in full operation by August 7th, using Zero, Four Thirty Hours as the fucking jump off time. Colonel, you need to nab this little cock sucker's ass for the President, sir. We'll be working on a twelve hour, than six hour step up time schedule; the first twelve hours will be used as observation and possible easy snatch operations of the damn human target, at eighteen hours plus into the mission, Colonel. It'll then be accomplished by an all out assault on the building in question and a hard snatch of the intended target, sir.

"If this isn't possible for your troops to accomplish, after twenty two hours plus into the operation, this mission goes to a Search and Splatter operation, Colonel Leadbetter. If we're forced to go this route sir, I want pictures of the execution of this lousy prick for the President's benefit. At twenty four hours plus zero into the operation, your troops will be withdrawn from the field of operations, with no if ands or buts about it, Colonel. The computers drop the success rate down to near zero at this time sir. These time lines will be rigorously adhered to by you and your troops, Colonel. Because that's the way I have your support systems set up for you and the troops. Any deviation from this plan will cause major problems for all concerned. Do I make myself perfectly clear on what I want accomplished on this operation, Colonel Leadbetter?"

"Yes sir, understood as received sir." The Colonel replied in a quick and confident tone.

"Then there's no sense wasting any more time speaking with me on this subject, Colonel Leadbetter. Get it going Colonel, we trained these specialized troops to be No Fail Teams, so I expect this operation to be a successful one as ordered sir. I want constant updated reports from you every three hours during the entire length of this operation, sir. I'll be spending my time in my office, so I'll be easy to make contact with any time you have need of me, sir. Good luck on this mission Colonel Leadbetter. You have the best of the best with you, so they better accomplish this damn mission the way it's drawn up on the table, sir." The General did not wait for the Colonel to respond to his last words, knowing he was pressed for time with the President.

Colonel Bruce Leadbetter jumped to his feet after speaking to General White, and he rushed out of his office and headed straight for the Humvee parked just outside his door. He started it, gunned the engine and took off for the loading area for the troops. By the time he arrived, Lieutenant Walker's crew was just starting to assemble in the area. Curses, gripes, and jokes constantly filled the air, as the upset Colonel rapidly approached the elite troops.

Other soldiers from the Marine base milled about the loading area, to watch what was going on with the soldiers gathered on the tarmac. A second General walked up to the men, and ordered them away from the site, keeping the mission locked in security. The other General replaced the troops, and he watched as the elite special operations soldiers mounted up for their latest mission.

The Mutt, forever standing by Walker's side, immediately noticed the unfamiliar General watching them, and he drew Walker's attention over to the other officer.

"Holy shit, that stinking dude's got the whole fucking Milky Way plastered all over his frigging chest, man." Lieutenant Walker grumbled as he passed his MP-5 automatic weapon over to Mother Flanagan who was waiting inside the parked humvee.

"At least this bird's a made man. He's got combat ribbons in that mess of salad dressing. That makes him A Number One in my book." The Mutt added as he saluted the other General.

The General stiffened up then snapped off a sharp salute to the young officer. He smiled pleasantly because this soldier took the time to offer him a curiosity.

Colonel Leadbetter pulled up to the lead of the column of humvees, and spotted the General and automatically saluted him, and then he barked new orders at his troops. "C'mon people, what the hell do you people think this shit is for the love of God, a fucking social gathering or something like that, get mounted up in them damn machines people." Colonel Leadbetter climbed on the roof of the hard shell jeep, and he waited for the last soldiers to pile into the waiting vehicles. When the Colonel's Grungie pulled up, Sergeant Kirkpatrick jumped in and he took his seat as driver. When the troops were mounted, the Colonel jumped off the machine, and pounded on the metal roof as he stood on the running board and bellowed at his driver. "Get going Sergeant while we have these shitbirds ready to go, mister."

CHAPTER TWENTY FOUR

THE MASSIVE MILITARY BASE FORT BRAGG, NORTH CAROLINA

The long column of humvees from Camp Lejeune was guided around the outside of the massive Fort Bragg Military Base under full security, and were allowed to enter the base from the rear near the so called Green Monster area shared by Pope Air Force Base and Fort Bragg alike. A humvee from the 101St, Screaming Eagles sharing the base, escorted the specialized Marine troops to their final destination on the large Army Base. Officers from Fort Bragg surrounded the first transport aircraft to catch a glimpse of these special operation troops, as they quickly boarded the aircraft for their upcoming mission. Colonel Leadbetter had Sergeant Kirkpatrick pull in front of the transport, and he jumped back on the roof of his jeep and snarled at his troopers. "Okay, everyone, gather round, I have last minute orders. C'mon people and move like you have a fucking reason to live. Sergeant Flanagan, get your slimy ass over here will ya before I hop you in the fucking can, mister."

When the troops were gathered around Colonel Leadbetter's humvee and they quieted down, he began speaking to the specialized soldiers. "Okay troops, here are some last minute orders for you shits to digest." The moment Colonel Leadbetter issued the orders, the officers from the Army Base not involved in his mission quickly disappeared. They knew they might be breaching the mission security if they remained and listened to the Colonel's orders.

"Before I left Camp Lejeune, I spoke to the head cheese in Washington. General White informed me we have top priory on this matter at hand. Full and complete support, and full cover for fucking extraction, whether it be hot or cold, people. This is a full body assault, your mission is to capture this stinking turd, and get his ass the hell out of his little love nest, so he can stand trial back here in the United States. The General also warned me the President wants this guy so bad he can actually taste it. That means we're under orders to capture him alive if at all possible. We have twenty four hours operation light in which to accomplish this mission. At the end of that time, we have to get the hell out of camel land. We have two fucking options left opened here, pardon me people, three. We can make an easy snatch and scoot with our baggage.

"Mid-way through the damn mission, it turns into a high risk invasion of the suspected building, and a tough capture and scoot of our intended target from that point forward. I need not remind any of you turds here of the fucking problems you'll be facing out in the field of action, if we're forced to breach the damn building where our luggage is supposed to be hiding in, dammit. Nearing the twenty four hour mark of the operation, this mission shifts into locate and destroy target with pictures. The General won't be too upset with any of you guys if General Hassan al-Zahar gets in the way of a drive by bullet either in the action, people.

"I'll transmit the signal when this mission goes to a search and destroy operation, when the allotted time is used up by you people. I don't mind telling you jackrabbits your government spent a major fucking fortune training you pissants for just this type of damn mission. That means everyone, included myself, will be extremely disappointed if this damn mission breaks down to a damn execution out in the field mission. I want this lousy bugger's ass taken alive, because I want the privilege of dragging his ass before General White. I also want to see the face of General White when he gets nose to nose with our baggage, and he gives him a piece of his mind. If you people give me this privilege, I'll take my own pictures of the confrontation and share them with all you people later on of the encounter.

"This is the first mission I'm aware of, where we'll have the full military support, but I don't want to involve the other services in our little party if we don't have to, people. This is a special ops mission plain and simple, and I intend to keep it that way throughout the entire operation. I want to add a few other items to the mid part of our mission, people. If, by some freak of chance, we're forced to breach the god damn building, no one is to stand in your way. Got that people? Anyone caught up in your sights is to be turned into body part donors. No fricking hesitation, you're to take out anyone and everyone if it becomes necessary on this mission and just spotting someone not from our unit is enough to send him on his way to Paradise. Just think of yourself as a fucking hammer, and everyone else you see is a stinking nail. Drive them into the ground.

"Mind you people, I'd prefer you just wound or otherwise disable the other occupants of the damn structure, but don't waste any time on them though. You know who our target is, and I want him at the cost of anyone else found inside the damn target building. Anyone who dares challenge you people is to be sent on the long dirt nap, period people. I don't give a flying fuck if Saddam Hussein himself is hiding inside the fricking building on you. Especially if he's in the damn building, he's not to see another god damn day's light if you get him in your sights. He's just as important a target as is our missing terrorist turd, people."

Wacko raised his hand, and he began to jump up and down while standing in place.

The Colonel spotted the excited soldier and barked at him nastily. "This isn't a fucking school around here, asshole. Put your damn hand down and call out your god damn question, if that's what is on your stinking mind, puke. But I warn you though, if this is a break balls question, you're going to find yourself running along the outside of the aircraft to get to your damn mission, buster." Colonel Leadbetter warned him in no uncertain terms.

Wacko immediately lowered his hand and tried his best to hide behind the other soldier standing directly in front of him on line.

"You fucking people are going to be the fricking death of me yet, dammit. Don't any you shitbirds ever take anything seriously around here anymore, for the love of God? I don't know about you bunch of damn alcoholics, misfits and bitches. Dammit to hell." Colonel Leadbetter growled as he held Wacko in his harsh glare for a long moment.

"Hey Colonel Leadbetter, I ain't no damn alcoholic sir. I'm a stinking drunk sir, plain and simple. Them damn alcoholics hafta attend all those boring ass meetings all the fucking time, sir." Wacko complained back to the Colonel's grip aimed at him.

Lieutenant Walker spoke over Wacko's busting of the Colonel's horns. "Colonel Leadbetter Sir, how the hell are we going to get inside Iraq for this damn mission, sir?"

"Holy shit, an intelligent question asked by one of you yahoos. Who would have thunk it possible. Lieutenant Walker, I won't go into that part of our mission right now. We'll talk more about this shit while we're in flight for our destination, sir. If there are no more questions from any of you flaming assholes, we have a fucking turd we have to flush out of his stinking rathole in sand land, people. The President wants this, the General wants this and the people of the United States wants this, so that means I want it. And, if I want it, it will happen or I'll leave the lot of you assholes in sand land and you can walk back to the United States from there if you fail." Colonel Leadbetter growled, as he waited for any more questions to be asked of him.

The Colonel looked over the anxious soldiers standing before him, and when no one else offered up a question or another suggestion, he turned to Sergeant Kirkpatrick and ordered him. "Okay Sergeant, it's time we load this pack of shit into them damn waiting trash haulers (transport aircraft), and get them on their way out to sand land, mister."

Sergeant Kirkpatrick snapped to attention, and he saluted the angry Colonel sharply. Once he received the return salute from the Colonel, he turned his attention to the troops, and bitched at them. "Okay people, you heard the Colonel. Let's get on board them damn things, so we can get on with our mission, and capture this little rat bastard for our President, people. Time's a wasting and we have to move out, now people."

The group of elite soldiers picked up their equipment and looped it over their shoulders effortlessly, as they quickly lined up in two separate lines and headed up the tail ramp of the transport aircraft. All the while they were boarding the transport planes, many of the elite soldiers complained at the Sergeant watching them get on board the aircraft.

For the first time in his life, Sergeant John Kirkpatrick felt the elite group of soldiers was finally accepting him in their ranks, and he took the horn busting as just that. Now he realized these outstanding soldiers busted everyone's horns they respected. He smiled as he watched the elite group of soldiers hustling up the tail ramps of the waiting aircraft. He knew with the confidence the soldiers were displaying before him and the other officers of the group, Colonel al-Adwani had no chance in hell of surviving this mission once they went after him.

Colonel Leadbetter got in the first aircraft, along with Lieutenant Walker, and most of the other officers and squad leaders of the specialized unit going on this mission. He wanted to speak more with Walker while they were in flight, until he felt Walker completely understood his orders, and what was expected from his troops on this operation. The Colonel also wanted this operation to go off like clock work, with no mess up where he would be forced to place more soldiers on the ground in Iraq, to support the soldiers on the mission. He wanted this missing terrorist more than he wanted leave time. He did not inform the rest of the soldiers, but he vowed to himself his troops were going to capture this terrorist alive if he had anything to do with it.

KUWAIT INTERNATIONAL AIRPORT, KUWAIT CITY

The United States military transport aircraft carrying the elite troops known as the MNRRF, Multi National Rapid Response Force. Flew through the night and found them circled in the transport aircraft over the Kuwaiti International Airport, just before six a.m. the following morning. When the pilot informed the troops they were about to land, the conversations shifted from general talk, to any new ideas of what they might employ during this current mission to snatch the missing terrorist, and bring him out of Iraq in one piece.

The transport planes landed without a hitch and a number of Kuwaiti owned military type humvees were parked on the tarmac, waiting to move the specialized troops off the airfield as quickly as possible, before anyone grew suspicious of their presence in the tiny Arab Kingdom. The Kuwaiti government was informed about the special operation, and they immediately began their campaign of confusion, by announcing the American soldiers were coming to their country, to begin training to protect Kuwait against any further attacks from Saddam's evil forces.

This story worked because few reporters bothered to hang around the airfield when the military transport aircraft landed. When they saw how few American troops were debarking the massive aircraft, the reporters quickly grew bored with the action and they slowly filtered back into the capital in search of better stories to follow up on.

Colonel Bruce Leadbetter got off the aircraft first, and was complaining at this time of year, the desert was as dry as a popcorn fart in an oven. The rest of the elite troops followed the Colonel to the column of waiting humvees. When the soldiers were assembled, the Colonel gave orders for them to climb on board the machines. When the humvees were loaded down with the elite soldiers, he placed Walker in command of the troops he was taking out to the old desert Storm Base Ramble stationed at the Saudi Arabian town of Al-Athamin. Colonel Leadbetter busied himself with gathering up the remaining troops that were not an active part of the mission, and had them hang around until the Navy Sea Stallions came in to take them out to the Carrier Washington. The Colonel watched with pride as Walker's humvees left his area.

Lieutenant Robert Walker riding in the first humvee was busy egging the driver to get a move on it quicker than he was driving. The driver bitched back at Walker they could only get over to the border during daylight. Then they would have to wait until dark, so they could sneak into Saudi Arabia, and make for the town of Al-Athamin, using the cover of darkness to hide their move into the Saudi Arabian desert. The American driver griped there was no sense speeding to the secluded base, because it was still light in the desert until nearly eight p.m.

Walker realized the driver was right, and he dropped back in his seat and stared at the flat, lifeless plain of unending sand. To his surprise, there were many destroyed Iraqi tanks and armored vehicles still dotting the barren landscape, left to die the slow death of slowly rusting away in the sand, and being picked clean of any worth by the children or Arabs roaming the desert, carving a harsh life out of the unforgiving land. A few soldiers spotted unexploded munitions lying out in the open right on the surface of the sand in plain sight, most were American and allied bombs and spent artillery rounds dropped on the dug in Iraqi troops.

Many abandoned bunkers once used by the Iraqi invaders of Kuwait, were marked out clearly with small red flags. Most were left opened to the ravages of the desert, other bunkers were concrete over, to seal inside any possible chemical and biological weapons trapped forever inside the cement tomb. Some land mine fields not yet deactivated by American troops sent to Kuwait for just this purpose were also clearly marked so no one wandered around in them.

The Mutt, (Lieutenant Frank Hall) leaned forward in his seat and tapped Walker on the shoulder and then pointed to a rusting T-72 Russian built Iraqi marked tank, obviously destroyed by what appeared to have been the tank killing A-10 Warthog. The sixty five ton tank had both tracks blown off the dead machine, and they were unraveled before its body. Its huge turret laid some fifteen feet away from the behemoth body of the tank resting on its side.

The cannon bent out to a ninety degrees angle, obviously receiving the full weight of the turret, as it tumbled in the air from the force of the exploding tank. An ugly hole eight inches wide was ripped into the thick steel hide of the turret. More holes were carved deeply in the steel carcass of the once great war machine itself, mostly where the crew would have been housed inside the war machine. It was easy to tell the tank was picked clean by the Nomad desert wanderers, and other scavengers who roamed the desert at night looking for anything of worth.

"I bet no stinking sand niggers got outta that fucking machine alive judging by the tank's condition, Walker. It's too chewed up for anyone to have been able to survive the attack, man." The Mutt offered as he stared at the dead tank and then he added to his gripe. "You can see where the fucking 30 mm rounds so easily ripped the damn pig apart, man."

Walker looked at the rusting old tank, but he did not comment on the mess. It was not necessary for any words from him. One look at the once fearsome deadly war machine, and you could easily tell no tankers made it out of the war machine before it was killed. Enemy soldiers or not, it still hurt any troops when a soldier dies for the beliefs of their country.

The long column of Kuwaiti humvees finally reached the border of Saudi Arabia just before eight p.m. The eerie shadows of the desert were growing fast and making the desert look worse than it was. When it was dark enough to continue further towards their destination, the drivers floored the engines of the powerful war machines, and they cut over the Saudi Arabia, Kuwait border. Two hours later they saw the first signs of the old special operations military base constructed in Saudi Arabia. A mere dugout that once was the home of the Special Forces Units involved in the Operation Desert Storm action was still mainly left intact.

Walker saw a few Arab people hanging around the closed base, and wondered what they were doing at the old site. He tapped his helmet radio and said in a low tone to the rest of his troops in his machine. "Okay look alive people, we got us some fucking movers out there, and I don't like it one fucking bit. As of this time, I have no idea if they're hostile Injins or not. Keep your fucking eyes open, and your hammers cocked, locked and ready to rock people."

The humvees cautiously circled the large dugout position, in case there was an ambush setup by any enemy soldiers against them. The instant the war machines came to a sliding stop, the twenty soldiers plus Walker rapidly piled out of the machine, and the soldiers aimed their weapons threateningly at the strangers roaming around the old military base.

An American Military Officer station there to secure the abandoned military base in advance before the specialized troops arrived on site, came charging out of a tent yelling as he held his hands in the air. "Whoa, whoa, whoa, hold on there, don't shoot at them damn troops. These people are friendlies, they were sent out here by the Saudi King, to help prepare meals before you people leap off on your mission. C'mon troops, there are some hot meals waiting for you guys. You're not going anywhere until Zero Hour anyway. You people have less than two hours to prepare for your operation so rest up some. I suggest you make the best of it while you're marking off time. I have orders to make certain you people soup up, (drink plenty of water) fill up, and know what you're doing before heading out to complete your operation. Hey you, you standing there in the lead of the other troops, are you the man?"

"Ask your fucking mama, sir." Walker snapped back harshly at him, even before he realized he was speaking to a Full Bird Colonel.

"Funny, very fucking funny, get your damn ass over here double quick, Mr. Wiseguy. I want to speak with you further mister." The insulted Colonel ordered Walker.

Walker knew Zero Hour was at midnight, as he headed for the angry officer. He issued the troops some quick hand signals, and they relaxed. Most were starving, and none of the soldiers knew when they would enjoy another hot meal in the next few days. The meat was goat, there was bread, pitas. There were also a mess of dates and other fruits, as well as some milk and other crap. Soda was plenty, Pepsi, along with endless chilled bottled water to take with them.

The Army Colonel wanted to make certain this group of elite soldiers were the ones he was supposed to linkup with. When he was certain these were the troops he was expecting, he dismissed Walker. When he was free, the other concerned soldiers quickly gathered around their present commanding officer, and they began jaw jacking at Walker at the same time.

The Mutt and Neck complained the most because they wanted some cold beers to down. But they also knew they were not going to be enjoying any beers in the Arab lands. Ice cold Buds were waiting for them back in the land of the free and the home of the brave.

"Hey man, there's something fucking alive moving around in my stinking food, Lieutenant." The massive soldier nicknamed No Neck, griped as he held his dish out from his body, and he moved the bug around in his food with his spoon, trying to show the Mutt the small cockroach was snitching some food on him. Even though his head was constantly pounding, he refused to inform Walker about the pain, for fear he might force him to remain behind with the support troops for the operation, because of the injury he suffered during their bar fight.

"Well big man, you can play with the damn thing all you want, but I don't want you eating the damn bug, or making a fucking fido (pet) out of it, Neck." Walker said as he grunted at the massive man, and then he carefully studied his actions for a few moments. He was trying to make certain the huge soldier was not suffering any ill effects from the concussion he received during their little bar fight a number of weeks ago back on the Island of Marathon.

The rest of the specialized soldiers laughed at Neck's complaint about the bug in his food.

As Walker's troops ate and got themselves in the right frame of mind for their upcoming mission, conversations were quite or not at all. As the soldiers worked out what the Colonel ordered, a stream of quick moving vehicles sped towards the closed military base. Walker looked up and knew they were his machines the soldiers were to use in the infiltration of Iraq, and capture his target. Colonel Leadbetter informed him earlier in the day he would be employing the desert fast track vehicles for this operation into Iraq.

Three light weight Nordac NMC-40 Warrior pipe light weight vehicles pulled to the side of the dugout and parked there. The machines were nothing more than fancy souped up dune buggies with a large engine mounted on a simple pipe frame, with a pipe roll cage to protect the soldiers riding in the machine. It was armed with a 50 caliber machine gun mounted on what was its roof. It was one of the fastest of the fast attack, strike/light forces vehicle family.

Walker grinned when he saw the fine fighting machines stop alongside the dugout. He was disappointed all the buildings were removed from the old military base, and his troops were exposed to the harsh conditions of the desert. Three other of the same type vehicles pulled up behind the Chenowths. These were the FAV Fast Attack Vehicles commonly used by the Army. They were nothing more than heavily beefed up jeeps with strong engines, suspension and roll bars. They were also armed with fifty caliber machine guns mounted on the top of the roll bar as well. Three M-998 series HMMWV, Highly Mobility Multi-purpose Wheeled Vehicles filled out the rest of the quick strike attack force as they parked behind the light weight jeeps.

These machines were designated to carry the elite soldier's equipment, extra ammunition and the rest of the troops of the strike team. They were likewise armed with a turret type mounted 50 caliber machine gun on its roof. The Humvees were completely enclosed with oversized and wide, deep thread tires, and well protected against land mines with extra steel plating welded to the bottom of the fast track machines. The engines were also goosed up for extra power, so they could keep up with the explosive speed of the much lighter weight Fast Attack Vehicles.

The radio the squad was going to employ for communication with Colonel Leadbetter who'll be stationed on board the Aircraft Carrier George Washington was the lightweight Panther 2000-V man pack transceiver. It was a frequency hopping radio satellite linkup, which made it nearly impossible for any listening devices to locate, or unscramble the coded unit communications of the assault team, and their support backup crews.

The Mutt held a plate of meat stuffed to overflowing in both hands, and sat without his shirt on, even though it was cold at night in the desert.

He stabbed a chunk of goat meat with the plastic fork, and pointed at one of the light weight fast sand buggies with it, and said with a mouth full of half chewed meat. "Hey Homes, it looks like we're gonna finally have some fucking fun on the stinking beach with those little babies there. I hope to hell there are some loose A-rab broads hanging around where we're heading, Walker. I always wanted to try and ride one of them fucking things in the stinking sand. But the fricking hot shot brass back home would not trust me with one of their precious little fucking machines to play wit, man.

"They said something about me being shit ass blind crazy, and they wouldn't trust me with any of their stinking little play toys, man. Some shit there huh Walker? Come to think of it man. The bastards also said they wouldn't trust me with any of their stinking daughters either in the same conversation, man. I can kill for the dirty bastards, but I can't drive their damn toys, or screw around with their stinking daughters either, Homes."

"I got some bad news for your ass dog man. If you find any stinking A-rab broads hanging around where we're going, man. They're gonna have fucking teeth like you have never saw before in your wasted life man, and they'll know how the fuck to use them on ya dopey ass, buddy. Any stinking broads we come across out there in sand land, would rather skin your fricking mixed ass alive, just as soon as look at you man. So keep your fucking dick in your stinking pants, and your finger on the damn trigger on this one, man." Walker warned his lifelong friend in no uncertain terms.

"Amen to that fricking shit there, fellow sand bag." Some other soldier offered him.

When Walker finished eating, he called the other officers of his group to him, and then he went over some last minute details of the mission. "Captain Wilson, you got the shit duty of remaining behind with the stinking vehicles. I know this is a suck ass duty for ya sir, but this operation's nothing more than a shit magnet anyway, Captain. We'll move up to within three miles of the town of Dawral, our Intel picked out an ancient, dried up wadi where we're gonna park the damn vehicles. They'll be well protected from prying eyes there. You'll have a radio with you, if we call for an E-vac, (Emergency Evacuation) you'll get those machines out to us on the quick enough and get us the hell outta there, Captain. Colonel

Leadbetter gave me word you're to take out anyone snooping around that's not in our fucking uniforms, Captain. Any fucking hot extraction will bring us out to the Washington for debriefing and evaluation of the damn mission back to our home base of operations, sir."

"That's good enough for me for this operation, Lieutenant Walker Sir." Captain Wilson replied as he followed Walker's finger across the map, until it stopped at where the ancient wadi was displayed on it. Even though the Captain out ranked Walker, he did not have a problem with him being in command of the troops for this mission, or even himself.

"I hate being on some damn swabbie tub on the fucking water, man!" Neck growled, remembering how seasick he got on the tin can (Destroyer) on their mission to help defend Taiwan a few years back from China's invasion of the small Island.

"Hey stupid if you were born to be fucking hanged whaddaya fraid of drowning for, man? Enough joking around for crap sake because this shit's fucking serious, people. Okay, we have three EXR's (Extraction Rendezvous) marked out clearly on your funny papers (maps). Here, here, and here, if we find ourselves being forced to separate for any fucking reason whatsoever out in the field, we go into another mode of EandE Escape and Evasion, and then we'll bug the hell outta here faster than sliding on owl shit. The separated teams will make it to one of the three EXR's, which ever one is closer to you at the time or during any pull back order, and then call in for an EXFIL from a possible hot pickup zone. Remember the Eleventh Commandment when out in the field people, Thou shall survive. Any shits get it here, we're gonna sell their stinking stuff to some fucking turd pushers (queers) back home in the damn States, and they're gonna use it for some weird stinking sex acts, tell the troops so.

"We're gonna stalk this stinking turd for a coupla hours, to see if we can possibly pick him up nice, clean and easy, and then we can get the fuck outta here before any damn sand swimmers even knows what the hell went down round them, Captain. If not, we're going in after the lousy bastard and things will get rather messy for us if we go this route during this damn operation. I know the stinking Colonel gave us a three point mission here. But I have no fucking intention of resorting to a Locate and Splatter mission on this one. The Boss wants this bastard brought back to the United States alive, and that's exactly what we're gonna do on this mission if I have any say about it. Even if we have to miss our cut off time, and we get stuck walk out of this stinking desert by ankle express while carrying our turd on a stick. Everyone got the fucking order?"

The small group of officers nodded in agreement with Walker's last orders.

"Fine then that just about covers my intentions on this stinking mission, people. You guys hafta make damn certain the troops under your command have enough to drink and eat before we jump off for this damn operation. Don't take any guff from any these pukes. Any of them give you a hard time about any order, you tell'em you're gonna report them to my ass. That should be more than enough to cut any flack off from the jackass. I don't need anyone petering out on us, because they're fucking thirsty or hungry on this operation, until we have completed the damn thing successfully, Captain Wilson Sir." Walker next checked his watch, it was ten forty p.m., and he went on with his orders to the other officers.

"We have another hour and twenty minutes before jump off time comes a calling, people. Mutt, you're gonna be in command of the backup troops for this mess, if and when we have to penetrate the stinking building on this damn lousy turd hunt. Get back to your people and make certain their weapons are checked and double checked, and that they have enough fucking ammo, and know where the hell the three EXRs are located on their damn maps. That's our only safety line if this mission goes tits up on us, and we have to engage the stinking enemy in a series of shoot and scoot maneuvers." Walker quickly finished his orders, and then he had to goose the officers up by jerking his hands up to make them head back to the troops.

The Mutt remained with Walker, because his people were going to be involved with Walker's troops throughout the entire mission. Each officer and NCO was going to command a six man hit team, leaving Mother Flanagan and Buckethead as their floaters for the operation, to perform backup duties and support with their M-60 heavy machine guns. The remaining five troops were scheduled to stay behind with Captain Wilson, to help protecting their escape vehicles, and also prepared to pick up the troops if the operation collapsed in around them.

When the time was near for the American soldiers to go in action, the troops quickly gathered around Walker again to hear who was going where on the mission. The Lieutenant looked at the many staring faces and saw nothing but pure confidence and anger locked in their eyes, and then he announced hotly to the gathered elite soldiers. "Listen up people, Ghost, Wacko, Snatch, McNip, and CoCo-G, you people are with me. Mutt, your Unit will consist of Blood Clot, Siberia, Blind Date, Roach, and the Neck. Hunter, you, Baby Tee, Ice, Boot Camp, Sun Tan and Six Pack, are your Unit, man. Mother Flanagan, you and Buckethead are the floaters for this mission with the M-60s for any backup support we might need during the damn operation. Captain Wilson, you have Just Bob, Weird Bill, Four F, Three Martines and Caviar..."

"Hey Lieutenant, what the hell's this shit all about, sir? I don't mean to correct you any about your orders Lieutenant, but I believe you have everything sealed up tight than two coats of paint, but your math's all fucking wrong, sir. We only have a twenty man hit unit for this mission, and you're calling out twenty six troops in all, Lieutenant." Captain Wilson complained as he tried to count the soldiers milling around him for a second time.

"I see you're not as observant as I had hoped you were, Captain Wilson. You didn't notice we have ourselves a coupla stow-a-ways on board with us for this mess, and we woulda had a shitload more if Colonel Leadbetter didn't stop the rest of the troops under his command from hitching a ride along with us when we first moved out, sir." Walker smirked at the concerned officer, who looked like he was just smacked in the face with a rotten egg.

Captain Wilson counted heads using his finger this time, while pointing at the many concerned faces staring back at him. When he finished counting the troops, he bitched at the Lieutenant. "Sonofabitch, you're right Lieutenant. The Colonel's going to have some heads when we get back to the real world, because of these damn hitch-hikers to this mess, sir."

"Not really sir, he gave me the nod when he saw the troops I didn't call out to come along on this mission, sneak into our humvees with us, sir. Look Captain, I'm sorry I'm sticking you with most of the FNGs (Fucking new Guys) to the Unit, sir. But I wanna keep them outta the soup until I know I can trust them when crunch time comes a knocking on any mission we're sent out on, sir. I don't need them shaking like a fucking turtle trying to dry hump a stinking bone dome when the shooting starts against us out there, sir."

"I can't say I'm too unhappy having the extra soldiers along with us on this mission, Lieutenant Walker Sir." Captain Wilson offered as he smirked at the Lieutenant.

"We're all glad to have the extra help with us, Captain Wilson," Walker snapped hotly, and then he added. "Everyone here knows who the fuck they're assigned to, right people?"

A choir of 'yes sir' was grumbled by the troops back at Walker.

"Hey Walker, I'd like to pitch a bitch at ya man." Weird Bill piped up.

Walker gave out with a disgusted sigh and then snapped at Bill. "What the hell's up your ass now, buddy? You're too damn green to this stinking outfit to pit a bitch at anyone in the Unit, buddy. You gotta get bloody on a mission before you can pitch a bitch at anyone connected too our Unit, asshole." Walker knew he was going to hear some shit from at least one of the new guys, because of his orders for all of them to remain behind with the escape vehicles.

"Hey Lieutenant, you just say you wanna keep our fucking asses outta the stinking fire until we can prove to you we can handle whatever the hell comes our fucking way during any operation we're working on with the rest of you guys, sir. What's up with that line of shit Lieutenant? How the fuck can we possibly prove to you and everyone else from the Unit that we're as good as anyone else in this damn outfit, sir. If we can't get some trigger time on this mission along with the rest of the soldiers from the Unit, sir?" Weird Bill complained at Walker.

"That's a pretty good bitch there you just fired off at my stinking ass, my friend. But I ain't got the stinking time or patience to get in a friggin pissing contest with you over my fucking decision and orders, buddy. You're raising fricking demons here that are betta off left sleeping, Bill. It's time to take you for a little force march through reality, my friend. You become a tried and true soldier when the first fucking bullet coming whizzing by your fricking noggin and you see your buddy in the same foxhole with you with half his fricking noggin blown away. That's when old glory, heroism, sacrifice, duty, honor and country you were taught that makes a true soldier, comes shitting outta ya fucking ass like soup, and you're scared shitless and looking for a god damn place to hide your stinking ass in until the shooting is over, man.

"Death changes the name of the friggin game rather quickly, and the soldier. The chips stack up and you find your God real quick out there, buddy. Then, you're a true and tried fucking soldier in my world my friend. You wanna prove to me how much of a fricking man you really are, man? How big your stinking balls are to my ass my friend? Fine, do as you're fucking ordered and shove the bitch in the damn shitter. I don't give a flying crap if you're related to Jesus Christ, and you have a direct pipeline to God Almighty, you'll do as I ordered, or I'll fucking bleed ya, and leave ya here for the damn scavengers to feast on, man. Once this mission's over with, you'll be given the credit you deserve, and you'll never be another REMF, (Rear Echelon Mother Fucker) no matter how much you beg for the position again, buster. Remember this pal, be damn careful what you wish for around here, you might just fucking get it friend."

Walker turned away from the seething new soldier and announced to the rest of the troops. "Okay you pack of shitbirds, you got away with it once already today, but there'll be no more jumping over to another unit, unless the one you're with gets chopped up on your ass. I warn you people, I won't be as friendly as the fucking Colonel was, if I find any of you not with your assigned Unit. I need to know where everyone is at all times during this entire operation, so I can properly direct any support we might need out there. You ain't with your damn Unit then you're gonna fuck up the mission on the rest of us, and that hurts everyone involved with this damn mess. By the way, since you have a fucking case of the ass with this mission Bill, you're now GRREG puke on this stinking op, buster. Any questions, wants and needs or other bitches' now is the time to air the damn thing, once the operation begins, all talking is ended, people?" Walker warned the rest of the troops involved with the operation.

"What the hell does GRREG mean, Walker! I never heard of that shit before today man." Bill snarled angrily at him, still pissed off he was not getting any respect from the young Lieutenant.

"It's Lieutenant Walker to you buster, if you wanna assume that fucking tone of voice with my damn ass mister, and it's 'Sir' at the beginning and end of any further fucking grips you aim at my ass as well, buster. GRREG is Graves Registration for the Unit, and you're stuck with the stinking job whether you like it or not, fucker." Lieutenant Walker hissed at the new soldier as he held him in his angry glare to see if he hand anymore gripes to pitch at him.

"Oh shit man, no fucking way in hell do I wanna pull that fucked up duty on this operation, Lieutenant Walker Sir. I can't hack that shit, yes sir I can kill with any man, but deal with the dead, no way in hell do I wanna get stuck with that duty man." Weird Bill growled out as he glared angrily back at his commanding officer for a hot moment.

"Anymore fucking grips from you, and you're gonna head the fucking list, mister. There's two fucking things you can do about it, nothing, and eat it man. So dump your stinking bitch in the damn shitter, buster." Walker raised his voice as he ordered the soldier to shut it up.

The Mutt noticed Walker was getting seriously pissed off at Bill, and he shifted his weight on his feet to get the Lieutenant's attention, and hopefully break off the heated confrontation going on between the two angry soldiers. "Hey Walker, I ain't too fucking happy wit going out on this stinking mission, witout our stinking body armor on our stinking asses for protection, man. Why the hell did the stinking government spend all that fucking money on the damn shit for, if they're not gonna supply us wit the damn crap when we need it the crap the most, man? My ass ain't fricking bulletproof you know my friend. Man, it's like three feet down a fucking cow's throat out here. I can't see my stinking hand in front of my damn face any longer, man."

"We want it fucking dark as possible man, because we do our best work in the fucking dark, bullet stopper. I hear your grip there Mutt, but we're gonna be on a fast track operation on this one, and our heavy body armor would only serve to slow us down on the mission, and that's why we ain't got the damn armor with us on this one, buddy. That means we're gonna hafta be doubly careful and quick on this stinking mission, people. Besides Mutt, you look so damn good dressed in your peachy looking fucking DCU's, (Desert Camouflage Uniforms) they almost make you look like a real fucking soldier there, buddy. I'd be happy if you acted like one for once in your stinking life while we're out on a stinking mission, Homes." Walker snapped hotly at the Mutt, and then he turned his back on his long time friend, knowing the Mutt was going to be hot under the collar for the attack on his soldiering.

"Hey Homes, was that a shot you just fired off at my stinking ass? Shit man, I think that was a fucking slug there man. Are you trying to start something you can't handle here, Home Boy. Remember pal who is the one always pulling your fat outta the stinking fire when we were living back on the stinking mean streets. Here, I got your fucking soldier right here Homes, and don't forget it." The Mutt growled as he grabbed his crotch and shook his dick through his pants.

"Hey Mutt, you're the only fricking slob I know who was arrested for assault with a dead weapon, honey. You keep tugging on that there little thing of yours like that, and you're going to jerk the damn thing off ya self honey." Baby Tee offered as she shook her hips back at him.

"Now that's a damn slug. I know a fucking slug when I hear one bitch, and that was definitely one of them, dammit. You again Baby Tee huh, keep it up bitch and I'm gonna get a little insulted around here honey. I have feelings you know, and they get hurt pretty damn easy whenever someone's dumping on me like you're doing now, bitch." The Mutt looked at Baby Tee, and then he shot her one of his famous smiles.

"Don't try and shit a shitter mister. To have feelings baby, you have to have a conscious, and you haven't heard for your conscious since you defiled your first woman on this earth many, many, years ago, Mutt." Ice, Sergeant Diane Morrison added as she fell in line with Baby Tee.

"Okay boys and girls, can the fucking shit and pay attention to the things at hand huh, I got some news for the Mutt. If you're having problems with your DCU's you're bitching bout, you're gonna cry like a stinking baby who just had his stinking crayons taken away from him, when I clue you in on this next pail of shit we gotta do for this damn operation, man. Once we're at the Iraqi village of Dawral, we're all gonna get stuck wearing those smelly ass A-rab Thobe things, if you people remember right that's the Nomads desert robes and Kaffiyeh, the A-rab headdress. And if you think I stink when I get hot, man. Just wait till you get a whiff of those little babies' people. I heard they were soaked in camel piss for a stinking week, before being issued to us for use on this operation, people." Lieutenant Walker bitched at the troopers this time as he looked from one face to the other in the group of soldiers.

"Why would anyone want anything smelling that fucking bad to be put on their asses for?" the huge soldier branded No Neck asked while getting into the conversation.

"Because you big genetic experiment gone fucking haywire. The worse you smell in this stinking country, the less anyone is gonna challenge your ass for any papers and ID's, and any uther crap like that." Walker shot back as he made his way for the first buggy.

"Man, what the fuck's up your fricking ass tonight, huh Walker? I was only asking a stinking question of ya man. That was bullshit and bad manners you just shot back at my stinking ass, man." Neck complained as he stared at the Lieutenant.

"You have to understand something bout our fearless leader here, Neck." Baby Tee said while getting on Walker's ass the instant she saw an opening to jump on the well liked soldier. "He's the type of guy who'll shoot at the welcoming wagon when it comes driving down his street. I heard a story about him just the other day. I was told he took a shit on his neighbor's property, just because his neighbor's dog took a dump on his property back in the real world, Neck."

CHAPTER TWENTY FIVE

Lieutenant Robert Walker turned his head and glared at Baby Tee, actually making her step away from his side. She never saw the terrible look he just fired off at her, before.

The Mutt rushed to catch up with Walker, once in step with the young Lieutenant the Mutt shoved him with his shoulder and moaned at him at the same time. "Hey Walker, I love being here sucking up the fucking sand and soon sun, man. It makes my fricking day for my friggin ass. You think the lousy little dude might be behind this turd we're searching for?"

The Lieutenant stopped walking and turned and looked at the Mutt for a brief second before complaining at him. "I guess I'm gonna start having some fricking trouble with you too now huh? Whatdaya think I am a fucking mind reader or something round here, man? Who the hell are you talking about now dog man? What lousy little dude are you talking about, man?"

"You know the stinking dude I mean Walker, the dopey Saudi Arabian dude who has a fricking hardon for anything with the stars and stripes printed on it, Homes." The Mutt smirked.

"You mean that Usama Bin Laden dude, asshole?" Lieutenant Walker grunted at the Mutt.

"Yeah, that's the scumbag dude I'm talking about man." The Mutt replied with a grin.

"No fucking idea man, but if that stinking prick's behind this mess then he's gonna pay through the fricking eyeballs for it, Homes. Along with anyone else who might be involved in this damn mess is gonna pay big

EAGLE'S NEST

time for it, man." Walker growled as he hoisted his weapon up and slapped the side of it. He then climbed into the buggy and the Ghost driving this time started it up. The young Lieutenant stood in the machine and poked his head above the protective roll bar cage and bellowed at the rest of his troops. "Saddle up people, off we go on this stinking turd hunt. The first guy to get his hands on this lousy little prick's stinking ass gets a case of ice cold fucking Bud when we get back to the real world."

Wacko jumped in the back of Walker's machine, and started to strap himself in, and then he cocked the M-50 machine gun and set a round in the chamber. Mutt, Blood Clot and Siberia got in the second machine, and Snatch, McNip and CoCo-G took the third buggy over. Hunter, Baby Tee, Buckethead and Ice got in one of the jeeps, with Blind Date, Roach, Mother Flanagan and Neck taking over the second one. Boot Camp, Sun Tan and Six Pack took over the third vehicle over. Captain Wilson and Just Bob took the first M998 HMMWV, with Weird Bill and Four F taking the second machine, Three Martines and Caviar starting up the last HMMWV.

At exactly midnight, Lieutenant Walker's column shot crossed the Saudi Arabian border into the vastness of the Iraqi desert. The route they were scheduled to take to their target area was designed to keep them from stumbling over any possible roaming Iraqi civilians or military troops stationed in the desert. The motors were almost silent, as the oversized tires kicked up a small sandstorm of their own, behind them as the machine's tires spun on the loose sand. A mile into the trip, the drivers moved to a left and right column to stop eating so much of the sand being kicked up by the speeding vehicle in front of them. It was figured it would take the specialized soldiers over two hours to reach the dried up wadi, and then at least another two hours to walk to the small Iraqi town of Dawral through the deep desert.

An hour and forty five minutes into the operation, Lieutenant Walker spotted the walls of the ancient wadi ahead of his machine. He stuck his arm out and waved it towards the wadi shelter. His vehicle turned and pulled into the wide deep depression, with thirty feet of sand piled up on either side of the depression once carved out by the strong flow of water. His machine stopped in the middle of the wadi, and the rest of the machines pulled up on either side of his buggy. He jumped out, followed closely by the Mutt, Captain Wilson and the Hunter.

Walker scouted out the wide depression, and then he announced to the other officer with him. "Say Captain Wilson, since you're the man who is gonna be protecting our stinking machines for us back here, it's up to you on how you wanna deploy the damn things out for the easiest way to protect them, sir. Each vehicle has camouflage netting with it, sir. You're to cover the machines over with it, and then you and your people will hunker down and wait for our return, or you call for help for our asses if we run into any problems with the damn op, sir. Air support's a Nine, One, One call away, Captain. If you're threatened, send a Nine, One, One out, and the sky will be fulla our fucking fly jockeys, sir. The rest of you shits, unload your equipment and take what you'll need for the mission and let's get going. I wanna be..."

Walker's conversation was cut off by a fast mover (fighter aircraft) detected rapidly closing in on their position. All eyes went towards the black sky, as they waited to see if they were spotted by a possible enemy aircraft. This day was picked out for the mission because of the lack of stars, and a weak sliver of a moon. The ever alert Ghost hustled up the side of a high sand dune and he checked the sky, and then called out. "Hey Walker, I see the stinking bird, it looks like a fucking F-18 Hornet, or maybe ever the older F-15 Eagle rapidly closing in on our position, sir. I see a pair of thrusters burning up the fucking sky, man."

"No chance it's any fucking Iraqi crap coming in at us, huh Ghost?" Walker bellowed.

"No way in hell man, this pilot knows what the hell's he's doing alright, and he's obviously using terrain following radar and is night capable of flying. Besides man, the Iraqi's don't have anything that spits out a dual flame like this baby doing, Lieutenant. Man, he's glued right to the fucking ground and kicking up a sand storm behind him." The Ghost reported as he had to bend over backwards to follow the aircraft as it ripped through the sky directly over his position.

"It's a fucking Hornet Walker!" the Ghost screamed over the deafening roar of the engines.

The go fast aircraft did a high over end loop around, and then dipped down and waved its wings at the American troops gathered below him that the pilot picked up in his night vision field. The sleek aircraft disappeared as quickly as it had appeared, so as not to draw any special attention to where the pilot was flying and why.

"Whatdaya make of that load of shit, Lieutenant? You think the damn mission was canceled on our asses, sir?" Captain Wilson asked Lieutenant Walker with deep concern lacing his tone.

"Hold your fucking water will ya, Captain Wilson. I think that was just an information pass for us sir, to sort of let us know that we have a ready air cap already protecting our stinking asses down here, sir." Walker growled as he watched the twin flames from the American warplane quickly disappear into the pitch darkness of the night, and then he added to his words for the concerned Captain. "Besides Captain, if the stinking mission was canceled on us, we woulda had a buster signal transmitted to us from Colonel Leadbetter the second the damn thing was canceled, sir. We gotta shove off now sir, time's a wasting and we gotta get a jump on this damn operation if we want it to be successful, sir."

Lieutenant Walker waited until his troops gathered into a loose formation around him, and then they slowly moved out together by what the soldiers commonly referred to as the ankle express. Each soldier with the young military officer had a pack containing the Arab robes they would wear when they reached the Iraqi village of Dawral. Walker could still smell the terrible stink from his garment, right through the heavy field pack.

The night time desert temperature was already down to a freezing fifty nine degrees Fahrenheit, and the elite American soldiers were shivering like hell as they continued heading for the little Iraqi village of Dawral. The Lieutenant could not figure it out, the desert was so cold at night, but it was going to be at least a hundred and fifteen degrees Fahrenheit tomorrow, and they'll be sweating their asses off and wishing for the cool of the night to come around again. He found himself wishing he could split the temperature up, so it was more bearable for them to carry out their present mission in both the day and night.

About midway to Dawral, the Mutt heard a camel suddenly blare angrily and he immediately dropped down to the ground and checked out the area before him. By the time he turned around to the other soldiers behind him, they were already belly to the ground aiming their weapons in the darkness towards where the sound was coming from. The Mutt picked up Lieutenant Walker and he crawled over to him on his belly to report what he just heard.

"You see anything hanging around out there Homes? I just heard a fucking camel cry out man. Someone's walking round out there and I can't see fucking shit in front of my stinking puss." The Mutt groused at Walker with some concern.

"Over there Mutt, the best I can tell it looks like a fucking caravan of stinking Nomads, or some other Arab bastards humping round out there in the darkness, Homes. The stinking dark's working against us on this one, and these guys must have eyes like a stinking Eagle, man."

"You think the sonofabitches mighta spotted us out here Walker?" the Mutt asked as he watched the group of Arabs moving about a hundred yards from them.

"Why the fuck do ya think their damn camels just squawked for dog man? Yeah, as sure as shit flows down hill they know we're out here man. You can't put nothing past these wiseass fucking sand dwelling bastards out here in their land of sand, man. I don't see them bastards making any changes in their fricking direction though, so I think they believe we're a fucking Iraqi military patrol or something like that, man. I'm certain the camel jockeys came across other Iraqi patrols out here in the deep desert before this." Walker chambered a round in his weapon, just in case they were challenged by the fearsome Nomad Tribe of the desert. He heard many stories of how great a warrior these desert wanderers were when it came down to fighting.

"Weren't most of the stinking Nomad bands helping our people out during the fucking Desert Storm war games, Road Kill?" The Mutt asked him as he stared at the string of camels and riders silhouetted by what little light was coming from the stars and a slit of a moon.

"Yep, and the only thing I fear is if these stinking pukes take a notion to eliminate what they may believe is a fricking Iraqi military patrol just for the hell of it, man. Make sure everyone's ready for a stinking fight if these lousy pudheads try something against us."

"You gotta be fucking shitting me Homes. You think anyone behind us ain't ready to off these lousy motherfucking sand suckas if they even look at us in the wrong way, Walker." The Mutt offered sarcastically as he

EAGLE'S NEST

looked over his shoulder, and he picked up the Ghost aiming his weapon at the camel drivers also.

"Yeah, I guess that was a pretty dumb order at that Mutt." Walker griped as he continued to watch the long caravan of Nomads, camels, and small carts suddenly increase their pace a little, and leave their field of vision rapidly. The American troops remained lying on the ground until the entire caravan of Nomads were completely out of sight on them. Even though it was dark, the Nomads were still outlined pretty well by the little light cast from the moon reflecting off the sands of the desert, and the natural light of the sands.

"Walker, we betta get a stinking move on it man. We're beginning to fall a little behind our time schedule already man. We're fucking piss poor on the time element out here man. I don't wanna end up walking into this stinking village right in the middle of the fucking day, Homes." The Mutt remarked as he got up to one knee and gave a last quick glance at the Nomads leaving his field of vision from a standing position this time.

"Yeah, they're out of fucking range already, so let's get going man. Pass the word to the others to keep their eyes open in case the stinking pukes double back, or they set up an ambush along the way against us, man." Walker got up, followed by the rest of the troops in his group. They moved like a Unit just itching for a fight. The troops paired off and held their weapons at the ready. Walker and the Mutt took the point, but the Ghost and Hunter moved up and they relieved the other two soldiers from point duty. They were the official pointmen of the outfit.

Lieutenant Robert Walker dropped back some to allow the pair of extremely dangerous soldiers do their act that they were so used to doing for the Unit. He checked his watch, it was Zero, Three, Forty Hundred Hours. The Mutt was correct, they fell behind their time schedule some. The young Lieutenant scanned the far off distance and noticed a slight glow over a sand dune, and he took it for granted the glow was coming from the lights of the small Iraqi village of Dawral. The Lieutenant pointed to it with the barrel of the weapon, showing the Mutt the direction they were heading in now.

By Zero, Four Hundred Hours, Walker waved his arm over his head, and the American troops again dropped to the sand. The Lieutenant saw the first building of the tiny Arab village. He tried to spot the Ghost and Hunter ahead of him as they worked their way nearer to the village. Although he could not see the two point soldiers working, he knew this was what they were up to. At this point, he needed up to date intelligence on the Iraqi town and its occupants, before he gave the order to move into the village and snatch their missing turd. The most important thing he had to know now was, if this village was the one they were searching for. According to his GPS, (Global Positioning System) and map reference, this was the town alright. But until he knew for certain, he was not going to give the order to move to it. Lieutenant Walker checked his position for a second time with his GPS. They were where they were supposed to be at this time.

For what seemed like hours to Walker, he waited for the first report to come in from either of his two point soldiers, and he was growing angrier with each passing second because they did not bother to check in with him as yet. It was only a half an hour when he finally picked up the Ghost and Hunter working their way skillfully back towards his current position. The exhausted Ghost slid down the sand dune Walker and the other soldiers were using to hide behind. The Hunter remained positioned on the top, standing watch to make certain no one spotted them while they were moving around in the desert and checking out the small village.

When the Ghost stopped sliding on the sand, he automatically lit up a cigarette while cupping the flame with his hand to hide the glow from his lighter. He then leaned his back on the sand dune and exhaled the choking smoke and then caught his breath.

"Whaddaya got for me man?" Walker demanded from his dangerous pointman.

"That town's Dawral okay Walker, we saw the fucking name plastered round the stinking dump enough times to ID the dump, man. It's a damn good thing Colonel Leadbetter gave us the name written out in stinking Arabic before we left on the fricking mission, man. Or we couldn't have made a positive ID of the fucking dump without it, man. The place is as dead as a stinking door knob at that man. There's only one street paved, and that's the main street. It looks like the other roads are made up of compressed sand as far as I can tell in the damn darkness, Walker. We didn't see a fucking soul out while we were in there either, and there were just a few civilian vehicles parked in and around the stinking dump, man. The town's piss poor Lieutenant.

"We went all the way in to the center of the stinking town wearing these smelly damn things you issued to us before we shipped out on this damn operation, man." The Ghost pulled on the Arab robe and then added to his angry words to his commanding officer. "I think we found the lousy rat's nest alright Walker. It's the only fricking building in the whole town that had anything in the way of any stinking military trucks parked in front of, or near the dump, man. The inside of the damn building's lit up like a stinking Christmas tree though, Lieutenant. I saw plenty of fricking organ donors moving about inside and around the lousy dump, sir."

"Can you give me an accurate number on the organ donors you picked up inside the military building you scoped out in the damn town, Ghost?" Walker asked, knowing the Ghost used the military slang for the enemy by branding them organ donors.

"Naw, we couldn't see enough of the stinking pukes to get a good count on the lousy bastards at this time, Walker. But the dopey little pricks we made a good MOE (Mark One Eyeball, visual contact) with were dressed in Iraqi military uniforms, and they were moving around as if they had a real purpose in life, good buddy. Man, I'd give my left stinking nut for a lousy cup of lifer's juice right about now, Lieutenant."

"Give me the stinking lowdown on the damn building and town and forget about a cup of coffee for now, and any fucking suggestions you might have figured out on how we're gonna hit the damn building, if and when it comes down to that move, mister. Security, you know the fucking routine and what I need from your ass, Ghost. When we pull off this fucking mission, I'll drown you in stinking coffee and beer at the same time, man." Lieutenant Walker grumbled as he took Casper's cigarette from his hand, and took a good pull from it, before handing it back to the other soldier, and then he waited for the Ghost's reply.

"Right Walker, it's a fucking two story dump made out of mostly their shit mud brick crap they use for construction in this wasted country, man. The only one in the whole damn town I saw built that sturdy, Walker. I'd say it's around two hundred and fifty to three thousand square feet large on each floor of the stinking dump. The first floor seems to be their friggin main offices, storage rooms and other crap like that, man. The second floor is probably the living area for the dopey little turds in the stinking dump. We couldn't get a good eye up there though. The place also has three doors on the first level leading to the outside of the damn building.

"I didn't locate any stinking doors on the second floor leading to the outside of the stinking building, man. That means if we hit the lousy dump, we'll easily trap anyone on the second floor up there, Homes. There are also nine windows on the first floor we'll hafta fucking secure in the opening attack on the stinking dump, if we have to go this route that is, Walker. Two of the windows aren't large enough for anyone to get the hell outta the damn things easy enuf, so they're real low on the security list, Lieutenant.

"I did however locate a fucking machine gun nest setup on the damn roof of the dump that seemed to be able to cover any approach of the structure, but no one was anywhere near the damn thing, Walker. It seems to be an abandoned defense system set up and left over during the Desert Storm bombing of Baghdad, Walker. That means there's either a door or some kind of scuttle to the roof from the inside of the damn building, man. When we finally hit the stinking building, if someone gets up on the roof, they could fuck us up pretty damn good while we're working on the stinking ground, Walker.

"Someone hasta get their ass up there and make sure our turd doesn't get out of the fucking building that way, and he secures the nest and make certain none of the other soft targets gets their stinking hands on that damn gun. I got right up to the damn building and actually peeked in and saw a few AK's and RPG's, (Rocket Propelled Grenades) leaning up against a wall. I suggest that's the first room we think about securing on our opening hit against the place, if we attack it that is, man. I think it's the armory judging from what I was able to pickup stacked inside this one room, man. There's some small crappy brush planted round the building which will offer us some sort of cover when, and if we hit the damn building under a hot entry, Walker. The building's also surrounded by a six foot metal fence that's in piss poor condition." The Ghost took another pull from his cigarette, and then continued his report to the young Lieutenant.

"The damn fence is rusted up pretty bad man, and it seems to have been hit a number of times by our people during the Desert Storm engagement, and it has never been bothered to be repaired by these lazy ass fucks. There are some areas in the fence where we can breach it with no trouble at all Walker, and some sections of the damn thing are completely missing anyhow, man. These lousy pukes show no fricking fear of us coming afta the lousy little turd hiding inside the damn dump, man. There's also a large pile of rubble and other crap stacked up outside the east side of the damn building. Evidently, it was war damaged crap from during the bombing of the little village, and is under reconstruction now I guess, from what I was able to see of the area.

"Walker, I scouted the rubble pile out close and I didn't see anything hid in or near it, man. It's just building rubble and other crap of no use to anyone in the village. There's an old Russian T-55 tank parked in the rear of the building, the damn thing hasn't seen any action in so long, it's rusted solid in fucking place. There's no guards posted outside the compound either. Like I said man, these dopey bastards don't seem to be on guard against a possible snatch and scoot of their king rat hiding in there, Lieutenant. I picked up a pair of Iraqi guards standing a sloppy post in the hallway of the building inside. They were completely demoralized and one dopey ass guard had his weapon leaning up against the fucking wall, and the uther guard held his weapon under his arm like it was a fricking Playboy magazine, Homes. We can take the both of them asses out quick and easy enuf before they even know what's happening around them Walker."

"What's the best fucking way to hit the stinking building, Ghost?" Walker asked his trooper.

"Dead nuts head on man, right through the front door of the stinking dump, Walker. I guess you should have some of the guys stationed at each window for a little extra support, and then just plow right on through the damn door like the Marines looking for a stinking Virgin, and takeover the whole damn place nice and easily, man. The staircase going up to the second floor of the dump is narrow as shit, and it's missing its fucking hand rail, Lieutenant. So that's gonna stop anyone from running down them in any kinda rush against us, Homes. If we hit them hard, we'll bottleneck the lot of them on the second floor, and if they don't have anything in the way of serious weapons on that floor then they're gonna be shit outta luck and we'll own them outright, and then we can pick them apart at our stinking leisure, Walker.

"We can have the two people we'll leave guarding the stinking windows I take as the armory, to enter the dump through that way Walker. Those two soldiers can secure the Iraqi soldier's horde of weapons for us, man. The way I see it Walker, there ain't no sense being a fucking soldier, if you don't have the stinking weapons needed to protect your ass with when the war comes searching for your ass, man. Unarmed, the Iraqi's are just a pack of dumb fucking civilians caught with their stinking thumbs up their asses, man. If we go at it and cut off their damn weapons then we'll own their asses." The dangerous pointman reported to Walker.

"I hear you there Ghost. Is this gonna work for us, head on I mean man?" Walker asked him.

"Hey man, was George a King, and am I handsome and you ugly? Of course it is gonna fucking work out real good and easy for us if we hit the dump the way I just suggested to you, Walker." The Ghost smirked as he put out his cigarette in the soft sand by his boot.

"Funny, you know something Ghost, there are twenty thousand fucking comedians outta work right now man, and here you are trying out for one of the dumb fucks, shitbird. Okay people, here's what we're gonna do then. We'll set up shop in the damn village in different locations, and see if we can get a clear eyeball on our missing turd moving round in there. If we spot the dopey prick easy enuf, but he offers us no real opportunity to nab him quickly. We'll tough it out for up to twelve hours and afta that time we'll make our hard entry into the stinking dump right through the front door as the Ghost had just suggested. I wanna get this damn prick real quick, and then get the fuck outta sand land toot sweet people."

"I'm all for that line of bullshit man." The Ghost replied with a snap as he lit a second butt.

"Okay Ghost, I want you and the Hunter to get yourselves back in there and do some more recon of the damn town for our asses. We'll make our first entry into the fricking village at exactly Zero, Six Hundred Hours today, man. We're gonna make like a pack of stinking Arab Nomads looking for something to eat or steal in there. I think if we hafta go in the damn building, we'll put that charge off until say Twenty Two Hundred Hours later on today, people. That way we'll enjoy the cover of darkness working on our side, and everyone we trap inside the damn building will be more interested in bedding down for the fricking night and hopefully, not expecting any stinking trouble from us and they call it a day in there."

"You got it sand hog." The Ghost snapped as he pulled his weapon to his chest, and scurried up the side of the small sand dune they were using for cover from anyone moving around in the town. Walker watched the Ghost trudging up the sand dune, and then struggling to get a good foot hold in the rapidly shifting soft sand under his feet. Then the Ghost and Hunter took off towards the town again, with Walker smiling when he saw the other troops gathered around him and they listened to everything the Ghost and he spoke of about the small Arab village.

"Okay people, here's what we're gonna do on this shit filled operation, we're gonna split up and do a little walk about in the stinking village for ourselves, foot stompers. I want everyone inside the damn town, in case we can make an easy and quick snatch of the stinking prick we want, and we need any extra protection while pulling back with our package in hand. We're gonna keep a close eye out for our missing turd in there. If he makes it impossible for us to snag his fricking ass real easy like then we're gonna drift over to the damn building as it gets dark out. Wacko, Snatch, McNip and CoCo, you fucking guys cover the damn windows of the building if we have to hit the dump. Sun Tan, you'll get your ass up on the damn roof of the stinking building and secure the fricking weapon up there, and make damn certain our little turd doesn't escape our snatch and scoot of his ass operation that way.

"Six Pack, you and Ice will cover the other windows on the first floor of the damn building. Mutt, Blood Clot, Siberia, Blind Date, Baby Tee, Roach, Neck, Mother and Buckethead will follow me in if we have to assault the stinking building on this operation. I'm taking most of the female fighters with me on this one. So they don't stand out so much while walking around the damn town. Any Arab women not working for their fricking husbands are subject to suspicion in this fucked up land of sand and arrogant assholes. The Ghost and Hunter will be our floaters to lend extra support to any dumb troops who get bogged down by any enemy fire..."

"What about me Homes? Whaddaya want me to do on this little ole turkey shoot of ours, Lieutenant Walker? You kinda left me out of your orders you know, man." Boot Camp complained as he pointed to himself with his thumb and then waited for Walker's reply.

"Oh Christ, I forgot all about your dumb ass, Homes. You better paint your stinking ass white so I can see ya in the fucking darkness, Boot Camp. I guess you'll come with me inside the damn building, man." Walker warned the soldier who just complained to him.

"Shit man, I hadta fucking ask for this stinking trouble, man." Boot Camp bitched, causing the Mutt and Six Pack to punch him in the arms.

"Hey man, take it easy with them punches I ain't got no damn body armor on to protect my ass from your punches, them fucking punches just hurt like hell, Homes."

"How the hell are we supposed to act when we're moving round in the stinking town, Lieutenant? While we're waiting to either snatch this dumb ass Colonel al-Adwani shit, or we hit the damn building with our people in force, Walker?" Baby Tee asked the young Lieutenant as she held him in her gaze for the moment.

"You're ordered to act like the rest of them stinking A-rab shits usually do in this damn crap filled stinking country, baby. Like you have nothing else to do, and all the stinking time in the world to do it in, and maybe you should look like you're trying to steal something from them assholes in there for crap sake. That should do the trick and keep anyone who might become suspicious of you from bugging your pretty little ass in there, baby sister. If some Iraqi asshole challenges ya in any way, shape, or form Baby. You're to take him out immediately if you can't bluff your way out of it one way or the uther, little sister.

"Use your K-bar and slit the bugger's stinking throat, and then dump his wasted body in the shadows of a friggin building or something else you can hide it in or under or behind. Make certain you hide the body good so no one else can find it easy. If you find you're up against the fricking wall, open up and the rest of us will come to your aide, and then we'll level the stinking village and take our fucking missing turd home nice and easy, feet up if necessary.

"Each one of you pukes have the wireless radios you guys removed from our helmets on ya person before we left on this turd hunt, so we'll communicate inter-squad easily with them. Does anyone have any questions about their orders bring them up now or forever hold your water?"

When no one from the group of elite soldiers replied to his last question, Walker added as if it was an afterthought to the concerned soldiers. "We have less than an hour before we take a stinking stroll in the little rat's nest, and we get sorta familiar with the fricking area and dumb shits in there. I wanna fucking walk in the village at exactly Zero, Six Hundred Hours, that way it's just getting light out, and the dopey bastards in there are kinda waking up, and they don't know what they're doing as yet, people. If at any point you feel you're drawing any attention to yourselves by hanging round in there where you're hunkered down, you're to move away and drift out of the damn town slow and easy like people.

"Then you'll inform me you're out of the area. We'll assemble back here at Eighteen Hundred Hours if we couldn't snatch our damn turd target by that time, troops. Then, we'll wait for darkness and assault the dump at Twenty Two Hundred Hours and get the dirty bastard outta there the hard way. Suck air for the next hour and soup up, and then we'll move out. Sun Tan!"

"Yo!" The young black soldier replied back to Lieutenant Walker's calling out his name.

"Yo your mama buster, you'll be the first one to head out if and when we decide to hit the damn building. You'll cut out at Zero Five Hundred Hours and find a way to scale the side of the damn building and take up position on the roof of the structure. I want that fucking machine gun nest secured, or put out of service before we go after the damn building. Got it tripwire?" Walker snapped as he stared in the face of the young black soldier.

"CFB Lieutenant Walker." (Clear as a Fucking Bell) Sun Tan smirked as he smiled back at Walker, and then he added as if he was hit with an afterthought. "Hey man if there's any fucking possible way for me to get my stinking black ass up on top of that fricking building, I'll sure as hell find the way to do it for ya, Walker."

"Yeah Walker, it should be pretty easy for Sun Tan to get his lousy ass on any roof, Homes. He had plenty of fucking experience living in the stinking Bronx, man." Mother barked at him.

"Whaddaya mean by that fucking bullshit remark white boy?" Sun Tan growled angrily, as he looked at the usually mild mannered and calm Mother Flanagan.

"Step back Homes, I was only paying your sagging ass a stinking compliment here, man. Wasn't it you who once told me you and your hood brothers owned the fucking roves of the stinking city projects? From there you guys always kept an eye on the cops, and knew where they were heading, even before they knew it, man?" Mother Flanagan offered to the angry looking black soldier, and then he shot him a quick smile.

"Yeah, yeah you're right man. I forgot all about that stinking shit man." Sun Tan griped.

"So this gave you the fucking expertise you needed to carry out your part of this damn mission, you asshole you. That's all I meant by that fucking remark, Homes." Mother Flanagan moved his hands apart, and then he shrugged at Sun Tan.

"I got it man." Sun Tan replied as he shook his head, pleased with the explanation by the soldier branded Mother Flanagan. He really did not want to get in an argument with this soldier, he was far too dangerous to bug that way.

ZERO, SIX HUNDRED HOURS IRAQI TIME. AUGUST 7th, 1999. THE IRAQI TOWN OF DAWRAL

Lieutenant Robert Walker checked his watch for the umpteenth time, and then he called out low to the rest of the soldiers bunched up with him, after he realized it was nearly time to go in against the village. "Okay, unass yourselves people, saddle up, let's get going and see what the fuck this A-rab bug nest has in store for our stinking asses in there. Remember people, maintain radio contact regularly and often while moving about inside the damn town."

Mother Flanagan moved to Walker's side. He was the one who earlier escorted Sun Tan over to the outskirts of the small Iraqi village nearly an hour before, so he could carry out his orders.

"How the hell is Sun Tan making out with getting his stinking ass on top of the fricking building, Mother? Were you keeping an eye on his ass, man?" Walker asked as he buried his cigarette butt in the soft sand, and then he started up the side of the small sand dune himself.

"That stinking little jig-a-boo climbed up the side of the fucking building like he was walking on the damn side walk, Walker. I never saw a man who could squirrel his way up the side of a stinking building like he did over an hour ago, man. I stayed nearby until I saw him cross over the roof, and he start to screw round with the fucking machine gun stationed up there, man. By this time I'm certain he has the roof and weapon secured for us, sir."

"Great, that's one less shitting thing we hafta worry about on this damn turd hunt, Mother." Walker snorted as he turned to make certain everyone fell in step with him.

"You know something Lieutenant Walker I've been doing a helluva lot of thinking about this lousy mission we're on lately, man. If we're successful with getting this fricking lousy little turd the hell outta here, and bring him back to the States in one stinking piece, man. Our shit won't stink for some time to come on us, man. Hell man, they might even give us a stinking fist full of fucking medals for our friggin trouble over here, Homes." Mother Flanagan offered to the young Lieutenant with a sort of smirk on his lips.

"Oh yeah, and they'll put my stinking puss on a fucking stamp too while they're at it, Mother. Fuck the fricking medals crap Homes. Let's go get this turd, and then put some gone between us and this fricking miserable little country of sand, man." Walker grunted as he started heading towards the intended target with the rest of the elite soldiers following closely behind him.

"You got that right Homes." Mother Flanagan replied as he followed Walker to the smallish Iraqi town. Before the troops left the States, they attended daily classes taught by a number of Iraqi defectors from their country, when it was clear President Saddam Hussein was going to survive the war with the United States and the other Coalition Forces supporting them. These Iraqi's in hiding taught the elite troops how to act properly while carrying out their mission in Iraq. They made certain Walker and his people, know how to go through all the motions of the well feared Nomad warriors, whenever they entered a village to place the fear of God in any possible Iraqi troops stationed there or civilians living in the town they entered.

When Walker's troops were within a quarter of a mile of the Arab village, he lifted a fold in his robe and hissed into the small crystal of his radio. "Okay boys and girls, let's split up here in twos and threes, and head for your assigned positions in the damn village. Remember people, look like you have a fucking purpose in there, and you'll take the stinking head offa anyone who bugs ya asses for any reason on ya. Nomads are the most feared people in this world by these gutless pukes, so let's act accordingly in there so we can get this damn thing done, people."

By the time the inserted mixed batch of troops successfully reached the first building of the village, the small town was just starting to show the first signs of waking up from its night's sleep. A few Arab male inhabitants of the village gathered at a local café, and they were busy sharing cups of bitter tea, and nibbling on dates that seemed to be too rotten to be eaten by anyone and expect to live. The Arab men stared at Walker, the Mutt, Mother Flanagan and Neck, as they entered the village on foot from the south end. Walker's face was nearly completely covered with a full growth of beard, and the points seemed like they could pierce steel.

When the Arab men recognized the desert robes of the well feared Nomad Tribes, they immediately broke off eye contact with the few strangers. Fearing a confrontation from the usually quarrelsome Arabs would take place, if they continued to stare at the Nomad group coming into their village from the vastness of the deep desert.

"Hey Walker, whaddaya do to that little sucker, man? Whatever the hell it was, you just scared the living shit right outta the stinking little prick, man. I though the fricking soft target was gonna wet himself when you just looked at his stinking ass, Homes." The Mutt complained to his lifelong friend as he closed the distance separating him from Walker's side.

"I just glanced at the lousy little tent peg, that's all I did to the sonofabitch, Mutt. But it was enough for him not to bug us any, man." Walker griped back at the other soldier.

"That seems like it was more than enough to do it to the man, Walker. I was on the receiving end of some of those stinking glances you usually give out more times than I'd like to admit to, and I know what the hell's going through the stupid assholes head right about now, Walker." The Mutt retorted, and then he chuckled at his friend as he caught up to him now.

Walker and his crew went the closest to the military building in question, stopping at a second small cafe to kill off a little more time, and taking cups of tea with them, while leaving the establishment without paying for the teas. The owner of the Iraqi cafe did not raise a protest against their actions, he was more than pleased that was all these supposed Nomads stole from his place of business, or damaged it on him.

The Lieutenant squatted down like most normal Arab men of the country did, just off the side of the main road and sipped on the terrible tasting dark tea while staring at the target building sitting directly across from where he was squatting. The Mutt, Mother and Neck circled him, and they squatted down with him as well. They spoke low in the hastily taught Arab language.

Two Iraqi military types suddenly rushed out of the building, and stopped long enough to look at the four strange looking though to be Arab men huddled together directly across the street from their building, and then the enemy soldiers chose to ignore Walker's small group. When the Iraqi soldiers pegged the American soldiers as Nomads, they hurried away from the small group without challenging them. Walker smiled, realizing none of these so called once feared Iraqi soldiers, wanted to cross swords with any Nomad Arabs of their land.

"Man, if you ever wanted to takeover this stinking dump on these dopey little bastards, all you hafta do is dress like these fucking Nomad creeps, and you can own the whole fucking shit hole lock, stock, and fucking barrel, man. These fricking so called Iraqi soldiers still have no damn backbones and they still give up their lousy weapons to little girls if they threaten the soldiers." Neck snorted as he placed his tea aside. He could not stand the terrible taste of the nasty brew anyhow, and he was done with trying to drink it for show for the Arabs in the town.

Walker did not reply to Neck's comment, he was looking over the rim of the cup, checking on the Iraqi soldiers he saw roaming around the town as they took up their assigned positions around the village. Mutt's duty was to stare at the building, and spot their target if it was at all possible.

By nine o'clock in the morning, the tiny village was humming with the usual sounds and activity accustom to any Arab town in the Middle East. Babies cried, men haggled and argued with one another while they drank their bitter tea, mother's screamed at their children and loud Arab music filled the streets of the town. Small tables were set up outside some of the homes, and homemade wears and food were placed on display for sale. This caused even more curses to be screamed by the merchants at the buyers trying to get the stuff for next to nothing. Wonderful odors of cooking soon filled the air of the streets of the village, making the exhausted and bored to death American soldier's bellies ache for want of some real food to enjoy.

Music filtered out of some of the homes, and women could be heard singing with the Arab tunes. Most Arab men of the village already left for their daily work, leaving the town overflowing with women and young children. The children roamed the streets begging money from any passerby's they happened across. Some young Arab kids received a kick in the seat of their pants for their troubles, from the men upset because the pesky children were interfering with their usual routine of work for the day.

Neck moved a little closer to Walker, and pointed at an incident taking place across the street from where they were huddled up with his chin, and he complained nastily at his commanding officer. "Hey Walker, didja see that sucka punch that poor kid square in the fricking noggin just now? Man, I thought he was going down for the stinking count from the heavy blow, Walker. If we go hot on this fucking mission, I'm gonna make it my fucking business to plant a cap right between the eyes of that sucka for hitting the poor kid like he did, man. I don't understand how the hell that stinking dude could punch some kid in the head like that."

"If we go hot on this damn mission, you can do whatever the fuck you wanna do to the fricking dude. Just don't forget about our main part of this mission, buddy." Walker warned the soldier as he looked to where an old man beat a child beggar.

CHAPTER TWENTY SIX

The extremely dangerous soldier known as the Hunter and Baby Tee separated from the rest of the group of American soldiers entering the Arab village, and they headed for the east side of the target building. Here, most of the military trucks in the village were parked. A number of Iraqi soldiers milled around the parked machines, smoking and looking at the young Arab women as they passed by them dressed in their Kajubas, the black robe and hood. Only the women's eyes and the bridge of their nose showed from the Kajubas. But this was more than enough to warn the looker that the young woman he was looking at was a real beauty. Lieutenant Walker always said there was something captivating about the eyes of most beautiful Arab women. It showed their inner soul of beauty and kindness shining brightly in their eyes.

"Hey Walker, why do the Arab women hafta dress in those damn Kajubas, man? They hide what the women look like, buddy. I can't see what any of these Arab chicks look like dressed in their garb. Why do the men want to hide their women like they do all the time, man?"

"I don't know if this is true or not, but I heard the reason the women wear those heavy Kajubas is it goes back to when God drove the bad Angles out of Heaven for having sexual relations with the earth women. The Arab men started to dress their women in the heavy robes to hide the fact the ones walking around in the robes were women, and the men were protecting their wives from the bad Angels having sex with them. Who knows, but that's what I heard anyway, buddy."

One Iraqi soldier leaning against a parked half track Russian made vehicle saw the two Nomads looking at them, and he drew them to his partner's attention. The second soldier griped at his fellow soldiers. "They're only a pair of filthy Nomads jackals who have slimed their way out of the vast desert to invade our peaceful village, so the fools can steal from us hard working men. It's far best for us to have nothing to do with the lowly troublemakers my brother. Allah knows how to handle such trash to the Arab lands, my faithful follower of the Qu'ran."

"Yes, Allah be praised for His great wisdom, but they're coming much too close to our vehicles and I don't like it one bit. I think the dirty animals are up to no good on this god cursed day, my brother. They're probably looking to steal something from us as they are always trying to do, any time they enter our peaceful village. Why Allah allows such waste to live and continue to pollute our sacred lands is beyond my limited understanding. Such filth has no right or claim to continue to walk the great lands that Muhammad's feet once trotted upon."

"Yes and when are these loathsome dogs of the desert not up to no good here, and not looking to steal something from us, Ahmed? That is how they live and survive in the vastness of the deep desert, fool." The second soldier offered, choosing to ignore the filthy Badawiyin warriors.

"Still my faithful brother from the desert sands, I don't like that filth being so near to our military equipment and myself. I don't trust them in the least my brother. Allah knows we have enough trouble getting our much needed supplies and equipment for ourselves from headquarters in Baghdad lately. We can ill afford to have any of it being stolen by the likes of these lowly dog eaters from the vast desert. We should drive them from our village."

"I agree with you Ahmed. I myself don't particularly like them being too near us. I can smell their foul stink from where we stand. But what are you going to do about them, my brother?"

"I think I'm going to challenge the foul fools and at least move them off, so we can rest a little easy without being forced to keep our eyes on the likes of these lowly animals, my faithful Arab brother." The first guard complained to the other soldier as he stared at the supposed Nomads.

"Be my guest fool, but leave your worthless ration card behind with me, fool. Because when they kill you for daring to bother them like you threaten, I'll not be forced to remove it from your pocket when we finally find your body cut up into so many small pieces, that we'll not be able to recognize your foul remains properly my foolish brother who does not know when to mind his own business, while we're doing guard duty for our General, you fool."

"I don't fear these filthy people of the vast desert who owe no allegiance to our great country in the same way you obviously do, Jawad. I think they should all be rotting away in the Abu Ghraib prison for the many crimes these desert rats commit against us all the time. Let the Secret Intelligence Guards of Baghdad deal with the filthy dogs of the desert properly, and purge all our deserts once and for all of these lowly jackal's foul presence."

"Ahmed, I fear you're getting all worked up over nothing really, my foolish brother and fellow soldiers. Look, they are already leaving our presence now, fool. Just our mere presence standing across from the worthless fools seems to have been more than enough to stop them from thinking about stealing anything of worth from us they might have leveled their worthless eyes upon for today at least." The second Iraqi guard offered, as he cautiously watched the two believed to be Nomads move away from their position and military vehicles and equipment.

"Yes, they're leaving at that, but they're only moving to another spot where they can steal from someone else who lives in the village, once they're out of our sight and we're no longer protecting the people of our village they wish to steal from, my brother. I'm still going to challenge them over being in our village, Jawad. Are you going to come with me as I try to get these filthy dog eaters to leave our village in peace on this most foul of days?"

"No Ahmed I'm not coming with you to bother them! I am happy where I stand guard duty. The lowly desert dogs have done nothing wrong for me to hassle them. Just leave them go in peace and don't seek any trouble where there is none lying, Ahmed. It's far too dangerous to bother someone such as these dangerous fools, my foolish brother." Jawad growled at his fellow soldiers as he flung his cigarette to the floor, and then he stared at his partner, trying to stop him from aggravating the thought to be Nomads visiting their village. To his surprise, all he saw was the back of Ahmed's head, as he went after the two desert wanderers with a purpose in his steps.

The Hunter and Baby Tee had their MP-5 automatic weapons hidden under the many folds of their filthy desert Arab robes. When the Hunter noticed one of the Iraqi guards giving them some attention, he decided to move away until the two enemy soldiers went back in the building to eat, or be relieved from their duty. Then the pair of American soldiers moved away from the street with the military building taking up most of the block in the town. Out of the corner of his eye, the Hunter picked up they were suddenly being trailed by one of the guards they just passed. He watched the Iraqi soldier out of the corner of his eye and when he was certain they were being trailed, he warned his fellow soldier with him.

"Hey Tee, we got us a fucking follower, lady. If he challenges our asses, you do all the damn talking for the both us, if he has to go. I'll do him before he knows what hit him, honey."

Tee nodded as they increased their pace more away from the two Iraqi soldiers.

The trailing Iraqi guard quickened his pace in an effort to try and keep up with the moving Nomads, and then he was forced to actually run, to try and catch up to the two. When he was near, he called out in a commanding tone to the two believed to be Nomads nearly running from him now. "Salam Alaikum my desert brothers." Peace be upon you.

The Hunter growled over his shoulder without looking back at the Iraqi soldier, offering them his friendship. "Yes, and may a camel give birth in your foul tent, fool," in Arabic.

This response from the two supposed Nomads did not seem to upset the trailing Iraqi guard in the least, because if these thought to be Nomads replied in any other manner to him. The Iraqi guard would have instantly grown more suspicious of the two.

"Halt fools, I order you to stop where you are, I wish to speak to you filth of the burning desert sands. Stop moving away from me!" Ahmed growled nastily as he unslung his automatic weapon, and moved it around to a more threatening position across his chest.

Baby Tee stopped walking away from the Iraqi soldier, but the Hunter continued to walk a few steps further from them. Unseen by the Iraqi guard, the Hunter's right hand closed around the handle of his hidden K-bar blade in his robe. With a slight movement of his arm, he freed the razor sharp deadly blade from its sheath under his robe. He then worked the blade through the many folds of his smelling robe, until it was free enough from the fabric of the garment to be used as the deadly weapon that it was, if it was needed at an instant's movement by him.

"I just ordered you two desert dogs to stop where you are you two god cursed fools, or I'll be forced to shoot the both of you for disobeying my order." Ahmed warned nastily as he quickly brought his weapon up to his shoulder, and aimed it right at the Hunter's back, because he was still walking slowly from the Iraqi soldier. He closed in on the smaller of the two Arabs, and then the soldier looked into the staring eyes, and realized the one he was looking at was a woman.

"By the sacred gray beard of the great Prophet himself, what manner of foul deception is this cursed game you play against me, loathsome lowly woman? Since when is a lowly Arab woman allowed to walk along even with her faithful husband or mate, upon the sacred sands of the desert, you filth wander through? You should be walking five paces behind him, so I would've known immediately that you were a lowly and foul woman, and the leader is the one I should be speaking with. Why are you dressed in a male's garments anyhow, filthy pig born from camel piss?" Ahmed growled harshly as he roughly yanked open Baby Tee's robe, to make certain that she was indeed a woman he was growling at.

"You, you over there, you, the big one, you come back here and explain this immediately to me. Or I'll shoot the both of you, and leave your foul and desecrated bones lying in the sands to be picked clean by your lowly brothers and sisters of the desert, the hated jackals." Ahmed snarled angrily as he made more threatening motions at Hunter with the barrel of his weapon.

The Hunter knew he had to do something, and do it in a hurry or this confrontation was going to get quickly out of hand on him. Or the entire mission was going to be uncovered by this nosy young Iraqi soldier threatening him. He turned and took his time walking back to the angry acting guard. His K-bar blade was held at the ready and just as he stood right next to the unsuspecting angry Iraqi soldier, the guard's eyes suddenly flared open. Then, the look of death slowly clouded over them as Ahmed turned, and then he stared open mouthed at the young and pretty female Arab standing so near him, as blood slowly dripped from the corner of his mouth. The guard's hands went to his belly as Tee removed her blade from the soldier's body.

The Hunter looked at Baby Tee and saw she had her K-bar locked in her right hand, with raw blood dripping from the very tip of it. She stared into the eyes of the Hunter, drawing strength from him as she watched the Iraqi soldier drop down to the ground.

Ahmed dropped his weapon as his hands went to the gaping wound so violently ripped into the side of his body. His eyes registered he had just received a death wound to his body, and nothing would change his fate now. Slowly, he sank down to his knees, his hands covering the wound and he was trying desperately to stop the heavy bleeding from the wound. When he was on his knees and struggling to breathe and remain alive, he tried to say something, call out an alarm. But nothing came out of his mouth but raw blood as he suddenly fell forward and landing on his face, dead as his last breath came out of his blood soaked mouth in a rattle.

The Hunter saw the look of terror locked in Baby Tee's eyes, and he offered to help calm her down some. "Hey baby you did real well with that lousy bastard, honey. Cold fucking blooded good, girl. We gotta ditch the stinking body, and hope no one misses the flaming asshole, or finds this damn puke until after we get our missing turd, and make like fucking ghosts and disappear from this lousy dump here, honey. C'mon little sister, you hafta help me with his body, get hold of yourself and help me with this prick, baby."

"What are we going to do with him? Oh look, I have his blood on my hand, Hunter." Baby Tee cried as she wiped at the blood as if it burned her hand, as she added nearly in a whisper to her fellow soldier. "I can't believe I did him in with my knife like that Hunter. Oh God forgive me please. I just killed another human being with my hands, Hunter."

"Tighten up your pretty little ass some Baby Tee. I don't need you going to pieces on me at this stinking time, honey. You did what you hadda do to the little fuck, girl. You're a fucking soldier, so start acting like one and give me a fricking hand with his frigging body, baby. You take his feet, I got his stinking arms, and we'll hide this damn puke's body where he can't be found easily, little sister. Besides, you didn't kill him with your hands you stabbed the sonofabitch dead with your stinking knife, baby girl."

The two elite American soldiers dragged the dead Iraqi guard's body into a narrow alleyway separating two dilapidated houses. They found a pile of garbage and building debris dumped in the back yard, and they quickly covered over the body with it. But before he left, the Hunter urinated on the pile of garbage covering the body. Not to dishonor the dead Iraqi soldier, but to make anyone hesitate digging into the pile of garbage to find anything, or the body on them.

Baby Tee had to turn her back on him, because of what the Hunter did to the body of another soldier. When he was finished, he grabbed Baby Tee by the arm and pulled her out of the area as quickly as he could move her along. The two American soldiers drifted around the small town, spotting some of their fellow soldiers spread throughout the village. No other elite soldiers had a problem with any of the Iraqi troops roaming around the small town at will, or the inhabitants of the village for that matter. When he was able to, the Hunter made contact with Walker. He tapped the crystal of his mike and whispered into it. "Hey Walker."

"Go, who the hell is speaking?" Lieutenant Walker grumbled back in his radio mike.

"Hunter man, I gotta speak with you Lieutenant." The pointman replied, as he kept his eye glued on Baby Tee for the time being.

"What's up, you spot our stinking turd yet, man?" Walker questioned the Hunter.

"Negative on that last Lieutenant, but we just had a slight problem over here though, man." The Hunter reported to Walker.

"Like what? What fucking slight problem didja get involved in for crap sake, soldier?" Walker growled into the radio mike, fearing there was trouble for the mission.

"Like Baby Tee just iced off a fucking nosy ass Iraqi soldier, she did it real cold blooded and professional like, man. She's some kinda ass kicking soldier, Walker. She can play in my fricking sand box anytime she wants to play in it, Homes. With her protecting your back, you have nothing to worry about I tell ya man. She's that good a stinking soldier, Walker." The Hunter reported proudly to his commanding officer over the radio.

"You don't hafta try and sell her to me buddy, I know she's good. Did anyone fucking see her do the lousy cocksucka in, Hunter?" Walker demanded to know from the other soldier.

"Negative on that last Walker, we're still secured and ready to rock, man." The dangerous pointman replied confidently to the concerned Lieutenant.

"Whatdidja do with the stinking body of the dead puke, Hunter?" Walker showed no emotion at all over the death of the young Iraqi trooper defending the village.

"It's well hidden in a fucking crapola pile, Homes. No one's gonna find the damn thing, until we're stinking history from this place and the body starts stinking, man."

"You think we should pull back and wait for the cover of darkness, and then hit the stinking building in light of this slight problem you two just dealt with, Hunter? Now that you two were forced to engage with one of the enemy soldiers in the village, Hunter?"

"Negative on that one, Walker like I just said man, we're still a secured and active mission, Lieutenant. I'd like to find this stinking turd, without having to assault the damn building and ripping this damn town apart in the process, Walker. I don't need another stinking war on my damn hands here, man." The Hunter bitched as he took a second to scan the area surrounding them, to make certain no one else spotted what they just did to the enemy soldier.

"Agreed Hunter, look, I want you and Tee to get the hell outta the area for a little while man. Head back to the stinking sand dune and look after Tee. Get her something to eat and drink. I'm sure she's not feeling too good after offing that stinking slug like she just did man and..." Walker's communication was suddenly interrupted by Tee's voice.

"Eighty six that crap Walker, I'm cocked, locked, and ready to fucking rock mister."

"I didn't think you'd be anything but that Baby. You're worth your dog tags honey. But I still want you to pull back for a while and regroup a little. Hunter will know when you're ready to return to duty, and then he'll drag your pretty little ass back here to complete your mission with the rest of us, trooper. There's no dishonor in pulling back for a little while and sucking up some fresh air, Baby. You did more than your fair share for this stinking mission already. You just blue crossed your first fucking bad guy on this damn operation, baby girl." Walker actually ordered the young and pretty female soldier over his radio set.

"Okay man, we're heading back to the sand dune for a quick breather I guess, Walker." The Hunter interrupted, knowing Walker wanted Baby

Tee to catch her breath, so she would be ready to work if and when the crunch time came.

Walker broke off their communication, and then waited until he picked up both the Hunter and Baby Tee working their way back out of the little Iraqi town, before he finally let out his breath and placed his attention back on this operation when someone else cut in.

"Walker! Walker! Come in Walker!" The Ghost growled kind of excitedly in his radio.

"Go talker." Walker replied, not knowing who it was making contact with him this time.

"Walker, Ghost! I have a positive MOE (Mark One Eyeball) on our missing fucking turd pile, Homes. I just picked the lousy bastard up in his turd house, man."

"Out fucking standing Ghost, where the hell's the ball sack hiding, man?"

"I spotted the lousy little prick walking around on the first floor of the stinking building, Homes. It looks like he's being trailed around by two well armed and alert Iraqi guards wherever he goes inside the building. I believe they'll trail him even outside the dump, if the shithead leaves the building for any reason, man. That's gonna complicate things a might." The Ghost reported as he pulled away from the window they pegged to be the armory of the target building.

"You see anyone else hanging around with our stinking turd inside the damn dump, Homes?" Walker asked him as he tried to locate the Ghost working near the building.

"Sure do Walker. He's practically holding fucking hands with that other stinking dude Colonel Leadbetter said he wouldn't be too upset, if he accidently gets caught up in our cross hairs a little during any action we take against these lousy cocksuckers in there, man. They look like a pair of stinking Twinkies, they're moving so close to one another in there man."

"You mean this General Hassan al-Zahar fucker, Ghost?" Walker asked the more dangerous of the two pointmen from their unit.

"Yeah, that's the lousy dude hanging around with our stinking target, Walker."

"Good work there Ghost. Here's what I want ya to do now man. Keep your eyeballs glued to the ass of our dumb loony tune in there, soldier. Let me know what he's up to whenever possible, man. If he makes any fucking motions to leave the stinking building, I wanna know about it before he leaves the dump. Also Ghost and this is important man. I want you to get a good head count of the pack of turds moving around inside the damn building. I'd like to know exactly what we're going up against in there, if and when we have to assault the damn building, man."

"Easy, too easy, you got it Walker. Color me gone." He cried as he broke communication.

"Okay, the rest of you puds listen up. Hunker down in positions for the time being and the Ghost just located our package. We got the dirty bastard. We'll wait and see if the lousy prick leaves the fucking building, so we can do an easy snatch and scoot of the bastard's ass."

Walker looked at his watch, it was eleven ten a.m., and then offered to the troops still listening to him over the small radio. "Look people, we have plenty of time left to make an easy snatch and scoot of the little prick. I wanna try and get him outside the building somehow. We hafta be real patience until we get the stinking prick, or our time runs out on us on the operation, and we hafta then shift to the second phase of this stinking operation. Everyone okay with these last orders I just issued you turds?" Walker counted the soft blows coming into the radio, and when he counted and he knew everyone responded to his last order of the troops, he ended their talk. He then turned to the Mutt and bitched at him.

"I guess you heard my orders dog man? The stinking Ghost has the damn turd locked up in his sights. Now, all we hafta do is sit tight and wait him outta the damn dump. At least we know for certain the lousy bastard is inside the stinking village, that's half of the damn mission, man."

"Alls I know is I'm getting fricking hungry, Homes." The Mutt replied with a smirk to Walker.

"Eat a fucking bug will ya dog man." Walker fired back angrily as he tried his best to locate the Ghost busy working over the target building, and then he continued his complaint against the Mutt. "I told you fucks to munch down on food when we had the stinking chance to eat as much food you wanted to eat in peace, man. You got any of them damn Meals Refused by Ethiopians (MRE) with ya stupid? I hope you were smart enuf to take some of them with ya, buddy?"

"Yeah, I got a B and D wit me man." (Hot dogs and beans) The Mutt bitched at Walker.

"Well drop back some and eat the shit then stupid, just stop crying in the breast milk will ya man." Lieutenant Walker snapped back at his lifelong friend.

"Cold? You want me to eat this shit cold, man? This shit isn't fit to eat even when it's hot, but cold it could be deadly, man." The Mutt retorted as he smiled at Walker.

"Don't eat it then! I don't give a shit either way. But stop bugging my ass bout your damn stomach will ya. I ain't got the time for this kinda crap, Homes. Drop back outta sight and eat the crap anyway you wanna eat it without a flame. Alls I know, if we go hot you betta not get caught with a hot dog sticking outta your damn chops, or I'll shoot it out of it for ya myself, stupid." He warned as he stared in Mutt's eyes while waiting for him to do something about his gripe.

"Fuck it man, I guess I'll wait till this stinking mission's over with, Lieutenant hot shot." The Mutt complained at Walker as he fumbled around with his MP-5 moving around under his robe.

"Hey munch hound, it's only gonna last for twenty four stinking hours, man. You can't wait until then to stuff your stinking face with some damn food, Homes?" Neck grumbled hotly, as he took the Mutt's position next to Walker, when he moved back a little from him.

"Wow, will you look at who all of a sudden got some fucking smart on me, man. You betta back outta a conversation that doesn't concern your ass, big man." The Mutt growled angrily, as he tried to get comfortable with his weapon still moving around under his desert robe on him.

"I am smart Homes, it's just you never noticed it before this time, Homes."

"Yeah, and this shit's coming from someone who don't know what the hell silver dollars are made from, people." Mother Flanagan offered, never leaving a chance to take a slug at any other soldier from the outfit go by him.

"Can the shit and get fucking serious people. Hold on a sec, I got traffic coming in."

"Walker!" The call was nearly a whisper in the ear set of his radio.

"Ghost?" Walker asked more than he said to the new talker on the radio.

"Yeah man, it's me Walker." Ghost replied as he made himself comfortable for the moment.

"Whaddaya got for me man?" Walker bitched back at him angrily.

"Hold on for a sec man, I got me some fucking movement up here. I have a number of movers Walker. It looks like our soft target's preparing to leave the damn building on us, Homes. He's busy gathering up some papers, and his lousy bodyguards seem to be getting excited too, hot in fact man. There he goes he's leaving the office with his fag General pal by his side, man. The guards are trailing the both of them out like little puppy dogs, man. Walker, it looks like they're heading for the front door of the stinking dump, man. Yeah, they're going outside now..."

"Break off your communication and get your fucking head down, Ghost. I got an eyeball on the motherfucker myself now, man. We got the bastard from here. He's with the damn General and a pair of his fucking bodyguards. You're right on target with your report, Ghost. All troops listen up, our fricking target is out in the open, so be alert. We might get this puke and bug the hell outta here faster than we first thought people." Walker wove his radio around his arm, so the mike ended up wrapped around his wrist. He was able to speak to the troops, while making it seem he was scratching an itch on his arm at the same time.

Iraqi General al-Zahar came out of his headquarters first. He did not seem very worried about any hints of danger being displayed against him, as he took the time to stretch his arms over his head and he yawned like he had no cares in the world. His face wore the fuck you look most of the Iraqi soldiers always wore, whenever they were anywhere near civilians of their country. The Iraqi General was followed closely by Colonel al-Adwani, who was walking a few steps behind him. The Colonel was flanked by the other two Iraqi guards who seemed to be well on alert, and they also acted like they knew what they were doing with protecting the two officers. The Iraqi General barely glanced at the four Arab men squatting across the road from his building.

"Hey Walker, should we make the fucking snatch now of the damn prick, man? Or do you wanna wait first, and see what the dopey little prick is up to first out here buddy." Neck asked as he tried to work his weapon into a better firing position under his heavy robe now.

"I guess now seems to be as good a time as any to take the fuck out. I'm getting kinda tired of sitting on my duff in this smelly ass thing while beating my stinking meat like this, man. All troops, get ready, we're gonna make our move on the fucking dude." Walker was just about to stand up when Mother Flanagan suddenly grabbed him by the arm and yanked him back down to a squatting position, as he kept his eyes glued on the four Iraqi soldiers.

"Hold on a sec Walker, we have a moving vehicle coming in on us now, man. A pair of them in fact man. They're heading right for the front of the stinking building, and our damn target looks like he's waiting for the vehicles to come for him, Homes."

"Hey Walker, I spotted two troop movers leaving from the rear parking lot of the stinking dump, man. They're loaded down with a shitload of extra troops. It seems like the lone car parked back here is starting up as well, man. Stand pact until I can make out what the fucking A-rabs are up to back here, man." Wacko called over the radio from the other side of the building.

"Shit! Dammit!" Walker growled in his radio, as he dropped down and stared as the Iraqi military vehicles pulling in front of the building. The troop carriers had four other soldiers packed in each machine and that made ten troops, the General and their target leaving the place.

The vehicles stopped in front of the Arab General. He climbed in the staff car, as if he was mad at the world. He was followed by Colonel al-Adwani, and the two Iraqi guards. The troop carriers remained idling behind the staff car and the armed troops seemed bored to death.

"Shit, buster, your signal is now buster people. This is the holy shit factor we were so damn worried about. We hafta hold off, or we're gonna end up dick deep in screaming Iraqi soldiers running around like flaming assholes, people. We missed the damn easy shot at our target, it looks like we hafta wait until our dumb slug returns from wherever the hell he's going, and we can make the stinking snatch on his ass then people."

When the Iraqi military vehicles left the site, Walker was on the radio again. "Turd hunters listen up close. You're ordered to drop back to the damn sand dune two atta time and take a couple moments to rest, and eat something if you wanna choke down any food. Let's hope this is a short leave for our stinking target, people. This is something that wasn't figured into the damn equation for this operation. Him leaving the site and not returning in our window of operations, we're not prepared to make a moving snatch of the lousy little dickhead out in the stinking field, people. We might as well use this time to get something to eat and rest a little for ourselves. Sun Tan, you're to stand your post until we call an end to this fucked up mission for crap sake. You got some food with ya ass, man?"

"Roger that last, I'm here for the fucking duration. I got some MRE's with me Walker."

"Good, eat, drink plenty of water and be on the alert at all times up there, man. I want you to call us when our fricking target returns to this stinking dump. There's no sense in all of us hanging around this shit filled little A-rab village, and possibly giving away our mission when our target isn't even near the stinking place. Shit, this mission's getting fucked up real fast on us dammit, and it betta get unfucked in a hurry it up, or we're not gonna be able to make our snatch of the lousy little prick. Then we're gonna end up looking like the south end of a north bound horse on this stinking operation. All troops pull back to A, and we'll see what turns up next for us on this damn mission, people."

Lieutenant Walker, Mother Flanagan, Neck and the Mutt held back for a few moments, until Walker was certain all his other people left the target area, and the soldiers headed out of the tiny Iraqi village. It was nothing for visiting Nomads to drift in and out of a village at will, when they were looking to rest from their long treks through the burning hot deep desert sands.

By the time Walker and the rest of the group of specialized soldiers under his command made it back to the small sand dune, the other soldiers were already eating and drinking water. Some of the troopers were exchanging their gathered Intel about the small Arab village, and the Iraqi troops they picked up moving around in the town with each other. Walker slid down the side of the dune, and he ended up sitting between Snatch and Wacko. The Lieutenant looked at the Wacker and bitched at him. "It was a good thing you spotted those two troop movers out there man, or we woulda ended up right in the middle of a fricking heavy shoot out with the lousy pricks that we weren't prepared to engage, man."

EAGLE'S NEST

Mother Flanagan and the Mutt entered the sand dune area next, the Mutt was already ripping into his MRE he was that hungry as he asked Walker with a mouth full of food he was chewing away on. "What are we gonna do now, oh fearless leader of mine?"

"I'll tell you what the hell we're gonna do now Homes. We're gonna sit tight for the time being, and see what turns up next with this stinking turd package. Sun Tan will let us know if and when our stinking target returns to his fricking little rat's nest here, man." Walker growled as he watched some of his troops eating their MRE's.

"And, if the stinking little dude doesn't return to the damn village in the time we have allotted to us, what the fuck are we gonna do then, man?" The Mutt asked of Walker as he shoved more food from his MRE in his mouth, and then he started chewing the hard food loudly.

"Then we're fucked right up the stinking asshole, man. If he doesn't return within our window of opportunity then I guess I'll make contact with Colonel Leadbetter, and see what the fuck he wants us to do with this snatch and scoot operation next, buddy." Walker replied in a disgusted tone to his friend as he looked him right in the eyes.

"Call the fuckwad now and see what the hell's up wit him Walker!" the Mutt snapped as he heated what was left of his MRE over a steno pot.

"Good idea there dog man. Hey Roach, set up the fucking satellite linkup for me will ya man." Walker ordered their SATCOM operator.

Two seconds later the Roach called back to the young Lieutenant. "Ready for ya Walker."

Walker went to the uplink, and tapped in his code. Almost instantly, Colonel Leadbetter's voice filled the radio. "Walker! Tell me you got me the sonofabitch already mister."

"That's a negative on that last request Colonel Leadbetter Sir. We know where he is alright, but our stinking target left his little rat's nest in a vehicle protected by a gaggle of Iraqi soldiers. He was too well protected for us to try and make an in the open snatch of the lousy prick without getting involved in a helluva firefight with the Iraqi soldiers, sir. We're now stuck waiting for his ass to return to his nest, sir. What are our orders in case the fucking puke doesn't return in our allotted time limit, Colonel Leadbetter Sir?" Walker asked his commanding officer.

"Shittt... If the fuck doesn't return within the time limit set, you're ordered to pull back at Twenty Four Hours plus Zero as you were ordered when you first headed out on this damn operation, Walker. If you can't make the damn snatch of the fuck by that time, I'm prepared to send in an F-18, and have him level the fucking building when the prick finally returns to it, mister. I don't give a rat's ass if the pilot has to level the entire stinking town to take this lousy fuck out for us, soldier. I don't have the authority to extend the fricking time limit on this mission any longer than it's already stated by Command, Lieutenant Walker Sir."

"But I wanna take the motherfucker ourselves, Colonel. I don't want the flying jockies picked up the stinking slack for us, sir." Walker bitched back at the Colonel.

"So do I Walker. But I just told you I can't possibly extend any further time on the ground for your troops for this damn mission on my own accord, mister. If you can't make a fucking snatch and scoot in the time allotted to your troops to operate then the mission's a buster and then it's going to be turned over to the damn fly boys, and they'll pick up our slack..."

"In a pig's fucking ear those stinking Navy fly boy pukes are gonna takeover my mission on us, Colonel!" Walker hissed in the radio, as he tightened his grip on the small receiver.

"Well then Lieutenant Walker, if you don't want the damn fly boys to get involved in your little mission, mister. Then I suggest to you that you carry out your orders as received, and stop bugging my ass over it on this here stinking radio, mister." He could not hide the smile he was enjoying, he knew what he was doing, lighting a fire under Walker's ass. But he wanted this mission, and he wanted Colonel al-Adwani more than he wanted his next rate increase.

"I'm gonna get this lousy motherfucker myself Colonel Leadbetter, even if I have to go right into the mother of all heat, and make my snatch of the lousy little bastard in the heart of Iraq, sir. Colonel Leadbetter Sir, I don't want you calling in a hammer signal on my ass on this one, sir. I'm telling ya right here and now Colonel, I'm gonna ignore the fucking buster signal if you transmit it out on us, sir. Give some excuse for not transmitting the buster signal against us if you hafta, sir. If we run over our time limit sir, we'll remain active on our own and we'll walk out of this damn desert dragging our fucking turd along with us by ourselves, Colonel Leadbetter."

"That sounds pretty good to me Walker. But what about any extra support you might need on your pull out of the damn target zone, mister? After the time limit has run its course on ya, I'll immediately lose all our stinking backup support for the entire mission, Lieutenant." Walker's commanding officer warned him in no uncertain terms over the small radio unit.

"Fuck our stinking backup support system then if we can't keep the shit, Colonel Leadbetter. We don't need any stinking support from anyone else on this damn operation, and we never did from the beginning, sir. We're fucking soldier's sir, and we'll make our own damn support if we need any stinking support Colonel Leadbetter." Walker growled hotly in his radio this time.

"Roger on that last response Walker. I'll refrain from transmitting any Hammer signal out on you and your soldiers in the field, buster. But I sure hope you know what the hell you're doing out there Lieutenant. I'll tell you this much mister, if you happen to go over the allotted time limit on this operation, and you continue on with your ordered mission, buster. I'll get you and your motley crew so fucking drunk when you come walking out of that stinking land with your turd in hand that it'll take weeks for you people to sober up any. Err... one thing else I have to inform you of Walker. If you have to go it alone on this damn mission, I'll do my best to keep some sort of ready air cap and extraction and backup support set in place for you people. I assure you Walker, you won't have to walk out of the entire desert by ankle express on this one, mister. Do I make myself perfectly clear on this subject to you, soldier?"

"CFB Colonel Leadbetter. I'm taking it you're giving me a round-about green light to extend our mission until completed if necessary, sir."

"Not on your fucking life mister. I just told you I don't have the fricking authority to extend the mission time for you out in the field, asshole. All I'm saying is, if for some unknown reason to me, we lose communication and you can't receive the Hammer signal. I'll do my best to extract you people from sand land. But only if you have our target in custody, soldier. Walker, if you fail this mission, you'll have to hot foot it out of the damn desert on your own. Might I add, under the eyes of the Navy fly jocks as they fly cover over your failing ass, soldier."

"You keep beating me over the fucking head with these stinking Navy pukes like you're doing here Colonel Leadbetter, and I'm gonna stick them lousy pukes right up your fricking ass on you sideways when I see ya ass again, sir." Lieutenant Walker warned his commanding officer nastily over the radio, growing hot over the constant references of the navy pilots supporting his operation, by the smug sounding Colonel on the radio.

"It's up your ass Colonel, Sir, to you mister. If you don't want the damn flying assholes to embarrass ya damn ass on this stinking operation like they're prepared to do, buster. Then I suggest you finish your stinking mission as ordered and in the time allotted to you to complete this minor operation, Walker! Out!" The Marine Colonel broke off the communication before Walker could bitch further at him. He leaned back in his chair and flipped his feet up on the metal table of the Carrier, and he clasped his hands behind his head and placed the widest grin on his face as in his mind could see the fuming Walker getting on his soldiers.

Sergeant Kirkpatrick was standing by the Colonel's side and smirked to his commander. "Was that a wise idea to rile Walker up like that when he's out on a mission, sir? He's going to come back here looking to take some heads at the conclusion of this operation, sir."

"It's the only way I saw in making the dumb shit angry enough to complete his damn mission as ordered, Sergeant." The wise Colonel replied while wearing the snug look.

"I agree with you there sir. But I think you better keep Walker and his people far away from any Navy personnel for a week or two, to give him some time to cool down a little, Colonel."

"Hmmmm... that's a good idea, make a memo to me remind me of that fact later, Sergeant."

Walker was so angry when he returned to the troops they easily saw it etched on his face. No one wanted to be the first to speak to the angry looking Lieutenant. After about five minutes, the Mutt piped up. "Well man, what the hell did the hot shot Colonel have to say, Homes?"

"I'll tell you what the motherfucker had to say, dog man. He said if we can't complete our fucking mission as ordered, he's gonna send in the stinking Navy pukes, and they'll pick up our slack for us because we didn't finish our operation as ordered, buster."

"Fuck that load of bullshit man let's go get the fucking turd now then, Walker." Neck complained as he flung open his robe and pulled out his MP-5 and added to his angry words. "I ain't gonna let some damn Navy fucks take any of my stinking glory away from me, man."

CHAPTER TWENTY SEVEN

2:35 P.M. IRAQI TIME AT THE VILLAGE OF DAWRAL

Lieutenant Robert Walker got angrier with each passing second of time. He believed the Iraqi Colonel al-Adwani was not going to return to the General's headquarters before their mission ran its course. He tried to figure out another way his troops could track Colonel al-Adwani down to where he went, and then they could make the snatch of him even if he had to pull it off right in the streets of downtown Baghdad. He smashed his umpteenth cigarette into the sand when he heard the soft blow come in on his radio. He jumped as he replied. "Sun Tan?"

"The one and only Walker." Sun Tan was up he was unaware of their latest orders.

"Fuck you, what's going on out there man?" Walker growled at the soldier over the radio.

"Hey Walker, back offa me some will ya man. After all, I was only put together with one fucking screw, man." Sun Tan complained as he tried to see where Walker was in the desert.

"You don't make your fucking report to me quicker than a fricking hurry it up. I'm gonna come back in that stinking little village, and I'm gonna climb up the side of that damn building myself, and throw your black ass offa the damn roof on ya, buster. Whaddaya got going down for me Homes?" Walker growled in the radio at the other soldier in the field.

"Man Walker, you betta go get yourself some fucking raw meat to gnaw on for a little while will ya buddy. I see the three vehicles that left the village earlier today, returning as of this time man. They're just about ready to enter the stinking village from north side your position, man. Whaddaya want me to do about it sir? The vehicles are just about to enter the stinking village."

"Keep your stinking eyeballs glued on the damn vehicles and let me know if our friggin target's returning to his stinking little rat's nest along with the rest of them lousy Iraqi slugs, man. I'm gonna get the rest of our people up and in gear again. We're leaving for the damn village right now as soon as I can get them moving again man." Walker nearly roared in his radio as he gave the rest of the soldiers with him the nod to get them moving again.

"Roger that last Walker." Sun Tan broke off his communication and raised his field glasses to his eyes and trained them on the lead Iraqi staff car, as the vehicle slowly entered the small village. He could not see into the car, so he had to wait until it stopped in front of the building, and dumped off its passengers riding inside the vehicle. He was sweating as he stared at what was going on in front of the target building now.

Walker jumped to his feet while calling to the rest of the soldiers with him. "Let's get fucking hot people. It looks like our stinking turds coming back home and this is gonna be our last stinking chance to flush him down the shitter like the turd he is. I want this mutherfucker, and I want him alive at that, and we have little time left to make the stinking snatch and scoot of the damn prick. I promise you people, we're not going home until I have his scrawny little neck wrapped up tight in my fucking hands, and his stinking eyeballs are bulging outta their damn eye sockets as I squeeze his neck for all I'm worth dammit."

The rest of the elite soldiers closely followed Walker up the side of the sand dune. They walked at a fast but in a controlled and steady pace towards the little Arab town, and the soldiers separated when Walker gave them the quick hand signal to do so. He was a thousand yards from entering the village when Sun Tan blew in the radio again. He instantly stopped moving forward, and then he keyed his mike. "What the fuck's up now Sun Tan, dammit?" He barked back in the small radio crystal and then he looked at the building the soldier was on top of.

"Our stinking scumbag just got outta his fucking vehicle, Homes. I couldn't make a positive ID before this time on the lousy bastard, because I couldn't see into the damn car his ass was riding in, man. He's already inside the damn building though Walker. Sorry man, I couldn't do anything about it, I hadda make certain he was in the car before I reported back to you, man. I was worried the bastard wasn't in the vehicle and we were gonna get stuck looking for the fuck somewhere in Baghdad." Sun Tan complained as he kept his field glasses trained on the target.

"It's not your fault man, you had to make certain he was in the damn vehicle for us first, Homes. If I don't see an easy way to snatch the lousy motherfucker then I'm gonna shift this mission from a snatch and scoot over to a smash and snatch without waiting for time to run out on the damn operation, man. I can't take another damn chance of this lousy turd leaving the damn village before we get at his ass, and he never returns to the dump until we're forced to break off the mission all together, and allow the flying jockstraps to finish it for us."

"Understood that last as received Lieutenant Walker, whatdaya want me to do from up here to support the operation, man?" Sun Tan asked his commanding officer as he looked over the edge of the building, and easily spotted his other troops moving in the village again.

"When we make our stinking move on the damn target, whether that be a clean snatch, or we're forced to assault the damn building in the process. Your responsibility is to make certain no one escapes through the roof area of the structure on us, buster. Once we're inside the building, you're to make sure no one traps us in our own set up buddy. When you feel everything's secured in the stinking building, get the hell offa the fricking roof the easiest way you can, and then linkup with the rest of us inside the structure. I want everyone with us when we bug the hell outta this damn dump, Sun Tan. Make certain that fucking machine gun's disabled before you leave your position on the roof of that dump, asshole."

"You got it Walker. It's already history up here, fellow killer." Sun Tan replied in his radio.

Walker waved his hand, and the elite troops entered the village. The Ghost and Hunter were already working in the village, and the Ghost gave Walker a quick warning over the radio.

"Hey Walker, I have two, I repeat man, two Iraqi soldiers walking around in this dump like they have a real purpose in mind, man. I think they're looking for the damn turd Baby Tee iced off before, man. They look like their plenty hot of the missing dude, Lieutenant."

"This fucking mission's going to hell in a damn hand bag in one helluva rush on our stinking asses, man. Trail the damn pukes, and if you think they're about to discover the one Tee offed, you're to take them out quick and silently. Keep your eye glued on 'em, and if you think they're ready to make an alarm, off them immediately. Better yet, just off the damn fuckers, and take them outta the picture nice and easy, you two. I don't need a fucking squad of enemy soldiers searching the stinking village, while we're still trying to make a snatch of this lousy prick here, man." Walker bitched back at the Ghost.

"Consider them on their way to Paradise, Walker." The Ghost hissed in his radio.

Walker shook his head he was extremely upset at what was happening to his mission.

The Ghost and Hunter trailed the two Iraqi soldiers making it obvious they were searching for the missing guard in the town. When the two soldiers neared the alley the Hunter stashed the body in, the two American soldiers rapidly closed in on the pair. They walked up behind the Iraqi guards, and the Hunter suddenly pointed down the alley excitedly.

"What do you think these two pieces of filth from the desert sands want of us, Jawad? We must keep our eyes on these desert rats or they'll steal right from your pocket." His new partner asked him as they kept a close eye on the Hunter and the way he was acting.

"I have no idea of what is causing these worthless animals to act such foolishness, but I do know Ahmed was going to ask a few of these lowly jackal's some questions. Now, the great fool's missing and I am in fear for his foul life. I told the foolish camel eater not to bother these god cursed Nomads who have entered our village over the past day. You never know how these lowly jackals will react to questioning them. They cannot be trusted for one second in time, my brother." Jawad growled as he stared in the beard covered face of the Hunter.

"What in Muhammad's great name is it you want from us, you great fool of the burning desert sands?" Jawal's partner asked the excited acting American soldier.

The Hunter was making like he could not speak, and he continued to point down the alley.

"Maybe the filthy fool saw what has happened to Ahmed. Knowing him, he has probably found himself a lowly woman, and he's taking his pleasure with her down this alley, Jawad."

"Maybe so, but these two don't look like the ones that Ahemd went after. One was much small than these two are, my faithful brother. Let us see what we can find in the cursed alley." Jawad grumbled at his fellow soldier as he and Fasial cautiously entered the narrow alley, with their weapons level before them and held at the ready. Slowly, they placed one foot in front of the other, and both of them were scared of what might be waiting for them at the end of the alley.

"Do you think we should allow the filthy Nomads to lead the way for us, my brother? I mean, maybe this is an ambush waiting ahead of us prepared by these filthy Nomads who are always angry at everyone in the world, Jawad?" The one soldier said to the other with fear in his voice.

"That is a good idea Fasial we'll allow these hated fools to lead the way for us. That way, if there is trouble ahead of us, these two worthless fools will be the ones who'll walk into it before we do." Jawad waved the two Nomads following them in the alley, to move to the front of them by using the barrel of his weapon to make his intention known to the two American soldiers. The Iraqi guards remained at the ready as the thought to be Nomads moved towards them.

The Hunter nodded to the two enemy Iraqi soldiers, to inform them he understood what they wanted from him, as he slowly closed in on the unsuspecting Iraqi soldiers. When he and the Ghost were about abreast of the both Iraqi soldiers, the Hunter acted first against them. He ripped out his K-bar and swung it at the lead Iraqi soldier. The blade easily ripped into the soft flesh of Jawad's throat. Jawad instantly dropped his weapon, as both his hands went up to his throat in a wasted effort to try and stop the bleeding and save his life. The second Iraqi soldier did not have a chance to move as he watched the savage death his partner just suffered.

Fasial stood with his eyes open wide as he just kind of stared at his brother Iraqi soldier slowly sagging down to the floor, drowning on his own blood that was pouring out of the nasty wound and his mouth at the same time. Fasial never expected to see death visited so curly upon one of his fellow soldier's right before his eyes like this. But before he could even react against the terrible murder of his fellow Iraqi soldier, the Ghost jumped behind him and held his head locked between his arms. With a swift movement of the Ghost's powerful arms, Fasial's neck easily cracked under the heavy pressure, instantly killing the young Iraqi soldier. The Ghost hung onto the body until he was certain the Iraqi soldier was dead, and then he released him.

The Hunter looked at the Ghost, his K-bar still dripping with Jawad's blood and he offered his fellow soldier. "Man that was colder than the other side of a fucking pillow there, Ghost. I never offed a fucking man with my bare hands like you just did yet, Ghost."

"It's all in the fucking wrist action man. You make contact with Walker and I'll dump the damn bodies of these two asses for us." The Ghost offered as he grabbed the legs of Fasial, and then he dragged his body deeper into the alley so he could hide the body in the garbage.

The Hunter blew twice into the radio then he waited for Walker to reply to his call.

"Walker!" The Lieutenant snapped in the radio the moment he heard someone blow in it.

"Hunter here man." The second pointman said in the radio receiver.

"How didja make out with your little problem there man?" Walker demanded from the soldier.

"Scratch two fucking loony tunes from the face of the earth man, and that makes three bad guys outta the damn picture for us to be forced to deal with already, Walker. We keep this shit up, and there's gonna be no one left inside that stinking dump to protect out fucking turd."

"Cool deal Hunter. Has the Ghost picked up anymore personnel in the damn building?"

"Dunno, here, you speak to him for yourself man. He can tell ya if he spotted anymore of these cocksuckers floating around in there himself, man." The Hunter offered to Lieutenant Walker.

"Ghost here." He said as he took over for the Hunter and spoke to Walker on the radio.

"You pick up anymore stinking organ donors inside of the damn building, Homes?"

"No, but I'm certain there are a few more we didn't pick up yet, hiding in there Walker."

"Your best guest then on the stinking number of fucking targets still hanging round inside the fricking building, Ghost?" Walker snarled at the dangerous soldier.

"I'd say there can't be anymore than fifteen other targets left inside, and that's including our stinking turd we're out here looking to take into custody, man."

"Okay, then we're gonna take up new positions and wait this lousy bastard outta the stinking dump. I'm gonna change the attack time on us though. Since the damn time line is so short and inflexible on us, here is what we're gonna do now buddy. If we can't make an easy snatch of this stinking dude, I'm gonna move the timeline for assaulting the fucking building up to Twenty Hundred Hours. I think this is a good time to hit the dump, because I feel most of the dopey bastards in there will be relaxing their guard and preparing for their night's sleep.

"I wanna believe most of the damn civilians of this stinking village will be so fucking wrapped up in doing whatever the hell they do at night while preparing to sleep that they won't be the least bit interested in what the fuck's happening outside their damn homes against them. They're probably scared shitless of their damn military anyway, man. I'm sure as hell they're used to weapon fire going off at all times of the day and night around here anyway, Ghost. All the dopey bastards are gonna end up doing is hiding under their stinking beds until it's all over with out here anyway. You know when we hit the damn building, we're gonna hafta hit it fast, hard and savagely, and then get the hell outta here before any of his stinking reinforcements from Baghdad arrive on the fucking scene against us, and they try and free our stinking turd and wipe us out in the process, man." Walker added as he explained his thoughts to the Ghost.

"You seem like you're beginning to lean more towards we being forced to assault the damn building, with each passing second we're stuck hanging around in this fucking A-rab village, Walker." The Ghost complained, as the Hunter hid the second body for him.

"I am Ghost, I intend to snatch our stinking turd if he shows his face a second time, even if he has all the damn Iraqi troops hanging around inside that building surrounding his ass. I can't afford to allow him to leave the damn village for a second time. We might not get him back again. If the lousy turd doesn't show by Twenty Hundred, we're going after his stinking ass."

"I read you loud and clear on this one, Homes. What do you want us to do now Walker?"

"Ghost, can you and the Hunter get near the damn building without being detected by the shits. If you can then get us more Intel, scope out the stinking place for me from top to bottom if at all possible. Keep it going until we decide if and when to assault the dump. If you see our damn turd heading for the door, let me know A-SAP man. Err... one uther thing to keep in mind man, and this goes for everyone listening to my words on this fucked up mission. From this point forward people, if anyone is able to eliminate any fucking enemy support from the building moving around in the town, you're to do it, no questions asked troops." Walker ordered his soldiers.

"Do you want us to ice them off for good man, or do you want us to just take them out of the picture for a little while, Walker?" Blind Date offered, as she cut into the conversation this time.

"I understand what Colonel Leadbetter told you people about that last question when we first left on this stinking mission. But I'm changing the fucking orders as of this point for all of us, people. Take them out, I don't need someone I'm taking for granted as being out of the fucking picture, suddenly turning up again and bit me on the stinking ass when we're locked in the heat of battle with any of their stinking pals trapped inside the damn building. We'll try like hell to keep the damn civilian causalities down to an absolute minimum though throughout the rest of the entire operation if possible. But it's open season for anyone else who happens to be dressed in a stinking Iraqi military uniform, or if anyone else in the damn village is stupid enuf to challenge us in any way, shape or form, people. They die where they complain."

4:20 P.M. IRAQI TIME, AUGUST 7th, 1999.
THE IRAQI VILLAGE OF DAWRAL

Lieutenant Robert Walker looked at his watch every couple of minutes now. He was trying to actually will the time to move along faster than it was moving for him and the rest of his troops. He was hoping the Iraqi Colonel al-Adwani would come out of the building for a smoke break or something, so they could make an easy snatch on him and then leave the small village.

He hated being a slave to time. He operated so much better when he did not have to worry about how long it would take him to finish up with a mission. When he had all the time he needed, it enabled him to pick and choose the right place and time to carry out his orders. On this operation, he might be forced to tangle up with a bunch of heavily armed well trained Iraqi soldiers, to get at his target. For the past few minutes, he considered killing his target outright and be done with it and get home. If he was going to be forced to keep an eye on his watch, a quick locate and splatter mission, would serve his troops and this operation better.

Again, he looked at his watch and cursed the slow moving time. He then glanced back at the building their target was using as his nest. He was actually tried to see through the walls as his mind screamed for Colonel al-Adwani to come out of the building for a cigarette, or anything else so they could make their easier snatch of him. Then bug the hell out of Iraq, before anyone knew his troops were even there.

The Mutt heard the curse and saw the concentration in his friend's eyes and asked Walker with concern in his tone. "What's the hell's doing man?"

"I hate this stinking shit of being forced to sit on my damn ass, while watching fucking rocks grow out there for crap sake, man. I wish to hell and back again that those fricking puds back at Fort Fumble would understand this shit, that we're damn action soldiers! Not fucking flag poles sitters eating up fricking time and sucking up the stinking sand and sun like we're doing at this time, dammit." Walker complained at his other Lieutenant angrily.

"I hear ya loud and clear Walker. But there's no fucking cook book for this damn mess we're involved in on this stinking operation, Homes." The Mutt offered sarcastically as he tapped out a cigarette, and then offered it to Walker.

"I'm telling ya Mutt, the second we make a stinking snatch of this lousy little prick, I'm gonna take off like my ass is shooting fucking sparks, man. So you betta stay real close to my ass, or you're gonna lose me in the damn dust I'm gonna create while leaving this stinking place, man." Walker growled and refused the offered cigarette from his lifelong friend, as he tried to locate the Ghost who was the closest of his soldiers to the target building, and their missing Iraqi Colonel.

When Walker could not pick up the Ghost moving around anywhere in the village, he turned back to the Mutt and complained at the soldier. "Do you see anything of the damn Ghost out there? Shit he must be well dug in, I can't see him anywhere in this fricking dump."

"I watched him weasel his way in the area like a fricking cat trying to sneak his way passed a sleeping dog with one eye open, a few minutes ago buddy. He's some fucking shit man."

"Yeah, but what's he up to now is the real question here, Mutt? I haven't heard crapola from him in quite a while, and I need fucking Intel in a fast hurry." Walker bitched.

"I dunno where he's at right now Walker. But you can bet the damn bank on it, he's doing his own version of Evil fucking Kenival out there man." The Mutt snorted with a quick laugh.

The Lieutenant's radio suddenly squawked, and some soldier barked in it. "Hey Walker!"

"Go talker." Walker snapped in the radio, getting upset with everyone bothering him.

"It's Ice honey I have two packages out in the open sir. What are my orders Walker?"

"Who's with ya out there Ice?" Walker growled at her over the radio.

"Six Pack, Boot Camp, and the Hunter is hanging around here some place with me darling."

"Can you take out the fucking packages without detection?" Walker asked the female soldier.

"Easy. That's a Roger on that last, honey." Ice purred back in the radio at Walker.

"Then I want you to take the two of them out nice and real quiet like I just ordered you people to do, girl. The less stinking enemy troops we have inside, and hanging around the damn building when we finally go after the damn thing. The better off we're all gonna be on this stinking mission when we finally go hot against the damn structure, baby sister. If you take them out, make certain you hide their bodies real good, honey." Walker warned the female soldier.

"Roger, I copy that last loud and clear baby. Consider them out of the picture Walker."

Walker turned towards where he knew Ice and the other soldiers took up positions, and he watched for them to make their move on the Iraqi guards they just signaled out for death over his radio. He easily picked up the pair of enemy movers, and concentrated his attention on their movements, until he saw Ice and Six Pack closing in on the two unsuspecting Iraqi targets. He smiled when he saw Ice move at the Iraqi guards with her robe hanging open. From his position, he could see her breasts that instantly got the Iraqi guard's full attention. Despite all the crap the Arabs usually gave the rest of the world about seeing naked women and the sight actually insulting them. Soldiers were soldiers all over the world, and when they saw Ice, the two asses acted like any other soldiers did, they stared at her nakedness.

Neck, the Mutt and Mother Flanagan closed in on Walker with Neck complaining at him as soon as he got up to his side. "Hey man, you think we should get our stinking asses over there and give them uther guys a stinking hand with the two Iraqi slugs, Walker?"

"Naw, dump that thought outta your stinking mind man, Ice can handle it alright for herself, man. I wouldn't want her aiming her anger at my sagging ass for a stinking second, man. She's cold fucking blooded and she'll get the job done for us, buddy." Walker replied as he continued to watch, and then he picked up the Hunter and Six Pack also closing in on the two unsuspecting enemy guards. Boot Camp made himself scarce because he was black, and he knew if the Iraqi guards saw him hanging around, they would be suspicious of him immediately.

While Ice allowed the two Iraqi guards to paw her body, the Hunter silently snuck up behind the two guards, and grabbed one of them around the neck and choked him until he stopped moving in his hands. Before the other guard even had a chance to react against the Hunter's attack on his fellow soldier, Six Pack had him and he was choking the life out of him.

Walker kept his attention glued to the action taking place on the south side of the target building, and only breathed normally again when he picked up the Hunter drag the body still locked in his arms, towards a military vehicle that seemed long time disabled. Six Pack was right behind him dragging the second dead Iraqi soldier with him. Ice was busy covering her body with the desert robe as the other two soldiers hide the bodies of the Iraqis, and the Ghost was standing on the side ready to lend a hand to any of the soldiers who need some help.

Ice picked up the dropped weapons from the dead Iraqi guards, and anything else they might have lost as they quickly died in her soldier's hands. She also took the time to kick the slight mounds of sand raised up by the struggling feet over around, and smoothed the ground back to its normal state before the slight scuffle. When she tossed the enemy weapons inside the disabled military van along with the bodies of the two Iraqi soldiers after emptying the weapons of ammunition, Ice blew in the radio and reported their success to Walker.

"Go Ice." Walker grumbled in the radio then waited for Ice to report.

"Ooooo baby you recognized my blow, I'm impressed, how sweet of you, Walker." She purred into the radio while smiling, and she told him they killed the enemy threat against them.

The Mutt cut in and smirked. "Why wouldn't he recognize your blow, honey? You had your mouth on his dick more times than enough for him to recognize it in a fucking wind storm."

"Ooooo, that had to be the forever angry Mutt getting on me this time." Ice shot back at him.

"Ice! I'm gonna stick a sausage down your damn throat, and a hungry dog up your ass if you don't get on with your fucking report to me, and be damn quick about it while you're at it, girl. How the hell didja make out with those two Iraqi shits, baby?" Walker hissed harshly, while drawing in air and fuming with energy.

"You know something Walker you're getting to be just like your little psychopathic friend you always hang around with lately, honey." Ice purred again, refusing to give into the anger Walker was emitting against her over the communication radio.

"Ice, you're screwing around with my damn ass baby girl, and you betta stop it right now if you know what's good for your purdy little ass. What status girl?"

"Gees Walker! Take it for a fact, two more bag guys are in for the long dirt nap here honey. They're history as ordered, baby. Hey Walker, I thought we had orders to just disable these ugly dudes and not take them out during this operation, honey?" Ice remarked as she looked up from her radio and looked towards where she knew Walker and the others were at.

"You did baby, you disabled them so they'll never be any future problems to us. Spread your people out there some Ice. I don't want anyone bunching up like you guys are starting to do, and possibly drawing added attention to them for the rest of this stinking mission."

"Will do as ordered, Walker honey." Ice replied to Lieutenant Walker over the radio.

Walker watched as the trio of special operations soldiers disappeared into the dark shadows cast by the target building. The Mutt lightly tapped Walker on the leg, and he held up five fingers. Indicating to Walker they already eliminated five enemy Iraqi guards from the village.

Walker nodded back to the Mutt as he did the math in his head. The Ghost reported he picked up twelve other Iraqi guards, and figured there might be as many as three more he did not detect, not counting the Commanding General, and their target still hanging around inside the building they were preparing to assault. If they already eliminated five of the enemy soldiers then they only had at the most, ten more enemy Iraqi guards to worry about on this mission. With each enemy soldier they took out before they jumped off to assault the building, the odds of completing the mission successfully, improved drastically for the specialized American soldiers.

Walker drew in his breath, every muscle in his body ached as his tightly bunched up muscles collected lactic acid from lack of movement. As he, the Mutt, Neck and Mother Flanagan sat across the street from the Iraqi General's headquarters. The young Lieutenant stretched his leg out before him, and then he tightened his muscles in an effort to try and get the circulation moving again in them, so he could act when he wanted to jump off at their target.

Neck mumbled just over a whisper to his commanding officer. "Hey Walker, it's getting pretty fricking late you know, man. I don't think our miserable little turd's gonna come out of his stinking rat's nest any time soon for us, buddy. I guess we're gonna get stuck going in there after the dopey little bastard, if we're ever gonna get at the lousy prick."

Walker looked to the sky and watched the sun rushing down for its long night's sleep. He looked at his watch and was surprised it was already nearing six p.m. He again tapped his mike and growled at his pointman. "Ghost!"

"Go Walker, what's up, man?" he replied as he looked towards where Lieutenant Walker was stationed.

"You see hide or hair of our fucking scumbag hanging around in there at this time man?"

"Negative on that last Walker, the scumbag's hiding inside his stinking dump like a fricking deer tick on a dog's ass, Homes. You want I should get any nearer to the damn building, and see if I can locate where the fuck he's hiding in there, Lieutenant?"

"Negative on that last Ghost, stay where you are for the time being. Err... I want you to locate the room this prick might be using for his protection. It'll help out better if we know where the hell he's staying when we hit the fucking dump, soldier." Walker warned the Ghost.

"Positive we're going in after the dirty bastard in there then, huh Walker?" the Ghost grumbled, allowing a hint of anger to enter his voice.

"Unless you can find another way to have the prick take a night time stroll for us, man."

"Fuck! I really hate this damn shit you know man." The Ghost growled in his radio.

"Agreed man." Walker fired back at him over the radio.

"Walker, I'm gonna drop back some and see if I can get an easy eyeball on our stinking target, if he's still hanging around somewhere on the second floor of the fricking dump, man. The first floor is just about fucking empty of all the little surrender monkeys, buddy. I guess the lousy A-rabs are upstairs bending a stinking knee on their prayer rugs, man."

"You do what you gotta do to gather that damn Intel I need for my ass, Ghost."

"Will do as ordered Homes." The Ghost broke off the connection with Walker and skillfully began to work his way a little further away from the target building. The second floor was lit up pretty well, and it took a few seconds for him to spot the missing Colonel al-Adwani, just as he happened to move in front of the window for a quick second. As he stared at the figure pacing back and forth in the room obviously screaming at someone he was unable to see at the moment in the room with him. Suddenly, he was surprised to see a naked woman pass before the window he was staring at in a flash. "Sonofabitch." He grumbled as he enjoyed the quick little show, and then he lightly tapped his mike to report back to Walker.

"Walker!" The Ghost mumbled in the radio again.

"Go Ghost. Didja see anything of our missing turd in there?" Walker snarled at him hotly.

"I just located the room our target's using for his little fun and games in there, man."

"I take it he's not alone in that room then, from what you're saying to me? What's up man?"

"You're right as always, he's not alone man, he's got some dizzy bitch running around naked as the day she was born with him, and he was really lacing into her for some reason and..."

"I got dibs on the hen when we hit the damn building." The Mutt offered as he got excited.

Walker ignored the Mutt's remark as he gave him a nasty glance, as the Ghost finished up his report. "Hey man, our stinking turd is in what I take to be the second room just to the left of the main staircase of the dump to the rear of the stinking building, man. He's really fucked if we can trap his ass upstairs in the room, pal. There's only one window in the damn room, but it's at least a twenty foot drop to the stinking ground, and I believe he'd never use it for an escape route against our attack against him, man. The package is out in the open and well within range of my weapon at this time. I got a good eye on stinking target Lieutenant you want me to off the little dick, so we can be home before the sun comes up?"

"Your target qualifies and I'd gladly give my left nut to give that damn order for you to drop the rotten mutherfucker where he stands, Ghost. But our orders are to try and take the lousy prick alive if at all possible man, and that's exactly what we're gonna do with this messed up stinking operation, man. We have to try and take him in alive or the stinking Colonel's gonna eat the lot of ya alive, buddy." Walker repeated to the dangerous soldier.

"Walker! How copy?" A new voice suddenly called over the radio in a rather excited tone.

"Signal down, signal down, lost copy. Repeat all after how, dammit!" Walker growled back over the new interruption.

"Corrected. How copy now?"

"Copy all, go with your report."

"Walker, there's four Iraqi guards pouring out of the stinking building like the dump's on fricking fire man. They're acting like they have a real purpose in their actions, honey. I believe they're looking for the two guards we just took out of the picture a few moments ago." Ice reported, trying to keep the excitement out of her tone while reporting to her commander.

"Can you and the others take the new jerks out nice and quietly like, honey?" Lieutenant Walker asked the female soldier.

"Not without getting involved in a mini war with the bastards if we try, Walker. They're too alert and on the move to do a sneak up and kill against them, honey." Ice replied as she wiggled a little deeper into the shadows she was using for cover.

"Shit, fuck, okay, I'll try and get some more guys out to your position to lend you a hand with controlling the damn situation. If you get involved in a firefight, I'm gonna used the rest of the group and your action as cover to hit the stinking building and get our fucking target either in custody or kill the lousy fuck. I think we're rapidly running outta fricking time around here, baby. God dammit, I didn't wanna hit the stinking dump in the fricking daylight like this. It aids them more than it does us for fuck sake. We're gonna be lit up like stinking Christmas trees out here while we're assaulting the damn building and..."

"Wait a minute Walker, I have an idea. Do you mind if I try something before you go hot and heavy on them first?" Ice offered as she caught an idea and wanted to run it before Walker.

"Whadaya wanna try and do with these lousy pricks, Ice? At this point I'm open to any and all suggestion if it'll help with this operation, baby." Lieutenant Walker asked Ice over the radio.

"There's no time to explain to you honey, they're almost right on top of me." Ice broke off her communication with Walker, and then she reached out and yanked the Hunter out of the shadows and forced him to lie down on the ground flat on his back. As the Hunter got down, Ice flung off her robe, and she whipped off her shirt and pants and straddled the Hunter's legs, and then she began to moan as she wiggled over his groin. As she dry humped the Hunter, she leaned near his ear and whispered to him. "Hunter, whose ever name these two turds call out, I want you to grunt and then ignore them and make like you're screwing the hell out of me, stupid."

"Got'cha loud and clear baby girl, you want me to open my robe for you, baby?"

"Nice try there buster, we're not here for a good time, I'm only doing this to insure the success of the damn mission, asshole. But if it works, I'll fuck you bowl legged when we get back to the real world mister. Make it look good though Hunter or we're going to end up as supper for these bastards, honey." Ice warned the soldier who was her partner for the operation.

"You got yourself a stinking deal on that offer, baby." The Hunter grinned from ear to ear as he took both of Ice' breasts in his hands, and began to work them over with his fingers.

As the Iraqi guards continued to pour wildly out of the target building, they immediately separated to each side of the building, and then they began to work over the bushes surrounding the south side of the structure. Two of the Iraqi guards started to call out the names of the missing guards, as the other soldiers assumed a sort of backup and support role for the other searching Iraqi soldiers.

"Salama, Bashir, where the devil are you two fools at. You fools have failed to report in for food and prayer. General al-Zahar is most upset with you two, and he has sent us out here to see if you two soldiers are alright. Reply to my words or we'll fire in the underbrush to flush you out fools. Salama, Bashir, where are you two fools and why don't you answer me?"

The Hunter froze up a bit, but Ice continued to move over his legs and moan. Her commotion drew the attention of a few of the searching Iraqi guards, and the two calling out the names of their missing fellow soldiers, moved a little closer to what they believed was a struggle taking place near the side of the General's headquarters. With their weapons held at the ready, and aimed at the shadow they saw a number of feet before them, the soldiers cautiously closed in for the kill against someone who might be attacking one of their fellow soldiers. Again, the leading Iraqi guard called out in a commanding tone. "Salama, Bashir, is that you over there? Are you two fools alright? What are you two god cursed fools doing out there in the shadows?"

Ice had to actually pinch the Hunter in the side hard, to make him make a sound in response to the Iraqi soldier speaking to them. He grunted against the pain of the pinch and jump at the same time. Ice ignored the presence of the guards, and she continued working over the Hunter.

"What are you two doing over there, fool? Is that you Bashir? Speak to me at once, fool."

Evidently, the Hunter sounded more like the one Iraqi soldier called Bashir, than he did of the other missing Iraqi soldier, and he grunted again deeply in an Arab tone. "Yes."

"Elif air ab tizak! (A thousand dicks in your ass!) What are you doing over there, fool?" The once scared Iraqi guard suddenly saw the naked woman straddling his friend's legs, and he could not keep the smile off his lips, as he offered with a smirk as he let down his guard some now. "Sadeeky, (friend) you have chanced the great wrath of the well feared General al-Zahar, for sharing your foul essence with this lowly and foul zarba (shit) of the great desert.

"General al-Zahar has issued new orders for us to have nothing to do with these filthy desert Nomads who have invaded our sacred village for most of this foul day. Tomorrow the General intends to arrest all the lowly Nomads still hanging around the village, and then question them to try and find what has happened to the three fools, Jawad, Ahmed and Fasial. Those three soldiers are still missing and the angry General believes that they were killed by the desert trash like the one you are having fun with. If the General knew you were with this filth koos (cunt), he would separate your golden zib (penis) from your foolish body."

The Hunter went to reply, but Ice quickly covered his mouth with hers, so all he could do was make a muffled sound at the Iraqi guard. She was afraid he would not be able to pull off the Arabic accent properly, or sound enough like this Bashir to pull off their bluff further.

"Ahhhh... Waj ab zibik! (An infection to your dick!) Hamal, will you look at the great desert fool there, he grunts like a rutting pig wallowing around in his own sweet filth. I say we leave him to the fate of Mohammed and the General who will skin him alive, because this terrible crime he has committed against his orders and his Commanding Officer. If the great fool wants to place his life on the line, just to enjoy this foul female jackal of the night's pleasures. Then I say we should leave him to enjoy his future foul fate. If the General ever finds out what the great fool is up to, he'll open his back with the lash for his terrible sins, and then have him suffer the death of a thousand cuts, and put this little sharmoota haygana (horny bitch) to death."

The second Iraqi soldier complained as he tugged on the arm of the first Iraqi soldier. He was upset his prayers were interrupted by the angry General, as he ordered them out to find the two missing guards. The remaining guards dropped their weapons down to their sides, and were busy trying to see what the young naked woman looked like in the dark shadows of the building.

"Bashir, I'll do you a great favor and inform General al-Zahar that you and Salama are walking the furthest rim of our defenses, and have decided to ignore food and Salah.(Prayers) He's going to be extremely angry with both of you fools, but he'll understand your attention to duty. Enjoy yourself fool, I hope your snake does not fall off in the morning, allowing that infidel pig enjoy her ride at your foolish expense. You own me Bashir, if she is that good, you must force her to remain and fetch me, so that I might enjoy the warmth of a woman on this cold desert night. I'll make her mos zibby. (suck my dick) It has been much too long since the last time I parted a woman's lips with my zib. Look at the filthy sharmoota, she must have a kis (vagina) vast enough to swallow up all the sands of the great desert." The Iraqi guard hovered while waiting for a reply from Bashir, still not certain that everything was alright with him.

Again, Ice had to pinch the Hunter on the side to make him jump and grunt out.

"Ahhhh... the lucky fool of a milkless whore, she must be the ride of a well trained camel on a star filled night, to make you grunt like that, Sadeeky. Remember Bashir, if you wish my silence as your ally, when you finish with this god cursed pig you are enjoying, you must force her to remain so I might partake in her foul pleasures myself, fool."

Before Ice had a chance to pinch him for a third time, he grunted on his own as he suddenly thrust his rearend up, to show the two soldiers how much he was enjoying this temptress.

"Let us leave these two miserable mutis (jackasses) to their sinful act and fate, my faithful Arab brother. Although I don't see him around here anywhere, Salama must also be with another one of these filthy Nomad kelbeh. (dog bitch) Come on Munif, if we remain here any longer than this time, the next thing you know, the god cursed Bashir will be begging

476

you for your honorable permission to nikomak (fuck your mother). I still do not believe these two worthless fools will risk the General's angry by doing what they are doing with these filthy pigs."

The other two Iraqi soldiers laughed over the older guard's ugly comment. They both then turned and left who they believed was Bashir to enjoy his young Arab woman. Laughing and passing even more crude remarks back and forth as the small group of Iraqi guards went back into the building, so they could report to their commanding officer the two missing guards were okay and only carrying out their orders.

When Ice realized the Iraqi guards left the area and went back into the target building again, she got off the Hunter's lap. He reached up and took a last grab of her perfect breasts. Ice slapped his hand away as she grumbled at him. "That's all you get for the time being, Mr. Wiseguy. We have to report back to Walker and inform him that everything's cool over here with us honey, before he has a damn puppy on us you know."

The Hunter got up on one elbow and enjoyed the great show Ice gave him, as she struggled to get back into her sweat soaked shirt and pants, and then she crawl back into the God awful smelling and heavy Arab desert robe of the Nomad Tribes.

"You know Ice there's something about the stinking smell of these fricking robes that's starting to get to my ass, honey. I think these dopey ass A-rab bastards might have something here with the damn things, baby." The Hunter offered the female soldier.

"You know something, you're starting to get as disgusting as the Mutt is all of the sudden, Hunter. If you enjoy screwing anyone that stinks as bad as I do right now mister. Then I really feel sorry for the women of the real world when you get let loose on them again back in the States, Hunter. What are you going to do with the women of our country? You know they won't stand for anyone smelling as bad as we do right now for a minute, mister."

Boot Camp and Six Pack remained hiding in the shadows cast by the target building, and they kept a sharp eye on the two Arab soldiers, and the action going on between Ice and the Hunter doing their act on the ground. They were ready to cut down the two Iraqi guards if they were foolish enough to challenge Ice and the Hunter in any way, and then fight their way back to Walker and the rest of the other trooper's sides. When the Iraqi guards were far enough away not to hear any of their comments, Boot Camp moved up to the Hunter and complained at him. "Hey white boy, is there any way this big ass nigger can get in on some of that fine white Ice action you were just enjoying, man? I'd really like to try her on for size myself, man."

Ice gave him a terrible look and then she flipped Boot Camp the bird as she quickly finished dressing and then regrouped with the other soldiers.

"Hey white girl, is that an offer or a request you just offered me there, honey?" Boot Camp moaned sarcastically at her, as he licked his lips and stared at Ice for a long moment.

"Fuck you and the horse you just rode in on, you big pig you. When you learn how to properly speak to a lady, you might get a little more action from us ladies, stupid." Ice growled hotly at Boot Camp as she slipped in her robe. When she was done dressing, she blew in the radio.

"Go Ice. Report baby girl!" Walker was tense waiting to find out what was going on.

"Everything's cool as my name Walker, we got everything under control here honey."

"How the hell didja pull this one off, Ice?" Walker asked the young and pretty female soldier.

"That's a trade secret I'll guard to my death, Walker baby." Ice purred back in the radio.

"You certain those stinking Iraqi pukes won't come back on you before we jump off honey?"

"Not on your life Walker." Ice fired right back at Walker over the radio.

"I don't know how you did it baby, but you received an A for effort in my fucking book, honey." Walker groaned and then he looked to the sky and noticed it was getting darker. He looked at his watch again, it was ten to seven. He could not believe the time was going by so slow and then he griped to the Mutt.

"Man, the fucking time's going by as slow as shit coming outta a stinking coke bottle."

The Mutt glanced at his watch, and then announced. "We got seventy minutes till jump off time Walker. Suck air and relax some, or they're gonna hafta bury you standing up, Homes."

CHAPTER TWENTY EIGHT

Neck spotted, and then he pointed to three young Arab kids as they slowly walked down the block shoving each other and laughing, all were boys, and the oldest boy could not have been more than thirteen years old. All the kids were armed, one of them with a beat up and obviously not working RPG (Rocket Propelled Grenade) and carrying no rounds for the deadly weapon. The other two young boys both carried AK-47s and one boy had two straps loaded with extra ammunition criss crossing his small body. Neck mumbled at Walker as he kept his eyes locked on the three kids. "Man, that's some fucking shit over there, huh Road Kill?"

"Bet the fricking bank on it man. No wonder why this screwing up stinking nation is so twisted up, buddy." Walker growled as he stared at the young kids until they were out of sight, and then he added to the massive soldier hunkered down by his side. "Their stinking parents must give them the damn weapons for their fricking birthday right from stinking birth, man. I bet the little pukes know exactly how the hell to use them damn things too, big guy."

"This fricking god forgotten country has no chance in hell of ever coming outta the damn stone ages, Walker. How the hell could they if they allow their damn kids to walk around the lousy streets armed with loaded automatic weapons as they're doing, man?" Neck growled bitterly as he tried to get a last look at the kids as they disappeared.

"Say Walker, all these dumb fucks are doing is fostering the next damn generation of hatred and stupid blind ass killers, man. I don't know why the fuck we don't just leave the damn assholes alone and let them devour each other, until there are not enough of the stupid fucks left alive to make a fricking working nation with, man. You know that's what they would be doing if we didn't keep sticking our stinking noses into their damn business and this screwed up country, man." Mother Flanagan complained as he fished around for a cigarette, and he caught himself before he freed one to enjoy.

"Walker." Another voice came in over Lieutenant Walker's radio this time.

"Shut the hell up people, someone's trying to make contact with us here. Go talker."

"Ghost here Homes! I got an easy eyeball on our fucking target, it seems like he's having himself a little patty cake with that hen I told you about before, man. He hasn't left the stinking bedroom since my last report. Walker, from what I can see of it, it looks like everyone inside the building is just marking time until they turn in for the night. I can see into a coupla rooms and the dopey turds are lying down on their damn beds, or screwing round with their stinking computers and uther crap in there. I only picked up the few guards assigned to our damn turd that still have weapons with them. I say fuck the time crap, and let's hit the lousy turds right now, man. If we go active, we can easily catch them with their stinking pants down, especially our bird."

"Hang in there man, I already made the time of the hit, and that's when we're jumping off, period. I changed it so many fucking times now, if I try and change it once more I'd get confused myself, dammit. You're doing real well at keeping a MOE on our damn pigeon and when we go, we'll know where the lousy little prick is in there."

"You got it for now man, will follow my orders as received, Walker."

"This fricking mess is beginning to smell like a stinking pail of dirty diapers, people. I hate this crap, I was bred for fighting, not sitting on my fricking duff watching this little turd enjoying himself in there with his damn little honey." Walker griped to no one in particular.

Time continued to drag along at a snail's pace and as it grew closer to their jump off time, the Lieutenant and the rest of his troops began taking up their new positions for the opening assault on the building. Slowly, every soldier from the group of elite troopers went to their assigned positions and then waited. Walker watched as Wacko, Snatch, McNip and CoCo-G closed in on the windows on the north side of the target building, while Six Pack and Ice moved near the windows on the south side of the structure. The Ghost went after the window he thought lead to the Iraqi armory. The Hunter backed up Ice and Six Pack. When the troops were close enough to react when the time came, Walker leaned back and took a quick breath for himself.

"Man Walker, those fucking people are good, damn good man. Look at them setting up out there." The Mutt remarked as he kept a close eye on the troops moving against the building.

"That's why we got'em with us Homes. They're the fricking best of the best, man."

As Walker, the Mutt, Neck and Mother Flanagan remained stationed directly across the street from the target building, the other soldiers of the group involved in the frontal charge, slowly came walking down the street as if they owned it. Blood Clot was in the lead of the rest of the troopers, and he was barely recognizable with the oversized robe hiding his normal features. Siberia and Blind Date was walking behind him. Baby Tee and Roach followed the other four American soldiers, but not too closely though. Buckethead and Boot Camp brought up the rear of the group. No matter what was draped over Bucket's huge body, his mere presence was more than threatening enough as he stumbled down the road with the other soldiers.

Walker checked his watch again because time was his master for this mission. Seeing the time his heartbeat increased, until he could actually hear it thumping in his ears. It was ten minutes before eight p.m., and their time to act. Blood Clot lead the group until the Mutt took it over on him, he glanced back at Walker and quickly opened and closed his hand twice, to inform Blood Clot they were ten minutes from the assault on the target building.

Walker blew in the radio then he growled deeply in it. "Ghost!"

"Go man." He instantly replied as he kept his eyes glued on the building now.

"What's the stinking status inside the damn building, buddy? We're bout to make our move on the damn thing, Ghost?" Walker demanded from the trooper.

"Walker, I have no eye on any soft targets hanging around the armory area of the building, but I got a clear eyeball deeper in the damn building. All I can see is the two lousy dudes standing post like they're waiting for a stinking cab to pick them up by the staircase leading to the second floor of the fucking structure. One ass is even smoking a stinking butt and the uther guy seems to have his mind off in lala land, man. Some fricking security they adopted in there, Homes."

"They're making it all that much easier for us to capture our damn turd alive, man. Make contact with me if something changes on us inside the damn building. I gotta know what the fuck to expect when we do our crash and bang against the damn thing, man."

"Got'cha Walker, will do as ordered man." The Ghost reported back to Walker.

Walker turned his attention to Sun Tan still guarding his position on the roof of the target building. He smiled when he saw the soldier moving around cautiously, and then he attacked the three radio antennas, completely disabling any communication between General al-Zahar's headquarters and Baghdad command. The Lieutenant looked to where Wacko and the other soldiers were stationed. He saw Wacko order Snatch to rip out the radios in the Iraqi vehicles. "Nice going there on your part Wacker." He mumbled loud enough for the Mutt to hear him.

"Yeah, he's really on his damn toes tonight, man. Say Walker, are we still gonna make the big crash through the stinking main door of this stinking dump, or are you gonna allow that fricking privilege to go to Blood Clot and the troops wit him this time around, Homes?" the Mutt asked, as he continued to stare at the front door of the target building.

"C'mon Mutt and use your damn head for something more than just a fricking hat rack will ya. The only stinking reason Blood Clot's on this operation in the first place, is because he's the only friggin medic I feel can carry his own weight when the crunch time comes a knocking against us, man. You and me are gonna hit the damn door. I'll crash into it and drop to the floor while you, Mother and Neck cover me and take out the stinking guards standing duty by the damn staircase." Walker explained to the Mutt who was glued to every word Walker told him.

"Cool deal man. I kinda like it that way Homes." The Mutt replied with a grin.

EAGLE'S NEST

Walker checked his watch again it was five minutes to eight and jump off time. He looked at the many faces of the soldiers staring at him and then he announced to the worried looking soldiers. "Okay dog man, swing your weapon around because it's time to get hot, man." When he gave this order, the Mutt, Mother Flanagan and Neck fumbled with their heavy desert robes, working their weapons over to the front of their bodies.

The group of specialized soldiers opened the robes and made it easy for the weapons to slip out of them when they went in action against the building and enemy troops trapped inside. The other troops were kind a staring at Walker and when they played with their robes, the other troopers did likewise. Making certain they could get at their weapons easily when needed.

The young and elite American soldiers were suffering from anxiety as they prepared to attack the target building. Walker saw the massive soldier Neck staring at the structure as if he was going to eat it, and felt he was getting too far into the black or kill zone on him. He slapped Neck on the back to break his deadly stare of the structure and thoughts.

"Holy shit motherfucker, don't do that fucking crap to my ass man. I nearly shit myself dammit." Neck complained as he ripped his eyes from the structure and looked at Walker.

"Relax big guy, it'll be over quicker than you think man." Walker snapped back at his friend.

"Yeah man, all I want is some stinking gone between me and this fucking miserable place, Walker. I really hate the fricking desert man." Neck griped as he shifted his weight on his legs to get in a better position to begin his attack against the building.

Walker decided to remind the other soldiers of an important item before they moved out against their intended target. He blew in the radio and offered barely over a whisper to the rest of his troops. "Remember people, you don't have your stinking body armor on, so you're not bulletproof for this damn mission. Keep on your damn toes and protect one another's back as always. We don't leave anyone behind people."

With this said, Walker got on his feet, and slowly started to cross the only paved street in the entire Iraqi village. The Mutt was right on his heels and mumbled after Walker in a Russian accent. "Good, now we go and kill moose and squirrel."

"You know you're fricking nuts dog man and you're getting worse with each passing day, man." He groaned without even looking back at the Mutt. When Walker was about half way across the street, he increased his pace some. In three quick strides, he was running flat out. His heavy desert robe flew off his shoulders, and his MP-5 locked in his hands.

The Mutt, Neck and Mother Flanagan charged for the building directly behind Walker.

Walker jumped up the set of three steps in one stride, and crashed his shoulder and full body weight against the old wood door of the building. The sheer force of his weight alone smashing in the old door sent it splintering from its hinges. The move was so sudden and quick and hard hitting that it completely caught the two young Iraqi guards inside the building completely off guard. They both stood staring at this large crazy looking man who just shattered their door down, with their mouths hanging open, and they were frozen in place. The Iraqi soldiers actually seemed scared to move before this young wild man now aiming a weapon at them.

The Mutt and Neck entered the door next, and they blasted the two stunned Iraqi guards. He hit the first one in the chest with a short burst of three rounds, and then he went to his right and dropped down to his knee and hissed. "Clear on the fucking right people." As the Iraqi guard he fired on left his feet, his body went somersaulting backwards until it crashed to the floor.

Neck hit the second guard with a longer burst, and then when to his left and surveyed the area before him, and then announced in a loud clear tone. "Clear on the left man."

His enemy Iraqi soldier went falling off to his right side dropping the weapon he was trying so desperately to aim at the sudden intruders. He was dead before his body hit the floor.

Mother Flanagan remained standing in the shattered doorway, ready to take out any other enemy soldiers who tried to attack his fellow soldiers now lying on the floor after killing the two Iraqi guards. Mother Flanagan sent a spray of rounds up the staircase and walls, to stop any Iraqi soldiers now trapped upstairs from getting the jump on his fellow soldiers from above them. The way the American soldiers so quickly and violently assaulted the building, forced the soldiers to hit the place in a two prong

EAGLE'S NEST

effort this time. The American troops were going to secure the entire first floor of the structure first, and then they would go after the Iraqi soldiers now trapped on the second floor of the building, and hope they could be out of the area before any possible enemy reinforcements dispatched from Baghdad arrived on the scene, and they ended up in an all out shooting war with the newly arriving enemy soldiers.

Walker chose this mode of attacking the building area, because there were no hostages involved in this hard hitting action, and if their target was killed in the action. He planned to take his head back to the United States, so the President could piss on it if he wanted to.

At the same instant the Lieutenant and the rest of the other soldiers hit the front door of the building the American troops stationed by the windows of the structure, smashed them out and then quickly climbed into the building from many different rooms. Weapon fire and crash bangs, (stun grenades) popped off here and there inside the building, and a flood of Arab curses quickly filled the air. As the Iraqi soldiers suddenly found themselves trapped in their rooms under attack, and they were being slaughtered by the sudden attackers.

Neck moved deeper into the building and was suddenly hit in the arm by an Iraqi soldier's round, as he tried to escape a room the American troops hit from the outside. Neck looked at his bleeding arm and growled angrily. "Not a fucking again dammit! Walker's gonna skin my sagging ass alive for getting tagged on this operation, dammit." He glared at the Iraqi guard who seemed like he was waiting for the huge invader to drop down from the wound. Neck clamped his jaw shut and glared at the stunned Iraqi soldier and then opened fire on him. He raked the entire body of the enemy soldier with the M-60 machine gun. He grinned as he watched the dead man dance on his feet, as the heavy rounds ripped into his body.

"Shoot me will ya you dopey little fucking bastard! Now I gotta explain to that pain in the ass Walker how I got myself shot again on another fricking operation, dammit. Crap, Walker's gonna be fit to be tied when he finds this shit out, you mutherfucker you." Neck growled as he moved a little deeper into the building looking for more targets to hit.

The Ghost secured the room he took to be the armory for the Iraqi soldiers in the building, and then he planted a number of detonation charges, enough to blow the room into the next world. Ice smashed the window she was assigned to with the butt of her weapon, and then she was just about ready to pitch a stun grenade into the room. She did not notice the Iraqi soldier hiding in the room she was attacking. The guard fired at the shattering window, striking Ice high on the shoulder and sending her flying backwards from the force of the round hitting her body.

The Hunter was right by her side in a flash, and he fired in the room while emptying his entire clip at the trapped enemy soldier who just tagged his partner. He instantly ejected this empty clip and slammed a second one home. His burst took out the enemy soldier who just wounded Ice. When he was certain no one else was hiding in the room, he quickly attended to Ice's serious wound. She was in a lot of pain, but not out of the battle. The Hunter ripped the top of her shirt open, and applied a field pressure dressing to the injury, and then he pulled her to her feet and shoved her through the window of the building. He did not want to leave her sitting on the ground outside of the building in the dirt, because he wanted to keep his eye on her.

"Owe you big dumb jerk you, take it easy on me will you please. Or I'll smack you right in that thick gob of yours if you don't take care with me, mister." Ice warned the Hunter as he placed his hand on her rearend, and he almost heaved her right into the opening of the shattered window.

"Walker!" The Hunter roared in his radio receiver when he got inside the building.

"Hunter?" Walker growled in his radio just as angrily as the voice yelling at him.

"Yeah man." He replied to Walker over his radio.

"Go. What's going down by you, trooper?" Walker said as he calmed down a little.

"Ice just got friggin tagged man, she's okay but she's wounded and in a helluva shitty mood at the same time, Homes. I'm gonna stay with her man, we successfully secured our area of responsibility for this fucked up operation, Walker. We're in the room, and we're working our way towards the stinking hallway towards your position at this very moment, Homes."

Walker was mad as hell Ice was tagged by one on the enemy soldiers in the building, as he growled back at the Hunter. "You stay with her man, if she fades out on ya ass, loop her over your damn shoulder and take her back to the fucking sand dune and wait for us there, man. We'll use the sand dune as our rallying point and for our..."

Three rounds suddenly went whizzing by Walker's head, forcing him to duck down and yell at the same time in his radio at the other soldiers with him. "Someone betta shoot that lousy mutherfucker will you please! He nearly parted my fucking head for my stinking ass, dammit. I can't get an eyeball on the lousy bastard, get the sonofabitch now dammit!"

"I just hit him Walker." The Roach screamed back in his radio and then he added for his commanding officer. "I shot the motherfucker right in the damn eye for ya, Walker."

"Well shoot him better will ya fucker, he's still firing at us you damn asshole you. Put some fucking ammunition on his damn ass for me, buster!" Walker growled as he pulled a stun grenade out from his vest and pitched it towards where the unseen enemy just fired at him from. It went off with a blinding flash and a heavy percussion, but no one screamed out. Informing him that the Roach had successfully took out the enemy shooter in the building.

Upstairs inside the structure, General al-Zahar rushed out of his room and he took up his position of defense at the head of the stairway, and he fired down at the many shapes of the invading soldiers darting by the opening on the first floor. He was fuming with rage, because he was caught out of position with just his 9 mm pistol locked in his hands for battle. He had no doubt in his mind these invaders were there to get Colonel al-Adwani. An Iraqi guard suddenly rushed by General al-Zahar's side, and fired down the stairs with an AK-47. The General savagely yanked the guard's Kalashnikov Assault weapon from the soldier's hands, and then he hissed at the young soldier. "Go get on the radio to Baghdad and inform the fools there that we have desperate need of reinforcement soldiers here. Tell them what is going on here that we're under attack by a group of unknown soldiers, and get us some help out here quick, fool."

"General al-Zahar, whoever attacked us, has successfully destroyed all our communications between us and Baghdad to and from our headquarters from the outside of the building, sir. I already tried to make contact with Baghdad Command, but all our communications are down across the board, and it's completely impossible for me to raise anyone from Baghdad, sir."

"These lowly attackers have to be the cursed American animals, you jackal ass you. Did you try the portable radio in my private quarters, fool?

The American fools were unable to disarm my portable radio, get on that machine and order reinforcements here immediately." General al-Zahar hissed angrily as he glared at the young Iraqi soldier hovering over him.

"No my General, by Allah's great mercy, I have forgotten about your private radio setup in your room, sir." The young soldier replied as his eyes lightened up, showing the Iraqi General the soldier felt their situation wasn't as hopeless as he first thought it was.

"Go get in there then and get us some help out here, you great fool you. Give me the extra clips for this god cursed weapon of yours that you have in your belt, jackal. Must I tell you everything, you young son of a lowly camel eater you? Get in my room and demand help out here." General al-Zahar snarled hotly, trying his best to get the young soldier in gear.

The scared Iraqi guard handed General al-Zahar the loaded clips for his weapon he had tucked in his belt, and then he backed up and headed for General al-Zahar's private sleeping room.

General al-Zahar felt a lot better about him now that he had an automatic weapon locked in his hands, and he was ready to fight the invading American soldiers on better terms. The Iraqi General began to fire down the steps in short, controlled bursts at anything he saw moving around on the first floor. General al-Zahar was successful in pinning the American attackers down for the time being. But it was not for too long a time though.

The Iraqi guard got to the General's radio and made contact with Iraqi headquarters situated in the heart of Baghdad. When he gave out the alarm to the headquarters, many Iraqi soldiers immediately began piling into the waiting troop carriers moved up to the command center when the call for reinforcements came in. But their orders were held up until their Commanding General first made contact with President Saddam Hussein, and he gave the final word for them to move out against the invaders. No one in Iraq did anything without Saddam Hussein's approval. A General rushed in Saddam's private sleeping quarters and informed the President of Iraq that General al-Zahar and his troops were under attack by some unknown forces in Dawral, and that the General was requesting they send out reinforcements and help from them.

President Saddam Hussein sat up in bed and thought for a moment, and then he barked nastily at the young soldier. "Leave the filthy god cursed camel spider to his foul fate. This will teach him and any other foul cursed soldier in my country never to dare go against my wishes and command. General al-Zahar no longer matters to the people of Iraq, and to me, General. Leave my room at once and have your soldiers stand down until I decide otherwise, fool."

"But President Saddam, General al-Zahar has informed us they were under attack by who he believed are American troops. American soldiers are once again invading our Iraqi soil, sir. It's our sacred duty to Allah to go to the General's aid immediately sir, and kill these god cursed hated invaders of our country, sir."

Iraqi President Saddam Hussein glared harshly at the scared and demanding General for a long moment, but said nothing more to him. This informed the soldier he was not going to come to the aid of General al-Zahar and his trapped troops, and their conversation was over with at this point and time. Unable to get President Saddam's approval for any reinforcements to move out to support al-Zahar, the General bowed his head slightly to his President, and then he backed out of his private living quarters. When the General was out of the room, one of Saddam's Republican Guard bodyguards offered to him with a smirk.

"That was very wise my President, for I fear it's like you stated, sir. The great wisdom of Allah will find a way to punish this renegade officer who dared to embarrass you in front of the peoples of Iraq, and the world, sir. It's good you didn't send us out to arrest the rebel General al-Zahar earlier today as was suggested. Or he would not be involved in this attack by the possible American troops now. You always said the hated American soldiers will come for the great fool Colonel al-Adwani, and it was his god cursed fault for not killing himself, when his mission failed you on his orders to assassinate the worthless American President, sir. You told me when the American soldiers come they'll settle with General al-Zahar for you, sir. You have the wisdom of the great Prophet himself, to have foreseen this attack on the fools, sir. Now I know why you have allowed this lowly filthy camel eater to live, sir."

Saddam completely ignored his guard's remarks, as he simply rolled over and went back to sleep, but not before allowing a slight smile that sealed General al-Zahar's fate.

DAWRAL

Colonel al-Adwani was enjoying Rasha's outstanding pleasures a second time in their room in the General's headquarters, when he heard the heavy weapon fire erupt inside the building. He leaped off her and got behind the bed, using it and her for cover. He grabbed Rasha by the hair and forced her to remain naked on the bed. He was going to use her for a distraction against what was happening in the building. The scared Colonel had no doubt in his mind that the soldiers attacking them were American troops sent to Iraq to take him as a captive and bring him back to the United States. He checked his nine millimeter pistol for ammunition. He had a loaded clip, but no extra rounds for the weapon on his person or in his room. He cursed himself for leaving the AK-47 given to him by General al-Zahar, downstairs.

The Iraqi soldier reported back to General al-Zahar he was unable to get a confirmation from headquarters that President Saddam Hussein was dispatching reinforcement soldiers to aid them in this desperate fight. He offered his fears that Hussein was punishing him, by allowing the American soldiers to destroy them in their headquarters.

General al-Zahar cursed himself and his worthless President as he went back to firing at the shadows he spotted moving about on the first floor of his building. He also realized Saddam Hussein was going to allow them to fight to the death on their own. And if he survived this action, he swore to himself he was going to organize his remaining troops, and march them in the heart of Baghdad, and kill the coward commanding Iraq, and drag his dead body through the streets of the city, so the children can pitch stones at it.

The extremely upset Colonel al-Adwani held Rasha tightly by the hair with one hand, and he aimed his weapon at the closed door of his room with the other. She struggled desperately to get free of the fuming Colonel's harsh grasp of her hair, but she stopped her movements the instant when the Colonel smacked her hard on the top of the head with the heel of his weapon. Al-Adwani could actually feel the building shaking under his feet from the many stun grenades still exploding downstairs in their building. He scanned the small room, hoping he might have had the smarts to have brought a second machine gun inside his room, and he might have forgotten about it until now. There was nothing but his pistol in the room he was trapped in, and he cursed himself again as he continued to stare at his closed door.

Walker and his elite troops ran all over the first floor of the General's headquarters, killing any Iraqi soldiers they come across hiding inside the building. As Baby Tee ran down the hallway and passed by an open door, an Iraqi guard hiding inside the room suddenly charged out of it at the same time, and he crashed head long into her body, and sending both of them tumbling to the floor. By the time Baby Tee stopped rolling on the floor she had her K-bar blade out and she held it at the ready to defend herself against the enemy soldier's attack. She ended up in a crouched and good attacking position, ready to spring into action against the stunned young Iraqi guard who was still struggling to get to his feet.

The Iraqi soldier was careless, and he lost his weapon in the hard tumble, and when he saw the young female soldier glaring wildly at him with the knife held in her hands. He raised his hands over his head and surrendered to the fuming young American female soldier.

The Mutt saw the action going on between Baby Tee and the Iraqi soldier, and he rushed down the hall to assist Baby Tee. He did not hesitate in the least as he ran up to the Iraqi soldier, and fired two rounds right in his face. The Iraqi guard went flying back and up against the wall, and then his body sagged slowly down to his knees, and then he fell forwards towards the floor, dead before his eyes closed for the last time.

"What the fuck did you do that for stupid? He was giving up to me when you shot him dead Mutt. Jesus Christ Almighty man, you didn't have to kill the sonofabitch, Mutt! I had the soldier completely under control and you had to pop him off, dammit. Hell, is Walker going to be plenty pissed off at you for this one, baby." Baby Tee complained angrily at him, as she stared at the dead Iraqi soldier lying on the floor at her feet.

"You heard the fucking orders from Walker, sister. No fricking prisoners on this damn mission honey. We have orders to splash anyone we come across inside this dump, sister." The Mutt growled harshly as he checked Baby Tee's condition. When he saw that she was unhurt, he continued his wild charge down the hallway, firing at anything dressed in an Iraqi uniform.

Baby Tee watched the Mutt run away screaming and firing like a wild man and she shook her head at him slowly. She knew he was right, but she still didn't like killing anyone in cold blood.

The Mutt ran down the narrow hall and crashed into an off side room of the building. CoCo-G caught up with the Mutt and acted as his backup. When he smashed the door off its hinges, he saw what he believed was an enemy soldier standing in the room, and he was aiming a weapon at him, and he emptied his weapon at the standing figure he caught up in his sight. CoCo tried to squeeze into the room with the Mutt, and flipped the light on and saw what the excited soldier fired at, and laughed at him over his mistake. The Mutt stood staring at a full length mirror which he shattered with his rounds. He turned to CoCo and warned him in no uncertain terms.

"You tell anyone about this fucking mess up of mine buddy, and I'll beat you to..."

"Oh yeah man, I'm gonna send a bunch of fucking postcards out about it to everyone I fucking know, asshole. It coulda happened to any one of us during a hot entry into a compromised room, Homes." CoCo fired back as he turned and headed back to the war.

For the most part, Walker and the other American soldiers left the enemy soldiers still trapped on the second floor alone, until they completely secured the entire first floor area of the structure in question first. Slowly, the smoke and weapon fire lessened on the first floor, and Walker was finally able to see the area around him pretty well. He took a few quick breaths in, and then barked in his radio at the rest of the soldiers in the building with him. "I need a fucking head count on all downed fucking organ donors in this dump, people. One of you guys run around and get me that accurate count on the dead. I don't need any fucking smoke blown up my stinking ass by doubling up on counting the dead enemy soldiers either man."

Walker leaned up against the wall and took a brief second to himself and lit up a cigarette, and then blew the smoke over his head and relaxed a little. The Mutt again worked his way to him and spoke in a controlled tone of voice to him.

"Man, we really took it to these stinking jay birds trapped in here, Homes. Talk about getting caught while fricking sleeping on the job man, these dumb shits were no fun at all Walker they went down without a stinking fight. Hey Walker, you wanna buy a stinking Iraqi weapon I just found in here lying on the floor, it's never been fired and only dropped once, man." The Mutt bragged as he turned and looked at Walker for the moment.

A shattered piece of thick wallboard suddenly fell away from the wall, and it bounced off the top of the Mutt's head, causing Walker to grin at his lifelong friend as he stared at him.

"I'm so damn glad that my pain amuses you so fucking much here Homes. Remind me to laugh at you the next time you try and stop a bullet with your fucking ass, man." The Mutt gripped at him as he rubbed the top of his head, and then he checked his hand for signs of blood.

"I wish we had some fricking bone domes (Helmets) with us, stupid. Touchy, touchy, touchy, you betta get out there and kill somebody so you get in a much better fucking mood around here, man. You got any clean underwear on, buddy?" Walker asked the Mutt as he continued to grin at the man and waited for his reply.

"Not anymore Homes." The Mutt retorted with a smirk to Walker.

The large soldier branded Neck, caught up with Walker and crouched down on one knee and griped at him. "Hey man, I'm really glad I made this stinking little journey back to fucking sand land along with the rest of you stinking people, man."

"You're hit man you're fucking bleeding from the damn arm, man." The Mutt snapped as he aimed his chin at Neck's massive arm to draw attention to Neck's slight wound.

"I saw it it's just a stinking nick man." Neck grumbled back, trying to ignore the wound.

"Fuck that line of bullshit tent peg, we're in the fucking arm pit of the stinking world over here, and even a damn hang nail here will fester up on you and get infected in this damn dump, stupid. Go get Blood Clot to have a look at your wound for you, Neck. It seems like we got the first floor of the stinking building secured now, so you betta make certain you take the fricking time to have Blood Clot check out your damn wound for ya, stupid. I don't need you bleeding to death on me out in the damn field, you asshole you. You're just too fucking big to carry your fat ass outta this stinking place, man. I'd need a front end loader to lug your ass outta here if you drop down on me. How many fricking times do I hafta tell you to not get wounded by any of these damn slugs we're after in here, stupid? Dammit you're thick asshole."

"C'mon Walker, whaddaya think I am dammit, a stinking girl who's gonna pass out at the first sight of blood, man?" Neck growled as he swiped as the blood freely running down his arm.

Walker was about to say something else to the huge Neck, when Blind Date walked up behind Neck, and she smacked him upside the head with her hand, and then she complained bitterly as she warned him. "A girl huh? Well Mister Big Ass soldier, I got some sad news for you, you big dumb shit you. We girls take pain a helluva lot better than any of you so called He-men type soldiers do. You better watch your step around here mister, before you finding yourself holding your nuts in your lousy hand for your dumping on us girls from the outfit like this, big boy."

Walker took a closer look at Neck's arm. Neck was right, it did not seem that bad a wound, but nevertheless it was still bleeding and he wanted that stopped immediately as he bellowed out. "Hey Blood Clot." He growled at the Unit's only medic.

"Here Walker. What's up sir?" The medic replied to Lieutenant Walker's calling him.

"Get your ass over here on the double quick man, and check out Neck's arm. Any of you other turds hit or utherwise injured? Where the hell is Ice, I know she's wounded, god dammit."

Blood Clot almost had to climb over the other soldiers clogging up the narrow hall to get at Neck and check him out. When he passed by Walker, the medic reported about Ice's wound. "Hey Walker, I got to Ice already man, she's hurt but not bad enough to stop her from fighting any, sir. I gave her a shot to help her take the stinking pain better, and a booster shot to give her a little extra strength, and I dressed the wound for her afta cleaning it, man. It stopped bleeding already Lieutenant. She still combat capable and on the fucking hunt for us, Homes."

"Out fucking standing man, get working on the big nudge then Blood Clot. I have a stinking feeling we're gonna need every swinging dick and bouncing tit we brought along on this little old turkey shoot with us, man." Walker snapped as he watched Blood Clot go to work on Neck's slightly injured arm. He was right, the wound was nothing to get overly concerned over, and Neck was gripping all the while Blood Clot worked on his arm.

CHAPTER TWENTY NINE

B lood Clot ripped the sleeve off Neck's DCU's, as he grumbled at the much large soldier, and he also grinned at him at the same time. "Oh, you poor little baby got himself a little bitty boo boo here I see, huh big man? I'm gonna give you a pretty little bandage to cover your itty bitty stinking wound with here, my friend."

"Look here blood sucker, I'll give you a little bitty fucking boo boo around your fucking eye if you don't shut the fuck up and fix my damn arm up good and proper for my stinking ass in a hurry it up, asshole. Even though there's a low in the fighting, it's gonna heat up again and I wanna be in the middle of the fighting, soldier." Neck growled angrily at Blood Clot as he did his work on his wounded arm.

"Yeah yeah big man, didn't anyone ever tell you that you're supposed to duck the fuck outta the stinking way of an incoming round, you big dumb slug you. One of these days you'll understand that big man." The medic grumbled at the big man as he continued to grin at him.

"How is the dopey bullet stopper doing Blood Clot? I need his ass active when we assault the second floor of this fucking dump." Lieutenant Robert Walker growled as he lit up another cigarette, and then continued to watch Blood Clot working on his wounded soldier.

"He's doing fine as can be expected sir, there's nothing much here to really worry about though, Lieutenant. I'll know a lot more when I get a better look at the damn wound once we're the hell outta here and I can work on it properly, sir."

By this time all the shooting ended on the first floor of the Iraqi General's headquarters, and most of the smoke and dust lightened up enough, so the American soldiers could see what was going on about them. Every once in a while there would be some firing coming down from the second floor area, but Walker gathered the rest of his elite soldiers around him well out of the way of the new weapon fire.

"He's gonna be fine Lieutenant, the bullet just barely broke the skin on the big dumb jerk, Lieutenant Walker." Blood Clot offered as he sprayed a disinfectant over the wound on Neck's arm, and then covered it with a dressing and taped it down on Neck's arm.

The Mutt closed in as did the rest of the soldiers, when General al-Zahar fired a short burst of rounds at something he thought he picked up moving around downstairs in the building.

Lieutenant Frank Hall, the Mutt was the only one who dared to speak to Walker as if challenging him as he griped at him. "Playful little bastards aren't they, Homes. Okay Kemosabe, how the hell do you propose we get up there and do the rest of these lousy little pricks in, and then make the stinking snatch of our little shit and then get the fuck outta here, man? I'm getting kinda tired of this fricking turd hunt already. I wanna go home and get blind stinking drunk and make love to Blind Date in a real bed this time, man. You know there must be a small Army of screaming Iraqi assholes on their way here from fricking Baghdad to get at our damn asses, and eat us up alive by now. Even though we disabled their known radios and uther communications abilities, one of those stinking turds up there must have a portable radio with'em, and he already made contact with the mother of all rat nests in Baghdad, Walker. We betta do something, and do it fast at that man, before we all find ourselves dick deep in a bunch of new, fanatical screaming A-rabs looking to make it to Paradise for themselves, man."

More weapon fire from General al-Zahar forced the American soldiers to duck down a second time, and then move a little further away from the staircase.

Walker remained leaning up against the wall wearing a shit eating grin, as he said nothing to the Mutt's last gripe, instead he just stared at the complaining Mutt while grinning at him.

EAGLE'S NEST

"Look at the damn fuck he must have something in his stinking pants giving him some pleasure while we're laboring around with these damn Iraqi dudes in here." The soldier branded the Roach complained as he ground his heel into the wood floor, to display he was getting really pissed off over the way the operation was being handled by Lieutenant Walker.

Walker's eyes suddenly glazed over with anger as he snarled harshly at the Roach. "I hope that little stunt of yours betta not have been fricking aimed at my stinking ass there, Homes? If it was pal, I'm gonna rip out your eyes then I'm gonna piss in the empty sockets of your skull for ya, buddy. I'm not here to take any stinking guff from any of you fricking slugs around here, man."

The Roach put his eyes down in a submissive response to Walker's angry threat.

"I didn't think so buster. Where the hell's the Ghost hiding at around here dammit?" Walker snapped, noticing the Ghost was missing from the rest of the group.

"I think he's off to see the stinking wizard, Homes. You never know what the hell that one's up to during most of our operations, man." The Mutt reported to his commanding officer.

"Dammit to hell and all the way back again. I though I told everyone to stick to fucking gether on this operation, dammit. So we don't lose anyone in this stinking mess for Christ sake." Walker roared at the soldiers gathered around him.

"Calm the fuck down some will ya Walker. I got the fricking count on all the hard rocks (dead bodies) we just stacked up so far. We got six down, nine more to go inside this damn dump, man. These damn turds were no fun at all Walker. They dropped like stinking pigeon shit round here, Homes." The Ghost bitched as he joined up with the rest of the group of soldiers.

"That means the bulk of the fucking fighting is still waiting for our asses upstairs of this stinking dump." Walker bitched as he threw his cigarette to the floor, and then stepped on it.

"Yeah man, but you gotta remember they're the ones not heavily armed, Walker. We got their stinking armory intact man, and it seems there were only a few racks missing any damn weapons, man. I checked out the soft targets we got down here man, and I counted three of the missing AK's, and that leaves two more weapons still missing, and I believe they're with the stinking turds up there, Homes. I have no way of knowing what small arms they might have with them though, Lieutenant. How the hell are we gonna hit them, they have the betta elevated position on us Walker?" The Ghost asked as he lit up a cigarette for himself now.

Again, Walker allowed the grin to cross his lips. He knew he gave orders to Sun Tan, and those orders were to create the diversion Walker and his troops needed to assault the stairway, and get at the Iraqi soldiers and their target hiding upstairs in the building as he offered. "What's the status of the fucking armory?"

"I'll answer that question, but only after you clue me in on what the hell's making you act like you're getting the blowjob of your stinking life, buster." The Ghost snorted at the young military officer as he stared at Walker's face, and then he added to his words aimed at him. "You put us in the fricking pickle jar by not going after everyone trapped inside this building at the same time on this operation you know, Homes. Now we're stuck with trying to root the sucker's outta their little stinking ratholes in here, Walker."

"I have a little surprise waiting for those stupid turds hiding up there on the second floor of this dump, Ghost. That's why I'm smiling like this man, I got it covered for you tent pegs, so don't worry about it people."

"Uh-oh, in that case man, I got the armory all wired up for fricking sound, man. Next stop for that mess, the Twilight Zone, Homes." The Ghost announced with a grin, while relaxing some.

"Good work there Ghost, when we leave this stinking dump with our little package all trussed up like a stinking Christmas ham in tow. I want you to blow that shithole sky high for us, man." Walker ordered the other soldier.

"You got it Walker." The Ghost replied proudly to Walker's last orders.

"Oh for Christ sake people, what the hell do I have to do to hear this damn plan of yours, Walker? Blow the shit out of you or something, mister?" Baby Tee suddenly complained in a huff as she kicked Walker on the side of his leg, and then she glared at him.

"That's a good start if you're offering there you know, Tee. I could sure use a blow job right about now, baby." Walker retorted with a wide grin aimed at the pretty young female soldier.

"C'mon Walker, we're wasting valuable time here man. You know Baghdad hasta be sending out a mess of damn reinforcement troops to help protect their lousy puke General here, man. We gotta get the hell outta this stinking place ten minutes ago, Homes." The Mutt growled at Walker, and then he waited for him to go into his act again.

Walker suddenly blew in his radio, and then he barked in it at the soldier stationed on the roof of the structure. "Sun Tan! You still breathing up there, buster?"

"Yo." The soldier replied from his position on the roof of the structure.

"You ready, the Injins down here are getting a little restless on my stinking ass, man." Walker informed his ace in the hole on the roof of the structure.

"Just say the word and it happens right now, Homes. I'm ready to carry out my end of this operation, sir." Sun Tan replied to Walker's question.

"Word." Walker growled in the radio as he kept his eye glued on the Mutt.

"Moving out now, Walker." Sun Tan replied to his new orders as he went in action.

"Okay people, unass yourselves, it's time to place the period at the end of this damn sentence around here, guys." Walker used his powerful back to shove himself off the wall he was leaning against, and then placed his weapon in the attack position in his hands and headed for the staircase leading up to the second floor of the structure.

"Whaddaya you think, Lieutenant. Whaddaya want us to do Walker? You seem like you're gonna do all the bad guys up there in all by your stinking self when we begin our attack against the dumb shits up there, man." Neck complained as he checked the job Blood Clot done on his injured arm, and nodded in approval towards the company medic.

"First off buster, I don't think out loud. What I know is, we're gonna move out and take up our new positions by the stairs heading up just out of reach of the turd shooting down at us guys. When Sun Tan creates his little diversion up there, we're gonna make our stinking move on them up there, people." Walker offered to the rest of his troops.

"Now you're talking some real soldiering for us stinking pukes here, man. Let's go get us some stinking trigger time against these scumbags, people." Baby Tee offered as she lifted her weapon around to its proper firing position, and then she added to her words to her commanding officer. "I'll tell you this much Walker baby, if this little plan of yours works like you think it will. I'm going to give you the blowjob of your natural life, honey."

Walker's troops circled around the staircase just out of sight of General al-Zahar's aim and weapon fire. The Iraqi Commander heard the American soldiers suddenly rapidly moving around downstairs, and he automatically fired a warning burst down at where he felt the American soldiers were bunching up against him. Now, he was trying to conserve his ammunition running low on him.

When the elite soldiers were set in their proper position for attack, Walker hissed into his radio one word. "Now." Then he concentrated his attention towards the staircase leading to the second floor of the compromised building.

Instantly, the machine gun stationed on the roof of the target building exploded, drawing General al-Zahar's attention along with everyone with him towards the roof above them. Sun Tan rolled two fragmentation grenades down the scuttle leading to the second floor. The force of the grenades blew the door of the scuttle off, sending it flying across the narrow hallway. This action forced General al-Zahar to fire at what he perceived was a roof penetration of his headquarters, and the more immediate threat against him and the rest of his soldiers trapped on the second floor of the structure with him. The scuttle area was instantly flooded by AK fire, accompanied by small arms fire by the trapped soldiers.

Sun Tan smiled as he pulled the pin on two stun grenades this time, and then he dropped them down the scuttle. This drew even more weapons fire from the trapped Iraqi soldiers aimed at the small closet from the second floor of the building. The narrow upstairs hallway filled with choking smoke, and the percussion and flash of the grenades going off inside the narrow scuttle.

General al-Zahar was forced to protect two areas from attack against him now. He turned to the one he felt was the most immediate threat to his life at the moment. He moved away from the stairwell, and headed closer to the scuttle area. He tried to look into the destroyed opening to see the first of the enemy soldiers, as they dropped down from the rooftop to attack him. He could not see anything, and he was forced to wait for the inevitable to happen.

The Iraqi civilian residents in Dawral automatically closed their doors and windows, and they moved away from the fronts of their homes to the rear of their homes and hid. They had no idea what was going on in their little town, and they were scared to death by the heavy automatic weapons fire going off about them. Curses, and bitter complaints of stopping the weapons fire, were called out from some of the civilians hiding in their homes. Many believed the Americans were attacking their country to punish their foolish President again. There was nothing they could possibly do to help out the situation, so the civilians just hid in their homes, forsaking their village to the destruction they knew the American soldiers would visit upon it.

When the stun grenades exploded inside the narrow scuttle shaft with a deafening roar, Walker waved his MP-5 at the Mutt and Mother Flanagan, and they both charged up the stairs without thought or hesitation. They did not encounter any enemy fire aimed at them, so they held their fire as they headed for the top of the landing of the second floor. When the Mutt reached the top, he dropped down on the steps and looked down the hallway. An Iraqi soldier suddenly fired at him with a nine mm pistol, the round missed him but it caused the Mutt to fire in his direction. Mother Flanagan leaned up against the wall, and cautiously walked up the steps alongside the prone Mutt, and fired the heavy M-60 machine gun down the hall blind in the other direction, to try and stop them from getting caught in any enemy crossfire.

The two Iraqi guards that accompanied General al-Zahar to protect the scuttle area of the structure, dropped down to the ground hit by the rounds being fired at them from Mother Flanagan's weapon. General al-Zahar jumped behind the two dead soldiers, using their bodies as cover, and he fired at the stairway area now. Mother Flanagan's fire killed the hidden Iraqi soldier in the other direction, and then he turned to lend his fire support to that of the Mutt's.

General al-Zahar had to stop firing because he ran out of rounds in his weapon, and he ejected the empty clip from his weapon, and then slammed his remaining loaded clip home. But the enemy fire coming at him now was so heavy he was forced to stay low until it stopped, or at least it lessened up some, so he could take a chance to return his fire at the enemy American soldiers hiding on the stairwell to the second floor.

Rasha soon regained her consciousness, as she was still forced to remain lying on the bed naked by Colonel al-Adwani's free hand holding on her down by her long hair. She got scared to death by the overwhelming amount of heavy weapon fire going off in the hallway just outside their door, and she began to desperately fight with Colonel al-Adwani again to be released. So she could at least better defend herself some.

Colonel al-Adwani roughly yanked her back on the bed by the hair, and slammed her in the face this time with the side of the pistol. When she was knocked out cold again and he pulled her to the center of the bed. Then he dropped down to the floor by the side of the bed and waited. He knew these American soldiers were after him.

Lieutenant Walker gave another quick movement of his weapon, and Baby Tee and Neck ran up the steps next. Baby Tee jumped over the prone Mutt, and rolled onto the landing and into a room that had its door blown off by the intense weapon's fire going off on the second floor of the building. She immediately checked the room out for any enemy soldiers hiding inside it. Seeing none, she poked her head back out in the hall and fired in the direction the Mutt, Mother Flanagan and now Neck straddling the Mutt still lying on the steps, fired in. Their combined fire was successfully pinning down General al-Zahar and the two Iraqi guards still alive with him. In all, the initial attack killed three more enemy guards, and it pinned down another three defending Iraqi soldiers, including General al-Zahar on the second floor.

The Iraqi soldier who went for the General's radio moments ago, soon returned to the room and he tried again to convince Baghdad Command to send supporting troops out to assist them in this attack by the American soldiers. When the soldier gave up trying to get reinforcements out of Baghdad, he poked his head out of the room and fired at the stairway with his nine mm pistol. His fire instantly drew a wave of lead aimed directly at him. The bullets easily ripped through the wall, door and floor, catching the Iraqi soldier in the heavy hail of death. He tumbled to the floor, hit five times by the return fire from the invading American troops.

"Move fucking up dammit! I want everyone up there right now for crap sake! We gotta get our stinking turd before he does something stupid, and he gets his lousy ass tagged, and then we gotta bug the hell outta this place faster than fast enuf, people." Lieutenant Walker yelled out at the top of his lungs as he got up, and then he also charged up the stairs, followed by the rest of the soldiers of the elite forces bunched up on the first floor of the structure with him. He waited before allowing the elite troops to stack up on the stairs, until he was certain there was no hand grenades in the Iraqi defenders hands. When he realized there was mostly small arms fire aimed at his troops, he decided to commit the rest of his troops to the action.

When the weapon fire stopped coming at the scuttle opening, the American soldier branded Sun Tan cautiously dropped the nine feet down into the narrow opening. He fell to the floor in the closet type structure and used his back against the wall to stop him fall again, he got up on one knee and ten he peeked out of the all but destroyed door frame. Bullets from his own troops were bouncing all around him, and he had to move to the side of the opening to not be hit by his own troop's heavy weapon fire now. The concerned soldier carefully looked out of the closet opening until he spotted the two Iraqi soldier's firing at his fellow troops still bunched up on the stairwell.

Sun Tan aimed his weapon at the first Iraqi guard and fired a short, three round burst at his body. The Iraqi soldier went flying backwards, but Sun Tan did not waste any time watching the soldier slump down to the floor dead. He instantly went after the second Iraqi guard still firing at his fellow soldiers. He fired another short three round burst and killed the second guard who was trying to turn and fire at who was firing at him from behind.

This dead Iraqi soldier fell right across General al-Zahar's body, and the Iraqi General pulled and pushed the body of this dead soldier on top of the other body he was using for cover, and then he turned to his back and fired at the dark shape of the soldier trapped in the narrow scuttle, killing his soldiers from behind him. The General sent five rounds into the opening of the scuttle, hitting Sun Tan with two of them, one in the chest and the other in his neck. Sun Tan dropped down slowly he was dead as his body came to rest on the floor of the narrow closet.

Walker actually ran over the back of the Mutt, and came to a stop on the landing on one knee. He saw the Iraqi soldier firing behind him, and knew he was shooting at Sun Tan. He cursed as he opened fire at the Iraqi soldier shooting at one of his own troops. "Get that mutherfukka at the end of the fucking hallway will ya. He's killing our fucking people, dammit!"

Walker's yell made his troops on the landing fire at General al-Zahar, as he fired at Sun Tan.

The fuming Lieutenant fired as he screamed as he charged wildly at the enemy General, hitting General al-Zahar high up on the shoulder, and driving him backwards some and away from his long weapon, and the bodies he was hiding behind. When he saw the Iraqi shooter go down, he charged right at him. Roaring as he charged the enemy soldier.

Although wounded but the wound was not a life threatening one, General al-Zahar instinctively reached for his pistol lying on the floor under his body. But Walker was on the enemy soldier before he was able to remove the weapon out from under the weight of his body. He kicked the weapon free from his hand as the Iraqi General was able to move it to a firing position, and then kicked the Iraqi General right in the face with his boot, knocking General al-Zahar out cold for the moment.

Walker did not stop as he continued on, until he was looking in the closet that served as the scuttle for the roof area of the building. He cursed when he saw Sun Tan's body lying on his back inside it. One look instantly informed the Lieutenant that Sun Tan was dead.

Many of Walker's troops moved down the hall to check on Sun Tan's, (Sergeant Clifford Saldinger's) condition. Walker turned to them and hissed angrily at the concerned soldiers. "Sun Tan's done for it people, and this fucking prick lying here did him in, dammit."

The shooting stopped for a moment and Buckethead lifted his heavy M-60 machine gun to his hip and aimed it directly at the prone body of General al-Zahar, and then he bellowed to the rest of the elite soldiers standing with him. "Okay people, let's ice this lousy motherfucker's ass and get it over with once and for all. He killed one of us, dammit! That makes him fair game for our fucking revenge, people."

"Let's find out who the fuck this stinking little prick is first, and then we'll ice off the fricking scumbag good and proper, people." Walker said as he looked down the hall, and then he complained at his other soldiers gathering round him. "You fucking birds are starting to bunch up again on my ass, and I don't like it and you people know betta than that, you pack of flaming assholes. We still have a bunch of uther bad guys in here that have to be neutralized. Get on them while I find out who the fuck this lousy motherfucking puke is."

The remaining American soldiers fanned out and started to check out each of the other rooms still protected by closed doors intact. One by one, a soldier from Walker's group would kick down a door while his backup immediately tossed a stun grenade into the darken room. The soldiers were trying to locate and take Colonel al-Adwani in custody alive.

"C'mon Walker, we ain't got the stinking time to waste on this fricking sucka like this, man. Those stinking reinforcement troops from Baghdad hafta be half way on their fucking way here by now, dammit. Let's just kill the dirty little scumbag and then let's get this damn Colonel al-Adwani prick and bug the hell outta this stinking land of sand once and for all, man. I'm sick and tired of walking around in the sand of this dump already, man." The Mutt complained bitterly at Walker as he also leveled his weapon at the prone Iraqi General al-Zahar's face, and then he took careful aim at between his eyes.

"Back the fuck off some dickhead I gotta see who the hell this bag of shit is first, before we ice his ass, man." Walker bent down and pulled General al-Zahar up by his hair, and he shook his head violently by it until his eyes fluttered open. When Walker saw he was half alert, he snarled into the Iraqi soldier's face. "You just cost me one damn good soldier mutherfucker, so you betta get yourself real smart in a fast fricking hurry it up and answer my fucking questions before I skin your ass alive, man. Who the fuck are you ball sack?"

General al-Zahar looked deeply into the enraged and burning eyes of the young American soldier for a long moment, before saying to him just as nastily as this soldier was addressing him in perfect English. "Take your god cursed foul hands off me immediately, or I'll have you hanged by your filthy feet. I'm a very important General in the Iraqi military, and any harm to me will be answered by thousands of Iraqi soldiers seeking their revenge upon the heads of you and every one of your lowly soldiers who have invaded my country again, American soldier. It shall be the civilians of your foul country, who'll pay dearly for any and all harm that befalls me and the rest of my troops."

"You're pissing up the wrong fricking tree here fella, but I must admit it buster. You got me shaking in my boots the way you're barking at my ass like that, man. Damn, I think I mighta just shit myself over the stinking wasted threats you're aiming at my ass, buster. I'll repeat to you in case you didn't hear me right the first time around, scumbag. Then, I'm gonna take your fucking head offa your damn shoulders for you, and then I'll piss down your stinking throat for ya ass, pal. Who the fuck are you, Mac?" Walker growled right in General al-Zahar's face as he pulled his head up so close that General al-Zahar actually felt the brush of Walker's beard, and his breath on his cheek.

General al-Zahar announced proudly, while trying to show absolutely no fear whatsoever towards this young and most threatening and huge American figure, who was glaring wildly back at him. "Filthy American pig, I am General Hassan al-Zahar of the well feared Republican Guard of Iraq, and I demand to know why you filthy infidels and jackals chose to attack me in my own homeland, American jackal. This is an invasion of the independent nation of Iraq that you and the rest of your cursed lowly gangsters have committed here. I shall bring charges against you and your foul nation, and all the hated soldiers involved in this uncalled for invasion of Iraq in the United Nations, and then I'll allow them fools to melt out your just and final punishment for this god cursed invasion of Iraq. I'll have you lowly sons of camels hunted down like the dog eaters and criminals you are, and then be brought to justice for this..."

"Hey man I just farted mutherfucka, and that's as close as I'm gonna get to my giving a shit over the load of crap you're aiming at my ass. It's too bad for you that you're who you say you are, you asshole you." Walker released the hold on General al-Zahar's hair, and rose to his feet and hissed down at the Iraqi. "Look scumbag, I have a hundred stinking reasons to send you on your fucking way to Paradise, pal. My government informed me they wouldn't be too upset if you got a fatal boo boo during this operation, man.

"You know, like hit by a fricking drive by bullet or something like that, fucker. But the best reason I can come up with to give me a clear conscious for offing your stinking ass, buddy. Is you just dusted off one of my favorite turds, man. You're now just meat for the worms, scumbag. Give my regards to Muhammad, maybe you can explain to Him why you're such a cold blooded murderer, prick face. Allah might not be done with you buster, but I sure as hell am, pal!" Walker leveled his MP-5 at General al-Zahar's chest and fired until his clip was empty, splattering his body all over the second floor landing.

"Whoa, that was real cold blooded dude. He's deada than fucking Elvis, man. I wished you woulda gave me the stinking honor of offing the lousy little scumbag though, Walker. Sun Tan was a brother, and his death shoulda been revenged by another stinking brother, man." The Mutt complained as he fired a few extra rounds into al-Zahar's body, just to satisfy his own need for revenge against the dead man.

Lieutenant Walker did not respond to the Mutt's angry words, as he kicked General al-Zahar's body out of anger for the last time, and then he shoved the Mutt forward with his weapon, forcing him to turn with the pressure he forced on him. As he headed towards the rest of the gathered troops, he realized too many of the soldiers were bunched up again in one area, while leaving his flank area relatively unguarded and unprotected, and he bitched at the rest of the specialized soldiers. "Look people, we have most everything under fucking control here. Bucket, I want you to take Blind Date, Roach, Siberia, CoCo and Snatch and linkup with the stinking Hunter and the Ghost stationed outside the damn building, and setup in order to betta defend our fucking position against any possible Tango (Enemy) reinforcements coming from Baghdad to help these cocksuckers out here, man.

"Grab Sun Tan's body while you're at it and get him outside and prepare him properly for travel, man. We don't leave our wounded or dead behind to be picked apart by these fucking lousy sand swimming bastards. No telling if they might cook and eat his ass. The rest of you slugs, we're gonna bust into the rest of the rooms on this floor and find our missing fucking turd. The faster we get this lousy dude in our custody, the faster we can get the hell outta this stinking dump once and for all. Let's get fucking hot people as much as it seems like it, the stinking game's not over for our asses just yet, people. Charlie Mike (Continue Mission)."

Walker watched as both the Roach and CoCo took Sun Tan's body carefully out of the narrow scuttle with respect, and then they carried him out of the building with them. All the time he watched, he kept an ear open to listen for any outside weapons fire. He was surprised no Iraqi reinforcements from Baghdad had showed up at their position after all the time he was working inside the General's headquarters. He felt they were no more than fifteen minutes away from the nearest Iraqi Military Base stationed just outside the country's capital city. He was not sorry the enemy reinforcements were dragging their feet with getting to the other Iraqi soldiers he was slaughtering, and he was starting to lean towards the belief that maybe the reinforcement soldiers were afraid to engage his small invasion force.

When the soldiers picked to protect the troops were outside the building, Walker barked at his remaining troops inside the structure. "I want three man teams hitting the damn rooms left unsearched on this fucking floor. Remember, we wanna take this fucking turd alive if possible, and let the President take a shit on his stinking puss if he wants too. Let's get a fucking move on it we're doing pretty well so far. If we have to fight any reinforcements, everything's gonna get worse that a shit sandwich on a humid day. Okay, let's move out people! And remember, there's no Chicken Switch (Abort Button) for this operation, we have to see it to its conclusion."

Walker looked down the hallway he knew was not fully secured yet, and counted four closed doors remaining secured. He basically knew the room Colonel al-Adwani was hiding in, but he had to clear out all the other rooms before they hit his. In case there might be any Iraqi stragglers hiding in any of the other rooms. He did not need any unaccounted enemy Iraqi soldiers coming popping out of a room after they passed by it, and creating new problems for them.

"Baby Tee, how the fuck you doing honey?" Walker asked the pretty female soldier.

"Hot as a firecracker as always, Walker baby. Why honey?" She questioned Walker.

"As you always are baby. I want you, McNip, and Wacko to hit the first closed door on the left hand side of the stinking hall, little sister. Mutt, you, Neck and Mother Flanagan leap frog by Tee's team, and you guys hit the second fucking closed door on the right side of the damn hall, and make your hot entry into that fucking room. We'll jump over the third room, and Boot Camp, you and Ice. Hey how the hell you doing Ice? How's your stinking wound doing, sister?"

"I'm still able to pull my weight around here, if that's what you're asking me, Walker."

Some of the specialized soldiers called out 'Ooorah', to Ice's defiant response to Walker.

"Fine, then you help Boot Camp and Blood Clot out clearing the last room of this dump out for me, honey. I'm depending on you to keep those two assholes outta any fucking trouble, sister. I don't need any more of our people going down because of this damn turd hunt, girl. When we have these rooms secured, Neck and Mother will regroup with me, and we'll hit the last room and collect our little missing shithead. Then we'll get the hell outta here, I'm getting kinda tired with sucking up all the sand in this dump anyway. Mutt, once your team secures the second room, you're form up on me, and we'll hit door three and collect out stinking prize. Let's get moving people, our job isn't finished yet."

"That's great with my ass Walker, I was gonna ask Ice to marry me anyway you know man. It's cool to work with her purdy little ass on any mission, Walker. She's a real good soldier, man." Blood Clot offered as he moved nearer to Ice's side. He was joking, but he wanted to be with her so he could keep a close eye on her wound, and how she was doing during this engagement. Walker knew right off what Blood Clot was doing, and that's why he assigned him to Ice's squad in the first place.

Ice turned to Blood Clot and offered to him with a beautiful smile. "I'm warning you Blood Clot. Don't get too involved with me honey. I'll only cheat on you baby."

"That's okay, just as long as you don't tell anyone about it, baby." Blood Clot retorted with a warm smile at the wounded female soldier.

"I'm so happy I made this little journey to sand land, I could just drop a fucking log right here, man. The wolf's gonna prowl to fucking night, and the stinking monkey is gonna pay for it real bad, people." The Mutt snarled and chambered a round as he slammed a fresh clip in his weapon after ejecting the half empty one and added. "Let's go get us this lousy little fuck."

Walker held back a little and provided backup for the other attacking groups, as he watched the units quickly move out to hit their assigned rooms. Once Baby Tee, McNip and Wacko aligned themselves properly against the wall near the first door, he tensed up a little. He watched as the team made their HEAT or High Entry Assault Team attack of the room, and the remaining teams leap frog over the rest of the first assaulting team.

Baby Tee was positioned just to the right of the closed door and she was leaning against the wall, she removed a stun grenade from her Alice harness and pulled the pin on it. When she was ready, McNip got in front of the door and prepared to tackle the door like an offensive linebacker would attack a fleeing quarterback on the ballfield. Baby Tee gave him the quick nod, and McNip crashed into the door, his weight easily ripping the door from it hinges.

McNip allowed his momentum to carry him forward and he fell into the dark room, and instantly dropped to the floor, and then Baby Tee pitched in the stun grenade in right behind him. Wacko followed the grenade in the room, and he fired into the mayhem, before the two Iraqi soldiers trapped inside the room had a chance to react against the sudden and violent intrusion. Wacko's rounds ripped into the two enemy guard's bodies, killing both of them, before the Iraqi defenders could even aim properly at the prone McNip lying on the floor.

"Good job Wacker, you just iced the two turds hiding in there, man." McNip groaned from the floor, and then he gave the thumbs up signal to the other soldier, and McNip then rolled over on his side, and looked up at the rather excited Wacko. Baby Tee was still standing directly behind McNip, and she was already checking the room out with her sharp eyes. She wanted to make certain there were no other enemy Iraqi guards still hiding inside the room against them.

The Mutt, Neck and Mother Flanagan gathered by the second closed door, as the last assault team passed them and took up positions by the remaining closed door. He was picked to attack this door, because he was larger than Mother, and Mother Flanagan was going to be the killer this time, and the Neck the pitcher of the stun grenades into the room. The assault went off like clockwork, with the Mutt ending up lying on the floor, and Mother spraying the interior of the room with heavy arms fire. No enemy troops were hiding in this room.

When Colonel al-Adwani heard weapon fire in the room directly next to his, he again thumped Rasha on the head with the heel of his weapon, to make certain she was still out cold. He was prepared to throw Rasha's body at the attacking American soldiers, so he could get a clear shot at at least one of the Americans, before he was killed in the fight against the hated invaders. The Iraqi Colonel believed the Americans were there to kill him, not to take him prisoner and bring him back to the United States to stand trial. Once he was certain Rasha was unconscious again, he released his grip on her hair and dropped down behind the bed. Using Rasha's body not only for a diversion, but also as a sort of human shield from the bullets he knew was going to be soon searching for his body in the room.

As the heavy weapon fire next door stopped, Colonel al-Adwani cursed Saddam Hussein, his country, and most of all, the United States for commanding such a powerful military presence not only inside his country, but over the entire Middle East. He drew in his breath while trying to get his breathing and trembling hands under control. He carefully poked his head just above the bed, and aimed his weapon at the door to his room, and then he waited for the assault of his room and against him began. He had no doubt the enemy soldiers would check this room because they were sweeping the entire second floor of the building.

Sweat poured down his face and in Colonel al-Adwani burning eyes, as he strained to keep his emotions in check and his hands steady. In his mind, he already saw the hated American soldiers smashing down his door, and firing wildly at him. This terrible thought fueled his mounting rage against the invaders. He made up his mind if he was going to die on this night he was going to take as many American lives he could with him. He thought of offering Muhammad the souls of the cursed American troops he was prepared to kill, hoping this would force Muhammad to open the gates of Paradise for him, and raise him to the level of a hero in the afterlife. As he set him mind to defend himself, the American soldiers outside went about their deadly business of eliminating all support Colonel al-Adwani hoped would come to his aide.

The Iraqi Colonel al-Adwani thought about throwing himself out the window of the second floor, hoping to survive the fall and landing on his feel, and then make good his escape to the vastness that made up the Iraqi desert. He got up and cautiously went over to the window, always checking behind him as he moved in the large room, in case the American soldiers charged in, before he was protected. He cursed when he noticed more of what he took as the American soldiers running around outside the building, as if they were not afraid of nothing, and taking up new positions of defense around his building. By their actions, he realized they were American troops, because all the time he lived in Iraq, he never saw any of his troops act in such a professional manner.

Residing himself he was trapped inside the building he reluctantly returned to the bed, after fighting the overwhelming want to fire at the American soldiers he picked up moving about outside the building. After checking on Rasha to make certain she was still unconscious, he dropped to the floor again, and readied himself to defend his life against these invading infidels.

Gone from his mind was the glory of dying for his cause, and for Allah's sake. His mind raced wildly, searching for a possible way out of his present dilemma, for a second he actually thought about waking Rasha, and then order her help protect his life. But judging by her past actions of late, he knew he could no longer trust her, or rely on her support. The Iraqi Colonel believed once Rasha saw the American soldiers attacking them she would turn on him, offering his life to the American troops for her own. He looked at her lying unconscious on the bed with loathing etching his eyes, hating her, and also blaming her for the terrible position he found himself trapped in with the invading troops gathering in the hallway before his room.

Colonel al-Adwani hated Rasha as much as he hated President Saddam Hussein and General al-Zahar now. He did not realize it, but he hated everything and one, especially the United States and her soldiers. His whole life was built upon many years around hatred, until he knew no other emotion. He enjoyed no other emotion, and this was his sole driving force in life. He wanted to take his revenge against the world for the life he was forced to endure while living in Iraq. A life of wants and constant disappointments, a life so cruelly filled with no home life, his wife and children had no love for him, and murder and deceit replaced their love and respect. Again, the Colonel drew in his breath to help steady his rattled nerves as he prepared his mind and body for the inevitable, his own death, and the blessed release it offered from the hatred of his life.

Outside the room in the hallway, when the Mutt, Neck, and Mother Flanagan disappeared in the room they were assigned to secure, Lieutenant Walker moved up and took position by the room he was certain the wanted Colonel al-Adwani was hiding in. The Lieutenant waited and watched as Ice and her team setup to hit the remaining room. Ice was the pitcher of the stun grenades this time around, while Boot Camp aligned his massive body up with the closed door. Blood Clot was the sprayer of death on this assault team.

Boot Camp launched his body at the closed door, knocking it down and splintering the wooden door, and the attacking soldier ended up lying on the shattered door remains on the floor. Instantly, Ice tossed a stun grenade into the small room. Blood Clot then charged in the room also and fired a spray of round. He actually ran over the back of Boot Camp who was still lying on the floor, to gain entry into the room. There was some return fire this time.

There were two young Iraqi soldiers hiding inside this room, along with the last missing AK-47 assault Kalashnikov rifle. The two enemy soldiers were set and ready for the American assault team to hit their room, and the one fired wildly at the charging figure of a soldier crashing into the room. If everything when off as prepared for by the Iraqi soldiers hold up inside the room, Blood Clot would have surely found himself caught up in their line of deadly fire. But when Ice heard the first round from the AK go off, she immediately reacted and sent her foot flying into the dark room.

The blow from her foot hitting Blood Clot on the back and sending him falling forward almost right on top of the prone Boot Camp, saving his life. Ice instantly reacted by tossing another stun grenade deeper into the dark room, actually having it land behind the two Iraqi defenders. Ice next spun her MP-5 around her body and caught it in a good firing position. She jumped in the door and fired into the boiling massive of smoke billowing up in the confining narrow room.

Windows shattered in the room from the bouncing rounds, and the percussion from the stun grenades going off, as the furniture was violently ripped apart in the smallish room, and anything made of glass, shattered. Even the walls of the room were destroyed by the hard hitting action. Screams from the two Iraqi soldiers, mixed in with those of the American attackers, as both sides tried to muster their inner strength, and continue the fighting against each other. The dancing of her weapon in her arms caused Ice's wound to hurt her like hell again. But she was not going to allow it to stop her from firing no matter what, until she was certain the threat against her two fellow soldiers in the room was handled. Ice stared intensely into the dark room as she continued to fire in it. She was searching for any sign of the two Iraqi soldiers moving around inside it.

Blood Clot decided to roll off Boot Camp's back, and then he got up on his side and started to fire at the muzzle flashes he picked up going off inside the room, and hidden in the cloud of smoke filling it. Blood Clot's nose bled from the heavy percussion of the stun grenades going off inside the room as was Boot Camp's, but he ignored the blood as his eyes, his weapon and his rounds searched the darkness of the room for the enemy shooters who fired at them. His fire drew the Iraqi soldier's weapon's fire from the door to the room, giving Ice the opportunity to easily locate and then kill the enemy shooter, or shooters.

Ice saw the muzzle flashes from the enemy's weapon as the Iraqi soldier turned to what he conceived as the more immediate threat against his life, Blood Clot. Ice was in control of herself and her weapon, as she carefully aimed and then she squeezed the trigger. Her MP-5 danced violently in her arms again, as it spat out the little harbingers of death. As she emptied her entire clip, the return fire from the Iraqi soldier ended when she saw his weapon go flying in the air, as his body went tumbling backwards and his limp body crash into the far wall of the room. The Iraqi soldier was dead long before his body stopped twitching its dance of death.

When Blood Clot saw the Iraqi soldier get knocked down by Ice's weapon fire, he immediately went in action himself, and he turned to the second Iraqi guard still firing into the chaos and madness of the room with a pistol. This guard held one ear with his free hand, while he had his eyes closed and fired wildly, allowing his weapon to be forced up and down and side to side by his firing blindly. This Iraqi soldier was scared to death, and Blood Clot knew this nut was not going to hit anyone by firing the way he was doing, only by dumb luck would ever make him successful. Blood Clot carefully aimed at the Iraqi fool, and then he squeezed off a control burst of five rounds, instantly killing the last Iraqi soldier defending the compromised room, and ending the mini war going on inside the all but destroyed room.

Boot Camp rolled over on his right side, and then he got up on one knee and crawled over to the shattered door frame over the rubble covering the floor. He poked his head in the hallway, and gave Walker the thumbs up signal as he sucked in large amounts of fresh air in his lungs, and then he said with a smirk. "Hey man, they're dropping like fricking pigeon shit in here my friend. They ain't any fucking fun at all man the assholes die to damn easy Homes."

While Boot Camp complained to Walker, he also made certain he did not call out any soldier's name, for fear of any living Iraqi soldiers hearing it, and then be able to identify the soldiers later on as Americans, once they left the area after they took the Iraqi Colonel in custody. Ice and Blood Clot were busy securing the last room, and he made sure no one else was hiding in the room that could possibly harm them.

The assaults on the rooms on the second floor of the Iraqi General's headquarters, seemed to take a short life time to accomplish, but in reality it was over in less than a heartbeat. When Lieutenant Walker was certain all the other rooms of the building but his were secured. He made a few quick hand movements, and the Mutt, Mother Flanagan and Neck immediately moved over to his side, to assist him and his assault on the remaining room in the building.

Just as Walker was about to throw himself against the closed door, his radio went off, startling him for a brief moment, and also causing him to bitch at the talker over it. "For Christ sake, what the fuck is this now, dammit! You just broke my fricking concentration on what the fuck I was doing over here, dammit." He nearly roared in a low tone in the radio.

"Take it fucking easy Lieutenant it's me Hunter, man." The pointman replied in his radio.

"Shit, okay, are you taking any pop out there man? Are the stinking enemy reinforcements from the mother of all rat's nest hitting your position yet, man? Are they on their way here?" Lieutenant Walker asked, fearing the Hunter was reporting he was engaging a large number of enemy troops sent out to assist General al-Zahar and his trapped troops from Baghdad.

"No man, and that's what's bugging the living shit outta my ass on me, man. I don't have any fricking tickies (lunatics) crawling all over my damn ass out here yet, Homes. Walker, I see no one coming from fricking Baghdad towards us either man. I can see the damn lights from the stinking capital, but I see no movement of any troops heading our way yet, man. I wonder if the king shit back there in Baghdad is gonna allow these dopey little turds to bite the fucking bullet, without offering them any possible support, man. If he does, it's a pretty unique way to eliminate your stinking competition in this madhouse of a shit filled nation, Homes. This stinking little prick running this back asswards country, is colder than I thought he was, man. I don't know how the hell the dumb shit's gonna ever command his stinking troops any longer, if he refuses to come to their damn aide when needed, Lieutenant. This madman is even worse that I first thought he was, man. He sucks shit outta a dead dog's ass, Walker."

"Are you complaining about his lack of support for his lousy troops for this operation, Hunter?" Walker smirked in his radio at the point soldier.

"No way in hell am I complaining about the head asshole not wanting to help out his fellow stinking soldiers we're taking out of the picture here, Walker. I'm just wondering what the fuck's going on around here, that's all man." The Hunter replied a little excited, as he continued to scan the area leading from Baghdad, to where he was standing.

"Look pal, you're not out there to wonder about any stinking thing around here but the success of our fucking operation, or use your fucking head for that matter, buddy. You're out there to protect our stinking flank for this damn mission, and to also make certain we don't get cut off from each uther either, man. I was just about to go after our missing package in this stinking dump before you interrupted my ass, soldier." Lieutenant Walker bitched hotly at the other pointman stationed outside the building.

"Then why the fuck are you wasting your time talking with me for, get to it then Walker. And while you're at it my friend, try and find a little personality in the process, man." The Hunter grumbled angrily over his radio as he broke off the communication with the Lieutenant operating inside the building.

CHAPTER THIRTY

Lieutenant Robert Walker ignored the mild rebuff just fired at him from the angry Hunter, as he prepared to assault the door again. This time he was stopped by the Mutt, who held his hand out in front of Walker's face.

"What the fuck's this shit about now Homes! What's bugging your stinking ass now, buddy?" He growled as he glared in the eyes of the Mutt as he waited for him to talk up.

He tried a quick smile on Walker, but he quickly realized it was a waste of time, and he offered in a rush of words. "Hey Walker, if we go charging wildly into that damn room, man. I don't see how in the hell we're gonna take this stinking slob in alive, Homes. He's gonna force us to off his fucking ass if we do it that way, man. I know I would if I was in his position, rather than becoming some stinking prisoner for us."

"You go a point, whaddaya suggest we do about it dog man?" He grumbled, while thinking to himself that the Mutt was probably right in his way of thinking on this assault of the room.

"Why the hell don't you try and talk the dumb prick outta his fricking rat's nest first, Homes. Promise the dumb mutherfucker the stinking world, if it'll get the lousy little prick outta there in one piece for us, man. We gotta try and take him in a fucking live, Road Kill." The Mutt tried a second smile on Walker, and this time he smiled back. The Mutt was also using the soldier's unit tag names so the Iraqi Colonel did not pick up any of their true names.

Walker thought about what the Mutt offered for a moment, and then decided. He backed off a few feet from the door, and then he looked at Neck ordered. "Mutt got himself a good idea for the first time in his stinking life, man. Neck, get over to the left side of the door and stand ready with your deer slayer shotgun, man. Mother, you and the Mutt get over to the right of it and give me some stinking elbow room while you're at it. I'm gonna try and talk this flaming asshole the hell outta there in one fucking piece. If he's stupid about it man, I want Neck to blow a fucking hole in the damn door, and then you and the Mutt toss in a few crash bangs. (Stun grenades) If the dopey ass doesn't wanna come out of there real peaceful like, once those babies go off we'll assault the damn room against him.

"If we crash into the room, I want everyone to hold their stinking fire until the last possible moment. Don't get me wrong troops I don't want anyone taking a fucking round for God and old glory here. I wanna try and take this lousy little prick in alive if at all possible. But if any of you don't like the stinking position you might find yourselves in inside the room, take the stinking prick out toot sweet, and we'll take his head back to the Boss, and let him piss on it if he wants."

Walker stopped giving out orders and stood in front of the last closed door on the second floor landing of the target building, just as the Neck unslung his standby weapon, a Savage, ten gauge pump shotgun, loaded with double odd buck. He set the weapon in place against his shoulder and carefully aimed it at the center of the door, and then he waited for Walker's signal to fire. Walker moved a little further away from the door, in case the Neck had to fire his weapon at it. He knew the scatter shot Neck had loaded in the weapon would flare out, and he did not want to get hit by any heavy lead pellets while he waited to get in the room.

Walker was not a fool by any means of the word, and he knew better than to stand directly in front of a closed door, trying to talk some possibly heavily armed lunatic on the other side of that door, out of the room peaceful like. He moved to his right side of the door, and joined the Mutt and Mother Flanagan, using the wall of the hallway as a sort of safety barrier between them and the Iraqi Colonel hiding in the last unsecured room on the second floor of the dead Iraqi General's headquarters. This fool was thought to be heavily armed and extremely dangerous, and he was waiting for them to attack the door against him, so he could fire and try and kill a few of them before he was killed by their weapon fire. Walker drew in a breath, and then he bellowed out at the Iraqi Colonel known to be trapped inside the room in a commanding tone.

Lieutenant Robert Walker moved to where the Mutt, (Lieutenant Frank Hall), and Mother Flanagan, (Sergeant Richard Flanagan) stood in the narrow hall, and they both gave him the room he needed to get around them easily. He leaned closer to the door hiding Colonel al-Adwani from view, and banged on it heavily with his fist. The banging echoed throughout the hall and upstairs, as Walker called out in a husky tone. "Hey shithead trapped inside the room, I know you're in there fucker. I wanna talk to ya face to face like man. I think enough people died already on this stinking day, for us to wanna put a period to the end of the killing. There's no reason for you to add yourself to the fricking mix, man. C'mon Colonel al-Adwani, give it up for me will ya man." He banged on the door again and then waited for a reply.

When Colonel al-Adwani heard the American voice in the hall calling out to him, he ducked behind the bed, and concentrated his aim at the center of the door, expecting the foolish American to come crashing through the door at any moment. He was stunned this enemy soldier knew his name and rank, and found himself wondering why he was offering him life during this situation. Taking a second to think about it, the reason seeped in his mind and he growled barely over a whisper. "These god cursed kaniths (fuckers) want to take me alive, so they can bring me to their cursed country. To be paraded before the gawking American pigs like a trophy before their fools of civilians, so they can throw rocks at me before they kill me. I have sad news for these foolish American soldiers. They'll never take me out of my country alive, never. I am no one's trophy, to be showed off before their gawking civilians before they kill me."

Colonel al-Adwani's mind scream in his ears not to allow himself to be taken alive by the American troops obviously gathered outside his room, no matter what he had to do to avoid being captured by them. Sweating and shaking hands forced al-Adwani to shift his weapon to his left hand, while he wiped his right hand on the sheet of the bed by the unconscious Rasha's head. Only when Walker pounded on the door for a third time, did his thoughts come back to reality, and what was threatening him from outside in the hall of a building. He drew in his breath deeply, and then he called out as nastily as he could at the voice on the other side of the door.

"Blif air ab tizak!" Al-Adwani barked out, and then he fired three rounds from his nine mm pistol through the door, hoping to hit the American soldier speaking to him from the hallway.

The bullets ripping through the interior door, and caused Walker to jump back a few feet more, as he leaned against the wall for added protection, and then he turned to the Mutt and asked him. "What the fuck did the dirty little bastard say to my ass, man? This fricking pigeon shit gibberish they speak around here, don't make any stinking sense to me buddy."

The Mutt shrugged his shoulders at Walker, because he did not know what the enemy Colonel said to him. But Mother Flanagan leaned away from the wall so he could see around the Mutt, and looked at Walker as he answered the question he just asked the Mutt. "Hey man, the dopey little turd told you a thousand dicks in your ass, man."

"Oooooh brother, I'd bet that'd hurt ya, big guy. What are you going to do now, oh fearless leader?" Baby Tee offered with a sexy purr over the unit radio, as she listened to every word being said by the other soldiers about to make their last forced entry in the room.

"That's from someone who knows how it must feel I bet." The Mutt fired back in his radio at the female soldier.

"Fuck you in the ear and I said ear, Mutt. When this mess is over with buddy, I'm going to kick the crap out of you all by myself, dog man." Baby Tee growled nastily in the radio at the soldier, highly upset over the way the Mutt just spoke to her over the small radio.

"Anytime, anywhere Baby." The Mutt retorted with a huge grin.

"Jesus Christ man, can't you ever be serious for once in your wasted life, man? Cut out all the bullshit will ya man, we got us a fucking problem here Mutt." Walker again leaned against the wall trying to figure out his next move. He had al-Adwani where he wanted him, isolated, and locked in a controlled no win situation, and he did not want to lose him after accomplishing so much during this mission. He again turned to the Mutt and warned. "I'm gonna try this shit once more and see where it gets me with the dumb mutherfucker in there man, hey Neck."

"Yo man I got ya man. What's up, sir?" The large soldier replied to Walker as he leaned away from the wall to see his face from the other side of the door they were about to hit.

Walker glared at the huge man because he hated the word 'yo' with a passion, and then he continued in a whisper at the huge man. "I'm gonna wrap on the fricking door again. If the dopey fuck replies in the same way he did the first time around, I don't want ya to wait any longer, man. Blow a fricking hole in that damn door as soon as you hear the fuck's stupid reply to my ass, man." Lieutenant Walker turned back to Mother Flanagan and the Mutt and added to his orders for the other soldiers.

"Mutt, once Neck opens a fricking hole in the damn door I want you and Mother to flood it with crash bangs. I want four in there before the first one pops off you guys. Everyone in that damn room has to be put to fucking sleep before we make entry into the damn place. It's the only way we're gonna get this lousy little prick outta there alive and in one piece, maybe he might be bent up a little. But who the fuck cares about that as long as he's still alive and kicking and we can drag his stinking ass back to the States for the Boss, man. We have permission to bend him up a might by General White, but he wants him still breathing if at all possible."

The Mutt and Mother Flanagan nodded at their commanding officer, and then he turned to Neck, and nodded at him. The Mutt and Mother looped their weapons over their backs to get them out of their way, and then they removed a pair of stun grenades apiece from their Alice straps and pulled the pins on the grenades, and held them ready one in each hand. They moved slightly away from the wall, so they could get by Walker, and pitch the grenades into the opening Neck was going to force in the door.

He moved nearer to the door and then he reached out and banged on it again from the hinge side, and then he took a quick step back a few feet, in case the Iraqi Colonel fired at the door a second time, as he called out to the trapped Iraqi Officer. "That was pretty fucking stupid on your damn part there, Colonel al-Adwani. I'm trying to keep your ass alive and you're trying to force me to take you out if you continue to fire a weapon at me, buddy. C'mon man, I thought you were smarta than that, Colonel. Look, I don't wanna kill ya ass in there man. I just wanna talk to you for a few minutes that's all Colonel. What the hell are you afraid of to just talk to me for a few moments, man?"

"Bouse Tizi! Foolish American filth, if you want me come get me, even if you only want to talk with me. I know how you cursed American jackals talk to someone, I saw how you American dogs talk to soldiers you hold prisoner in our jails in Iraq. You and your foul jackal friends better be prepared to meet your God. I'm prepared to kill anyone who tries to enter this foul room, American jackal. Go back to your god cursed country of lowly infidels, and report to your dung eating President, that Colonel, Abdulaziz Majd al-Adwani, was not afraid to die as the soldier I am, for what I believed in, filth born from a camel's arse." Al-Adwani fired at the door, one round. He was getting real low on ammunition, and he was trying to save some of what little ammunition he had for the fight of his life. He stared at the door, waiting for their next move from the American soldiers in the hallway.

Walker shook his head at the display of balls al-Adwani offered as he held up his hand and he stopped Neck from firing at the door. Then he turned to Mother Flanagan and asked him. "What the fuck does Ballsie frigging Tazi mean? I wish these lousy little cocksuckers would talk English and make it easy for my ass."

"You said it wrong man, but it roughly means kiss my ass though, Road Kill." Flanagan smiled at Walker as he saw the expression change on his face, and he knew Walker was fuming at the Iraqi dude trapped in the room, and he wanted him in the worse way now.

"This lousy cocksucka in there got himself a pair of stinking balls alright. Neck, I'm gonna try this once more on the damn asshole, man. If it doesn't work, do it and we'll go in and get the dumb fuck the hell outta there." Walker ordered Neck on the other side of the door over the radio. He was using the radio to communicate with Neck, because he was at least seven feet away from him, and he did not want the Iraqi to hear what he was telling him to do next.

Neck nodded as his hands tightened on the shotgun as he aimed it at the door before him.

"Hey Colonel, you have a real good fucking way with all the stinking big words pal. It's nice to know you use the right lingo from my so called land of sin, buddy. I'm really impressed by your stinking balls, man. Real tough, but it still doesn't change the reason why I'm out here, Colonel al-Adwani. Alls I want is your signature on a slip of paper, stating you masterminded the fucking attack on my Boss. If you give me that much pal, I'll let you live and be outta your hair and this country of yours quicker than the sweat can dry on your stinking face, man. Whaddaya say to my offer pal? You wanna make this mess easier on everyone concerned out here or what?" He stepped away from the door again in case al-Adwani fired a third time. He waited for what seemed like a short lifetime for the Iraqi to reply to his last offer.

For a brief second, al-Adwani thought about what Walker offered him. True, he wanted to live and do another attack against the United States' interests. But his mind warned him the American soldiers would never have chanced invading his country, just to get a slip of paper with his name printed on it. Admitting he was the one who ordered the death of their hated and cursed President. He knew if he gave the American soldiers what they wanted from him, they would kill him, or maybe drag him back to the United States to stand trial.

The confused Iraqi Colonel had no intention of spending the rest of his life rotting in an American jail, as the old Sheik was doing. He ejected his clip, and counted four rounds remaining in it. He slammed the clip back home and aimed at the door, knowing he only had five rounds left to protect his life, and then he called out angrily. "Ebh el Metanaka, filthy American dog. I have no intention of surrendering to you Kanith. (Fucker) I'll fight you to my death for the sake of Allah, and my country's fate, fool."

Walker leaned forward until he could see Mother's face. Once looking at him Flanagan replied, knowing what Walker wanted from him. "He called you a sonofabitch, Homes."

"This bastard has all the stinking words right, man. Let's see if he has the fricking balls to carry out his damn threats against my ass. I want you guys to try and crease (wound) the lousy bastard when we go in, people." Walker turned from Mother and nodded at Neck.

Neck shoved his large frame away from the wall by his powerful shoulders, and then he fired two rounds from his shotgun at the closed door. In a flash, there was a hole blasted in the center of the door large enough to stick your head in it. When Neck fired, the Mutt and Flanagan charged passed the door, and they pitched their stun grenades in the hole, and then they ran to the other side of the door in the hall.

The shotgun blast to the door, forced al-Adwani to duck below the bed frame he was using for cover, but he recovered quickly and fired at the dark shapes he spotted passing swiftly by the hole blasted in the door. He emptied his weapon without thought of conserving one round to take his own life with, before the blast from the stun grenades robbed him of his consciousness. When the first grenade went off inside the small room, the blast picked up and it threw al-Adwani away from behind the bed, as the bed was lifted and rolled up on its side, and spilled Rasha's body on the floor on top of the prone al-Adwani.

The metal spring frame remained locked in the heavier bed frame. The three follow on explosions covered both al-Adwani and Rasha with debris blown apart from the force of the grenades going off inside the room, knocking al-Adwani momentarily unconscious, and placing Rasha deeper in her own stupor.

The second the grenades went off, Walker pushed off the wall, and he jumped in front of the door and crashed in the all but shattered door with his shoulder and body weight. The damaged door splintered under his weight so easy that he never lost his balance or footing. He darted in the smoke filled room with his MP-5 held at the ready, looking for where al-Adwani was hiding. He was followed closely in by the Mutt, Flanagan and Neck. The rest of the soldiers gathered in the hall, rushed to the door to lend support to the team penetrating the room. Inside, the room was a mess, choking and burning smoke added to the problems the soldiers were having with locating Colonel al-Adwani's body.

Walker went to his left, while the Mutt went to his right, and Mother Flanagan remained standing in the doorway, ready to sweep the room with his heavy M-60, if anyone dared to attack his two fellow soldiers who just forced their way inside the room. He was not going to allow Walker or the Mutt to become causalities during this operation, for the sake of this Iraqi Colonel who tried to off his President.

Seeing no one moving around freely in the destroyed room, the Mutt moved deeper in first, roughly kicking and shoving debris out of his way with his feet, as he moved into the disheveled room. Walker moved towards the upturned bed, and picked up al-Adwani's body crunched up against the far wall, along with part of the ripped apart mattress lying across his legs.

Al-Adwani was bleeding from the nose and mouth, and from many nicks and cuts he received from the power of the four stun grenades going off in the room. Walker never saw Rasha's body because it was covered over by the ripped and smelling mattress from the overturned bed. A few small fires added to the smoke assaulting the American soldier's lungs and eyes.

"Hey Mutt, I got the lousy bastard over here man! He looks like he's down and out for the stinking count though man. The bastard's still breathing good enuf on his own man." Walker called out as he moved swiftly in on the prone body of al-Adwani. He saw his weapon lying by his leg and he kicked it away from al-Adwani's hand and reach, and then he dropped down and placed his knee in the throat of the unconscious terrorist.

The Mutt moved nearer to Walker and kicked at the overturned mattress, to make certain al-Adwani did not have a second weapon hidden on his person, or under the mattress and in reach. He was the first one to see the leg of a female sticking out from under the mattress, and he called out to warn the other soldiers of a second person in the room. "Hey Road Kill, I got a second A-rab turd lying here man."

The Mutt warned Walker as he aimed his weapon at what he thought would be the upper body of the person he could not see yet.

Mother Flanagan ran over to the Mutt's side, and helped him pull the double size mattress out of the way, and off the downed female Arab. When the Mutt saw the body of the naked woman, he mumbled at the other soldiers in the destroyed room. "Well will you look at this little gift we just got ourselves here man. It looks like the Iraqi turd left us a fucking present to have some fun with, guys. At least I'm gonna have a little play time with her before we leave this shit filled dump of nothing but sand and angry people, Homes." The Mutt started fumbling around with the buttons of his uniform.

"Knock it off dog man we ain't got time for that kinda shit." Walker complained as he removed his knee from the Arab male's neck, and checked on al-Adwani's condition. He wanted to make sure he was still alive. He checked the pulse on his neck, and found a good strong beat from it and he smiled, relieved the Iraqi Colonel was still alive.

"Awe C'mon man alls I wanna do is rip me off a little piece of trim here, and then leave this bitch A-rab with something to remember me by for the rest of her stinking life, Homes." The Mutt griped at Walker as he tried a quick but wasted smile on him.

"You touch that bitch with anything of yours and I'll put a cap in your ass, mista. I'm not fooling around with you Mutt. I really mean it, if you touch that poor woman, I'll never allow you to forget it." Blind Date growled in her heavily French accent, as she stepped inside the room, and then she aimed her weapon right at the Mutt's rearend, to get her point across to her man, as she continued to glare at him, daring him to touch the woman.

"Dammit, this is the last time I bring my main squeeze to a party like this, guys." The Mutt complained as he reached down and roughly pulled Rasha's limp form out from under the overturned bed by her leg, and then he remarked to the rest of the soldiers in the room as he pitched her forward. "Man, will ya look at this pretty little A-rab bitch, she's a real beaut, I gots ta have me some of this to try on for some fun, man."

"And, I gots to put a cap in your ass if you try that shit on her I told you, mista." Blind Date warned for a second time as she tried to mimic some of the Mutt words, this time displaying sheer anger in her tone and showing the Mutt she really meant business.

"Man what big confetti they throw around here." Neck remarked as he had to step aside or Rasha's body would have crashed into him as he added. "Well, if the Mutt not allowed to have some of this pretty little A-rab bitch's ass. I'm sure as hell gonna rip me off a little piece of this shit, man. I ain't got no woman to answer to on this stinking mission, people." The Neck complained as he moved in on Rasha's naked body, and crudely grabbed her breasts with both hands and stared kneading them in front of the rest of the soldiers.

"The same thing goes for you too big man, you touch that poor woman again and I'll put a cap in your big ass, mista." Blind Date warned Neck as angrily, as she turned her weapon on him.

"Well what the hell's this stinking shit about lady, she your stinking twin sister from another mother or sumthin around here, honey?" Neck growled at the pretty French soldier as he released his grip on Rasha's breasts and glared at Blind Date.

"Look stupid, we didn't come here to rape their woman, we came here for that slug lying on the floor. Now we have the bastard, we're going to start acting as civil as possible to anyone left behind alive, mista." Blind Date hissed and then she turned to Walker looking for his support.

"You heard the Date, people. No one screws around with the A-rab woman. Handcuff her yes, blindfold her damn right, and then dump her stinking ass on top of the stinking mattress, and leave her ass the fuck alone. Mutt, help me with this stinking package of shit here, buster. I think the poor fella was taken with a fucking dizzy spell, man." Walker grabbed al-Adwani by the throat, and shook him roughly by it. He knew al-Adwani was still alive, because he saw his chest raising and falling with each breath he drew in, and he still had a good pulse.

"C'mon you stinking scumbag and open them fucking eyes of yours and wake up, before I allow the stinking Mutt to rape your damn ass in here, man." Walker shook Colonel al-Adwani savagely until his eyes finally fluttered open.

"I don't wanna do him unless you shave the dumb fuck first, man." The Mutt complained as he kept his eyes glued on the young Arab woman just dumped on top of the mattress.

"That's betta scumbag, now get on your fucking knees and lock your stinking hands behind your head, you lousy little puke!" Walker roughly shoved the barrel of his weapon in al-Adwani's face, digging it harshly into his cheek to cause him extra pain, as he continued with his orders to the stunned Iraqi Colonel. "You listen up real fucking careful like sucka, you just give me a fricking reason to off your stinking ass, and I'll blow your friggin head clear into tomorrow for ya, if you don't follow all my orders, pal. You'll do everything I tell ya to do, or you're gonna experience fucking pain like you never believed possible in your wasted life, buddy."

Walker pulled al-Adwani forward by his neck and kicked him hard in the small of the back, as he barked again at the Iraqi Colonel. "On your fucking knees I told ya buster, and lock them hands behind your head. Before I change my mind just for the hell of it, and I kill ya nice and quick, and then I'll take your damn head back to my Boss, so I can show him we got ya stinking ass, pal. You know if you're not whole, you'll never gonna get into Paradise stupid, and I'll cut your fricking balls off for ya, and feed the damn things to a stinking dog and I'll stuff your dead ass inside a stinking pig skin and bury you in it, just to keep you from making it to your damn Paradise world, buster." Walker savagely pulled the Iraqi Colonel's body to his knees with his powerful hands.

Colonel al-Adwani was forced to walk forward on his knees a few steps, to stop himself from falling forward because of Walker's rough shove on his body. The angry Iraqi simply refused to allow himself to fall forward to the ground before these American soldiers. When al-Adwani regained his balance, he did as ordered by the extremely angry American soldier and put his hands behind his head. Then he arched his back so he was a more comfortable on his knees.

Al-Adwani allowed his mind to believe he would be treated well in the United States, go through a mocked criminal trial, and then be classified as a soldier of war and treated as one. He had to do something because of the savage way this young American soldier was treating him, and he had no doubt in his mind this wild soldier would kill him in a most barbarous way at a drop of a hat, if he offered any resistance to his orders. Colonel al-Adwani heard a terrible sound of something being ripped behind him, and froze while he waited for his fate to befall him.

Al-Adwani watched out of the corner of his eye, as two American soldiers roughly dragged Rasha's limp body off the mattress across the rubble covered floor, and then they crudely yank her hands behind her back and cuff them together on her. The soldiers allowed their hands to explore every inch of Rasha's naked body, as they dumped her back on the upturned bed and metal springs again.

"Get me some pictures of that fucking A-rab bitch for our files back in the States, Mutt." Walker snorted nastily, keeping a close eye on the Iraqi Colonel at the same time.

The Mutt pulled out the small pocket camera he always carried, and snapped a number of pictures of Rasha from every angle, especially of her face. She was dropped down on the bed in such a terrible position it exposed every bit of her body to the small camera's lens.

"Jesus Christ, at least close her damn legs some will ya please." Baby Tee cried in an angry voice, embarrassed at the ugly way Rasha's body was being photographed by the grunting Mutt.

"Man, you stinking hens are taking all the damn fun outta this fricking mission. First I can't touch her stinking body, now I can't even take me some photos of this bitch for my private collection, man." The

Mutt complained as he pulled Rasha's legs closer together, and then he took a few more pictures of her. When the photos were done, the soldiers secured her body so she could not move a muscle.

Colonel al-Adwani stared in disbelief as two American soldiers wrapped the wide duck tape around Rasha's mouth and eyes. Around and around the soldiers ran the thick tape over her face and hair, leaving just enough of her nose out of the wrapping so she could breathe without too much trouble. One of the wild acting soldiers wanted to tape her legs to the bed posts, but the female soldiers helping them ordered her legs together, and they taped them together around the ankles. Al-Adwani could not help but feel a bit sorry for Rasha he knew the pain she was going to suffer when she tried to get the heavy tape from her hair and bare skin.

When Rasha's body was secured properly, a soldier dumped water from his canteen over her head and face, bringing her around. Rasha's eyes shot open under the tape, she could not see the blazing eyes of hatred the soldier called No Neck was glaring at her with. When he was certain he had her attention, Neck warned in a threatening voice. "Now look here sister, you're under fucking arrest. Try something stupid against us, and I'm gonna take fucking pleasure showing you the error in your ways of thinking, honey." Neck reached out and grabbed her breast roughly, and rolled it in his hand to get his point across as he added. "You feel me here bitch?"

Rasha nodded yes fearfully at the unseen and extremely angry sounding American soldier.

"This one's fucking secured good and proper, Road Kill." Neck announced to his commander, using his unit tag name because he did not want to identify any soldiers to the Arab bitch they were going to leave alive behind when they left the Iraqi village.

"Good, now we can take care of this uther turd." Walker replied as he stepped aside and allowed Neck and the Mutt to secure al-Adwani. All the while the soldiers worked on the Iraqi Colonel, Walker kept his weapon trained on the back of the head of the helpless al-Adwani.

More ripping of duck tape scared al-Adwani again, as the Mutt shoved his hat over the Iraqi's face, and held it there and Neck ran the tape over his head, securing the hat in place, blinding al-Adwani, and making it nearly impossible for him to speak and hard for him to breathe.

Colonel al-Adwani's hands were ripped from atop his head, and roughly yanked down behind his back, as the Mutt handcuffed them. Clipping the metal military cuffs tighter than needed to sort of get some revenge against the Iraqi Officer out of his system. He next kicked al-Adwani's legs together with his foot, and used a pair of heavy leg irons to secure them, making it impossible for him to do anything but what he was told to do by the Americans.

When al-Adwani was secured, Walker moved to his side and roughly pulled the Colonel to his feet by the arm and shoulder, and then hissed in his ear in a low snarl. "Okay turd, we're getting the hell outta this fucking rat's nest real quick like man. Remember scumbag, give me a reason, any fucking reason, and I'll rip ya ass apart with my bare hands, buddy. You got it sucka? Blood Clot, you wanna give this turd something to make him more agreeable to work with, man."

Colonel al-Adwani could only nod yes he understood the warning aimed at him.

"Great, now we understand each uther well enough, let's get going scumbag." Walker watched as Blood Clot loaded up al-Adwani with drugs to make him easier to control, and then he tapped his mike with his finger and barked in it. "Hey Ghost?"

"Go Road Kill." The Ghost replied as he looked at the building, trying to see Walker inside it.

"What's the fucking deal out there man? Are you taking any pop by any bad guys?"

"Nope, I don't think anyone's coming to help out this lousy prick, Road Kill." He reported to his commander.

"Great, get ready man we're coming out with this bag of shit. We got the lousy little stinking turd and he's in one fricking piece, man."

"Out fucking standing Road Kill. We're moving to the front of the building as of now man. We jumped started a few Russian built shit buggies, so we can now drive out to our machines in the desert, and blow this fucking shit filled nation once and for all, man."

"Good thinking Ghost, have them waiting by the front doors of this dump when we get out there. I wanna get the hell outta here as quickly as possible. What about Sun Tan's body?" Walker did not wait for a reply as he turned to al-Adwani and snarled at him. "Hear that prick. Not even your own shit filled stinking President thinks enough of your slimy ass to come to your aide, buster. You're going back to the United States to stand trial for your sins against my President, fella. Then, it's gonna be up to the American infidels as you like to call us, to place the period to the end of your worthless fucking life, sucka."

"I got Sun Tan's body placed in the first machine we started up, Road Kill." The Ghost reported, not knowing he was not paying attention to him any longer.

Walker shoved al-Adwani towards the door using his weapon to move him along with.

The Mutt stayed behind with Rasha for a few seconds longer, and warned her in as nasty a tone as he could speak at her. "Now you look here bitch, we're gonna leave ya pretty little ass behind breathing and alive. You're the only one left alive in this entire dump, so appreciate the fact, honey. Do nothing and you'll live long enuf to raise yourself a few rug rats. Do anything stupid, and I'm sure as hell gonna hate like fuck killing your little ass. But I'll do it without thought, if you force me to do it baby. You see bitch, I'd much rather fuck a woman, than waste her pretty little ass. Is any of this shit getting through to that hate filled A-rab brain of yours, bitch?"

Rasha swallowed, and then she replied the best she could through the thick tape. "Yes I make no further trouble for you. Leave my county!" Rasha tried to pull her body from the Mutt's probing, insulting hands. All the time he was warning her, he was playing with her breasts.

The Mutt had a little bit of a problem understanding most of Rasha's words, they were nothing more than a mumble of garbled words, blurred because of Rasha's Arab accent, but he got the gist of them and replied. "That's real fine baby. You remember this as long as you live bitch. This American pig is gonna allow you to live until the next time you hurt any Americans. Then I'll be back here, and have some real fun with your stinking body, before I cut it up into little pieces on ya ass and feed it to your desert scavengers, honey." He released her breasts, and leaned closer to Rasha's face. He slowly licked the side of her cheek, the only thing he could thing of doing to insult her further, as he added to his nasty warning. "Remember my breath baby, if you ever come back to the United States.

It is gonna be the last thing you'll ever smell in your fucking life, before you're off to greet Muhammad, bitch."

Rasha actually shuttered from the terrible threat, and the harsh and chilling way it was delivered against her. She made up her mind she was not going to be a terrorist any longer, she felt she was now too well known and compromised to the Americans, to be an effective agent against them any longer.

Walker and Neck nearly carried the drugged al-Adwani down the stairs, and out the front door of the building. He noticed the vehicles waiting for them outside the main door of the nearly destroyed building, and he smiled as he shoved al-Adwani roughly forward. Some of the local residents of the town strolled out of their homes when the weapon fire stopped, to see what was going on in their village. They saw strange soldiers dragging another man towards the vehicles, and they figured the feared Republican Guard just arrested someone from inside the building, and they were now taking him to his death.

"Hey Road Kill, we betta get a step on it man. It seems like the king rat decided to send out some soldiers for this rat bastard here after all, Homes." The Ghost pointed with his chin towards three fast moving vehicles flying across the desert towards Dawral.

Walker looked behind him and noticed the large cloud of dust being raised by the rapidly moving vehicles, and cursed. "Dammit." Walker growled as he ordered the other soldiers into the aged Soviet made troop transports, and then he bitched at a few troopers. "Mother, you and Buckethead get in the last vehicle, and keep them fucking bastards offa our asses as long as you can, man. We gotta get the hell outta here double quick guys."

When the soldiers were out of the crumbling building and in the vehicles, they pulled out just as the pursuing Iraqi machines entered the far end of the village from the east side of town. Walker's troops had no idea the Iraqi troops were part of General al-Zahar's units returning from a normal patrol the General sent them out on earlier in the day. Walker did not realize Colonel Hamoodi al-Qaysi was among the soldiers who returned to the town. Al-Zahar sent him out on the patrol to get him out of the village, because he knew the other Iraqi Colonel hated al-Adwani with a passion, and he was looking for any reason to kill his spy Colonel.

EAGLE'S NEST

The respected Iraqi General wanted the other Colonel out of the way for the time being.

When the arriving Iraqi troops saw the other vehicles pulling away from the front of the building they used as their headquarters, and smoke pouring out of the shattered building. They realized something was wrong in the town, and they automatically opened fire on the retreating troops and vehicles. Mother Flanagan and Buckethead returned fire on the enemy soldiers at the same time, raking the leading machine with machine gun fire from their M-60s. Two Iraqi vehicle's engines erupted in steam, as the radiators were ripped open by their heavy rounds.

"There's no sense waiting any longer, pop that fucking armory Ghost!" Walker roared.

With a press of a button a thunderous explosion followed. The side of the building exploded in a ball of flame and tumbling debris. Then the weakened structure collapsed in on itself. What Walker did not realize, was Rasha was still inside the building, and she died in the explosions ripping the building apart.

The newly arrived Iraqi troops poured out of their disabled vehicles, and continued firing at the retreating machines as they disappeared out of the town. The Iraqis were forced to duck down as building debris from their headquarters pelted them as it returned to earth. Colonel al-Qaysi got out of his machine and he did not flinch as their headquarters exploded close of him. He stood in the middle of the road with his hands resting threateningly on his hips, as he watched with anger as the vehicles carrying the Americans and al-Adwani, leave his town. As he watched the vehicles leave, he cursed the American soldiers as he roared at them at the top of his lungs.

"You foolish god cursed American jackals have won this round of the game of life and death. But if you think you'll place that great fool of a Colonel you have taken with you on trial in your cursed country. I have sad news for you hated Americans. I'll stop you, and in my stopping you, you'll lose many foul judges and police officers in my attack and revenge on you the next time we shall meet. Allah will guide my hand and make my aim true. I'll kill every one of you American fools who have invaded my country, this I swear to the Almighty Allah. I'm coming to the United States, and I'll have my revenge on all your worthless heads, infidels."

The remaining Iraqi vehicle still working, pulled up alongside the Iraqi troops shooting at the fleeing American soldiers. But the driver did not pursue the unknown group of retreating soldiers, as he parked his vehicle behind the two disabled troop transports. This was because Colonel al-Qaysi had not ordered them to do so. Flames also blocked his way momentarily, and the driver used this excuse to break off his pursuit of the foreign invaders.

Mother Flanagan and Buckethead slapped forearms together, to celebrate them stopping the trailing enemy soldiers in their tracks, and then Mother reported to Walker. "That fucking did it Road Kill. It seems these damn pukes still have no stomach for real fighting, man."

As Walker's troops left the village with many residents standing in the road, or along what resembled a sidewalk, waved and smiled at the retreating soldiers. Colonel al-Qaysi watched as the villagers waved at the fleeing Americans. He cursed and it was at this point he decided to kill everyone living in the village. He continued to stare at the vehicles as they left the outskirts of the village. All the while he was trying to control the rage within his heart, until he was finally able to get his revenge on all these hated American soldiers.

The Mutt leaned nearer to Walker, and grumbled at him over the roar from the engine of the machine. "Look at these stupid assholes, will ya man. They're so fricking confused they think we're their own fucking soldiers leaving them, the dopey bastards."

Walker did not reply, instead, he made contact with Captain Wilson, stationed with their return vehicles. "This is Sand Flea. Over."

"Road Kill?" The Captain replied in his radio in an excited tone.

"Yep, the one and only man, and we got the little slimy stinking bastard with us, and he's in one piece too, sir. We're coming to ya right now Captain. Be fucking ready to pull out the instant we get there and get on board our stinking machines and get outta here."

Captain Wilson used the unit names of the soldiers he was speaking to over the radio, and cut Colonel Leadbetter's name off so no one who might be monitoring their communications could pick up the names of any specially trained soldiers involved in the snatch and scoot operation in Iraq of al-Adwani. "You got it Road Kill. Hey Road Kill, our Commander has been busting my horns for the last few hours, wanting to know how you people were doing out there, and where you were..." Captain Wilson's communication was interrupted by Colonel Leadbetter, as he growled in the radio.

"Road Kill!" Colonel Leadbetter was also using the tag names.

"The one and only." The young Lieutenant smirked in his radio in reply, instantly recognizing Leadbetter's harsh voice as it barked at him.

"Funny! Real funny buster! You're a real fucking Jerk Benny there, Road Kill. You got our fucking package wrapped up like a Christmas gift, wiseguy?" He snorted in the radio he was choking to death in his hands.

"Yes sir, he's sitting alongside me Colonel, and he's alive and kicking, sir. But I'm afraid he's a might beat up some, sir. We had to use a little force on the bastard to make him understand he was to come along with us, nice and peaceful like Colonel." Walker replied to the Colonel.

"Outstanding, I don't give a shit how messed up he might be, you get his fucking ass here, and I'll take it from there soldier. Are you receiving pop from any Iraqi soldiers, mister?"

"Negative on that last sir. We had a little trouble leaving Dawral though, but it's all over now sir. Some Iraqi soldiers tried to stop us from leaving the village, sir. They didn't get very far with that move though sir." Walker reported with a deep sigh of sheer exhaustion.

"Look overhead Road Kill." The Colonel ordered Walker over the radio.

Walker looked into the brightening sky, and smiled. Three F-18s were flying overhead, and taking up position to escort them safely out of the Iraqi desert.

"Those fly boys are going to stay with ya ass all the way until you're back in Saudi Arabia, nice and safe and sound, Road Kill. I have transportation waiting there for your ass, mister. You did an outstanding job on this one. Good work soldier, give the rest of your troops a well done from me, Captain." The Colonel smiled in the radio now.

"I got me a fucking raise Colonel?" The new Captain replied with surprise in the radio.

"Yep, but don't let it go to your head, asshole. You're over two fucking hours passed your scheduled break off time, and we're going to have a nice little in your face discussion about your failure to complete your mission, under the prescribed time limit I set for the operation, mister. Have you taken any dead or wounded during this screwed up operation?" The Colonel demanded to know from him.

"Yes sir, I'm afraid we lost one man in the op, sir. We're bringing him home, Colonel." Captain Walker replied, and then he broke off the communication when he saw the light from Captain Wilson's vehicles in the distance before them. The new Captain ordered the machines started up, and they were coming out to meet up with Walker's crew.

The Mutt slapped Walker on the back, and then griped at the new young Captain. "Don't take it too fucking hard Homes. You know Leadbetter had to find something to get on our asses about, man. We're going home Walker, this fucking game is over buddy, we accomplished what we were sent out to do, man."

"Yeah." Was the only thing Walker snapped back at his friend, as he watched Captain Wilson's vehicles rapidly closing on them. He allowed his thought to drift to Sergeant Dorothy Ramirez and to the child she had growing in her, and he smiled. He finally allowed himself to think about real world thoughts and pleasures. He was dying to hold Ramirez in his arms, and make love to her again and watch as his child grew in her body. He was dying to see what his son would look like, who he would resemble, Ramirez or him. For some reason, he knew she was carrying a boy in her. The rest of the elite soldiers settled down in the machines and allowed them to relax a little, all wanting to be home and get on with their lives in the civilized world.

Iraqi Colonel Hamoodi al-Qaysi turned away from the fleeing vehicles with the American soldiers in them, he could no longer see any of them in the small sand storm the vehicles kicked up. But as he turned away, the angry colonel again vowed his revenge against the American soldiers leaving his country in the vehicles they stolen from him.

"Hey Walker, Blood Clot."

"Go Blood Clot, what's up?"

"It's Ice, she's going bad on me, I don't like the way she looks man."

"Crap, I forgot about her being hit, is she dying?"